select
editions

Reader's
Digest

Reader's Digest

The condensations in this volume
are published with the consent of the authors
and the publishers © 2010 Reader's Digest, Inc.

www.readersdigest.co.uk

Published in the United Kingdom by Vivat Direct Limited
(t/a Reader's Digest), 157 Edgware Road, London W2 2HR

Printed in Germany
ISBN 978 0 276 44441 8

**select
editions**

THE READER'S DIGEST ASSOCIATION, INC.

contents

author in focus

'**You are about to travel** to Edgecombe St Mary, a small village in the English countryside, filled with rolling hills, thatched cottages, and a cast of characters both hilariously original and as familiar as the members of your own family . . .' It is with these words that Helen Simonson, author of *Major Pettigrew's Last Stand*, introduces her debut novel on her website, www.helensimonson.com. We would only add that the Major himself is an endearing character who you'll find hard to forget: a pillar of wisdom, broad-mindedness and more.

in the spotlight

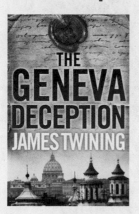

We love to find books that not only entertain but also provide what we call a 'plus factor'. In our terms, that means an insight into some facet of life that you may not have come across before. In this collection of Select Editions, James Twining brings you this 'plus factor' in plenty, with a novel that is based on extensive research into the black market in rare antiquities. Did you know, for instance, that the Italians actually have a special name for the thieves who dig them up? They call them *tombaroli*, derived from *tomba* or 'tomb' in Italian. Find out more about the tomb robbers and art thieves who steal or trade in priceless treasures at www.jamestwining.com.

THE
GENEVA
DECEPTION

JAMES TWINING

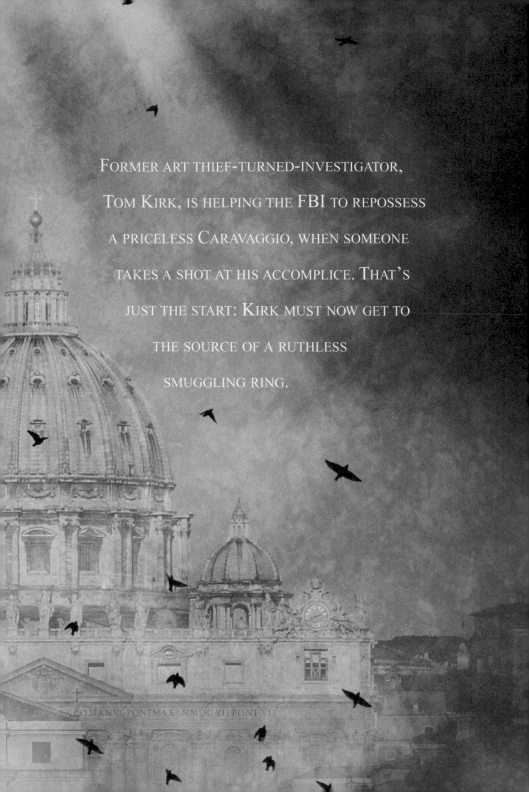

Former art thief-turned-investigator, Tom Kirk, is helping the FBI to repossess a priceless Caravaggio, when someone takes a shot at his accomplice. That's just the start: Kirk must now get to the source of a ruthless smuggling ring.

PROLOGUE

Ponte Duca d'Aosta, Rome

The cold kiss roused him. A teasing, tentative embrace, it nibbled playfully at his ear and then, growing in confidence, slipped down to nuzzle against his naked throat.

Eyes screwed shut, cheek pressed against the wooden decking, Luca Cavalli knew that he should enjoy this moment while it lasted. So he lay there, cradled by the darkness, the gentle swell of the river rocking him softly. He concentrated on keeping the steady cadence of his breathing constant. So they wouldn't notice he was awake.

Ahead of him, near the bow, a small pool of rainwater had gathered. He could hear it sloshing from side to side under the duckboards as the boat swayed, smell the rainbow shimmer of engine oil dancing across its surface, the heady scent catching in the back of his throat like an exotic perfume. He had a strange, uncontrollable urge to swallow, to taste the raw truth of the moment while he still could.

The momentary stutter in his breathing's rhythmic beat was all it took. Immediately, the thin lips resting against his skin parted with a snarl, and the sharp teeth of the knife's serrated edge bit into him savagely. He was hauled upright, eyes blinking, shoulders burning where his wrists had been zip-locked behind his back.

There were three of them in all. One at the helm, his slab hands gripping the wheel. One perched on the bench opposite, a gun wedged into the waistband of his jeans. One hugging him close, the knife he had caressed his cheek with only a few moments before now pressed hard against his belly.

They were silent, although there was something noisily boastful about their lack of disguise, as if they wanted him to know that they would never be caught, never be picked up out of a line-up.

Cavalli glanced over the side of the boat and saw that the river was engorged and running fast. He realised then that the engine wasn't running, and that this whole time they had been carried forward noiselessly on the river's powerful muscle as it flexed its way through the city.

The current carried them towards the Ponte Sant' Angelo and the carved angels lining its balustrades as if gathered to hear his final confession. Abruptly, the helmsman whistled and a light flashed twice from the bridge. Someone was expecting them.

Immediately the engine kicked into life and the helmsman steered them towards the left-hand arch. As they passed under it, the helmsman jammed the throttle into reverse and edged the boat against the massive stone pier. He nodded at the others and they leapt forward to secure the boat to the iron rings embedded in the wall. Then he switched the engine off.

A bright orange rope came hissing out of the darkness, the excess coiling in the prow. The helmsman stepped forward and tugged on it to check it was secure, then found the end. It had already been tied into a noose.

Now, as he understood that there was to be no last-minute reprieve, Cavalli felt afraid. Desperate words began to form in his mouth, screams rose from his stomach. But no sound came out, as if he had somehow been bound into the same demonic vow of silence as his captors.

Hauling him out of his seat, the two other men dragged him over to where the helmsman was looping the surplus rope round his arm, and forced him onto his knees. The noose was snapped over his head and then jerked tight, the knot biting into the nape of his neck. Then he was silently lifted to the side and carefully lowered into the freezing water.

He gasped, the change in temperature winding him. Without warning, the river grabbed on to him, nudging him along slowly at first and then tugging at his ankles with increasing insistence. He drew further away, as the rope gently uncoiled in the water.

It snapped tight. Choking, his body swung round until he was half in and half out of the water, the current hauling at his legs, the rope lifting his head and upper body out of the river, the tension wringing the water from the fibres. He kicked out frantically, but rather than free himself, all he managed to do was flip himself onto his front so that he was face down over the water. Slowly, and with his reflection staring remorselessly back up at him from the river's dark mirror, Cavalli watched himself hang.

PART ONE

Arlington National Cemetery, Washington DC

One by one, the limousines drew up, disgorged their occupants onto the sodden grass, and then pulled away to a respectful distance.

A handful of secret-service agents were patrolling the space between the burial site and the road. Their unsmiling presence made Tom Kirk feel uncomfortable, even though he knew it shouldn't. After all, it had been nearly two years since he'd crossed over to the other side of the law. Two years since he'd teamed up with Archie Connolly, his former fence, to help recover art rather than steal it. Clearly it was going to take much longer than that to shake off instincts acquired in a lifetime on the run.

There were three rows of seats arranged in a horseshoe round the flag-draped coffin, and five further rows of people standing behind these. A pretty good turnout, considering the weather. Trent Clayton Jackson Duval III had been an important man—a senator and a war hero. Tom and Archie had stayed back, sheltering under the generous spread of a blossoming tree halfway up the slope that climbed gently to the left of the grave. From his vantage point, Tom recognised a few of the faces sheltering under the thicket of black umbrellas, although most were strangers to him.

As they watched, the carefully choreographed ceremony unfolded beneath them. The horse-drawn caisson winding its way up the hill, followed by a riderless horse. The presenting of arms by the military escort. The transport of the coffin to the grave by eight members of the 101st Airborne Division, Tom's grandfather's old unit. The final adjustments to the flag to ensure that it was centred.

'Who's the bird?' Archie sniffed. In his mid-forties, about five foot ten and unshaven with close-cropped blond hair, he had the square-shouldered, rough confidence of someone who didn't mind using their fists to start or settle an argument. This was at odds with the patrician elegance of his clothes, however: a three-button dark grey Anderson & Sheppard suit, crisp white Turnbull & Asser shirt, and black silk tie hinting at a rather more refined temperament. Tom knew that many struggled to reconcile this apparent incongruity, although the truth was that both were valid. It was only a short distance from the trestle tables of Bermondsey Market to

Mayfair's panelled auction rooms, but for Archie it had been a difficult journey that had required this expensive camouflage to travel undetected.

'Miss Texas,' Tom answered, knowing that his eye would have been drawn to the platinum blonde in the front row. 'Or she was a few years ago. The senator upgraded after meeting her on the campaign trail. He left her everything.'

'I'll bet he did, the dirty old bastard.' Archie grinned.

The corners of Tom's mouth twitched but he said nothing, finding himself wondering if her dark Jackie O glasses were to hide her tears or to mask the fact that she had none. The chaplain started the service.

'You sure you don't want to head down?' Archie was holding up a Malacca-handled Brigg umbrella.

'This is close enough.'

'Bloody long way to come if all we're going to do is stand up here getting pissed on,' Archie sniffed. 'They invited you, didn't they?'

'They were being polite. They never thought I'd actually show. I'm not welcome here. Not really.'

The empty caisson pulled away, the horses' hooves clattering noisily.

'I thought he liked you?'

'He helped me,' Tom said slowly. 'Took me in after my mother died, put me through school, recommended me to the NSA. But after I left the Agency . . . well. We hadn't spoken in twelve years.'

'Then tell me again why the bloody hell we're here?' Archie moaned.

Tom hesitated. The truth was that, even now, he wasn't entirely sure. Partly, it had just seemed like the proper thing to do. But probably more important was the feeling that his mother would have wanted him to come. Expected it, insisted on it. To him, therefore, this was perhaps less about paying his respects to his grandfather than it was a way of remembering her.

'You didn't have to come,' Tom reminded him sharply.

'What, and miss the chance to work on my tan?' Archie winked. 'Don't be daft. That's what mates are for.'

They stood in silence, the priest's faint voice and the congregation's murmured responses carrying to them on the damp breeze. As the service droned mournfully towards its conclusion, a man stepped out from the crowd and signalled up at them with a snatched half-wave. Tom and Archie swapped a puzzled look as he clambered up the grass towards them.

'Mr Kirk?' he called out hopefully as he approached. 'Mr Thomas Kirk?'

Short and worryingly overweight, he wore a large pair of tortoiseshell glasses that he kept pushing back up his blunt nose.

'I recognised you from your photo,' he huffed as he drew closer.

'I don't think . . .?' Tom began, trying to place the man's face.

'Larry Hewson,' he announced, his tone and eagerly outstretched hand suggesting that he expected them to recognise the name. 'From Ogilvy, Myers and Gray—the Duval family attorneys,' Hewson explained. '*I* sent you the invitation.'

'What do you want?' Archie challenged.

'Meet Archie Connolly,' Tom introduced him. 'My business partner.'

Below them, the chaplain had stepped back from the casket, allowing the senior NCO and seven riflemen to step forward and turn to the half right.

'Ready,' he ordered. Each rifleman moved his safety to the fire position.

'It's a delicate matter,' Hewson said in a low voice. 'It concerns your grandfather's will.'

'Aim,' the NCO called. The men shouldered their weapons.

'His will?' Archie asked with a frown. 'I thought he'd left the lot to Miss 32F down there?'

'Fire.' Each man quickly squeezed the trigger, the sharp crack of the blank round piercing the gloom. Twice more the order to aim and fire came, twice more the shots rang out across the silent cemetery. Hewson waited impatiently for their echo to die down before continuing.

'The senator did indeed alter his will to ensure that Ms Mills was the principal beneficiary of his estate,' he confirmed. 'But at the same time, he identified a small object that he wished to leave to you.'

A bugler had stepped forward and was now playing taps, the mournful melody swirling around them. As the last note faded away, one of the casket party stepped forward and began to fold the flag draped over the coffin to form a triangular bundle, before handing it to the chaplain. The chaplain stepped over to where the main family party was seated and handed the flag to the senator's wife.

'I believe it had been given to him by your mother,' Hewson added.

'My mother?' Tom's eyes snapped back to Hewson's. 'What is it?'

'I'm afraid I don't know,' Hewson shrugged as the ceremony ended. The congregation rapidly thinned, most hurrying back to their cars, a few pausing to talk. 'The terms of the will are quite strict. No one is to open the box and I am to hand it to you in person. That's why—'

'Tom!' Archie interrupted, grabbing Tom's arm. Tom followed his puzzled gaze and saw that a figure had appeared at the crest of the hill above them. It was a woman dressed in a red coat, the headlights of the car parked behind her silhouetting her against the dark sky in an ethereal white glow.

'That's why I sent you the invitation,' Hewson repeated, raising his voice slightly as Tom turned away from him. 'I've taken the liberty of reserving a suite at the George where we can finalise all the paperwork.'

'Isn't that . . .?' Archie's eyes narrowed, his tone incredulous.

'Otherwise I'm happy to arrange a meeting at our offices in New York tomorrow, if that works better,' Hewson called out insistently, growing increasingly frustrated, it seemed, at being ignored. 'Mr Kirk?'

'Yes . . .' Tom returned the woman's wave, Hewson's voice barely registering any more. 'It's her.'

Via del Gesù, Rome

Ignoring her phone's shrill call, Allegra Damico grabbed the double espresso off the counter and stepped back outside into the fading light. Answering it wouldn't make her get there any quicker. And if they wanted her to make any sense after the day she'd just had, she needed the caffeine more than they needed her to be on time. She walked down the Via del Gesù, then turned right onto the Corso Vittorio Emanuele, cupping the coffee in both hands and blowing on it, her reflection catching in the shop windows.

She owed her athletic frame to her father, an architect who had met her mother when he was working as a tour guide in Naples and she, a Danish student, was backpacking across Europe. Allegra had inherited both his olive skin and quick temper and her mother's high cheekbones and the sort of curling strawberry-blonde hair that the rich housewives who stalked the Via dei Condotti spent hundreds of euros trying to conjure from a bottle. Nowhere was this genetic compromise more arrestingly reflected than in her mismatched eyes—one crystal blue, the other an earthy brown.

Lifting her nose from the cup, she frowned, suddenly aware that despite the time of day, dawn seemed to be breaking ahead of her, its golden glow bronzing the sky. She quickened her pace, taking this unnatural event and the growing wail of sirens as an ominous portent of what lay in wait.

Her instincts were soon proved right. The Largo di Torre Argentina had been barricaded off, a disco frenzy of blue and red lights dancing across the walls of the surrounding buildings. A curious crowd had gathered on one side of the metal railings, straining to see into the square. On the other side loomed a determined cordon of state police. A police helicopter circled overhead and a searchlight shone down from its belly, its beam picking out a spot that Allegra couldn't yet see.

Her phone rang again. This time she answered it.

'*Pronto.* Yes, sir, I'm here . . . I'm sorry, but I came as soon as I could . . . I'll meet him at the northeast corner in three minutes . . . *Ciao.*'

She extracted her badge from her rear jeans pocket and, taking a deep breath, plunged into the crowd and elbowed her way to the front. Once there, she identified herself and an officer unhooked one of the barriers.

She headed through the gap towards the fenced-off sunken area that dominated the middle of the square. She could see now that this was the epicentre of the synthetic dawn she had witnessed earlier, a series of large mobile floodlights having been wheeled into place along its perimeter.

'Lieutenant Damico?'

A man had appeared at the top of a makeshift set of steps that led down to the large sunken tract of land. She nodded and held out her ID.

'You're a woman.'

'Unless you know something I don't.'

About six foot three, he must have weighed seventeen stone, most of it muscle. He was wearing dark blue trousers, a grey jacket and a garish tie that could only have been a gift from his children at Christmas. She guessed he was in his late fifties; his once square face was rounding softly at the edges, black hair swept across his scalp to mask his baldness.

'Major Enrico Salvatore.' He grudgingly shook her hand. 'Sorry about . . . we don't see too many women in the GICO.'

She just about managed to stop herself from rolling her eyes. GICO—properly known as the Gruppo d'Investigazione sulla Criminalità Organizzata—the special corps of the Guardia di Finanza which dealt with organised crime. And by reputation an old-school unit that frequented the same strip joints as the people they were supposedly trying to lock up.

'So what's the deal?' she asked. Her boss hadn't told her anything.

'You know this place?' he asked, gesturing anxiously at the sunken area behind him.

'Of course.' She shrugged. 'It's the "Area Sacra".'

'Go on.'

'It contains the remains of four Roman temples unearthed during an excavation project ordered by Mussolini in the 1920s. They were built between the fourth and second centuries BC. Each one has—'

'Fine, fine . . .' He held his hands up for her to stop, his relieved tone giving her the impression that she had just successfully passed some sort of audition without entirely being sure what role she was being considered for. He turned to make his way back down the steps. 'Save the rest for the boss.'

The large site was enclosed by an elegant series of brick archways that formed a retaining wall for the streets some fifteen or so feet above. Bleached white by the floodlights' glare, a forensic search team was strung out across it, inching their way forward on their hands and knees.

Immediately to her right, Allegra knew, was the Temple of Giuturna—a shallow flight of brick steps leading up to a rectangular area edged by a row of Corinthian columns of differing heights. Further along the paved walkway was a circular temple where only six tufa stone columns remained standing, a few surviving bases and sections from the other missing pillars poking up like rotting teeth.

Salvatore steered her over rough ground and half-formed brick walls towards a large structure made of scaffolding and covered in white plastic sheeting, the sort of makeshift shelter erected by archaeologists to protect an area of a site that they were excavating.

'I'd stay out of the way until the colonel calls you over,' Salvatore suggested, pausing on the threshold to the shelter.

'The colonel?'

'Colonel Gallo. The head of GICO,' he explained in a hushed tone. 'He'll call you over when he's ready.'

'Great.' She nodded, her tight smile masking a desperate urge to make some pointed observation about the irony of having been harried halfway across the city only to be kept waiting.

'And I'd lose that if I were you, too,' he muttered, nodding at her cup. 'It's probably better he doesn't know you stopped off for a coffee.'

Taking a deep breath, she theatrically placed the cup on the ground, and then looked up with a forced smile.

'Happy now?'

'Ecstatic.'

Greeting the two uniformed men guarding the entrance with a nod, Salvatore held a plastic flap in the sidewall open and they stepped inside. It revealed a long, narrow space, the scaffolding forming a sturdily symmetrical endoskeleton over which the white sheeting had been draped.

Salvatore motioned at a crumbling pediment, his gesture suggesting that he wanted her to sit there until she was called forward, then made his way towards a small group of men standing in a semicircle fifteen or so feet in front of her. Making a point of remaining standing, she counted the minutes as they ticked past—first one, then three, then five. Nothing. In fact no one had even turned round to acknowledge that she was there. Pursing her lips, she set off towards them. Busy was one thing, rude was another.

Seeing her approaching, Salvatore frantically signalled at her to stay back. She ignored him, but then stopped anyway, the colour draining from her face as a sudden gap revealed what they had been shielding from view.

It was a corpse. A man. A half-naked man. Arms spread-eagled, legs pinned together, he had been lashed to a makeshift wooden cross with steel wire. Allegra glanced away, horrified, but almost immediately looked back, the gruesome scene exercising a strange, magnetic pull. For as if drawn from some cursed, demonic ritual, the cross had been inverted.

He had been crucified upside down.

Arlington National Cemetery, Washington DC

'You sure about this?' Special Agent Bryan Stokes stepped out of the car behind her, his tone making his doubts clear.

'Absolutely,' Jennifer Browne nodded, as she watched Tom set off up the hill towards them. Despite his tall, athletic frame there was something almost feline about the way he moved. He had seemed pleased to see her, his initial surprise having melted into a warm smile and an eager wave. That was something, at least.

'So what's the deal with you two?' Stokes wedged a golf umbrella against his shoulder with his chin and flicked a manila file open. Jennifer guessed that Stokes had been born frowning, deep lines furrowing a wide, flat forehead. In his early forties, he was dressed in a severe charcoal suit and black tie that had dropped away from his collar.

'There is no deal,' she said, looking away in case he noticed her smile. 'We've worked a couple of cases together, that's all.'

'It says here he was CIA?'

'Senator Duval was on the Senate Intelligence Committee and recommended him,' she explained. 'They recruited him into a black-ops industrial-espionage unit. When they shut it down five years later, Kirk went into business for himself, switching from technical blueprints and experimental formulas to fine art and jewellery.'

'Was he any good?'

'The best in the business. Or so they said.'

'And the guy with him?'

'Archie Connolly. His former fence. Now his business partner. And his best friend, to the extent he allows himself to have one.'

It had been Jennifer's idea to come here, of course. Immmigration had flagged Tom's name up when he'd landed at Dulles and it hadn't taken her much to figure out where he'd be headed. But now that she was actually here, she was surprised at how she was feeling. Excited to be seeing Tom again after almost a year, certainly. But there was also a nagging sense of nervousness and apprehension that she couldn't quite explain.

'And now they've gone straight?'

'I'm not sure that someone like Tom can ever go straight,' she mused. 'Not in the way you and I mean it. The problem is, he's seen too many supposedly straight people do crooked things to think those sorts of labels matter. He just does what he thinks is right.'

'And you're sure about this?' Stokes pressed again, her explanation seeming to have, if anything, heightened his initial misgivings.

She didn't bother replying. Instead she stepped forward to greet Tom, who had reached the final incline that led up to where they were waiting. Tom, however, hesitated, his eyes flicking to Stokes.

'Tom.' She held out her hand. It felt wrong, too formal, but with Stokes hovering she didn't have much choice. Besides, what was the alternative? A hug? A kiss? That also didn't seem right after eleven months.

'Special Agent Browne.' Tom shook her hand with a brief nod, having clearly decided to ape her stilted greeting. He looked healthier than when she had last seen him, his handsome, angular face having lost some of its pallor, his coral-blue eyes clear and alive.

'This is Special Agent Stokes.'

'Agent Stokes.' Tom nodded a greeting.

Stokes grunted something indistinct in reply.

'Come to pay your respects?' Tom asked.

'We need some help on a case,' Jennifer began hesitantly.

'You mean this wasn't a coincidence?'

Despite his sarcastic tone, she sensed a slight tension lurking behind his smile. Annoyance, perhaps, that she was only there because she wanted something. Or was that just her projecting her own guilty feelings?

'*I* need your help,' she said.

There was a pause, his smile fading. 'What have you got?'

'Why don't we get in . . .' She held the Chevrolet Suburban's rear door open. 'There's something I want to show you. It'll only take a few minutes.'

Tom hesitated for a moment. Then, shrugging, he followed Jennifer into the back, while Stokes climbed into the driver's seat.

'Recognise this?' She handed him a photograph sealed inside a clear plastic evidence bag. It showed a nativity scene, an exhausted Mary staring blankly at the Christ child lying on the straw in front of her, an angel plunging dramatically overhead. Unusually, in the foreground a spiky-haired youth, his back to the viewer and one foot touching the baby, had turned to face an aged Joseph, his face tortured by a mischievous disbelief.

'Caravaggio. *The Nativity with San Lorenzo and San Francesco.*' Tom pointed at the two other men in the painting gazing adoringly at the infant. 'Painted in 1609 for the Oratory of San Lorenzo in Palermo, Sicily. Missing since 1969. Where did you get it?'

'Special Agent Stokes is from our Vegas field office,' she explained. 'A week ago he took a call from Myron Kezman.'

'The casino owner?' Tom asked in surprise.

'The photo arrived in his personal mail. It had a New York postmark,' Stokes said. 'We've checked the envelope for prints and DNA. It was clean.'

'There was a phone number on the back of the photo,' Jennifer continued. 'When Kezman called it there was a recorded message at the other end. It only played once before the number was disconnected.'

'What did it say?'

'According to Kezman it made him a simple offer. The painting for twenty million dollars. And then a different phone number to dial if he was interested in making the trade.'

'That's when Kezman called us in,' Stokes said. 'This time we taped the call. It was another message setting out the instructions for the exchange.'

'And then they called you?' Tom turned to Jennifer.

'The Caravaggio is on the FBI Art Crime Team's top ten list of missing art works, so it automatically got referred our way,' she confirmed. 'I got pulled off a case to help handle it. I've been camping out in an office here in DC, so when I saw that you'd been flagged up at Dulles . . .'

'You thought that maybe I could handle the exchange for you.'

'How the hell did you . . .?' Stokes eyed him suspiciously.

'Because you've never dealt with anything like this before.' Tom shrugged. 'Because you know that these types of gigs never go down quite like you plan them. Because you know I might spot something you won't.'

'That's pretty much it, I guess.' Stokes nodded with a grudging smile.

'When's this happening?'

'Tonight in Vegas. On the main floor at the Amalfi. Kezman's joint.'

'That's smart. Busy. Exposed. Multiple escape routes.'

'So you'll do it?' Jennifer asked hopefully.

There was a sharp rap on the window. Tom lowered it and Archie peered in, the rain dripping off his umbrella.

'Very bloody cosy,' he observed with a wry smile. 'Not interrupting anything, am I?'

'I don't think you two have ever actually met before, have you?' Tom asked, sitting back so Jennifer could lean across him and shake his hand.

'Not properly.' She smiled.

'What do you want with my boy this time?' Archie sniffed.

'The *Nativity* has turned up,' Tom answered for her. 'They want me to fly to Vegas with them to help handle the exchange.'

'I'll bet they do. What's our take?'

Tom looked at Jennifer and then at Stokes, who shrugged sheepishly.

'Looks like the usual fee,' he said with a smile. 'Attaboys all round.'

'Well, bollocks to that, then,' Archie sniffed. 'You and I are meant to be meeting Dom in Zurich tomorrow night to see a real client. One that pays.'

Tom nodded slowly. Archie had a point.

He turned back to Jennifer. 'Who'll handle the exchange if I don't?'

'Me, I guess,' she replied with a shrug. 'At least, that was the plan until you flashed up on the system.'

There was a long silence, Tom looking first at Jennifer, then Stokes.

He turned back to Archie. 'Why don't I meet you in Zurich tomorrow?'

'Oh, for fuck's sake, Tom,' Archie protested. 'I don't know why I bother sometimes.'

'One night. That's all,' Tom reassured him. 'I'll be on the first flight out.'

'Fine,' Archie sighed. 'But you can deal with Hewson.' Archie stepped back and pointed down the slope towards a lonely figure who appeared to be patiently waiting for them to return. 'He's doing my bloody head in.'

'Whatever he's got for me, it's waited this long'—Tom sat back with a shrug—'it can wait a day longer.'

Largo di Torre Argentina, Rome

Allegra could just about make out one of the men's low voices. A pathologist, she guessed.

'Cause of death? Well, I'll only know when I open him up. But at a guess, oedema of the brain. Terrible way to go.'

'How long has he been here?' the man next to him asked. From his flinty, aggressive tone, Allegra knew immediately that this had to be Gallo.

'All day. Possibly longer. It was a cold night and that would have slowed decomposition.'

'And no one saw him until now?' Gallo snapped, his voice disbelieving.

'No one works here at the weekend,' Salvatore explained in an apologetic tone. 'And you couldn't see him from the street.'

'Terrible way to go,' the pathologist repeated, shaking his head. 'It would have taken hours for him to die. And right until the end he would have been able to hear people walking around the site and the cars coming and going overhead, and not been able to move or call for help.'

'You think I give a shit about how this bastard died?' Gallo snorted dismissively. 'Don't forget who he was or who he worked for. All I want to know is who killed him and why like this. The last thing I need is some sort of vigilante stalking the streets of Rome re-enacting satanic rituals.'

'Actually, Colonel, it's Christian, not satanic,' Allegra interrupted.

'What?' Gallo rounded on her, looking her up and down with a disdainful expression. He was six feet tall and powerfully built, with a strong, tanned face covered in carefully trimmed stubble. About forty-five or so, she guessed, he was wearing the uniform of a colonel in the Guardia di Finanza. He had chin-length steel-grey hair that parted down the centre of his head and fell either side of his face, forcing him to sweep it back out of his eyes every so often.

'The inverted crucifixion,' she explained, ignoring the look on Salvatore's face. 'It's taken from the Acts of Peter in the Apocrypha. According to the text, when the Roman authorities sentenced Peter to death, he asked to be crucified head down, so as not to imitate Christ's passing.'

Gallo's eyes narrowed. 'Thank you for the Sunday-school lesson, Miss . . .'

'Lieutenant. Damico.'

'The antiquities expert you asked for, Colonel,' Salvatore added quickly.

'You work at the university?' Gallo asked.

'I used to be a lecturer in art and antiquities at La Sapienza, yes. Now I'm in the TPA,' she added, using the acronym for the Nucleo Tutela Patrimonio Artistico, the special corps within the Carabinieri tasked with protecting and recovering stolen art.

He looked her up and down again, then shrugged. 'Well, you'll have to do, I suppose,' he said. 'I take it you know who I am?'

She nodded, although part of her was itching to say no, just to see the look on his face. Gallo jabbed his finger at the man next to him.

'This is Dottore Giovanni la Fabro from the coroner's office, and this is, or was, Adriano Ricci, an enforcer for the De Luca family.'

Allegra nodded again. The GICO's involvement was suddenly a lot clearer. The De Luca family were believed to run the Banda della Magliana, one of Rome's most notorious criminal organisations.

Gallo stepped back and introduced the corpse with a sweep of his hand. Ricci's wrists and ankles were bleeding where the chicken wire used to bind him to the cross had bitten into his flesh.

'Why am I here?' she asked with a shudder, glancing back to Gallo.

'This—' He snapped his flashlight on to illuminate Ricci's face.

For a few moments she couldn't make out what he was pointing to, her attention grabbed by Ricci's staring, bloodshot eyes. But then she saw it. A black shape, a disc of some sort, lurking in the roof of Ricci's mouth.

'What is it?' she breathed.

'That's what you're meant to be telling me,' Gallo shot back.

'Can I see it, then?'

Gallo snapped his fingers and la Fabro handed him a pair of tweezers. He levered the object free and then carefully deposited it inside an evidence bag.

'I thought it might be some sort of antique coin,' Salvatore suggested eagerly over her shoulder. 'It seems to have markings etched into it.'

'The ancient Romans used to put a bronze coin in the mouths of their dead to pay Charon to ferry their souls across the Styx to the Underworld,' she said slowly. 'But I don't think that's what this is.'

'Why not?'

'Feel the weight, it's lead. That's too soft to be used in everyday coinage.'

'Then what about the engraving?' Gallo asked impatiently.

She traced the symbol that had been inlaid into the coin with her finger. It showed two snakes intertwined round a clenched fist, like the seal from some medieval coat of arms.

'I don't know,' she said with an apologetic shrug. 'But whatever this is, it's not an antique nor, I would say, particularly valuable.'

'Well, that was useful.' Gallo glared angrily at Salvatore and turned his back on Allegra as if she had suddenly vanished. 'We've wasted enough time. Let's just get him bagged up and out of here so the forensic boys can move in,' Gallo ordered. 'Then I want a priest or a cardinal or somebody else in sandals down here to tell me more about—'

'It can't be a coincidence that they killed him here, though, can it, Colonel?' Allegra called after him.

Gallo spun round angrily. 'What the hell are you talking about?'

'I mean that Ricci isn't the first person to be killed here,' she explained, a tremor of excitement in her voice. 'I mean that in 44 BC, Julius Caesar was assassinated on almost this exact same spot.'

The Getty Villa, Malibu, California

Verity Bruce had been looking forward to this day for a while. For nearly three years, to be precise. That's how long it had been since she had first been shown the dog-eared Polaroid in a smoky Viennese café, first been winded by the adrenaline punch of excitement at what was on offer.

She'd shaken on the deal there and then, knowing that the director would back her judgment. The trustees had taken a little more convincing, but then they didn't know the period as she did. Once they'd understood the magnitude of the find, they'd bitten and bitten hard, sharing her mounting frustration at the years lost to the scientists as test upon test had heaped delay upon deferral. And then, of course, the lumbering wheels of international bureaucracy had begun to turn, adding months to the process. Today, finally, the waiting ended.

She positioned herself in front of the full-length mirror on the back of her office door. Had the intervening years between that first encounter and today's unveiling aged her? A little, perhaps, around her fern-green eyes and in the tiny fissures that had begun to fleck her top lip. Ever since she'd turned forty-five, the years seemed to weigh a little heavier on her face. But, she reminded herself as she put the finishing touches to her make-up, it wasn't as if she'd lost her looks. And she still had great legs too.

'They're ready for you.'

One of the Getty PR girls had edged tentatively into the room. Verity couldn't remember her name, but then all these girls looked the same to her—blonde, smiley, skinny.

'Let's do it,' she said, slipping her leather jacket over a black Chanel dress. It was an unlikely combination, deliberately chosen to further fuel the quirky image she'd cultivated over the years. If you wanted to get ahead in the hushed and dusty corridors of curatorial academia without waiting to be as old as the exhibits themselves, it paid to get noticed. She certainly wasn't about to tone things down now. After all, this was a $10 million acquisition and the *Los Angeles Times* would be taking pictures.

The small group of donors, experts and journalists that she and the director had hand picked for this private viewing to gather maximum pre-launch coverage was gathered expectantly in the auditorium. The figure had been draped in a black cloth and placed in the middle of the floor so that people had to circle round it. Snatching a glass of Laurent-Perrier Rosé from a tray at the door, Verity swept inside and began to work the room, shaking the hands of some, kissing the cheeks of others.

'Ladies and gentlemen . . .' The director had stepped into the middle of the room. 'Ladies and gentlemen, if I could have your attention, please,' he called, ushering the audience closer. The lights dimmed. 'Today marks the culmination of a remarkable journey that began over two thousand five hundred years ago in ancient Greece. A journey that ends here, in Malibu. Because today, I am delighted to unveil the Getty Villa's latest acquisition, in my opinion one of the most important works of art to enter the United States since the Second World War.'

With a flourish, the cloth slipped to the floor. Under a lone spotlight stood a seven-foot-tall marble sculpture of a young boy, his left foot forward, arms at his sides, head and eyes looking straight ahead. There was a ripple of appreciative, even shocked recognition.

Verity stepped forward. 'This uniquely preserved example of a Greek kouros has been dated to around 540 BC,' she began, standing on the other side of the statue from the director. 'As many of you know, although inspired by the god Apollo, a kouros was not intended to represent an individual youth but the *idea* of youth itself, and was used in ancient Greece both as a dedication to the gods in sanctuaries and as a funerary monument. Our tests show that this example has been hewn from dolomite marble from the Cape Vathy quarry on the island of Thassos.'

She continued in her usual authoritative style, enjoying herself more and more as she got into her stride: its provenance from the private collection of a Swiss physician; the exhaustive scientific tests that had revealed a thin film of calcite coating its surface resulting from hundreds, if not thousands of years of natural lichen growth; the stylistic features linking it to the Anavyssos Youth in the National Museum in Athens. In short, a masterpiece.

Her speech drew to a close. Acknowledging the applause with a nod, she retreated to allow people forward for a closer look.

At first all went well, a few people nodding appreciatively at the sculpture's elegant lines, others seeking her out to offer muted words of congratulations. But then she sensed the mood darkening as a few of the guests eyed the statue with a strange look and whispered excitedly to each other.

Thierry Normand from the Ecole Française d'Athènes was the first to break ranks. 'Doesn't the use of Thassian marble strike you as anomalous?'

'And what about the absence of paint?' Eleanor Grant from the University of Chicago added. 'As far as I know, all other kouroi, with the possible exception of the Melos kouros, show traces of paint.'

'Well, of course we considered—' Verity began with a weak smile, forcing herself not to sound defensive.

'I'm sorry, Verity,' Sir John Sykes, Lincoln professor of classical archaeology and art at Oxford University, interrupted. 'It just isn't right. The hair is pure early sixth-century BC, as you say, but the face and abdomen are clearly much later. And I've only seen feet and a base like that in Boeotia. The science can only tell you so much. You have to rely on the aesthetics, on what you can see. To me, this is almost verging on pastiche.'

'Well, I'm sorry, Sir John, but we couldn't disagree more . . .' Verity began angrily, looking to the director for support.

'Actually, Sir John, the word I'd use,' Professor Vivienne Foyle of the Institute of Fine Arts at New York University added, 'is *fresh*.'

The loaded meaning of the word was clear. Foyle was suggesting that the statue was in fact a forgery. Verity was reeling, but the mood in the room was now such that she knew she had no chance of sensibly arguing her case.

The interrogation continued. How was it that such an exceptional piece had only surfaced now? What due diligence had been carried out on its provenance? She barely heard them, her ears filled with the dull pulse of her mounting rage. She nodded and smiled and shrugged at what seemed opportune moments, not trusting herself to open her mouth without swearing. A further ten minutes of this torture had to be endured before the director finally saw fit to bring an end to her ordeal.

'Fresh? I'll give that senile old bitch fresh,' she muttered angrily as she stalked back to her office. 'Sonya?'

'I'm Cynthia,' the PR girl chirped, skipping to keep up with her.

'Whatever. Get me Earl Faulks on the phone. I don't care where he is. I don't care what he's doing. Just get him for me. In fact, I don't want to speak to him, I want to see him. Here. Tomorrow.'

Over Nebraska

Kezman's private jet was a potent introduction to the Vegas experience: snow-white leather seats, leopard-skin carpets, mahogany panelling the

length of the cabin like the interior of a prewar liner, a small glass bar lit
with blue neon. At the front, over the cockpit door, hung a photo of
Kezman, all teeth and tan, gazing down on them benevolently.

Tom, lost in thought, had immediately settled back into his seat, politely
declining the offer of a drink from the stewardess. Head turned to the
window, gaze fixed on some distant point on the horizon, he barely noticed
the plane take off, let alone Jennifer move to the seat opposite him.

'You're still wearing it, then?' she asked, head tilted to one side so that
her curling mass of black hair covered the top of her right shoulder. Five
feet nine, slim with milky brown skin, she had lustrous hazel eyes and was
wearing her usual office camouflage of black trouser suit and cream silk
blouse.

He glanced down at the 1934 stainless-steel Brancard Rolex Prince on
his wrist. It had been a gift from the FBI for Tom's help on the first case he'd
worked on with Jennifer, although Tom suspected that the decision to offer
it to him, and the choice of watch, had been all hers.

'Why?' He turned to face her with a smile. 'Do you want it back?'

'Not unless you're having second thoughts.'

'Should I be?'

'You just seem a bit . . . distracted,' she ventured.

'Not really. I guess I was just thinking about today.'

'About your grandfather?'

'About some of the people there. About my family, or what's left of it.
About how little I know them and they know me.'

'You're a difficult person to get to know, Tom,' she said gently.

'Even for you?' He turned back to her with a hopeful smile.

'Maybe especially for me,' she shot back, an edge to her voice that was at
once resigned and accusing.

He understood what she meant, although she had got closer to him than
most over the years. Not that things had started well between them when
they had first met, necessity strong-arming their initial instinctive mutual
suspicion into a fragile working relationship. Yet from this unpromising
beginning a friendship had slowly evolved, until their growing attraction for
each other had found its voice in one unplanned night together.

Since then, the intervening years and a subsequent case had given them
both the opportunity at different times to try and revive those feelings and
build on that night. But for whatever reason, the other person had never
quite been in the same place—Tom initially unwilling to open up, Jennifer

subsequently worried about getting hurt. Even so, the memory had left its mark on both of them.

'How have you been?' Tom asked, deliberately moving the focus of the conversation away from himself. Jennifer glanced over his shoulder before answering. Stokes was asleep, his head lolling onto his shoulder.

'Were you annoyed I came?' She answered with a question of her own.

'I was disappointed you didn't come alone,' he admitted.

'This is Stokes's case,' she said with an apologetic shrug. 'I couldn't have come without him.'

'That's not what I meant.'

'You should have told me you were coming.'

'I didn't know I was until I was on the plane,' he protested.

'You could have called,' she insisted.

'Would you have called me if you hadn't needed my help?'

'Probably not,' she conceded.

It was strange, Tom mused. They weren't dating, hadn't spoken in almost a year, and yet they seemed to be locked into a lovers' awkward conversation, both of them fumbling around what they really wanted to say.

There was a long silence.

'What do you know about the painting?' Tom picked up the photo from the table between them and studied it through the plastic.

'It was one of four that Caravaggio completed in Sicily in 1609. We have it down as being worth twenty million dollars, but it would go for much more.'

'What about the theft itself?'

'October the 16th, 1969. The crime reports say that the thieves cut it out of its frame over the altar of the Oratory of San Lorenzo in Palermo with razor blades and escaped in a truck. Probably a three-man team. At the time, people blamed the Mafia.'

'It's always looked to me like an amateur job,' Tom replied with a shake of his head. 'Local crooks who'd thought through everything except how they were going to sell it. If the Sicilian Mafia have got it now, it's because no one else was buying or because they decided to just take it.'

'And no one's ever seen it since.'

'I've heard rumours over the years,' Tom sighed. 'That it had surfaced in Rome, or maybe even been destroyed in the Naples earthquake in 1980.'

'What do you think?'

'If you ask me, it's been with the Mafia the whole time. Probably traded between *capos* as a gift or part payment on a deal.'

'Which would mean that the Mafia are behind the sale now?'

'If not, then someone who has stolen it from them. Either way, they'll be dangerous. If we're lucky, they'll just run if they smell trouble. If we're not, they'll start shooting.' A pause. 'That's why I came.'

'I can look after myself,' she said pointedly, irritated, it seemed, by what he was implying. 'I didn't ask you here to watch my back.'

'I'm here because I know how these people think,' Tom insisted. 'And the only back that will need watching is mine.'

Amalfi Hotel and Casino, Las Vegas

Ever since going freelance, Kyle Foster had never met or even spoken to his handler. It was safer that way. For both of them. Besides, all he needed was a name, a photograph and 50 per cent of his fee in his Cayman Islands account. Why complicate things with a face or a voice when he could just email the details through?

His PDA vibrated on the table in front of him, breaking into his thoughts. He sat forward, muting the TV so he could concentrate on the message.

Beneath a photo was a simple message: *Target confirmed arriving LAS tonight. Terminate with extreme prejudice.*

Good, he thought, climbing onto the bed. He hated being kept waiting, especially now the minibar was running dry and he'd cycled through the porn channels.

Unscrewing the ceiling grille, he lifted down the US Navy Mark 12 Special Purpose Rifle from where he'd hidden it inside the duct and began to disassemble it. Laying a hotel hand-towel down next to the parts, he carefully arranged the pieces on it and then rolled it into a bundle and placed it in his backpack.

McCarran International Airport, Las Vegas

'Kezman's laying it on pretty thick,' Tom observed as the plane taxied to a halt. A stretched white Hummer was waiting to greet them, its neon undercarriage staining the apron blue. 'First the jet. Now this. What does he want?'

'A friendly word with the Nevada Gaming Control Board,' Stokes growled, as he pushed past Tom and stepped through the doorway. An unmarked FBI escort vehicle was drawn up behind the limo and he gestured at them to follow. 'One of his pit bosses was caught dealing ecstasy to some college kids and he doesn't want to lose his gaming licence.'

An envelope was waiting for them on the white leather seat, together with three glasses and a bottle of Cristal on ice. To Jennifer's surprise, it was addressed to her. She opened it with a puzzled frown.

'Status update from my other case,' she explained as she flicked through it, guessing that someone in the escort vehicle must have been entrusted with it to pass on to her. Nodding, Stokes shuffled further along the seat towards the driver and reached for his phone.

'Bad news?' Tom asked eventually. 'Anything I can help with?'

She paused, her eyes locked with his. Discussing a live investigation with a civilian wasn't exactly standard procedure but she had learned to value his opinion. Besides, who would know? Certainly not Stokes, whom she could overhear noisily checking on the money.

'A few weeks ago the Customs boys in Norfolk got a tip-off about a shipment of car parts out of Hamburg,' she began. 'When they opened the container everything looked fine, but something weird showed up on the X-ray.'

'A marzipan layer?' Tom guessed.

'Exactly. Car parts stacked at the front and round the sides. A smaller crate hidden in the middle filled with furniture.'

'Furniture?' Tom frowned.

'Eileen Gray. Ten to fifteen million dollars' worth.'

Tom whistled. Eileen Gray art deco furniture was as rare as it was expensive.

'They boxed it back up and then followed the shipment via a freight-forwarding service to an Italian art dealer in Queens. He started squealing the minute they kicked down the door. He thought they were a hit squad. I don't think anyone's ever been so relieved to see a badge. It turns out that he's been smuggling pieces for a high-end antiquities trafficking ring for years. The furniture was a little side deal he'd cooked up for himself. He thought they'd found out.'

'What sort of antiquities?' Tom asked.

'Statues, vases, plates, jewellery, even entire frescoes. Most of it illegally excavated from Roman and Etruscan tombs. That's when they called me in.'

'My mother used to be an antiquities dealer,' Tom sighed. 'I remember her once describing grave-robbing as the world's second oldest profession.'

'You're talking about tomb robbers?'

Tom nodded. 'In Italy they call them *tombaroli*, in Peru *huaceros*.

Mexico, Cambodia, China, Iraq. As long as there are people prepared to buy pieces without asking difficult questions about where they've come from, there'll be others only too happy to dig them up. But Italy is ground zero, the *Terra Santa* of the tomb-robbing world. It's got over forty UNESCO World Heritage Sites and the remains of about five different civilisations.' A pause. 'Did your guy ID any of his buyers?'

She gave a firm shake of her head. 'His job was to get the stuff through Customs. He never had any idea where it was coming from or going to. But he did give us another name. Someone in the organisation who had broken cover a few weeks before, looking to bring something across. We passed it on to the Italians and they said they'd check him out. The State Department's been working on them to make sure they keep us in the loop, but they're playing hard to get.'

'Does this outfit have a name?'

'We're not sure. When we went through his trash, we found two bags of shredded paper. Most of it was unusable, but the lab guys were able to piece together one yellow sheet, because the coloured strips stood out from everything else. It was mainly covered in doodles but in one corner he'd written the words Delian League and then sketched out a sort of symbol underneath. Two snakes wrapped round a clenched fist.'

'Means nothing to me.' Tom shook his head.

'Well, it means something to him because he's clammed up since we showed it to him. Won't even talk to his attorney. But we found his bank records too and I think that the Delian League is—'

She broke off as Stokes ended his call and shuffled back towards them.

'The money's ready. Las Vegas and Metro are playing ball. Looks like we're all set.'

They turned onto Las Vegas Boulevard, a grinning cowboy on an overhead billboard welcoming them to the home of the seven-day weekend. The different hotel resorts galloped past in a single garish streak of light, like an overexposed photograph of a merry-go-round.

'We're here,' Stokes called as the limo turned in under a monumental arch topped by two rearing lions.

Despite its name, the Amalfi seemed to have been inspired by Florentine rather than Neapolitan architecture, although rendered on such a scale as to make the Duomo look like a concession stand. It was the Palazzo Strozzi on steroids, a massive, fortress-like structure made from Indiana limestone and Ohio sandstone.

Rather than pull round to the covered main entrance, their car headed to the left and then dipped into an underground car park.

'The high-rollers' entrance,' Stokes explained. 'Some of these guys don't want to risk getting jumped between the car and hotel.'

Tom laughed. 'They're more likely to be robbed inside than out there.'

The Pantheon, Rome

Different day. Different place. And yet it seemed to Allegra that there was something strangely familiar about the way things were playing out—the unexpected phone call. The barked summons. The police barricades across the streets. The swelling crowd. The helicopter hovering overhead. The TV crews prowling like hyenas around a kill. Her being late.

As she made her way onto the Piazza della Rotunda it started to spit with rain. The Pantheon loomed ahead of her, the classical elegance of the three rows of granite columns that supported its front portico compromised by the hulking, barrel-shaped building behind it.

Allegra walked up to the portico, stooping under the police tape that had been strung between the columns, and made her way inside the rotunda, her shoes squeaking on the ancient marble. Almost immediately she paused, her eyes drawn to the pale beam of the helicopter's searchlight funnelled through the circular opening at the apex of the dome. A slanting column of light had formed between the ceiling and the altar, sparks of rain fluttering around it like fireflies trapped in a glass jar.

'Are you coming in, or just going to stand there like a retard?' Salvatore sounded even more put upon than he had yesterday.

'"Hello" would be nice.'

'You're late. And Gallo's not happy.'

'He doesn't exactly strike me as the happy type.'

He eyed her unblinkingly, looking both appalled and yet also slightly envious of her brazen tone. He gave a resigned shrug.

'Suit yourself.'

There were about fifteen, maybe even twenty people inside, some in uniform interrogating the security guards who'd been covering the night shift, others in hooded white evidence suits taking photographs or examining the floor around the altar, which was obscured by some makeshift screens. Gallo, in a suit this time, was waiting for her next to Raphael's tomb. As Salvatore had warned her, he was in a dark mood.

'Nice of you to show up.'

'Nice of you to ask me.'

Gallo paused, lips pursed, as if he couldn't quite decide if he found her insolent or amusing.

'What can you tell me about this place?' he snapped. 'Is there anything I should know about it? Anything that might tie it to last night's body?'

'The Pantheon was built by Hadrian in about 125 AD, so there's no obvious connection to Caesar, if that's what you mean,' she began with a shrug. 'Then again, although it's been a church since the seventh century, the Pantheon used to be a pagan temple, just like the ones in the Area Sacra.'

'Hardly conclusive,' Gallo sniffed.

'No,' she agreed with a firm shake of her head.

'Then what do you make of this?'

At a flick of his wrist, two forensic officers rolled away the screens. A body was lying on the altar, naked from the waist up. His bearded face was turned towards them, eyes gaping open with shock. Two gleaming white shop mannequins were standing at his head—one small and hunched, the other taller—and staring down at the corpse. Both were unclothed, with moulded blank features and no hair, although the smooth hump of their breasts marked them out as female.

The taller mannequin had been arranged so that her left hand was gripping the man's hair and the right holding a short sword embedded in a deep gash in the victim's neck. The blood had gushed from his wound, cascading to the floor where it had pooled and solidified into a brackish lake.

It was a carefully arranged, almost ritualistic scene. And one that, for a reason Allegra couldn't quite put her finger on, seemed strangely familiar.

'Who is it?'

'Don't you recognise him?' Salvatore, looking surprised, had ventured forward to her side. 'His brother's always on TV. He looks just like him.'

'Why, who's his brother?' she asked.

'Annibale Argento,' Salvatore explained. 'The Sicilian deputy. The stiff is his twin brother, Gio, otherwise known as Giulio.'

'Hannibal and Julius,' Gallo nodded. 'There's your damn Caesar connection. And we found this in his mouth.' Gallo held up a clear plastic evidence bag. She knew, almost without looking, what it contained.

Amalfi Hotel and Casino, Las Vegas

Kezman's private elevator opened on to a tennis-court-sized room, rainbows cloaking the lush tropical gardens that could be glimpsed through the open windows where floodlights shimmered through a cooling mist.

Glancing up, Tom could see that the soaring ceilings had been draped in what looked like black satin, three huge chandeliers flowering from within their luxuriant folds. The only furniture, if you could call it that, was a 1926 Hispano-Suiza H6 parked about two-thirds of the way down, a mass of gleaming chrome and polished black metal.

'You're here. Good.'

A man had come in off the balcony, a radio in one hand, a mobile phone in the other. Short and wiry, his olive skin was pockmarked by acne scars, his black hair shaved almost to his skull.

'Tom, this is Special Agent Carlos Ortiz.' They shook hands as Jennnifer introduced them. 'I've borrowed him from my other case for a few days.'

'I hope you're half as good as she says you are,' Ortiz sniffed. Tom glanced questioningly at Jennifer, who gave him an awkward shrug. 'Did you get the envelope from the State Department?'

'Yeah.' She nodded. 'Let's talk about that later. How long have we got?'

'It's set for midnight, so just under an hour,' he replied.

'Everyone's already in place,' Stokes added. 'I got six agents on the floor at the tables and playing the slots, and another four on the front and rear doors. Metro and SWAT are holding back two blocks south.'

'What about the money?' Tom asked.

'In the vault in two suitcases,' Stokes reassured him. 'Unmarked, non-sequential notes, just like they asked. They'll bring it out when we're ready.'

'Let's get you miked up,' Ortiz said.

He led Tom over to the car, which Tom suddenly realised had been turned into a desk, the seats ripped out and the roof and one side cut away and replaced with a black marble slab.

'I guess rich people are always looking for new ways to spend their money, right?' Ortiz winked.

He removed a small transmitter unit from the briefcase and helped Tom fix it to his inner thigh, hiding the microphone under his shirt.

'If anyone finds that, they're looking for a date not a wire,' Ortiz joked once he was happy that it was secure and working. He checked his watch. 'Let's go. Kezman asked to see you downstairs before we hit the floor.'

They stepped back inside the elevator and it headed down automatically, stopping at the mezzanine level, close to the Amalfi's private art gallery.

'He suggested we wait for him inside,' Ortiz said, nodding at the two security guards posted either side of the entrance as he walked past.

The gallery consisted of a series of rooms containing twenty or so paintings, as well as a number of small abstract sculptures. It was an impressive collection, bringing to mind the recent newspaper headlines when Kezman had broken his own auction record for the highest amount ever paid for a painting. Tom's eyes sought out the Picasso he'd bought on that occasion in amongst the works by Cézanne, Gauguin, Van Gogh and Matisse.

'What do you know about him?' Tom asked.

'He's rich and he's smart,' Jennifer replied. 'In thirty years he's gone from running a diner in Jersey to being the biggest player on the Strip.'

'As well as the Amalfi, he owns three other places in Vegas, two in Atlantic City and one in Macau,' Stokes added.

'And he's clean?' Tom asked.

'As anyone can be in this town,' Stokes replied with a smile. 'He mixes with a pretty colourful crowd, but so far he seems to check out.'

'He used to collect cars, but art is his new passion now,' Jennifer added. 'He's become a major donor to both the Met and the Getty.'

'Which is your favourite?'

Kezman had breezed into the room wearing sunglasses, a gleaming white smile and a tuxedo. He was closely flanked by an unsmiling male assistant clutching a briefcase.

Kezman was in his mid-fifties or thereabouts, and shorter than Tom had expected. The photo on his jet had clearly been taken several years before, his brown hair now receding and greying at the temples. The energy in his voice and movements, however, was undimmed; his weight shifted from foot to foot like a boxer, his head jerking erratically as he looked around the room. He answered his own question before anyone else had a chance to respond.

'Mine's the Picasso, and not just because I paid a hundred and thirty-nine million dollars for it. He was a genius. A self-made man. A visionary.'

Tom smiled. It was hard to know whether Kezman was talking about himself or Picasso.

'Mr Kezman, this is—'

'Tom Kirk, I know.' He grinned. 'Luckily the FBI doesn't have a monopoly on information. At least not yet. I like to know who's on my plane.'

Tom stepped forward to shake his hand, but Kezman waved him back.

'Stay where I can see you, goddammit,' he barked.

Tom suddenly understood why Kezman was wearing sunglasses and moving his head so erratically—he was blind, or very nearly so. His aide was presumably there to help steer him in the right direction as he navigated through the hotel.

'Retinitis pigmentosa,' Kezman confirmed. 'The closer I get to things, the less I can see. And one day even that . . .' His voice tailed off.

'I'm sorry,' Tom said. He didn't know him, but he meant it all the same.

'Why? It's not your fault,' Kezman shrugged. 'Besides, in a way, it's a gift. After all, would I have started my collection if I hadn't known I was going blind? Sometimes, it's only when you are about to lose something that you really begin to understand what it's worth.'

There was a silence, which Ortiz broke with a forced cough. 'As I have discussed with your head of security, the plan is for Mr Kirk to take the money down to the casino floor and wait there for them to make contact.'

'It's unlikely they'll bring the painting with them,' Jennifer added. 'So we expect them to either provide us with a location, which we will then check out before handing over the money, or lead us to it so that we can make the exchange there.'

'Either way, we'll follow them to make sure we grab them, the painting and the money,' Stokes said confidently. 'Once again, Mr Kezman, the government is very grateful for your cooperation in this matter . . .'

'Don't mention it.' Kezman waved Stokes's thanks away with a sweep of his hand. 'You just make sure no one gets hurt.'

IT WAS FUNNY HOW people conditioned themselves to only ever see what they wanted to, Foster mused. Ask anyone who wears a watch with Roman numerals how the number four is written on it and they'll say IV. All those years that they've been looking at it, checking the time, and they've never actually noticed that it's IIII. That it's always IIII on a watch, because IV would be too easily confused with VI. That their brains have tricked them into seeing what they expect to. It was pathetic really.

Like tonight. The security detail at the staff entrance of the casino had barely glanced at his badly fitting uniform and tampered badge before waving him through. He looked the part, so why see something that you've convinced yourself isn't there? He, on the other hand, had immediately picked out the FBI agents as they loitered near the entrance or perched unconvincingly in front of the slot machines.

He stopped next to an anonymous-looking red door. Quickly picking the locks, he opened the door on to a dimly lit stairwell that he slipped into, wedging a fire extinguisher between the base of the door and the bottom step of the metal staircase to stop anyone coming in after him. The staircase led up to the observation deck—a series of cramped, interconnecting gantries hidden in the ceiling void that stretched over the entire casino floor.

Although in theory these were to allow maintenance staff to service the casino's complex lighting grid and vast network of air-conditioning ducts, the careful positioning of two-way mirrors and air vents also allowed casino security to spy on people.

As Foster had expected, the gantries were empty. He took up his position, removed the rolled-up towel from his backpack, and unrolled it. Piece by piece he began to reassemble his rifle, the parts sliding into place with a satisfying click. With the infrared sight fitted he hesitated momentarily, toying with the suppressor before slipping it into his top pocket.

No suppressor. Not tonight. He wanted everyone to hear the shot, to be paralysed by its angry roar, and then to run. To run screaming.

The Pantheon, Rome

Allegra was sheltering in the portico, grateful for the coffee Salvatore had conjured up for her and for the fresh air.

'So it's the same coin?' Gallo materialised at her side.

'It's the same.' She nodded.

'So it's the same killer?'

'There are some obvious similarities,' she began hesitantly, surprised that Gallo even cared what she thought. 'The lead discs. The proximity of the two murder scenes. The pagan temples. The connection to Caesar. But . . . the way they were killed. I'm not a profiler, but there's no consistency between the two murders. They look different. They feel different.'

'I agree. Two murders. Two killers.' Gallo held up photographs of the two crime scenes side by side as if to prove his point.

Allegra glanced at the photos and jumped. There was something in the crime scenes, something she'd not noticed before, but which, when framed within the photographs' white borders, was now glaringly obvious.

'Where's your car?'

'Over there—' He pointed out a dark blue BMW.

'Come on!' She stepped out into the rain, then turned and motioned impatiently at him to follow when she realised he hadn't moved.

'Where to?'

'The Palazzo Barberini,' she said.

A few moments later, Gallo gunned out of the square down the Via del

Seminario, the Carabinieri clearing a path for him through the crowd. As soon as they were clear, he accelerated, siren blazing as he carved his way through the rush-hour traffic to the main entrance at the top of the hill. The drive was chained off, although the Galleria Nazionale d'Arte Antica, the museum that occupied the former papal residence, was clearly open.

'Damn these peasants,' Gallo muttered, leaning on his horn, until a guard appeared and let them through.

They lurched forward, the gravel spitting out from under their tyres as they shot round to the far side of the fountain.

'First floor,' Allegra called as she jumped out and headed through the arched entrance.

'Police,' Gallo called, waving his badge at the astonished museum staff.

Allegra sprinted through first one room, then another, her eyes skipping over the paintings, not entirely sure where it was, but knowing it was here somewhere. Filippo Lippi, Piero di Cosimo . . . no, not here. Next room. Tintoretto, Bronzino . . . still nothing. Carry on through. Guercino . . .

'There,' she called triumphantly, pointing at the wall.

'*Ammazza!*' Gallo swore, stepping past her for a closer look.

The large painting showed a bearded man being decapitated by a woman, a sword in her right hand, his hair firmly gripped in her left. He was naked, his face contorted into a scream, the blood spurting onto a white sheet. Next to the woman stood an old woman, her hands gripping the hem of her mistress's dress to keep it clear of the blood.

Gallo held the photograph of the Pantheon crime scene up next to it. There was no question it had been staged to mirror the painting.

'*Judith and Holofernes*,' Allegra said slowly. 'It was only when I saw the photos that I made the connection.'

'And Ricci?'

'*The Crucifixion of Saint Peter* in the Cerasi Chapel in Santa Maria del Popolo,' she confirmed. 'That's what links your two murders, Colonel. The killers are re-enacting scenes from Caravaggio paintings.'

Amalfi Hotel and Casino, Las Vegas

Tom had insisted on getting down onto the floor early, guessing that whoever had been sent to meet him would already be in position and that it would help if it looked as though he was keen to do the deal. And it gave them a chance to see the money. It was at Tom's feet now—$20 million in cash, neatly packed into two aluminium suitcases.

He looked around the blinking, cavernous floor to get his bearings. The place was packed. He spotted Jennifer at the bar to his left, nursing a soft drink. Ortiz, meanwhile, was to his right, pretending to play video poker and losing badly. Stokes, he knew, was in the back with the casino's head of security, watching the screens and coordinating the other agents. In front of him was a roulette table, where the animated abandon with which a noticeably younger crowd was flinging chips onto the baize contrasted with the silent, mesmerised application of the older people on the slots.

There. A man with his back to him at the neighbouring blackjack table, his head snapping back a little too fast to suggest the glance he had just given him had been accidental. And again, only this time he didn't break eye contact. He knew Tom had seen him. He was getting up. This was it.

'Blackjack table,' Tom muttered into his mike. 'White hair, black . . .' His voice tailed off as the man turned round and nodded.

Dressed in a black suit, he was about five feet ten with a curling mop of white hair and a farmer's sun-blushed cheeks. But it was the white band encircling his neck that had drawn Tom's attention.

'He's a priest,' Tom breathed in disbelief, as much to himself as anyone.

As the man advanced towards him, Tom was reassured that, as Jennifer had predicted, he wasn't carrying anything that might have contained the painting. That would have marked him and whoever he was working for as amateurs, and amateurs were unpredictable and more easily spooked. Instead, slung over his left shoulder was a tired leather satchel.

They met in the middle of the main aisle. Saying nothing, the priest reached into his bag and handed Tom a series of photographs. They showed the *Nativity*, but in more detail this time, with close-ups of the faces and hands, always the hardest things to paint. From what Tom could tell, the brushwork looked genuine, and although the canvas had been slightly damaged over the years, overall the condition was very good.

There was no sign of a signature, but Tom took that as further proof of the painting's probable authenticity. As far as he knew, Caravaggio had only ever signed one painting, *The Beheading of the Baptist*, where he had marked an M for Merisi, his family name, in the blood spilling from John the Baptist's neck.

'I need to see it,' Tom said.

'Is that the money?' the priest replied, Tom detecting an Italian accent.

'Twenty million dollars,' he confirmed, tapping a case with his foot.

'*Bene, bene.*' The priest nodded. 'Good.' There was an anxious edge to the man's voice that surprised Tom. For a pro he seemed a little tense.

'I need to see the painting first,' Tom reminded him.

'Of course,' the priest said. 'It's not far. You have a car?'

'The money's going nowhere until I see the painting,' Tom warned him.

'Don't worry,' the priest immediately reassured him. 'We have a deal. You have the money, I have the painting, we have a deal, yes?'

'We have a deal,' Tom agreed.

'You want this painting, yes?'

'As much as you want the money,' Tom answered with a puzzled smile. It was a strange question. Why else would he be there? 'My car's in the garage.'

'It has been a long time. You will be the first, the first in many years to see it.' His eyes flicked over Tom's shoulder as he spoke and then back again. 'It is still beautiful, despite everything it has been through.'

Tom felt his stomach tightening. Something wasn't right. First a hint of nervousness. Now an abrupt shift from urgency to an almost languid calm as if . . . as if he was trying to waste time so that somewhere else—

A shot rang out, its whiplash crack cutting through the casino's raucous din. Tom staggered back, the world suddenly slowing, as if someone was holding the movie projector to stop the reel from turning. There was a terrified scream, one voice triggering another and that one two more until a sustained, shrieking lament filled the air.

Tom glanced instinctively to his left. Jennifer was lying on the floor. Her blouse was blotted poppy red.

Institute for Religious Works, Via della Stazione Vaticana, Rome

As the six men opposite him bowed their heads, Antonio Santos picked up his spoon and studied the hallmarks. To the left he recognised the symbol of the Papal State, and next to it the initials NL—Lorenzini Nicola, an Italian silversmith active in the mid-eighteenth century, if he wasn't mistaken.

'*Nos miseri homines et egeni, pro cibis quos nobis ad corporis subsidium benigne es largitus . . .*' Archbishop Ancelotti intoned grace, his voice rising and falling as if he was reciting some mediaeval incantation. ' . . . *Per Jesum Christum Dominum nostrum. Amen.*'

'Amen,' Santos agreed enthusiastically.

Ancelotti looked up and nodded at the two young priests standing near the door to serve breakfast. He was wearing a black simar with amaranth-red piping and buttons together with a purple fascia and zucchetto.

A large gold pectoral cross dangled from his neck. The other five men sitting either side of him were similarly dressed, although, as cardinals, their buttons, sashes and skullcaps were scarlet.

'Thank you for coming, Antonio,' Ancelotti said. 'I apologise for the short notice.'

'Not at all, Your Grace,' Santos said with a generous shrug, holding his hand over his coffee as one of the priests went to add cream. 'I apologise for being late. The Carabinieri seem to have closed off half the city. My driver told me that they've found a body in the Pantheon.'

'Dear, dear,' Ancelotti tutted. 'We live in such wicked times. Jam?'

'No, thank you.' Santos gave a tight smile. 'I don't eat breakfast.'

'You should, you should,' Ancelotti admonished him. 'Most important meal of the day. Now, does everyone have what they need?'

Seeing that they did, he waved at the two priests to retire to the outer room, then turned back to face Santos.

'I believe you know everyone here?'

He nodded. Cardinals Villot, Neuman, Simoes, Pisani and Carter. The Oversight Commission of the Istituto per le Opere di Religione. The Vatican Bank.

'Your eminences,' he said, bowing his head.

'Antonio, we asked you here today in our capacity as the largest shareholder in the Banco Rosalia,' Ancelotti began.

'Largest and most important shareholder,' Santos added generously, sipping his coffee. 'We are, after all, working to help finance God's work.'

'Ah, yes, God's work.' Ancelotti clasped his hands together as if in prayer. 'Which is, as I'm sure you understand, why we need to be especially vigilant.'

'I'm not sure I do understand, Your Grace,' Santos said with a frown, placing his cup back down on the table. 'Vigilant for what?'

'For anything that could harm the reputation of the Church, of course.'

'Your year-end accounts are almost a month overdue,' Cardinal Villot said in an accusing tone.

'As I've already explained to Archbishop Ancelotti, there are a number of small, purely technical matters that the auditors have . . .'

'We've also heard your liquidity position's deteriorated,' Cardinal Carter added, his voice equally sharp.

'Not to mention the provisions on your real-estate portfolio,' Cardinal Neuman chimed.

Santos took a deep breath. 'A number of banks have withdrawn their funding lines, yes, but that's to be expected with the squeeze that the whole market is feeling. We still have more than enough headroom, given our deposit and capital base.'

'I think what we're suggesting is that a short, sharp financial review would help allay our concerns,' Ancelotti said in a gentle tone.

'What sort of a financial review?'

'We'd probably start with a quick canter through your latest management accounts and bank statements,' Ancelotti said breezily. 'We have a small team of accountants we like to use for this sort of thing. They'll be in and out in a few weeks. You won't even notice they're there.'

A pause. 'When would you like them to start?'

'Is the day after tomorrow too soon?' Ancelotti asked. Santos noticed that the archibishop's eyes were locked on to his, as if to gauge his reaction.

'Of course not,' Santos replied with a confident smile. 'That gives me enough time to brief the team so that we can make sure that we have a room set aside and all the documentation prepared.'

'Excellent, excellent.' Ancelotti stood up to signal that the meeting was over and leaned across the table to shake his hand. 'I knew you'd understand.'

A few minutes later Santos was down on the street in the rain, angrily loosening his collar as he flicked a tin open and pushed one, then two pieces of liquorice into his mouth. Then he reached for his phone.

'We're fucked,' he barked into it the moment it was answered. 'Ancelotti and his performing monkeys want to audit the bank . . . I don't know what they know, but they must know something, and even if they don't, it won't take more than a few days for them to figure everything out . . . I need to bail. How much would I have if I liquidated everything? . . . Is that it?' He swore angrily, earning himself a disapproving look from two nuns walking past. 'That's not enough,' he continued. 'Hold on, I've got another call.' He switched lines. '*Pronto?*'

'It's done,' a voice rasped.

'Are you sure?' Santos sheltered inside a doorway.

'It's done,' the voice repeated. The line went dead.

Smiling, Santos went to switch back to the first caller before pausing, a thought occurring to him. He helped himself to more liquorice as the idea slowly took shape. It had only ever been part of the set-up, but why not? The trick was getting to it, but if he could . . . the Serbians would take it off his hands. They were always in the market for that sort of thing.

Amalfi Hotel and Casino, Las Vegas

Kicking their stools out from under them, people began to run, half-drunk cocktails collapsing to the floor and neatly stacked piles of chips swooning onto the baize as gamblers clambered over each other.

Tom fought his way across to Jennifer, Ortiz a few feet behind him. She was still alive, thank God, her eyes wide with shock, but still alive. He ripped her blouse open, saw the blood frothing from under her left breast.

'It's OK,' Tom reassured her, leaning close so she could hear him. She nodded, lifted her head as if to speak, then fell back.

'Where's she hit?' Ortiz fell onto his knees next to him as the fire alarm sounded.

'Get an ambulance here,' Tom shouted back over the noise, ripping his jacket off and folding it into a makeshift pillow. 'Press down.' He grabbed Ortiz's hand and jammed it hard against the wound, then leaned across and snatched his Beretta out from under his arm.

'Where the hell are you going?' Ortiz called after him.

'To find the shooter.'

He leapt up onto the roulette table, knowing from the location of her wound and the direction she'd been facing that the gunman must have been positioned somewhere ahead of her. Scanning the floor, he suddenly noticed a shimmer of glass under the stampeding crowd's feet. He glanced up at the ceiling and saw that a single mirrored panel was missing from its reflective surface.

Tom leapt down and grabbed a passing security guard.

'The observation deck,' Tom shouted. 'How do I get up there?'

The guard paused, transfixed by the gun in Tom's left hand, then pointed unsteadily at a set of double doors on the other side of the floor.

'Through there,' he stuttered.

Snatching the guard's security pass off his belt, Tom fought his way through to the doors he had indicated and swiped them open. He found himself in a long, white service corridor lit by overhead strip lighting and lined on both sides by a series of identical red doors. A steady stream of people were half walking, half running towards him—casino staff ordered to evacuate the building, judging from their identical red Mao jackets.

Tom walked against the flow, scanning for a pair of shoes, or a uniform, or a face that didn't quite fit. Ahead of him, about two-thirds of the way down the corridor, a door opened and a man wearing a baseball cap stepped out. Tom noticed him immediately. It was his studied calmness that gave him away. His calmness and the detached expression on his face.

He seemed to notice Tom at almost the same time because, grimacing, he turned and retreated back inside, locking the door behind him. Tom sprinted down the corridor after him, tried the handle and then stepped back and pumped four shots into the locks. With a kick, the door splintered open.

Carefully covering the angles above him, Tom made his way up the stairs into the shadows of the observation deck, his eyes adjusting to the darkness. He felt the shooter before he saw him, the metal walkways shuddering under his heavy step as he sprinted away along the gantries. Tom took aim and fired three times, then twice more, a couple of the bullets sparking brightly where they struck the steel supports. But the man barely broke his stride, turning sharply to his left and then to his right.

Tom set off after him. Up ahead the gunman paused and then in an instant was over the side of the gantry and dangling down over the suspended ceiling below. Tom again took aim, and fired twice, this time catching the gunman in his shoulder. With a pained yell he let go, crashing through the mirrored ceiling and vanishing from sight.

Tom sprinted across to the same point and then lowered himself down as far as he could before dropping through the hole onto a blackjack table.

'Where did he go?' he asked the dealer, who was staring at him open-mouthed.

The man pointed dumbly towards the exit. Tom looked up and saw the gunman almost at the door. Tom again pulled the trigger, the bullet skimming the man's head. Tom leapt down and followed the gunman outside, determined not to lose him. But rather than melt away into the panicked crowd that had swamped the forecourt, the man seemed to be waiting for him. For an instant, they stood about twenty feet apart, their eyes locked. Tom, his gun raised, finger-tested the trigger spring's resistance. But before he could take the shot, a hand gripped his arm and pulled him back.

'Not here,' Stokes yelled. 'Are you crazy? You'll hit someone.'

Tom angrily shook him off, took aim and fired. The gun clicked, empty. With a wink, the killer turned and dived into the frothing sea of people. In an instant, he was gone.

'Where's the back-up? They need to set up a perimeter,' Tom ordered.

'It's a little late for that.' Stokes shrugged helplessly at the mob that had spilled out onto the Strip, bringing the traffic to a standstill as they surged across the road, trying to get as far away from the Amalfi as they could.

Tom glared resentfully at the crowd, wanting Stokes to be wrong but knowing he wasn't. What made it worse was that the gunman had played him. He'd seen Tom was carrying a Beretta, counted the shots until he'd known it was empty, then waited for him. Taunted him.

Tom's thoughts snapped back to Jennifer. 'How is she?'

'The paramedics are with her now,' Stokes reassured him, before lowering his gaze. 'She's lost a lot of blood. They're taking her up onto the roof for a medevac.'

'Get me up there,' Tom barked.

They ran back into the casino and, using the card Tom had taken from the security guard, rode up to the top floor.

'What happened to the priest?' Tom asked as the levels pinged past.

'We lost him too,' Stokes admitted. 'Soon as everyone started running, he vanished. The money's safe, though.'

'You think I give a shit about the money?' Tom hissed.

The doors opened and they sprinted up the final two flights of the service staircase to a metal door that Tom swiped open. The helicopter was already there. Jennifer was being loaded into the rear by two paramedics, a drip attached to her arm and an oxygen mask over her face. Ortiz was crouching on the ground, his shirt covered in her blood, his head in his hands.

'I'm going with her,' Tom shouted over the throb of the engines.

Head down, he sprinted across the pad and hauled himself in behind the stretcher, slamming the door shut after him. The pitch of the engines deepened as the pilot throttled up and with a lurch they rose into the sky.

'How is she?' Tom called to one of the medics as they hooked her up to a mobile ECG, her pulse registering with a green blip on the screen and a sharp tone—Beep . . . beep . . . beep.

'She's lost a lot of blood . . . we need to get her into theatre a.s.a.p.'

'Is she conscious?'

'In and out. Try talking to her. Keep her awake.'

Tom shuffled forward until he was sitting next to Jennifer's head. Her eyes flickered open and he was certain that he saw a smile of recognition tremble across her face.

'Hold on, Jen,' he whispered. 'We'll be there soon.'

She nodded weakly. He brushed the hair out of her eyes.

'You're going to be OK. I'll make sure you're OK.'

He smiled at her reassuringly. He felt her hand reach for his and press something hard and rectangular into it, her grip tightening as she pulled him closer, her mouth moving under the oxygen mask. He bent over her, straining to hear her voice. He caught something, the fragment of a word, perhaps more, and then her eyes closed again and her grip loosened, allowing him to slip what she had given him into his pocket.

'Come on, Jen,' Tom called, shaking her arm gently at first and then with increasing urgency. 'We're nearly there now. You're going to be OK. You just need to keep listening to me. Listen to my voice.'

But there was no reaction and all he could hear was the gradual, almost imperceptible lengthening of the gaps between each tone of the ECG.

'Help her,' Tom shouted angrily to the paramedics. 'Do something.'

They swapped a glance, one of them wiping the back of his hand across his brow. 'We've done what we can.'

Tom leaned forward, his lips brushing against her cheek.

'Stay with me,' he whispered.

For a second he could have sworn that her breathing quickened. Then the machine gave a piercing shriek. The monitor showed a perfectly flat line.

PART TWO

Via Luigi Galvani, Testaccio, Rome

The speaker crackled into life. '*Mitto tibi navem prora puppique carentem.*'

Allegra hesitated. She understood the Latin, of course—I send you a ship lacking stern and bow. But what did it mean? How could a ship not have a stern and a bow? Unless . . . unless it was referring to something else. To the front and the back? The beginning and the end? Latin for ship was *navem*, so if it was missing its beginning and its end, its first and last letters perhaps . . .

'*Ave*,' she replied with a smile. Latin for hello.

'*Ave*, indeed,' the voice replied with a chuckle. 'Although I can't claim the credit this time. That was one of Cicero's.'

The door buzzed open and Allegra made her way to the lift, smiling. She'd first met Aurelio Eco at La Sapienza, before heading off to Columbia for her master's, where he'd been a visiting professor in the university's antiquities department. Before that, he'd spent fifteen years as the director of the Villa Giulia, Rome's foremost Etruscan museum. These posts seemed to have provided him with an inexhaustible supply of riddles, which he delighted in asking her as a condition of entry to his apartment.

As usual the door was open and the kettle boiling. She made herself a strong black coffee and Aurelio an Earl Grey tea with lemon.

He was waiting for her in his high-backed leather chair, the split in the seat covered by a red-and-white kaffiyeh purchased during an exchange posting to Jordan. His dusty office was full of such mementos—photographs of him at various digs over the decades, framed maps and faded prints, fragments of inscribed Roman tablets, shards of Etruscan pottery.

Despite his cheerfulness on the intercom, Aurelio now seemed to have sunk into what Allegra could only describe as a sulk, his bottom lip jutting out, brows furrowed.

'Maybe you shouldn't come any more,' he sighed. 'Spend time with your real friends, instead, people your own age.'

'Don't start that again,' she sighed. 'I've told you, I'm too busy to have any friends. Besides, I like old things.' She winked.

Approaching seventy, Aurelio had no family left now. Allegra had therefore taken it upon herself to look in on him whenever she knew she would be in the area.

'But you said you'd be here for lunch,' he continued. 'You're late.'

'And whose fault is that?'

He grinned, his sulk vanishing. He had a kindly face, with large light brown eyes, a beaked nose and leathered skin.

'So they did call you?' he crowed. 'The GICO wanted an antiquities expert. The university put them on to me. I told them I'd retired and recommended you instead.'

'I knew it!' she said. 'Did they tell you what they wanted?'

'Of course not. It's the GICO. They never tell you anything.'

With a deep breath, Allegra recounted the events of the past twenty-three hours. Aurelio listened intently until she had finished.

'Anything to go on?' he asked hopefully.

'Plenty. Just no idea where to start,' she sighed. 'Which reminds me. Both victims had what looked like an antique coin in their mouths.'

'To pay Charon,' Aurelio guessed immediately.

'That's what I thought. Except it wasn't a coin. It was a lead disc. I wondered if there was some other reference to the classical world.'

'Lead?' Aurelio frowned. 'That's unusual but not unprecedented,' he said. 'Can you reach that red book down for me?'

She handed the book to him and he leafed slowly through it.

'Here.' He fixed her with a knowing smile. '*Threatened by the Persian empire, several Greek states came together in the fifth century* BC *to form a military alliance under the leadership of the Athenians,*' he read. '*Members had to contribute ships or money, and in return the alliance agreed to protect their territory. Symbolically, upon joining, representatives of the member states had to throw a piece of metal into the sea.*'

'Lead,' Allegra breathed. He nodded.

'*Normally a piece of lead. The alliance was to last until it floated to the surface again.*'

There was a pause, as she reflected on this. 'And you think . . .?'

'You asked about a link between lead and the classical world.' He smiled. 'Thinking's your job.'

'What was the name of this alliance?'

'They called themselves the Delian League.'

J. Edgar Hoover Building, FBI headquarters, Washington DC

The door buzzed open. Tom didn't bother to look round. He could tell from Ortiz's shuffling steps and Stokes's heavier, wider stride who it was.

'How long are you going to keep me here?' he demanded angrily.

'A federal agent's been killed, Mr Kirk,' Stokes replied icily. He dragged a chair out from under the table and straddled it. 'So we're going to keep you here pretty much as long as we like.'

'You don't have to tell me she was killed, you pompous bastard,' Tom hissed. 'I was holding her hand when she died, remember?'

In a way he was glad that Stokes was acting like this. It gave him a reason to be angry, to give himself over to his rage. Better that than allow his sadness to envelop him and feel the paralysing arms of grief tighten around him as he analysed what he could and should have done to save her.

'If we're going to catch the people who did this, we're going to need your help.' Ortiz had adopted a more conciliatory tone.

'You're not going to catch anyone, stuck down here,' Tom retorted. 'We should be in Vegas. The longer we talk, the colder the trail.'

'There is a team on the ground there already, reporting directly to FBI Director Green,' Stokes said.

'To FBI Director Green?' Tom asked, momentarily encouraged. He knew Jack Green, or at least had met him a few times when working with Jennifer. He had first-hand experience of the help Tom had given the Bureau in the past. 'I want to talk to him. Does he know I'm here?'

Ortiz's eyes flickered towards the large mirror that took up most of the left-hand wall. Tom's heart sank. Not only did Green know he was here, but, judging from the uncomfortable expression on Ortiz's face, he was probably watching. Jennifer's death had clearly reset the clock. Until they knew what had happened, he wasn't going to qualify for any special treatment.

'You can talk to us instead,' Stokes snapped. 'Tell us what happened.'

'You know what happened. You were there. You saw the whole thing.'

'All I know is that twelve hours after Browne brought you into the case, she was dead.'

'You think I had something to do with it?' Tom's anger was momentarily overwhelmed by incredulity.

'Twenty million dollars is a lot of money.' Stokes's eyes narrowed accusingly. 'Even for you.'

'So that's your theory? That this was a botched heist?' Tom wasn't sure whether Stokes was being deliberately provocative or just plain stupid.

'I think that shooting a federal agent is a pretty good diversion. If one of our agents hadn't secured the suitcases, who's to say—'

'If all they'd wanted was a diversion, they could have shot anyone in that place,' Tom countered. 'Except they didn't. They chose Jennifer. Maybe you should be asking yourselves why.'

'What are you talking about?' Stokes said impatiently.

'Jennifer told me that two weeks ago she'd stumbled across an antiquities smuggling ring,' Tom said. 'Then, out of the blue, a long-lost Caravaggio shows up. One of the few works in the world guaranteed to ensure that Jennifer gets the call. You think that's a coincidence?'

'You don't?' Ortiz asked him with a frown.

'I did until last night.' Tom shrugged. 'But now I'm thinking that it was all a set-up. That that's why the priest started stalling. Because he was expecting Jennifer. Because he wanted to give the gunman enough time to find her.'

'This was about the money, and you know it,' Stokes said with a dismissive wave of his hand.

'Jennifer told me that the dealer you arrested in Queens had given you a name. Someone in Italy,' Tom said to Ortiz, ignoring Stokes. 'Who was he? Did he have any ties to the Mafia?'

'That's classified,' Stokes said angrily.

'The Mafia control the illegal antiquities business in Italy,' Tom said. 'They decide who can dig where, and take a cut on everything that comes out of the ground. It's worth millions to them. The same Mafia who, if you believe the rumours, have been holding the Caravaggio all these years.'

'What are you saying?' Ortiz asked, ignoring Stokes's venomous gaze.

'I'm saying it was a professional hit. I'm saying that something she'd stumbled across had made her a threat and that the painting was just a way of flushing her out into the open.'

'If you're right . . .' Ortiz said slowly.

'If I'm right, then we're already too late to catch the killer. You can run a DNA test on the blood traces, but people like that are ghosts. You'll get nothing. But I might still be able to find whoever ordered the hit. Let me see her files,' Tom said to Ortiz. 'I can go places you can't, speak to people you don't know. But I need to move fast. I need to move now.'

Ortiz hesitated, his eyes again flickering towards the mirror.

'Yeah, sure!' Stokes gave a rasping laugh.

'Then either charge me with something, or let me go,' Tom shouted angrily, rising to his feet. 'Right now you're just wasting my time.'

'You're going nowhere, Kirk,' Stokes said coldly, standing up and swiping the door open.

'I'm sorry, man,' Ortiz shrugged, joining him in the doorway. 'But he's right. This is how it's got to be.'

The door sealed shut behind them and the electronic reader flashed from green to red.

Tom reached into his trouser pocket and felt the hard outline of the swipe card Jennifer had pressed into his hand in the helicopter. Even then, as she lay dying, she'd known how this would play out. Even then, she'd known what he would have to do.

Ospedale Fatebenefratelli, Isola Tiberina, Rome

Allegra had left Aurelio in yet another of his sulks. She had arrived late and was now leaving early, he had complained as she saw herself out. No matter. All would be forgiven and forgotten by tomorrow, she knew.

Allegra wasn't sure whether the link between the lead discs and the Delian League was meaningful or not, but one thing that she was certain about was that Gallo would want to know about it a.s.a.p. His phone appeared to have been switched off, but according to his assistant he was at the mortuary, where she would catch him if she hurried.

Having signed in, she headed down to the basement. A young man wearing a white lab coat was manning the reception desk.

'Colonel Gallo?' she asked, flicking her ID open.

'You just missed him,' he replied. 'Signor Santos is still here, though.'

'Who?'

'He came in for the formal ID on Argento.'

She glanced at the door he had indicated and with a curious frown stepped towards it. Peering through the porthole she could see that it opened onto a large rectangular room. On the left-hand wall was a series of evenly spaced square aluminium doors, each with a large levered handle and a name-tag slot. One of the doors was open; the drawer had been pulled out. A man was standing to one side of it, his back to her.

She pushed the door open. 'Signor Santos?'

Santos turned slowly at the sound of her voice. He was in his late forties and looked slim and fit, with a tanned face and teeth the colour of polished ivory. His close-cropped dark hair was sprinkled with silver. He was immaculately dressed in a navy blazer and white flannel trousers.

He gave her a wary look that prompted her into an explanation.

'Lieutenant Allegra Damico,' she introduced herself, holding out her ID. 'I'm working with Colonel Gallo.'

'I see.' He smiled. 'Apologies. I thought you might be from the press. They're looking for an opportunity to snatch a photograph of an elected official grieving over his brother's butchered corpse. I'm here to make sure they don't get that chance.'

'Deputy Argento asked you to identify his brother's body instead of him?' she guessed.

'Actually, Colonel Gallo suggested it,' he corrected her. 'He thought it might help . . . simplify matters.'

'How did you know the victim?'

'My apologies.' Santos stepped forward, his hand rising. 'I haven't introduced myself. I am Antonio Santos, president of the Banco Rosalia.' He handed her his business card. 'Gio used to work for me.'

Allegra moved over to stand on the other side of the open drawer.

Giulio Argento was lying in between them, shrouded by a white sheet apart from his uncovered face.

'Liquorice?'

She refused. There seemed something strangely inappropriate about the way Santos was shaking the ornate tin over Argento's body.

'I read that Roman soldiers could go for ten days without eating or drinking with liquorice in their rations,' he said, popping two pieces into his mouth and then slipping the tin back into his pocket.

Allegra nodded. 'So, what did Signor Argento do for you?' she asked.

'God's work.'

'In a bank?' She sounded more sceptical than she had intended.

'The Vatican Bank is our largest shareholder,' he explained. 'We take deposits in the normal way and then lend money at subsidised rates to worthy projects that might not otherwise get funding. Gio had responsibility for managing the relationships with some of our larger accounts.'

'So no reason to think that anyone would want to—'

'This?' Santos gestured with disgust. 'This is the devil's work. The irony was that, despite working for us, Gio was not a believer. He used to say that life was too short to waste it worrying about what might happen when he was dead. At times like this, when it almost seems that God has deserted us, I almost understand what he meant.'

Folding the sheet back over Argento's face, Santos made the sign of the cross and then eased the drawer back into the wall and swung the door shut.

Allegra turned to leave, then paused. 'I wonder, did he ever mention an organisation or group called the Delian League?'

'The Delian League? Not as far as I remember.' Santos shook his head, frowning in thought. 'Why, who are they? Do you think they . . .?'

'It's just a name I've come across,' she reassured him with a smile. 'It probably means nothing. Shall I see you out?'

A Mercedes with diplomatic plates was waiting for Santos on the street outside. The chauffeur jogged round and held the rear door open for him.

'A small perk of the job,' Santos smiled as he shook her hand.

He slipped inside and settled back into his seat. As the car drew away, he reached for his phone.

'You know who it is. Don't hang up,' Santos said carefully when the number he had dialled was answered. 'I need a favour. And then I'm gone. For good this time, you have my word.'

Hotel Bel-Air, Los Angeles
Verity always sat at the same table for breakfast. In the far left corner, under the awning, behind a swaying screen of bamboo grass. It was close enough to the entrance to be seen by anyone coming in, sheltered enough not to be bothered by anyone walking past.

'Good morning, Ms Bruce.' Philippe, the maître d', bounded up to her. 'Your guest is already here.'

She pushed her sunglasses back onto her head with a frown and followed his gaze to where Earl Faulks was sitting waiting for her.

Faulks had just turned fifty but was still striking in a gaunt, patrician sort of way, with dark hooded eyes that seemed to blink in slow motion looming above a long oval face and aquiline nose, and silver hair swept back off a pale face. He was wearing a dark blue linen suit, white Charvet shirt with a cutaway collar, Cartier knot cuff links and one of his trademark bow ties.

'Verity! Looking gorgeous as always.'

He rose with a smile to greet her, leaning heavily on an umbrella, an almost permanent accessory since a riding accident a few years ago. She ignored him and sat down, a waiter pushing her chair in for her. The maître d' snapped her napkin onto her lap before taking their orders.

Verity reached into her handbag and took out an art deco silver cigarette case. Opening it carefully, she tipped the thirty or so vitamin pills and herbal supplements it contained into a small pile on her side plate.

'Verity, darling, if you go on being this healthy, it'll kill you,' Faulks warned as the waiter arrived with mineral water and a pot of tea.

'I'm not talking to you, Earl,' she replied.

'You were the one who wanted to meet,' he reminded her. 'I was packing for the Caribbean.'

She ignored him, although she couldn't help but feel a pang of envy. Faulks seemed to ride effortlessly in the slipstream of the super rich as their sumptuous caravan processed around the world: Gstaad in February, the Bahamas in March, London in June, Italy for the summer . . . She began to take her pills in silence, washing each one down with a mouthful of water and a sharp jerk of her head.

'Fine, you win,' Faulks said eventually. 'What do you want me to do? Apologise? Wear a hair shirt? Walk up the Via Dolorosa on my knees?'

'Any of those would be a start.' She glared at him. 'Have you any idea of the embarrassment you've caused me?'

'You have nothing to be embarrassed about,' he assured her.

'Tell that to Thierry Normand and Sir John Sykes. According to them, I paid you ten million dollars for something that was at best "anomalous", at worst a "pastiche".'

'Pastiche?' Faulks snorted. 'Did you tell them about the test results? Don't they know it's impossible to fake that sort of calcification?'

'By then they weren't listening.'

'You mean they didn't want to hear,' he corrected her. 'Don't you see,

Verity, darling, that they're all jealous of your success. The kouros was a smart buy. Don't you think the Met would have made a move if they'd been given even half a chance? The problem here isn't the kouros,' he insisted. 'The problem is people's unwillingness to accept that their carefully constructed picture of how Greek sculpture developed over the centuries might need to be rewritten. They should be thanking you for opening their eyes. Instead, they're seeking to discredit you, just as the Church did with Galileo.'

She nodded, rather liking this image of herself as an academic revolutionary that the establishment was desperate to silence.

'I agree with you. If I didn't, the kouros would already be on its way back to Geneva. But even if they're wrong, it'll take years for them to admit it. Meanwhile the director can't look me in the eye and the trustees have asked for a second round of tests. What if something else comes out?'

'Nothing else will come out,' Faulks said, his voice hard. 'Not unless someone's planning to talk. And nobody's planning to talk, are they, Verity?'

It was phrased as a question, but there was no doubting that he was giving her a very clear instruction. Maybe even a warning.

'Why would I risk everything we've achieved?' she said quickly.

'You wouldn't,' he said, his eyes locked unblinkingly with hers. 'But others . . . Well, I don't like to be disappointed.'

There was an icy edge to his voice and she gulped down a few more pills. Almost immediately, however, Faulks's face thawed into a warm smile.

'Anyway, let's not worry about that now. I understand that you're upset. And I want to make it up to you. What are you doing tomorrow?'

'Tomorrow?' She frowned. 'I'll be in Madrid. The US ambassador is hosting a cultural exchange. Why?'

'There's something I want to show you.' He reached inside his jacket and handed her a Polaroid. 'I was hoping you might come to Geneva.'

'Do you really think that the director is going to let me buy anything from you again?' she asked, taking the photo from him with a shrug.

'You won't have to. It'll come to you as a donation.'

She glanced down at the photo, then heard herself gasp.

'Is it . . .?' she whispered, her mouth suddenly dry, her hands trembling.

'Genuine? Absolutely,' he reassured her. 'I've seen it myself.'

'Who's it by?'

'Come now, Verity—450 BC? Can't you guess?'

There was a pause. 'Where is it now?'

'On its way to me.'

'Provenance?'

'Private Lebanese collection since the 1890s. I have the documentation.'

Another pause as she carefully placed the photograph on the table, sipped some water and then looked up hungrily. 'I have to see it.'

Headquarters of the Guardia di Finanza, Viale XXI Aprile, Rome

The headquarters of the Guardia di Finanza was located to the northeast of the city centre, just beyond the Porta Pia. It occupied a Spanish-looking building, with shutters at every window and its walls painted a dusty yellow and rich ochre colour.

In a way, Allegra reflected as she stepped out of her taxi, it was better for her to catch up with Gallo here, rather than at the mortuary. This was where the physical evidence from the two murders was being kept, giving her the opportunity to have another look at the lead discs in the light of what Aurelio had told her and to get her story straight before seeing him.

The duty officer buzzed her in and directed her towards the basement. Following the signs, she found the evidence store. It was secured by a steel door with a lock but no handle, suggesting that it could only be opened from the inside. Next to it, a low counter had been chopped out of the reinforced concrete wall. An elderly officer was sitting on the other side behind a screen of bulletproof glass. Allegra knocked on the window and then placed her ID flat against it.

'You're a long way from home, Lieutenant.' The man gave her a quizzical look. His badge identified him as Enrico Gambetta.

'I've been seconded on to the Argento case with Colonel Gallo,' she explained.

'So he got my message?' he asked excitedly. 'He sent you to see me.'

'Your message?' She frowned.

'About the other murder.'

'I haven't spoken to him all afternoon,' she said. 'I was just hoping to take another look at the lead discs from the Argento and Ricci killings.'

'The lead disc—exactly!' He beamed. 'Now, I can't really let you sign it out, but . . .' He paused, clearly trying to decide what to do. 'Wait there.'

A few moments later there was the sound of bolts being thrown back and the steel door opened. Gambetta ushered her inside.

'Are you sure I'm allowed to . . .?' she began, frowning.

'I won't tell if you won't,' he whispered, as if afraid of being overheard. 'But I need to show somebody. Are you carrying?'

'Yes.' She swept her jacket back to reveal the gun holstered to her waist.

'Pick it up on your way out.' He tapped his desk.

'Of course.'

The room was divided into five aisles by a series of floor-to-ceiling metal shelving units. Gambetta led her down the second aisle. Allegra could see that the shelves were crammed with thousands of cardboard boxes and plastic evidence bags, each sealed and identified by a tag.

'They think that all we do down here all day is sit on our arses and read the paper,' Gambetta moaned, grabbing hold of a small set of steps and wheeling them ahead of him. 'They forget that we have to check every piece of evidence in, and every piece out.'

The neon tube above where he had stopped was failing, the light stuttering on and off, creating a strange strobing effect. Climbing up the steps, he retrieved a box marked *Cavalli* and dated March 15.

'Most of the time they barely know what the people in their own teams are doing, let alone the other units,' he called back excitedly over his shoulder. 'That's why they missed it.'

'It's the Ricci and Argento cases I'm interested in,' she reminded him, but he had already placed the box on the top step and ripped the seal off.

'Three murders in three days. They may have me stuck down here, but I'm not stupid.' He tapped the side of his head with a grin.

'Three murders?' She frowned.

'I left the details on Gallo's answer machine: Luca Cavalli. A lawyer from Melfi they found hanging from the Ponte Sant'Angelo with this in one of his pockets.' He reached into the box and handed her a clear evidence bag. It contained a lead disc. And engraved on one side, just about visible in the flickering light, was the outline of two snakes and a clenched fist.

J. Edgar Hoover Building, FBI headquarters, Washington DC

Tom had given them half an hour or so before making his move. Long enough for Ortiz, Stokes and whoever else had been lurking on the other side of the two-way mirror to have dispersed, but not so long for them to feel the need to check up on him again.

He flashed Jennifer's pass through the reader. The device beeped and the magnetic seal was released. News of Jennifer's death would still barely have reached the Bureau's higher grades, let alone filtered down to the foot soldiers who manned the IT and security systems. That gave him a small window of opportunity that would last until someone triggered whatever protocol disabled her access rights and log-ons.

He ripped the fire-evacuation instructions off the back of the door and stepped out into a corridor. Not wanting to appear lost, he turned to his right and followed the arrows on the map towards what looked like the main emergency stairwell.

Just before he reached it, however, he came across an open doorway. Glancing inside, he could see that someone had left a blue FBI jacket hanging over the back of a chair. Darting inside, he slipped the jacket on as a rudimentary disguise, then dialled the operator using the internal phone.

'I'm trying to find Jennifer Browne's office,' he explained when the call was answered. 'She's normally based in New York, but she's been spending some time here lately. I wanted to swing by and surprise her.'

'Let's see,' the voice came back. 'Browne, Jennifer. Oh, yeah, she's got her calls diverting to Phil Tucker's office up on five while he's on leave.'

Memorising the room number, Tom stepped back out into the corridor and headed for the stairwell. He knew that this was a long shot, but he'd rather take his chances out here than sit in a dark room while Jennifer's killer slipped even further over the horizon. He owed her that at least.

Clearing the call, the operator immediately dialled another extension.

'Yes, good morning, sir, it's the switchboard. I'm sorry to bother you, but you asked that we should let you know if anyone asked for the location of Special Agent Browne's office. Well, someone just did.'

Headquarters of the Guardia di Finanza, Viale XXI Aprile, Rome

'When was this?' Allegra asked, returning the bag containing the lead disc.

'March the 15th,' Gambetta replied, placing it carefully back in the box.

'The fifteenth of March?' she shot back incredulously. 'Are you sure?'

'That's what it said in the case file,' he confirmed, looking startled by her reaction. 'Why?'

The 15th was the Ides of March, the same day that Caesar had been killed over two thousand years before. Cavalli and Ricci's murders weren't just linked by the lead disc. They were echoes of each other.

'Who found him?' she asked, ignoring his question.

'River police on a routine patrol. He was hanging from one of the statues on the bridge—the Angel with the Cross, from what I can remember. Their first thought was that it was a suicide, until some bright spark pointed out that his wrists were tied behind his back. Not to mention that the rope would have decapitated him if he'd jumped from that height.'

'You mean he was deliberately lowered into the water?' Allegra asked.

'The current there is quite strong. Whoever killed him clearly wanted to draw it out. Make sure he suffered.'

'Why's the GDF involved? It sounds like one for the local Questura.'

'It was, until they impounded his Maserati near the Due Ponti metro and found fifty thousand euro in counterfeit notes lining the spare wheel. Anything to do with currency fraud gets referred here.'

'Do you mind if I have a quick look through the rest of Cavalli's stuff?'

'Of course not. Here, I'll move it over there where you can see properly.' He scooped the box up and led her further down the aisle to where a battered Anglepoise lamp had been arranged on a folding table. 'That's better.'

'Much,' she smiled. 'You've been incredibly—'

There was a rap against the counter window at the far end of the room. Gambetta placed his fingers against his lips.

'Wait here,' he whispered conspiratorially. 'I'll get rid of them.'

He went back to the entrance, leaving Allegra to go through the rest of the contents of the box. Much of it was what you'd expect to find in someone's pockets: a mobile phone, some loose change, reading glasses, a wallet. There was a nice watch too—round and simple with a white face, black Roman numerals and a scrolling date. Unusually, apart from the Greek letter gamma engraved on the back of the stainless-steel case, it seemed to have no make or logo marked anywhere on it, featuring instead a distinctive bright orange second hand. Finally there was a set of keys— house and car, judging from the Maserati key fob.

An angry shout made her glance up towards the entrance. Gambetta seemed to be having an argument with the person on the other side of the window. As she watched, he stepped away from the window, unclipped his keys from his belt, and waved at her to get back.

Allegra didn't have to be told what to do. Still clutching Cavalli's keys, she retreated to the far end of the aisle and hid. Gambetta had done her a favour by letting her in here and the last thing she wanted to do was get him in trouble. Even so, she couldn't resist peering round the edge of the pier as he unbolted the door.

She never even saw the gun, the rolling echo of the shot's silenced thump breaking over her like a wave before she realised what was happening. The next thing she knew, Gambetta was staggering back, his arms flailing. He swayed unsteadily for a few moments longer, desperately trying to stay on his feet. Then, with a bellow, he crashed to the concrete floor.

J. Edgar Hoover Building, FBI headquarters, Washington DC

The room where Jennifer had been camping out was essentially a glass box, albeit one with a view of 9th Street. Unlike the rooms that flanked it, however, its door was shut and all the blinds drawn. It suited Tom well, concealing him from view once he had satisfied himself that no one was watching him and slipped inside.

Almost immediately, his heart sank. Perhaps without realising it until now, he had secretly been hoping to find a bit more of Jennifer here, even though this had only ever been a temporary home for her. Instead it boasted a sterile anonymity that was only partly lifted by Tucker's scattered photographs and personal trinkets. Then again, there was no debating who was responsible for the lipstick-smeared rim of the polystyrene cup that was still nestling in the bin.

The safe was in a cupboard under the bookshelf. With a weary sigh, he saw that it was protected by both a password and voice-recognition software. Tricky, unless . . . He glanced up at her desk hopefully. The light on her phone was glowing red to indicate that somebody had left her a voicemail. With any luck, that meant that she'd recorded a greeting.

He picked the phone up and dialled Jennifer's extension.

'You've reached Special Agent Jennifer Browne in the FBI's Art Crime Team . . .' Tom's stomach flipped over at the sound of her voice. She sounded so close, so real that for a moment it was almost as if . . . He needed to stay focused. He replaced the handset. That would do.

Now for the password. He opened each of the desk drawers. The third drawer down yielded a small make-up bag and within that, a powder brush.

Kneeling next to the safe, he dusted the brush over the keys and then blew away the excess. The result allowed him to see which keys had been most heavily used, the powder sticking more thickly to the sweat left there.

This highlighted the letters A, C, R, V, G, I and O. Tom jotted them down on a piece of paper, knowing that they formed an anagram of some other word. The key was to try and get inside Jennifer's head. A name, a place, a person . . . Tom smiled, seeing that the last three letters had given him an obvious clue. G, I, O—Caravaggio, perhaps? He typed the word in and one of the two lights flashed green.

Reaching the phone down from the desk, he listened to the greeting a few more times to get a feel for exactly when Jennifer said her name. Then, just at the right moment, he placed the handset against the microphone before quickly snatching it away again. The second light flashed green. With a whirr, the door sprang open.

He reached inside and pulled out a handful of files. He flicked through them, discarding them all apart from one that Jennifer had initialled in her characteristically slanting hand.

Sitting at the desk, he scanned through the file, quickly recognising in the typed pages and photographs the details of the case that Jennifer had laid out for him on their way to Vegas. The Customs tip-off. The raid on the warehouse and the discovery of an Aladdin's cave of illegally exported antiquities. The dealer's confession. A copy of his doodled sketch of the two snakes wrapped round a clenched fist, the symbol of the so-called Delian League. Bank statements. An auction catalogue. And, of course, the name provided by the dealer that Jennifer had passed on to the Italian authorities, who had rewarded her with an address in Rome and a promise to follow up: Luca Cavalli. It wasn't much, but it was a start.

Closing the file, he stood up, only to brush against the mouse as he turned to leave. The log-on screen immediately flickered on. He stared at it for a few moments and then, shrugging, sat down again. It was worth a try.

Headquarters of the Guardia di Finanza, Viale XXI Aprile, Rome

Allegra snatched her head back, heart thudding, fist clenched, the teeth of Cavalli's keys biting into her palm. Gambetta shot, right in front of her, in the Guardia di Finanza headquarters. It was impossible. But she'd seen it.

She knew she needed to stay calm, think through her options. Not that she had many. Not with her gun stranded on Gambetta's desk and only the length of the room separating her from the killer. Perhaps if she was quiet, she reasoned, he wouldn't even realise . . .

The sudden hiss of polyester on concrete interrupted her thoughts. She frowned, at first unable to place the noise, until with a sickening lurch of her stomach she realised that it was the sound of Gambetta's corpse being dragged towards her.

She knew immediately what she had to do. Move. Move now while the killer was still far enough away not to see or hear her. All she had to do was figure out which aisle he was coming down; then she'd be able to creep back to the entrance up one of the other ones. At least, that was the idea.

She shut her eyes and concentrated on the noise of Gambetta's uniform catching on the tiny imperfections in the concrete, knowing that she had to be absolutely sure. Then, when it seemed that he must be almost on top of her, she opened them again. The second aisle. The one she'd been standing in a few moments before when looking through Cavalli's evidence box.

Taking a deep breath, she edged her head round the pier and peeked along the first aisle. It was empty. Crouching down, she slipped her shoes off and began to creep towards the exit. But she'd scarcely gone ten yards before suddenly she paused. She could see the killer.

Not his face, but his back, through a narrow gap between the shelves as he dragged Gambetta towards her. A glimpse of his face was all she needed. Just enough to be able to give a description.

She edged carefully forward, trying to find a place where she could stand up without being seen, occasionally seeing the killer's leg and his black shoes through the shelving as he backed towards her. Then, when he was almost parallel to her, Gambetta's feet fell to the floor with an echoing thud.

Sensing her chance, she slowly straightened up. Through a narrow slit between two boxes, she could see his face, or rather the outline of it, the overhead neon tube having blinked off yet again. Holding her breath, she waited until the light stuttered on again and the image strobed briefly across her retina until it finally settled. It was Gallo.

She instinctively snatched her head back, but the sudden blur of movement must have caught his eye because he called out angrily.

There was no time to think. No time to do anything. Except run. Run to the door, throw the bolts back, tumble through it, stumble up the steps and stagger out into the street, gasping with shock. The world on its head.

J. Edgar Hoover Building, FBI headquarters, Washington DC

Tom found Jennifer's password taped to the underside of the stapler. No great mystery there. It was always the same in these large organisations. Obsessed by security, IT insisted on people using 'strong' passwords that had to be changed every five minutes, and then claimed to be surprised when people wrote them down. He typed the password in and hit the enter key. Almost immediately the screen went blue. Then it sounded a long, strident beep. Finally it flashed up a message: *Password not recognised. Please remain at your desk and an IT security representative will be with you shortly.*

The phone started to ring. Tom checked the display and saw that it was

Stokes, presumably tipped off by some clever piece of software that some-one was trying to access Jennifer's account. The Bureau was clearly more nimble and joined up than Tom had given them credit for.

Shoving the file under his jacket, he leapt across to the door and gingerly lifted the blind. Checking that no one was coming, he slipped out of the office and headed back towards the stairs.

Almost immediately he jumped back. The stairwell thundered with the sound of heavy footsteps and urgent shouts. He glanced around, looking for somewhere to hide. But before he could move, he felt a heavy hand grip his shoulder. He spun round. It was Ortiz, his chest heaving.

'This way,' he wheezed, urging him towards an open office. 'Quickly.'

Tom hesitated for a fraction of a second, but the lack of a better option quickly made up his mind for him. Following him inside, he watched as Ortiz shut the door behind him and let the blinds drop.

'Can you really find them?' he panted, peering through a narrow crack as a group of armed men, led by Stokes, charged towards Jennifer's office.

'What?' Tom asked, not sure he'd heard right.

'Jennifer's killers? Can you find them?' Ortiz repeated.

'I can.' Tom nodded. 'If I can get out of here, I can find them.'

Ortiz stared at him unblinkingly. 'What will you do?'

'Whatever I have to,' Tom reassured him in a cold voice. 'What you can't. What Jennifer deserves.'

Ortiz nodded slowly. 'Good.' He stepped forward and pressed his card into Tom's hand. 'Just call me when it's done.' He reached out and flicked the fire-alarm switch. The siren's shrill cry split the air.

'Go,' he said. 'Get outside with everyone else before I change my mind.'

With a nod, Tom sprinted back towards the stairwell. Taking the steps two at a time, he raced down towards the ground floor. As he cleared the first-floor landing, he was forced to slow to a walk, the crowd backing up ahead of him. Peering over their heads, he saw that a line of security guards was checking everyone's ID before allowing them to leave the building. Had Stokes tipped them off? Tom had to do something quickly.

Waiting until he was almost at the bottom of the penultimate flight of stairs, Tom deliberately tripped the man ahead of him and, with a sharp shove, sent him crashing into the wall opposite. He smacked into it with a sickening crunch and a deep gash opened up in his forehead, the blood streaming down his face.

'Let me through,' Tom called, hauling the dazed man to his feet and throwing his arm round his shoulder. 'Let me through.'

Seeing Tom staggering towards them, one of the guards stepped forward and supported the injured man on the other side. Together they lifted him along the narrow path that had opened through the middle of the crowd.

'He needs a doctor,' Tom called urgently. 'He's losing a lot of blood.'

'This way, sir.'

The line of guards parted to let them through. Another officer escorted them clear as he radioed for a medic. They sat the still groggy man down on the pavement until an ambulance arrived moments later. The paramedics jumped out and threw a foil blanket round the man's shoulders. Tom stepped back, leaving the two guards to crowd round with words of advice. Then, seeing that no one was watching, he turned and walked away.

Standing at a seventh-storey window, FBI Director Green watched Tom disappear down D Street with a smile. He knew Kirk well enough to guess that he'd find a way out of that room and that, when he did, he'd head straight for Browne's safe. The truth was that Kirk was her best chance now. While the Bureau was worrying about who was going to get blamed for one of its most promising young agents getting killed, Kirk would be out there making things happen. Browne had trusted Kirk with her life many times before now. It seemed only right to trust him with her death too.

Viale XXI Aprile, Rome

Panting, Allegra sprinted onto the Via Gaetano Moroni and then right on to Via Luigi Pigorini. Gallo . . . a killer? It made no sense. It was impossible. But how could she ignore what she'd seen?

She found her stride, her ragged breathing slowly falling into a more comfortable rhythm, her thoughts settling. Had Gallo seen her face? She wasn't sure. Either way, it wouldn't take him long to pull the security footage. The only thing that mattered now was getting as far away from him as she could. She flagged down a taxi and gave him Aurelio's address.

At least Gallo's motives seemed clear. He'd killed Gambetta so that he couldn't tell anyone else about his discovery of the links between the murders. Why else would he have paused under the faltering neon light where Gambetta had taken Cavalli's evidence box down from its shelf? He'd been looking for the lead disc, so that no one else would make the connection.

'What number?' the driver called over his shoulder ten minutes later.

'Drive to the end,' she ordered. 'Here, this will do.'

Paying him, she got out and walked towards Aurelio's apartment.

'*Ego sum principium mundi et finis saeculorum attamen non sum deus,*' came the voice from the speaker.

'Not now, Aurelio,' Allegra snapped. 'Just let me in.'

There was the briefest of pauses. Then the door buzzed open. She made her way to the lift. Aurelio was waiting for her on the landing.

'What's happened?' he asked as she stepped out.

'I'm in trouble.'

'I can see that. Come in.'

He led her silently into his office and perched anxiously on one arm of his leather chair. Speaking in as dispassionate a tone as she could, she described what she'd seen. When she finished, there was a long silence.

'It's my fault.' Aurelio spoke in a whisper. 'If I'd known . . . I should never have got you involved with any of this.'

'If you want to blame someone, blame Gallo,' she insisted.

'I know someone. A detective in the police,' Aurelio volunteered. 'I could call him and—'

'No,' she cut him off with a firm shake of her head. 'No police. Not until I understand what's going on. Not until I know who I can trust.'

'Then what do you need?'

'A place to stay. A coffee. Some answers.'

'The first two I can help with. The third . . . well, the third we might have to work on together.'

'Two out of three's a good start.' She bent down and planted a grateful kiss on his forehead.

'I should offer to make the coffee more often.' He grinned. 'Here, sit.' Aurelio stood up and pulled her towards his chair. 'Rest.'

She shut her eyes and tried to clear her mind, finding the merry clink of crockery as Aurelio busied himself in the kitchen strangely comforting. But almost immediately her eyes snapped open. Rest? How could she rest, after what she'd just seen?

She jumped up and padded cautiously to the window, standing to one side so she could check the street below without being seen. It was empty. Good. As far as she knew, she'd never spoken to anyone on the team about her friendship with Aurelio, so there was no reason to think Gallo's men would come looking for her here. Not that she was in a position to put up much of a fight if they did, given that she was unarmed.

The realisation made her feel strangely vulnerable. If only . . . She had a sudden thought and glanced across at Aurelio's desk. Somewhere inside it, she seemed to remember, he had a gun. She crossed over to the desk, noticing the typed notes for a lecture that according to the cover page Aurelio was giving at the Galleria Doria Pamphilj the following day. She tried each of the overflowing drawers in turn, her fingers eventually closing round the weapon at the back of the third drawer.

She slid out the eight-round magazine. It was full and the gun itself was well maintained. Satisfied, she slapped the magazine home.

She walked into the kitchen. To her surprise it was empty. The kettle was boiling on the stove. Frowning, she turned the hob off, then stepped back into the hall.

'Aurelio?' she called, reaching warily for the gun.

There was no answer, although she thought she heard his voice coming from his bedroom. She stepped over to it, a narrow slit of light bisecting the worn floorboards where the door hadn't quite been pulled to. She pressed her ear against the crack and then froze. He was talking about her.

'Yes, she's here now,' she heard him say in an urgent voice. 'Of course I can keep her here. Why, what do you need her for?'

She backed away, the gun raised towards the door, her face pale, heart pounding, the blood screaming in her ears. First Gallo. Now Aurelio too?

Her eyes stinging, she turned and stumbled out of the apartment, down the stairs and onto the street, not knowing if she was crying from sadness or anger.

Vicolo dei Panieri, Trastevere, Rome

Tom had booked himself on to the afternoon flight out of DC, taking the obvious precaution of using another name. He never travelled without at least two changes of identity stitched into his bag's lining and luckily the FBI had not thought to check whether he had left anything with the concierge at the hotel he'd been staying in the previous night.

He'd managed to snatch a few hours' sleep, and then spent the rest of the flight reading through Jennifer's file in a bit more detail. As his taxi swept into the city he phoned Archie.

'Tom?' Archie rasped, jet lag and what Tom guessed had probably been a heavy night at the hotel bar combining to give his voice a ragged croak. 'What time is it? Where the hell are you?'

'Rome,' Tom answered.

'Rome?' he repeated sleepily. 'What are you doing in Rome? You're meant to be in Zurich.'

'Jennifer's dead,' Tom said sharply. 'It was a set-up. The Caravaggio. The exchange. They were waiting for us.'

'Shit.' Any hint of tiredness had evaporated from Archie's voice. 'What happened?'

'Sniper,' Tom said. 'Professional job.'

'You're sure she was the target?'

'Pretty sure. Have you ever heard of an antiquities-smuggling operation called the Delian League?'

'No. Why? Is that who you think did it?'

'That's what I'm in Rome to find out. That's why I need you in Geneva.'

'Of course,' Archie replied instantly. 'Whatever you need, mate.'

'There's a sale at Sotheby's this afternoon,' Tom said, glancing down at the circled entry in the Geneva auction catalogue that had been included in Jennifer's file. 'One of the lots is a statue of Artemis. It looks like Jennifer thought it was important. I want to know why.'

'No worries,' Archie reassured him. 'What about you? What's in Rome?'

'A name. Luca Cavalli. He was fingered by someone Jennifer arrested in New York. I thought I'd start with him and work my way back up the ladder.'

'Tom . . .' Archie spoke haltingly, for once lost for words. 'Listen, mate, I know you two were . . . I'm really sorry. Are you going to be all right?'

'I'll be fine,' Tom said. 'Just call me on this number when you get there.'

About fifteen minutes later the taxi pulled up. Tom stepped out.

The wide, cobbled street was largely populated by neat four-storey buildings with symmetrical balconies and brightly coloured plaster walls. Cavalli's house, by contrast, was a feral, hulking shape. Long and only two storeys high, its stonework was grey and wizened by age.

Hitching his bag across his shoulders and checking that the street was empty, Tom clambered quickly up the drainpipe, glad that he had changed out of his suit. Reaching across to the window, he could see that although it was closed, the frame was warped and the latch loose. Pushing a knife into a narrow gap, he levered the blade back and forth, so that the latch slowly worked itself free, until it popped open and he was able to clamber inside.

He found himself in what he assumed was a bedroom. The contents of the wardrobe had been swept onto the floor, the bed propped against the wall and the chest flipped onto its back, its emptied drawers at its side.

He exited the bedroom onto a glass and stainless-steel walkway that ran the length of the building and looked down on to a wide, double-height living space. He stepped past a bathroom and another bedroom that had been similarly turned upside down.

Then he made his way down to the ground floor. Here, the brutality of the assault was, if anything, even more marked—the large plasma screen had been lifted off its brackets and broken almost in two across a chair, the seats and backs of the leather furniture slashed open, the coffee table overturned and the bookcase forced onto its front, its contents crushed underneath.

A sudden noise from the front door made Tom look up. Someone was coming in. The bottom lock was clunking open, the key now slipping into the top one. He knew immediately he wouldn't have time to make it back upstairs. That left him only one option.

The door opened. Someone stepped inside and quickly eased it shut behind them. They paused. Then, with careful, hesitant footsteps, they walked down the small entrance hallway towards him.

His back pressed to the wall, Tom waited until the intruder was almost level with him and then leapt out, sending their gun spinning across the floor with a chop to the wrist. Rather than press his advantage, however, Tom paused, surprised by the realisation that it was a woman. This hesitation was all the invitation she needed to turn and crash her right fist into his jaw, the force of the blow sending him staggering back with a grunt. Spinning round, she stretched towards the gun, but Tom stuck out a leg and tripped her, sending her sprawling headlong into an upturned chair. By the time she was on her feet, the gun was in Tom's hands and aimed at her stomach.

'*Trovisi giù,*' he wheezed. Her chest heaving, she gave him a long, hate-filled look and then lay face down on the floor as he'd ordered. Tom quickly patted her down, finding her wallet in her jeans pocket.

'*Siedasi là,*' he ordered as he opened it, waving the gun at a chair. Her eyes burning, she pulled herself to her feet, righted the chair he had indicated, and then sat in it.

'*Una poliziotta?*' he asked in surprise, at the sight of her ID. Tall and obviously strong, she was wearing jeans, a tight brown leather jacket and red ballet-style pumps. She was also very striking, with olive skin, a jet-black bob that was cut in a square fringe around her face and mismatched blue and brown eyes embedded within a smoky-grey eye shadow. There was something odd about her appearance, though. Something that Tom couldn't quite put his finger on yet, that didn't quite fit.

'Congratulations,' she replied. 'You've managed to assault a police offi-cer and trespass on a crime scene before most people have got out of bed.'

'Where did you learn English?' Tom's Italian was good, but her English, while slightly accented, was almost faultless.

She ignored him. 'Put the gun down.'

'You tell me what you're doing here and I'll think about it,' he offered.

'Who are you working for? Gallo?' she shot back, ignoring his question.

'Who's Gallo?'

'He didn't send you?' There was hope as well as disbelief in her voice.

'Nobody *sent* me,' he said. 'I work for myself. I'm looking for Cavalli.'

A pause. 'Cavalli's dead. He was murdered. Four days ago.'

'Shit.' Tom gave a long sigh. Cavalli had been his main hope of working his way back to whoever had ordered the hit. 'I wanted to talk to him.'

'About what?'

'This for a start.' Tom held up the photocopy of the symbol of the two snakes wrapped round a clenched fist. 'I hoped he might . . .'

'Where did you get that?' she gasped.

'You've seen it before?'

'C-cavalli,' she stammered. 'They found a lead disc in his pocket. That was engraved on it!'

'Do you know what it means?' Tom pressed.

'It means that you've got about five minutes to get out of here before someone comes looking for me.'

Tom studied her face for a few moments. She was bluffing.

'Why wait?' he said, offering her his phone. 'Call it in.'

She gazed at the handset for a few moments, then lifted her eyes to his.

Tom smiled. 'No one even knows you're here, do they?'

She ignored his question, although the momentary flicker of indecision across her otherwise resolute face effectively answered it for him.

'Just let me go,' she said. 'You're in enough shit as it is.'

Tom was about to reply when he paused, having suddenly realised what it was about her appearance that had been troubling him earlier. It was her hair, or rather the ragged way it had been cut. She'd clearly cut it herself. Recently. Probably dyed it too, given its unnaturally deep lustre.

'Where did you put the empty dye bottles?' he asked. 'And the hair you cut off. Did you lose them somewhere safe? Because if whoever's looking for you finds them, it won't take them long to figure out what you look like now.'

Allegra gave him a long, curious look. 'Who are you?'

'Someone who can help,' Tom said with a tight smile. 'Because right now, I'm guessing you're in a lot more shit than me.'

Leaning forward, he offered the gun to her, handle first.

Headquarters of the Guardia di Finanza, Viale XXI Aprile, Rome

'Colonel? We've got her.'

'About time!' Gallo grabbed his jacket off the back of his chair, pausing in front of the mirror to centre his tie. 'Her phone?'

'She switched it on about ten minutes ago,' Salvatore nodded. 'The signal's been triangulated to a street in Trastevere.'

'Cavalli's house?' Gallo snapped.

'Could be.'

Gallo turned and gave Salvatore a sharp clap on the back. 'Well done.'

Fixing his peaked cap on his head, Gallo strode towards the lift. Twenty seconds later they walked outside towards two waiting cars. They climbed in, and Gallo turned the key in the ignition.

'We also know where she stayed last night,' Salvatore said. 'A hotel out near the airport. The manager saw her picture this morning and called it in.'

'They ran the story?'

Salvatore reached across to the back seat and handed Gallo a copy of that morning's *La Repubblica*. Allegra's face dominated the front page under a single shouted headline: 'Killer Cop on the Run.'

Gallo scanned through the article. He wouldn't normally have leaked the details of a case, but the more people who knew what Allegra looked like, the better. As long as he found her first.

'What about Professor Eco?' Gallo asked.

'According to him, she took off before telling him anything.'

'I want him watched anyway,' Gallo insisted. 'Just in case she tries to contact him again.'

'She's probably armed now, by the way. Eco had a gun. Illegal. Says he can't find it any more.'

'Even better.' Gallo gave a satisfied nod. 'Gives us an excuse to go in heavy.' Smiling, he punched the siren on.

Vicolo dei Panieri, Travestere, Rome

Allegra wasn't about to take any chances. Snatching the gun from Tom's grasp, she turned it back on him. Unflustered, he settled into a chair.

'How can you help me?' she demanded.

There was a pause. 'Thirty-six hours ago a friend was murdered,' he said eventually. 'Shot by a sniper in a casino in Vegas. I think this person was killed because they were closing in on someone.'

'"Closing in"? What was he, a cop?' Allegra guessed.

'*She* was FBI,' he corrected her. 'Special Agent Jennifer Browne. Cavalli was fingered by a man she arrested in New York. A dealer for a tombaroli smuggling ring. She found a drawing of the symbol I showed you in his trash. I've got the case file, if you want to see it,' he offered, leaning forward to reach into his bag.

'Wait,' she said sharply. 'Kick it over here.'

With a shrug, he placed his bag on the floor and slid it towards her with his foot. Keeping her eyes fixed on him, she felt inside it and pulled out a thick file. Seeing the FBI crest, she shot him a questioning look.

'Don't tell me you're FBI too?'

'No,' he admitted.

'Then where did you get this?'

A pause. 'I borrowed it.'

'You borrowed it?' She gave him a disbelieving smile. 'From the FBI?'

'When one agent gets killed, another one gets blamed,' he said, an impatient edge to his voice for the first time. 'Everyone was too busy covering their own ass to worry about finding Jennifer's killer. I did what I had to do.'

'And came here? Why? What were you hoping to find?'

'I don't know. Something that might tell me why Jennifer was murdered, or what this symbol means, or who the Delian League is.'

'The Delian League?' she shot back. 'What do you know about them?'

'Not as much as you, by the sound of things,' he replied.

'I just know what it used to be,' she said. 'An association of city states in ancient Greece. A military alliance, formed to protect themselves from the Spartans,' she explained. 'The members used to throw lead into the sea when they joined, to symbolise that their friendship would last until it floated back to the surface.'

'Lead. Like the engraved disc you found on Cavalli?'

'Not just on Cavalli,' she admitted. 'There have been two other murders: Adriano Ricci, an enforcer for the De Luca crime family, and Giulio Argento, who worked for the Banco Rosalia, a subsidiary of the Vatican Bank. The discs were found with them too.'

'The same killer, right?'

Allegra's eyes snapped to the door before she could answer, the sound of approaching sirens lifting her to her feet.

'You must have been followed.' Tom glared at her accusingly.

She ignored him, instead picking up a chair and swinging it hard against one of the sliding glass doors. They leapt through the frame as they heard three, maybe four cars roar up the street outside.

'Here—' Tom cradled his hands and gave Allegra a boost, then reached up so she could help haul him up onto the garden wall beside her.

'You'll slow me down,' she said with a firm shake of her head.

'You need me,' Tom insisted.

'I've done OK so far,' she said, readying herself to jump down.

'Really? Then how do you explain that?' Tom glanced towards the muffled sound of the police banging on the front door. 'Let me guess. You turned your phone on just before you got here, right?'

'How did you know . . .?' she breathed, Tom's question pulling her back from the edge. She had briefly switched it on. Just long enough to see if Aurelio had left her a message. Something, anything, that might explain what she had overheard.

'It only takes a few seconds to triangulate a phone signal. You led them straight here.'

She took a deep breath. 'Who *are* you?'

'Someone who knows what it's like to be on the run,' he shot back. 'Someone who knows what it takes to keep running fast enough to stay alive.' Sighing heavily, she reached down, her hand clutching on to his.

THEY HAD FOUND a battered old Fiat a few streets from Cavalli's house. It was coated in a thick layer of rain-streaked dirt that suggested that it hadn't been used for weeks, and so was unlikely to be missed.

'What are you doing?' he asked as she suddenly cut across the Ponte Principe Amedeo and pulled in on the Largo dei Fiorentini. 'We can't stop here. We're still too close. If anyone's seen us . . .'

'If you want to get out, now's your chance,' she snapped, leaning across him and pushing his door open. 'Otherwise, I want some answers.'

'What sort of answers?'

'How about a name?'

He sighed, then slammed the door shut.

'It's Tom. Tom Kirk.' He held out his hand so that she had to shake it rather formally. 'Can we do the rest of the Q and A somewhere else?'

'You said you knew what it was like to be on the run. Why? Who are you?' she demanded.

'You really want to do this here?' he asked. She returned his stare. 'Fine,' he said eventually with a resigned sigh. 'I . . . I used to be a thief.'

'A thief?' She smiled indulgently before realising that he wasn't joking. 'What sort of thief?'

'Art mainly. Jewellery too. Whatever paid.'

'And now?'

'Now I help recover pieces, advise museums on security, that sort of thing,' he replied.

'What's any of that got to do with Cavalli?'

'I told you. Jennifer had asked me to help her on a case before she was killed. Cavalli was the best lead I had as to who might have ordered the hit. Why, what's Cavalli to you?'

'It's what he is to Gallo that I care about.' Allegra turned back to face the front, her hands clutching the wheel.

'Who's Gallo?' Tom frowned. 'The person you're running from?'

'Colonel Massimo Gallo,' she intoned in a bitter voice. 'Head of the GICO—the organised-crime unit of the Ministry of Finance—and the officer in charge of the two Caravaggio killings.'

'What?'

'The other murders I told you about,' she explained. 'Ricci and Argento. Their deaths had been staged to mirror two Caravaggio paintings.'

'Jennifer was lured to Las Vegas to help recover a Caravaggio stolen in the 1960s,' Tom explained.

There was a pause as she let this sink in. First the symbol. Then the mention of the Delian League. Now Caravaggio. Surely these couldn't all be coincidences? Speaking quickly and confidently, she plunged into an account of the past few days.

'Somehow, it's all linked,' Tom said slowly when she had finished. 'The murders, Caravaggio, the symbol . . . we just need to find out how.'

'Is that all?' she said with a bitter laugh.

'I know someone who might be able to help.'

ALLEGRA HEARD the Trevi Fountain before she saw it, a delirious, ecstatic roar of water that crashed and foamed over gnarled travertine rocks and carved foliage, tumbling in a joyful cascade into the open embrace of the wide basin below. Despite the relatively early hour, the tourists were already out in force, some seated on the steps that encircled the basin's low stage, others facing the opposite direction and flinging coins over their shoulders in the hope of securing their return to the Eternal City.

'Was there a Trevi family?' Tom asked as they paused in front of it.

'Trevi comes from *tre vie*, the three streets that meet here,' she told him. 'Are we here for a history lesson or to actually see someone?'

'That depends on whether you can keep a secret,' he said with a shrug.

'Oh, come on,' she snorted impatiently. 'How old are you, ten?'

Tom turned to face her. 'You can't tell anyone about what you see. Yes or no?' he insisted.

There was a pause. Then she gave a grudging nod. 'Yes, fine, whatever.'

'Come on. It's this way.'

He led her to the right to the Via della Stamperia, where a small doorway had been set into the side wall of the building directly behind the fountain. He knocked sharply against the weather-worn door.

A few moments later it opened to reveal a young Chinese man dressed in black, his hair standing off his head as if he had been electrocuted.

'I'm here to see Johnny,' Tom announced. 'Tell him it's Felix.'

The man gave them a cursory look, then shut the door again.

'Felix?' Allegra shot him a questioning look.

'It's a name people used to know me by when I was still in the game. I try not to use it any more, but it's how a lot of people still know me.'

'The game?' She gave a hollow laugh. 'Is that a word people like you use to make you feel better about breaking the law?'

The door reopened before Tom had a chance to answer. The man ushered them inside and then marched them along a low passageway, through a second door and then up a shallow flight of steps into a narrow room.

'Where are we?' Allegra hissed.

'Listen,' Tom replied.

Allegra suddenly realised that she could hear the muffled roar of water through the thick walls.

'We're behind the fountain,' she breathed.

'The Trevi was pretty much tacked on to the façade of the Palazzo Poli when they built it,' Tom explained as the man ordered them up the stairs with a grunt. 'This space was bricked off as a maintenance shaft, to provide access to the roof and the plumbing in the basement. Johnny cut a deal with the mayor to rent the attic.'

'You're kidding, right?'

'Why? How else do you think he paid for his re-election campaign?'

They climbed to the first floor, then to the next. The fountain's low rumble slowly faded, until it was little more than a distant hum. In its place, however, Allegra was increasingly aware of a whirring, rhythmical clattering noise. She glanced at Tom for an explanation, but he said nothing.

Another man was waiting to greet them on the second-floor landing, a machine gun slung across his oversized Lakers shirt. He signalled at them to raise their arms and then quickly patted them down, confiscating Tom's bag and Allegra's gun and keys. Then he nodded at them to follow him to the foot of the next flight of stairs, where an armoured steel door and two more guards blocked their way. Unprompted, the door buzzed open.

They made their way upstairs to a long, narrow attic room that seemed to run the width of the entire building. A line of squat windows squinted down on to the square below. And running down the centre of the room, hissing and rattling like an old steam engine, was a huge printing press.

'The sound of the fountain masks the noise of the machine,' Tom called to Allegra over the press's raucous clatter as she approached it. 'It's actually five separate machines, laid out end to end. A Simultan to print the background colours and patterns. An intaglio machine for the major design elements. A letterpress for the serial numbers. An offset press for the overcoating. And a guillotine right at the end to cut the sheets to size.'

Allegra stepped closer to the press, trying to catch what was coming off the machine's whirling drum, then looked back to Tom in shock.

'Money?'

'Euros.' He nodded. 'Johnny runs one of the world's biggest counterfeiting operations outside of China.'

'Johnny who?' she asked, looking back along the room and noticing the small army of people in blue overalls tending silently to the press.

'Johnny Li. His father is Li Kai-Fu. Runs one of the most powerful Triad gangs in Hong Kong,' Tom explained. 'A couple of years ago he posted his five sons around the world, via Cambridge, to help grow the family business. Johnny's here, Paul's in San Francisco, Ringo's in Buenos Aires—'

'He moved to Rio,' a voice interrupted him. 'Better weather.'

'Johnny!' Tom turned to greet the voice with a warm smile.

Li was young, perhaps only in his late twenties, with long dark hair, a pierced lip and a dotted line tattooed round his neck as if to show where to cut. He was dressed in a white Armani T-shirt, expensively ripped Versace jeans with a stainless-steel key chain looping down one leg, and Prada trainers. He was flanked by two unsmiling guards and balancing Allegra's gun in his hand as if trying to guess its weight, his face creased into an unwelcoming scowl.

'What do you want, Felix?' He had a strong English accent.

'Bad time?' Tom frowned, clearly surprised by his tone.

'What do you expect when you turn up at my place with a cop?' Li snapped, stabbing a rolled-up newspaper towards him. 'Even if she is bent.'

Tom took the paper off him and scanned the front page, then handed it to Allegra with an awkward look. She didn't have to read much beyond the headline to understand why. Gallo was pinning Gambetta's death on her. Beneath her photograph was an article describing her 'murderous rampage'. She felt suddenly dizzy, as if the floor was moving under her.

'She's with me now,' he said.

'What do you want?' Li shot back, flashing Allegra a suspicious glance.

'Your help.'

'I thought you'd retired?' Li's question sounded more like an accusation.

'A friend of mine has been killed. We're both after the people who did it.'

Li paused, glancing at Tom and Allegra in turn. Then he handed Allegra her gun back with a grudging nod.

'What do you want to know?'

Tom handed Li the drawing of the symbol.

'What can you tell me about this?'

Li took it over to an architect's desk and angled it under the light. He glanced up at them with a wary look.

'Is this who you think killed your friend?'

'You know what it means?' Allegra asked excitedly.

'Of course I do,' he snorted. 'It's the symbol of the Delian League.'

'Who runs it?' Tom pressed.

Li sat back. 'Come on, Tom. You know that's not how things work.' He smiled indulgently as if gently scolding a child. 'I'm running a business here, not a charity. Even for deserving causes like you.'

'How much?' Tom asked wearily.

'Normally twenty-five thousand euro,' Li said, picking at his fingernails. 'But for you and your friend I'm going to round it up to fifty.'

'Fifty thousand!' Allegra exclaimed.

'I can get it.' Tom nodded. 'But it's going to take some time.'

'I can wait.' Li shrugged.

'Well, we can't,' Tom insisted. 'I'll have to owe you.'

'No deal.' Li shook his head. 'Not if you're going up against the League. I want my money before they kill you.'

'Come on, Johnny,' Tom pleaded. 'You know I'm good for it.'

'What about a down-payment? You must have something on you? That watch, for example.' Li nodded towards Tom's wrist.

'It's not for sale,' Tom insisted, quickly pulling his sleeve down.

'Think of it as a deposit,' Li suggested. 'You can have it back when you bring me the cash.'

Tom said nothing, then gave a resigned shrug. 'Fine.' Sighing heavily, he took the watch off. 'But I want it back.'

'I'll look after it,' Li reassured him, fastening it carefully to his wrist.

'Let's start with the Delian League,' Allegra suggested. 'Who are they?'

'The Delian League controls the illegal antiquities trade in Italy,' Li answered simply. 'Has done since the early 1970s. Nothing leaves the country without going through them.'

'And the tombaroli? Where do they fit in?'

'They control the supply,' Li explained. 'Most of them are freelance. But since the major antiquities buyers are foreign, the League controls access to the demand. The tombaroli either have to sell to them, or not sell at all.'

'Don't the Mafia mind the League operating on their turf?' Tom asked.

'The League *is* the Mafia,' Li laughed. 'That's what the two snakes represent—one for the Cosa Nostra, one for the Banda della Magliana.'

'The Banda della Magliana is run by the De Luca family,' Allegra explained, glancing at Tom. 'They're who Ricci worked for.'

'The story I heard was that when the Cosa Nostra realised there was money to be made in looting antiquities, they teamed up with the Banda, who controlled all the valuable Etruscan sites around Rome, on the basis that they would make more money if they operated as a cartel. The League's been so successful that most of the other families have sold them access rights to their territories in return for a share of the profits.'

'Who runs it now?' Tom asked. 'Where can we find them?'

Li tapped his finger slowly against his lips. 'I can't tell you that.'

Tom gave a hollow laugh. 'Can't or won't?'

'It's nothing personal, Felix,' Li said with a shrug. 'I just want my money. And if I give you everything now, I know I'll never see it.'

'We had a deal,' Allegra said angrily. Li had tricked them.

'We still do,' Li insisted. 'Come back tomorrow with the fifty K and I'll tell you what side of the bed they all sleep on.'

'We need to know now,' Allegra snapped.

Another pause. 'What about the car?' Li asked.

'What car?' Tom frowned.

'Cavalli's Maserati,' Allegra breathed, as she recognised the set of keys that Li had produced from his pocket as the ones that had been confiscated from her on the way in.

'Do you have it?' Li pressed.

'No, but I know where it is,' she replied warily. 'It's in the pound. Why?'

'New deal,' Li offered, sliding the keys towards her. 'The car instead of the cash.'

TEN MINUTES LATER they were back in the Fiat, skirting the eastern rim of the Piazza del Popolo.

'Who gave the watch to you?' Allegra asked.

A pained look flickered across Tom's face. 'Jennifer.'

'I'm sorry. I didn't realise . . .'

'We didn't have much choice,' Tom said, sighing. 'Besides, as long as we can get him the car, he'll give it back.'

'It shouldn't be too hard,' she said. 'Three, four guards at most. Why does he want it?' She frowned, checking her mirrors as she turned onto the Lungotevere Arnaldo da Brescia.

'He collects cars,' Tom explained. 'Has about forty of them in an underground garage somewhere near Trajan's Column. None of them paid for.'

They followed the river in silence, heading north against the traffic as the road flexed round the river bank's smooth contours.

'Tell me more about the Banda della Magliana,' Tom said.

'There are five major Mafia organisations in Italy,' Allegra said. 'The Cosa Nostra and Stidda in Sicily, the Camorra in Naples, the Sacra Corona Unita in Apulia and the 'Ndrangheta in Calabria. The Banda della Magliana was a smaller outfit based in Rome and controlled by the De Luca family.'

'Was?'

'You might remember that they were linked to a series of political assassinations and bombings between the 1970s and the 1990s. But since then they've been pretty quiet.'

'And Ricci worked for them?' Tom asked.

'Gallo said he was an enforcer. As far as I know the family's still controlled by Giovanni De Luca, although no one's seen him for years.'

'What about the Cosa Nostra, the Banda della Magliana's partner in the Delian League? Who heads them up?'

'Lorenzo Moretti. Or at least that's the rumour. It's not the sort of thing you put on your business card.'

The car pound occupied a large, anonymously grey multistorey building at the end of a tree-lined residential street. Two guards were stationed at each of the two sentry posts that flanked the entry and exit ramps.

'*Buongiorno.*' Allegra flashed a broad smile and her badge in the same instant, snapping it shut before they could get a good look at her name or the picture. 'Sorry to disturb you,' she continued, 'but my friend has had his car stolen.'

The two men glanced at Tom accusingly.

'It's probably in a container to Morocco by now,' one of them suggested.

'That's what I told him,' Allegra agreed. 'Only one of his neighbours says they saw it being towed. And this is the closest pound to where he lives.'

'If it's been towed it will be on the database,' one of the officers said to Tom. 'Pay the release fee and you can have it back.'

'He's already looked and it's not there,' she said with a shrug. 'He thinks that someone might have made a mistake and entered the wrong plates.'

'Really?' The men eyed him as they would a glass of corked wine.

'He's English,' she murmured, giving him the sort of weary look a mother might give a naughty child. The officers nodded in sudden understanding, a sympathetic look crossing their faces. 'Is there any chance we can go up and take a quick look to see if it's here? I'd really appreciate it.'

The two men glanced at each other and then shrugged their agreement.

'When did it go missing?' one of them asked her, ignoring Tom.

'Around March the 15th.'

'We store all the cars in the order they get brought here,' the first officer explained, pointing at a map of the complex that had been taped to the counter. 'Cars for that week should be around here—in the blue quadrant on the third floor. The lift's down there on the right.'

A few moments later the lift doors pinged shut behind them.

'You enjoyed that, didn't you?' Tom said in a reproachful tone.

'It could have been worse,' she said with an amused smile. 'I could have told them you were American.'

The lift opened onto the southern end of the third floor. It was a dark, depressing place; most of the neon tubes were missing or broken. The floor was divided by lines of concrete pillars into three long aisles, with cars parked along both sides. They made their way over to the area pointed out by the guard. Allegra took out the keys and pressed the unlock button. Cavalli's car eagerly identified itself with a double flash of its indicators—a souped-up Maserati Granturismo, worth almost double what Johnny was asking for it.

'What are you doing?' Tom called in a low voice as Allegra opened the boot and leaned inside. 'It must have been searched already.'

'That doesn't mean they found anything,' she replied, her voice muffled.

She stood up, triumphantly holding a small piece of pottery that had been nestling in a fold in the grey blanket that covered the boot floor. It featured a bearded man's face painted in red against a black background.

'It's a vase fragment. Probably Apulian, which dates it to between 430 and 300 BC. I'd guess it was part of a *krater*, a bowl used—'

'For mixing wine and water,' Tom said, grinning at her obvious surprise. 'My parents were art dealers. My mother specialised in antiquities. I guess I was a good listener.'

'Notice anything strange?' she asked, handing it to him with a nod.

'The edges are sharp.' He frowned, drawing his finger over one of them.

'Sharp and clean,' she agreed. 'Which means the break is recent.'

'It was done after it was dug up?' Tom gave her a puzzled look.

'I mean it was done on purpose,' she shot back. Tom detected a hint of anger in her voice. 'See how they've been careful not to damage the painted area so they can restore it.'

'You mean it's been smashed so it can be stuck back together again?'

'It makes it easier to smuggle,' she explained. 'Unfortunately, we see it all the time. The fragments are called orphans. The dealers can sometimes make more money selling them off individually than they would get for an intact piece, because they can raise the price as the collector or museum gets more and more desperate to buy all the pieces. And of course, by the time the vase is fully restored, no one can track where or who they bought each fragment from. Everyone's protected.'

'Then Cavalli must have been working either with or for the League,' Tom said grimly as she dropped the boot lid. 'Perhaps they found out that the FBI had his name and killed him before he could talk?'

The noise of an engine starting echoed up to them from one of the lower floors, and drew a worried glance from Tom towards the exit.

'We should go.' He opened the passenger door to get in, but immediately staggered back, coughing as a choking chemical smell clawed at his throat.

'You OK?' Allegra called out in concern.

'It's been sprayed with a fire extinguisher,' he croaked. 'Old trick. The foam destroys any fingerprint or DNA evidence.'

'Which Cavalli's killers would only have done if they'd been in the car,' Allegra said thoughtfully, opening the driver's side door and standing back to let the fumes clear.

'Where did they find the car keys?' he asked, rubbing his eyes.

'In his pocket. Why?'

'I'm just wondering if he was driving. Based on that I'd guess he was. I doubt his killers drove him out to wherever the car was dumped and then planted the keys on him before killing him.'

'What does it matter either way?'

Taking a deep breath, Tom disappeared inside the car. Leaning over the passenger seat, he plunged his hand down the back of the driver's seat. Feeling around with his fingertips, he pulled out first some loose change, then a pack of matches and finally, pushed right down, a folded Polaroid.

'If Cavalli was driving, that's about the only place he would have been able to hide something once he realised what was going on,' he explained. 'Here.' He leant over the roof and handed the photo to her. 'Any ideas?'

'Some sort of statue fragment,' she said. 'Greek, I'd guess, although—'

She was interrupted by a shout.

'*Rimanete dove siete!*' Stay where you are!

Spinning round, Allegra recognised the two officers they had talked their way past downstairs. One was hunched over the wheel of the blue Fiat squad car that had ghosted up the ramp behind them, its headlights now blazing through the darkness. The other was standing next to it, gun drawn.

'We found the car.' Allegra stepped towards him with a smile, switching back into Italian. 'My friend just needs to pay . . .'

'I said stay where you are,' the officer barked, his trigger finger twitching.

'I don't think he's buying it any more,' Tom whispered.

'No,' she agreed. 'Get in!'

Diving through the open doors, she jammed the key in the ignition, fired up the engine and selected reverse. Tom jumped in alongside her, the crack of a gunshot whistling overhead. The car leapt backwards and swung out.

'You're facing the wrong way,' Tom shouted. Their windscreen was now in the glare of the squad car's headlights as it accelerated towards them.

'Don't tell me how to drive,' she retorted indignantly, turning to look back over her shoulder. 'If I'd tried to reverse out the other way, I'd have wrapped it round the pillar.'

She stamped on the pedal, the car springing backwards and then yawing wildly as she fought to keep it straight. Tyres screaming, they rounded the corner and then doubled back on themselves, the engine protesting with an angry whine as they sped down the central aisle, the revs climbing steeply.

Another shot rang out. One of their headlights exploded.

'Head down a floor,' Tom suggested. 'Try and get far enough ahead of them to flip it round.'

She cannoned the wrong way onto the up ramp, using the ramp's curved walls to guide herself down to the second level.

'Someone's coming up the other way,' Tom warned her as a second squad car, siren pulsing, stormed up the ramp towards them.

She steered them off the ramp onto the flat. From behind came the angry squeal of brakes as the squad car chasing them fishtailed to avoid colliding with the second police car coming up the other way. Allegra sensed her opportunity. Leaning on the clutch, she yanked on the handbrake and jerked the wheel hard to spin them round so that they were facing forward, then shoved the car into gear and accelerated away along the left-hand aisle.

'You've got one right behind, one to the right,' Tom shouted over the engine noise, pointing to where the second car was now speeding down the central aisle, roughly parallel to them.

'They're going to try and cut us off at the end,' she guessed. 'Hold on.'

Checking in her mirror to see how close the car behind was, she stamped on the brake. The car juddered to a halt, forcing their pursuers to run into the back of them, the impact knocking them five or six feet forward and wrenching their boot open. What damage they had sustained was as nothing compared to the Fiat, however, which had, unsurprisingly, come off second best with both front tyres burst, the engine block almost in the front seat, and the bonnet concertinaed back on itself.

Allegra glanced across at Tom with a satisfied grin, but he was pointing at the second police car, which was already at the far end of the second aisle and rounding the corner towards them.

'Here comes the cavalry.'

Dropping the Maserati into gear, she pulled forward and cut through a gap in the parked cars to her right to reach the central aisle and then span round, so that she was facing back towards the exit ramp.

'What are you doing?' he asked with a frown.

'Enjoying myself,' she breathed.

Gunning the motor hard, she took off, glancing across at the squad car racing down the adjacent aisle to make sure she was far enough ahead.

She steered away from the line of cars to her right and then carved back in, ramming an Alfa square on. It jumped forward, colliding with the VW parked opposite it, which in turn T-boned the squad car as it came past, sending it ploughing into the line of parked cars on the far side of the aisle.

There was an abrupt, empty moment of calm. The squad car's blue light pulsed weakly in the gloom. Then a jarring chorus of car alarms kicked in, roused by the force of the crash.

'Where did you learn to drive like that?' Tom asked.

'Rush hour in Rome.' She smiled, breathing hard.

'Do you think Johnny will notice the damage?'

She glanced in the mirror and saw the boot lid flapping around behind them like a loose sail, then looked along the crumpled bonnet at the cloud of steam rising from the cracked radiator.

'It'll polish out.' She grinned.

Reversing out, the steering pulling heavily to the right, she nursed the car down the exit ramp and then made her way out onto the street.

Deposito Eroli, Via Eroli, Rome

'I thought you told these idiots to hold off until we got here?' Gallo said in an accusing tone as Salvatore hurried towards him.

Misfortune was snapping at his heels, it seemed. First the triangulation of Allegra's mobile-phone signal, only for her to have vanished by the time they got there. Then a sighting reported by the officers here, only for her to slip through his fingers a second time.

'I did,' Salvatore sighed wearily. 'Apparently they were trying to lock down the area in case they drove off.'

'Lock down the area? The stupid bastards have been watching too much TV.' Gallo glowered at the two men in neck braces being stretchered past him into a waiting ambulance. 'It's just as well she's put them in hospital. She's saved me the trouble.' Cursing under his breath, he lit a cigarette.

'You mean *they* saved you the trouble,' Salvatore corrected him.

'She wasn't alone?' Gallo glanced up, surprised.

'There was a man.'

'What man?'

'Not sure yet.'

A pause, as Gallo let this sink in. 'What were they doing here?'

'They were seen opening up a black Maserati. Registration number . . . JT14 9VT,' Salvatore read from his notebook. 'Cavalli's.'

Gallo span round to face him. 'Cavalli's?' he spat. 'What the hell was she looking for?' He glared at the building behind him as if it was somehow at fault and owed him an answer. To his surprise, it gave him one.

'There must be a camera up there!' He pointed at the lens fixed above the entrance. 'Get me the disk.'

A few minutes later they were seated round a small monitor in the sentry post, Salvatore forwarding to the time of the last entry in the log. For ten, maybe twenty seconds the grainy black-and-white footage showed nothing but parked cars, but then, just as Gallo was about to hit the fast-forward button again, two people appeared in the shot.

'That's not her,' Salvatore said with a shake of his head.

'Yes it is,' Gallo breathed. 'She's cut her hair. Dyed it, too. Clever girl.' His face broke into a grudging smile. 'And who are you?' He hit the pause button, trying to make out the face of the man walking next to her.

'Never seen him before,' Salvatore shrugged.

'Get a print of this off to the lab when we've finished,' Gallo ordered, starting the disk again. 'Get them to run it through the system. Interpol too.'

'Where did she get his car keys?' Salvatore asked with a frown as they watched Allegra beep the car open and then step round to the boot.

'Evidence room. They were probably on the same set as—' Gallo broke off with a frown as he saw Allegra retrieve something from the boot. He paused the footage again. 'What the hell is that?'

'Christ knows.' Salvatore shrugged. 'The picture's too dark. I'll ask the lab to see what they can do with it.'

'I thought you said that car had been searched?' Gallo barked angrily.

'I—I thought it had,' Salvatore stammered. Coughing nervously, he restarted the film only to pause it himself a few moments later.

'He's got something too,' he said, squinting as he tried to make out the image. 'Looks like . . . a piece of paper. Or maybe a photo?'

'I want the names of whoever searched that car,' Gallo said through gritted teeth. 'Put out a revised description of Damico and get something worked up for this guy,' he ordered. 'Then—'

'Colonel, we've found the car!' A young officer had appeared at the door, breathing hard. 'Abandoned in the Borghese Gardens.'

'And Lieutenant Damico?'

'No sign of her, I'm afraid.'

Salvatore stood up, giving Gallo an expectant look.

'Go.' He nodded. 'Find her. She can't have got far if she's on foot.'

Gallo waited until the room was empty and then dialled a number.

'It's me.' He lit another cigarette and took a long drag. 'We just missed her again . . . She came looking for Cavalli's car. She found something he'd hidden in it . . . If I had to guess, a photograph.' Another pause as he listened, his expression hardening. 'How should I know what was on it?' he said angrily. 'I was rather hoping you could tell me.'

Spagna Metropolitana station, Rome

The train galloped into the station, the doors hissed open and a muscular human wave swept Tom and Allegra through the tunnels and up the escalators, until it broke as it reached the street above, beaching them in the shadow of the Spanish Steps.

'Let's head into the centre,' Tom said, shaking off the street hawkers tugging at his sleeve. 'Stick with the crowds.'

Ten minutes later they were opposite each other in a cubicle at the rear of a bar on the Piazza Campo Marzio, tucking into pastries and espressos.

'So what are we going to do about Johnny?' Allegra asked.

'What can we do?' Tom shrugged. 'Even if we hadn't trashed the car, the cops will be all over it by now. We're just going to have to wait until Archie calls and then pay Johnny the cash instead.'

'Archie?'

'My business partner,' Tom explained. 'He's on his way to Geneva, but he knows people here. The sort of people who can lend us fifty grand without asking too many questions.'

'Show me that photo again,' Allegra said.

Reaching into his pocket, Tom laid the Polaroid down between them. It showed a sculpted man's face against a black background, a jagged edge marking where part of his chin and left cheek had broken off.

'It looks like marble. A statue fragment,' she said slowly, turning it to face her. 'Beautifully carved . . . Almost certainly looted.'

'How can you tell?'

'Tomb-robbers always use Polaroids. They can't be as easily emailed around as digital photos, allowing you to keep track of who has seen what.'

'Are you sure it's marble?' Tom frowned. 'It looks pretty thin. Almost like some sort of mask.'

'You're right,' she said, peering at the image. 'Strange. To be honest, I've never really seen anything like it before.'

'Then we need to find someone who has. Cavalli must have hidden the photo for a reason.'

'Well, the obvious person is—' Allegra began, breaking off as she realised what she was saying.

'Your friend the professor?' Tom guessed.

'I wasn't thinking.' She shook her head. 'There's no way I'm—'

'You won't have to. I'll do the talking. Where can I find him?'

'Forget it, Gallo will have someone watching his apartment.'

'He must go out?'

'Not if he can avoid—' She gripped Tom's arm. 'What time is it?'

He glanced up at the clock on the wall.

'Just after ten. Why?' Tom asked as she excitedly stuffed the photograph into her pocket.

'He's giving a lecture this morning,' she exclaimed. 'I saw his notes yesterday. Eleven o'clock at the Galleria Doria Pamphilj.'

Piazza del Collegio Romano, Rome

Aurelio Eco paused on the entrance steps to the Doria Pamphilj and snatched a glance over his shoulder. Gallo's men weren't even trying to pretend they weren't following him now. Two of them had parked near where he'd been dropped off by his taxi and were following on foot about thirty feet behind. He felt more prisoner than protected, despite what they'd told him. With a helpless shrug, he placed his hand on the door and heaved it open.

'*Buongiorno, Professore,*' the guard on reception welcomed him cheerily.

He was early, but then he liked to leave himself enough time to check the room and have a final read through his notes.

Stepping out of the lift, he limped through the Poussin and Velvet rooms to the ballroom, where giltwood and red velvet chairs had already been laid out. Enough seating for fifty, he noted with a smile.

'Are you alone?'

He turned to see a man closing the door behind him and turning the key in the lock.

'The lecture doesn't start until eleven,' he replied warily.

'Are you alone, Aurelio?' A woman stood framed in the doorway to the small ballroom, her face stone, her voice like ice.

'Allegra?' Aurelio gasped. 'Is that you? What have you done to yourself?'

'How many men followed you here?' Tom growled in Italian.

Aurelio's eyes flicked back to him. 'Two,' he stuttered. 'Gallo's. They've been watching me ever since . . .'

'Ever since you betrayed me?' Allegra hissed. It was strange. She'd felt many things for Aurelio since yesterday afternoon. Sadness, disbelief, confusion. But now that he was actually standing in front of her, it was anger, instinctive and uncontained, that had come most naturally.

'We haven't got time for that now,' Tom warned her, bolting shut the door that gave onto the adjacent ballroom. 'Just show it to him.'

'I'm sorry, Allegra. I'm so sorry,' Aurelio whispered. 'I should have told you. I should have told you everything a long time ago.'

'Save it,' she snapped, then pressed the photo into his hands. 'What is it?'

He gazed down at the picture, then looked up, open-mouthed.

'Is this real?' he croaked.

'It looks Greek,' Allegra prompted. 'I thought the marble could be from Pentelikon.'

'Greek, yes, but that's not marble.' He shook his head excitedly, his eyes locking with hers. 'It's ivory.'

'Ivory?' she repeated breathlessly. It was obvious, now he'd mentioned it. Obvious and yet impossible.

'It's a mask from a chryselephantine statue,' Aurelio confirmed. 'Circa 400 to 500 BC. Probably of Apollo.' A pause. 'Are you sure this is real?' he asked again.

'Chryselephantine means gold and ivory in Greek,' Allegra explained in English, seeing the confused look on Tom's face. 'They used to fix carved slabs of ivory onto a wooden frame for the head, hands and feet, and then beat sheets of gold leaf onto the rest to form the clothes, armour and hair.'

'It's rare?'

'It's a miracle,' Aurelio replied in a hushed tone. 'There used to be seventy-four of them in Rome, but they all vanished when it was sacked by the Barbarians in 410 AD. Apart from two fire-damaged examples found in Greece and a fragment in the Vatican Museum, not a single piece has survived. Certainly nothing of this size and quality.'

Their eyes all shot to the door as someone tried the handle.

'Time to go,' Tom said firmly, snatching back the photo. 'The private apartments should still be clear. We can go out the same way we came in.'

'Wait,' Aurelio called after them. 'Don't you want to know who it's by?'

'You can tell that from a photo?' Allegra frowned.

'Not definitively,' he admitted. 'But if I had to guess . . . there's only one sculptor from that period that we know of who was capable of something of that quality. The same person who carved the statue of Athena in the Parthenon.'

'Phidias?' Allegra guessed, her mouth suddenly dry.

'Who else?' He nodded excitedly. 'Don't you see, Allegra? It's a miracle.'

'Let's go,' Tom repeated, grabbing Allegra's arm. The door was now shaking violently. But she wrestled herself free, determined to ask the one question that she most wanted answered.

'Why did you do it, Aurelio? Has Gallo got something on you?'

'Gallo? I'd never even heard of him until yesterday,' he protested.

'Then who were you on the phone to?'

There was a long pause, Aurelio's lips quivering. 'The League.'

'The Delian League?' she breathed, not sure which was worse—Aurelio working with Gallo, as she'd first assumed, or this?

'They said they wouldn't hurt you. That they just wanted to see what you knew,' he pleaded. 'I wanted to tell you everything. Have done for a long time. When you told me about the lead discs and the killings . . . I tried to point you in the right direction. But I was afraid.'

Abruptly, the noise outside stopped.

'They'll be back with a key,' urged Tom. 'Come on!'

'You could have trusted me,' she insisted. 'I could have helped you.'

'It was too late for that. It's been thirty years. They'd kept records of everything I'd ever done for them. The false attributions, the inflated valuations, the invented provenances. I needed the money. I needed the money to finance my work. Who else was going to pay? The university? Pah!'

'Who are they?' she pressed. 'Give me a name.'

'There was a dealer who I met a few times,' he muttered. 'An American called Faulks. Everyone else was just a voice on the phone. Believe me, Allegra, I tried to get out so many times. But the older I got, the harder it became to throw everything away. My books, my research—everything I'd ever worked for . . . It would all have been for nothing if they'd leaked my involvement. I had no choice. My reputation was all I had left.'

'No,' she said, with a broken smile. 'You had me.'

Quai du Mont Blanc, Geneva

There was a definite spring in Earl Faulks's step that morning. Things were going well. Much better, in fact, than he had anticipated. His courier had cleared the border at Lake Lugano that morning and was due down at the Free Port anytime now. In Rome, meanwhile, events were unfolding far more quickly and dramatically than he had ever dreamed would be possible.

There had been that unhelpful little episode with the kouros at the Getty, of course, although for the moment at least, tempers seemed to have cooled. Having seen the ivory mask, Verity had understood that there was a far greater prize at stake here than a dry academic debate over a statue's marble type and muscle tone. She was due in from Madrid the following day.

Until then he had an auction to prepare for. On cue, his car drew up outside Sotheby's. He sat back, waiting for his chauffeur to jog round and open his door, but then waved him away when his phone began to ring. An American number that he didn't recognise.

'Faulks.'

'This is Kezman,' the voice replied.

'Mr Kezman. Thank you for returning my call. I wasn't expecting to hear from you so late.'

'I'm in the casino business. This is early,' he growled. 'If you've got something to sell, sell it.'

'Fair enough. Here's the pitch: seven and a half million and your name in lights.'

'My name's in ten-foot neon out on the Strip already.' Kezman gave an impatient laugh. 'Tell me about the money.'

'Seven and a half million dollars,' Faulks repeated slowly. 'Risk-free.'

'Go on.'

Faulks smiled. He had his attention now.

'An item has come into my possession. An item of immense historical and cultural significance. I want you to buy it for ten million dollars.'

'Sure. Why not make it twenty?' Kezman gave a hollow laugh.

'Then you're going to donate it to Verity Bruce at the Getty,' Faulks continued, ignoring the interruption. 'She will value it at fifty million, its true price. This will lead the IRS . . .'

'To give me a seventeen-and-a-half-million tax credit for having made a fifty-million-dollar charitable donation,' Kezman breathed, his flippant tone vanishing.

'Which, subtracting the ten you will have paid me, nets out at a seven-and-a-half-million profit, courtesy of Uncle Sam. Not to mention the PR value of the coverage that will be triggered by your generosity.'

'How firm is the valuation?'

'Verity Bruce is due here tomorrow to authenticate the piece. Something this rare isn't affected by short-term economic factors. The value will hold.'

Kezman was silent for a few moments. Faulks waited, knowing that his next question would reveal how well he'd played his hand.

'When would you need the money?'

'A few days. A week at most.'

'If Verity OKs it, I'm in,' Kezman confirmed. 'Just get her to call me when she's seen it.'

'Wait! Don't you even want to know what it is?' Faulks asked.

A pause. 'Will I make any more if I do?'

'No,' Faulks conceded.

'Then why should I care?'

Via del Governo Vecchio, Rome

The streets were dark and narrow, the buildings seeming to arch together over Tom and Allegra's heads like trees kissing over a country lane. It was busy too, with people picking their way along the narrow pavements.

Allegra was silent. She was hurting, Tom knew. He tried to think of something to say that might comfort her. But he couldn't. The truth was that in time the floodwaters of her anger and confusion would recede, leaving behind them the tidemark of lost friendship with Aurelio.

'What other Phidias pieces are there?' he asked.

'There's a torso of Athena in the Ecole des Beaux-Arts in Paris that's been attributed to him,' she replied. 'And they found a cup inscribed with his name in the ruins of the workshop at Olympia where he assembled the statue of Zeus.'

'But nothing like the mask?'

'Not even close.' She shook her head. 'If Aurelio's right, it's priceless.'

'Everything has a price,' Tom smiled. 'The trick is finding someone willing to pay it.'

'Maybe that's what Cavalli was doing the night he was killed,' she said. 'Meeting a buyer. Or at least someone he thought was a buyer.'

'It would explain why he had the Polaroid on him,' Tom agreed. 'And why he hid it when he realised what they really wanted.'

'But not where he got the mask from in the first place.' Allegra paused, frowning, as the road brought them out onto the Piazza Ponte Sant'Angelo. 'What are we doing here?'

'Isn't this where you said Cavalli was killed?' Tom asked.

'Yes, but . . .'

'I thought we should take a look.'

A steady two-way traffic of pedestrians was streaming over the bridge's polished cobbles, the hands and faces of the statues lining the parapet seeming strangely animated under the sun's flickering caress, as if they were waving them forward.

'Where did they find him?' Tom asked.

'In the river. Hanging from one of the statues.'

'Killed on the anniversary of Caesar's murder, only for Ricci to be murdered on the site of Caesar's assassination,' he said thoughtfully.

'With both Ricci's and Argento's deaths staged as a re-enactment of a Caravaggio painting.' She nodded impatiently. 'We've been through this.'

'I know.' He shrugged. 'It's just that everything about these murders has been so deliberate. The dates, the locations, the arrangement of the bodies. It's almost as if . . . they weren't just killings.'

'Then what were they?'

Tom paused before answering. In the distance the glorious dome of St Peter's rose into the sky. Around it swarmed a flock of pigeons, their solid mass wheeling and circling like a shroud caught in the wind.

'Messages,' he said. 'Maybe someone was trying to have a conversation.'

'If you're right, it started with Cavalli,' she said slowly.

'Exactly. So why kill him here? Why this bridge?'

'It was originally built to connect the city to Hadrian's Mausoleum. And in the sixteenth and seventeenth centuries, famously of course, they used to display the bodies of executed prisoners along it as a warning.'

'A warning to whom?' Tom frowned, then nodded at the weathered shapes looming over them. 'What about the statues? Do they mean anything?'

'Each angel is holding an object from the Passion. Cavalli's rope was tied to the one holding a cross.'

'Which was then echoed by Ricci's inverted crucifixion and Argento being found in a church.'

'That's not the only thing,' Allegra added excitedly, a thought having just occurred to her. 'Cavalli's not the first person to have been killed here. A noblewoman called Beatrice Cenci was tortured and put to death on the Piazza Ponte Sant'Angelo in 1599,' she explained.

'What had she done?'

'Murdered her father.'

'Patricide. Treason. Maybe that's it. Maybe Cavalli had betrayed the

League and this was his punishment?' He gave a deep sigh, then turned to her with a shrug. 'Your guess is as good as mine. Come on, let's try and call Archie. He should have landed by now.'

They turned and walked to the end of the bridge. Tom reached for his phone as they waited for a break in the traffic. But before they could cross, a large armoured truck gunned down the road towards them. Two men jumped down, one holding what Tom recognised as what the Sicilian Mafia called a *lupara*—a traditional break-open-design shotgun.

A woman behind screamed and Tom could hear the fumbling scramble of panicked feet behind him as people scattered.

'Get in,' one of the men barked.

LOOKING AROUND HIM, Tom could see that the truck's interior had been furnished like an expensive office. To his left a red leather sofa abutted what he assumed was a toilet cubicle, its door latched shut. In the far right-hand corner stood an elegant cherrywood desk on which a brass banker's lamp illuminated a laptop and a police scanner spitting static. Opposite the sofa was a rack, which contained four MP5 submachine guns, half a dozen Glock 17 pistols and a pair of Remington 1100 shotguns.

The gears crunched and the truck swayed forward. The gunman, who had followed them inside, waved at them to sit down and then instructed them to handcuff themselves to the hoop bolted to the wall above them so that their arms were held above their heads. Stepping forward, he made sure that the ratchets were tight against their wrists and then emptied their pockets and Tom's bag, pausing over the FBI file and the Polaroid of the ivory mask.

There was the muffled sound of the toilet flushing. The latch clicked open and a man walked out. Tall and square-faced, he had a thinning head of hair that rose in white waves at the front and then foundered into a black expanse at the rear. He was smartly dressed in a grey Armani suit and gaudy Versace tie with matching pocket handkerchief.

The guard handed him the file and the Polaroid. He glanced at each of them, then sat down.

'Welcome to Rome, Signor Kirk.' He spoke in a thick accent, his eyes fixing them with a cold gaze.

'You know him?' Allegra's voice was both angry and disbelieving.

Tom frowned as he tried to place the face, then shook his head.

'He's Giovanni De Luca,' Allegra said unsmilingly. 'The head of the Banda della Magliana.'

Tom's eyes flickered in recognition. So much for tracking the Delian League down and the element of surprise. Instead, one half of it had come looking for them and sprung its own trap.

'Felix doesn't know me,' De Luca said. 'But I had the pleasure of meeting his mother once.'

'My mother?' Tom breathed, astonished.

'A fundraising dinner many years ago. A beautiful woman, if I may say so. A terrible loss. Of course, it was only years later that I heard of you.'

'Heard what, exactly?' Allegra asked, eyeing Tom with the same suspicious look she'd had back in Cavalli's house when she'd first met him.

'It's hard to be good at what Felix does without word getting out. He has a special talent.'

'Had,' Tom corrected him. 'I got out a few years ago.'

'And yet, from what I hear, you're still running.'

'What is this about?' Tom asked impatiently. His arms were beginning to ache and every gear change and bump in the road was making the cuffs saw a little deeper into his wrists.

'What's this?' De Luca waved the photo at him.

'We found it in Cavalli's car. We think he was trying to sell it.'

'What do you know about Cavalli?' De Luca shot back, spitting the name out in a way that revealed more than he had probably intended.

Tom nodded slowly, immediately guessing at the truth.

'Why did you kill him?'

De Luca paused, then inclined his head in a small bow.

'Strictly speaking, the river killed him.'

'Did he work for you?'

'Pfff! He was one of Moretti's.'

Moretti. Tom recognised the name as the person Allegra had identified as supposedly heading up the *other* half of the Delian League.

'What had he done?' Allegra asked.

'I only kill for two reasons. Theft and disloyalty.' De Luca counted them off on his fingers. 'In Cavalli's case, he was guilty of both.'

'You mean he'd betrayed the League?' Tom asked.

'It seemed fitting to mark his treachery on the spot of an earlier treason,' De Luca nodded, confirming what they'd already guessed on the bridge.

'And Ricci?' Allegra asked.

'I took care of Cavalli to protect the League. But Moretti thought I was about to make a move on the whole operation.' De Luca's tone hardened.

'He had Ricci killed to warn me off. Argento was me evening the score.'

Tom nodded as the realisation dawned that far from being a conversation the careful echoing and symbolism of the various deaths had in fact been the opening shots of a very public, very acrimonious divorce.

'And now it seems my accountant in Monaco has disappeared,' he continued. 'Well, if Moretti wants a war, I'm ready for him.'

'What did Jennifer Browne have to do with your war?' Tom demanded angrily.

'Who?' De Luca frowned.

'The FBI agent you had killed in Vegas.'

'What FBI agent?'

'Don't lie to me,' Tom shouted, his wrists straining against the handcuffs.

'Cavalli was going to sing, so I clipped his wings,' De Luca said in a low voice. 'Ricci and Argento—that's just business between Moretti and me. I had nothing to do with killing any FBI agent. I've never even heard of her.'

'She was closing in on the Delian League, so you had her taken out,' Tom insisted.

'Is that what this is about? Is that why you're here?' De Luca picked up the FBI file and glanced at its cover with a puzzled shrug. 'Well, then maybe somebody did us a favour. Either way, I never ordered the hit.'

'Well, somebody in the League did,' Tom insisted. 'And I'll take you all down to find them, if I have to.'

There was a pause. De Luca blew out the sides of his cheeks, clearly mulling something over. Then he nodded. 'Yes. I expect you probably would.'

Tom felt the needle before he saw it, a sharp stab of pain in his neck. Allegra was next, her head slumping forward as he felt the room begin to spin and darken. The last thing he was aware of was De Luca's voice.

'Do give my best to your mother.'

Sotheby's auction rooms, Quai du Mont Blanc, Geneva

Short, perhaps only four feet high, she was dressed in a simple tunic that hung from her body in smooth folds; a hunting strap ran down from her shoulder and across her breasts. Gazing straight ahead, she wore a slight smile. Her arms were cut off at the elbows.

'Statue of the goddess Artemis, fourth century BC,' Archie murmured to himself as he looked down at the auction catalogue.

Glancing up, he caught sight of Dominique de Lecourt standing near the entrance. Seeing her now, blonde hair cascading onto her delicate shoulders, it struck him that her pale, oval face mirrored something of the goddess Artemis's cold, sculpted and remote beauty. There was a parallel too, between the statue's simple tunic and her tailored linen dress. But any resemblance was only a fleeting one, the illusion shattered by her Ducati biker jacket and the way her blue eyes glittered with a wild freedom that the marble sculpture would never taste.

Still only twenty-five, her age hadn't prevented her from successfully running Tom's antiques business, having helped him transfer it from Geneva to London after his father died.

Archie nodded at her as Earl Faulks turned to leave the room, leaning heavily on his umbrella. Even if the auctioneer hadn't accepted the carefully folded €500 note to finger him as the lot's seller, Archie would have guessed it was him. It wasn't just that he had returned four times during the viewing period that had marked him out, but the look he had given anyone who had strayed too close to the statue.

Seeing Archie's signal, Dominique set off, bumping into Faulks heavily as they crossed.

'*Pardon*,' she apologised.

'That's quite all right,' Faulks snapped, a cold smile flickering across his face before, with a curt nod, he limped on.

'Go,' she whispered as she walked past Archie, their hands briefly touching as she handed him Faulks's PDA.

Turning to face the wall, Archie popped off the rear cover, removed the battery and then slipped out the SIM card. Sliding it into a reader connected to a micro-computer, he scanned its contents. The software quickly identified the IMSI number, before girding itself to decrypt its ki code.

Archie glanced up at Dominique, who had moved back towards the entrance and was signalling at him to hurry. He gave a grim nod, his heart racing, but the program was still churning as it tried to break the 128-bit encryption, numbers scrolling frantically across the screen.

He looked up again, and cursed when he saw that she was now mouthing that Faulks was leaving. Damn! He'd counted on him staying for the auction itself. He looked back down at the computer. Still nothing. Dominique was looking desperate now. Back to the screen again. Done.

Snatching the SIM card out of the reader, he hurried to the door, fumbling as he slid it back into Faulks's phone and fitted the battery and cover. He crossed Dominique, their hands briefly touching again as he slipped her the micro-computer, leaving her the task of programming a new card.

'He's outside,' she breathed.

Archie sprinted into the hall, down the stairs and through the main entrance. Faulks was settling back in the rear seat of a silver Bentley.

'Excuse me, mate,' Archie panted, rapping sharply on the window.

The window sank and Faulks fixed him with a suspicious look.

'You dropped this.'

Faulks looked at the phone, patted his pockets, then glanced up at Archie.

'Thank you,' he said, his wary look fading into a grateful smile. Taking it with a nod, he sat back, the window smoothly sealing itself shut.

As the car accelerated away, Dominique appeared at Archie's shoulder.

'All sorted?' he puffed.

'We've got him.' She nodded, handing him the newly cloned phone.

Near Anguillara Sabazia, northwest of Rome

Tom's eyes flickered open. The room slowly came into focus. Allegra was lying on the tiled floor next to him. Still breathing.

Gingerly pulling himself upright, he sat with his back against the wall, trying not to vomit. The drugs had left him dizzy and with a bitter taste at the back of his throat. Worse still was the headache centred behind his right eye. Within seconds he'd fainted back to sleep.

'Tom?'

Allegra had rolled over onto her side to face him. She looked worried and he wondered how long she had been calling his name.

He groaned as he sat up, his neck stiff.

'What time is it?' she asked.

He checked his watch, then remembered with a rueful grimace that it was still wrapped round Johnny Li's tattooed wrist.

'No idea.'

'*Merda.*' She rubbed her hands wearily across her face, then sat up next to him. 'Where do you think they've taken us?'

Tom looked around with a frown. They were at one end of a windowless room that had been almost entirely swallowed by what appeared to be a large swimming pool. Five feet deep, sixty feet long and thirty feet across, it was lined with white tiles. Water spilled with a gurgling noise over the edges into an overflow trench. Underwater lights cast a shimmering flicker onto the white-washed concrete walls.

Standing up, Tom walked unsteadily to the edge. His eyes adjusting, it took him a few moments to realise that the dark shapes lurking under the water's silvered surface were rows of antique vases and jars.

'It's a chemical bath,' he said, pointing at the blue drums that explained the slight burning sensation in his eyes.

'I've seen something like this before,' Allegra nodded, joining him. 'But not this big. Not even close.'

'Over there.' Tom pointed hopefully at a door on the far side of the pool.

They passed through into a large room, its tiled walls lined with glass-fronted cabinets that contained a rainbow array of paints and chemicals in tins and jars. Beneath these, running along each wall, were polished stainless-steel counters loaded with microscopes, centrifuges, test-tube racks, scales, shakers and other pieces of laboratory equipment.

'Cleaning, touching-up, repairs, open-heart surgery . . .' Tom pursed his lips. 'This is a tombaroli restoration outfit.'

'On an industrial scale,' she agreed, with anger in her voice.

There was another unlocked door, which gave, in turn, on to a third room. Here there was a more rustic feel, the ceiling supported by parallel lines of closely spaced wooden beams. Semicircular iron-framed windows were set into the stone walls at above head height and welded shut. A flight of stone steps led upstairs to another door. Predictably, this one was locked.

Shrugging dejectedly, Tom made his way back down. Allegra was waiting for him, silently pointing, her outstretched arm quivering with rage.

Looking around, he could see the paved floor was covered in a foaming sea of dirty newspapers, wooden crates and old fruit and shoe boxes, some stacked into neat piles, others split open or listing dangerously where the cardboard had collapsed under their combined weight. He only had to open a few to guess at the contents of all the others—antique vases still covered in dirt, loose jumbles of glass and Etruscan jewellery, envelopes bulging with Roman coins. In the corner was what had once been an entire fresco, chain-sawed into laptop-sized chunks, presumably to make them easier to move and sell.

'How could they do this?' Allegra breathed.

'Because none of this has any value to them other than what they can sell it for. Because they don't care. Look.'

He nodded with disgust towards one of the shoe boxes. It was stuffed with rings and human bones, the tombaroli having simply snapped off the fingers of the dead to save time.

'You think this is where Cavalli got the ivory mask?' she asked.

'I doubt it. Whoever owns this place must work for De Luca, and he didn't look like he'd ever seen the mask before.'

'He may not have seen it, but he might have found out that Cavalli was ripping him off,' she suggested. 'Theft and disloyalty, remember? According to De Luca, Cavalli was guilty of both. Maybe Cavalli was trying to sell the mask behind the League's back.'

'So De Luca killed Cavalli, Moretti evened the score by murdering Ricci, and then De Luca struck back by executing Argento. He was right. We've stumbled into a war.'

'That must be why they both put the lead discs on the bodies. Remember I told you that the original Delian League was to have lasted as long as the lead its members had thrown into the sea didn't rise to the surface? The discs were to signal that this new alliance was fracturing.'

'None of which explains who ordered the hit on Jennifer or why.' He sighed impatiently.

'She must have meant a lot to you,' Allegra said gently. 'For you to have come all this way. For you to be risking so much.'

'She trusted me to do the right thing,' Tom answered with a half-smile. 'That's more than most have ever—'

He broke off as the door above them was unbolted and thrown open. A man stood silhouetted in the doorway, his long shadow stretching down the stairs towards them. He was holding a hip-flask.

'Let's go for a drive.'

Banco Rosalia, Via Boncompagni, Rome

'So? How much are we down?' Santos sniffed, helping himself to a half-tumbler of Limoncello from the drinks trolley.

Alfredo Geri looked up from his laptop, frowning slightly. His thin black hair was slicked down against his marbled scalp, his face bleached a cadaverous shade of white by lack of sleep and sunlight.

'Now I've had a chance to look properly . . . eight . . . maybe nine hundred million. Euro.'

'Eight or nine hundred million euro.' Santos closed his eyes and sighed heavily, then reached for his tin of liquorice and popped the lid. 'And how about the League's deposits and investments?' he asked hopefully.

'Antonio, the bank's entire capital base is gone.' Geri spoke slowly. 'It's all gone. Everything.'

Santos knocked the Limoncello back.

'Good. It makes things easier. This way I only need to worry about myself. Where did I come out in the end?'

'I've liquidated what I can.' Geri sounded apologetic. 'Most of it at a loss. But the bulk of your portfolio would take weeks if not months to sell.'

'How much?' Santos snapped.

'Three, maybe four million.'

'That barely gets me a chalet,' Santos said with a hollow laugh. 'What about the money-market positions?'

'Already included, minus what you had to sell to fund your fun and games in Las Vegas last week,' Geri reminded him in a reproachful tone.

'Fine.' Santos stood up. 'It is what it is and what it is . . . is not enough. I need the painting.'

'You've found a buyer?'

'The Serbs are lined up to take it off my hands for twenty million,' Santos said with a smile. 'I'm flying out to meet them later tonight.'

'And the watches?'

'I've got one already and another on its way. I'll get the third on the night from De Luca or Moretti. They always wear theirs.'

'They won't let you get away with it,' Geri pointed out, closing his file.

'They won't be able to stop me if they're dead.' Santos shrugged, moving round to stand behind him.

'For every person you kill, the League will send two more. You can't kill them all. Eventually they'll find you.'

'How?' Santos shrugged. 'The world's a large place. And you're the only other person who knows where I'm going.'

'Well, you know I'll never tell them,' Geri reassured him.

'Oh, I know.' Santos smiled.

In an instant, he had locked his left arm round Geri's throat and pulled him clear of the table. Geri lashed out with his legs, catching the edge of his file and sending it cartwheeling to the floor. Then with his right hand, Santos reached round and grabbed Geri's chin. With a sharp jerk, he snapped his neck.

Near Anguillara Sabazia, northwest of Rome

'Drink?' Fabio Contarelli had turned in the passenger seat to face them, battered hip-flask in hand. In his mid-forties, short and pot-bellied, he had a warm, jovial manner. His weather-worn face was brown and cracked, although his green eyes shone, as if he was permanently on the verge of playing a practical joke. There was certainly little there to suggest that he had been responsible for the horrors Allegra and Tom had witnessed in the basement of his house.

'*No*,' Allegra refused. Tom did the same. Contarelli shrugged and took a swig himself, turning back to face the road as the mud-flecked Land Cruiser danced over the potholes.

'How long have you been a tombarolo?' Tom asked.

'Since I was a boy,' Contarelli said proudly. 'It's in the blood, you see. I used to come out to these fields with my father. In those days the earth would be littered with fragments of pottery and broken statues surfaced by the farmers' ploughs. That's when I realised there was another world under there. I sold what I found in the market, used the money to buy some books, got smarter about what pieces were and how much they were worth, climbed through the ranks. Now I'm a *Capo di Zona* and it's the only life I know.'

'And you always go out at night?'

'It depends on the site. For some of the larger ones, we offer the landowner a share in the profits. Then my boys turn up in the day with a bulldozer. If anyone asks, we tell them we're working on a construction project. If they ask again, we pay them off. Or shut them up.'

Allegra felt her anger rising, momentarily blinding her to the danger they were in and to the armed man seated in the back with her and Tom. This wasn't just tomb-robbing. It was cultural vandalism: Contarelli's brutal methods probably destroyed as much as he found.

'So you've never been caught?' Tom asked.

'The Carabinieri need to find us before they can catch us,' he explained with a grin. 'They do their best, but there are thousands of tombs and villas buried out here and they can't be everywhere at once.'

'Why do you do it?' Allegra snapped. 'Haven't you made enough money?'

'I don't do it for the money, my dear. Archaeology is my addiction,' he explained, his eyes shining. 'The thrill of finding a tomb, the adrenaline rush as you crawl inside, the fear of being caught . . .'

'What you do is not archaeology,' Allegra protested. 'It's rape. You take innocence and corrupt it, turning beauty into a bauble for the rich to decorate their mantelpieces with.'

'I bring history back from the dead,' he shot back, his face hardening. 'I restore artefacts from thousands of years of neglect. I provide them with a home. A home where they will go on display and be appreciated, rather than languish in some museum's basement storeroom. Is that rape?'

'What about *your* basement and the fresco we saw, hacked into pieces?' she retorted. 'Or the fingers ripped from the dead. Is that archaeology?'

Contarelli, face now like thunder, eyed her coldly.

'Stop the car,' he ordered the driver tonelessly. 'We'll walk from here.'

THEY HAD PARKED at the end of a rutted track and then set out across the fields on foot, Contarelli leading the way, his two men at the rear. Tom and Allegra had been roped together by their wrists, Tom's tied behind his back, Allegra's fixed in front of her so that she could follow behind.

'Where are you taking us?' Tom demanded. The hopelessness of their situation was growing with every step. Over this rough ground, roped together, they had no chance of escaping.

Contarelli turned to face him. 'Don De Luca told me you were interested in understanding what we do.'

'I think I've got the general idea, thanks.' Tom gave a tight smile. 'We can make our own way back from here.'

Contarelli gave one of his booming laughs and strode on.

'It takes us two nights to break into a tomb normally. On the first night we clear away the entrance and let whatever's inside oxidise and harden. Then on the second night we come back and take what we can before dawn. Usually I never come back a third time. It's too risky. But I've made an exception for you.'

He stopped and signalled at someone standing beneath a low hillock covered in trees. The man was leaning wearily on a shovel and had clearly been waiting for them. As they approached him and the dark passage he had uncovered, he waved back, jumping down to greet them.

'It's an Etruscan burial chamber,' Allegra breathed.

Contarelli turned, smiling. 'You see,' he said with a pained sigh. 'That's the type of cleverness that's got you both killed.'

Before Tom could move, a plastic hood was placed over his head by one of the men standing behind him and he was forced to his knees. Working quickly, they deftly passed a length of duct tape several times round his neck, sealing the bag against his skin. He felt himself being lifted and then dragged along the tomb's short corridor into the Stygian darkness of the burial chamber. Moments later Allegra was thrown down onto the damp earth next to him, struggling furiously.

'Compliments of Don De Luca,' Contarelli intoned from somewhere above them, his disembodied voice echoing off the tomb's domed roof.

For a few moments Tom could hear nothing apart from the rattle of his own breathing and Allegra's muffled shouts. But then came the muted sound of steel against stone. They were filling the entrance in.

THEY DIDN'T HAVE LONG, Tom knew. Each breath used a little more of the oxygen sealed within the bag. He could already feel the plastic rubbing against his face and hear it crinkling every time he inhaled. In a few minutes the air would all be gone and then the CO_2 levels in his blood would rise, shutting down first his brain's cerebral cortex and then the medulla.

It was a cruel death—light-headedness, followed by nausea, then unconsciousness. And finally oblivion.

Lying next to him, Allegra was still shouting, using up her air far more quickly than she should. He'd have to get to her first. He shuffled back towards her, feeling for her with his hands, which were still tied behind his back. Touching her arm, he bent forward and pulled himself round with his feet until he made contact with the hood's surface. She seemed to guess what he was doing, because she went quiet and bent towards him until he was able to feel the outline of her mouth.

Digging his finger hard into the shallow depression formed between the hard edges of her teeth, he gouged the thick plastic with his nail, weakening it until it suddenly gave way. There was a loud whistling noise as Allegra sucked air greedily through the small hole.

But the effort had cost Tom more than he'd expected. He felt lightheaded. He didn't have long before he went under. Thirty seconds at most. He bent his head towards where he guessed Allegra's hands had been retied behind her back so that she could feel for his mouth. With her longer nails, it took far less time for her to rupture the plastic. The chamber's stale air tasted sweet to Tom's starving lungs.

'Where are your hands?' he called through the darkness.

Feeling for her wrists, he carefully picked away at the knot. Little by little he was able to loosen it and then undo it completely. Sitting up, Allegra returned the favour. As soon as he was free they hugged with relief—relative strangers brought close by the intimacy of fear.

'Which way's the entrance?' Tom asked as he broke away and ripped the remainder of the plastic hood from his neck.

'We should be able to find it if we feel our way along the walls,' she replied. 'Perhaps if we . . . What's this?'

A light clicked on, forcing Tom to shield his eyes as it was pointed at him. Allegra turned it away with an apology. It appeared that Contarelli had left them a torch. Perhaps he was trying to help them escape? The thought filled Tom with hope.

He glanced around excitedly, noting the low domed roof above them and the earthen floor littered with pottery fragments.

'That way.' Allegra pointed towards the tunnel that led to the entrance.

He crawled hopefully down it, but soon found his path blocked. As the shovelling sound earlier had suggested, the entrance had been filled in. And not just with earth, but with a massive stone plug that they must have brought there with this purpose in mind.

'We should have left the bags on,' Allegra said in a shaky voice. 'I'd rather suffocate quickly than starve down here.'

'I wouldn't worry about starving,' Tom said with a grim smile. 'I'd say we have six hours of air, eight max.'

'That's reassuring.' She gave a short laugh, then frowned as her torch picked out a dull metal object lying near the entrance.

It was a Glock 17. Tom picked it up and checked the magazine. It contained two bullets. Contarelli, it seemed, was offering them a way out.

Avenue Krieg, Geneva

'This can't be it,' Dominique whispered. Normally Archie would have agreed with her—a half-empty building with a broken lift, shabby communal areas, half the light bulbs blown and the nameplate hanging loose didn't seem to fit with what he'd seen of Faulks. But the porter he'd bribed in the Sotheby's loading bay had been adamant that this was the right address for the company who'd sold the Artemis. In fact, he'd proved it.

'He showed me the bloody receipt,' Archie grunted as he tried to force the final locking pin out of the way. 'Galeries Dassin is registered here.'

'It just doesn't feel right,' she said. 'We should have spoken to Tom.'

'I've been trying to get him on the blower all day,' Archie reminded her sharply, his tone reflecting his concern. It wasn't like Tom to be out of touch this long. 'Besides . . .' With a final effort, the pin fell into place and the lock clicked open. 'We're in now. We might as well have a butcher's.'

Pulling their masks down over their faces, they slipped inside. The suite consisted of a large open-plan space with four desks in it, a small kitchen, a meeting room and what Archie guessed was the owner's personal office.

'Still sure this is the right place?' Dominique whispered as her torch picked out bookcases overflowing with legal and tax reference books.

'I'll have a quick shifty in there,' Archie suggested, nodding towards the office. 'You have a look through this lot.'

The office was dominated by a vast desk. Behind this ran mahogany shelves loaded with books and photo frames. Archie absent-mindedly picked up one of the photo frames, then frowned. Rather than be confronted by Faulks's patrician scowl as he had expected, he instead found himself staring at a heavily overweight man in swimming trunks trying to pour himself into a wet suit.

Replacing it with a shudder, Archie turned his attention to two filing cabinets in the corner. Opening the drawers in turn, he walked his fingers along the tabs until he found one marked Galeries Dassin.

'I've got something,' he called in a low voice, carrying it to the entrance. Dominique looked up from where she had been leafing through the papers arranged on one of the desks. '*Galeries Dassin*,' he read, flicking through a few of the pages. '*Registered address, 13 Avenue Krieg.* That's here. *Fiduciary owner, Jerome Carvel.*' He glanced up at the door and saw the same name picked out on it in black letters. 'That's him.'

'What's a fiduciary owner?' Dominique asked.

'Someone who deals with all the administrative bollocks, as opposed to the beneficial owner, who calls the shots and makes the serious wonga and who in this particular instance is . . .' He'd found a shareholder contract and flipped to the signature page. 'Earl Faulks. Carvel's a front.'

'Why bother?'

'Fuck knows. But if I had to guess, to hide . . .' Archie paused, struck by a thought. 'Who bought the Artemis again?'

Dominique had approached the auctioneer after the sale and expressed an interest in buying the statue from its new owner. Sensing the opportunity to make another fee, the auctioneer had volunteered their name and offered to broker the deal.

'It was a commission bid for Xenephon Trading.'

Archie vanished back inside the office, returning a few moments later clutching another file.

'*Xenephon Trading*,' he read. '*Fiduciary owner, Jerome Carvel. Beneficial owner . . . Earl Faulks.*' He looked up at her triumphantly.

'He bought it from himself?' Dominique exclaimed. 'That makes no sense. He'd be paying buyers' and sellers' commission on the deal.'

'Are those invoices?' Archie nodded at the papers she'd been sorting through.

She nodded. 'Last month's auction.'

'Anywhere Xenephon is the buyer?' Archie went to stand next to her.

Gripping her torch in one hand, she quickly counted them up. 'There's one here. Two . . . three . . . four . . . five. And look who's on the other side of the deal here and here: Galeries Dassin.'

'Who's Melfi Export?' Archie tapped his finger on the page with a frown.

Without waiting for an answer, he disappeared back into the office, returning a few moments later with a third file and a solemn expression.

'*Melfi Export. Fiduciary owner, Jerome Carvel. Beneficial owner . . . Earl Faulks*. It's the same story—he's selling with one company and buying with another. It makes no sense.'

'He must be getting something from it,' she pointed out.

'Well, I don't see what, apart from a load of paperwork.'

Dominique turned to him excitedly. 'That's it. He's doing it for the paperwork. It's a laundering scam. First he puts an item up for auction. Then he buys it back under another name. Finally he sells it on to a real buyer, only this time with a manufactured provenance, courtesy of an official auction-house invoice and valuation certificate.'

'Maybe it's not just about provenance,' Archie said with a slow nod. 'Arms dealers get around embargoes by selling weapons down a network of shell companies and middlemen, so that by the time the shipment gets to the intended customer, no one can tie the final transaction back to the original seller. It's called triangulation. Faulks could be pulling the same stunt here to cover his tracks.'

Near Anguillara Sabazia, northwest of Rome

They had run out of conversation a while ago. Now they were sitting in silence, locked into their own thoughts, hugging their knees for warmth. The torch nestled on the ground between them.

He'd faced death before. But never with the resigned acceptance and powerlessness he felt now. The walls were rock solid, the domed roof unyielding, the entrance sealed. They had no tools, no way of communicating with the outside world, no answers. Nothing except for the two bullets that lay side by side in the torch's pale wash.

Allegra's voice broke the cloying silence. 'When we first met at Cavalli's and you handed me the gun,' she reminded him, 'how did you know I wouldn't just shoot you?'

'I didn't.'

'Then why did you trust me?'

'I didn't.' Tom grinned. 'I took the clip out before I gave you the gun. You couldn't have shot me if you'd wanted to . . .'

'Why, you . . .' Allegra's face broke into a wide smile. Then she paused, her chin raised like a foxhound that has caught a scent. 'What's that?'

Tom listened, at first not hearing anything, but then making out what seemed to be the faint rattle of an engine.

'They're coming back,' Allegra exclaimed.

The ground was now shaking with a dull throb and the occasional sound of a muffled voice reached them. Readying himself, Tom took aim at the stone plug that was blocking the entrance, determined to take Contarelli, or whichever of his men he sent ahead of him, down with them.

Ten or so minutes later the massive stone began to move. A harsh, lightning strike of light flooded down the entrance corridor, washing over them and making them blink. On its heels came the thunder of what Tom realised was a helicopter.

For a few moments nothing happened. Then a figure appeared at the tunnel entrance, a black silhouette against the floodlit backdrop.

'Tom Kirk? Allegra Damico? *Andiamo*,' he said, reaching towards them.

They swapped a look. Tom slowly lowered the gun.

'What's going on?' Allegra shouted through the noise.

'I don't know,' Tom called back. 'But it beats being in here.'

Crawling forward, they emerged gratefully into the night, brushing the earth from their clothes and hands as they stood up. But whatever relief they felt at escaping was soon tempered by the realisation that their three liberators were all dressed in black paramilitary clothing—ski masks, fatigues, bulletproof vests, field boots, guns strapped to their thighs.

'Go.' The man who had helped them to their feet ushered them towards a black Agusta Bell 412EP, which had landed about thirty feet away, its spotlight trained on the tomb's entrance, the wash of its rotors backcombing the grass. A fourth man was waiting for them in the cockpit.

'Get in,' the first man shouted over the roar of the engine, handing them each a set of headphones. 'Don't worry. We'll put everything back here so they won't know you've gone.'

Slamming the door, he stepped back and gave the pilot the thumbs-up. Throttling up, the helicopter lurched unsteadily off the ground, dipped its rotors and then climbed at a steep angle into the sky.

'Military?' Allegra's voice hummed in Tom's ear.

'I don't know,' he replied, glancing round. 'Their equipment's standard Italian army issue. Could be special forces or some sort of private militia?'

'Right now, I'm not sure I even care,' she said. 'The further we can get . . .' Her voice tailed off as she noticed the envelope that had been left on the bench opposite. It was addressed to them. She ripped it open and emptied the contents into her lap: about €20,000 in a neat bundle, a set of car keys and five black-and-white photographs of a fire-ravaged apartment attached to a press release from the Monaco Police.

'What does it say?' Allegra frowned, handing it to him.

'They're looking for a missing person,' Tom translated. 'An Irish banker called Ronan D'Arcy. It says no one's seen them since D'Arcy's apartment caught fire two days ago. Looks like somebody wants us to take a closer look.' His eyes narrowed as he studied the third photograph again, a small object having caught his eye. Had the police noticed that yet? he wondered.

'De Luca?' she suggested. 'Remember he told us that his accountant in Monaco had disappeared?'

'Why have Contarelli bury us, only to dig us up a few hours later?'

'But who else would have known where to find us?'

Tom shrugged. She had a point, although right now he was less concerned with who had rescued them than why, and what they wanted.

The pilot's voice broke into their conversation. 'What's our heading? My orders are to take you anywhere within operational range.'

'Anywhere?' Tom asked in surprise. He'd assumed that whoever had set them free was planning to have them brought to him.

'Anywhere,' the pilot confirmed. 'As soon as we land, you're free to go.' He reached back and handed them two Swiss passports made out in false names.

Allegra pulled her headset off and yelled into Tom's ear so she couldn't be overheard. 'What do you want to do?'

He removed his headset. 'If we want out, then this is it,' he called back. 'A chance to walk away while we still can.'

'Walk away to what? Until I can prove what Gallo's up to, I've nothing to walk away to.'

Tom slipped his headset back on.

'Can we make it to Monte Carlo?'

'Of course,' the pilot confirmed. 'What do you need?'

Tom paused before answering. 'A suit for me. Three buttons and a double vent. A dress for the lady. Black. Size eight.'

PART THREE

Monte Carlo, Monaco

The city had appeared out of the night, a stepped pyramid of lights that clung to the steep mountainside with concrete claws, its jaws open to the sea. The helicopter banked to the left and climbed over the yachts anchored in the harbour before swooping back towards the heliport, a narrow cantilevered shelf that hung over the water. It landed with a bump and then dusted off again as soon as their feet had hit the tarmac.

The heliport was shut for the night, but someone had seen to it that the gate was left unlocked. The keys left for them in the envelope opened an X5 parked on the street outside the deserted terminal building. Inside, Allegra found a bag of casual clothes and two suit carriers—one containing Tom's shirt and suit, the other a knee-length black dress that they had clearly managed to lay their hands on in the hour or so it had taken them to fly here. Shoes, underwear, cuff links, comb, make-up—they'd thought of everything. These people, whoever they were, knew what they were doing.

'Ladies first?' Tom offered, closing the door and turning his back.

It was only when she undressed that she realised how filthy she was; her face, arms and clothes were covered in dirt and grazes. Grabbing some wipes, she cleaned herself up as best she could, applied some make-up and then wriggled into the dress. She checked herself in the mirror before she got out. Not bad, apart from her hair, which would need six months and several very expensive haircuts to get it looking even half decent.

She swapped places with Tom, hoping that his raised eyebrows were a sign of silent appreciation. Five minutes later and he too was ready to go.

'Want to drive?' Tom offered, holding out the keys. 'Only this time you have to promise not to crash into anything.'

She refused with a smile. 'What's the fun in that?'

The casino was only a short drive from the heliport, although, in a country of only 485 acres, everything was, almost by definition, close to everything else. It was still busy. Turning in by the central fountain, they waited in line behind a Bentley Continental for the valet to take their car.

The casino itself was an elaborate baroque building. The floodlights had given it a rather gaudy appearance, clothing it in amber in some places and gold in others, while a lush green copper roof was just about visible through the gaps between the towers. A central clock, supported by two bronze angels, indicated it had just gone 3 a.m.

'You still haven't told me why we're here,' Allegra complained as Tom led her into the marble entrance hall to the ticket office.

He glanced across with an indulgent smile as he paid their entrance fee.

'To play blackjack, of course.'

As THEY WALKED THROUGH the casino, Tom found his thoughts drawn back to the Amalfi. It was as if he were watching a film. The echo of the shot being fired, Jennifer crumpling to the floor, that first, disbelieving scream. A film that he could play, pause, forward and rewind at any time, although it would never allow him to go further back than the crack of the gunshot. That's when everything had started.

'Tom?' The mirrored room slowly came back into focus and he saw Allegra's hand laid in concern on his shoulder. 'Are you OK?'

'I'm fine.'

He sat at an empty blackjack table and placed a €5,000 chip on the box in front of him. 'Deal me in.'

The croupier looked up and smiled. In his early forties, he was a tall, precise man, gaunt and with a pianist's long, cantilevered fingers.

'Monsieur Kirk. Very good to see you again.'

He dealt him a king and a five.

'You too, Nico. *Carte.*'

'You don't twist on fifteen,' Allegra whispered to him. 'Even I know that.'

'Seven,' the croupier intoned. 'Twenty-two.' He scooped the cards and Tom's chip off the baize.

'See?' Allegra exclaimed.

'I've come for my gear,' Tom said in a low voice, placing another €5,000 chip down. 'Is it still here?'

'Of course.' Nico nodded, dealing him an ace and a seven.

'Eighteen. You need to stick again,' Allegra urged. Tom ignored her.

'*Carte.*'

The croupier deftly flicked an eight over to him.

'Twenty-six.'

Allegra tutted angrily.

'You don't like losing, do you?' Tom said, amused by her expression.

.85825255.255

'I don't like losing stupidly,' she corrected him.

'Perhaps madame is right,' the croupier ventured. 'Have you tried the Roulette Anglaise?'

'Actually, I was hoping to bump into an old friend here. Ronan D'Arcy. Know him?'

The croupier nodded. 'He's been in a few times. Good tipper.'

'Any idea where I can find him?'

Nico shook his head. 'No one's seen him since the fire.'

'Where did he live?'

'Up on the Boulevard de Suisse. You can't miss it.'

'Can you get me in?'

The croupier checked that no one was listening, then nodded. 'Meet me in the Café de Paris in ten minutes.'

'I'll need a couple of phones too,' Tom added. 'Here.' He threw another €5,000 chip down. 'For your trouble.'

'*Merci, monsieur*, but four should cover everything.' He slid a €1,000 chip back, then signalled at the floor manager that he needed to be relieved.

'You lost both those hands on purpose, didn't you?' Allegra muttered as they made their way back towards the entrance.

'He charges a ten-thousand-euro fee for looking after this.' He held up the chip that the croupier had given him. Two numbers had been scratched on its reverse. 'Come on.'

Reaching the main entrance lobby, Tom led her over to the far side of the galleried space, where a mirrored door on the right-hand side of the room gave onto a marble staircase. They headed down it until they eventually found themselves in a narrow corridor that led to the men's toilets.

Checking that they hadn't been followed, Tom opened the small cupboard under the stairs and removed an *Hors Service* sign. Pinning the sign to the door, he cordoned the toilet entrance off and then disappeared inside, reappearing a few moments later with a smile.

'It's empty.'

'Is that good?' she asked, as she followed him inside.

The room was as he remembered it: four wooden stalls painted a pale yellow to his right, six porcelain urinals separated by frosted-glass screens to his left. The walls were covered in grey marble tiles.

'Six across, three down.' He showed her the numbers scratched onto the chip and then turned to face the urinals and began to count, starting in the far left corner and moving six tiles across, then dropping three tiles down. 'I make it this one,' he said, pointing at a tile over the third urinal.

Snatching up the fire extinguisher hanging just inside the door, he swung it hard against the tile they had picked out. There was a clunk as it caved in.

'It's hollow,' Allegra breathed.

Tom swung the extinguisher against the wall again and the hole widened as the tiles around the opening fell away until he had revealed a rectangular space. He reached into the space and hauled out a large black holdall.

'How long's that been here?'

'Three or four years?' he guessed. 'Nico paid off the builder the casino hired to re-tile this room. It was Archie's idea. A precaution. Enough to get us operational again if we ever had to cut and run. He chose here and a few other places around the world where we had people we could trust.'

Allegra leaned forward as he unzipped the bag. 'What's inside?'

'Batteries, tools, drill, borescope, magnetic rig, backpack . . .' he said, sorting through its contents. '. . . money, guns,' he continued, taking one of the two Glocks out, checking the magazine was full and placing it in his pocket.

'And this?' Allegra asked, frowning as she took out a small object the size of a cigarette packet.

'Location transmitter. Three-mile radius.' He pulled out the receiver, slotted a fresh battery in place and then turned it on to show her. 'Stick it on, if you like. At least that way I won't lose you.'

'Don't worry, you won't get rid of me that easily.' She smiled, tossing it back.

'Good. Then you can give me a hand with this. Nico will be waiting.'

THEY PULLED IN a little way beyond D'Arcy's building. Nico had been right—you couldn't miss it. Not only was a police car parked outside on the narrow one-way street, but the upper storeys of the otherwise cream apartment block were scorched and coated with ash.

Tom gave Allegra a few minutes to struggle out of her dress and heels and into the casual clothes that had been left for them in the car, and then rapped impatiently on the window. She lowered it and he thrust the second Glock and a couple of spare clips through the gap.

'Are there actually any bullets in this one?' she asked sceptically.

'Let's not find out.' He winked.

'*Bonsoir.*' A junior officer from Monaco's small police force rose from behind the reception desk and greeted them warmly.

'Thierry Landry. Caroline Morel. From the palace,' Tom snapped in French, each of them flashing the passes that Nico had produced for them. 'We'd like to see D'Arcy's apartment.'

'Yes, sir, madam,' the officer stuttered. 'Of course. The elevator's still out, but I can escort you up the stairs to the penthouse.'

'No need,' Tom insisted. 'We were never here. You never saw us.'

'Saw what, sir?' The officer winked, then froze, as if realising that this was probably against royal protocol. To his visible relief, Tom smiled back.

'Exactly.'

They climbed the stairs in silence, the fire's charred scent growing stronger and the floor getting wetter as water dripped through from the ceiling. On the third floor, Tom stopped and swung his backpack off his shoulder. Reaching inside, he took out a small device that he stuck onto the wall at about knee height, then turned on.

'Motion sensor,' he explained, holding out a small receiver that Allegra guessed would sound if anyone broke the transmitter's infrared beam.

They emerged on the top landing. The fire's pungent incense was so heavy that Allegra could almost taste the ash sticking to the back of her throat. Tom flicked his torch on and the beam settled on the door to D'Arcy's apartment, which had been unscrewed from its hinges and placed against the wall.

'Quarter-inch steel and a four-bar locking mechanism,' Tom observed slowly. 'Either he knew his attackers or someone let them in.'

They stepped inside the apartment onto a sodden carpet of ash and charred debris. The walls had been licked black by the cruel flames and the ceiling almost entirely consumed, so that Allegra could see through it to the roof's steel ribs and, beyond them, the sky.

'This looks like where it started.' She picked her way over the wreckage to a room that looked out over the harbour. The fire here seemed to have been particularly intense. The steel beams overhead were twisted and tortured, and opaque pools of molten glass had formed under the windows. There was also some evidence of the beginnings of a forensic examination: equipment set up on a low trestle table and mobile lighting arranged in the room's corners.

'Probably here,' Tom agreed, pointing his torch at a dark mound that was pressed up against what was left of a bookcase. 'As you'd expect.'

'What do you mean?'

Tom reached into his backpack and pulled out one of the photographs that had been left for them in the helicopter. 'What do you see?'

She studied it carefully and noticed a rectangular shape on the photo that her torch revealed to be a metal grille set into the wall at about head height.

'What's that?' she asked with a frown.

'That's what I wondered too,' Tom muttered. He stepped closer and rubbed gently against a section of the wall. Through the damp layer of soot, a narrow groove slowly revealed itself. 'A panic room,' he said. 'The grille must be for an air intake that would have been concealed by the bookcase. D'Arcy hasn't disappeared. He never even left his apartment.'

'Can you open it?'

'Half-inch steel, at a guess.' Tom rapped his knuckles against the door. 'Electromagnetic locking system. Assuming they've cut the mains power, the locking mechanism will release itself as soon as the batteries run out, typically about forty-eight hours after they kick in.'

'Which is still at least twelve hours away,' she calculated, thinking back to the time of the fire given in the missing persons report. 'We can't hang around here until then.'

'We won't have to. Here, give me a hand clearing this away.'

Reaching up, they ripped what was left of the bookcase to the floor.

'There would have been an external keypad, but that must have melted in the fire,' Tom explained. 'But there's usually a failsafe too—a secondary pad that they conceal inside the room's walls in case of an emergency. That should have been insulated from the heat.' Stepping forward, he carefully ran his hands across the filthy steel walls at about waist height. 'Here.'

He spat into his hand and wiped the dirt away to reveal a rectangular access panel that he quickly unscrewed.

'It's still working,' Allegra said with relief as she shone her torch into the recess and made out the keypad's illuminated buttons.

Tom reached into his bag and pulled out a small device that looked like a calculator. Levering the fascia off the keypad to reveal the circuit board, he knelt down next to it and connected his device. Immediately the screen lit up and numbers scrolled across it in seemingly random patterns until, one by one, it began to lock them down. These then flashed up on the keypad's display, hesitantly at first and then with increasing speed, until the full combination flashed up green: 180373.

With a hydraulic sigh, the panic room's door rolled back.

Allegra approached the open doorway, then staggered back.

'*Cazzo!*' she swore, her hand over her mouth.

D'Arcy was lying slumped in the corner. Head lolling against his chest, his eyes bulging as if someone had tried to pop them out onto his cheek. He had already begun to bloat in the heat and the sickly-sweet stench of rotting meat washed over them.

Breathing through his mouth, Tom stepped inside the cramped space. Allegra followed close behind.

'The smoke would have killed him,' Tom guessed. 'Then he must have started to cook in the heat.'

'*Cazzo*,' she breathed to herself again.

Glancing around, it seemed clear that D'Arcy had taken to using the room for storage. Filing boxes were stacked to the ceiling against the far wall.

Tom lifted down a box and opened it. Inside were four or five lever-arch files, neatly arranged by year, containing hundreds of invoices.

'Private jet hire. Hotel suites. Yacht charter agreements,' Allegra read, opening the most recent file and turning the pages.

'Anything linking him to De Luca?' Tom asked, opening a second box.

'Nothing obvious. Trade confirmations, derivatives contracts, settlement details, account statements . . .' She flicked through a couple of the folders.

'This one's the same,' Tom agreed, having heaved a third box to the floor.

'Look at this, though,' Allegra said, having come across a thick wedge of bank statements. 'Every time his trading account went over ten million, the surplus was transferred back to an account at the Banco Rosalia.'

'Wasn't that where Argento worked?'

'Exactly. Which ties D'Arcy back to the other killings.'

'Except there's nothing here that links his death to either Caesar or Caravaggio,' Tom pointed out. 'Why would Moretti break the pattern?'

'Maybe he didn't. Maybe D'Arcy locked himself in here before Moretti could get to him,' she suggested.

Tom nodded, although he wasn't convinced. Compared to what he'd heard about the other murders, this one seemed rushed and unplanned. Different.

'What do you know about the Banco Rosalia?' he asked.

'Nothing really.' She shrugged. 'Small bank, majority-owned by the Vatican. I met the guy who runs it at the morgue, ID-ing Argento's body.'

'We should take the disks.' Tom pointed at a stack of DVDs that he guessed were server back-ups. 'If the bank's involved, the money trail might show us how.'

'What about him?' She motioned towards D'Arcy's distended corpse.

'We'll re-seal the door and leave him for the cops to find,' he said. 'There's nothing he can tell them that we—' He broke off, having just caught sight of D'Arcy's wrist.

'What's up?'

Tom knelt down and gingerly lifted D'Arcy's arm.

'His watch,' he breathed as he tried to get at the fastening. 'It's a Ziff.'

'A Ziff?'

'Max Ziff. A watchmaker. A genius. He only makes three, maybe four pieces a year. They sell for hundreds of thousands. Sometimes millions.'

'How can you tell it's one of his?' She crouched down next to him.

'The orange second hand,' he explained as the catch came free and the strap peeled away, leaving a deep welt in the skin. 'That's his signature. He fits one to every watch he makes.'

'I've seen one of these before,' she frowned, reaching for it.

'Are you sure it was a Ziff?' he asked with a sceptical look.

'It wasn't *a* Ziff. It was the *same* Ziff,' she insisted. 'It was in Cavalli's evidence box. White face with no make on it, steel case, roman numerals, orange second hand and . . .' She flipped it over. 'Yes. Engraved Greek letter on the back. Only this is delta. Cavalli's was gamma.'

Tom shook his head in surprise. 'It must have been a special commission. He normally only makes one of anything.'

'Then we should talk to him,' Allegra suggested. 'If it's unusual, he might remember who ordered it and where we can find them.'

'We'd have to go and see him. He doesn't have a phone.'

'Where?'

'Geneva. We could drive there in a few hours and Archie could—' A sharp electronic tone broke into the conversation. 'Someone's coming.'

They leapt towards the exit, Allegra pausing only to hit the close button and snatch her hand out of the way as the door slammed shut. Working quickly, Tom stuffed the keypad back into the recess and screwed the access panel on, rubbing soot over it so that it blended in with the rest of the wall.

'Outside,' Allegra mouthed, dragging him onto the balcony. Moments later, his back pressed against the stone, Tom heard someone crunching through the ash and debris, entering the room and then stopping. Reaching into his backpack for his gun, he flicked the safety off. Allegra, standing on the other side of the doorway, did the same.

'It's Orlando,' a voice rasped in Italian. Tom frowned. He sounded strangely familiar. 'No, it's still shut . . .' A pause as he listened to whatever was being said at the other end of the phone. 'They've cleared away what was left of the bookcase, so they must know it's there . . .' Another pause. Tom was still trying to place a voice that he was now convinced he'd heard only recently. 'I'll make sure we have someone here when it's opened. Otherwise there's someone in the morgue . . . We've got an agreement . . . Don't worry, everything's set up. I'll be back before they land.'

The call ended and the footsteps retreated across the room towards the stairs. A few minutes later the motion sensor beeped again and Allegra let out a relieved sigh. Tom, however, was already halfway across the room.

'Where are you going?' she called after him in a low voice. 'Tom!'

Tom span round. 'It's the priest from the Amalfi,' he spat angrily. 'The one sent to handle the Caravaggio exchange. I recognised his voice.'

Barrelling through the doorway, Tom took the stairs as quickly as he dared, Allegra on his heels. The priest connected whatever had happened here to both the killings in Rome and Jennifer's death. He could lead Tom to whoever had ordered the hit. Tom couldn't let him get away.

A few minutes later they emerged into the lobby.

'Which way did he go?' Tom barked at the officer, whose smile had faded as he caught sight of the expression on Tom's soot-smudged face.

'Who?' he stuttered.

'The man who just came down ahead of us,' Tom snapped impatiently.

'No one else has been in since you went up,' the officer replied in an apologetic voice, as if he was somehow at fault.

'He must have come in another way,' Allegra immediately guessed. 'Probably jumped across from a balcony next door.'

They stepped through the sliding glass doors just as the garage entrance on the adjacent building rattled open. A blood-red Alfa Romeo MiTo raced up the slope from the underground car park. As they sprinted to their car Tom glimpsed the driver as he accelerated down the street.

'Are you sure it's him?' Allegra asked as she buckled herself in, bracing an arm against the dash as the car leapt away.

'I remember every voice, every glance, every face from that night,' Tom insisted. 'It was him. And if he's here, whoever sent him might be too.'

They caught up with the Alfa near the casino. Dropping back to a safe distance, Tom followed him down the hill and through the underpass back towards the port. Pulling in, they watched as he parked and made his way down to the water, where a launch was waiting for him.

'Drive to the end,' Allegra suggested. 'Then we can see where he's going.'

With a nod Tom headed for the harbour wall and then got out, pausing to grab a set of night-vision goggles out of his bag. Putting them on, he tracked the small craft as it cut across the waves to an enormous yacht moored in the middle of the bay.

'*Il Sogno Blu*,' Tom read the name painted across its bows. 'The Blue Dream. Out of Georgetown.' A pause. 'We need to get out to it.'

Allegra pointed back over his shoulder. 'What about one of those?'

They ran down the ramp onto a pontoon where three small tenders had been tied up. The keys to the second one were attached to a champagne cork in a watertight storage compartment under the instrument panel. A few minutes later they were slapping across the waves towards the yacht.

'This will do,' Tom called over the noise of the outboard as they approached. 'If we get any closer, they'll hear us. I'll swim the rest.'

She killed the engine, then went and stood over him as he took his soot-stained tie off and loosened his collar.

'You don't know who's on board or how many of them there are,' she pointed out, the wind whipping her hair.

'I know that someone on that ship helped kill Jennifer.' He kicked his shoes off and stood up, looping the night-vision goggles over one arm.

'I'm coming with you,' she insisted.

'You need to stay with the boat,' he pointed out, handing her both the phones the croupier had given him and D'Arcy's watch. 'Otherwise it'll drift and neither of us will make it back.'

She eyed him angrily. 'I thought we were in this together.'

'We are. But this is something I have to do alone.'

There was a long silence. Then Allegra stepped unsmilingly to one side. Tom squeezed past her and lowered himself into the water.

'Look, I'm not stupid. I'll be careful. Just give me twenty minutes, thirty max. Enough time to see who's on board and what they're doing here.'

Lips pursed, she gave a grudging nod.

Turning, Tom kicked out for the yacht with a powerful stroke. Even so, it took him ten minutes to cover the 150 yards, his clothes dragging him back and a slight current throwing him off his bearing.

Up close, the yacht was even larger than it had appeared from the shore—perhaps 400 feet long, with sheer white sides that rose above him like an ice shelf. Tom counted five decks, capped by a mushrooming radar and comms array that wouldn't have been out of place on an aircraft carrier.

The launch had been moored to a landing platform that folded down out of the stern. Swimming round to it, Tom hauled himself on board and then carefully climbed across onto the ship itself.

Quickly drying himself on one of the neatly folded towels monogrammed with the yacht's name, he buttoned his jacket and turned the collar up to conceal as much of his white shirt as he could. Then he slipped his NV goggles over his head and turned them on. With a low hum, night became day, albeit one with a stark green tint.

Stealthily, Tom made his way up a succession of steep teak-lined staircases to the main deck, the only one with any lights on. Finding the port gangway empty, he made his way forward along it, keeping below the windows. Two doors had been left open about halfway along. The glow spilled out onto the polished decking, making his goggles flare. Switching them off, he edged his head round the first opening. It gave onto a panelled dining room, the table set for the following morning's breakfast.

The second open doorway revealed the main sitting room. Hanging over the mantelpiece was a painting that Tom recognised as *The View of the Sea at Scheveningen*, stolen from the Van Gogh Museum in Amsterdam. There was champagne cooling in an ice bucket and an empty bottle of '78 Château Margaux stood next to a full decanter.

Turning the goggles back on, Tom continued along the gangway, wondering if he should head down below. But before he could do anything, a door ahead of him opened. He froze in the shadow of a bulkhead. A man stepped out, talking on his phone. Tom's heart jumped. It was the priest, his mouth twisted into a cruel laugh, but recognisably the same man he'd faced in the casino—medium build, white, wavy hair, ruddy cheeks.

Even as Jennifer's image filled his mind, he felt anger flood through him, and sensed his chest tightening and his jaw clenching. Before he knew it, he was clutching his gun, her name on his lips and death in his heart.

IT HADN'T TAKEN Allegra long to decide to ignore Tom's instructions and follow him on board. There'd been something in his eyes that had suggested he would need her help—not to deal with whoever was on board, but to protect him from himself.

Having approached from behind so that the wind would carry the engine's echo away from the yacht, Allegra pulled alongside the launch and lashed the tender to it. She paused for a few moments, waiting for an angry shout and for an armed welcoming party to materialise. But none came.

Climbing onto the landing platform, she made her way up to the main deck. Unlike Tom, she had no night-vision equipment, so had to feel her way through the darkness. Even so, Tom was proving relatively easy to track, as the deck was still damp wherever he had paused for more than a few seconds.

Moving as quickly as she dared, she edged forward, ducking under windows and darting across the open doorways until she had almost reached the sundeck area, which took up the entire front third of this level. At its centre was a helipad that she realised parted to reveal a swimming pool.

In the same instant she saw Tom ahead of her, crouched in the shadows of the side rail, his gun in his hand. She followed his aim and saw a man standing at the bow, looking out to sea, talking into his phone. Leaping forward, she placed her hand on Tom's shoulder. He spun round to face her, a strange, empty expression on his face as if he was in some sort of trance.

'Not now,' she whispered. 'Not here.'

For a few moments it was almost as if he didn't recognise her, before his face broke with surprise, and then a flash of anger.

'What . . .?'

She held her finger to her lips, then pointed towards the top deck. An armed guard was leaning back casually against the railings above them blowing smoke rings. Tom blinked and then glanced across at her, his eyes betraying a flicker of understanding.

She motioned for him to follow her and the second door she tried opened into a small gymnasium.

'Are you trying to get yourself killed?' she hissed at him as soon as the door had shut.

'I . . .' he faltered. 'It's him. He set her up!'

'*He* doesn't matter. What's important is finding out who sent him.'

'I saw him and I . . .' Another long pause, until finally he said, 'You're right. I wasn't . . .'

'Let's just get off this thing before they find us.'

Checking that the gangway was still empty, Allegra led him back towards the stern. But they were only about halfway along it when the sound of running feet forced them to dive through the open sitting-room door and crouch behind the sofa, guns drawn. As three men tore past, the approaching thump of rotor blades explained the sudden commotion.

'Someone's landing,' Allegra breathed.

'Which must be what all this is for,' Tom said, pointing at the carefully prepared drinks and glasses. 'We need to . . . What the hell are you doing?'

'Inviting us to the party,' she said with a wink. Having taken out both the phones Tom had handed her earlier, she used one to dial the other and then slid it out of sight under the coffee table. 'At least until the battery runs out.'

With the phone hidden and still transmitting, they made their way back along the gangway, then down the staircase to the landing platform. The helicopter's low rumble was now a fast-closing thunder. As it landed, they cast off, using the engine noise as cover to throttle up and spin away towards the harbour.

SANTOS POURED the Margaux into four large glasses. It pained him to share a bottle as good as this at the best of times, but to split it with two former members of the Serbian special forces seemed positively criminal. Then again, they would recognise the Margaux for what it cost, even if they couldn't taste why it was worth it. And that was half the point in serving it.

'Nice boat,' Asim whistled. 'Yours?'

He was the older of the two and clearly in charge, squat and square-headed, with a buzz cut and a bayonet scar across one cheek.

'Borrowed from one of my investors,' Santos replied, sitting down opposite them. 'How was your flight?'

'No problem,' Dejan, the second Serb, replied.

Compared to Asim, he was tall and gaunt, with curly black hair that he had slicked back against his head.

'Good,' Santos replied. 'You're welcome to stay the night, of course.'

'Thank you, but no,' Dejan said. 'Our orders are to agree deal and return.'

'We do have a deal, then?'

'Fifteen million dollars,' Asim confirmed.

'You said twenty on the phone,' Santos retorted angrily. 'It's worth at least twenty. I wouldn't have invited you here for fifteen.'

'Fifteen is new price,' Asim said stonily. 'Or you find someone else with money so quick.'

There was a pause as Santos stared angrily at each of the Serbs in turn. With Ancelotti's team of accountants due to start on his books any day, he was out of options. He glanced across at Orlando, who shrugged helplessly.

'Fine. Fifteen,' Santos spat. 'In cash.'

'You understand the consequences if you are not able to deliver . . .'

'We'll deliver,' Santos said firmly, standing up.

'Then we look forward to your call,' Dejan shrugged, draining his glass. 'Tomorrow, as agreed.'

Santos showed them to the door, waited until their footsteps had melted into the engine whine of the waiting helicopter, then swore.

'We could find another buyer,' Orlando suggested.

'Not at this short notice, and the bastards know it,' Santos said angrily. 'It's tomorrow night or never.'

'De Luca and Moretti agreed to the meet?'

'I told them that things had got out of hand,' Santos nodded. 'That business was suffering. Then offered to broker a settlement. They didn't take much convincing. Usual place. No weapons, no men. It'll be our only chance to get the watches and the painting in the same room.'

'As long as we can get D'Arcy's.'

'We only need three,' Santos said. 'We've got Cavalli's already and Moretti and De Luca should both be wearing theirs. D'Arcy's is back-up.'

'They'll come after you. They'll come after us both.'

'They'll have to find me first.' Santos shrugged. 'Besides, life's too short to waste it worrying about being dead.'

'Amen,' Orlando nodded, topping up their glasses.

'ARE YOU SURE that was him?'

'I'm telling you, it's Antonio Santos,' she breathed. 'The Chairman of the Banco Rosalia. He said exactly the same thing about life being too short when he was identifying Argento's body.'

'It wouldn't exactly be the first time a Vatican-funded bank has been a front for the Mafia,' Tom conceded with a shrug.

'Do you think he ordered the hit on Jennifer?'

'The priest clearly works for him and, by the sound of it, he had access to the Caravaggio too,' Tom nodded darkly.

'But why would he have done it?'

'My guess is that she found something during that raid on the dealer in New York. Something that implicated the Banco Rosalia or that tied him back to the League. Something worth killing her for.'

'Even if we could prove that, he's got a Vatican passport,' she reminded him with a shake of her head. 'He can't be prosecuted.'

'Maybe if we can get to the painting before him, he won't have to be. The Serbs will take care of him for us if he doesn't deliver.'

'At least now we know why D'Arcy's murder didn't match any of the other killings,' she said. 'It had nothing to do with the League's vendetta. Santos killed him for his watch.'

'They link everything,' Tom agreed.

'Moretti, De Luca, D'Arcy.' She counted the watches off on her fingers.

'Cavalli,' Tom finished the list for her.

'That must have been what Gallo was looking for when he killed Gambetta. He's been working for Santos all along.'

'But why? How can a watch help get to a painting?'

'Even if we knew, we still don't know where the painting is.'

'Ziff's our best hope,' Tom said. 'He'll know why Santos needs them.'

Lake Geneva, Switzerland

It was a six-hour drive to Geneva, the road snaking up into the hills behind Monte Carlo and then along the motorway into Italy, before turning north and plunging into the Alps.

Allegra had soon drifted off, leaving Tom to take the first shift, although she had at least managed to share what she remembered about Santos before her tiredness had finally caught up with her. Eventually, about three hours in, Tom had turned off at a service station near Aosta on the A5, hungry and needing to stretch his legs before swapping over.

While Allegra queued for the toilet, Tom got them both a coffee from a machine and a couple of pastries. Then he called Archie.

'Where the fuck have you been?' Archie greeted him angrily. 'I've been trying to call since lunchtime yesterday.'

'I had to swap phones. It's a long story.'

'Then make it a good one. Dom was worried. We both were.'

'We think Jennifer was killed because she was investigating a Mafia-controlled antiquities-smuggling ring called the Delian League,' Tom explained, mouthing Archie's name to Allegra as she returned.

'*We?* Who the bloody hell is "we"?'

Tom sighed. Step by step, he ran through the events of the last day or so. Then it was Archie's turn to explain how it seemed that the Artemis Tom had asked them to look into had been bought by a company controlled by the same person who had sold it in the first place.

'Our guess is that it's part of an elaborate laundering scam,' Archie added. 'You ever heard of an antiquities dealer called Faulks?'

'Faulks,' Tom exclaimed. 'Earl Faulks? Aurelio mentioned his name. Where he is now?'

'His car had Geneva plates, so I'm guessing he's based here.'

'See if you can find him. When we've finished with Ziff, I'll call you. We can pay him a visit together.'

A COUPLE OF HOURS LATER they drew up at the lake's edge. A yacht was skating across the water's glassy surface, its sail snapping in the breeze.

Getting out, they walked up to the gates of a large three-storey redbrick building with steep gabled roofs. Set high up and back from the road behind iron railings, it appeared to be empty, with grey shutters drawn across the mullioned windows, walls choking with ivy, the gardens wild and overgrown.

'The Georges d'Ammon Asylum for the Insane?' Allegra read the polished brass nameplate and then shot Tom a questioning look.

'Used to be,' Tom affirmed, rolling his shoulders to try and ease the stiffness in his back. 'That's why Ziff bought it. He thought it was funny.'

'What's the joke?'

'That anyone who spends their life watching the seconds tick away is bound to go mad eventually.' A pause. 'Swiss humour. It takes some getting used to.'

Tom pressed the buzzer. No answer. He tried again, holding it down longer this time. Still nothing.

'Maybe he's out,' Allegra ventured.

'He never goes out,' Tom said with a shake of his head. 'He's just being difficult. Show him the watch.'

She held D'Arcy's watch up to the security camera. A few seconds passed, and then the gate buzzed open.

They made their way up the steep drive, the gravel crunching underfoot. The front door was open and they stepped inside, finding themselves in a large entrance hall lit by a flickering emergency-exit sign.

Her eyes adjusting to the gloom, Allegra could see that the room rose to the full height of the building. An oak staircase zigzagged its way up to each floor, capped off by a glass cupola far overhead. To their right was what had clearly once been the reception desk, the yellowing visitors' book still open at the last entry. A straitjacket had been left slung over the back of a wheelchair at the foot of the staircase.

'Up here,' a voice called.

Allegra looked up and saw a man peering down at them over the second-floor banisters. They made their way up to him.

'So you've come to visit at last, Felix?' Ziff grinned manically, thrusting his hand towards them as they stepped on to a landing. He spoke quickly and with a thick German accent.

'A promise is a promise.' Tom smiled, shaking his hand. 'Max, this is Allegra Damico.'

'Friend of yours?' Ziff asked without looking at her.

'I wouldn't have brought her here otherwise,' Tom reassured him.

Ziff considered this for a few seconds, then gave a high-pitched, almost nervous laugh that flitted up and down a scale.

'No, of course not. *Wilkommen.*'

Ziff stepped forward into the light. He was tall, perhaps six feet three, but slight, his reedy frame looking as though it would bend in a strong wind, dyed black hair thinning and cropped short. His features were equally delicate, almost feminine, his face dominated by a neatly trimmed moustache. He was wearing a white apron over green tweed trousers, gleaming brown brogues and an open-necked check shirt worn with a yellow cravat. His sleeves were rolled up so Allegra could see his thin wrists. Strangely, given his occupation, he wasn't wearing a watch.

She shook his hand, his skin feeling unnaturally slick, until she realised that he was wearing latex gloves.

Ziff turned back to Tom. 'Now tell me, Felix. What brings you here?'

ZIFF LED THEM THROUGH a set of double doors into a corridor, its grey linoleum unfurling towards a fire escape. He stopped at the first door on the left and opened it to reveal one of the asylum's former wards.

It seemed that nothing had been touched, until Ziff flicked a power switch and Allegra suddenly realised that all the beds were missing and that in their place, lined up between floral curtains dangling listlessly from aluminium tracks, were pinball machines. Sixteen of them in all, eight running down each side of the room, backboards flashing, lanes pulsing, drop targets blinking and bumpers sparking as they flickered into life. Allegra read the names of a few as she walked past—'Flash Gordon', 'Playboy', 'Close Encounters of the Third Kind', 'The Twilight Zone'—their titles evocative of a distant, almost forgotten childhood.

'They're all vintage,' Ziff explained proudly, stepping slowly past them like a doctor doing his rounds. 'Each one is for a private commission I've completed. A tombstone, if you like. So I don't forget.'

He stopped by a battered wooden desk marooned in the middle of the ward. Its top was covered in red felt, worn and stained in places with oil. A large magnifying lamp was clamped to one edge. He sat down in front of a steel tray containing the disembodied guts of a Breguet, a 20x loupe and several jeweller's screwdrivers. Other tools had been laid out in the drawers of a small wheeled cabinet to his right—case openers, tweezers, screwdrivers, watch hammers, pliers, brushes, knives.

'Show me,' Ziff said, pushing the tray out of the way and putting on an almost comically large pair of black square-framed glasses.

Allegra handed him the watch and he angled the magnifying lamp down over it, peering through the glass.

'Oh, yes.' His face broke into a smile. 'Hello, old friend.'

'You recognise it?'

'Wouldn't you recognise one of your own children?' Ziff asked impatiently. 'Especially one as special as this.'

'What do you mean?' Tom shot back eagerly.

'Each of my watches is normally unique,' Ziff explained. 'A one-off. But in this case, the client ordered six identical pieces.'

'Six?' Allegra repeated excitedly. They knew of four already. That left two others still unaccounted for.

'They're numbered,' Ziff continued, pointing at the delta symbol engraved on the back of the case. 'Platinum bezel, stainless-steel case, ivory face, self-winding, water resistant to thirty metres . . .' He balanced it in his hand as if weighing it. 'A good watch.'

'Who was the client?' Tom asked.

Ziff looked at him with an indulgent smile, slipping his glasses up onto his forehead. 'Felix, you know better than that. My clients pay for their confidentiality, the same as yours.'

'Please, Max,' Tom pleaded. 'It's important. I have to know.'

Ziff paused before answering, his eyes blinking, then slipped his glasses back onto his nose and stood up.

'Do you like pinball?'

'We're not here to play pinball,' Tom said sharply. 'We're here to—'

'"Straight Flush" is a classic,' Ziff interrupted, crossing over to the door. 'Why don't you have a game while you're waiting?'

'Waiting for what?' Tom called after him, but Ziff was already out of the room, the sprung door easing itself shut behind him.

Allegra turned towards the machine he had pointed out. It appeared to be one of the oldest and most basic in the room. She frowned. It wasn't an obvious recommendation, compared to some of the more exciting games in the room, but then again she had detected an insistent tone in his voice that had made her wonder if there was something there he wanted them to see.

'Can you open it?' she asked, pointing at the metal panel on the front of the machine that contained the coin slot.

'Of course.' Tom squatted down next to her with a puzzled frown, reaching into his coat for a small pouch of lock-picking tools.

'He said that each machine was for a job he'd completed,' she reminded him as he deftly released the lock and opened the door, allowing her to reach into the void under the playing surface. 'I just wondered—'

Her voice broke off as her fingers closed on an envelope of some sort. Pulling it out, she opened it. It contained several sheets of paper.

'It's the original invoice,' she exclaimed. 'Six watches. Three hundred thousand dollars,' she read. 'A lot of money, thirty years ago.'

'A lot of money today.' Tom smiled. 'Who was the client?'

'See for yourself.'

Allegra handed him the sheet, her eyes blazing with excitement.

'*E. Faulks & Co.*,' Tom read. 'And there's a billing address down at the Free Port. Good. I'll ask Archie to meet us there.'

'That's strange,' she said. 'There's another invoice here. Same address, only twelve years later.'

'But that would make seven watches.' Tom frowned. 'Ziff only mentioned six.'

Before she could even attempt an explanation, she heard the whistled strains of the overture from *Carmen* echoing along the corridor outside. Snatching the invoice from Tom's hand, she slipped it back in the envelope, shoved it inside the machine and shut the door.

'Magnets,' Ziff announced as he sauntered in, excitedly waving several sheets of paper over his head. 'I knew they were down there somewhere.'

'What?'

Picking D'Arcy's watch up, Ziff held it over the tray containing the watch he was working on. Two small screws leapt through the air and glued themselves to the bezel.

'See. Each watch has a small electromagnet built into it powered by the self-winding mechanism,' he explained, opening the file and pointing at a set of technical drawings. 'They were all set at slightly different resistances.'

'What for?'

'A locking mechanism, I think. They never said exactly what.'

Allegra swapped a meaningful glance with Tom. So this was why Santos needed the watches. Together, they formed a key that opened wherever the Caravaggio was being stored.

'Normally I destroy the drawings once a job is completed, but this was the first time I had used silicon-based parts and I thought they might be useful. Turns out it was just as well. The client lost one of the watches and asked for a replacement. The epsilon watch, I think. Without these I might have struggled to replicate it.'

Allegra took a deep breath. That explained the second invoice. More importantly, it meant that there were seven numbered watches out there somewhere. Each the same and yet subtly different. Each presumably entrusted to a different key member of the Delian League.

'By the way, what was your score?' Ziff jerked his head towards the 'Straight Flush' pinball machine he had pointed out earlier.

'Ask us tomorrow,' Tom answered with a smile.

Free Port Compound, Geneva
The Free Port was a sprawling agglomeration of warehouses lurking in the shadow of the airport's perimeter fence. For the most part, its business was entirely legitimate, the facilities providing importers and exporters with a holding area through which goods could be shipped or stored, with duty only being paid when items officially 'entered' the country.

The problem, as Tom explained to Allegra on the drive there, lay in the Free Port's insistence on operating under a code of secrecy. This allowed cargo to be shipped into Switzerland, sold on and then exported again with only the most cursory official records kept of what was being sold or who it was being sold to. The Free Port's entrenched position at the crossroads of the trade in illicit art and antiques seemed to be holding firm.

'There's Archie and Dom.' Tom pointed at the two figures waiting in the car park of the warehouse mentioned on the invoice.

'Tom!' Dominique wrapped her arms round Tom's neck as they got out. 'I'm so sorry about what happened to . . . I'm so sorry.'

'Yeah.' Archie coughed awkwardly, lowering his eyes.

No one could bring themselves to say Jennifer's name, Tom noticed. Afraid of upsetting him. Afraid of what he might do or say.

'This is Allegra Damico,' Tom said, turning to introduce her.

She nodded hello, Tom realising from their awkward greetings that they were all probably feeling a bit uncomfortable. Dom and Archie at Allegra stepping inside their tight little circle, Allegra at being outnumbered, with only Tom providing the delicate thread that bound them all together.

'How was Max?' Archie asked. 'Still bonkers?'

'Getting worse,' Tom sighed. 'Although we did manage to find out why Santos needs the watches.'

'They contain small electromagnets that open some sort of lock,' Allegra jumped in. 'Presumably to wherever the painting's being kept.'

'Faulks commissioned seven of them,' Tom continued. 'So as well as the four we know about, there are three more out there somewhere, which might give us a chance to get to the painting before Santos.' He glanced sceptically at the squat, square building behind them. 'So, this is it?'

'It's scheduled for demolition later in the year,' Archie nodded. 'Faulks and a few other tenants who are due to move out at the end of the month are the only people left inside.'

'He's got a suite of rooms on the third floor,' Dominique added. 'He's due back at around four for a meeting with Verity Bruce.'

'The curator of antiquities at the Getty?' Allegra frowned in surprise. 'What's she doing here?'

'Having lunch at the Perle du Lac anytime now and then doing the usual rounds of the major dealers.'

'How do you . . .?' Allegra's question faded away as she saw the phone in Dominique's hand.

'We cloned his SIM. I've got it set up to mirror his calendar entries and record every call he makes.'

'Well, if they're due back here at four, that gives us . . . just under four hours to get inside, have a look around and get out,' Tom said.

'I've rented some space on the same floor as Faulks.' Archie held out a key. 'Bloke on the desk thought I was loopy, given they're shutting down, but it's ours for the next two weeks.'

They signed in, the register suggesting that they were the only people there. The guard was all smiles, the momentary flurry of activity clearly a welcome respite from the silent contemplation of empty CCTV screens. To Archie's amusement he seemed to take a particular shine to Dominique.

'You're well in,' he grinned as they made their way to the lift.

'Lucky me.'

'Archie's got a point,' Tom said. 'Why don't you stay down here and keep him busy?'

She gave Tom an injured look. 'Please tell me you're joking.'

'Just until we can get inside.'

She glared at Archie, who was trying not to laugh, then turned wearily back towards the reception as they got into the lift.

A few moments later they stepped out onto a wide corridor that led off left and right. Steel doors were set into the walls at irregular intervals, identified only by numbers, not company names. They followed the signs to corridor twelve and then stopped outside room seventeen.

'This is it,' Archie confirmed.

The offices were secured by three locks—a central one, common to every door, and two heavy-duty padlocks at the top and bottom. Working quickly, Tom placed a tension wrench in the lower half of the keyhole and placed some light clockwise pressure on it. Then he slipped his pick into the top of the lock and, feeling for each pin, pushed them up out of the way one by one. In little over a minute all three locks had been released.

Grabbing the handle, Tom fractionally eased the door open and looked along its frame, then shut it again.

'Alarmed?' Archie guessed.

'Contact switch,' Tom said, glancing up at the camera at the end of the corridor and hoping that Dominique was working her magic.

'Can't you get round it?' Allegra asked.

'The contact at the top of the door is held shut by a magnet,' Tom explained. 'If we open the door, the magnet moves out of range and the switch opens and breaks the circuit. We need another magnet to hold the switch in place while we open the door.'

'I'll go and get your gear out of the car,' Archie volunteered.

'Can't we just use this?' Allegra held up D'Arcy's watch, her eyebrows raised into a question. 'It's magnetised, isn't it?'

Tom turned to Archie with a questioning smile.

'Yeah, well, I can't think of everything, can I?' Archie sniffed grudgingly.

Restaurant La Perle du Lac, Geneva

'You found it!'

Faulks leant on his umbrella to stand up as the maître d' escorted Verity along the terrace to the table. She was wearing a black dress and a denim jacket and clutching a red Birkin to match her shoes.

'Earl, darling,' she gushed. They air-kissed noisily. 'Sorry I'm late. Spanish air-traffic control was on strike again. I just got in.'

'Allow me.' He stepped forward and pushed her chair in for her.

'What are we celebrating?' She clapped her hands excitedly as the waiter stepped forward and poured them both a glass of the Pol Roger Cuvée Sir Winston Churchill that Faulks had ordered.

'I always drink champagne for lunch. Don't you?'

'Oh, Earl, you're such a tease.' She took a sip. 'You know this is my favourite.' She looked at him with a suspicious smile. 'Are you trying to soften me up?'

'As if I'd dare!' He grinned. The waiter materialised expectantly at their table. 'I recommend the pigeon breast.'

Their order taken, the waiter backed away.

Verity fixed him with a casual look. 'Do you have it?'

There. The question he'd been waiting for.

'I have it,' he confirmed. 'It arrived yesterday. I unpacked it myself.'

'And you have a buyer?' she asked. 'Because after the kouros, the trustees have asked for a review of our acquisitions policy. They're even talking about establishing some sort of unofficial blacklist. It's madness.'

'I have a buyer,' he reassured her. 'And provided you value the mask at the agreed figure, he will happily donate it to the Getty as we discussed.'

'Of course, of course,' she said, seeming relieved.

'What about Director Bury?' It was Faulks's turn to sound concerned.

'If it's in the condition you say it is and I confirm that it's by Phidias, he'll submit the acquisition papers to the trustees himself.'

'My buyer has promised me the money by the end of the week if you green-light it. It could be in California by the end of the month.'

'I just wish we hadn't arranged all these meetings today,' she sighed. 'Four o'clock seems like a long way away.'

'Then I've got some good news for you,' Faulks smiled. 'I bumped into Julian Simmons from the Galerie Orientale on the way in and he wants to cancel. We should be able to head over there by around three.'

'Two and a half hours.' She checked her watch with a smile. 'I suppose that's not too long to wait after two and a half thousand years.'

Free Port Compound, Geneva

'What a shithole,' Archie moaned.

Tom had to agree. Withered carpet, wilting curtains, a row of steel cupboards lining the wall. There was something irredeemably depressing about the room's utilitarian ugliness. Sighing, he opened one of the cupboards and then stepped back, open-mouthed.

'Look at this.'

The shelves were overflowing with antiquities. Vases, statues, bronzes, frescoes, mosaics, glassware, faience animals, jewellery . . .

'This one's the same,' Allegra said, opening the one next to him.

There was a gentle knock at the door. Using D'Arcy's watch again, Tom let Dominique in.

'You're just in time,' Tom said. 'We were about to have a look next door.'

They stepped through into the adjacent room. The lights flickered on to reveal another Aladdin's cave of antiquities, although here stored with rather less care—a wooden Egyptian sarcophagus sawn into pieces, vases covered in dirt, cylinder seals from Iraq wrapped in newspaper, bronze statues from India propped up against the wall . . .

'He's got stuff here from all over,' Archie noted. 'Fakes too.' He pointed at two identical Cycladic statues of a harp player. 'The original's in Athens.'

But Tom wasn't listening, having seen the large safe at the far end of the room. He tried the handle, more in hope than expectation. It was locked.

'Over here.'

Allegra was standing at the threshold of a third room, much smaller than the others, but no less surprising. For where they had been flooded with antiquities, this was drowning in documentation—Polaroids, invoices, valuation certificates, consignment notes, shipping manifests, certificates of authenticity. All carefully filed away in archive boxes.

The photographs told their own grim story. One set showed an Attic kylix covered in dirt and in pieces in the boot of a car, then the same object cleaned and partially restored, then fully restored with all the cracks painted, and finally on display in some unnamed museum, Faulks standing next to the display case like a proud father showing off a newborn baby.

'Like Lazarus raised from the dead,' Allegra murmured.

'With the evidence to prove it,' Dominique added. She'd found several boxes crammed with index cards. Written on each one was a meticulous record of a sale—the date of the transaction, the object sold, the price paid, the name of the customer. 'The Getty, the Met . . .' she said, flicking through the first few cards. 'This goes back fifteen, twenty years . . .'

'So he could remind himself how clever he was?' Tom suggested. 'He just never counted on anyone finding it.'

'Does it matter?' Dominique said impatiently. 'It's quarter to one. That means we've only got just over three hours until Faulks gets back.' She went to get Tom's equipment from the car.

'Just about enough time to get his safe open,' Tom said with a smile.

Five feet tall and three feet across, the safe had a hulking presence. A five-spoke gold-plated handle jutted out of its belly, the Cyclops eye of a combination lock glowering above it.

'It's a Champion Crown,' Tom said, rubbing his chin wearily.

'Is that bad?' asked Allegra.

'Two-and-one-eighth-inch-thick composite-concrete walls with ten-gauge steel on the outside and sixteen-gauge on the inside. A concrete door secured by twenty one-and-a-half-inch active bolts. Internal ball-bearing hinges. Sargent and Greenleaf combination dial with a hundred million potential combinations . . .' Tom sighed. 'It's about as bad as it gets.'

'So you can't open it?' Allegra said.

'Everything can be opened, given the right equipment and enough time,' Archie reassured her. 'You just need to know where to drill.'

'Manufacturers build in a drill point to most types of safes,' Tom explained. 'A specific place where locksmiths can more easily drill through the door and, for a safe like this, a hole in the glass plate to get at the lock. They vary by make and model, and if you get it wrong . . .'

'Then your only option is a side entry.' Archie dragged three crates out of the way to give them access to the safe's flanks.

Dominique re-entered, breathing heavily as she hauled Tom's equipment bag behind her.

'Did you get lost?' Tom asked, surprised it had taken her so long.

'I got out at two by mistake,' she panted. 'I was banging on the door like an idiot until I realised I was on the wrong floor. They all look the same.'

Tom unzipped the bag and carefully lifted out the magnetic drill rig.

'What about all that?' Allegra asked, nodding towards the paperwork in the third room. 'It's proof of every deal the Delian League has ever done. We can't just leave it. There's enough in there to bring the whole organisation down and implicate everyone who has ever dealt with them.'

'Have you seen how much of that shit there is?' Archie snorted.

'Let's photograph some of it,' she suggested. 'We've got three hours . . .'

'Two hours,' Dominique corrected her.

'What?' Tom's head snapped round. 'You said . . .'

'According to his calendar, Faulks just cancelled his last meeting,' she explained. 'That means he could be here anytime after three.'

'Shit.' Archie shot Tom a questioning glance. 'Can you do it?'

'No way.' Tom shook his head emphatically, running his fingers through his hair. 'It's a three-hour job. Two and a half if we're lucky.'

'Then we need to buy you some more time,' Archie said. 'Find a way to keep Faulks away from here until we've finished.'

'Can you get to the surveillance cameras?' Allegra asked.

'The patch panel's probably next to the server room downstairs,' Dominique said with a nod. 'Why?'

'It's just . . . I might have an idea. Well, it was your idea really.'

'My idea?' Dominique looked surprised.

'Only it'll never work.'

'Perfect!' Archie grinned. 'The best ideas never do.'

'ARE WE HERE?' Verity glanced up at the warehouse's rusted façade with a dubious expression.

'Don't sound so disappointed,' Faulks laughed. 'Most people don't even know I have this place, let alone get to come inside.'

'In that case I'm honoured.' She smiled.

Logan, Faulks's driver and bodyguard, stepped round and opened her door. But as Verity went to get out, Faulks placed his hand on her arm.

'Can you give me five minutes? I want to make sure everything's set up.'

'Of course.' She sat back with a smile although there was no disguising the impatience in her voice. 'There are a few calls I need to make anyway.'

Nodding his thanks, Faulks led Logan inside.

'New tenants, Stefan?' Faulks asked as they both signed in. He was surprised to see four names above his.

The guard leaned forward with a grin. 'Just until the end of the month,' he whispered excitedly. 'They're making a porno and wanted somewhere . . . discreet. You should see the two girls they've got! The director said I could go and watch them shoot a couple of scenes later this week.'

Faulks mustered a thin smile. 'How nice for you.'

They took the lift to the third floor and traced a familiar path round to corridor twelve, stopping outside Faulks's suite. Unlocking the door, he stepped inside and then stopped.

'That's funny,' he muttered. 'The alarm's off. I was sure I'd . . .'

Logan drew his gun and stepped protectively in front of him.

'Wait here.' Treading carefully, he stepped over to the door to the middle room, eased it open and then peered inside. His gun dropped.

'Boss, you'd better come 'n' see.'

Faulks stepped past him with a frown, then froze. It was empty. Gutted.

The crates, the boxes, the vases, the statues, the safe—everything had gone.

He felt suddenly faint, the room spinning around him. He limped back into the first room and threw open one of the cupboards. Empty. The next one was the same. And the one after that. They were all empty.

'You've been fuckin' turned over,' Logan growled.

Faulks couldn't speak. He staggered to the table, his legs threatening to give way under him at any minute. What about the files? Somehow he found the strength to limp through to the third room, Logan following behind. Faulks stopped on the threshold, not needing to go inside to see that this room too had been stripped bare.

He had the strange sensation of drowning, of the air being squeezed from his lungs. And then he was falling, legs tumbling away from underneath him, back sliding down the wall. Gone. Gone. Everything gone.

'Earl?' He heard Verity's voice echoing towards him. 'You said five minutes, so I thought I'd come up. Is everything OK?'

'HE'S GONE INSIDE.' Archie let himself back into the room with a relieved smile. 'I've left Dom watching the stairs. How are you getting on?'

'Any minute now,' Tom replied, the air thick with the smell of oil, burnt steel and hot machine parts.

Allegra had been right. Her idea had had no reason to work. And yet, like all good ideas, there had been an elegance and simplicity to it that had at least given it a fighting chance of success.

'Dominique said all the floors look the same,' Allegra had reminded them. 'Maybe we could trick Faulks into getting off on the second floor.'

'It might work,' Tom had said, immediately catching on. 'We could rig the lift, swap over the wall signs and door numbers, and then use the forklift to move all his furniture downstairs so that when he goes inside his first thought will be that he's been robbed.'

'I'll reroute the camera feed so the guard can't see us,' Dominique had suggested. 'And we could fix the alarm cover panel to the wall so it at least looks the same.'

'How are you getting on with the photos?' Tom now called to Allegra, stopping to allow the power drill to cool.

'I've got a system going'—she poked her head into the room—'I won't get them all, but I'll get enough.'

'Anything that might tell us where the League is meeting tonight?'

'No, but I'll keep looking.'

At last the drill punched through the steel of the safe.

'That's it,' Tom called, fumbling for the off switch.

'Here.' Archie handed him a small monitor which he taped to the side of the safe and then connected to the borescope. The screen flickered with light, indicating it was working.

'Ready?' Tom looked up with a hopeful smile at Allegra, who had run across to join them. She nodded silently as he blew against the hole to cool the scorched metal and then slipped the cable inside.

'Look,' she gasped almost immediately. The outline of a white face was framed on the small screen like a human skull. 'It's the ivory mask. Cavalli must have sent it here before he was killed.'

'They must have been working together,' agreed Tom. 'Cavalli supplying the antiquities and Faulks providing the buyers. That way, they didn't have to split the profits with the Delian League.'

'Faulks doesn't have to split anything with anyone now that Cavalli's dead,' Allegra observed wryly.

'Pretty convenient,' Tom agreed. 'It wouldn't surprise me if—' He broke off, a thought occurring to him. Of course. It had been so simple. And once Faulks had realised how much the mask was worth, so necessary.

'Oi, you two,' Archie interrupted. 'Holmes and bloody Watson. Do you mind if we get a move on?'

Tom winked at Allegra, then nodded. He was right.

Looking back to the screen to get his bearings, he bent the cable towards the left and found the back of the safe door. Then he slowly moved it along until he was roughly behind the combination dial.

'There it is,' Archie said sharply.

'There what is?' Allegra leaned closer with a frown.

'The key-change hole,' Archie explained. 'Every combination safe comes with a special key that you insert in that hole when the safe's open to change the code.'

They watched the image silently. The camera's proximity made the tiny hole look surprisingly large on the screen, the cable catching on its edge as Tom tried to nudge it inside.

'Shit,' he hissed, as the cable slipped past yet again. 'It keeps sliding off.'

Dominique came in, out of breath from having run up the stairs.

'How much time have we got?' Tom barked without looking up.

'About as much time as it takes them to look out of the window and realise they're only two floors up. How are we doing?'

'Shit,' Tom swore as the camera skated past the hole again.

'Why don't you try coming in from underneath?' Archie suggested. 'You might catch against the upper lip.'

'I don't see why that will . . .' Tom glanced up at Archie with a sheepish smile. It had worked first time.

The screen now showed a fuzzy image of the lock mechanism—four wheels, each with a notch that had to be aligned so that the locking gate could fall into them.

'Someone's going to have to turn the dial for me,' Tom said. Allegra immediately stepped forward and crouched down next to him.

'Which way?'

'Clockwise. You need to pick up all the wheels first.'

Allegra turned the lock. The picture showing the drive cam gathered up each of the four wheels one by one until they were all going round.

'Slowly,' Tom said, as he saw the notch on the first wheel at the bottom right of the screen moving upwards.

'Stop!' Archie called as the notch reached the twelve o'clock position. Fifteen. 'Now back the other way.'

Allegra turned the dial back, again slowing as the notch appeared on the second wheel and then stopping when Archie called to her. Seventy-one. Then came sixteen.

'The last number's ten,' Tom guessed.

'How do you know?' Dominique asked with a frown.

'Fifteen seventy-one to sixteen ten,' Tom explained with a smile. 'Caravaggio's dates.'

As Tom pulled the borescope out of the hole, Allegra turned the dial to the final number and then tried the gold-plated wheel in the middle of the door. It turned easily, the handle vibrating with a dull clunk as the bolts slid back. Standing up, she tugged on the door. The airtight seal at first resisted her until, with a swooshing noise, it swept open.

The safe had a red velour interior and four shelves containing an eclectic assortment of items—twenty or so antique dinner plates, a set of red figure vases, notebooks, some files, a few maps. And of course the ivory mask.

Tom's attention, however, was drawn to a rectangular black velvet box, monogrammed with a by now familiar symbol: the clenched fist and entwined snakes of the Delian League. It opened to reveal a cream silk interior moulded to house six watches. Two of the spaces were occupied.

'Epsilon and zeta,' Allegra said, taking them out and turning them over so that they could see the Greek letters engraved into their backs.

'Which gives us the three we need,' Tom said, sliding D'Arcy's watch into place and then snapping the case shut. 'Let's just see if there's anything in here that tells us where they're meeting tonight.'

'What about this?' Archie asked, carefully sliding out the small packing crate containing the ivory mask.

'Leave it,' Tom said with a shake of his head.

'Leave it? Are you joking? This thing's worth a bloody fortune.'

'Not to us it isn't. Besides, the less we take, the more chance that Faulks won't even realise we've been here.'

FAULKS'S INITIAL SHOCK had given way to a bewildered incredulity. It was impossible. The stock. The documentation. The safe. Everything gone. Spirited away. Everything. Thousands of items. Tens of millions of dollars. How had they got in? How had they got away without being seen?

'Did you tell anyone you were coming here?' Faulks spun round to face Verity, jabbing his umbrella at her accusingly.

'Of course not,' she insisted. 'How could I? I've never been here before.'

He glared at her, his disbelief having slipped into anger. She gave a sharp intake of breath, her eyes widening in understanding.

'Oh my God, Earl, have you been robbed?'

Logan reappeared and jerked his head to indicate that they needed to talk. Alone.

'Give me a minute, Verity,' Faulks said, following Logan back out into the first room and closing the door behind him.

'The guard downstairs hasnae seen nothing,' Logan said in a low voice. 'Nor had the one on the night shift when we called him.'

'Not unless they're both in on it together,' Faulks pointed out.

'Aye, well, I'd know if he was.' Logan gave him a tight smile.

Looking down, Faulks noticed that the Scotsman's knuckles were grazed and that there was a faint spray of blood on his collar. He felt a little better.

'What about the surveillance footage?'

'Backed up remotely. I've asked for a copy. It'll be here in an hour.'

'Anyone else in the building?'

'Just the people who moved in today.'

Faulks snorted. 'Well, there you go, then.'

'There's only four o' them and they signed in at twelve thirty,' Logan pointed out. 'Shiftin' all tha' would have tak'n them days.'

'And he didn't hear the alarm go off?'

'No.'

'Bastards must have disabled it,' Faulks hissed, striding over to the control panel next to the main entrance and smacking it angrily. 'What's the point in paying for—'

He broke off as the keypad fell away from the wall and crashed onto the floor. Frowning, he bent down to pick it up, then noticed the two pieces of black tape that had been securing it to the wall.

'Jesus,' he swore. 'It's a dummy. We're in the wrong goddamned room.'

Turning, he limped back out onto the corridor. He made his way to the fire escape and leaned over the banisters, following the staircase as it snaked its way down to the floor below and then . . . to the ground floor.

With Logan at his shoulder, Faulks climbed the staircase as fast as he could, then stepped out onto the empty corridor and turned towards his offices. Here the nature of the deception became abundantly clear—all the signs and door numbers were missing, having presumably been removed and reattached on the floor below to confuse him.

He flung the door to his offices open. Apart from the cupboards down the right-hand wall, the room was empty and almost unrecognisable without its furniture, carpet or curtains.

And standing at its centre was a woman.

'SO WHAT NOW?' Dominique asked.

'I'm not sure,' Tom admitted, sliding into the seat next to her. 'We still don't know where they're meeting.' He craned his neck for a view of the entrance. 'What's taking them so long?'

'Look, here he comes!' Dominique pointed with relief as Archie exited the building and jogged over to the car.

'Yeah, but why's he on his own?' Tom frowned.

Archie threw the door open and climbed in. 'Close one. Nearly bumped into Faulks coming up the stairs. I think he's finally twigged.'

'Where's Allegra?' Tom asked in an urgent voice.

'Allegra?' Archie looked around. 'I thought she was with you?'

'Well, she's not,' Tom shot back.

'When did you last see her?'

'Upstairs. She was helping me pack up my kit. I handed her the . . .' He paused, a sudden thought occurring to him. Flinging the door open, he raced round to the back of the car and popped the boot.

'What are you looking for?' Archie asked as he rooted through his bag.

'This,' Tom said, holding up the receiver for the location beacon.

He turned it on. A faint pulse of light confirmed what he had already guessed. The transmitter was about fifty yards directly in front of him.

'She's still inside.'

'What the hell's she doing?' Archie's voice was caught somewhere between surprise and admiration.

'Playing the only card we have left.'

FAULKS PAUSED on the threshold. 'Who the hell are you?'

'Everything's here,' she reassured him. 'I just wanted to make sure I got your attention.'

'Congratulations. You've got it,' he snarled, motioning at Logan to grab her, while he checked the cupboards and stuck his head into the next room.

Unbelievably, everything did indeed seem to be there. The empty desolation of a few minutes ago was quickly replaced by a warm wave of relief.

'Who are you?' he repeated.

'Lieutenant Allegra Damico. An officer with the TPA. I have some information for the Delian League.'

'Who?'

'I think we're a little beyond that,' she said, nodding in the direction of the documentation in the small room.

'Earl, are you in here?'

Faulks's head snapped round at the sound of Verity's approaching voice.

'Damn,' he swore, then turned back to Allegra with an impatient shrug. He didn't have time for this. Not today of all days. But after the lengths she'd gone to . . . there was no telling what she knew or who she'd told. He had to be sure. The League had to be sure. 'You're right. We're way beyond that.'

Stepping forward, he grabbed the end of his umbrella and swung its handle hard against her temple. Groaning, she went limp in Logan's arms.

'Take her to the back and keep her quiet,' he hissed. 'When we're finished here, load her up with the rest of the shipment.'

Turning on his heel, he walked back out onto the corridor. Verity was marching towards him, her face drawn into a scowl.

'Earl, I don't know what you're playing at, but . . .'

'Verity, I can't begin to tell you how sorry I am,' he apologised. 'There's been a mistake. And it's entirely my fault. We were on the wrong floor!' He laughed lustily. 'Can you believe it? It must be old age. I'm losing it.'

'The wrong floor?' she repeated unsmilingly.

'The landlord needed access to my old offices, so they've moved me up here,' he explained. 'I'm so used to going to the second floor that I didn't even think about it. I'm so sorry.'

'So everything's here?' She glanced past him with a sceptical frown.

'Absolutely.' He gave an emphatic nod. 'Thank God, because for a terrible moment I thought . . .'

'I know. Me too.' She let out a nervous, hesitant laugh. He forced himself to join in.

Ushering her in, he led her through to the middle room. Verity murmured with appreciation at some of the items she could see stacked there.

'Good God, Earl, this is wonderful.'

'Even better, it's all for sale,' he reminded her with a smile as he crouched next to the safe, flicked the dial and heaved it open.

'Is that it?' Verity said, pulling on a pair of white cotton gloves.

'That's it.' Sliding the shallow box out, he carefully placed it on top of a packing crate. Removing his jacket, he draped it over another crate so that its scarlet lining covered it. Then he gingerly removed the mask and set it on top of the lining, the pale ivory leaping off the red material. Finally he stepped back and ushered her forward.

Verity carefully picked the mask up. She raised it level with her face, eyes unblinking, her breathing quickening, hands trembling. She gave a long sigh of pleasure and lowered it unsteadily back into its straw bed.

'So? What do you think?' Faulks asked.

Verity made to speak, but no sound came out, her lips trembling, tears welling in her eyes.

'It's so beautiful,' she breathed eventually. 'It's like . . . it's like gazing into the eyes of God.'

'Attribution?'

'Assuming the dating is right . . .'

'Oh, it's right.'

'Then Phidias. Phidias, Phidias!' Her voice built to an ecstatic crescendo. 'We would have heard of any other sculptor from that period of this quality.'

'Then I hope you won't mind confirming that to my buyer?' Faulks pulled out his phone and searched for a number. 'Or the valuation you'll put on it once he donates it to you?'

'Of course,' she enthused, snatching the phone from him as soon as it started ringing. 'What's his name?'

Over Milan, Italy

Coming round, Allegra lifted her head and then sank back with a pained cry. There was something above her preventing her from sitting up. Something smooth and flat and . . . wooden. She moved her hands gingerly across it. It was a box. She was lying in a wooden box.

The last thing she remembered was Faulks, wild-eyed, raising his umbrella above her and then . . . darkness. Darkness, the smell of straw, a dog barking, something hard and uneven underneath her, her head throbbing where he'd struck her. And in the background a low, incessant drone. She was on a plane. Lying in a wooden box in the hold of a plane.

She nervously patted her inner thigh, and then sighed with relief. The location transmitter was still there—taped to her skin at the top of her leg.

She'd taken a big risk, she knew. But as soon as it had become clear that there was nothing in either Faulks's papers or the safe that was going to give them even the slightest hint as to where the League was meeting that night, she'd known what she had to do. Grab the transmitter and some tape out of the bag. Hold back amid the confusion of their hurried retreat. And then try to talk or shock Faulks into delivering her to the League himself. It was that or give up on getting to the painting before Santos could hand it to the Serbs.

Protestant Cemetery, Rome

'I've lost her,' Tom barked.

'What do you mean, you've lost her?' Archie grabbed the receiver from him and shook it. 'She was just there.'

'Well, she isn't now,' Tom shot back, his anger betraying his concern.

Until now, Allegra had proved surprisingly easy to track. Her signal had led them to the cargo terminal at Geneva airport, where they had observed Faulks's driver overseeing several large crates being loaded onto a plane bound for Rome. It hadn't taken much imagination to deduce that she had been placed inside one of them. They had therefore immediately booked themselves on to an earlier flight to ensure that they would already be in position to pick up the signal again by the time her plane landed. From there they had tracked her to the Protestant Cemetery.

Sheltered by regimented lines of mourning cypresses and Mediterranean pines, the cemetery nestled on the slope of the Aventine Hill in the shadow of the Pyramid of Caius Cestius and the adjacent Aurelian walls. Even by moonlight, Tom had been able to see that it was populated by an eclectic tangle of stone monuments, graves and family vaults, separated by long grass woven with wild flowers.

'Where was the last reading from?' Dominique asked, ever practical.

'Over there.' Tom immediately broke into a loping run, navigating his way around the tombs. Then, just as he was about to emerge into one of the wide avenues that cut across the cemetery, he felt Archie's hand grab his shoulder and force him to the ground.

'Get down,' he hissed.

Three men had emerged from the trees ahead of them, their machine guns glinting black in the moonlight, torch beams slicing the darkness. Moving quickly, they glided over to a large family vault. As Tom watched, they ghosted up its steps and vanished inside.

'She must be in there,' Tom guessed, standing up.

The vault was a small rectangular building designed to echo a Roman temple. The handsome bronze door had a single name carved over it: *Merisi*. Tom pointed at it with a smile as they crept towards it.

'What?' Dominique whispered.

'Merisi was Caravaggio's real name.'

They paused, straining to hear a voice or a sound from inside. But nothing came apart from the silent echo of darkness.

With a determined nod at the others, Tom carefully eased the door open with one hand, his gun in the other. This and three other 'clean' weapons had been sourced by Archie from Johnny Li while they had been watching the hangar at Rome airport. The price had been steep but Johnny had at least held his half of their earlier bargain and returned Tom's watch.

Inside, a thin carpet of dirt and leaves covered the black-and-white mosaic floor. At the far end stood a black marble altar with the name *Merisi* again picked out in bronze letters above a date—1696. Above it, suspended from the wall, was a crucifix.

The room was empty.

'Where the hell have they gone?' Archie exclaimed.

Tom examined the floor with a frown. 'How did they expect to bury anyone in here? It's a family vault. There should be a slab or something that can be lifted up.'

'No inscriptions either,' Archie chimed in. 'Not even a full set of dates.'

'The one that's here doesn't fit,' Dominique pointed out. 'This graveyard wasn't used until the 1730s. No one would have been buried here in 1696.'

'It could be a birth year,' Tom suggested, crouching down in front of the altar. 'Maybe the second date has come away and . . .'

The words caught in his throat. As he'd rubbed the marble, his fingers had brushed against the final number, causing it to move slightly. He reached forward to turn it, the number spinning clockwise and then clicking into place once it was upside down so that it now read as a nine.

Archie frowned. 'But 1699 doesn't make no sense either.'

'Not 1699—1969,' Tom guessed, turning each of the previous three numbers so that they also clicked into place upside down. 'The year the Caravaggio was stolen.'

There was the dull thud of what sounded like a restraining bolt being drawn back from somewhere in front of them. Then the altar began to lift, pivoting high above their heads, stopping a few inches below the ceiling.

They jumped back, swapping a surprised look. Ahead of them, a flight of steps disappeared into the ground, leading down to a brick-lined corridor set on a shallow incline. It was dimly lit, the sodium lighting suspended from the vaulted ceiling at irregular intervals forming pallid pools of orange light that barely penetrated the cloying darkness.

Aiming their guns towards the darkness into which the three armed men had presumably disappeared, they crept down the tunnel. The passage traced a bewildering course as it zigzagged violently between the grave-yard's scattered crypts and burial chambers. Eventually, after about 200 yards, it ended, opening up into a subterranean network of interlinking rooms supported by steel props.

'It's Roman,' Dominique whispered, stooping to look at a section of the frescoed wall that hadn't crumbled away. 'Probably a private villa.'

Picking their way through the thicket of metal supports propping the roof up, they arrived at the main part of the buried villa, a tiled floor giving way to intricate mosaics featuring animals, plants, laurel-crowned gods and a dizzying array of boldly coloured geometric patterns.

An angry shout echoed towards them through the empty rooms.

'You think Santos is already here?' Dominique whispered.

'Allegra first,' Tom insisted. 'We worry about Santos and the painting when she's safe.'

They tiptoed carefully to the doorway of a small vaulted chamber. Crouching on the floor with their backs to them, checking their weapons and speaking in low, urgent voices, were the three men they'd seen earlier.

Tom locked eyes with Archie and Dominique; both of them nodded back. On a silent count of three, they leapt inside and caught the three men completely cold.

'*Tu?*' one of the men hissed as, one by one, Archie taped their hands behind their backs and then gagged them.

It was Orlando—the priest from the Amalfi. Tom returned his hateful glare unblinkingly. Strangely, the murderous rage that had enveloped him in Monte Carlo had vanished; he felt almost nothing for him now. Not compared to Santos. Not with Allegra's life at stake.

'I'll watch them,' Dominique reassured him, waving the men back into the corner of the room with her gun.

With a nod, Tom and Archie continued on, a bright light and the low rumble of voices drawing them to the next room, where they crouched on either side of the doorway.

'Look,' Archie whispered excitedly. Tom followed his gaze and saw that a large recess, perhaps nine feet high, six across and three deep, had been hacked out of the far wall. And, hanging within this, behind three inches of blast-proof glass, was the Caravaggio. It was unframed, although its lack of adornment seemed only to confirm its raw, natural power.

'There's Faulks,' Archie whispered.

At the centre of the room was a circular table inlaid with small squares of coloured marble. The man Archie had pointed out was clutching an umbrella and standing in front of three other men seated round the table.

'The guy on the left is De Luca,' Tom breathed. 'And the one in the middle who's speaking now—' He broke off, his chest tightening as he realised that this was the face of the man he'd overheard on the yacht in Monaco. The man who'd ordered Jennifer's death. 'That's Santos.'

'Which must make the other bloke Moretti,' Archie guessed, nodding towards a short man wearing glasses who was seated on the other side of Santos. He was wearing a grey cardigan and brown corduroy trousers, looking more like someone's grandfather than the head of one of the Mafia's most powerful families.

Tom nodded but looked past him, distracted by the gagged and bound figure he could see slumped in a chair to Faulks's left. It was Allegra. Still alive, thank God.

'She wants to speak to us,' Faulks was protesting. 'She said she had a message.'

'Of course she does,' Santos shot back in English, his tone at once angry and mocking. 'She's working on the Ricci and Argento cases.' He glanced across at De Luca. 'I thought you said you'd taken care of her?'

De Luca shrugged. 'I thought I had.'

'She managed to locate and break into my warehouse,' Faulks retorted.

'From what you've told us, she took nothing apart from your pride,' Santos reminded him. 'You should have taken care of her in Geneva. You have no business here.'

'In case you've forgotten, I have two seats on this council.' Faulks spoke in a cold tone. 'I have as much right to be here as anyone. If not more.'

'An accident of history that you delight in reminding us of,' said De Luca.

Santos took a deep breath. 'This meeting was called by the Moretti and De Luca families, as representatives of the founding members of the Delian League, to resolve their recent . . . disagreements. Disagreements that have led to two former members of this council not being here with us tonight.'

'We had nothing to do with D'Arcy's death,' Moretti insisted angrily.

'Cavalli was a traitor who deserved what he got,' De Luca retorted, both men standing up and squaring off.

'Enough!' Santos called out. Muttering, they both sat down. Santos turned back to face Faulks. 'They asked me here to help mediate a settlement. I let you know we were meeting as a courtesy. But, as I told you when we spoke, there was no need for you to come.'

Faulks looked at them, then nodded sullenly towards Allegra.

'Then what am I meant to do with her?'

'What you should have done already.'

'I dig bodies up, not bury them,' Faulks said through gritted teeth.

'Then I'll finish what you are too weak to begin,' Santos snapped, taking his gun out from under his jacket and aiming it at Allegra's head.

A shot rang out. Santos fell back with a cry, clutching his arm.

'Sit the fuck down. Nobody move!' Archie bellowed.

Tom pushed past him to Allegra, pulling the gag out of her mouth, then slicing her wrists free.

'Are you OK?' he breathed as she fell gratefully into his arms.

She nodded and gave him a weak smile. Turning, Tom scooped Santos's weapon off the floor and quickly searched the others.

'I'm bleeding,' Santos shrieked.

'It's a graze. You'll live,' Tom snapped.

'Pity,' Archie intoned behind him. Faulks's eyes widened in shocked recognition, although the others didn't seem to notice his expression.

'You have no idea what you've done,' Santos hissed through clenched teeth. 'You're both dead men.' He snatched a glance towards the entrance.

'Who are you?' Moretti demanded.

'He's Tom Kirk,' De Luca said slowly.

'Kirk?' Moretti gasped.

'Tom Kirk?' Faulks gave a disbelieving smile, his face turning grey.

Tom frowned, confused. Some people knew who he was, or at least who he had been. But that didn't usually warrant this sort of reaction.

'What do you want?' Santos demanded.

'The same as you,' Tom said simply. 'The Caravaggio.'

'You'll never get it out of there,' Faulks scoffed. 'Not without destroying it.'

'Even with these?' Tom asked, holding up the monogrammed case he'd taken from Faulks's safe. The dealer went pale, his eyes bulging. 'Here, you might as well collect them all up,' said Tom, tossing Allegra the box. 'Although it is only the three watches I need, isn't it?'

Moretti and De Luca swapped a dumbfounded look.

'How did you know?' De Luca asked as Allegra loosened his watch and then Moretti's, before finding the sixth in Santos's top pocket. 'Did your—'

'Santos has struck a deal to sell your painting,' Tom explained. 'We overheard him negotiating the terms yesterday. He let slip about the watches.'

Santos rose from his seat. '*Stronzata!*' he spat, his face stiff with anger.

'Bullshit. Really?' Tom smiled. 'Dom?' he called out.

A few moments later Dominique appeared, ushering Santos's three men ahead of her. Santos slumped back into his seat as she forced them onto the ground and made them sit with their hands on their heads.

'These men work for Santos. We found them next door. You were the only people standing between him and the fifteen million dollars his Serbian buyers have promised him for the painting.'

'He's lying,' Santos seethed, his eyes fixed on Tom. 'It's a trick. We all know to come to this place alone. I would never break our laws.'

'Can you open it?' Tom called across to Allegra, who was crouching in front of the case.

'There are six plates,' she said, pointing at the brass roundels set into the wall under the painting. 'Each one's engraved with a different Greek letter.'

Opening the box, she took out the first watch and carefully matched it to the corresponding plate, the case sinking into the crafted recess with a click. Then she repeated the exercise with another two watches and stood back. With a low hum, the thick glass slid three feet to the right, leaving an opening that she could step through.

'I'll give her a hand,' Archie volunteered, passing Tom his gun. He followed her through the gap into the narrow space behind the glass, and then helped her lift the unframed painting down. Carrying it back through with small, shuffling steps, they leaned it gently against the wall.

Tom stepped closer. He recognised the scene. It was exactly as he remembered it from the Polaroid Jennifer had shown him in her car. But there was no comparing that flat, lifeless image to the dramatic energy and dynamism of the original.

'Let's take it off the stretchers so we can roll it up,' Archie suggested.

'Be careful with it,' Moretti warned him.

Tom turned to De Luca. 'You know the FBI officer I asked you about, the one who was shot in Vegas three nights ago?' De Luca nodded with a puzzled frown. 'A few weeks back she got a tip-off about one of your US-based distributors. An antiquities dealer based in New York. Under questioning, he volunteered Luca Cavalli's name.'

'I knew Luca,' Moretti frowned. 'He was careful. He would never have revealed his name to someone that far down the organisation.'

'He didn't,' Tom agreed. 'Faulks did.'

'What?' Faulks gave a disbelieving laugh.

'We came across a photo of the ivory mask in Cavalli's car.' Allegra glanced up at De Luca. 'We found the original in Faulks's safe. It's worth millions. Tens of millions.'

'My guess is that Cavalli had been secretly bringing you pieces for years,' Tom said, turning to stand in front of Faulks. 'Pieces his men had dug up and that he had deliberately not declared to the League, so that you could sell them on and share the profits between you. But then one day he unearthed something really valuable, didn't he? Something unique. And you just couldn't help yourself. You got greedy.'

'Cavalli sent me the mask, it's true,' Faulks blustered, looking anxiously at De Luca and Moretti. 'A wonderful piece. But my intention was to split the proceeds with the League in the usual way after the sale. And not just the mask. I have the map showing the location of the site where he found it. Who knows what else might be down there?'

'Can you prove any of this?' De Luca challenged Allegra.

'Who told you that Cavalli had betrayed you?' Tom shot back.

De Luca paused, then pointed towards Faulks. 'He did.'

'I had no choice,' Faulks protested. 'It's true that Cavalli wanted me to deal with him direct. But when I refused he threatened to go public with everything he knew. What I told you was the truth. He was planning to betray you. You know yourself that your informants backed me up.'

'The FBI had Cavalli's name,' De Luca acknowledged, turning his gaze back to Tom. 'They wanted the authorities here to arrest him.'

'Cavalli was ripping you off, but I doubt he was going to go public with anything,' Tom said with a shrug. 'The simple truth is that Faulks wanted him out of the way so he could have the mask for himself. So he came up with a plan. First feed Cavalli's name to the New York dealer. Then sell the dealer out to the FBI to make sure he would talk. Finally accuse Cavalli of betraying you, knowing your police informants would confirm that the FBI was investigating him and that you would think he was collaborating.'

'This is crazy,' Faulks spluttered. 'I've never—'

'The clever thing was the way he set both sides of the League against each other,' Allegra mused, rising to her feet. 'He knew that Don Moretti would retaliate once you'd killed Cavalli, leaving him free to sell the painting for himself, while you were busy fighting each other.'

'That was never my intention,' Faulks pleaded angrily. 'Cavalli was a threat. I was simply acting in the best interests of the League.'

'Of course, while all this was going on, Santos was busy taking out a contract on my friend,' Tom continued, turning to face him. 'My guess is—'

'How much more of this do we have to listen to?' Santos interrupted, his palms raised disbelievingly to the ceiling. 'I've never—'

'*Basta*,' De Luca cut him off angrily. 'You'll have your chance.'

Santos sat back with a scowl, muttering to himself.

'My guess is that when Special Agent Browne searched the dealer's warehouse, she found something implicating the Banco Rosalia and started kicking the tyres,' Tom continued. 'When Santos realised that she was on to him, he had her taken out, using the prospect of recovering your Caravaggio to lure her to Las Vegas where he had a gunman waiting.'

'Is this true? You killed an FBI agent without our permission?' De Luca jumped to his feet, violence in his voice now.

'I did what I had to do to protect the League,' Santos protested.

'At first we thought everything was connected,' Allegra admitted. 'Then we realised that the Rome murders and the ivory mask had nothing to do with Jennifer's assassination, or with D'Arcy, who was killed for his watch.'

'The irony is that it was Faulks's tip-off about the dealer in New York that unknowingly led to the FBI looking into the Banco Rosalia in the first place,' Tom said with a rueful smile. 'Without that Jennifer would probably still be alive and—'

A single gunshot cut him off. Tom's head snapped towards the doorway. A uniformed policeman was standing there, gun pointed towards the roof, five, maybe eight armed police filtering into the room either side of him, machine guns braced against their shoulders.

'Colonel Gallo, thank God you're here!' Santos rose gratefully from his seat and stepped towards him, switching back to Italian.

'Sit down,' Gallo ordered him back.

'I've been kidnapped. Held against my will. Shot!' Santos held out his bloodied arm, his voice rising hysterically.

'Sit down, Santos, or I'll shoot you again myself,' Gallo warned him.

'This is an outrage,' Santos insisted. 'In case it's slipped your mind, Gallo, I have diplomatic immunity. I demand to be released immediately.'

'No one is going anywhere,' Gallo fired back. 'Get their weapons.' Two of his men quickly patted everyone down, tossing whatever they found into the far corner of the room. Santos sank into his chair. Gallo turned to Allegra. 'Lieutenant Damico, are you hurt?'

'N-n-no,' Allegra stammered, bewildered. This was the man she'd been running from; the man she'd seen execute Gambetta; the man who had supposedly supplied Santos with Cavalli's watch. And yet this same man was now holding Santos at gunpoint and asking if she was OK.

'Good.' Gallo twitched a smile. 'And what is this?' He kicked the rolled-up painting.

'The missing Caravaggio Nativity.'

'You're joking!' Placing his gun down next to him, Gallo knelt and unrolled the first few feet of the canvas before glancing up, shaking his head in wonder. 'My God, you're not.'

Without warning, Santos flew forward off his chair, snatched Gallo's gun up and before anyone had time to move, aimed it at his forehead.

'Back off,' he snarled as the armed police belatedly aimed their weapons at him. 'Put your guns on the floor or I'll kill him right here.'

The police ignored him, a few even taking a step closer. Santos immediately took shelter behind Gallo, pressing the gun to his temple.

'You know I'll do it,' he hissed. 'Tell them to back off.' From the wild look in his eyes, Allegra could tell that he meant it.

'Stand down,' Gallo said in a strangled voice. 'That's an order.'

One by one, the officers lowered their guns, placing them at their feet, and then backed away. Santos's three men rearmed themselves, Orlando leaping to Santos's side, the other two covering the rest of the room.

'Now get them out of here,' Santos roared, striking Gallo on the head with the heel of his gun.

'Fall back the way you came in,' Gallo ordered grudgingly, clutching his skull. 'Tell them what's happening.'

'Yes, tell them everything,' Santos called after them. 'And tell them that if anyone else comes down here, I'll kill everyone in this room.'

There was a pause as Santos waited for the room to empty. Allegra glanced at Tom, who gave her a grim smile. They were on their own.

'Get the painting,' Santos barked. 'Time to go.'

With Orlando standing guard, the two other men heaved the rolled-up canvas onto their shoulders and staggered towards the entrance. Still holding Gallo's neck in the crook of his arm, the gun pressed to his head, Santos backed across the room.

'I'll be seeing you soon, Antonio,' Moretti called after him.

Santos paused, then shoved Gallo into Orlando's arms and grabbed two grenades from the bag looped round Orlando's neck.

'I doubt it,' he said, smiling as he pulled the pins out and lobbed one, then the other, into the middle of the room.

The first grenade landed at Tom's feet. Without thinking, he snatched it up and ,with a deft snap of his wrist, flicked it through the gap in the glass-fronted display case where the painting had been hanging. Hitting the wall, it bounced a short way along the bottom and then exploded.

The room jumped around them, smoke and dust avalanching through the opening, a terrible, angry roar lifting them off their feet and knocking the wind out of them. But the armoured glass absorbed the brunt of the blast, its surface cracking but holding firm.

There was to be no such reprieve from the second grenade, however. Having struck the marble table, it bounced into Moretti's lap. As De Luca dived out of the way, it went off, cutting Moretti in half and sending a meteor shower of shrapnel across the room.

Tom looked up from where he had thrown himself to the floor, barely able to see through the thick smoke. Ears ringing, he staggered to his feet and made his way unsteadily towards where he had last seen Allegra and the others, tripping over De Luca, whose arm was hanging limply at his side, blood leaking from a deep gash to his head. The two halves of Moretti's body were lying next to him. It was a gruesome sight.

Coughing, he knelt by Allegra's side. She seemed OK if a little disorientated. But both Archie and Dominique were injured—Archie clutching the side of his face, the blood soaking through his fingers, while a shard of hot metal had embedded itself in Dominique's thigh.

'Are you OK?' Tom called.

'We'll be fine,' Archie said. 'Just go and shoot the bastard.'

Tom jumped across to the pile of guns discarded by Gallo's men, grabbing one and tossing another to Allegra, who was back on her feet.

'Let's go,' she said, her eyes filled with the same diamond-tipped determination he'd seen when she'd engineered their escape from the car park.

They sprinted back through the various decorated rooms towards the vaulted tunnel that led outside.

'Wait!' Allegra called. 'Can you feel that?'

He paused, and then realised what she meant. A fresh breeze was tickling his cheek. Santos must have found another way out.

Turning to her right, she led him along a narrow tunnel that rose in total darkness up a steep incline. Feeling his way along the brick walls, Tom followed closely behind, the breeze getting stronger, until they found themselves in a square chamber. Above them, an iron ladder climbed towards a patch of star-flecked sky. At the foot of the ladder, a body was lying on a bed of rubble. It was Gallo.

'He's alive,' Allegra said, kneeling next to him and pressing her fingers against his neck. Tom wasn't sure if she sounded relieved or disappointed. 'Santos must have thrown him back down the hole.' She pointed at the colonel's arm, which was bent at an unnatural angle.

Tom flew up the ladder, emerging under the disapproving glare of an angel that had escaped damage when Santos had smashed through the gravestone she had been guarding. Hauling himself clear, he reached down to help Allegra climb out. Flickering blue lights on the other side of the cemetery indicated where Gallo's man had congregated.

'Which way?'

Allegra's question was almost immediately answered by the sound of an engine being started. They ran to the cemetery wall, Allegra giving Tom a leg up, Tom then reaching down and hauling her up behind him. As he jumped down onto the pavement, an ambulance surged out of the darkness, headlights blazing, Santos hunched over the wheel.

Stepping into the road and taking careful aim, Tom unloaded a full clip into the ambulance's windscreen. Allegra, perched on the wall, did the same. But they both missed, forcing Tom to leap out of the way as the ambulance veered past.

'*Merda*,' Allegra swore.

Tom shook his head, popping out the magazine and checking it. 'He was coming straight towards me. He could only have been thirty feet away. Probably less.'

A sudden thought came to him. An impossible thought. And yet . . . it was the only explanation. He jumped down and raced back to the angel guarding the shattered gravestone. He lowered himself down the ladder.

'Don't move!'

Hearing the voice, Tom turned and saw that Gallo was conscious now, propped up against the wall and being attended by a medic. Four armed policemen were eyeing Tom suspiciously, their machine guns raised.

'It's OK,' Gallo rasped. 'He's with us. Her too.'

Tom looked up and saw that Allegra was climbing down towards them. The policemen relaxed, allowing their weapons to swing down.

'What the hell is going on?' Tom demanded angrily.

'What do you mean?' said Gallo, wincing as a medic prodded his shoulder.

'I mean this.' Stepping forward, Tom smashed his forearm into the bridge of a policeman's nose and wrenched the machine gun from the man's grasp as he staggered back, howling in pain.

'Tom, what are you doing?' Allegra gasped as he swung the weapon towards Gallo and flicked the safety off.

'Ask him,' he replied tonelessly, before pulling the trigger.

The gun jerked in his hand, the muzzle flash lighting the narrow tunnel like a strobe light, hot shell casings pinging off the walls, the noise crashing around them with a deafening echo.

Gallo returned Tom's accusing glare through the smoke. Unharmed.

'Blanks?' Allegra's face turned from horror to understanding.

Pushing the medic roughly away, Gallo heaved himself to his feet.

'We need to talk,' he growled.

Ponte Sant'Angelo, Rome

With his men forming a cordon at either end of the bridge, Gallo led them out to the middle, then turned to face them, his arm strapped across his chest where the medic had popped his shoulder back into its socket.

'This will do.'

'Where have you taken Archie and Dom?' Tom asked angrily.

'To hospital,' Gallo reassured him. 'My men will take you to them when we've finished.'

'The same men who attempted a rescue armed with blanks?' Allegra snorted. She didn't believe a word he said any more.

'It's complicated. There are powerful forces at work here.'

'What the hell are you talking about?' Tom demanded.

Gallo paused, turning to face down the river so that his back was to them.

'Santos is connected. Very well connected,' he began. 'It seems that, over the years, the Banco Rosalia has done a lot of favours for a lot of people.'

'What sort of people?' Allegra pressed.

'People he helped to evade tax and launder money. People who had relied on him to help fund their political campaigns. People who had profited from the sale of looted antiquities. *Important* people. People who couldn't risk Santos going down and taking them with him.'

'So these people—they're why you helped him get away?' Allegra's voice was heavy with disgust. 'They're why you watched him try to kill us.'

'He wanted it to look as though he'd had to shoot his way out,' said Gallo. 'I didn't know he was going to throw . . . That was . . . wrong.'

'How long has he had you on a leash?' Allegra asked. 'Since Cavalli was killed? Before?'

'I didn't even know who Cavalli was until I was put on to the Ricci case.' Gallo turned to face them again. 'I don't think Santos did either. But when Argento was killed, Santos grew worried that I might somehow connect the murders back to him or the Delian League. So he made some calls.'

'Who to?' Tom asked.

'I've already told you.' Gallo shrugged. 'People. All I know is that, when my orders came, they came from the top. The very top. Protect Santos. Keep a lid on things. Stop the case spiralling out of control.'

'What about Gambetta?' Allegra said. 'Did they tell you to kill him too?'

'I did what I had to do,' Gallo said defiantly. 'Santos had offered us a deal. Cavalli's watch in return for keeping a lid on everything he knew and a promise to leave the country. Gambetta was an old fool who was never going to keep quiet about evidence going missing. He was a necessary sacrifice.' A pause. 'He's not the first person to have died for his country.'

'A necessary sacrifice?' Allegra shook her head in disgust, a fist of anger clenching her stomach. 'This has nothing to do with patriotism. This is about rich, powerful people doing whatever it takes to protect themselves. This is about murder. You killed Gambetta for doing his job.'

'You don't understand,' Gallo shot back. 'I had my orders. The things Santos knows . . . this was a matter of national security. I had no choice.'

'You had a choice,' Allegra insisted. 'You just chose not to make it. You killed a man and framed me for it.'

'I was trying to protect you. Santos found out you were asking questions about the Delian League. He wanted you dealt with. Why do you think De Luca picked you up? I thought that if I blamed you for the killing and got your face in the papers, I might find you before he did . . . Look, maybe it was wrong of me. But you'll get a full retraction, an apology, your choice of assignments—'

'You disgust me. You and whoever it is who can decide that an old man should die to stop someone like Santos being caught.'

'I love my country,' Gallo insisted. 'I did what I had to do to protect it, and I'd do the same again. Anyway, I tried to put things right by saving you. Who do you think dug you out of that tomb?'

'That was you? How did you find us?'

'I had a back-up team watching Eco. They picked you up coming out of the gallery and followed you to where De Luca snatched you and then out to Contarelli's farmhouse. I sent my men in as soon as I could. Luckily, they weren't too late.'

'Luckily,' Allegra repeated in a sarcastic tone, the thought of the plastic bag slick and tight against her lips still making her stomach turn.

'So it was you who fed us the information about D'Arcy?' Tom asked.

'I knew that he worked for De Luca,' Gallo nodded. 'So when I heard about the fire and that he'd gone missing, I realised it was probably connected. I'd seen enough of Allegra to know that if I gave her the option, she'd follow up the lead herself rather than walk away.'

There was a long silence, Gallo glancing at each of them in turn.

'So what happens to Santos now?' Allegra asked eventually.

'He sells the painting and leaves the country. As long as he never comes back, we forget about him and move on.'

'And the Banco Rosalia?'

Gallo laughed. 'The Banco Rosalia is bankrupt. That's why he had to make a move for the painting. It was his last chance to get out with something before the news broke. Not that it ever will. The government and the Vatican have agreed to jointly underwrite the losses and quietly wind the business down to avoid any bad press. No one will ever know a thing.'

Allegra shook her head angrily. The hypocrisy and injustice of a world where a murderer like Santos was allowed to go free to protect a cabal of corrupt politicians and God knows who else, while Gambetta was . . . It made her feel dirty.

'What about De Luca and Faulks? Aren't you going to charge them?' Tom asked hopefully.

'What with?' Gallo shrugged. 'We know what Faulks does, but we've never had any proof that he's broken an Italian law on Italian soil. And as for De Luca—'

'Colonel!' He was interrupted by an officer signalling urgently from the end of the bridge. 'We've found them.'

SIRENS BLARING, they swept through the city, outriders clearing their path. Twenty minutes later they reached the Via Appia Antica.

'A local patrol unit ran their plates as they came past,' Gallo explained. 'They came up registered to a vehicle stolen last week in Milan. When they tried to stop them, the driver lost control and rolled it into a tree.'

Peering through the seats in front of her, Allegra could see a faint glow on the horizon. She looked across to Tom, who gave her an encouraging smile and then reached for her hand. She understood what he was trying to tell her. That this was nearly all over. That they'd almost won.

There were two fire crews on the scene but they were holding back.

'The fuel tank could go at any moment,' one of the crew explained to Gallo. 'We're just going to let it die down a bit.'

Allegra led Tom to the edge of the semicircle of policemen and passers-by that had formed around the burning ambulance. Deep ruts in the verge showed where the vehicle had careered off the road and into a ditch.

Abruptly, the fuel tank exploded, the ambulance jerking spasmodically. Sparks flitted through the air around them like fireflies.

Allegra glanced at Tom and followed his impassive gaze to the body that must have been thrown clear before the fire had broken out. It was the priest, Orlando. From the way he was lying it didn't look like he would be getting up again. She turned back to the ambulance, straining to see through the swirling flames and smoke, and caught the charred outline of a body in the driver's seat, head slumped forward, hands still gripping the wheel.

'Santos?' she asked Tom.

Tom shrugged and then turned away.

'If you want it to be.'

The Getty Villa, Malibu, California

One thing was certain—they had all been asked here to witness something special. The clue, as always, had been in the expense lavished on the engraved invitations, the quality of the champagne served at the welcoming reception and the bulging gift bags positioned next to the exit.

Without warning, the lights dimmed and three people stepped out onto the stage, one of them wearing sunglasses. The shortest person, a man, approached the lectern. A large screen behind him showed a close-up of his face—pink, fleshy and sweating.

'Ladies and gentlemen,' Director Bury began nervously. 'Ladies and gentlemen, it is my pleasure to welcome you here today to see what I believe is the single most important acquisition in the museum's history. Dr Bruce, please.'

He retreated a few steps and led the clapping as Verity stepped forward. She waited for the applause to die down, and then nodded. The stage was immediately plunged into darkness. Then a single spotlight came on, illuminating the jagged outline of a carved face. An ivory face. Behind them the screen was filled with its ghostly, sightless eyes.

The silence of anticipation gave way to an excited murmur.

'Thanks to the incredible generosity of Myron Kezman, a man of singular vision and exquisite taste whose philanthropy shines through these dark economic times,' Verity said, waving at a beaming Kezman to step forward, 'the Getty is proud to announce the acquisition of *The Phidias Apollo*, the only surviving work of possibly the greatest sculptor of the classical age.' She paused as the applause grew, unrestrained and exultant. 'As you can see, it is a uniquely well-preserved fragment of a chryselephantine sculpture of the Greek god Apollo. Dated to around 450 BC, it shows—'

'Verity Bruce?' A man in the front row had interrupted her. Standing up, he moved to the stage.

'If you don't mind, sir, I'll take questions at the end,' she said through a forced smile, eyeing him contemptuously.

'My name is Special Agent Carlos Ortiz, FBI,' the man announced, holding out his badge. 'And if you and Mr Kezman don't mind, you'll be taking my questions downtown.'

The audience turned in their seats as the doors at the back of the auditorium flew open. Four dark-suited men entered the room and fanned out.

'What is this?' she called out over the crowd's low, confused muttering, her expression caught somewhere between incredulity and indignation.

'I have a warrant for your arrest, along with Mr Myron Kezman and Earl Faulks,' Ortiz announced. Kezman said nothing, his indulgent smile having faded behind the blank mask of his sunglasses.

'On what charges?' Director Bury challenged him.

'Federal tax fraud, conspiracy to traffic in illegal antiquities and illegal possession of antiquities,' Ortiz fired back. 'But we're just getting started.'

'This is outrageous,' Verity erupted, shielding her face from the flash of press cameras. 'I have done nothing—'

She was interrupted by a commotion at the back of the room as a man tried to make a run for the exit, only to be brought down heavily by the outstretched leg of another member of the audience.

'It seems Mr Faulks is not as confident in his innocence as you appear to be in yours,' Ortiz observed wryly as two of his men pounced on Faulks's prone figure and hauled him to his feet. 'Cuff them.'

Verity and Kezman's shouted protests were drowned out by the hyena howl of the crowd as they leapt from their seats and surged forward to feast.

Amidst the commotion, a man and a woman slipped out, unobserved.

'HOW'S YOUR FOOT?' Allegra laughed as they made their way outside. A light breeze was blowing in from the Pacific and tugging at her hair, which was now its original colour once again.

'He was meant to trip over it, not step on it,' Tom grinned.

'Do you think they'll let him cut a deal?'

'Unlikely, given what you copied in his warehouse and the tape Dominique recorded of the three of them discussing the mechanics of the whole deal on the phone she and Archie cloned.'

They made their way down a ramp into a large rectangular courtyard.

'What do you think they'll do with the mask?' Allegra asked.

'Ortiz told me that the Italian government has drawn up a catalogue of forty artefacts acquired by or donated to the Getty over the past twenty years that they want returned. The mask is at the top of the list. And that's just the Getty. There are other museums, galleries, private collections . . . The fallout from this will take years to clear.'

'But nothing will change,' Allegra sighed. 'When the Delian League finally falls, others will just see it as an opportunity to step in and fill the vacuum.'

'You can't stop the supply,' Tom nodded. 'But if the publicity makes museums, collectors and auction houses clean up their act, it might choke the demand. With fewer buyers, there'll be less money and less incentive to dig. In time, things might just change.'

There was a silence. 'They buried Aurelio yesterday,' she said.

'I didn't know that . . .?'

'Some kids found his body washed up on the Isola Tiberina.'

'Murdered?'

'They don't think so.'

Tom placed his hand on her shoulder. She glanced up and then quickly looked down, her eyes glistening.

'I'm sorry.'

'I think he was too.'

'What's happened to Gallo?'

'Promoted, I expect.' She gave a hollow laugh. 'To be honest, I don't care. Him, the people he was protecting . . . they all disgust me.'

'But he kept his part of the deal?' Tom checked.

She nodded. 'All charges dropped. A formal apology. My pick of assignments. He even had my parking tickets cancelled.'

'So you'll stay?'

'I'll think about it,' she said. 'Not everyone's like him. Besides, I want to see Contarelli's face when I raid his place.' Tom grinned. 'What about you?'

'Me?' Tom gave a deep sigh. 'Archie's meeting me in New York for Jennifer's funeral. The FBI only released her body last week. After that . . . Who knows? I never like to plan too far ahead. Which way's the sea?'

They followed some steps down to a path.

'By the way, did you hear about the Caravaggio?' Allegra asked.

'Destroyed?' A hint of surprise in Tom's voice.

She shook her head. 'There wasn't any trace of it in the ambulance.'

'And Santos?'

'The DNA from the body at the wheel matched the sample the Vatican provided for him,' she said with a shrug. 'So that's case closed, I suppose.'

'Except you think he's still alive,' Tom guessed.

'I think if he's got any sense, he'll stay dead,' she said, the muscles in her jaw flexing with anger. 'Moretti's people are looking for him and the word is that De Luca's put a five-million-dollar ticket on his head.'

They reached a large lawned area and walked to its far wall, where there was a view out over the treetops to the sea.

'There's just one thing I still can't figure out,' Allegra said, hitching herself up onto the wall to face Tom. 'De Luca, D'Arcy, Moretti and

Cavalli had one watch each. Why did Faulks have two?'

'He said that he had two seats on the council,' Tom reminded her. 'Presumably to act as a counterweight between D'Arcy and De Luca on one hand and Cavalli and Moretti on the other. The watches went with the seats, I guess.'

'Except the League was formed by putting De Luca's and Moretti's two organisations together,' she said slowly. 'That must have meant that they would each have had their own dealer at one stage.'

'So what are you saying? That one of the watches used to belong to someone else?' Tom frowned as he considered this.

'De Luca did say that Faulks's two seats were an accident of history,' she said. 'What if the other dealer left? Faulks would have taken over his seat and his watch.'

'Unless the other dealer never handed the watch back. That might explain why Faulks had a replacement made,' Tom suggested. 'You could be right.'

Central Square, Casco Viejo, Panama
Antonio Santos, his arm in a sling, stood to one side and pressed the muzzle of his gun against the door at about head height.

'Who is it?'

'DHL,' a muffled voice called back. 'Package for Mr Stefano Romano.'

'Leave it outside.'

'I need a signature,' the voice called back.

Santos paused. He was expecting a couple of deliveries this week under that name, and it would be a shame if they got returned. On the other hand, he needed to be careful until he was certain that he had shaken everyone off the trail.

'Who is it from?' he asked, sliding his face across to the peephole.

A bored-looking man was standing on the landing dressed in a brown uniform. He was chewing gum.

'It's from Italy,' he replied, glancing at the stamps and then turning it over so that he could read the label on its back. 'Someone called Amarelli?'

Grinning, Santos tucked his gun into the back of his trousers, unbolted the door and threw it open.

'Amarelli liquorice from Calabria,' he explained, signing the form and eagerly ripping the box open. 'The best there is.' He flicked open a tin of Spezzata and crammed two pieces into his mouth. 'I've looked everywhere, but no one seems to stock it here. Lucky for me they do mail order.'

'Lucky for me too, Antonio,' the courier replied. 'Or I'd never have found you.'

His eyes widening as he realised his mistake, Santos immediately kicked the door shut and reached for his gun. But the man was too quick, stamping his foot in the jamb and then shouldering the door open, sending Santos reeling backwards. Swinging his gun out from behind him, Santos lined up a shot, but before he could pull the trigger a painful punch to the soft inside of his arm sent it rattling across the tiled floor, while a forearm smash to his neck sent him crashing to his knees.

Quickly checking that no one had heard them, the man eased the front door shut and then dragged Santos by his feet towards the kitchen. Once there he cuffed him, and then attached his wrists to a steel cable that he looped over the security bars covering the window.

'Wait. What's your name?' Santos croaked as he was forced to his feet.

'Foster,' the man replied as he tugged down hard on the cable, until Santos's hands were stretched high above his head, forcing him to stand on the balls of his feet to stop the cuffs biting into his wrists.

'Foster, whatever they're paying you, I'll double it,' he wheezed.

'You know how this works. Once I've taken a job, there's no backing out. It's why people hire me. It's why you hired me.'

'I don't even know you.'

'Sure you do.' Foster tied the cable to a radiator, twanging it to check that it was under tension. 'Las Vegas? The Amalfi? That *was* you, wasn't it?'

'The Amalfi?' Santos breathed. 'Please,' he whispered. 'There must be another way. Let me go. I'll disappear. They'll never know.'

'I'll know,' the man replied. 'Now, open wide.'

'What?'

Santos gave a muffled shout as a grenade was forced into his mouth and wedged between his jaws, his eyes wide and terrified.

'The person who sent me wanted you to know that he is a reasonable man. A civilised man. So, if you were to feel able to apologise . . .?'

Santos nodded furiously, the pain in his arms now making him feel faint.

'Good!' Foster reached forward, pulled the pin out and placed it on the counter. Then he took out a mobile phone, dialled a number and positioned it next to the pin. 'He's listening now.' Foster nodded at the phone. 'So when you're ready, just spit the grenade out and say your piece. Just remember— you'll need to speak quickly.'

EPILOGUE

Tarrytown, New York

This was how everything had started. A funeral. Black limos lining the road. A sea of unfamiliar faces. Secret-service agents patrolling the grounds. Guests seated in a horseshoe. The coffin draped with the Stars and Stripes. The service droning towards its muted conclusion.

For a moment it seemed to Tom that time had stood still. That he must have imagined everything. That any moment now Jennifer would appear out of the rain and wave at him to run up and see her. Except today there was no rain, no choreographed ceremony.

'Thanks for coming,' Tom whispered to Archie as FBI Director Green stepped forward and handed Jennifer's parents the neatly folded flag. Her father took it with a proud nod, clutching it to his chest, his left arm hugging her mother into his collar, her shoulders shaking.

The service ended and the congregation broke up. Tom had a sudden urge to go and introduce himself to Jennifer's parents, to let them know the part she'd played in his life and he in hers. But there seemed little point. They had no idea who he was.

'Come on, then. Let's go.'

He got up and made eye contact with FBI Director Green on the other side of the coffin. The sight of Tom caused him to mutter some instructions to his security detail and then step towards him. Tom met him halfway.

'Kirk.'

'Mr Director.'

'I thought you might like to know that Santos was killed yesterday. In Panama.'

Tom nodded slowly, a weight that he had scarcely been aware of slowly lifting from his shoulders.

'What about the shooter who killed Jennifer? This isn't over yet.'

'We're still working on it.' Green shrugged. 'As soon as we get a firm lead, I'll let you know.'

'And the ballistics results? I know someone who—'

'We'll find him. And when we do, I promise you that he'll feel the full force of—'

'Excuse me, but are you Tom Kirk?' Jennifer's father had appeared in front of them.

'Y—yes, I am,' Tom stammered. 'I'm so sorry . . .'

'I think . . . I think she would have wanted you to have this.'

Biting his lip to hold back his tears, he pressed the folded flag into Tom's hands and then fell back to his wife's side.

Tom and Green stood there silently, only a few feet apart, the material strangely warm against Tom's chest. Green glanced around, as if to check that no one was watching, then thrust out his hand.

'Thank you,' he said.

Tom hesitated for a few moments, then shook it.

The next instant Green was gone, caught up in a flurry of dark suits, Ray-Bans and clear plastic earpieces as he was bundled towards his car.

'You think he let you escape from the FBI building on purpose?' Archie murmured.

'I think I did exactly what he'd hoped I would,' said Tom. 'Come on. Let's get out of here.'

'Mr Kirk? Mr Kirk?'

A voice called out as they turned to leave. Tom's eyes narrowed, unable to place the man navigating his way through the crowd.

'Larry Hewson, from Ogilvy, Myers and Gray,' the man introduced himself enthusiastically. 'We met at your grandfather's funeral. I'm the Duval family—'

'Attorney, yes,' Tom suddenly remembered. 'How did you . . .?'

'Your associate was kind enough to suggest that I might find you here,' Hewson explained.

Tom fixed Archie with a questioning stare.

'He kept calling.' Archie shrugged. 'I didn't think he'd actually show up.'

'There's the small matter of your grandfather's will,' Hewson continued. 'As I explained to you when we last met, he specified that I was to pass on to you something that your mother had given him shortly before her death.'

'Yes, I remember.'

'This time I've brought all the paperwork with me. If you wouldn't mind just signing here—. Hewson produced a sheet of paper and a pen, and then held up his briefcase so that Tom could lean against it as he signed. 'Excellent,' he exclaimed, popping the briefcase's brass catches and taking out a small wooden box and an envelope, which he handed to Tom with a flourish. 'Then I will be on my way.'

With a nod, he filed away the signed sheet of paper and strode off towards his waiting car, snapping a phone to his cheek.

'What is it?' Archie asked in a curious voice.

'A letter from my mother,' Tom replied, the sight of his name written in faded black ink strangely familiar from hoarded postcards.

The envelope opened easily, revealing a white card dated to the year before she'd died, across which she'd scribbled a brief message:

Darling Tom

One day, when you're older, you might want some answers. And if you're reading this, it probably means I'm not there to give them. So what's inside this box might help. Whatever you find, don't think too badly of me. I always loved you. I still do.

Love Mummy

Tom turned away from Archie, his eyes hot and stinging, his throat tightening, and opened the box.

All of a sudden the events of the past few weeks came flooding back into sharp focus. De Luca's strange familiarity on meeting him, Faulks's open-mouthed surprise at the mention of his name, Santos's veiled questions. Because inside, nestling on a black velvet background, was a watch.

A watch with an ivory face and an orange second hand.

james twining

You have to hand it to author James Twining. If his central character, Tom Kirk, is the epitome of the dashing gentleman hero—suave, capable, cultured and daring—Twining himself tries to live up to the ideal in every way.

Educated, as an English gentleman should be, at Merchant Taylors' School, an impressive public school set in 250 acres of lakes and countryside, where Middlesex, Buckinghamshire and Hertfordshire meet, he won a place at Christ Church College, Oxford, to read French Literature. After three years, he graduated with a First Class degree and set his sights on a job in the high-risk world of the City of London. His impeccable record took him into the corporate finance department of SBC Warburg (now Warburg UBS). Here he learned to joust with the best in the cut-and-thrust of hostile bids and leveraged buy-outs. Cat-burglary it may not be, but nerves of steel are a prerequisite.

Twining further proved his entrepreneurial mettle and his bravery by setting up an e-procurement business called GroupTrade, with a friend. He sold the business in August 2002, but not before he and his co-founder had both been chosen to rank among eight 'Best of Young British' entrepreneurs in a *New Statesman* competition.

Still, our hero aimed for greater heights, this time as a published author. And it wasn't long before he found success with his first book, *The Double Eagle*, featured in Select Editions in 2005. He has since written three more Tom Kirk stories, of which *The Geneva Deception* is the most recent.

So what does Twining identify as the vital ingredients for a good book? 'A brilliant central character, a recognisable writing style (Fleming has short sentences and muscularity, Hammett has fantastic dialogue), some link to reality like a real event, character or detailed research, an inanimate object around which the human story revolves, and a news story that breaks as a result of the novel.'

Following his own instructions to the letter, Twining always brings fascinating real-life stories into his plots. In the past, he has researched, for instance, a long-forgotten and secret order of SS knights, a missing rare gold coin known as a Double Eagle, and the audacious theft of Leonardo da Vinci's masterpiece, the *Mona Lisa*, weaving all of them into exciting storylines. For this new book, he delved into the illegal international market for antiquities and its Italian suppliers, the *tombaroli* or 'tomb-robbers'. He discovered that one of the most infamous of these, Pietro Casasanta, worked for decades, between prison sentences, in the countryside around Rome, often going about his thefts in broad daylight by posing as a construction worker. One of Casasanta's most important finds was the very rare Apollo ivory mask, which he unearthed just yards from the Baths of Claudius, north of Rome. A unique life-size ivory head of Apollo, the Greek god of the sun, it is from a fifth century BC chryselephantine statue. Many experts believe that it was carved by the classical sculptor Phidias, considered to have perhaps been the greatest of all Ancient Greek sculptors. Such statues were incredibly rare, even in ancient times. The Apollo mask (pictured below) is featured in *The Geneva Deception* and is the main attraction of looted artefacts that have been returned to Italy and are on display at Rome's Quirinale Palace.

On his website, www.jamestwining.com, the author cheekily announces that he played for Arsenal football club, scored a hat trick in the North London Derby and turned down an opportunity to drive for the Ferrari F1 team in order to follow his true vocation as a writer! So, would the multi-talented, shape-shifting Mr Twining prefer the glamorous life of his fictional hero, or that of a paid-up member of the establishment?

'When I was growing up and people asked me what I wanted to be, I would always oblige by telling them what they wanted to hear: an accountant or a lawyer. The truth was, though, that from an early age I had harboured a secret ambition to become one of the world's greatest art thieves—dancing around infrared tripwires, abseiling down the sides of buildings, cracking open safes. In a way, Tom Kirk has been living in my thoughts since I was a child and has perhaps been at the root of my lifelong interest in art and antiques.'

Beneath the skin of every well-brought-up English gentleman, it seems, there is an adventurer just itching to get out—if only in the pages of a well-turned novel.

Major Pettigrew's Last Stand

Helen Simonson

'In the noisy world of today, it is a delight to find a novel that dares to assert itself quietly, with the lovely rhythm of Helen Simonson's funny, comforting and intelligent first novel—a modern-day story of love which takes everyone, grown children, villagers, and the main, participants, by surprise, as real love stories tend to do.'

Pulitzer prize-winning author,
Elizabeth Strout, on *Major Pettigrew's Last Stand*

Chapter 1

Major Pettigrew was still upset about the phone call from his brother's wife and so he answered the doorbell without thinking. On the damp bricks of the path stood Mrs Ali from the village shop. She gave only the faintest of starts, the merest arch of an eyebrow. A quick rush of embarrassment flooded the Major's cheeks and he smoothed helplessly at the lap of his crimson, clematis-patterned housecoat with hands that felt like spades.

'Ah,' he said.

'Major?'

'Mrs Ali?' There was a pause that seemed to expand slowly, like the universe, which, he had just read in the Sunday paper, was pushing itself apart as it aged.

'I came for the newspaper money. The paperboy is sick,' said Mrs Ali, drawing up her short frame to its greatest height and assuming a brisk tone, so different from the low, accented roundness of her voice when they discussed the texture and perfume of the teas she blended specially for him.

'Of course, I'm awfully sorry.' He had forgotten to put the week's money in an envelope under the outside doormat. He started fumbling for the pockets of his trousers, which were somewhere under the clematis. He felt his eyes watering. 'I'm sorry,' he repeated.

'Oh, not to worry,' she said, backing away. 'You can drop it in at the shop later.' As she turned away he was seized with an urgent need to explain.

'My brother died,' he said. She turned back. 'My brother died,' he repeated. 'I got the call this morning. I didn't have time.' The dawn chorus had still been chattering in the giant yew against the west wall of his cottage when the telephone rang. The Major, who had been up early to do his weekly housecleaning, now realised he had been sitting in a daze ever since. He gestured helplessly at his strange outfit and wiped a hand across his face. Suddenly his knees felt loose and he could sense the blood leaving his head. He felt his shoulder meet the door post unexpectedly and Mrs Ali was somehow at his side propping him upright.

'I think we'd better get you indoors and sitting down,' she said, her voice soft with concern. 'If you will allow me, I will fetch you some water.' Since most of the feeling seemed to have left his extremities, the Major had no choice but to comply. Mrs Ali guided him across the narrow hallway and deposited him in the wing chair tucked just inside the door of the bright, book-lined living room. It was his least favourite chair, lumpy-cushioned and hard, but he was in no position to complain.

'I FOUND THE GLASS on the draining board,' said Mrs Ali, presenting him with the tumbler in which he soaked his partial bridgework at night. The faint hint of spearmint made him gag. 'Are you feeling any better?'

'Yes, much better,' he said, his eyes swimming. 'It's very kind of you . . .'

'May I prepare you some tea?' Her offer made him feel frail and pitiful.

'Thank you,' he said. Anything to get her out of the room while he recovered some semblance of vigour and got rid of the housecoat.

It was strange, he thought, to listen again to a woman clattering teacups in the kitchen. On the mantelpiece his wife, Nancy, smiled from her photo. Six years she had been gone. Now Bertie was gone, too. They had left him all alone, the last family member of his generation.

Of course, there was Marjorie, his unpleasant sister-in-law; but, like his late parents, he had never fully accepted her. She had loud opinions and a North Country accent that scraped the eardrum like a dull razor. He hoped she would not look for any increase in familiarity now. He would ask her for a recent photo and, of course, Bertie's sporting gun. Their father had made it clear when he divided the pair between his sons that they were to be restored in the event of death, in order to be passed along intact within the family. The Major's own gun had lain solitary all these years in the double walnut box, a depression in the velvet lining indicating the absence of its mate. Now they would be restored to their full value—around £100,000 he imagined. Not that he would ever dream of selling. For a moment he saw himself quite clearly at the next shoot, coming up to the invited group, bearing the pair of guns casually broken over his arm.

'Good God, Pettigrew, is that a pair of Churchills?' someone would say—perhaps Lord Dagenham himself, if he was shooting with them that day—and he would casually look, as if he had forgotten, and reply, 'Yes, matched pair. Rather lovely walnut they used when these were made.'

A rattling against the doorjamb startled him out of this pleasant interlude. It was Mrs Ali with a heavy tea tray. She had taken off her green wool coat and draped her paisley shawl round the shoulders of a plain navy dress, worn over narrow black trousers. The Major realised that he had never seen Mrs Ali without the large, stiff apron she always wore in the shop.

'Let me help you with that.' He began to rise from the chair.

'Oh, I can manage perfectly well,' she said, and brought the tray to the nearby desk. 'You must rest. You're probably in shock.'

'It was unexpected, the telephone ringing so absurdly early. Not even six o'clock, you know. I believe they were all night at the hospital.'

'It was unexpected?'

'Heart attack. Quite massive apparently.' He brushed a hand over his bristled moustache, in thought. 'Funny, somehow you expect them to save heart attack victims these days. Always seem to on television.' Mrs Ali wobbled the spout of the teapot against a cup rim and it made a loud *chonk*. He recollected (too late) that her husband had also died of a heart attack. It was perhaps eighteen months or two years now. 'I'm sorry, that was thoughtless—' She interrupted him with a sympathetic wave of dismissal and continued to pour. 'He was a good man, your husband,' he added.

What he remembered most clearly was the large, quiet man's restraint. Things had not been altogether smooth after Mr Ali took over the village shop. On at least two occasions the Major had seen him calmly scraping spray paint from his new plate-glass windows. Several times Major Pettigrew had been in the store when young boys on a dare had dashed in and yelled, 'Pakis go home!' Mr Ali would only shake his head and smile while the Major would bluster and stammer apologies. The upper echelons of the village, led by the ladies of the various village committees, compensated for the rudeness of the lower by developing a widely advertised respect for Mr and Mrs Ali. The Major had heard many a lady speak proudly of 'our dear Pakistani friends at the shop' as proof that Edgecombe St Mary was a utopia of multicultural understanding.

'I am sorry I did not have an opportunity to meet your lovely wife,' said Mrs Ali, handing him a cup.

'Yes, she's been gone some six years now,' he said. 'Funny really, it seems like both an eternity and the blink of an eye all at the same time.'

'It is very dislocating,' she said. Her crisp enunciation struck him with the purity of a well-tuned bell. 'Sometimes my husband feels as close to me as you are now, and sometimes I am quite alone in the universe.'

'You have family, of course.'

'Yes, quite an extended family.' He detected a dryness in her tone. 'But it is not the same as the infinite bond between a husband and wife.'

'You express it perfectly,' he said. They drank their tea and he felt a sense of wonder that Mrs Ali should be revealed as a woman of such great understanding. 'About the housecoat,' he said.

'Housecoat?'

'The thing I was wearing.' He nodded to where it now lay in a basket of *National Geographic*s. 'It was my wife's favourite housecleaning attire. Sometimes I, well . . .'

'I have an old tweed jacket that my husband used to wear,' she said softly. 'Sometimes I put it on and take a walk round my garden.' She lowered her deep-brown eyes to the floor, as if she had said too much. 'Are you ready for more tea?' she asked, and held out her hand for his cup.

WHEN MRS ALI LEFT, she making her excuses for having invited herself into his home and he making his apologies for inconveniencing her with his dizzy spell, the Major donned his housecoat once more and went back to the small scullery beyond the kitchen to finish cleaning his gun. He was conscious of tightness around his head and a slight burn in the throat. This was the dull ache of grief in the real world; more dyspepsia than passion.

He had left a small china cup of mineral oil warming on its candle stand. He dipped his fingers in the hot oil and began to rub it slowly into the burled walnut root of the gun stock. As he relaxed into his task he felt his grief ease, making room for the tiniest flowering of a new curiosity.

Mrs Ali was, he half suspected, an educated woman, a person of culture. Nancy had been such a rare person, too, fond of books and of chamber concerts in village churches. But she had left him alone to endure the blunt tweedy concerns of the other women of their acquaintance, who talked horses and raffles at the hunt ball. Mrs Ali was more like Nancy. She was a butterfly to their scuffle of pigeons. He acknowledged a notion that he might wish to see Mrs Ali again outside the shop, and wondered whether this might be proof that he was not as ossified as his sixty-eight years might suggest.

Bolstered by this thought, he felt that he was up to the task of phoning his son, Roger, at his office in a tall glass tower in London's Docklands. He wiped his fingertips on a soft rag and peered at the innumerable chrome buttons on the cordless phone, a present from Roger. Its speed-dial and voice-activation capabilites were, Roger said, useful for the elderly. Major Pettigrew disagreed on both its ease of use and the designation of himself as old. It was frustratingly common that children were no sooner gone from the nest than they began to infantilise their own parents and wish them dead, or at least in assisted living. It was all very Greek, the Major thought. With an oily finger, he depressed the button marked '1—Roger Pettigrew, VP, Chelsea Equity Partners', which Roger had filled in with large, child-like print.

Roger had already heard.

'Jemima has taken on the call-making. The girl's hysterical, but there she is, calling everyone and his dog.'

'It helps to keep busy,' suggested the Major.

'More like wallowing in the whole bereaved-daughter role, if you ask me,' said Roger.

'That's unnecessary, Roger,' he said firmly. Really, his son was becoming as unedited as Marjorie's family. The City was full of blunt, arrogant young men these days and Roger, approaching thirty, showed few signs of evolving past their influence.

'Sorry, Dad. I'm very sorry about Uncle Bertie.' There was a pause.

'Will you come down the night before the funeral?' asked the Major.

'No, I'll take the train. There's a big flap on here. Two billion dollars, tricky buyout of the corporate bonds—and the client's nervous. I mean, it'll go in my calendar as a "must", but you never know. I might get stuck.' The Major wondered how he was usually featured in his son's calendar. He imagined himself flagged with a small yellow sticky note—important but not time sensitive, perhaps.

THE FUNERAL was set for Tuesday at four.

'It seemed good for most people,' Marjorie said on her second call. 'Jemima has her evening class on Mondays and I have a bridge tournament on Wednesday night.'

'Bertie would want you to carry on,' the Major replied, hearing a slightly acid tone creep into his voice. He was sure the funeral had also been scheduled round available beauty appointments. Marjorie would want to make sure her stiff wave of yellow hair was freshly sculpted.

'Yes. Is Roger going to drive you?'

'No, he'll come straight from London by train and take a taxi. I'll drive.'

'And you'll come back to the house afterwards, of course. We'll have drinks and a few nibbles. Nothing elaborate. And perhaps there is something of Bertie's you'd like to have. You must have a look.'

'That's extremely thoughtful of you,' he said, trying to dampen the eagerness that brightened his voice.

'Some *small* token, some memento. Bertie would have insisted.'

When the Major hung up the phone it was with a feeling of despair. She truly was a horrible woman. He sighed for poor Bertie and wondered whether he had ever regretted his choice of wife.

IT WAS ONLY a twenty-minute drive from Edgecombe St Mary to the nearby seaside town of Hazelbourne-on-Sea where Bertie and Marjorie lived. The town was always busy with shoppers and tourists, so the Major had determined to be on the road no later than one thirty. Yet here he was sitting in the car, in front of his house, unmoving. He worked to quell his panic with a series of deep breaths. It was not possible that he should miss his own brother's funeral and yet it was equally impossible to turn the ignition key.

There was a knock on the car window and he turned his head to see Mrs Ali, looking anxious. He took a deep breath and managed to land his fingers on the power window button.

'Are you all right, Major?' she asked.

'I think so,' he said. 'I was just catching my breath. Off to the funeral.'

'Yes, I know,' she said, 'but you're very pale. Are you all right to drive?'

'Hardly a choice, dear lady,' he said. 'Brother of the deceased.'

'Perhaps you'd better step out and get some fresh air for a minute,' she suggested. 'I have some cold ginger ale here that might do you good.' She was carrying a small basket in which he could see a slightly oily paper bag that suggested cakes, and a tall green bottle.

'Yes, perhaps for a minute,' he agreed, and stepped from the car. The basket, it turned out, was a small care package she had meant to leave on his doorstep for his return.

'I didn't know if you'd remember to eat,' she said as he drank the ginger ale. 'I myself did not consume anything for four days after my husband's funeral. I ended up in the hospital with dehydration.'

'It's very kind of you,' he said. He felt better for the cold drink but his body still ran with small tremors. He had to make it to the funeral somehow.

'I think I'd better see if there's a taxi available. I'm not sure I'm fit to drive.'

'That is not necessary,' she said, 'I'll drive you myself. I was on my way to Hazelbourne anyway.'

'Oh, I couldn't possibly . . .' he began. He didn't like being driven by a woman. He hated their cautious creeping about at intersections, their indifference to the nuances of gear changing, and their ignorance of the rearview mirror. Many an afternoon he had crept along the winding lanes behind some slow female driver who blithely bobbed her head to a pop radio station, her stuffed animals nodding their own heads in time on the rear shelf. 'I couldn't possibly,' he repeated.

'You must do me the honour of letting me be of service,' she said. 'My car is parked in the lane.'

SHE DROVE LIKE A MAN, aggressively changing gear into the turns, accelerating away, swinging the tiny blue Honda over the hills with relish. She had opened her window slightly and the rush of air blew ripples in her rose silk headscarf, and tossed stray black locks of hair across her face.

'How are you feeling?' she asked.

'I'm not feeling as washed-out as before,' he said. 'You drive very well.'

'I like to drive,' she said, smiling at him. 'Just me and the engine. No one to tell me what I should be doing. No accounts, no inventory—just the possibilities of the open road and many unseen destinations.'

'Quite,' he said. 'Have you made many road trips?'

'Oh, no,' she replied. 'There are so many places I would like to go. But there is the shop.'

'Perhaps your nephew will soon be able to run the shop by himself?'

She laughed a not altogether happy laugh. 'Oh, yes,' she said. 'One day soon he will be quite able to run the shop and I shall be superfluous.'

The nephew was a recent and not very pleasant addition to the village shop. He was a young man of twenty-five or so. He carried himself stiffly, a hint of insolence in his gaze, as if always prepared to meet some new insult.

'Will you retire?' he asked.

'It has been suggested,' she said. 'My husband's family lives up north and hope I will consent to live in their home.'

'No doubt a loving family will compensate for having to live in the north of England,' said Major Pettigrew, doubting his own words. 'I'm sure you will enjoy being the revered grandmother and matriarch.'

'I have produced no children of my own and my husband is dead,' she replied, her voice level. 'Thus I am more to be pitied than revered. I am expected to give up the shop to my nephew, who will then be able to afford to bring a very good wife from Pakistan. In exchange, I will be given the honour of taking care of the children of other family members.'

The Major was silent. He was at once appalled and also reluctant to hear any more. This was why people usually talked about the weather. 'They surely can't force you . . .' he began.

'Not legally,' she said. 'My wonderful Ahmed broke with family tradition to make sure the shop came to me. But what is the rule of law against the weight of family opinion?' She made a left turn, squeezing into a small gap in the hurtling traffic of the coast road. 'You Anglo-Saxons are lucky. You have largely broken away from such dependence on family. Each generation feels perfectly free to act alone and you are not afraid.'

'Quite,' said the Major, accepting the compliment automatically but not feeling at all sure that she was right.

When they arrived in Hazelbourne she dropped him off at the church, and he scribbled down his sister-in-law's address on a piece of paper.

'I expect we'll be done by six o'clock, if that's convenient?' he added.

'Certainly.' She took his hand a moment in hers. 'I wish you a strong heart and the love of family this afternoon.' The Major felt a warmth of emotion that he hoped he could keep alight as he faced the awful starkness of Bertie in a walnut box.

THE SERVICE WAS LARGELY the same mix of comedy and misery he remembered from Nancy's funeral. The church was large and dismal. The only comfort was the small satisfaction of seeing the service well attended.

Jemima and Marjorie both spoke. He expected to be derisive of their speeches, especially when Jemima announced a poem composed in her father's honour. But though the poem was indeed atrocious, her genuine grief transformed it into something moving, as was Marjorie's short and tearful goodbye to her husband.

After the service, shaking hands with people in the smoked-glass lobby, the Major had been touched by the appearance of several of his and Bertie's old friends, some of whom he had not seen in many years. Martin James, who had grown up with them both in Edgecombe, had driven over from Kent. Bertie's old neighbour, Alan Peters, who had a great golf handicap, had driven over from the other side of the county.

But there was no sign of Roger.

Chapter 2

Bertie's house—he supposed he should have to start thinking of it as Marjorie's house now—was a boxy split-level that Marjorie had managed to torque into some semblance of a Spanish villa. The lumpy brick pergola and wrought-iron railings of a roof-top patio crowned the attached double garage. The front garden was given over mostly to a gravel driveway that circled a spindly copper fountain in the shape of a very thin, naked young girl. The late afternoon was growing chilly, but upstairs on the second floor, Marjorie still had the doors from the tiled living room open to the roof-top patio. Marjorie's idea of 'nothing elaborate' was a huge banquet of spoon-dripping food—egg salad, lasagne, a wine-soaked chicken stew—served entirely on paper plates. All round the room people cradled sagging plates in their palms, plastic glasses and cups of tea set down haphazardly on window ledges.

Across the room the Major caught an undulation in the crowd and followed the stir to see Marjorie embracing Roger. His heart jumped to see his tall, brown-haired son. So he had come after all.

Roger made copious apologies for his lateness. He was charming and smooth in an expensive dark suit, unsuitable gaudy tie and narrow, highly polished shoes.

'Listen, Dad, Jemima had a word with me about Uncle Bertie's shotgun,' said Roger when they had a moment to sit down and talk.

'Yes, I was meaning to talk to Marjorie about it. But it's not really the time, is it?'

'They understand perfectly the value of it.'

'It's not a question of the money,' said the Major sternly. 'Our father was quite clear in his intentions that the pair be reunited.'

'Yes, Jemima feels the same,' said Roger. 'She says the market is red-hot right now. There aren't Churchills of this quality to be had for love or money.' The Major's smile became quite rigid as he anticipated the blow that was to come. 'So, Jemima and I think the most sensible course of action would be to sell them as a pair. Of course, it would be your money, Dad, but since you are planning to pass it on to me eventually, I assume, I could really do with it now.'

The Major said nothing. He concentrated on breathing. He had never really noticed how much mechanical effort was involved in maintaining the slow in-and-out of the lungs. Roger had the decency to squirm in his chair. He knew, thought the Major, exactly what he was asking.

'Excuse me, Ernest, there's a strange woman outside who says she's waiting for you,' said Marjorie, appearing suddenly. He looked up, coughing to hide his wet eyes. 'Are you expecting a dark woman in a Honda?'

'Oh, yes,' he said, 'that's Mrs Ali. She's come to pick me up.'

'In that case, you'd better have her come in and have some tea,' said Marjorie, her lips tight with disapproval.

'I'll do that, thank you,' said the Major, rising to his feet.

'Actually, Dad, I was hoping I could drive you home,' said Roger.

The Major was confused. 'But you came by train,' he said.

'Yes, that was the plan,' said Roger, 'but things changed. Sandy and I decided to drive down. She's looking at weekend cottages right now.'

'Weekend cottages?' It was too much to take in.

'Yes, Sandy thought since I had to come down anyway . . . I've been on at her about getting a place down here. We could be nearer to you.'

'A weekend cottage,' repeated the Major.

'I'm dying for you to meet her. She should be here any minute.' Roger scanned the room in case she had suddenly come in. 'She's American, from New York. She has a rather important job in the fashion business.'

'Mrs Ali is waiting for me,' said the Major. 'It would be rude—'

'Oh, I'm sure she'll understand,' interrupted Roger.

OUTSIDE, THE AIR was chill. The view of the town and the sea beyond was smudged round the edges with darkness. Mrs Ali had parked her Honda just inside the curly iron gates with their depictions of flying dolphins. She waved and stepped from the car to greet him.

'Mrs Ali, won't you come in and have some tea?' he said.

'No, thank you, Major, I don't want to intrude,' she said. 'But please don't rush on my account. I'm quite fine here.' She indicated a paperback book she was holding in her hand.

The Major was miserably confused. He was tempted to climb in the car and go right now. It would be early enough when they got back to invite Mrs Ali in for tea. Perhaps they could discuss her book.

'You're going to think me impossibly rude,' he said. 'But my son managed to come down after all, by car.'

'How lovely for you,' she said.

'Yes, and he would like—of course I told him I'd already arranged to go home with you . . .'

'No, no, you must go home with your son,' she said.

'I'm most awfully sorry,' he said. 'Are you sure you won't come in and have some tea?'

'No, thank you,' she said. 'I must be getting back.'

'I really am in your debt,' he said. 'I can't thank you enough for your gracious assistance.'

'It's nothing at all,' she said. 'Please don't mention it.' She gave him a slight bow, got in the car and reversed it in a tight circle that flung gravel in a wide arc. At the gate, the Honda braked to avoid the sweeping oval head-lights of a large black car, which slid up the driveway and parked in the large open space the other guests had politely left clear in front of the door.

The Major, trudging back up the gravel incline, arrived just as the driver opened her door. More from instinct than inclination, he held the door for her. She looked surprised and then smiled as she unfolded tanned legs from the close confines of the champagne leather cockpit.

'I'm not going to do that thing where I assume you're the butler and you turn out to be Lord So-and-So,' she said, smoothing down her plain black skirt. She wore it with a fitted black jacket worn over nothing—at least, no shirt was immediately visible in the cleavage area, which, due to her height and vertiginous heels, was almost at the Major's eye level.

'The name is Pettigrew,' he said. He was reluctant to admit anything more. He was still trying to process the American vowels.

'Well, that narrows it down to the right place,' she said. 'I'm Sandy Dunn. I'm a friend of Roger Pettigrew.'

'I believe he is talking to his aunt just now,' the Major said, looking over his shoulder at the open hallway. 'Perhaps I should get him for you?'

'Oh, just point me in his general direction,' she said, and moved past him. 'Nice to meet you, Mr Pettigrew.'

'It's Major, actually . . .' he said, but she was already gone, leaving a trail of citrus perfume in the air.

THE MAJOR FOUND HIMSELF loitering in the hall, unwilling to face what was inevitable upstairs. He would have to be formally introduced to the Amazon. He could not believe Roger had invited her. She would no doubt make out his prior reticence to be some sort of idiocy.

He sighed and trudged upstairs, where he saw Marjorie standing by the French doors with Roger and the American.

'Dad, I want you meet Sandy Dunn,' said Roger, when he had spotted him. 'Sandy's in fashion PR and special events. Her company works with all the important designers, you know.'

'Hi,' said Sandy, extending her hand. 'I knew I was right about the butler thing.' The Major shook her hand, and raised his eyebrows at Roger, signalling him to continue with the introduction, even though it was all in the wrong order. Roger only gave him a big vacant smile.

'Ernest Pettigrew,' said the Major. 'Major Ernest Pettigrew, Royal Sussex, retired.' He managed a small smile.

'Oh, yes. Sorry, Dad,' said Roger.

'It's nice to meet you properly, Ernest,' said Sandy. The Major winced at the casual use of his first name.

'Do you live in London?' asked the Major. He waited, stiff with concern, for any hint that they were living together.

'I have a small loft in Southwark,' she said. 'It's near the new Tate.'

'Oh, it's an enormous place,' said Roger, excitedly. 'The only problem is finding furniture on a big enough scale. She's having a sofa custom-made in Japan.' Marjorie looked impressed.

'I find G-Plan makes a good couch,' she said. Bertie and Marjorie had acquired most of their furniture from G-Plan—good solid upholstered couches and sturdy square-edged tables. 'Did you order it with slipcovers?'

'Goatskin,' said Roger. There was great pride in his voice. 'She saw my goatskin lounger and said I was ahead of the trend.'

The Major wondered whether it was possible he had been too strict with Roger as a child and thereby inspired his son to such excesses. Nancy, of course, had tried to spoil him rotten. He had been a late gift to them, born just as they had given up all hope of having children, and Nancy could never resist making that little face smile from ear to ear. It was he who had been forced to put a stop to many an extravagance.

'Roger really has an eye for design,' said Sandy. 'He could be a decorator.' Roger blushed.

'Really?' said the Major. 'That's quite an accusation.'

THEY LEFT SOON AFTER, Sandy handing her car keys to Roger to drive. She took the passenger side without comment, leaving the Major to sit in the back.

'I'm so sorry Roger was late today,' said Sandy, turning round to smile at him. Her bosom strained at the seat belt. 'We were looking at a cottage and the realtor—I mean the estate agent—was late.'

'Looking at a cottage?' the Major said. 'What about work?'

'No, that all got resolved,' said Roger, fixing his attention on the road. 'I told the client I had a funeral and he could push things back a day or get someone else.'

'So you looked at cottages?'

'It was my fault entirely, Ernest,' said Sandy. 'I thought I'd scheduled plenty of time to fit it in before I dropped Roger off at the church. The estate agent messed things up royally.'

'I'm going to complain to that agent tomorrow,' said Roger.

'No need to cause a ruckus, darling. Your Aunt Marjorie was extremely gracious about it.' Sandy put a hand on Roger's arm and smiled back at the Major. 'You all were.' The Major tried but failed to summon his rage. In his now sleepy state, he could come up with the thought only that this young woman must be very good at her public relations job.

'Touring cottages,' he murmured.

'We shouldn't have gone, I know, but these cottages get snapped right up,' said Sandy. 'Remember that cute place near Cromer?'

'We've only looked at a few places,' said Roger, his eyes giving an anxious glance in the rearview mirror. 'But this area is our priority.'

'I admit it's more convenient than the Norfolk Broads or the Cotswolds,' said Sandy. 'And, of course, for Roger you're the big attraction.'

'An attraction?' said the Major. 'If I'm to outrank Norfolk, perhaps I'd better start offering cream teas in the garden.'

'Dad!'

'Oh, your father is so funny,' said Sandy. 'I just love that dry humour.'

The Major said nothing. He relaxed his head against the leather seat and gave himself up to the soothing vibrations of the road. Soon he was dozing as Roger and Sandy talked together in low voices.

'HERE WE ARE,' said Roger. His voice was brisk. The Major blinked his eyes and struggled to pretend he had been awake the whole time. He had forgotten to leave a light on and the brick and tile façade of Rose Lodge was barely visible in the sliver of moonlight.

'What a charming house,' said Sandy. 'It's bigger than I expected.'

'Yes, there were what the Georgians called "improvements" to the original seventeenth-century house, which make it look more imposing than it is,' said the Major. 'You'll come in and have some tea, of course,' he added, opening his door.

'Actually, we won't, if you don't mind,' said Roger. 'We've got to get back to London to meet some friends for dinner.'

'But it'll be ten o'clock before you get there,' said the Major, feeling a ghost of indigestion just at the thought of eating so late.

Roger laughed. 'Not the way Sandy drives. I'll see you to the door.' He hopped out of the car. Sandy slid into the driver's seat, legs flashing like scimitars. She pressed something and the window whirred down.

'Good night, Ernest,' she said, holding out her hand. 'It was a pleasure.'

'Thank you,' said the Major. He dropped her hand and turned on his heel. Roger scurried behind him down the path.

'See you again soon,' called Sandy. The window purred shut.

'I can hardly wait,' mumbled the Major.

'Mind your step on the path, Dad,' said Roger behind him. 'You ought to get a security light, you know. One of those motion-activated ones.'

'What a splendid idea,' he replied. 'With all the rabbits round here it'll be like one of those discos you used to frequent.' He opened the door and was pleased that he found the light switch at first snap.

'Will you be OK, Dad?' He watched Roger hesitate, one hand on the doorjamb, his face showing the nervous uncertainty of a child who knows he has behaved badly.

'I'll be fine, thank you,' he said.

'OK, I'll call you tomorrow.'

'It's not necessary.'

'I want to,' insisted Roger. He stepped forward and the Major found himself teetering in an awkward angular hug. He gave a couple of tentative pats to Roger's back, then rested his hand for a moment and felt, in his son's knobby shoulder blade, the small child he had always loved.

'You'd better hurry,' he said, blinking hard. 'It's a long drive back to town.'

'I do worry about you, Dad.' Roger stepped away and became again the strange adult who existed mostly at the end of the telephone. 'Sandy and I will work out our schedules so we can come down and see you in a couple of weeks.'

'Sandy? Oh, right. That would be delightful.' Roger grinned and waved as he left, which reassured the Major that his dryness of tone had remained undetected. He waved back and watched his son leaving happy, convinced that his ageing father would be buoyed up by the prospect of the visit to come.

TWO DAYS PASSED before it occurred to the Major that Mrs Ali had not called in to check on him and that this had caused him a certain disappointment. The paperboy was quite well again, judging by the ferocity with which *The Times* was thrown at his front door. He had had his share of other visitors. Alice Pierce from next door had come round the day before with a hand-painted condolence card and a casserole dish of what she said was her famous organic vegetarian lasagne, and informed him that it was all over the village that he had lost his brother. That day, Daisy Green, the vicar's wife, had dropped by unannounced with her usual entourage of Alma Shaw and Grace de Vere, and insisted on making him a cup of tea in his own house.

It usually made the Major chuckle to see the trinity of ladies going about the business of controlling all social and civic life in the village. The ladies swam in Daisy's wake like frightened ducklings as she flew about offering unsolicited advice and issuing petty directives that somehow people found easier to follow than refuse. It amused him less that, treating their spinster friend as a project, Daisy and Alma had conspired to make a presentation of Grace. She was fully primped, her slightly elongated face made papery with pale powder and a girly pink lipstick, a coquettish scarf tied in a bow under her left ear as if she were off to a party. It was a shame because Grace was actually quite a sharp and pleasant woman, very knowl-edgeable about roses and local history.

While Daisy and Alma clattered the cups and banged the tray, Grace was left to keep him pinned in the living room with whispery conversation about the weather. He huffed in his chair with impatience until the tea was brought in.

'There's nothing like a good cup of tea from a real china pot, is there?' said Daisy, handing him his cup and saucer. 'Biscuit?'

'Thank you,' he said. They had brought him a tin of assorted 'luxury' biscuits with views of thatched cottages printed on the lid. He selected a shortbread biscuit and took a bite. The ladies settled themselves on chairs, smiling at him with compassion as if watching a starving cat lap from a saucer of milk.

'Was your brother older than you?' asked Grace.

'No—younger, actually, by two years.' There was a pause.

'He was ill for some time?' Grace asked, eyes wide with compassion.

'No, quite sudden, I'm afraid.'

'I'm so, so very sorry.' She fussed with her fingers at the large green stone brooch at her high-collared neck. The other ladies busied themselves with their teacups and there was a palpable desire in the room for the conversation to move on. Grace, however, could not find her way out.

'Was his family with him at the end?' she said, looking at him desperately. He was tempted to tell her that no, Bertie had died alone in an empty house and been discovered weeks later by the charlady from next door, in order to puncture the vapid conversation with the nail of deliberate cruelty.

'His wife was with him when they took him to the hospital and his daughter was able to see him for a few minutes, I understand,' he said.

'It must be a great comfort to you to know he died surrounded by family,' said Alma. The Major would have liked to reply that this was not so, that he was pierced with pain that no one had thought to call him until it was all over and he had missed saying goodbye to his brother. He wanted to spit this at them, but his tongue felt thick and useless.

'And, of course, he was surrounded by the comfort of the Lord,' said Daisy. The vicar's wife spoke in an awkward rush as if she were bringing up something vaguely impolite.

'Amen,' whispered Alma.

'Oh, go to hell,' whispered the Major into the translucent bottom of his teacup, covering his muttering with a cough.

LATER THAT AFTERNOON, the Major decided to take a short walk to the village. He might even stop at the village shop to purchase some tea. It would, he thought, give the busy Mrs Ali a chance to make her excuses for not coming to see him.

The walk down the narrow lane never ceased to give him pleasure. The dense hedges of privet, hawthorn and beech swelled together as fat and complacent as medieval burghers. The air was scented with their spicy dry fragrance, overlaid with the tang of animals in the fields behind the cottages. As he rounded a curve, the hedges gave way to the plain wire fence of a sheep field and allowed a view of twenty miles of Sussex countryside spreading beyond the roofs of the village below. Behind him, above his own house, the hills swelled upwards into the rabbit-cropped grass of the chalk downs. Below him, the Weald of Sussex cradled fields full of late rye and the acid yellow of mustard. He liked to pause at the stile, one foot up on the step, and drink in the landscape. Something—perhaps it was the quality of the light, or the infinite variety of greens in the trees and hedges—never failed to fill his heart with a love of the country that he would have been embarrassed to express aloud.

The shop lay only a few hundred yards downhill of his position, and the wonders of gravity helped him as he thrust away from the stile and continued to stride down the hill towards the village green.

The orange plastic sign, 'Supersaver SuperMart', winked in the low September sun. Mrs Ali's nephew was in the window, pasting up a large poster advertising a sale on canned peas; the Major hesitated in midstride. He would rather have waited until the nephew was not around. He did not like the young man's perpetual frown, which, he admitted might be the result of unfortunately prominent eyebrows. The shop bell's tinkle made the young man look up. He nodded and the Major gave a slightly smaller nod in return and looked round for Mrs Ali.

The store contained a single small counter and cash register up-front. Four narrow but clean aisles stretched back through the low-ceilinged rectangular room. They contained a well-stocked but plain selection of foods, and only the canisters of loose tea and a dish of homemade samosas hinted at Mrs Ali's exotic heritage. There was an awkward extension to the back that contained a small area of bulk items like dry dog food, potting soil and plastic-wrapped multipacks of Heinz baked beans. The Major couldn't imagine who purchased bulk items here. Everyone did their main shopping at the supermarket in Hazelbourne-on-Sea. For most people, the village shop was strictly for when one had run out of something, especially late at night. The Major noticed that they never thanked Mrs Ali for being open until eight on weeknights and also on Sunday mornings, but they loved to mumble about the prices being high.

He did not hear or sense Mrs Ali's presence in the empty store and so, rather than scour each aisle, the Major made his way as casually as possible towards the back, beyond which the shop office was hidden behind a curtain of stiff vertical vinyl panels.

He was inspecting prices when Mrs Ali finally appeared through the vinyl, carrying an armful of Halloween-themed boxes of mini apple pies.

'Major Pettigrew,' she said with surprise.

'Mrs Ali,' he replied. 'I just wanted to thank you for your kindness the other day.'

'No, no, it was nothing.' She seemed to want to wave her hands but, encumbered by the pies, she could only waggle her fingertips.

'And I wanted to apologise—' he began.

'Please don't mention it,' she said, and her face tightened as she looked past his shoulder. The Major felt between his shoulder blades the presence of the nephew and sensed that Mrs Ali did not wish him to go on with his apologies in front of him. He turned round.

'Again, I just wanted to thank you both for your kind condolences,' he said, particularly pleased with the 'both', which dropped in softly, like a perfectly putted golf ball. The nephew, stubbornly staying where he was, was forced to nod his head in appreciation.

'Anything we can do, you must just ask, Major,' said Mrs Ali. 'Beginning, perhaps, with some fresh tea?'

'I am running a little low,' said the Major.

'Very well.' She lifted her chin and spoke to the nephew. 'Abdul Wahid, would you fetch the rest of the Halloween specials and I'll take care of the Major's tea order?' She marched past both of them with her armful of boxes and the Major followed. The nephew scowled and then disappeared behind the vinyl curtain.

'My dear lady,' began the Major. 'Your kindness to me—'

'I would rather not discuss it in front of my nephew,' she whispered and a brief frown marred the smoothness of her oval face. 'He has recently returned from his studies in Pakistan and is not yet reacquainted with many things here.' She looked to make sure the nephew was out of earshot. 'He does not like it when I drive the car.'

'Oh.' It was slowly dawning on the Major that the nephew's concerns might include strange men such as himself.

'Not that I have any intention of paying the least heed, of course,' she said, and this time she smiled. 'I'm trying to re-educate him slowly. The young can be so stubborn.'

'Quite. I quite understand.'

'So if I can do anything for you, Major, you must just ask,' she said. Her eyes were so warm and brown, the expression of concern on her face so genuine, that the Major threw caution to the winds.

'Well, actually,' he stammered. 'I was wondering if you were going to town later this week. It's just that I'm still not feeling well enough to drive and I have to stop in and see the family solicitor.'

'I usually go in on Thursday afternoons but I can possibly—'

'Thursday would be fine,' said the Major quickly.

'I could pick you up around two o'clock?' she asked.

The Major, feeling very tactful, lowered his voice. 'Perhaps it would be most convenient if I waited at the bus stop—save you driving to me?'

'Yes, that would be perfectly convenient,' she said, and smiled. The

Major felt that he was in danger of smiling like a fool.

'See you Thursday, then,' he said. 'Thank you.' As he left the shop, it occurred to him that he had failed to buy any tea. It was just as well really, since he was quite amply stocked. As he strode back across the village green, he was aware of a lighter step and easier heart.

Chapter 3

Thursday morning, the Major surfaced from sleep to the sound of rain hammering at the eaves like fists. He cursed himself for having assumed the weather would be sunny. Perhaps it was the result of evolution, he thought—some adaptive gene that allowed the English to go on making blithe outdoor plans in the face of almost-certain rain. For sun was to have been his excuse to turn a borrowed car ride into something more. An invitation to walk the seafront would have been entirely appropriate, given the beauty of the day. Now a walk was out of the question and he was afraid that an invitation to afternoon tea in a hotel would reflect too much presumption. He sat up rather suddenly and the room swam round him. What if Mrs Ali used the rain as an excuse to telephone and cancel entirely? He would have to reschedule his meeting with his solicitor or drive himself.

Assuming she did not cancel, there were certain adjustments to be made to his wardrobe. He got up, slipped his feet into Moroccan leather slippers, and padded over to the large pine wardrobe. He had planned on a tweed jacket, wool slacks and a splash of celebratory aftershave. However, the tweed gave off a faint odour when moist, so he decided that today would be the perfect opportunity to wear the expensive acrylic sweater that Roger had given him last Christmas. He had thought its slim fit and black-on-black diamond pattern too young, but today he felt that a little youthful style might be just the thing to counter a potentially damp social setting.

He was unusually fidgety by lunch time and jumped when the phone rang. It was Alec Shaw, Alma's husband, wondering whether he was up to playing a round of golf despite the rain.

'I'm sorry I haven't called you before,' Alec said. 'Alma gave me a full report. Said you appeared to be holding up?'

'Yes, thank you,' he said.

'I should have called you sooner.' The Major smiled to hear Alec strangling himself on his own awkwardness. They had all stayed away, not just Alec, but Hugh Whetstone, who lived in the next lane, and the entire golf club group. He didn't mind. He had done the same in the past; kept away from the nuisance of other people's losses and let Nancy deal with it. It was understood that women dealt better with these situations.

'I have to pop into town and see the family solicitor,' he replied. 'Maybe next week?' He tried to play golf once a week—a challenge in the unpredictable autumn weather. With Bertie's death, he had not been near the club in nearly two weeks.

'Ground may be soggy today, anyway,' said Alec. 'I'll get us an early tee-off time for next week. See if we can't get in a full round before lunch.'

BY TWO O'CLOCK the clouds had given up their roiling and simply sat down on the land, transforming the rain into a grey fog. The Major stood in the bus shelter and watched as the small blue car came up over the swell of the hill. Mrs Ali pulled up and he saw her wide smile first and then the scarf of brilliant peacock blues and greens loose on her smooth black hair. She reached over to release the passenger door for him to climb in.

'I'm sorry, let me just move these,' she said, and scooped two or three plastic-covered library books out of his way.

'Let me hold those for you,' he said as he settled into the seat. She gave him the books and he was conscious of her long smooth fingers.

'Are we ready?' she asked.

'Yes, thank you. It's very kind of you.' He wanted to look at her but he was very aware of the narrow confines of the car. She put the car in gear and pulled away from the kerb. The Major fixed his gaze on the books: a Colette novel, de Maupassant stories, a poetry anthology. To the Major's surprise, the de Maupassant was in French.

'You certainly didn't get these books from the mobile library van,' he observed. Mrs Ali laughed and the Major thought it sounded like singing.

'I go to the library in town,' said Mrs Ali, calmly overtaking a towering hay wagon on the briefest stretch of open road between two blind curves, 'but even then I have to order most of what I want.'

'I've tried to order a book once or twice,' said the Major. 'I remember requesting a particular edition of Samuel Johnson's essays, and was disappointed that the librarian didn't seem to appreciate it at all. You'd think that after stamping the flyleaves of cheap novels all day, they'd relish the challenge of tracking down some wonderful old classic, wouldn't you?'

'Try ordering foreign languages,' said Mrs Ali.

'You speak other languages besides French?' asked the Major.

'My French is very bad,' she said. 'I'm more fluent in German. And Urdu, of course.'

'That's very impressive,' said the Major.

'And quite useless in the running of a shop,' said Mrs Ali with a sad smile.

'There's nothing useless about reading the classics,' said the Major, weighing the books in his hand. 'Too few people today appreciate and pursue the delights of civilised culture for its own sake.'

'Yes, it can be a lonely pursuit,' she said.

'Then we—the happy few—must stick together,' said the Major. She laughed, and, as the little car picked up speed, the Major felt that the afternoon was somehow already a success.

'Where would you like me to drop you?' she asked as they joined the slow curl of traffic into Hazelbourne.

'How about the seafront? Would that take you out of your way?'

'The seafront will be fine,' she said, and very soon pulled the car into the small pay-and-display car park right behind the beach. She left the engine running and added, 'Pick you up in an hour and a half?'

'That will be perfect,' he said, handing her the books and reaching to open the door. His mind raced with casual ways of requesting that she join him for tea, but he did not seem able to bring any of them to actual speech. He cursed himself for an idiot as she sped away again, waving.

THE OFFICES of Tewkesbury and Teale, Solicitors, were in a lemon-coloured Regency villa fronting onto a small square two streets behind the sea. The Tewkesburys had been lawyers here since before the turn of the last century and had been the Pettigrew family lawyers for nearly as long. Father, son and grandson had quietly given of their time to civic duties (free legal advice to the town council being just one of their causes), but had resisted all calls to stand for office, lead a committee or appear in the paper. As a boy, he remembered, he had been impressed by Tewkesbury's unhurried speech, sober clothes and heavy silver fob watch.

He had been puzzled, as had Bertie, when Tewkesbury took in Mortimer Teale as an associate. Teale had come out of nowhere to attach himself to the Tewkesbury daughter and only heir, Elizabeth. Mortimer favoured loud ties, liked his food to the point of fussiness, and bowed and scraped in front of clients in a way that gave the Major his only opportunity, outside the *Sunday Times* crossword, to use the word 'oleaginous'. He had married Elizabeth and had squatted like a well-fed cuckoo in the midst of the Tewkesbury clan until he had managed to bury old Tewkesbury.

The Major had considered finding himself a new solicitor but had not wanted to break with his own family's tradition, reminding himself that Mortimer had done nothing but excellent work, and that it was uncharitable to dislike a man for wearing purple spotted pocket squares and having sweaty palms.

'AH, MAJOR, so nice to see you even under such sad, sad conditions,' said Mortimer, advancing across the carpet of his office to clasp the Major's hand.

'Thank you.'

'Your brother was a fine man and it was a privilege to call him a friend.' Mortimer settled back down at his mahogany desk and waved at a club chair. 'Let's get this started, shall we?' He took a thin, cream-coloured file from a desk drawer and slid it across the vast expanse between them. Light fingermarks now decorated the plain typed page headed 'Last Will and Testament of Robert Carroll Pettigrew'.

'As you know, Bertie has named you the executor of this will. As executor, you will have a couple of bequests and small investment accounts to oversee, and for this you are entitled to a small compensation, expenses and so forth. You may wish to waive . . .'

'I'll just read it, then, shall I?' said the Major.

'Of course, of course. Just take your time.' Mortimer sat back and laced his hands across his bulging waistcoat as if preparing to take a nap, but his eyes remained sharply focused across the desk.

Bertie's will was only a page and a half long, with plenty of white space between the lines. His possessions were transferred to his loving wife and he asked his brother to be his executor in order to relieve her of administrative burdens during a difficult time. There was a small investment account set up for Jemima's son, Gregory, and any other grandchildren who might arrive later. There were also bequests to three charities. When he finished reading, the Major went back and read the will again, to make sure he hadn't missed a paragraph.

The will made no mention of any bequests of personal items, to anyone, offering only a single line: 'My wife may dispose of any and all personal effects as she deems fit. She knows my wishes in these matters.' In these few words, the Major sensed his brother's capitulation to his wife and an apology to himself.

'Are there not a couple of omissions?' he enquired at last.

'I think you'll find all the required language is there,' said Mortimer. The Major could see he had no intention of helping smooth over the awkwardness of asking about the Major's own interests.

'As you know, there is the matter of my father's sporting guns,' he said. He could feel his face flushing with heat, but he was determined to be direct. 'It was understood by all that the guns were to be reunited upon the death of either one of us, and I was under the impression that Bertie's will would contain explicit directions in this matter—as my own will does.'

'Ah,' said Mortimer slowly, and sighed.

'Those guns were passed on to us in trust by my father,' the Major said, drawing himself up as far as possible. 'It was his dying wish that we share in them during our lifetimes and that we reunite them to pass on down the generations. You know this as well as I.'

'Yes, that has always been my understanding,' agreed Mortimer. 'However, since your father gave you the guns in person, during his illness, there was no such direction in his will and therefore no obligation . . .'

'But I'm sure Bertie put it in his will,' he said, annoyed to find a begging tone creeping into his voice.

Mortimer did not answer at once. He gazed up at the brass chandelier as if searching for the exact phrasing of his next words. 'I can say very little,' he finally offered. 'Let us say only that the leaving of any specific assets away from a spouse may become an issue of loyalty for some couples.' He grimaced in conspiratorial fashion and the Major caught the faintest echo of Marjorie's shrill voice ringing off the panelling of the office.

'Everyone knows that gun is mine,' said the Major. He was hurt and angry to the point of feeling faint. 'It should have been mine in the first place, you know—oldest son and all that. Not that I ever begrudged Bertie his share, only he never was a shooting man.'

'Well, I think you should have a friendly chat with Marjorie about it,' said Mortimer. 'That way, we know there's no conflict of interest on your part. I must get the probate filed soon, so if you could get back to me . . .'

'And if she doesn't agree to give me the gun?' said the Major.

'Then, in the interest of expediting probate, I would advise you to decline the executor position.'

'I can't do that,' said the Major. 'It's my duty to Bertie.'

'Talk to Marjorie and call me as soon as you can,' said Mortimer, rising from his chair and holding out his hand. The Major also stood. He wished he had worn a suit now, instead of this ridiculous black sweater. It would have been more difficult for Mortimer to dismiss him like a schoolboy.

Stepping out of the office into the square, the Major was momentarily blinded. The fog had been pushed back from the sea, and the stucco fronts of the villas were drying to pale tones in the afternoon sunshine. He felt the sudden warmth relax his face. He breathed in and the salt water in the air seemed to wash away the smell of furniture wax and avarice that was Mortimer Teale's office.

To TELL MORTIMER that he had never begrudged Bertie the gun had been a lie. Sitting on the seafront, his back pressed against the wooden slats of a bench, the Major turned his face up to the sun and thought back to the day when his mother called him and Bertie into the dining room, where their father lay in a rented hospital bed wasting away from emphysema.

The Major was a second lieutenant by then, one year out of officer training, and he had been granted ten days' special leave. The time had seemed to flow slowly, a quiet eternity of whispers in the dining room, but while his mother and Bertie often crept away to their rooms to wet pillows with their tears, he preferred to read aloud at his father's bedside or help the private nurse in turning his emaciated body. At the end, his father sent for his two sons and his prized pair of Churchills.

'I want you to have these,' he said. He opened the brass lock and pushed back the lid of the double walnut box. The guns gleamed in their red velvet beds; the finely chased engraving on the silver action bore no tarnish.

'You don't have to do this now, Father,' he had said. But he had been eager; perhaps he had even stepped forward, half obscuring his younger brother.

'I wish them to go on down through the family,' said his father, looking with anxious eyes. 'Yet how could I possibly choose between my two boys and say one of you should have them?'

He looked to their mother, who took his hand and patted it gently. 'We want you to each have one, to keep his memory,' she said at last.

'Given to me by the maharajah from his own hand,' whispered their father. It was an old story so rubbed with retelling that the edges were blurry. A moment of bravery, an Indian prince honourable enough to reward a British officer's courageous service when all around were howling for Britain's eviction. It was his father's brush with greatness. The medals might desiccate in the attic, but the guns were always kept oiled and ready.

'But to break up a pair, Father?' He could not help blurting out the question, though he read its shallowness in his mother's blanched face.

'You can leave them to each other, to be passed along as a pair to the next generation—keep it in the Pettigrew name, of course.'

The guns were not listed as part of the estate, which was passed to his mother for her lifetime use and then to him, as the eldest son. Bertie was provided for out of small family trusts. By the time their mother died some twenty years later, the trusts had eroded to an embarrassing low. However, the house was decrepit too. There was rot in some of the seventeenth-century beams, its traditional Sussex brick-and-tile-hung exterior needed extensive repairs, and their mother owed the local council money. The house still looked substantial and genteel, but it was more of a liability than a grand inheritance, as he had told Bertie. He had offered his brother most of their mother's jewellery as a gesture. He had also tried to buy his brother out of the gun, both then and several other times over the years when Bertie had seemed hard up. His brother had always declined his offers.

The Major sighed. He was a man who always tried to do his duty without regard for gratitude or even acknowledgment. Surely he could not have inspired resentment from Bertie all these years?

'Ah, there you are, Major,' said a voice. He sat upright and blinked in the strong light. It was Mrs Ali, holding a large tote bag and a new library book. 'I didn't see you at the car park.'

'Oh, is that the time?' said the Major, looking in horror at his watch. 'I completely lost track. My dear lady, I am so horribly embarrassed to have kept you waiting.' Now that he had unconsciously achieved what he would never have dared to contrive deliberately, he was completely at a loss.

'It is not a problem,' she said. 'As the day has turned out so unexpectedly nicely, I thought I'd take a brief walk and maybe start my book.'

'I will, of course, pay for the car park.'

'It's really not necessary.'

'Then will you permit me to at least buy you a cup of tea?' he asked, so quickly that the words pushed and elbowed each other to get out of his mouth. She hesitated, so he added, 'Unless you're in a rush to get home, which I quite understand.'

'No, there is no rush,' she said. She looked left and right along the promenade. 'Perhaps, we could walk as far as the kiosk in the gardens?'

'That would be lovely,' he said.

THE PROMENADE formed a scrolling timeline of Hazelbourne-on-Sea's history. The net-drying sheds and the fishing boats drawn up on the shingle, where the Major had been sitting, were part of the old town, which huddled round small cobbled alleys lined with lopsided Tudor shops.

As one walked westwards, the town grew more prosperous. In the middle, copper roofs, white wooden walls and a curlicued wrought-iron structure sat out over the Channel like a big iced cake. Beyond the pier, the mansions and hotels became imposing. Between the hotels were open squares of villas or wide streets of elegant townhouse façades.

Beyond the appropriately named Grand Hotel, the town's march through history was abruptly interrupted by the sudden swell of the chalk cliffs into a vast headland. The Major, who often walked the entire promenade, never failed to ponder how this might represent something about the hubris of human progress and the refusal of nature to knuckle under.

Mrs Ali walked with a comfortable stride. The Major tried to fall in with her rhythm. He had forgotten how to let a woman dictate the pace.

'What book did you pick today?' he asked.

'Kipling,' she replied. 'It's a children's book, as the librarian took pains to inform me, but the stories are set in this area.' She showed him a copy of *Puck of Pook's Hill*, which the Major had read many times.

'I used to consider myself a bit of a Kipling enthusiast,' said the Major. 'I'm afraid he's rather an unfashionable choice these days, isn't he?'

'You mean not popular among us, the angry former natives?' she asked, with an arch of one eyebrow.

'No, of course not . . .' said the Major, not feeling equipped to respond to such a direct remark.

'I did give him up for many decades,' she said. 'He seemed such a part of those who refuse to reconsider what the Empire meant. But as I get older, I find myself insisting on my right to be philosophically sloppy. It's so hard to maintain that rigour of youth, isn't it?'

'I applaud your logic,' said the Major, swallowing any urge to defend the Empire his father had proudly served. 'The man wrote some thirty-five books—let them analyse the prose, not the politics.'

'Besides, it will drive my nephew crazy just to have him in the house,' Mrs Ali said with a slight smile.

The Major was not sure whether to ask more about the nephew. He was extremely curious, but it did not seem his place to enquire directly, so he said, 'Do you have other nephews and nieces?'

'There is only the one nephew. His parents, my husband's brother and his wife, have three daughters and six granddaughters.'

'Ah, so your nephew must be their golden boy?' said the Major.

'He was my golden boy, too, when he was little. I'm afraid that Ahmed and I spoiled him terribly.' She hugged her book a little tighter to her chest and sighed. 'We were not blessed with children of our own, and Abdul Wahid was the very image of my husband when he was small. He was a very smart boy, too, and sensitive. I thought he would be a poet one day.'

'A poet?' He tried to picture the angry young man writing verse.

'My brother-in-law put a stop to such nonsense once Abdul Wahid was old enough to help in one of their shops. I suppose I was naive. I wanted so much to share with him the world of books and of ideas.'

'A noble impulse,' said the Major. 'But I taught English at a boarding school after the army and I can tell you it's pretty much a lost cause, getting boys over ten to read. Most of them don't own a single book.'

'I cannot imagine,' she said. 'I was raised in a library of a thousand books.'

'Really?' He did not mean to sound so doubtful, but he had never heard of grocers owning large libraries.

'My father was an academic,' she said. 'He came after Partition to teach applied mathematics. My mother always said she was allowed to bring two cooking pots and a picture of her parents. All the other trunks contained books.' She sighed. 'They're all gone now. When he died, my uncles came from Pakistan to settle the estate. One day I came home from school and my mother and an aunt were washing all the empty shelves. My uncles had sold them by the foot. There was an odour of smoke in the air and when I ran to the window . . .' She paused and took a slow breath.

Memories were like tomb paintings, thought the Major, the colours still vivid no matter how many layers of dust and sand time deposited. She looked at him, her chin raised. 'I can't tell you the paralysing feeling, the shame of watching my uncles burning paperbacks in the garden incinerator.' Mrs Ali stopped and turned to look out over the sea, and the Major wondered whether he should pat her on the back.

'I'm so sorry,' he said.

'Oh, I can't believe I told you this,' she said, rubbing a corner of her eye. 'I apologise. I'm such a silly old woman these days.'

'My dear Mrs Ali, I would hardly refer to you as old,' he said. 'You are in what I would call the very prime flowering of mature womanhood.' It was a little grandiose but he hoped to surprise a blush. Instead she laughed.

'I have never heard anyone try to trowel such a thick layer of flattery on the wrinkles and fat deposits of advanced middle age, Major,' she said. 'I am fifty-eight years old and I think I have slipped beyond flowering. I can only hope now to dry out into one of those everlasting bouquets.'

'Well, I have ten years on you. I suppose that makes me a fossil.'

She laughed again, and the Major felt that there was no more important and fulfilling work than to make Mrs Ali laugh. His own troubles seemed to recede as their steps took them beyond the ice cream stalls and ticket booths of the pier, and into the public gardens.

At the far end of the gardens, on a small circular lawn that lay open to the sea on one side, a thin, dark-skinned boy of four or five was nudging a small red ball with his feet. When he gave the ball a sharp tap it bounced against a low bronze sign that said 'No Ball Playing' in raised, polished letters and then rolled towards the Major. Feeling jovial, the Major attempted to chip the ball back, but it bounced sideways off his foot, struck an ornamental boulder and rolled swiftly under a hedge of massed hydrangeas.

'Oi, there's no football allowed 'ere,' shouted a voice from a small green kiosk that offered tea and an assortment of cakes.

'Sorry, sorry,' said the Major, waving his hands to encompass both the grey-faced, plump lady behind the kiosk counter and the small boy, who stood looking at the bushes as if they were completely impenetrable. The Major hurried over to the hedge and looked for some flash of red.

'What kind of park is it if a six-year-old can't kick a football?' said a sharp voice. The Major glanced up to see a young woman who, though obviously of Indian origin, wore the universal uniform of the young and disenchanted. She was dressed in a rumpled parka the colour of an oil slick, and long striped leggings tucked into motorcycle boots. Her short hair stuck out in a halo of stiff tufts as if she had just crawled out of bed, and her face, which might have been pretty, was twisted with belligerence.

'There won't be no flowers left if all the kids trample about with balls all day,' said the kiosk lady. 'I don't know what it's like where you come from, but we try to keep things nice and genteel round here.'

'What d'you mean by that?' The young woman scowled.

'Don't get all shirty with me—I don't make the rules,' said the lady. The Major scooped up the ball and handed it to the boy.

'Thank you,' said the boy. 'I'm George, and I don't really like football.'

'I don't, either,' said the Major. 'Cricket is the only sport I follow.'

'Tiddlywinks is a sport, too,' said George with a serious expression.

'But Mum thought I might lose the bits if I brought them to the park.'

'Now that you bring it up,' said the Major, 'I've never seen a sign saying "No Tiddlywinking" in any park, so it might not be such a bad idea.' As he spoke, the young woman hurried over.

'George, I've told you a thousand times not to talk to strange men,' she said.

'I do apologise,' said the Major. 'It was entirely my fault, of course. Bit of a long time since I played any football.'

'Silly old cow ought to mind her own business,' said the young woman, loud enough to carry back to the kiosk.

'Very unfortunate,' said the Major in a noncommittal voice.

'The world is full of small ignorances,' said a quiet voice. Mrs Ali appeared at his elbow and gave the young woman a stern look. 'We must all do our best to ignore them and thereby keep them small, don't you think?' The Major braced himself for an abusive reply but to his surprise, the young woman gave a small smile instead.

'My mum always said things like that,' she said in a low voice.

'But of course we do not like to listen to our mothers,' said Mrs Ali, smiling. 'At least, not until long after we are mothers ourselves.'

'We have to go now, George. We'll be late for tea,' said the young woman. 'Say goodbye to the nice people.'

'I'm George, goodbye,' said the boy to Mrs Ali.

'I'm Mrs Ali, how do you do?' she replied. The young woman gave a start and seemed to hesitate for a moment, as if she wanted to speak, but then she appeared to decide against volunteering any further introductions, and set off with George towards the town.

'What an abrupt young woman,' said the Major.

Mrs Ali sighed. 'I rather admire such refusal to bow before authority, but I fear it makes for a very uncomfortable daily existence.'

At the kiosk, the lady was muttering something under her breath about people who thought they owned the place. The Major tightened his upright stance and spoke in his most imposing voice, 'Do my eyes deceive me or are those real mugs you're using for tea?' he said, pointing towards a row of thick earthenware mugs.

'I don't hold with them polystyrene things,' said the woman, softening her expression just a bit. 'Makes the tea taste like furniture polish.'

'How right you are,' said the Major. 'Could we have two teas, please?'

They drank their tea at a small iron table partly sheltered by an over-grown hydrangea, rusty with the drying blooms of autumn. They were quiet and, as the Major looked out to sea, he felt a small sense of contentment quite unfamiliar in his recent life. A gin and tonic at the golf club bar with Alec and the others did not inspire in him the happiness that now possessed him. He was struck then by the thought that he was often lonely, even in the midst of many friends. He exhaled and it must have come out as a sigh, for Mrs Ali looked up from sipping her tea.

'I'm sorry, I haven't asked you how you are doing,' she said. 'It must have been difficult today, dealing with the solicitor?'

'These things have to be taken care of,' he said. 'I am the executor for my brother, and unfortunately there are one or two things he left rather vague. I'm afraid it will require delicate negotiation on my part to make things come out right.'

'He is lucky to have an executor of your integrity,' she said.

'Nice of you to say so,' he said, trying to ignore a sudden twinge of guilt. 'I will do my best to be absolutely fair, of course.'

'But you need to act fast,' she continued. 'Before you can take inventory, the silver is gone, the linens have disappeared, and the little brass unicorn from his desk—worth nothing, except to you—poof! it's slipped into a pocket and no one can remember it when you ask.'

'Oh, I don't think my sister-in-law would stoop—'

'And everyone knows exactly what happened but no one will ever speak of it again, and the family goes on with its secrets invisible but irritating, like sand in a shoe.'

'There must be a law against it,' he said. Mrs Ali blinked at him, emerging from her own thoughts.

'Of course, there is the law of the land,' she said. 'But we have talked before of the pressures of the family.' The Major nodded. He thought Mrs Ali's face had clouded over, but perhaps it was just the day.

'Looks like we've had the best of the weather,' he said. 'Perhaps it's time we were heading back?'

The walk back to the car was silent and somewhat uncomfortable, as if they had trespassed too far into personal areas. As he walked, his head churned with the repeating phrase, 'I was wondering if you were planning to come to town next week?' but he could not bring himself to express it aloud. They reached the small blue car and a sharp sadness threatened him as Mrs Ali bent to unlock the door. He admired again her smooth brow and the brightness of her hair disappearing into her scarf. She looked up under his gaze and straightened up.

'Major,' she asked, 'I was wondering if it would be possible to consult you more about Mr Kipling when I've finished my book?' The sky began to spit fat drops of rain and a cold gust of wind whipped against his legs. The sadness vanished and he thought how glorious the day was.

'My dear lady, I would be absolutely delighted,' he said. 'I am completely at your disposal.'

Chapter 4

The golf club was built on the water side of the Downs, on a low promontory that ended in a roll of grass-backed dunes. The greens ranged in quality from thick green turf, clipped to perfection, to patchy brown areas, invaded by dune grass and prone to sudden spurts of sand whipped up into the face by wind gusts. The thirteenth hole was famous for Dame Eunice, a huge Romney Marsh ewe who kept the grass cropped to the limit of her rusty chain.

The Major, feeling his spirits lift with the early-morning light and the smell of the sea and the grass, gave Eunice a surreptitious pat as he shooed her away from the green where his ball lay near the southern edge. Alec was scything dune grass looking for his ball, the bald spot on his head shining in the chilly sunshine. The Major waited patiently, enjoying the low arc of the bay: miles of sand and water washed with silver by the cloudy light.

'Bloody grass. Cuts you to ribbons,' said Alec, stamping on a clump.

'Careful there, old chap,' said the Major. 'The ladies' environmental committee'll be after you.'

'Bloody women and their bloody dune habitats,' said Alec. The ladies of the club had become recent advocates for more responsible golf course management, putting up posters urging members to keep off the dunes and advising of wildlife nestings. Alma was one of the prime agitators.

'How is Alma?' asked the Major.

'Won't leave me in peace,' replied Alec. 'What with all the environmental nonsense and now the annual dance, she's just driving me crazy.'

'Ah, the annual dance. And what is our theme this year?' It was a source of annoyance to the Major that what had once been a refined black tie dance had been turned into a series of increasingly elaborate theme evenings.

'They haven't made the final decision,' said Alec. 'But I believe the working title is "Mogul Madness".'

'They will be hard-pressed to exceed the "Last Days of Pompeii",' said the Major, knowing he was being unkind. Last year's theme, combined with an open bar until midnight, had resulted in open debauchery and a ridiculous loosening of standards wholly unworthy of a golf club of pedigree.

'Don't remind me,' said Alec. 'I still have nightmares of being stuck inside that gladiator costume.'

'If only this year we could just go back to having an elegant dance,' said the Major. 'I'm tired of wearing my dinner suit and having people ask me what I'm supposed to be.'

'There's a meeting this morning to settle the issue,' said Alec. 'When we get in, you could pop your head round the door and suggest it.'

'Oh, I don't think so,' said the Major, horrified. 'Perhaps you could have a quiet word with Alma?' Alec merely snorted, took a ball out of his pocket, and dropped it over his shoulder onto the edge of the green.

'One-stroke penalty gives you four over par?' added the Major, writing in his tiny leather scorebook. He was a comfortable five strokes ahead.

'Let's say the winner talks to my wife,' said Alec, and grinned. The Major was stricken. He put away his notebook and lined up his shot. He hit it a little fast and too low, but the ball made a dive into the hole anyway.

'Oh, good shot,' said Alec.

THE GRILL BAR was a high-ceilinged Edwardian room, with French doors looking over the terrace and eighteenth hole. A series of mirrored doors at the east end hid an annexe with a stage, which was opened on the occasion of large tournaments as well as the annual dance. The wall of the long bar to the west end was hung with arched wood panelling on which racks of bottles were ranged below portraits of past club presidents.

'Good morning, gentlemen. The usual?' asked Tom the barman, a tumbler already poised under the optic of the green gin bottle.

'Make mine a half of lager instead, would you, Tom?' said the Major.

They ordered two thick ham and cheese sandwiches. Alec also put in his order for a piece of jam roly-poly since it was offered only on Fridays and tended to sell out.

They had barely settled onto a couple of bar stools when a foursome came in, laughing over some incident during their round. Reverend Green, the local vicar, and Hugh Whetstone the Major recognised, and he was surprised to see Lord Dagenham, who was very rarely at the club and whose atrocious playing made for some very awkward questions of etiquette. The fourth man was a stranger; something in his unfortunate pink golf shirt suggested to the Major that he might be an American. Two Americans in as many weeks was, he reflected, approaching an epidemic.

'Shaw, Major—how are you?' asked Dagenham, slapping Alec on the back and then clasping the Major firmly on the shoulder. 'Sorry to hear about your loss, Major. Damn shame to lose a good man like your brother.'

'Thank you, your lordship,' said the Major, standing up and inclining his head. 'You are very kind to say so.'

'Frank, allow me to present Major Ernest Pettigrew, formerly of the Royal Sussex, and Mr Alec Shaw—used to help run the Bank of England in his spare time. Gentlemen, this is Mr Frank Ferguson, from New Jersey.'

'How do you do,' said the Major.

'Frank is in real estate,' added Lord Dagenham. 'One of the largest resort and retail developers on the East Coast.'

'Oh, you're making too much of it, Double D,' said Ferguson. 'It's just a little family business I inherited from my dad.'

'You're in the building trade?' asked the Major.

'You got me pegged, Pettigrew,' said Ferguson, slapping him on the back. 'You Brits can smell a man's class like a bloodhound smells rabbit.'

'I didn't mean to imply anything . . .' the Major stumbled.

'Mr Ferguson can trace his lineage to the Ferguson clan of Argyll,' said Hugh Whetstone, who tried to ferret out the genealogy of everyone he met so he could use it against them later.

'Not that they were very happy to hear it,' Ferguson said. 'My ancestor faked his own death in the Crimea and ran off to Canada—gambling debts, so I believe. Still, they were pretty happy with my offer on the castle at Loch Brae. I'm going to look into restoring the shoot up there.'

'The Major is a shooting man, too.' said Lord Dagenham. 'Shoots with a very nice gun—a Purdey, isn't it, Major?'

'A Churchill, actually,' said the Major, slightly annoyed that Dagenham had automatically mentioned the more famous name. 'Lesser known, per-haps,' he added, 'but they've made their share of exquisite guns.'

'Nothing like the workmanship in an English gun,' said Ferguson. 'At least, that's what they say when they take a year to make you a pair.'

'Actually, I may be in the happy position of reuniting my pair.' The Major could not resist giving this information directly to Lord Dagenham.

'Well, of course,' said Lord Dagenham. 'You inherit the other one from your brother, don't you? Congratulations, old man.'

'It's not quite settled yet,' said the Major. 'My sister-in-law . . .'

'A matched pair of Churchills?' said the American, smiling at the Major with slightly increased interest.

'Yes, 1946 or thereabouts. Made for the Indian market,' said the Major, not allowing even a hint of pride to show through his modesty.

'I'd love to see them in action some time,' Ferguson said.

'The Major often comes over and has a go with us,' said Dagenham.

'Then I'm sure I'll be seeing you at Double D's shoot on the eleventh.'

Dagenham looked awkward and the Major held his breath. Lord Dagenham was now in the terrible position of having to explain to his American guest that the shooting party in question was strictly for business colleagues, mostly down from London for the day. It was appalling to see a good man so trapped by the ignorance of the bad-mannered.

'Of course you must come, Major,' said Dagenham at last. 'Not much of a challenge, though. We'll only be taking the ducks off the hill pond.'

Once a year, Dagenham held a shoot at a small pond tucked into a copse that crowned a low hill above the village. The gamekeeper and some hired helpers scared the ducks off the pond with yelling and by thrashing about with rakes and cricket bats. The birds would circle the copse once, squawking in protest, then fly back directly into the path of the guns, urged home by the gamekeeper's welcoming whistle. The Major's disappointment at never being invited to this more elaborate shoot, with its huge breakfast party at the Hall to follow, was slightly mitigated by his contempt for so-called sportsmen who needed wildfowl driven right onto the gun barrel.

'I'd be delighted to come,' said the Major, hoping that Marjorie could be persuaded to lend him Bertie's gun for the occasion.

'Ah, I think Tom has our table ready,' said Dagenham, ignoring the expressions of hope on the face of the vicar and Whetstone. 'Shall we?'

'See you on the eleventh, then,' said Ferguson, pumping the Major's hand. 'I'll be on you and those guns of yours like a bear on honey.'

'Thank you for the warning,' said the Major.

THE MAJOR'S CAR had already pulled up beside Marjorie's spindly fountain before second thoughts overwhelmed him. He should have telephoned before arriving. The fiction that he was welcome to drop in at any time could be maintained only as long as he never took Marjorie at her word.

He rang the doorbell and the chimes played their few bars of 'Joyful, Joyful', echoing away deep in the house. He rang again. Somewhere a door closed and at last heels clicked on tile and the door was unbolted. Jemima was dressed in grey sweatpants and a black sleeveless polo-neck top, with her hair pulled back under a white sweatband. She gave him a glare she might have given a door-to-door salesman or an evangelical proselytiser.

'Is Mother expecting you?' she asked. 'Only I just got her to lie down for a few minutes.'

'I'm afraid I drove over on the off chance,' he said. 'I can come back later.'

'I was just doing my healing yoga,' she said. 'But I suppose you'd better come in while I'm here. I don't want people bothering Mother when I'm not around.' She turned and went in, leaving the door for him to close.

'I SUPPOSE you'd like a cup of tea?' Jemima asked as they arrived in the kitchen. She put on the electric kettle and stood behind the U-shaped kitchen counter. 'Camomile, Blackberry Zinger or burdock?'

'I'll have real tea if you have it,' he said. She reached high into a cupboard and pulled out a tin of plain tea bags. She dropped one in a cup and poured boiling water up to the brim. It immediately began to give off a smell like wet laundry.

'How is your mother doing?' he asked.

'It's funny how people keep asking me that. "How's your poor mother?" they say, as if I'm just some disinterested observer.'

'How are you both doing?' he offered, biting back a more resentful retort. Her broad hint of people's insensitivity did not extend to asking how he was coping.

'She's been very agitated,' Jemima confided.

The Major jiggled the tea bag in the cup by its string. The swollen belly of the bag rolled in the brown water.

'Ernest, how lovely to see you. You should have called and let us know you were coming.' Marjorie came in wearing a voluminous black wool skirt and a ruffled blouse of black and purple that looked as if it had been whipped up out of funeral bunting. He stood, wondering whether to hug her, but she slipped behind the counter with Jemima and the two of them looked at him as if he had come to buy stamps at the post office.

'I'm sorry just to barge in like this, Marjorie,' he said, adopting a businesslike tone. 'But Mortimer Teale and I have begun the estate work and I did want to just clarify one or two little matters with you.'

'You know, Ernest, that I have no head for these things. I'm sure you can leave most of it to Mortimer. He's such a clever man.'

'That may be, but he is not a member of the family and therefore may not be able to interpret some of the will's intentions, so to speak.'

'I think my father's will is very straightforward,' said Jemima, her eye beady as a gull's. 'We don't need anyone upsetting Mother by raising questions for the sake of it.'

'Oh, Jemima, don't be rude to your uncle Ernest,' said Marjorie. 'He is one of our only friends now. We must depend on him to look after us.' She dabbed her eyes and gave a close approximation of a tremulous smile. The Major could see a hint of steely resolve burning under the smile, but it put him in an impossible position. He was quite unable to ask for his gun in the face of his brother's crying widow.

'Of course. Mortimer and I will file all the appropriate paperwork, nothing we can't resolve between us. I will take care of everything,' he promised.

'Thank you, Ernest,' she said, her voice faint.

'So what about the guns?' asked Jemima.

'We don't have to go into that now,' said Marjorie through compressed lips. 'Let's leave it until later, all right?'

'You know Anthony and I need the money right away, Mother. Private school isn't cheap, and we need to get a deposit down.'

'Am I to understand that you wish to discuss my father's sporting guns?' He tried to keep his voice as calm and clipped as that of a brigadier. 'I was, of course, not going to bring it up at this difficult time—'

'Yes, plenty of time later,' interjected Marjorie.

'And yet, since you bring it up, perhaps we should speak frankly on the subject—we're all family here,' he said. Jemima scowled at him. Marjorie looked back and forth between them both a few times before speaking.

'Well, Ernest, Jemima has suggested that we might do very well now, selling your father's guns as a pair.' He said nothing and she rushed on. 'I mean, if we sell yours and ours together—we might make quite a bit, and I would like to help Jemima with little Gregory's education.'

'Yours and ours?' he repeated, as he felt his vision shift in and out of focus.

'Apparently, they're not worth nearly as much separately.'

'Since you bring it up . . . I was under the impression . . . that Bertie and I had an understanding with each other . . .' He drew a breath and prepared to thrust himself even into the teeth of the frowning women before him. 'It was my understanding . . . It was our father's intention . . . that Bertie's gun should pass into my care . . . and vice versa . . . as circumstances should dictate.' There! The words had been cast at them like boulders from a catapult; now he could only brace himself for the counterattack.

'Dear me, I know you've always been very keen on having that old gun,' said Marjorie. For a moment the Major's heart leaped at her blushing confusion. Might he prevail?

'That, Mother, is exactly why I don't want you talking to anyone without me,' said Jemima. She rounded on the Major. 'She's not herself, as you can see, and I won't have people try to walk all over her, no matter if they are relatives.' The Major felt his neck swell with rage. It would serve Jemima right if he popped a blood vessel and collapsed there and then.

'I resent your implication,' he stammered.

'We've always known you were after my father's gun,' said Jemima. 'It wasn't enough that you took the house, the china, all the money—'

'Look here, I don't know what money you're referring to, but—'

'And then all those times you tried to con my father out of the one thing his father gave him.'

'Jemima, that's enough,' said Marjorie. She had the grace to blush but would not look at him. Could Bertie, the Major wondered, have harboured the same resentments all these years and never let it show?

'I did make monetary offers to Bertie over the years,' he conceded with a dry mouth. 'But I thought they were always fair market value.'

Jemima gave an unpleasant, porcine snort.

'I'm sure they were,' said Marjorie. 'Let's just all be sensible now and work this out together. Jemima says if we sell the pair, we'll get a lot more.'

'Perhaps I might make you some suitable offer myself,' said the Major, though he failed to see immediately how he might find such a substantial cash sum. Might he contemplate some kind of small mortgage on the house? This prompted a shiver of dismay.

'I couldn't possibly take money from you,' said Marjorie.

'In that case—'

'We'll just have to get the highest price we can,' said Marjorie.

'I think we should ring round the auction houses,' said Jemima. 'Get a few appraisals.'

'Look here,' said the Major. 'My father's Churchills are not being put on the block at public auction like some bankrupt farm equipment.'

'What else do you suggest?' asked Marjorie. The Major calmed his voice to a tone suitable for placating small, angry children.

'I would like you to give me an opportunity to look round a bit,' he said, improvising as he went. 'I actually met a wealthy American gun collector recently. As it happens, he is attending Lord Dagenham's shoot next month, when I would be able to show him how the guns perform as a pair.'

'How much will he pay?' asked Jemima.

'That, my dear Jemima, is a delicate subject best broached after the guns have been displayed to their finest advantage. I am afraid that Bertie's gun will probably need some restoration work first.'

'So I suppose we should just give you the gun right now?' asked Jemima.

'I think that would be best,' said the Major, ignoring her sarcasm. 'Of course, you could send it away to be restored, but I am in a position to effect a restoration myself at no cost.'

'That's very kind of you, Ernest,' said Marjorie.

'It is the least I can do,' said the Major. 'Bertie would expect no less.'

'Do you think he'd pay cash?' asked Jemima.

'I would think he might be so overwhelmed by the pageantry of the event to offer us any amount we name. On the other hand, he may not. I make no promises.' He tried to affect an air of disinterest, and felt almost confident that at any moment he would be loading Bertie's gun into the car and driving away. There was such greed shining in both pairs of eyes.

'Let's try it, then,' said Marjorie. 'I'd like to take a cruise this winter. You must take the gun with you and look it over, in case it needs to be sent somewhere. We don't want to waste any time.'

'It's in the boot cupboard with the cricket bats,' said Jemima. 'I'll get it.'

The Major reassured himself that he was largely telling the truth. He would be showing the guns to Ferguson, even though he had no intention of letting them be bought. Furthermore, he could hardly be expected to take the moral high road with people who would keep a fine sporting gun in the back of a shoe cupboard. He was, he decided, doing the same thing as rescuing a puppy from an abusive scrapyard owner.

'Here we are,' said Jemima, pointing a quilt-covered bundle at him. He took it from her, turning the barrel end towards the floor.

'Thank you,' he said. 'Thank you very much.'

IT WAS JUST a cup of tea and a chat. As the Major mounted the step stool for a better view of the top shelf of the china cupboard, he chided himself for fussing over the arrangements like some old maid. He was determined to be completely casual about Mrs Ali's visit. Her voice on the telephone

MAJOR PETTIGREW'S LAST STAND | 205

had asked in a most straightforward manner whether he might have any time on Sunday to offer her his insights on the Kipling book, which she had just finished. Sunday afternoons the shop was closed, and she usually had a couple of hours to herself. He had replied in a carefully offhand way that Sunday afternoon would suit him and that perhaps he would rustle up a cup of tea. She said she would come around four, if that was convenient.

He considered using the good china, but he did not feel he could pull off a casual image while bearing a tray loaded with fine, gold-rimmed antiques. Then he had remembered Nancy's cups. There were only two of them, bought at a flea market before she and he were married. Nancy had admired the unusually large blue and white cups, shaped like upside-down bells, accompanied by saucers deep enough to use as bowls. They were very old, and Nancy had got them cheap because they did not quite match.

She had made him tea in them one afternoon, just tea, carried carefully to the small deal table set by the window in her room. The landlady, who had been persuaded by his uniform and quiet manners that he was a gentle-man, allowed him to visit Nancy's room as long as he was gone by nightfall. They were used to making love in the strong afternoon sunlight, smothering their giggles whenever the landlady deliberately creaked the floorboards outside the door. But that day the room was tidy, the usual debris of books and paints cleared away, and Nancy, hair smoothed back into a loose pony-tail, had made them tea in the beautiful translucent cups, which made the cheap, loose tea glow like amber. She had poured him milk from a shot glass, careful not to splash, her movements as slow as a ceremony. He had lifted his cup and known, with a sudden clarity that did not frighten him as much as he might have expected, that it was time to ask her to marry him.

The cups trembled in his hands now as he put them carefully on the counter. As he reached for the saucers he wished he could ask Nancy whether it was all right to use them. He had never been one of those people who believed that the dead hung around, dispensing permissions and gener-ally providing watchdog services. Sometimes in church, when the organ swelled and the chorus of the hymn turned irritating neighbours into a brief community of raised hearts and simple voices, he envisaged her in the heaven he had learned about in childhood: a grassy place with blue sky and a light breeze. He saw Nancy strolling in a simple sheath dress, her shoes held in her hand and a shady tree beckoning her in the distance. The rest of the time he could not hold on to this vision and she was only gone, like Bertie, and he was left to struggle on alone in the awful empty space of unbelief.

The preparations for tea completed, the Major checked his watch. He had several hours before his guest arrived. He decided to spend the time taking his first good look at Bertie's gun.

HE HAD BEEN SITTING in the scullery, in the same fixed position, for at least ten minutes, staring at Bertie's gun lying on the counter. He straightened his shoulders and made a mental note not to waste any more time wondering why Bertie had neglected it all these years, and what it meant that the gun lay unwanted in a cupboard even as Bertie rejected cash offers from his own brother. Instead, he focused his attention on a dispassionate inspection of the parts that might need repair.

There were cracks in the grain, and the wood itself was grey and dry. The ivory cap on the butt was deeply yellowed. He cracked the action open and found the chambers dull but thankfully free of rust. The barrel looked straight, though it had a small grouping of rust spots, as if it had been grasped by a sweaty hand and not wiped down. The elaborate chase work, a royal eagle entwined with persimmon flowers, was black with tarnish. He rubbed a finger under the eagle's flailing talons and, sure enough, there was the trim and upright 'P' monogram, which his father had added. He hoped it was not hubris to experience a certain satisfaction that while maharajahs and their kingdoms might fade into oblivion, the Pettigrews soldiered on.

As he lit the candle to warm the oil and took his leather case of cleaning implements out of the drawer, he felt much more cheerful. He had only to strip the gun down and work at it piece by piece, for perhaps an hour a day, until it was rebuilt just the way it was intended to be. Immediately he felt the sense of calm that comes from having a well-designed routine.

WHEN THE PHONE RANG in the early afternoon, his cheerfulness overrode his natural sense of caution at hearing Roger's voice on the other end.

'I just called to tell you some exciting news. Sandy and I may have found a cottage on the Internet.'

'The Internet? I think you'd better be very careful, Roger. I hear there is nothing but con games and pornography on that thing.'

Roger laughed. 'Dad, it's a unique opportunity. This old woman has her aunt's cottage—rent with option to buy—and she doesn't want to use an estate agent. We have a chance to get it before someone makes her see what it's really worth. It sounds perfect, Dad, and it's only a few minute away, near Little Puddleton.'

'I really don't see why you need a cottage,' said the Major. He was familiar with Little Puddleton, a village whose large contingent of weekenders
had spawned several arty pottery shops and a coffee house selling hand-
roasted beans at exorbitant prices. 'You must know that you and your friend
would be perfectly welcome here at Rose Lodge,' he added.

'We talked about that,' said Roger. 'I told Sandy there was plenty of
room and I was sure you'd even consider sectioning off the back part of the
house to make a separate flat.'

'A separate flat?' said the Major.

'But Sandy said it might look like we're trying to shuffle you off into a
granny annexe, and we probably should get a place of our own for now.'

'How considerate,' said the Major, his voice an outraged squeak.

'Look, Dad, we'd really like you to come and see it with us and give us
your approval,' said Roger. 'Sandy has her eye on some cow barn near
Salisbury, too, but I'd much rather be near you.'

'Thank you,' said the Major, aware that Roger probably wanted money
more than advice; but then, Roger was just as likely to ask for money for
the cow barn in Salisbury, so perhaps he really did want to be close to
home. The Major's heart warmed at this flicker of filial affection.

'Sussex is a much easier drive, and if I put in a few years at your golf
club now, I may have a shot at membership in a serious club later on.'

'I don't quite follow you,' said the Major. The flicker of filial love went
out like a pilot light in a sudden draught.

'Well, if we go to Salisbury I'll have to be on waiting lists for golf there,
you see. But your club isn't considered too prestigious.'

'Is that supposed to be a compliment?' said the Major, trying to catch up.

'Look, Dad, can you come and help us meet Mrs Augerspier in Little
Puddleton on Thursday?' said Roger. 'We'll just give it the once-over—
nose around for dry rot and that sort of thing.'

'I have no expertise in these matters,' said the Major. 'I don't know what
has potential.'

'The potential's not the issue,' said Roger. 'The issue is the widowed Mrs
Augerspier. She wants to sell the cottage to the "right" people. I need you to
come with us and be your most distinguished and charming self.'

'So you would like me to come and kiss the hand of the poor widow like
some Continental gigolo until she accepts your meagre offer for a property
that probably represents her entire nest egg?' asked the Major.

'Exactly,' said Roger. 'Is Thursday at three good for you?'

MRS ALI WAS in the living room waiting for him to bring in the tea. He stuck his head round the door and paused to notice what a lovely picture she made as she sat in the old bay window, bent over a book of Sussex photographs. The sun, striking in through the glass, made the dust motes shimmer and edged her profile with a light gold brushstroke. She wore a shawl of deep rose draped about the shoulders of a wool crepe outfit in a blue as dark and soft as twilight.

'Milk or lemon?' he asked. She looked up and smiled.

'Lemon and a rather embarrassing amount of sugar,' she said. 'And when I visit friends with gardens, I sometimes beg them for a mint leaf.'

'A mint leaf?' he said. 'Spearmint? Or I also have some kind of purple oddity my wife swore was mint, but I've always been afraid to eat it.'

'It sounds intriguing,' she said. 'May I take a look at this strange plant?'

'Of course,' said the Major, grappling with the sudden change in programme. He had been saving an invitation to see the garden in case of a sudden lapse in conversation. And if they toured the garden now, the tea might become stewed and undrinkable.

'Just a quick peek, so the tea doesn't spoil,' she added, as if she had read his mind. 'But might I impose on you for a more complete tour later?'

'I would be delighted,' he said. 'If you'd like to step through the kitchen?'

By going through the kitchen and the narrow scullery, he reasoned, they could see the side garden, which contained the herbs and a small gooseberry patch, while leaving the full vista of the back gardens to be enjoyed later, from the dining room's French doors.

'This must be your alien mint,' Mrs Ali said, bending to rub between her fingers the ruched and puckered surface of a sturdy purplish plant. 'It does seem a bit overwhelming for your average cup of tea.'

'Yes, I've found it too pungent for anything,' said the Major.

'Oh, but I think it would be excellent for perfuming a hot bath,' said Mrs Ali. 'Very invigorating.'

'A bath?' said the Major. He fumbled to produce some further remark that might be suited to casual discussion of perfumed bathing. 'Rather like being a human tea bag, isn't it?' he said.

Mrs Ali laughed and tossed the leaf aside. 'You're quite right,' she said. 'And it's also an awful bother to pick all the soggy leaves out of the drain afterwards.' She bent down to pick two pale leaves of spearmint.

'Shall we go in and drink our tea while it's fresh?' he asked, waving his arm towards the house.

THE MAJOR POURED them each a second cup of tea and wished there were some way to stop the late afternoon light from travelling any farther across the living room. Any moment now and the golden bars would reach the bookcases on the far wall and reflect back at Mrs Ali the lateness of the hour. He feared she might be prompted to stop reading.

She had a low, clear reading voice and she read with obvious appreciation of the text. He had almost forgotten how to enjoy listening. During the dusty years of teaching at St Mark's preparatory school, his ears had become numb, rubbed down to nonvibrating nubs by the monotone voices of uncomprehending boys. But as Mrs Ali read from the fragments that she had marked out as having interested her, he thought that Kipling had never sounded so good. She was now quoting from one of his favourite stories, 'Old Men at Pevensey', which was set soon after the Norman Conquest and had always seemed to the Major to express something important about the foundations of the land.

'"I do not think for myself",' she read, quoting the knight De Aquila, master of Pevensey Castle, '"nor for our King, nor for your lands. I think for England, for whom neither King nor Baron thinks. I am not Norman, Sir Richard, nor Saxon, Sir Hugh. English am I."'

The Major gulped at his tea making an unfortunate slurp. It was embarrassing but served to quell the 'Here, here!' that had leaped unbidden to his lips. Mrs Ali looked up from her book and smiled.

'He writes characters of such idealism,' she said. 'To be as grizzled and worldly as this knight, and yet still so clear in one's passion and duty to the land, is that even possible now?'

'I know most people today would regard such love of country as ridiculously romantic and naive,' he said. 'Patriotism itself has been hijacked by scabby youths with jackboots and bad teeth. But I do believe that there are those few who continue to believe in the England that Kipling loved. Unfortunately, we are a dusty bunch of relics.'

'My father believed in such things,' she said. 'Just as Saxons and Normans became one English people, he never stopped believing that England would one day accept us, too. He was only waiting to be asked to saddle up and ride the beacons with De Aquila, as a real Englishman.'

'Good for him,' said the Major. 'Not that there's much call for actual beacon-watching these days. Not with nuclear bombs and such.'

'I was speaking metaphorically,' she said.

'Of course you were, dear lady,' he said, 'But how much more satisfying to think of him literally riding to the top of Devil's Dyke, flaming torch at the ready. The jingling of the harnesses, the thudding of hoofbeats, the cries of his fellow Englishmen, carrying the banner of St George . . .'

'I think he would have settled for not being so casually forgotten when the faculty agreed to meet for a drink at the local pub.'

'Ah,' said the Major. He would have liked to be able to make some soothing reply—something to the effect of how proud he would, himself, have been to partake of a glass of beer with her father. However, this was made impossible by the awkward fact that neither he, nor anyone else he knew, had ever thought to invite her husband for a drink in the pub. Of course he was probably a teetotaller, anyway. But none of these thoughts was in the least usable; the Major was mentally a hooked carp, its mouth opening and closing on the useless oxygen.

'He would have liked this room, my father.' He saw Mrs Ali's gaze taking in the inglenook fireplace, the tall bookcases on two walls, the comfortable sofa and unmatched armchairs, each with small table and good reading lamp to hand. 'It was always my dream that Ahmed and I would buy a small house one day—a real Sussex cottage, with a white boarded front and windows looking out on a garden.'

'I suppose it is very convenient, though, living above the shop?'

'Well, I've never minded it being a little cramped,' she said. 'But with my nephew staying . . . And then, there is little room for book shelves like these.' She smiled and he was happy that she shared his appreciation.

'My son thinks I should get rid of most of them,' the Major said. 'He thinks I need a wall free for an entertainment centre and a large TV.'

'It is a fact of life, I suppose, that the younger generation must try to take over and run the lives of their elders,' said Mrs Ali. 'My life is not my own since my nephew came to stay.'

'Even in your own home, they track you down with the telephone at all hours,' said the Major. 'I think my son tries to organise my life because it's easier than his own—gives him a sense of being in control of something in a world that is not quite ready to put him in charge.'

'That's very perceptive of you,' said Mrs Ali, considering a moment. 'What do we do to counteract this behaviour?'

'I'm considering running away to a quiet cottage in a secret location,' said the Major, 'and sending him news of my well-being by postcards forwarded on via Australia.'

She laughed. 'Perhaps I may join you?'

'You would be most welcome,' said the Major, and for a moment he saw a low thatched hut tucked behind a gorse-backed hill and a thin crescent of sandy beach filled with wild gulls. He and she returning from a long walk, to a lamp-lit room filled with books, a glass of wine on the table . . .

Conscious that he was dreaming again, he abruptly recalled his attention to the room, hoping Mrs Ali had not noticed. Roger always became impatient when he drifted off into thinking. But to his surprise, Mrs Ali was gazing out the window as if she, too, was lost in pleasant plans. He sat and enjoyed her profile for a moment: her straight nose, her strong chin, and, he noticed now, delicate ears under the thick hair. As if feeling the pressure of his gaze, she turned her eyes back to him.

'May I offer you the full garden tour?' he said.

THE FLOWERBEDS were struggling against the frowziness of autumn. Chrysanthemums held themselves erect in clumps of gold and red, but most of the roses were just hips, and the mats of dianthus sprawled onto the path like blue hair.

'I'm afraid the garden is not at its finest,' he said, following Mrs Ali as she walked slowly down the gravel path.

'Oh, but it's quite lovely,' she said. 'That purple flower on the wall is like an enormous jewel.' She pointed to where a late clematis spread its last five or six velvet flowers against the old brick wall.

'It was my grandmother who collected all our clematis plants,' said the Major. 'I've never been able to find out the name of this one but it's quite rare. We had to move it round the back in the late 1970s, when we caught someone prowling in the garden at midnight, secateurs in hand.'

'Plant burglary?'

'Yes, there was quite a rash of it,' he said. 'Part of a larger crisis in the culture, of course. My mother always blamed it on decimalisation.'

'Yes. It almost invites disaster, doesn't it, when people are asked to count by ten instead of twelve?' she said, smiling.

'You know, my wife used to laugh at me in just the same manner,' he said. 'She said if I maintained my aversion to change I risked being reincarnated as a granite post.'

'I'm so sorry—I didn't mean to offend you.'

'Not at all. I am delighted that we have progressed already to a level of . . .' He searched for the right word, recoiling from 'intimacy'. 'A level above mere pleasant acquaintance, perhaps.'

They were at the lower fence now, where the sheep field fell away down a small fold between two hills to a copse thick with oaks. Mrs Ali leaned her arms on the rail and considered the trees, which were now blending to a soft indigo in the fading light.

'It is so beautiful here,' she said at last, cupping her chin in one hand.

'Yes. I never tire of watching the evening sun leaving the fields.'

'I don't believe the greatest views in the world are great because they are vast or exotic,' she said. 'I think their power comes from the knowledge that they have been the same for a thousand years.'

'And yet how suddenly they can become new again when you see them through someone else's eyes,' he said. 'The eyes of a new friend, for example.' She turned to look at him, her face in shadow.

'It's funny,' she said, 'to be presented suddenly with the possibility of making new friends. One begins to accept, at a certain age, that one has already made all the friends to which one is entitled. One becomes used to them as a static set—with some attrition, of course. People move far away, they become busy with their lives . . .'

'Sometimes they leave us for good,' added the Major, feeling his throat constrict. 'Dashed inconsiderate of them, I say.' She made a small gesture, reaching out as if to lay a hand on his sleeve, but circled her hand away. He pressed the tip of his shoe into the soil as if he had spotted a thistle.

They began to walk back to the house, Mrs Ali drawing her shawl closer round her shoulders as the light faded.

'When Ahmed died, I realised that we had become almost alone together,' she said. 'Being busy with the shop, happy with each other's company—we had stopped making an effort to keep up with friends.'

'I suppose one does fall into a bit of a rut,' agreed the Major.

'And now, just when I am being asked to consider how and where I will spend the next chapter of my life,' she continued, 'I have not only had the pleasure of discussing books with you, but I have also been asked by Miss de Vere to assist her and her friends with a dance at a golf club. She has asked me to call up some people I know in town to get some ideas and prices for the food. The theme is Mogul Madness, I believe.'

The Major tried to mask his surprise by saying, 'The ladies are tireless. Many, many good works and all that sort of thing.' Mrs Ali's smile indicated that she understood him.

'Grace de Vere has always been very polite to me. I suppose I am wondering whether this might be a small opening for me to participate in the community. A way to spread some more roots.' They were at the front gate already, and the garden and lane were almost dark. The Major sensed that Mrs Ali was tethered to the village by only the slightest of connections. A little more pressure from her husband's family, another slight from an ungrateful villager, and she might be ripped away. Yet to persuade her to stay, just for the pleasure of having her nearby, seemed utterly selfish. He could not, in good conscience, promote any association with Daisy Green and her band of ladies. He could more easily recommend fence-hopping into the polar bear enclosure at Regent's Park zoo. She looked at him and he knew she would give his opinion weight.

'I have pledged my cooperation, too,' said the Major at last. 'I have agreed to attend the food tasting.' He paused. 'However, I must warn you that the committee's overabundance of enthusiasm, combined with a complete absence of knowledge, may produce some rather theatrical effects. I would hate for you to be offended in any way.'

'In that case, I shall tell Grace to count on us,' she said. 'Between the three of us, perhaps we can save the Mogul Empire from once again being destroyed.' The Major bit his tongue. As they shook hands and promised to meet again, he did not express his conviction that Daisy Green might represent a greater menace to the Mogul Empire than the conquering Rajput princes and the East India Company combined.

Chapter 5

The Taj Mahal Palace occupied a former police station. The redbrick building still bore the word 'Police' carved into the stone lintel of the front door, but it had been partially covered by a neon sign that flashed in succession the words 'Late Nite—Takeaway—Drinks'. A large painted sign bore the restaurant name and offered Sunday buffet lunches, halal meat and weddings. In order to back the car into a narrow space outside, the Major put his arm across the back of the passenger seat, a manoeuvre that caused Grace de Vere to shrink and blush as if he had dropped a hand on her thigh, while Mrs Ali smiled encouragingly at him from the back. The Major had tried to suggest they drive separately, since he had agreed to meet Roger in Little Puddleton right after, but Grace had expressed an immediate need to visit Little Puddleton's famous yarn shop, the Ginger Nook, and had insisted on making an outing of it. The Major managed to fit the car into the space in a single move.

A well-upholstered woman with a wide, smiling face and a flowing mustard-coloured shawl stood waiting for them in the glass doorway, waving a plump hand sparkling with rings.

'Ah, and here is my friend Mrs Rasool to greet us,' said Mrs Ali. 'She and her husband own two restaurants and a travel agency. They are quite the business tycoons.'

Mrs Ali got out of the car and disappeared into a mustard-coloured hug.

'Najwa, I'd like you to meet Major Pettigrew and Miss Grace de Vere,' said Mrs Ali, her arm still tucked in that of her friend.

'My husband, Mr Rasool, and I are delighted to have you grace our humble restaurant and catering hall,' said Mrs Rasool, greeting them with an enthusiastic grasping of both hands. 'We are quite the small operation—all homemade, you know—but we do silver service for five hundred people here. You must come in and see for yourself . . .' And she was already sweeping into the restaurant, waving for them to follow. The Major held the door for the ladies and followed them in.

Several tables in the cavernous restaurant were occupied. The Major noted the walls were a cheerful orange, and bright saffron silk curtains swagged the large iron-framed windows, which still had bars, relics of the former police station. To the Major's eye, the effect of the grand room was marred only by the effusive use of obviously plastic flowers gathered in swags of pink and mauve across the ceiling. Orange water lilies floated in the central tiled fountain, collecting by the overflow valve like dead koi.

Mrs Rasool led the way back to a large booth, partially screened by a carved wood panel and another huge silk curtain. As they approached, a thin man with sparse hair and a starched shirt stood up from where he was sitting with an elderly couple. He gave them a reserved bow.

'Mr Rasool, these are our guests, Major Pettigrew and Ms de Vere,' said Mrs Rasool.

'Most welcome,' said Mr Rasool. 'And may I introduce to you my parents and the founders of our business.' The old couple stood up and bowed.

'Pleased to meet you,' said the Major, leaning across the table to shake hands. He thought they resembled two halves of a walnut.

'Please sit down with us,' said Mr Rasool.

'Now, I hope Mrs Ali has explained that we are on a strict budget?' said

Grace, inching along the banquette as if it were made of Velcro. The Major tried to allow Mrs Ali to slide in, both to be polite and because he hated to be confined, but Mrs Rasool indicated that he should sit next to Grace. She and Mrs Ali took the outside chairs.

'Oh, please, please,' said Mr Rasool. 'No need to talk of business. First we must hope you enjoy our humble offerings. My wife has ordered a few small samples of food for you.' He clapped his hands together and two waiters came through the kitchen doors bearing silver trays covered with domed silver lids. They were followed by a pair of musicians, one with a hand drum and one with some kind of sitar, who began a spirited atonal song.

'We have musicians for you,' said Mrs Rasool. 'And I think you will be very happy with the decorations we have sourced.' As soon as she stopped speaking the old woman wagged her finger and spoke rapidly.

'My mother insists that first our guests must eat,' said Mr Rasool. 'It is an offence to talk business without offering hospitality.' The mother frowned as if a breach of decorum had already been committed.

'Well, perhaps just a little taste,' said Grace, pulling from her bag a small notebook and a thin silver pen. 'I really don't eat much at lunch time.'

THE DISHES CAME QUICKLY, small bowls of steaming food, blurry with colour and fragrant with spices. Grace nibbled her way through them all, pursing her lips in determination at some of the more dark and pungent offerings. The Major watched with amusement as she wrote them all down, her writing becoming more laboured as the food and several servings of gin punch made her sleepy. The Rasools and Mrs Ali drank only water.

'How do you spell "gosht"?' Grace asked for the third time. 'And this one is what meat?'

'Goat,' said Mr Rasool. 'It is the most traditional of ingredients.'

'But the chicken is very popular, too,' said Mrs Rasool.

'I wonder if it might be a little spicy for the main course,' said Grace, cupping her hand round her mouth as if making a small megaphone. 'What do you think, Major?'

'Anyone who doesn't find this delicious is a fool,' said the Major. He nodded his head fiercely at Mrs Rasool and Mrs Ali. 'However . . .' He was not sure how to express his conviction that the golf club crowd would throw a fit if served a rice-based main course instead of a slab of meat.

Mrs Rasool raised an eyebrow at him. 'However, it is perhaps not foolproof, so to speak?' she asked. The Major could only smile in vague apology.

'I understand perfectly,' said Mrs Rasool. She waved her hand and a waiter hurried into the kitchen. 'I'm sure you will approve of our more popular alternative.' The waiter returned at a run, with a silver salver that held a perfectly shaped individual Yorkshire pudding containing fragrant slices of pinkish beef. It sat on a pool of burgundy gravy and was accompanied by a dollop of cumin-scented yellow potatoes and a lettuce leaf holding slices of tomato, red onion and star fruit.

'It's quite perfect,' breathed Grace. 'Are the potatoes spicy?' The elder Mr Rasool muttered something to his son. Mrs Rasool gave a sharp laugh that was almost a hiss.

'Not at all.' Mrs Rasool smiled. 'So, I think we have agreed on the chicken skewers, samosas and chicken wings as passed hors d'oeuvres, and then the beef, and I suggest trifle for dessert.'

'Trifle?' said the Major.

'One of the more agreeable traditions that you left us,' said Mrs Rasool.

'Roast beef and trifle,' said Grace in a daze of food and punch. 'And all authentically Mogul, you say?'

'Of course,' said Mrs Rasool. 'Everyone will be very happy to dine like the Emperor Shah Jahan, and no one will find it too spicy.'

The Major could detect no hint of derision in Mrs Rasool's tone. She seemed completely happy to accommodate. Mr Rasool also nodded and made a few calculations in a black book. Only the old couple looked rather stern.

'Now, what can you suggest about decorations?' Grace said, and took another sip from her glass of punch.

'I was looking into it, as Mrs Ali asked,' said Mrs Rasool, 'and I was afraid it would all be very expensive.'

'But then we struck on a lucky coincidence,' added Mr Rasool. 'A distinguished friend offered to help.'

'Oh, really?' said Grace. 'Because our budget, as you know . . .'

'I know, I know,' said Mr Rasool. 'So let me introduce you to my friend, Mrs Khan. She is the wife of Dr Khan, a specialist at Hill Hospital. One of our most prominent families. She has her own decorating business.' He waved his hand and the Major looked to see two women who were sitting at a window table getting up. The older one waved back and spoke to her companion, who hurried out of the restaurant.

'Saadia Khan?' asked Mrs Ali quietly. 'Are you sure that's a good idea, Najwa?' Najwa Rasool gave a pained smile.

'My husband insists that she is very keen to help.'

'Oh, yes, Mrs Khan implied she might even help out on a complimentary basis,' said Mr Rasool. 'I believe her husband has many friends among the membership of your respected club.'

'Really?' said Grace. 'I haven't heard the name. Dr Khan, is it?'

'Yes, very prominent man. His wife is involved with many charities.'

Mrs Khan loomed impressively over the table. She wore a tweed suit with a heavy gold brooch on the lapel and a single ring on each hand, one a plain gold band and the other an enormous sapphire in a heavy gold setting. Her hair, in lacquered layers, reminded the Major of Britain's former lady prime minister. He struggled out of the banquette to stand by Mrs Ali's chair while the introductions were made.

'How do you do, Major? Do call me Sadie, everyone does,' said Mrs Khan with a big smile. 'And Miss de Vere, I believe we met at that awful Chamber of Commerce garden party last year?'

'Yes, yes, of course,' said Grace, in a voice that telegraphed her complete lack of such a recollection.

'Such a crush of people, but my husband feels we must support such basic institutions,' added Mrs Khan. She seemed to see Mrs Ali for the first time. 'Why, Jasmina, you are here, too?' she asked. The Major recognised the use of Mrs Ali's first name as a deliberate slight but he was very grateful finally to hear it.

'Saadia,' said Mrs Ali, inclining her head.

'What a treat it must be for you to be liberated from the shop counter,' added Mrs Khan. 'A small break from the frozen peas and newspapers?'

'I think you have some fabric samples to show us?' said Mrs Rasool.

'Yes,' said Mrs Khan. 'My assistant Noreen and her niece are bringing them now.' They watched Mrs Khan's lunch companion and a younger woman struggle through the heavy restaurant door with several armfuls of sample books and a small box of fabrics. A small boy followed, carrying a large book precariously in both arms. The Major recognised him immediately as the young boy from the Promenade. He felt a schoolboy flush of panic rise into his face at the possibility that his friendship with Mrs Ali would be exposed.

'Oh, my goodness, the niece has brought her boy,' said Mrs Khan in a loud whisper to Mrs Rasool. 'What was she thinking?'

'Don't be silly,' said Mrs Rasool. 'It will be perfectly all right.'

'What a darling little boy,' exclaimed Grace as the women dropped their heavy load onto a nearby table and the boy struggled to do the same.

'What's his name?' There was the briefest of pauses, as if introductions had not been expected. The woman named Noreen looked nervously at Mrs Khan, whose lips were pressed to a thin line.

'I couldn't just leave him in the car,' said the young woman, also looking at Saadia Khan, but with a face as fierce as her aunt's was meek.

'I believe his name is George,' said Mrs Ali, dispelling the tension. She went over to shake the boy's hand. 'We had the pleasure of meeting in the park. Did you manage to get your ball all the way home?'

The young woman frowned and swung George up onto her hip. 'He managed that day, but he lost it down a drain on the way to the shops the next day.' She said nothing to the Major, giving him only a brief nod. In an obvious effort to dress more conservatively, today she was wearing a long, shapeless black dress over leggings; the tone was spoiled only by violently crimson sneakers that laced up over the ankle.

'Jasmina, I believe Amina and George are from your home turf up north,' said Mrs Khan with a silky smile. 'Perhaps your families are acquainted?'

The Major couldn't tell whether Mrs Ali was amused or angry. She compressed her lips as if suppressing a chuckle, but her eyes flashed.

'I don't think so, Saadia,' she replied. The Major detected a deliberate avoidance of the name Sadie. 'It's a big place.'

'Actually, I think you might have a nephew my age who used to live there,' Amina put in, while her aunt Noreen trembled like a leaf.

'Well, perhaps, but he left a while ago,' said Mrs Ali with a hint of caution in her voice. 'He has been in Pakistan studying for some time.'

'And now I hear he is living with you,' said Mrs Khan.

'Shall we talk about decorations?' said Mrs Rasool, clearly uncomfortable with the conversation. 'Why don't you show us the table runner fabrics first, Mrs Khan?'

Mrs Khan, Mrs Rasool and Grace were soon over at the table arguing over the relative merits of the iridescent sorbet sheers and the heavy damasks. Amina and her aunt Noreen turned sample book pages in silence, the former with pressed lips. The Major regained his seat and the waiters brought glasses of hot tea. He watched as Mrs Ali invited George to climb up on her lap. She handed him a teaspoon dipped in honey and he gave it a cautious lick. 'George likes honey,' he said with a serious face. 'Is it organic?'

Mrs Ali laughed, and the Major said, 'Well, George, I've never seen anyone injecting bees with antibiotics.' George frowned at him, and for a moment the Major was reminded of Mrs Ali's dour nephew.

'Organic is better, Mum says.' He ran the spoon down the entire length of his tongue. 'My *nani* puts honey in her tea, but she died,' he added.

Mrs Ali bent her head to the top of his and gave his hair a brief kiss. 'That must make you and your mother sad,' she said.

'It makes us lonely,' said George. 'We're lonely in the world now.'

'You mean "alone"?' asked the Major, aware that he was being pedantic. He resisted the urge to ask about a father. These days it was better not to.

'Can I have more honey?' asked George, with a child's honest abruptness.

'Of course you can,' said Mrs Ali.

'I like you,' said George.

'Young man, you have very good taste,' said the Major.

GRACE CAME BACK to the booth beaming and informed the Major that Mrs Khan would lend them wall hangings and draperies and charge them at cost for fabric used as table runners, which were almost certain to get stained.

'The golf club is such an old and important institution in the area,' said Mrs Khan. 'And my husband has so many friends who are members. We are glad to help in any way.'

'I'm sure it will be appreciated,' said the Major. He raised his eyebrows at Grace who gave him a blank smile in return. 'Perhaps, Grace, you'd like to get final approval from your committee chairwoman?'

'What? Oh, yes, of course I should,' said Grace. 'Though I'm sure they'll be thrilled with everything.'

As the Major shook hands with Mrs Khan, he couldn't help feeling sorry for her. Regardless of her husband's prominence, or their generosity, he thought it quite unlikely that Daisy or the membership committee would have any interest in entertaining the question of their joining the club. He could only hope the committee would have the decency to refuse the Khans' generous offer and keep things properly separated with cash instead.

ON THE WAY to Little Puddleton, Grace elected to sit in the back of the car, where she sprawled at a strange angle and, after a few moments, declared herself to be feeling just the tiniest bit green.

'Would you like me to stop the car?' asked the Major, though he could manage only a halfhearted attempt at sincerity. It was getting close to three and he did not want to disappoint Roger by being late.

'No, no, I'll just rest my eyes,' said Grace in a whisper. 'I can't wait to show you the new alpaca yarns, Mrs Ali. It'll be the highlight of our afternoon.'

'I am to be converted to the joys of knitting.' Mrs Ali smiled at the Major.

'My condolences,' he said.

They made the long slow swoop downhill into Little Puddleton. The village green was as obsessively manicured as the Major remembered. Wooden posts with a fresh coat of whitewash held up a knee-high chain all round the edges of the cropped grass, and at one end was an elliptical duck pond, on which floated three bleached-looking swans. The cottages and houses of the village huddled together companionably. Windows twinkled with double glazing above window boxes foaming with painterly foliage.

The shops occupied a small street running away from the green. The Major pulled the car up in front of the Ginger Nook. Its brimming windows offered a cornucopia of cushion covers waiting to be cross-stitched, dolls' houses awaiting paint and furniture, and baskets of wool skeins in a rainbow of colours.

'Here we are,' said the Major, in what he hoped was a jolly, rallying tone. 'Shall we say I'll come back for you in one hour?' There was only a groan from the back seat. 'Or I can try to be quicker,' he said. 'My son just wants me to have a look at a cottage with him. Seems to think I could help make a good impression.'

'Grace, I think you'll feel much better in the fresh air,' added Mrs Ali, who had turned round in her seat and was staring with concern at Grace's grey face. 'I'll come round and help you out.'

'No, no,' whispered Grace. 'I can't get out here, not in front of everybody.' To the Major, the road appeared largely deserted.

'What should we do?' he asked Mrs Ali. It was nearly three and he was beginning to panic. 'I am already expected at Apple Cottage.'

'Why don't we all go there?' said Mrs Ali. 'You can go in, and I'll walk with Grace in the lane.

'Wouldn't you be happier sitting on the Green?' asked the Major.

'She might get cold,' said Mrs Ali. 'It would be better if we stay near the car, I think.' She looked at him rather sternly. 'If our presence in the vicinity won't spoil your good impression, of course?'

'Not at all,' said the Major, already imagining Roger's raised eyebrows.

APPLE COTTAGE was at the end of a small lane, which ended in a five-bar gate and a field. Sandy's Jaguar was parked by the field, leaving room for just one other car directly in front of the cottage's front gate. The Major had no choice but to draw up there.

'Here we are,' he said. 'I don't expect to be too long. I'll leave the car unlocked for you.'

'Yes, please go ahead,' said Mrs Ali. 'Grace will feel much better after a walk, I'm sure.' As the Major got out of the car, Grace was still groaning. He hurried through the gate of the cottage where Roger and Sandy were standing in the garden beside a third person: the widow Augerspier, he assumed.

Mrs Augerspier had a long face set in a slight frown, and lips that seemed thinned by sourness. She wore a stiff suit of black wool, and a brown felt hat that boasted black feathers sweeping in serried rows across her sunken forehead.

'Ah, my father was a colonel in the military,' she said when introduced. 'But he made his money in hats,' she added. 'My husband took over the business when my father died.'

'From military to millinery,' said the Major. Roger glared at him then turned a wide smile towards the dead crow on the widow's brow.

'Is that a real vintage hat?' asked Sandy. 'I just have to send a picture to my editor friend at *Vogue* magazine.'

'Yes, yes, I suppose it is now,' said the widow, tipping her head at a coquettish angle while Sandy snapped pictures with her mobile phone. 'My father made it for me for my mother's funeral. And last month I wore it to my aunt's funeral.' She took out a lace-edged handkerchief and wiped her nose.

'We're very sorry for your loss,' said Roger. 'And I'm sure Sandy would love to talk hats with you for hours, Mrs Augerspier, but may we see the inside of the cottage now? We would like to see it in the afternoon light.'

As FAR as the Major could determine, the cottage was a damp and unsuitable mess. The plaster bubbled suspiciously in several corners, the beams looked wormy, and the window frames were so buckled and twisted it looked as if the handmade glass might pop from the heavy leading with the slightest wind.

'It might be possible that I will sell some of the furnishings to the new tenants,' said Mrs Augerspier. 'If I get the right sort of people, of course.' The Major wondered why Roger nodded with such enthusiasm. The dead aunt's possessions ran to cheap pine furniture, seaside knick-knacks, and a collection of plates featuring scenes from famous movies.

In the large empty kitchen, a cheap, boxy extension from the 1950s, the Major peered round an open door into a mousy larder and counted eleven boxes of dried chicken soup on the otherwise empty shelves. It seemed sad that life should have gradually thinned out until so little remained.

'Oh, I wouldn't change a thing,' Sandy was saying. 'Only maybe I could fit a regular US-sized refrigerator into that back corner.'

'My aunt always found the refrigerator perfectly adequate,' said Mrs Augerspier, pulling aside the chequered curtains under the counter to show a small green fridge with a fringe of rust. 'But then young people today will insist on all that convenience food.'

'Oh, we're going to shop at all the local farm shops,' said Roger. 'There's nothing quite like fresh vegetables, is there?'

'Horribly overpriced, of course,' said the widow. 'Designed to rob the weekenders from London. I refuse to shop in them.'

'Oh,' said Roger. He flung a hopeless glance at the Major, who could only stifle a laugh.

'This is a very good table,' continued Mrs Augerspier, knocking on the plastic. 'I would be willing to sell the table.'

'I think we're going to commission an oak table from this great crafts-man I know,' said Sandy, turning the sink taps and examining the trickle of brown water that was produced.

'I would like to think of the table remaining here,' said the widow, as if she had not heard. 'I think it fits here.'

'Absolutely,' said Roger. 'We could have an oak table in the dining room instead, couldn't we, Sandy?'

'I will show you the bedroom,' said the widow. She unlatched a door and waved at them to follow her. Roger followed; as the Major stepped back to allow Sandy to pass, she whispered, 'Do you think the aunt died in her bed here?' She grinned at the Major as she went by. 'And do you think she'll let us buy the mattress?' The Major could not suppress a laugh.

As they prepared to mount the crooked stairs to the upper floor, Roger shot him a look like a Jack Russell terrier with urgent business. The Major recognised an appeal and was pleased to find he could still read his son's facial communications.

'My dear Mrs Augerspier,' said the Major, 'I was wondering whether you might consent to show me the garden. I'm sure these young people can look around upstairs by themselves.' The widow looked suspicious.

'I don't usually let people go unaccompanied,' Mrs Augerspier said. 'You can't be certain of anyone these days.'

'If I might vouch for the integrity of these particular young people,' said the Major. 'It would be so kind of you to indulge me with your companionship.' He extended an arm to the widow.

'I suppose it would be acceptable,' she said, taking it. 'One gets so few opportunities for refined conversation these days.'

'After you,' said the Major.

COMING FROM the musty cottage, the air smelled like pure oxygen. The Major took a grateful breath and was rewarded with the scent of box and hawthorn underlaid with a hint of damp oak leaves. Mrs Augerspier led the way to the main stretch of garden, which rose gently to one side of the cottage. Under a small arbour at the far end, Mrs Ali sat with Grace who, the Major noticed with alarm, was slumped with closed eyes against the seat. Mrs Ali seemed to be taking her pulse.

'People are so rude to come without an appointment,' said Mrs Augerspier, hurrying over the grass. 'And always they are not suitable,' she added.

'Oh, they're not here about the house,' said the Major, but the widow wasn't listening.

'The house is not available,' she called, flapping her hands as if to shoo away recalcitrant chickens. 'I must ask you to go now.' Grace opened her eyes and shrank back against the seat. Mrs Ali stood up as if to shield her from the angry bobbing figure rushing across the grass.

'It's all right, Mrs Augerspier,' said the Major, catching up at last. 'They're with me.' Grace threw him a grateful look.

'My friend Grace needed to sit down,' said Mrs Ali. 'We didn't think anyone would mind.' Grace hiccupped loudly.

'Well,' said the widow. 'Only I get the strangest people wandering in from the road.'

'Now that we have established our credentials, perhaps a glass of water?' asked Mrs Ali.

'Certainly,' said Mrs Augerspier. 'Wait here and I will bring it to you.' She hurried back towards the house, leaving an awkward silence.

'Dreadful woman,' said the Major at last. 'I'm so sorry.'

'Oh, no, please. I just had a bit of a reaction to the spices,' said Grace.

'I'm afraid we're not contributing to the good impression your son was anxious to make,' said Mrs Ali.

'Oh, not at all, not at all,' said the Major. 'Don't even think about it. He will be delighted to see you both.' He looked up to see a scowling Roger jogging up the lawn with a glass of water slopping over his hand.

'Mrs Augerspier said one of your friends needed a glass of water,' said Roger. In a quieter voice he added, 'You invited people along?'

'You remember Miss de Vere, Roger,' said the Major, passing the glass of water to Grace. 'And this is Mrs Ali from the village shop.'

'How do you do,' said Mrs Ali. 'We are so sorry to intrude.'

'Not at all. Only I do need to borrow my father for a few minutes.'

'I remember when you were just a little boy, Roger . . .' said Grace, wiping her eyes. 'Such a lovely little boy with all that unruly hair.'

'Is she drunk?' whispered Roger to the Major.

'Certainly not,' said the Major.

'Sorry, got to run, ladies,' said Roger, already turning away. As the Major found himself being hustled along back to the house, he heard his son hiss, 'How could you bring them here? Mrs Augerspier is all nervous now. We've gone from being the right sort of people to being a strange bunch with a circus of hangers-on. For God's sake, one's Pakistani and one's tipsy—what were you thinking?'

'You're being ridiculous,' said the Major. 'I won't have my friends subjected to such rudeness.'

'You promised to help me,' said Roger. He opened the cottage door and stood aside as if waiting to shepherd in a troublesome child. The Major fumed as he was marched in.

Sandy was sitting on the rickety sofa with a fixed smile on her face. Mrs Augerspier was peering from the window.

'It's just that I've been so nervous since that couple last week,' she said, holding her hand to her heart. Sandy nodded in apparent sympathy.

'Mrs Augerspier was just explaining to me about a very rude couple who came to see the cottage last week,' Sandy said.

'I told them only that since they were used to a warmer climate, I thought they'd find the cottage too damp. They were quite unreasonable about it.'

'Where were they from?' asked Roger.

'I think you said from Birmingham, Mrs A?' asked Sandy, her eyes stretched to wide innocence.

'But they were from the islands originally, the West Indies,' said Mrs Augerspier. 'Such rudeness—and from doctors, too.'

The Major looked at Roger whose mouth was open, making slight movements but no sound. Sandy looked unperturbed, enjoying herself even.

'Roger, have you finished looking round?' asked the Major. He hoped his abrupt tone would register his disapproval of the widow without creating a confrontation. Mrs Augerspier's smile indicated that he had failed.

'We really shouldn't take up too much of your time,' said Roger. He walked over to pat Sandy on the shoulder. 'Are you done, darling?'

'I could move in right now,' said Sandy. 'What's it going to be, Mrs A? Are we suitable, do you think?'

Mrs Augerspier smiled, but her eyes narrowed in an unpleasant fashion. 'It is important that I find just the right people . . .' she began.

Sandy turned to look at Roger and patted his hand like a mother to a small boy who has forgotten his manners.

'Oh, yes, I forgot,' said Roger. He dug in his coat pocket and flourished a cheque. 'My fiancée and I took the liberty of bringing a cashier's cheque for six months' rent just in case you could let us have it right away.' He handed the cheque to Mrs Augerspier, who appeared fascinated.

'Roger, are you sure you're not being too spontaneous?' asked the Major, his mind struggling to process the word 'fiancée'. He focused instead on watching the widow examine both the back and front of the cheque. Her eyes wobbled in delight. She pursed her lips and gave him a frown.

'Well, I believe I could agree to six months—on a trial basis,' she said. 'But it will take me a few days to pack up my dear aunt's personal effects.'

'Take all the time you need,' said Roger, shaking her hand. 'Now, what say we all go and have a cup of tea somewhere to seal the deal?'

'That sounds very lovely,' said Mrs Augerspier. 'I believe there's a local hotel that offers a wonderful afternoon tea—now where did I put my rental form?' The Major thought chewing stinging nettles and washing them down with a pint of ditch water might be more pleasant than watching the widow bob her feathers over a mountain of whipped cream.

'Major, you look as if you have some pressing engagement,' said Sandy, winking at him. Roger gave the Major a pleading glance.

'I think I must get the ladies home,' said the Major. 'Grace is quite unwell.'

Mrs Augerspier hovered by the doorway as Sandy and Roger signed the form and took the carbon copy. 'Of course you must get your friend home. We would not dream of dragging you to tea with us,' she said.

THE MAJOR was glad that the ladies were quiet on the drive back. He felt tired and his jaw ached. He realised it was clamped shut.

'Is something the matter, Major?' asked Mrs Ali. 'You seem upset.'

'Oh, no, I'm fine. Long day, though.'

'Your son rented the cottage, did he not?' she said.

'Oh, yes, yes, all signed and sealed. He's very happy about it.'

'How lovely for you,' she said.

'It was all a bit hasty,' said the Major, taking a right turn into the single-track short cut back to Edgecombe St Mary. 'Apparently they're engaged.'

'Then I offer you my congratulations, Major.'

'I just hope they know what they're getting into. All this renting cottages together. It seems so premature,' said the Major. 'However, Roger tells me that they should be able to buy the place eventually. He says it will be rather a smart investment.'

'When true love combines with clear financial motive,' said Mrs Ali, 'all objections must be swept away.'

'Is that a saying in your culture?' asked Grace. 'It seems very apt.'

'No, I'm just teasing the Major,' said Mrs Ali. 'I think the circumstances may prove to be less important than the fact that life is bringing your son and a future daughter-in-law closer to you, Major. It is an opportunity to be seized, is it not, Miss de Vere?'

'Oh, certainly,' said Grace. 'I wish I had children to come and live near me.' Her voice held a hint of a pain unconnected with digestive problems.

'I have tried to see my nephew's presence in such a light,' said Mrs Ali. 'Though the young do not always make it easy.'

'You must bring your son and his fiancée to the dance, Major,' said Grace. 'Introduce them to everyone. Everyone is always so relaxed and approachable when they're in costume, don't you think?'

'Yes, but they often don't remember you the next day, I find,' said the Major. Mrs Ali laughed.

'I suppose I'll wear my Victorian tea dress again,' said Grace. 'Maybe I can borrow a pith helmet or something.'

'If you would be interested, I would be more than happy to lend you a sari, or a tunic set and shawl,' said Mrs Ali. 'I have several very formal pieces, packed away in the attic somewhere, that I never use. I will look out a few things and drop them off for you to try.'

'Would you really? You are very kind,' said Grace. 'You must come and have tea with me so you can tell me what you think.'

'That would be lovely,' said Mrs Ali. 'I'm usually free on Sunday after-noons.' The Major felt his jaw compress again. Though he told himself to be happy that Mrs Ali was making other friends in the village, his heart cried out as the vision of another Sunday discussing Kipling faded.

PREPARATIONS FOR 'An Evening at the Mogul Court', as it was now called, were in full vulgar display as the Major arrived early for his round of golf with Alec the following Thursday. In the annexe beyond the Grill all the tables had been pushed aside to create rehearsal space in front of the stage. The girls of the luncheon staff, deep in concentration, were engaged in flinging scarves about and stamping their feet as if to crush earwigs. Amina, the young woman from the Taj Mahal restaurant, seemed to be teaching the group. George was ensconced on top of a steep pile of chairs, drawing with a fat coloured pencil in a thick sketchbook.

'Five, six, seven . . . hold the eight for two beats . . . stamp, stamp!' called Amina, leading with graceful steps from the front while the women lumbered behind her. The Major thought she might be better off turning round to watch them, but then perhaps that would be too painful. As he scanned the entire room in vain for a tea urn, trying to remain invisible, a cry went up from a large girl in the back row.

'I'm not doing this if people keep coming in looking at us. They told us it would be private.' The entire troupe glared as if the Major had invaded the ladies' locker room.

'Sorry, just looking for some tea,' said the Major.

'Girls, we have only a couple of weeks to do this,' said Amina, clapping her hands together. 'Let's take a five-minute tea break and then we'll talk about feeling the rhythm.' The Major had not expected to hear such a tone of authority coming from someone so scruffy and odd-looking. Even more surprising was how the girls shuffled so obediently back into the kitchen.

'Major Pettigrew, right?' said Amina. 'You were at the Taj Mahal with Miss de Vere and that Mrs Ali?'

'Nice to see you and George again,' said the Major, waving at the boy and not answering the particulars of her question. 'May I ask what you are attempting to do with our lovely ladies of the luncheon service?'

'I'm trying to teach them some basic routines for the big dance,' said Amina. 'Sadie told Miss de Vere I dance, and she asked me to help.'

'Oh, dear, I'm truly sorry,' said the Major. 'I can't believe she roped you into something so impossible.'

'They're not so bad if you don't ask them to do more than three different steps. So we'll be shaking a lot of hips, and using bigger scarves.'

'Yes, the more veils the better, I think,' said the Major.

'So, how well do you know Mrs Ali?' she asked abruptly.

'Mrs Ali runs a very nice shop,' said the Major, responding with automatic evasiveness. There was a brief pause. 'May I assume you are a dancer by profession?' he added, by way of turning the conversation.

'Dance, yoga, aerobics. Dance doesn't pay very well, so I teach whatever,' she said. 'Do you think she's nice, then, Mrs Ali? Because I was thinking of going over to see her. I heard she wants some part-time help in the shop.'

'You did?' The Major couldn't quite see her stacking tins of spaghetti rings. On the other hand, she could hardly be worse than the grumpy nephew. 'Mrs Ali's a lovely woman. Very nice shop,' he said again.

'Of course, it'd have to be school hours only.'

'I hope you get the job,' said the Major. He looked away towards the door and raised an eyebrow to acknowledge an imaginary passing acquaintance—an invisible Alec to help him escape the room. 'I must be getting along to find my partner.'

'D'you think you could give us a lift after your game?' said the young woman. The Major knew he should answer, but he had no idea how to parry such a bold request. He simply stared at her. 'Only it's two buses from here to Edgecombe,' she added. 'We'll probably have to hitchhike.'

'Oh, I couldn't let you do that,' said the Major. 'Not safe at all.'

'Thank you, then,' she said. 'I'll wait and go with you.'

'I may be some time,' he began.

'Oh, I've got plenty of work here,' she said, as the slack-postured lunch girls filed back from the kitchen. 'We'll wait for you in the lobby.' Several faces perked up as she said this and the Major had the horrible sensation of being caught making an assignation. He fled as fast as possible, determined to wait discreetly somewhere outside until Alec arrived.

AMINA AND GEORGE were not in the lobby when the Major finished his round. She was waiting for him in the car park, leaning on a concrete post with her arms wrapped across her chest. He noticed that she was not wearing a warm-enough coat and her hair had begun to wilt in the chill drizzle. George was squatting at her feet, trying to protect his book from the rain. There was no avoiding her, so the Major waved. Amina hoisted a huge backpack onto her thin shoulder and joined him at his car.

'I thought you must have gone,' he said as he unlocked the car.

'Got kicked out,' she said, tossing her heavy bag in the boot on top of his clubs. 'Some old git suggested we wait by the service entrance.'

'Oh, dear, I'm sure he wasn't trying to be offensive,' said the Major.

'Don't worry about it. I don't. They are bullies who expect you to slink away or tip your cap or something,' said Amina. 'When you spit back at them, they get all flustered. You ought to try it some time. It can be really funny.' There was a weary tone to her voice that made the Major doubt she found it as amusing as she claimed.

They drove in silence for a while and then she shifted in her seat to look at him. 'You're not going to ask me about George, are you?' she asked in a low voice.

'None of my business, young lady.'

'Women always ask. Men don't but you can see they've made up a whole story about me and George in their heads.' She turned away and placed her fingers where the rain ran sideways along the glass of her window.

'I'm not going to answer for men, or women, in general,' he said after a moment. 'But personally, I have never sought to burden other people with my life history and I have no intention of meddling in theirs.'

'But you're making judgments about people all the time—and if you don't know the whole story . . .'

'My dear young woman, of course we all make shallow and quite possibly erroneous judgments about each other. I'm sure, for example, that you already have me pegged as an old git, too, do you not?' She said nothing and he thought he detected a guilty smirk.

'But we have no right to demand more of each other, do we?' he continued. 'I mean, I'm sure your life is very complicated, but we are strangers, and you have no right to demand that I give it any thought.'

'I think everyone has the right to be shown respect,' she said.

'Ah, well, there you go.' He shook his head. 'Young people are always demanding respect instead of trying to earn it. In my day, respect was something to strive for. Something to be given, not taken.'

'You know, you should be an old git,' she said with a faint smile, 'but for some reason I like you.'

'Thank you,' he said, surprised. He was equally surprised to find that he felt pleased. There was something about this prickly young person that he also liked. However, it was with a feeling of relief that he pulled up the car in front of Mrs Ali's shop and let his passengers out.

'Do they have comics?' asked George.

'I've got no money, so just be a good boy and maybe when we get home I'll make you a cake,' said Amina.

'Good luck,' he called through the window as Amina paused in front of the shop, holding George by the hand. The face she turned to him was quite grey and frightened. He felt a dawning of suspicion that she was not going to the shop for a mere job interview.

He returned home and was putting the tea in the pot when his uneasiness about dropping the strange young woman and her son on Mrs Ali's doorstep was compounded by the horrible realisation that it was the third Thursday of the month. On that day, the bus company shifted all the afternoon buses to some mysterious other duties, and no one had been able to get a clear answer as to where they went.

The Major was sure that Amina had told George the truth when she said she had no money. He was certain she could not afford a taxi. With great reluctance, tinged with curiosity, he put the tea cosy on the pot and fetched his coat. He would have to offer to drive the pair back to town at least.

THROUGH THE DISTORTION of the plate-glass window he could see Mrs Ali. Her nephew stood rigid, which was hardly unusual, but he was staring past the Major's shoulder at some distant point outside the window. Amina looked down at her bright crimson boots, her shoulders sunk into an old woman's hunch that telegraphed defeat. This was no job interview. The Major was just thinking about sneaking away again when he was accosted by a loud voice.

'Major, yoo-hoo!' He turned round and was greeted with the sight of Daisy, Alma, Grace and Lord Dagenham's niece, Gertrude, crammed into Daisy's Mercedes. 'So happy to have spotted you, you're just the man we wanted to see,' added Daisy, as the four ladies emerged from the car. 'We couldn't wait to tell you all about the exciting new plan we came up with.'

The Major held the car door for Alma and bent to rescue a large yellow satin turban that had tumbled into a puddle.

'It involves you!' said Alma, as if the Major should feel pleased.

'Major, we have been debating whether our folk dancing was enough to set the theme of our evening,' said Daisy. 'Then this morning, while we were breakfasting at Lord Dagenham's, we came up with a delightful proposition.'

'It was a lovely breakfast, Gertrude,' said Alma to the niece. 'Such a delightful start to the day.'

'Thank you,' said Gertrude. 'I'm more used to grabbing a bacon sandwich in the stables than entertaining other ladies.'

'Ladies, ladies,' said Daisy. 'If we could stay on point?' She paused for effect. 'We've settled on a series of scenes—very tasteful—and we were discussing how to make them relevant.'

'Oh, you tell him, Grace—it was partly your idea,' added Alma.

'Well, we were just talking about local connections to India and I happened to mention your father. I didn't mean to suggest anything.'

'My father?' asked the Major.

'If I might explain,' said Daisy, quelling Grace with a lifted eyebrow. 'We were reminded of the story of your father and his brave service to the maharajah. It'll be the perfect core of our entertainment.'

'No, no, no,' the Major said. He felt quite faint at the idea. 'My father was in India in the thirties and early forties. He served at Partition. The Mogul Empire died out around 1750,' said the Major, his exasperation overcoming his politeness. 'So you see it doesn't go at all.'

'So we'll just change "Mogul" to "Maharajah" and celebrate how we gave India and Pakistan their independence,' said Daisy breezily. 'Now, Major, I understand you have possession of your father's guns? And what about some kind of dress uniform? I understand he was a colonel, wasn't he?'

'We'll need to find someone younger than you, Major, to play him, of course,' said Alma. 'And we'll need some men to play the murderous mob.'

'Maybe Roger, your son, would do it?' said Gertrude.

'Be a murderous mob?' asked the Major.

'No, be the colonel, of course,' said Gertrude.

'I'm sure the lunch girls have a few murderous-looking boyfriends between them to be our mob,' said Daisy.

'My father was a very private man,' said the Major. That the ladies could imagine that he or Roger would consent to appear in any sort of theatrical was beyond comprehension.

'My uncle thinks it's a wonderful story,' added Gertrude. 'He wants to present you with some kind of silver plate at the end of the speeches. Recognition of the Pettigrews' proud history, and so on. He'll be so disappointed if I have to tell him you declined his honour.' She looked at him with wide eyes and the Major fumbled unsuccessfully for words.

'Perhaps we should give the Major some time to absorb the idea,' said Grace, speaking up, defending him.

'Quite right, quite right,' said Daisy. 'We'll say no more right now, Major.' She looked at the windows of the shop and waved at Mrs Ali inside. 'Let's go in and secure Mrs Ali's help for the dance, shall we, ladies?'

'Why, that's Amina, the girl who's teaching our waitresses to dance,' said Gertrude. 'I wonder what on earth she's doing here in Edgecombe.'

'Perhaps now is not the best time,' said the Major, anxious to spare

Mrs Ali an assault by the ladies. 'I believe they have business together.'

'It's the perfect opportunity to speak to both of them,' said Daisy. 'Everybody in!' The Major was herded inside the shop along with the ladies. It was a tight squeeze around the counter area, and the Major found himself standing close to Mrs Ali.

'I'm sorry,' he whispered. 'I could not dissuade them from coming in.'

'Those that will come, will come,' she said in a tired voice. She looked at Amina, to whom Daisy was talking.

'What luck that you are here as well,' Daisy said to Amina. 'How is the dancing coming along?'

'Considering they all have two left feet and no sense of rhythm, it was going quite well,' said Amina. 'But I don't think your club manager will be letting me back in any time soon.'

'You mean the secretary?' said Gertrude. 'Yes, he was quite apoplectic on the phone.' She stopped to chuckle. 'But don't worry, I told him he must have more patience, considering your circumstances.'

'My circumstances?' said Amina.

'You know, single mother and all that,' said Gertrude. 'Afraid I laid it on a bit thick but we do hope you'll carry on. We need your talent. I think we can approve a little more money, given the bigger scope of the project.'

'You're dancing for money?' asked Mrs Ali's nephew.

'I'm only teaching a few routines,' she said.

'Oh, she's teaching our girls how to shake those hips,' said Alma. 'Such a wonderful display of your culture.' She smiled at Mrs Ali and her nephew. The nephew turned an ugly copper colour and rage flickered under his skin.

'Now, Mrs Ali, we were wondering whether we could prevail on you to attend the dance.'

'Well, I don't know,' said Mrs Ali. A sudden, shy pleasure lit her face.

'My aunt will not engage in public dancing,' said Abdul Wahid, his voice bubbling with anger. Daisy peered at him with condescension suitable only for shop assistants who might unwittingly forget their manners.

'We were not expecting her to dance,' she said.

'We wanted sort of a welcoming goddess, stationed near the hat stand,' said Alma. 'And Mrs Ali is so quintessentially Pakistani.'

'Actually, I'm from Cambridge,' said Mrs Ali in a mild voice. 'Never been farther abroad than the Isle of Wight.'

'Mrs Khan feels we need someone to welcome and to take the hats and coats,' said Daisy. 'She and her husband, Dr Khan, are coming as guests, so they can't do it. She suggested you, Mrs Ali.' Mrs Ali's face grew pale and the Major felt a rage climbing into his own throat.

'My aunt does not work at parties—' began the nephew, but the Major cleared his throat loudly enough that the young man stopped in surprise.

'She won't be available,' he said. They all looked at him, and he felt torn between a desire to run for the door and the need to stand up for his friend. 'I have already asked Mrs Ali to attend as my guest.'

'How extraordinary,' said Daisy, and she paused as if fully expecting him to reconsider. Mrs Ali's nephew looked at the Major as if he were a strange bug discovered in the bath. Alma could not disguise a look of shock. Grace turned away and appeared suddenly absorbed in a local newspaper. Mrs Ali blushed but held her chin in the air and looked straight at Daisy.

'I'm sure Mrs Ali will add a decorative note to the room anyway,' said Gertrude, stepping blunt but welcome into the awkward silence. 'We will be happy to have her as an ambassador at large, representing both Pakistan and Cambridge.' She smiled, and the Major realised he had underestimated the redheaded young woman's character. She seemed to have a certain authority and an edge of diplomacy that might drive Daisy insane eventually. He could only look forward to that day.

'Then there's no more to be done here,' said Daisy in a huffy voice. 'We must go over the plans and we must call the Major and arrange to search his house for uniforms and so on.'

'I will call Roger; he and I can work on the Major,' said Gertrude, giving him a conspiratorial smile. 'I'm sure he'll be itching to help.'

'Thank you for your quick thinking, Major,' said Mrs Ali when the ladies had left. To his surprise, she seemed to be moving him towards the door also. 'Did you need anything before you go?'

'I just came to see if Amina needed a lift back to town,' the Major said. 'There are no buses in the afternoon today.'

'I didn't know that,' said Amina. She looked at Mrs Ali. 'I had better go if the Major is willing to drive us home.'

'No, you must stay and we will talk some more,' said Mrs Ali.

'She should leave and go back to her mother,' said Abdul Wahid in a fierce, low voice.

'My mother died two months ago,' said Amina, speaking just to him. 'Thirty years in the same street, Abdul Wahid, and only six people came to the funeral. Why do you think that was?' Her voice cracked, but she refused to look away from him.

To break the painful silence, the Major asked, 'Where is George?'

'He's upstairs,' said Mrs Ali. 'I found him some books to look at.'

'I am sorry that your mother had to bear that shame,' said the nephew, turning his head away. 'But it was none of my doing.'

'That's what your family would say,' said the girl, tears now making tracks down her thin cheeks. She picked up her backpack. 'George and I will go now and you will never have to be bothered by us again.'

'Why did you have to come here at all?' he asked.

'I had to come and see for myself that you don't love me. I never believed them when they said you left of your own accord, but I see now that you are the product of your family, Abdul Wahid.'

'You should go,' said Abdul Wahid.

'No, no, you will stay and we will go upstairs and have something to eat,' said Mrs Ali. 'We will not leave things like this.' She looked flustered. 'Thank you for your offer, Major, but everything is fine. We will make our own arrangements.'

'If you're sure,' said the Major.

Mrs Ali moved towards the door and he had no choice but to follow. He added, in a whisper, 'Did I do wrong in bringing her here?'

'No, no, we are delighted to have them,' she said loudly. 'It turns out that they may be related to us.' A last puzzle piece slipped into place and the Major saw in his mind an image of little George frowning and looking so much like Abdul Wahid. He opened his mouth to speak, but Mrs Ali's face was a mask of exhausted politeness and he did not want to say something that might break the fragile veneer.

'Extra relatives are useful, I suppose—a bridge player at family parties, or another kidney donor,' he babbled. 'I congratulate you.' A small smile lifted her weary face for a moment. He wished he could hold her hand and ask her to unburden herself to him, but the nephew was still glowering.

'Thank you also for your chivalrous deception about the dance, Major,' she added. 'I'm sure the ladies meant well, but I am glad to decline their request.'

'I am hoping you will not prove me a liar, Mrs Ali,' he replied. 'It would be my honour and pleasure to escort you to the dance.'

'My aunt would not dream of attending,' said Abdul Wahid loudly.

'I will rule my own life, thank you, Abdul Wahid,' said Mrs Ali sharply, 'Major, I accept your kind invitation.'

'I'm much honoured,' said the Major.

'And I'm hoping we can continue to discuss literature on Sundays.'

Chapter 6

It was not cricket season, so the Major was confused for a moment by the muffled sound of wickets being hammered into turf. The sound shivered along the rise of Lord Dagenham's field, which ran along the bottom of his garden, and flushed a few pigeons from the copse. Carrying a mug of tea, and the morning paper under one arm, the Major went to investigate.

There was not much to see, only a tall man in rubber boots and a yellow waterproof coat consulting a theodolite and a clipboard while two others, following his directions, paced out lengths and hammered bits of orange-tipped wood into the rough grass.

'Major, don't let them see you,' said a disembodied voice in a loud stage whisper. The Major recognised the voice as belonging to Alice from next door, hiding behind the hedge.

'Don't look at me,' she said in an exasperated tone. 'Just keep looking about as if you were alone.'

'Good morning to you, Alice,' said the Major. 'Is there some reason we're being so covert?'

'Major, they're surveying for houses,' said Alice.

'But that can't be true,' said the Major. 'This is Lord Dagenham's land.'

'And Lord Dagenham intends to make a pretty penny from selling his land and building houses on it,' said Alice. 'Since they've seen you, you might as well go and interrogate them. See if they crack under direct confrontation.'

The Major walked round into the field and went to speak to the man in charge, who seemed perfectly pleasant as he shook hands but politely refused to explain his presence.

'I'm afraid it's all quite confidential,' he said. 'Client's all hush-hush.'

'I quite understand,' said the Major. 'Most people round here have a quite ridiculous dislike of any kind of change.'

'Well, exactly,' said the man.

'When I shoot with Dagenham on the eleventh, I'll have to ask him what he's up to and for a peek at the plans,' said the Major.

'I can't promise they'll have all the architectural plans by then,' said the man. 'I'm just the engineer. We have to do all the top fields, and then there's the traffic studies for the commercial area, which takes time.'

'Yes, of course. It will all take some months, I imagine.' The Major felt quite faint. 'What should I tell people if they ask?'

'If they're persistent, I tell 'em it's drains,' said the man.

'Thanks very much,' said the Major, turning away. 'I'll tell Lord Dagenham you're on top of things.'

Back behind his own gate, the Major felt a small spasm of grief. He had been feeling better in recent days and it was a surprise to find that his sorrow over his brother had not gone away but had been merely hiding somewhere, waiting to ambush him on just such an occasion. He felt his eyes water and he pressed the fingernails of his free hand into his palm to stop it. He was keenly aware of Alice, crouched behind the hedge.

'I'm afraid you might be right,' said the Major, being careful not to look down at her. 'It's houses for sure—and some commercial component.'

'Good God, it's a whole new town,' said Alice. 'We must take direct action right away.'

'You do what you must,' said the Major. 'I shall write a stern letter to the planning officer.'

THAT AFTERNOON, the Major walked down to the postbox with his letter and stood for some time, envelope in hand. Deciding, finally, that his words were adequately composed and the letter suitably concise and grave, he popped the envelope into the box. He had debated copying the letter directly to Lord Dagenham but decided that this might be put off, perhaps until a date after the duck shoot, without any serious moral compromise. The letter posted, he was free to look at the village shop and decide, as if hit by a sudden idea, to enquire after Mrs Ali and her nephew.

Inside the shop, Mrs Ali was seated at the counter pushing small squares of silk into the raffia baskets that she usually filled with sandalwood candles and packets of eucalyptus bath salts. Wrapped in cellophane and a silk bow, they were popular gifts.

'Those sell quite well, I believe,' he said, by way of greeting. Mrs Ali looked startled, as if she had not paid attention to the door's bell.

'Yes, they are the favourite last-minute purchase of people who have entirely forgotten the person for whom they must buy,' said Mrs Ali. She appeared agitated, twirling a completed basket at the end of her long slender fingers. 'There is profit in panic, I suppose.'

'You appeared to be somewhat in distress yesterday,' he said. 'I came to see whether everything was all right.'

'Things are . . . difficult,' she said at last. He waited for her to elaborate, finding himself curious in a way that was entirely unfamiliar.

'I've finished polishing the apples,' said a small voice. The boy, George, came from the back of the store holding a small green apple in his hand. 'This one is much smaller than the others,' he added.

'That is just much too small to sell, then,' said Mrs Ali. 'Would you like to eat it up for me?'

'Yes, please,' said George, grinning. 'I'll go and wash it.'

'I would say you have a special touch with children,' said the Major, once George had disappeared. 'However, in the case of straight bribery one should reserve judgment.' He had meant to make her laugh, but her face was grave.

'I have to tell you something,' she began. 'I'm not supposed to tell anyone, but if I do, perhaps it will help my confusion . . .' Her voice died away. He waited. 'Amina and George stayed with us last night,' she began. 'It turns out that George is my great-nephew. He is Abdul Wahid's son.'

'Is he indeed?' said the Major, feigning ignorance.

'How could I not have guessed, not have felt it?' she said. 'And yet now, with a word from Amina, I am welded to this small boy by a deep love.' She blinked, but a tear escaped and rolled down her left cheek. 'I cannot escape the fact that this brings shame on my family, and I would understand if you preferred not to continue our acquaintance.'

'Nonsense. Such a thought never crossed my mind,' said the Major. He could feel himself blushing at this small lie. He was doing his best to squelch the uncomfortable desire to slide out of the shop and free himself from what was, however you looked at it, a slightly sordid business.

'I knew Abdul Wahid was sent away because he was in love with some girl,' she said. 'But I never knew there was to be a child.'

'Did he know?' asked the Major.

'He says not.' Her face darkened. 'A family will do many things to protect their children, and I fear life has been made very difficult for this young woman.' There was silence as the Major searched in vain for some useful words of comfort. 'Anyway, they are here now, Amina and George, and I must make things right.'

'What will you do?' asked the Major. 'I mean, you hardly know anything about this young woman.'

'I know I must keep them here, while we find out,' Mrs Ali said, her chin lifting in an attractive arc of decisiveness. She was a woman on a mission.

'And if Abdul Wahid wants to continue sleeping in the car, so be it.'

'Sleeping in the car?'

'He insists he cannot sleep under my roof with an unmarried woman, so he slept in the car,' said Mrs Ali. 'I pointed out the obvious inconsistency in his thinking, but his new religiosity permits him to be stubborn.'

'But why have them stay at all?' asked the Major. 'Can't they just visit?'

'I fear if they go back to town, they may disappear again. Amina says her aunt is practically hysterical with people asking questions about her,' she said. 'So Abdul Wahid has threatened to go to town and ask the imam for a bed, which would mean our business would be the gossip of the entire community.' She covered her face with her hands and said softly, 'Why must he be so stubborn?'

'Look here, if it's really important to you to keep them all here, how about your nephew coming to stay with me for a few days?' The Major surprised himself with the offer, which seemed to emerge of its own accord. 'I have a spare room—he wouldn't be in my way.'

'Oh, Major, it is too much to expect,' said Mrs Ali. 'I could not trespass this way on your kindness.' Her face, however, had lit up with anticipation.

'Look, it's really no trouble,' he said. 'And if it helps you resolve this problem, I'm glad to be of service.'

'I will be entirely in your debt, Major.' She stood up from her stool, came close and laid her hand on his arm. 'I cannot express my gratitude.' The Major felt warmth spreading up his arm. He kept still for a moment, as if a butterfly had alighted on his elbow.

'Well, it's quite all right.' He gave her hand a quick squeeze.

'You are a most astonishing man,' she said, and he realised he had inspired a sense of trust and indebtedness that would make it entirely impossible for an honourable man to attempt to kiss her any time soon. He cursed himself for a fool.

IT WAS DARK when Abdul Wahid knocked at the door of Rose Lodge. He was carrying a few simple belongings rolled in a small prayer rug.

'Do come in,' said the Major.

'You are very kind,' said the young man, who wore the same frown as usual. He carefully removed his battered, brown slip-on shoes and placed them under the hallstand. The Major knew this was a sign of respect for his home, but he felt embarrassed by the intimacy of a stranger's feet in damp socks, and was glad his own feet were encased in stout wool slippers.

Leading the way upstairs, he showed the nephew to the spare room.

'Will this do?' he asked. The thin mattress, the pine chest of drawers and the single print of flowers on one wall seemed suitably monastic.

'You are too kind.' Abdul Wahid deposited his belongings on the bed.

'I hope you'll be warm enough,' the Major said.

Abdul Wahid sat on the edge of the bed, his hands on his knees, staring into thin air. 'She was always so beautiful,' he whispered. 'I could never think straight in her presence.'

'The window rattles a bit if the wind gets round this corner of the house,' the Major added, tightening the catch. He found himself slightly unnerved by the young man's intensity and decided to play the jovial host.

'They promised me I would forget her, and I did,' said the young man. 'But now she is here and my brain has been spinning all day.'

'Maybe it's a low-pressure system. My wife always got headaches when the barometer dropped.'

'It is a great relief to be in your home, Major,' said Abdul Wahid. The Major turned in surprise. 'To be once again in a sanctuary far from the voices of women is balm to the anguished soul.'

'I can't promise it will last,' said the Major. 'My neighbour Alice Pierce is rather fond of singing folk music to her garden plants. Thinks it makes them grow or something.' The Major had often wondered how a wailing rendition of 'Greensleeves' would encourage greater raspberry production but Alice did produce several kinds of fruit in pie-worthy quantities. 'No sense of pitch, but plenty of enthusiasm,' he added.

'Then I will add a prayer for rain to my devotions,' said Abdul Wahid. The Major could not determine whether this was intended humorously.

'I'll see you in the morning,' he said. 'I usually put on a pot of tea around six.' As he left his guest and proceeded down to the kitchen, he felt in his bones the exhaustion of such a strange turn of events.

And yet he could not help but register a certain sense of exhilaration at having thrust himself into the heart of Mrs Ali's life in such an extraordinary and spontaneous manner. He was tempted to celebrate his own boldness with a large glass of Scotch, but as he reached the kitchen he decided that a large glass of sodium bicarbonate would be more prudent.

SATURDAY MORNING was sunny and the Major was in the back garden, forking a pile of leaves into a wheelbarrow, when his son's raised voice from the house, followed by what sounded like a chair being overturned, caused him to drop the entire load with a half-formed oath. Having no idea that Roger would visit, the Major had not told him that he had a guest in the house.

As he hurried towards the back door, he cursed Roger for never bothering to phone before turning up. He had never seemed to find the right words to tell his son that his childhood home was no longer available to him at all hours. Now he would be stuck with Roger pouting as if he owned the place, and the Major and his guest were the interlopers.

As he reached the door, Roger came panting through, red-faced and furious. 'There's a man in the house claiming he's staying here,' said Roger. 'Sandy's keeping him talking but I've got the police on speed dial.'

'Oh, good heavens, don't call the police,' said the Major. 'That's just Abdul Wahid.'

'Abdul what?' said Roger. 'Who the hell is he? I almost hit him with a dining chair.'

'Are you mad? Why would you assume my guest is an intruder?'

'Is that any more absurd than assuming my father has suddenly become friendly with half the population of Pakistan?'

'And you left Sandy alone with my "intruder"?' asked the Major.

'Yes, she's keeping him occupied, talking to him about handmade clothing,' said Roger. 'Spotted that his scarf was some vintage tribal piece and quite calmed him down.'

'So much for chivalry,' said the Major.

'Well, as you said, he isn't dangerous. But what the hell is he doing here?'

'I am simply helping out a friend by putting up her nephew for a couple of days. It's a bit complicated,' said the Major.

He felt himself on shaky ground, not fully understanding what Mrs Ali was trying to accomplish in immediately moving Amina and George into the flat above the shop. She had stared hungrily at little George, and the Major had not recognised the look until later. It was the same look Nancy had sometimes given Roger, when she thought no one was looking. She had looked that way on the day of his birth and she had looked at him just the same as she lay wasting away in the hospital. In that bleach-scented room, Roger had chattered on about his own concerns as usual, as if a cheery recitation of his promotion prospects would wipe out the reality of her dying, and she had gazed at him as if to burn his face into her fading mind.

'Well, Sandy and I are here now, so you can use us as an excuse to get rid of him.'

'It would be entirely rude to "get rid" of him,' said the Major. 'He has accepted my invitation—an invitation I might not have made had I known you were coming down this weekend.'

'Look, I'm sure he's a perfectly nice chap, but you can't be too careful about foreigners, particularly at your age.'

'Would that apply equally to Americans?' asked the Major. 'Because I spot one of them now.' Sandy was standing in the doorway.

Roger greeted her with a kiss on the lips and an arm round the waist. 'Are you all right, darling?' he asked. 'Turns out Abdul is here at my father's invitation.'

'Of course he is,' said Sandy. She turned to the Major. 'Ernest, you have a lovely home.'

'Thank you,' said the Major.

'You can almost smell the centuries,' said Sandy, who was perfectly dressed for a literary version of the countryside. She wore high-heeled brown shoes, pale, well-pressed slacks, a shirt with autumn leaves printed on it and a cashmere sweater tied round her shoulders. She did not look ready to climb over a stile and walk through soggy sheep fields to the pub for lunch. A happy maliciousness prompted the Major to suggest just that.

'Let's celebrate the lovely surprise of your visit, shall we?' he said. 'I thought we'd walk down for lunch at the Royal Oak.'

'Actually we brought lunch with us,' said Roger. 'Picked up supplies at this great new place in Putney. Everything is flown in from France.'

'I hope you like truffle dust.' Sandy laughed. 'Roger had them powder everything but the madeleines.'

'Perhaps you'd like to invite that Abdul chap to join us, by way of apology,' added Roger, as if it were the Major who had created an offence.

'It's not polite to call him Abdul. It means servant,' said the Major. 'You should use the entire Abdul Wahid. It means Servant of God.'

'Touchy about it, is he?' said Roger. 'I suppose Mrs What's-Her-Name from the village shop told you that? The one you brought to the cottage to freak out Mrs Augerspier?'

'Your Mrs Augerspier is an objectionable woman—'

'That goes without saying, Dad.'

'Just because it goes without saying doesn't mean one shouldn't speak up, you know. Or at least refuse to do business with such a person.'

'There's no point in being confrontational and losing out on something lucrative, is there?' asked Roger. 'I mean, it is much more satisfying to beat them by getting the better end of the bargain.'

'On what philosophical basis does that idea rest?' asked the Major. Roger gave a vague wave of the hand and the Major saw him roll his eyes for Sandy's benefit.

'Oh, it's simple pragmatism, Dad. If we refused to do business with the morally questionable, the deal volume would drop in half and the good guys like us would end up poor. Then where would we all be?'

'On a nice dry spit of land known as the moral high ground?' suggested the Major.

ROGER AND SANDY went to fetch their hamper and the Major tried not to think of truffles, which he had always avoided because they stank. Abdul Wahid came out of the house. He was carrying a couple of religious texts tucked under his arm and was wearing the dour frown that the Major now understood was the result of excessive thinking rather than mere unpleasantness.

'Your son has come to stay,' said Abdul Wahid. 'I should leave.'

'Oh, no, no,' said the Major, who was growing used to Abdul Wahid's abrupt style of speaking and no longer found it offensive. 'There is no need for you to rush off. The room is yours as long as you want.'

'He has brought his fiancée with him, and you will need your guest room,' said Abdul Wahid. 'Your son was very clear that they will be staying with you for several weekends, until their cottage is made habitable.'

'Ah, will they?' said the Major. He could think of no immediate response. He doubted that the spare room would be required in this case, but he didn't want to place himself in the awkward position of having to make direct reference to his son's sleeping arrangements.

'I should return to the shop, and Amina and George should go back to her auntie in town,' said Abdul Wahid in a firm voice. 'This whole idea that we can be together again is just foolish.'

'There is no hurry to make decisions, is there?' said the Major. 'Look, why don't you stay to lunch and we could walk down together?' The Major was reluctant to let the young man precipitate some crisis. Moreover, he found himself eager to inflict his guest upon Roger—or perhaps to inflict them on each other, in the hope of jolting both out of their moral complacency. 'I would really like you to meet my son properly.'

Abdul Wahid gave a strange bleating sound and the Major realised he was actually laughing.

'Major, your son has brought an entire feast of pâtés, hams and other pig-related products. I barely escaped the kitchen with my faith.'

'I'm sure we can make you a cheese sandwich or something,' said the Major. Abdul Wahid shuffled his feet and the Major pressed his invitation home. 'I do wish you'd sit round the table with us.'

'I will, of course, defer to your wishes,' he said.

IN THE KITCHEN an unfamiliar cloth of blue-striped burlap had been laid across the table. His best wineglasses, the ones the Major brought out at Christmas, were laid out next to plastic plates in a lurid lime green. Strange mustards had been decanted into his china finger bowls while an unfamiliar vase like a tree root held a bunch of yellow calla lilies. They had kindled an unnecessary but attractive fire in the grate and the Major wondered whether they had purchased firewood in Putney as well.

'How many of us are there for lunch?' asked the Major. 'Is there a coach tour about to turn up?'

'Well, Dad, I planned for leftovers,' said Roger. 'That way you'll have some food for the week.'

'Ernest, do you have a corkscrew?' asked Sandy, and the Major's indignation at the suggestion that he needed to be provided with food was displaced by the need to head off a cultural misunderstanding.

'Abdul Wahid has consented to sit at the table with us, so perhaps I'll put on the kettle for tea and get us all a nice jug of lemon water,' said the Major.

Sandy paused, cradling a bottle of wine against one hip.

'Oh, I say, do we have to—' began Roger.

'Please do not mind me,' said Abdul Wahid. 'You must drink as you wish.'

'Good show, old man,' said Roger, smiling. 'If everyone would just show such good manners, we could solve the Middle East crisis tomorrow.'

'Do come and sit down by me, Abdul Wahid,' said Sandy. 'I want to ask you more about traditional weaving in Pakistan.'

'I won't be much help,' said Abdul Wahid. 'I was raised in England, and bought my scarf as a tourist in Lahore, in a department store.'

Sandy handed Roger her wine bottle as she sat down by Abdul Wahid.

'Now, Father, you surely aren't going to pass up a nice '75 Margaux,' said Roger. 'I picked it out especially for you.'

TWO LARGE GLASSES of decent claret in the middle of the day were not part of the Major's usual schedule. He had to admit that they imparted a rosy air to a luncheon that would otherwise have been stilted. Sandy's impeccably made-up face seemed softer in the haze of firelight and wine. Roger's brash commands—he had compelled them to swirl their wine round the glass and stick their noses in as if they had never tasted a decent vintage before— seemed almost endearing. Abdul Wahid gave no sign of derision, answering Sandy's questions with the politest of replies.

Roger was pointed in ignoring their guest and chattered on about the new cottage. In one week he and Sandy had apparently managed to engage the services of a carpenter and a team of painters.

'Not just any old painters, either,' said Roger. 'They're so in demand, doing galleries and restaurants. Sandy knows them through a friend.' He shot her a loving smile. 'She's the queen of the right connections.'

'Lots of connections, very few close friends,' said Sandy. The Major caught a hint of regret that sounded genuine. 'It's so refreshing just to sit around with family and friends, like we're doing now.'

'Have you two set a wedding date, or were you going to make that a surprise as well?' asked the Major. Roger looked down and crumbled bread on the side of his plate. Sandy took a long swallow of wine, which the Major observed with pleasure as a possible crack in her façade of perfection. There was a pause.

'Oh, goodness, no,' said Roger finally. 'We have no plans to get married any time soon, or I would have told you.'

'No plans?' asked the Major. 'I'm not sure I understand.'

'I mean, once you're married, people start thinking "family man", and before you know it your whole career smells of impending nappies,' said Roger, twirling the wine cork in his fingers.

Sandy paid close attention to her wineglass and said nothing.

'Marriage is a wonderful part of life,' said the Major. 'All this lack of commitment these days—doesn't it smack of weakness of character?'

'As one who has been weak,' said Abdul Wahid in a quiet voice, 'I can attest to you that it is not a path to happiness.'

'Oh, I didn't mean you, Abdul Wahid,' said the Major, horrified that he had unintentionally offended his guest. 'Not at all.'

'Sandy's her own boss, and she has no problem with it,' said Roger.

'It was my idea, actually,' said Sandy. 'My firm kept the whole visa thing dangling over my head, so getting engaged to a Brit seemed the ideal answer. I don't mean to offend you, Abdul Wahid.'

'I am not offended,' said Abdul Wahid. He blinked several times and took a deep breath. 'Only sometimes when we pick and choose among the rules, we discover later that we have set aside something precious in the process.'

'But everyone puts off marriage if they can,' said Roger.

'I must get back to the shop now.' Abdul Wahid stood up from the table and inclined his head to the Major and to Sandy. The Major rose to see him out of the room.

'What's his problem?' said Roger when the Major returned.

'Abdul Wahid has just discovered he has a son,' said the Major. 'It is a warning to all of us that unorthodox romantic arrangements are not without consequences.'

'I agree you're right, at least when it comes to the working classes and foreigners,' said Roger. 'Totally oblivious about birth control and things. But we're not like them, Sandy and I.'

'The human race is all the same when it comes to romantic relations,' said the Major.

'Look, we'll see how it goes with the cottage, Dad,' said Roger. 'Who knows, maybe in six months we'll be ready to commit.'

'To marriage?'

'Or at least to buying a place together,' said Roger. Sandy drained her wineglass and still said nothing.

AFTER LUNCH, the Major made a pot of tea and tried to dissuade Sandy from washing dishes.

'Please don't clear up,' he said. He still found all offers of help in the kitchen to be an embarrassment and a sign of pity.

'Oh, I love doing dishes,' said Sandy. 'I know you probably consider me a dreadful Yank but I'm so in love with the fact that people here are able to live in tiny houses and do chores without complicated appliances.'

'I should point out that Rose Lodge is considered rather spacious,' said the Major.

'Maybe I won't bother getting a dishwasher for the cottage,' she said. 'We'll just keep things authentic.' She laughed and the Major did not wince quite so much. Either he was getting used to her, or the claret had not yet worn off.

'I went down to the golf club last week to check out what's what,' said Roger, taking the dry tea towel the Major offered him but then sitting down at the table instead of helping.

'And what exactly was what?' asked the Major.

'That old secretary is a damn idiot. But I ran into Gertrude Dagenham-Smythe and she's getting her uncle to sponsor me,' said Roger.

'Lord Dagenham?'

'When she offered, I thought I might as well get sponsored by someone as high up the food chain as possible.'

'But you don't even know her,' said the Major.

'We've met her a few times in town,' said Sandy. 'She remembered Roger right away—joked about how she had had a crush on him.'

The Major had a sudden vision of a tall, thin girl with a blunt chin and green glasses who had haunted the lane one summer.

'Do you remember how she was always popping out of the hedge and presenting me with gifts?' said Roger. 'She was as plain as the back of a bus and I had to drive her off with a peashooter.'

'Roger!' said the Major. The young lady's status as Lord Dagenham's niece was enough to grant her a certain distinction, if not beauty.

'Oh, he's very attentive to her now,' said Sandy. 'She asked for his help with this dance and he agreed right away. Good thing I'm not the jealous type.'

'They've asked me to play Grandfather Pettigrew. It's unbelievably good luck.' Roger yawned again.

'I don't like our name being used as entertainment,' said the Major.

'It's a boost to my social career and it won't cost you a penny,' said Roger. 'Would you deny me that chance?'

'We'll look ridiculous,' said the Major.

'Everyone looks ridiculous in the country,' said Roger. 'The point is to join in so they don't suspect you.'

'Roger is even going shooting now,' said Sandy, as they took their tea into the living room. 'We had to spend three hours in a store on Jermyn Street, getting him the proper outfit.'

'An outfit?' asked the Major. 'I could have lent you a pair of breeches.'

'I got everything I needed, thanks,' said Roger. 'Except a gun, of course. I was hoping I could borrow yours and Uncle Bertie's.' The request was smoothly made, as if it was of no more significance to him than asking to borrow some spare wellies during a rainstorm. The Major set down his cup and saucer and pondered how to produce a response that would be blunt enough to make an impression on Roger.

'No.'

'I'm sorry?' said Roger.

'No, you may not borrow the guns,' said the Major.

'Why ever not?' asked Roger with round eyes. The Major was about to answer when he recognised that his son was tempting him into explanations. Explaining would then simply open negotiations.

'Let's not discuss it in front of our guest,' said the Major. 'It is out of the question.' Roger stood up so quickly that he slopped tea into his saucer.

'How come you always have to undermine me?' Roger asked. 'This is my career we're talking about.' He banged down his teacup and turned to look into the fireplace, clenching his hands together behind his back.

'I'm sure your host has arranged some perfectly adequate extra guns,' said the Major. 'Besides, as a novice, you would look ridiculous banging away with such a valuable pair. You would look absurd.'

'Thank you, Father,' said Roger. 'Nice of you to be as frank as usual about my limitations.'

'I'm sure your father didn't mean it that way,' said Sandy, who was remembering why business acquaintances were, after all, preferable to family.

'What kind of shoot is this, anyway?' asked the Major. 'If it's clay shooting, they often have just the right equipment.'

'No, actually it's a local country thing,' said Roger. 'I'm shooting with Lord Dagenham next week. Sorry, Dad, but it just came about and I couldn't exactly say no.'

'Of course not,' said the Major, stalling for time. He was mortified at the thought of Roger waving a shotgun around, and for just an instant he saw himself explaining a dead peacock on the lawn.

'I wanted to ask Gertrude about adding another person, but I believe only a certain number of guns can be accommodated,' said Roger. 'I thought it wasn't polite to press them.' He blushed and the Major saw with some wonder that embarrassment about one's relations went both up and down the generations.

'Oh, no need to worry about me,' said the Major. 'My old friend Dagenham asked me some time ago to come and help him beef up the line.' He paused for greatest effect. 'Said we needed some old hands to show you London chaps how it's done.'

'That's wonderful,' said Sandy. 'I'm so glad it all worked out.' She stood up, adding, 'Excuse me.'

'I'm looking forward to giving the old Churchills a good day's work,' said the Major, standing as Sandy left the room. 'You should stick with me, Roger, and that way I can toss a few extra birds in your bag if you need them.' Roger looked sick to his stomach, and the Major felt he might have gone too far with his ribbing.

'Actually, there's an American chap who's interested in buying them and I'm going to show them off as best I can,' the Major said.

'Really?' said Roger, looking more cheerful. 'That's excellent news. Jemima was starting to get worried that you'd run off with them.'

'You've been talking to Jemima behind my back?'

'Oh, it's not like that,' said Roger. 'It's more—since the funeral, you know, we thought it might be useful to keep in touch since we both have parents to take care of. She has her mother to worry about, and I—well, you seem all right now, but then so did Uncle Bertie. You never know when I might have to jump in and take care of things.'

'I am speechless with gratitude at your concern,' said the Major.

'Dad, that's not fair,' said Roger. 'I'm not like Jemima.'

'Oh, really?' said the Major.

'Look, all I'm asking for is that when you sell the guns, you consider giving me a bit of a windfall you don't even need,' continued Roger. 'You have no idea how expensive it is to be a success in the City. The clothes, the restaurants, the weekend house parties—you have to invest to get ahead these days.' He sat down and his shoulders slumped. For a moment he looked like a rumpled teenager.

'Perhaps you need to moderate your expectations a little,' said the Major, genuinely concerned. 'Life isn't all about flashy parties and rich people.'

'That's what they tell the people they don't invite,' said Roger, gloomily. Sandy came back down the stairs and they ceased speaking. A hint of fresh cologne and lipstick brightened the room.

'We should be going if we want to speak to the painters,' she said.

'You're right,' said Roger.

'You told Abdul Wahid you would probably be staying here?' said the Major. Roger and Sandy traded a guarded look. The Major felt like a small boy whose parents are trying to shield him from grown-up conversation.

'I did explain to him that we would need a place to stay while the cottage is under renovation,' said Roger. 'He quite understood that it wouldn't be convenient having us all here.'

'You are completely right,' said the Major. 'I'm sure you and Sandy will be much happier staying down at the pub.'

'Hang on a minute,' said Roger.

'You must ask the landlord for the blue room, my dear,' said the Major to Sandy. 'It has a four-poster and, I believe, one of those whirlpool tubs of which you Americans are so fond.'

'I'm not staying at the pub,' said Roger, his face a picture of outrage.

'It is true that the whirlpool tub does reverberate through the public end of the bar,' said the Major, as if pondering the subject deeply, and he noticed that Sandy was having a hard time keeping a straight face.

'You can't expect my fiancée to share this house with some strange shop-keeper's assistant from Pakistan,' Roger spluttered.

'I quite understand,' the Major said. 'Unfortunately I had already invited him to stay and it's not possible to throw him out because you disapprove.'

'For all we know, he could be a terrorist,' said Roger.

'Oh, for God's sake, Roger, go and see your painters before they have to rush off to touch up the Vatican or whatever,' said the Major, in a harsher tone than he had intended.

The Major was sad at his outburst. He wanted to feel the kind of close bond with Roger that Nancy had enjoyed. The truth was that now, without his wife to negotiate the space that they occupied as a family, he and Roger seemed to have little common ground. He sat at the table and felt the weight of this admission hang about his shoulders like a heavy, wet coat. In the shrunken world, without Nancy, without Bertie, it seemed very sad to be indifferent to one's own son.

Chapter 7

The cheap purple and green kite, purchased especially for the after-noon's expedition, fluttered against the Major's hand. He released the rudimentary catch on the spool and handed it to George.

'Ready to take it up?'

George took the spool and began to walk away from the Major, across the rabbit-cropped grass. The park, busy with families on this fine Sunday, occupied the whole top of the broad headland to the west of the town. It was good for kites but not so good for balls, many of which were at that very moment careening downhill towards the edge of the high cliff. Signs warned people that the white chalk face was always being slivered away by the action of the sea and the weather. Bunches of dead flowers made cryptic reference to the many people every year who chose this spot to plunge to their deaths on the jagged rocks below. Every mother in the park seemed to feel the need to call to her children to stay away from danger, forming a background chorus louder than the sea.

'If they are so afraid for their children, why did they come?' asked the Major, handing Mrs Ali the kite to launch. 'Are you ready, George?'

'Ready!' said George. Mrs Ali tossed the kite into the air, where it hovered for a fluttering moment and then, to the Major's immense satisfaction, soared into the sky.

'That's the ticket,' called the Major as George ran backwards, unspooling more line. 'More line, George, more line.'

'Don't go too far, George,' called Mrs Ali. Then she clapped a hand over her mouth and turned wide eyes of apology to the Major.

'Not you as well?' he said.

'I'm afraid it must be a trick of nature,' she said, laughing. 'The universal bond between all women and the children in their care.'

'More like the universal hysteria,' said the Major.

'Do you not find the view even the slightest bit disorientating?' asked Mrs Ali. 'I can almost feel the earth spinning beneath my feet.'

'That's the power of it,' said the Major. He looked out at the green cliff and the enormous bowl of sky and sea and reached for a quotation.

> Clean of officious fence or hedge,
> Half wild and wholly tame,
> The wise turf cloaks the white cliff edge,
> As when the Romans came.

'I expect Roman women also cried out to their children to be careful,' said Mrs Ali. 'Is that Kipling?'

'It is,' said the Major, pulling a small red volume from his pocket. 'It's called "Sussex" and I was hoping to share it with you over tea today.' She had called to cancel their planned reading, explaining that she had volunteered to take George out for the afternoon. The Major, refusing to be disappointed for a second Sunday, asked if he might come along.

When the kite had been tossed several dozen times into the air, and George had run until his legs were exhausted, the Major suggested that they get some tea. They settled, with tea and a plate of cakes, at a sheltered table on the terrace of the pub that was absurdly built right on the headland. George swallowed a bun almost whole and drank a glass of lemonade before wandering off to view a puppy being walked nearby.

'My nephew suggested we come here,' said Mrs Ali. 'He says he walks up here all the time after mosque because here he can imagine that Mecca is just over the horizon.'

'I think France might be in the way,' said the Major, squinting at the horizon and trying to imagine the correct bearing for Saudi Arabia. 'But on a spiritual level, there is something about the edge of the land that does make one feel closer to God. A sobering sense of one's own smallness, I think.'

'I was very glad he wanted George to see it,' she said. 'I think it is a good sign, don't you?' The Major thought it might have been a better sign had he shown George himself, but didn't want to spoil Mrs Ali's afternoon.

'I must thank you again for putting up my nephew,' she said. 'It has allowed George and Amina to be with us and has allowed Abdul Wahid to get to know his son. I am hoping he will come to see where his duty lies.'

The Major tested the colour of the tea and gave the pot a stir. 'I am glad he doesn't object to Amina being in the shop. Do you believe he loves her?'

'I know that they were very much in love before,' she said. 'I also know that the family has gone to many lengths to separate them.'

'He seems to believe that despite your good offices, your late husband's family will never accept Amina.'

Mrs Ali seemed anxious at this remark and hesitated before answering. 'I am afraid that I have been very selfish,' she said.

'I cannot allow you to suggest such a thing,' said the Major.

'It is true,' she said. 'I have told Abdul Wahid that I have written to the family—and I have written.' Here she paused again. She wrapped her arms round her chest and gazed out at the vista. She did not look at the Major as she continued. 'But each day I have been somehow too busy to post the letter.' She fumbled in a small handbag and withdrew a thin envelope, very creased and folded. The Major took it gently from her, and as their fingertips met, he felt a skip in his veins that could only be happiness.

'A letter unposted is a heavy burden,' he said.

'Each day that passes I feel heavier,' she said. 'I know things cannot go on as they are. But at the same time, each day I feel a lightness I had almost forgotten.' She gazed at George, who was crouching on the grass, talking to the boy with the puppy. 'I am afraid everything will be taken from me,' she said in a quiet voice.

'Perhaps your letter will meet with a more friendly reaction than you imagine,' said the Major.

'My faith does permit the occasional miracle,' said Mrs Ali, a wistful smile hovering on her lips. 'My hope is that Abdul Wahid's parents will see they have been unjust. Of course, if that fails, I am prepared to bargain on a more temporal level.'

'One really shouldn't have to bargain with one's family like a used-car salesman.' The Major sighed. With acknowledged cowardice, he had ignored two phone messages from Marjorie. He felt that he could no more hold off a confrontation about the guns than Mrs Ali could hope to hold back the fury of her family.

'Someone must stand up for George,' she said. 'It is not permitted in Islam to let a child carry the weight of a parent's shame on his shoulders. He had to witness his grandmother's funeral shunned by all but a handful of people. It was a great dishonour.'

'Terrible,' said the Major.

'I am afraid my husband's family may have increased the shame by spreading certain untruths,' said Mrs Ali. 'I know Abdul Wahid understands this, and I believe it will help him decide to put things right. I pin my hopes on him coming to see where his real duty lies.'

'He does seem fond of her and the boy,' said the Major.

'I am glad that you say that,' said Mrs Ali. 'I was hoping you might talk to him for me. I think he needs a man's perspective on this.'

'It's not really my place,' began the Major, horrified at the thought of talking about such intimate matters with the stubborn and reticent young man currently using his guest room.

'With your military background, you understand better than most men the concept of honour and pride,' said Mrs Ali. 'I am a woman and I would throw away every shred of pride to keep George with me. Abdul Wahid knows this and therefore mistrusts my ability to see his point of view.'

'I'm not an expert on the faith behind his sense of duty,' said the Major. 'I could not instruct him.' Yet he felt his opposition melting under the warm satisfaction of hearing Mrs Ali's compliment.

'I ask you only to talk to him as one honourable man to another,' said Mrs Ali, her brown eyes unwavering.

'I will do anything you ask,' he said, and he could read gratitude in her face. He wondered if he might also be seeing some happiness. He turned away as he added, 'You must know that I am entirely yours to command.'

'I see chivalry lives on,' she said.

'As long as there's no jousting involved, I'm your knight,' he said.

ON THE WAY BACK, George slept in the back seat, tired from all the running and filled with cake. The Major drove as scenic a route as possible; Mrs Ali seemed entranced by the high banks and snug cottages of the less-travelled lanes. She spotted an old round postbox at a crossroads and he stopped the car so she could post her letter. He held his breath as she stood for a moment, letter in hand, her head cocked in thought. As she dropped the envelope in the box, all the sun seemed to drain out of the afternoon.

THE QUESTION OF HOW to begin a casual conversation designed to persuade a young man to accept a stranger's guidance on life-altering decisions plagued the Major for several days. There seemed to be few opportunities, even if one could find the appropriate words. Abdul Wahid rose very early and left without so much as a cup of tea. He returned late most days, having already had his dinner at the shop, and slipped up at once to his room where he read from his small stack of religious books.

One evening, when it was raining, the Major found his chance. Abdul Wahid was delayed in the back hall by the need to shake out and hang up his dripping rain jacket. Sliding the kettle onto a hot plate on the Aga, the Major set the teapot in the middle of the table and put out two large mugs.

'Won't you join me in a mug of hot tea?' he asked as Abdul Wahid entered the kitchen. 'It's a rough night out there.'

'I do not want to give you any trouble, Major,' said Abdul Wahid, shivering. 'Your hospitality is already more than I deserve.'

'You would be doing me a great favour, sitting down for a while,' said the Major. 'I've been by myself all day today and I would like the company.' He poked the fire as if the matter were already settled. As he bent over the smoking logs, he realised that his suggestion of loneliness was true. Despite his attempts to maintain a vigorous structure of errands, golf games, visits and meetings, there were sometimes days like this one, filled with rain and touched with a gnawing sense of parts missing from life. He missed his wife. He even missed Roger and how the house used to ring to the kicking shoes of grubby boys playing up and down the stairs.

Abdul Wahid took a seat at the kitchen table and accepted a cup of tea. 'Thanks. It's pretty damp out tonight.'

'Yes, not too nice,' agreed the Major, wondering if they would be stuck for long in the inevitable loop of weather talk.

'It is funny that you are tired of spending the day alone,' said Abdul Wahid. 'While I am tired of being in a busy shop filled with chattering people all day. I would love more time for reading and for thinking.'

'Don't rush to trade places with an old man,' said the Major. 'Youth is a wonderful time of vigour and action. For collecting friends and experiences.'

'I miss being a student,' said Abdul Wahid. 'I miss the passionate discussions with my friends, and most of all the hours among the books.'

'Life does often get in the way of one's reading,' agreed the Major, and they drank their tea in silence as the logs cracked and spat in the fire.

'I am sorry to leave you to your solitary days, Major, but I have decided to move back to the shop,' said Abdul Wahid at length.

'Are you sure?' asked the Major. 'You're welcome to stay on here.'

'Thank you, Major, but I have decided to live in a small outbuilding we have behind the store,' said Abdul Wahid. 'It has a toilet and a window, and with a fresh coat of paint it will be a sanctuary until things are decided.'

'You haven't yet heard from your family, then,' said the Major.

'A letter has come,' replied Abdul Wahid.

'Ah,' said the Major. Abdul Wahid stared into the fire and said nothing, so, after an interminable pause, the Major added, 'Good news, I hope?'

'It appears the moral objections may be overcome,' said Abdul Wahid. He screwed his face up, as if tasting something sour.

'Well, that's wonderful,' said the Major. 'Soon you can be with your son, and maybe even live in the same house instead of the chicken shed.'

Abdul Wahid got up and walked over to the mantelpiece. 'I do not think you would be so quick to approve if it was your son,' he said. The Major frowned as he tried to quell the immediate recognition that the young man was right. He fumbled for a reply that would be true but also helpful. 'I do not mean to offend you,' added Abdul Wahid.

'Not at all,' said the Major. 'You are not wrong—at least, in the abstract. I would be unhappy to think of my son becoming entangled in such a way and many people, including myself, may be guilty of a certain smug feeling that it would never happen in our families.'

'I thought so,' said Abdul Wahid with a grimace.

'Now, don't you get offended, either,' said the Major. 'What I'm trying to say is that I think that is how everyone feels in the abstract. But then life hands you something concrete—something concrete like little George— and abstracts have to go out the window.'

'I did not expect my family to agree with anything my aunt proposed,' Abdul Wahid said, returning to his chair. 'And it's not that I don't want to marry Amina. In her presence, I'm lost to her. She has such eyes. And then she was always so funny and wild. She is like a streak of light, or maybe a blow to the head.' He smiled, as if remembering a particular blow.

'That sounds suspiciously like love to me,' said the Major.

'We are not expected to marry for love, Major,' said Abdul Wahid. 'I do not wish to be one of those men who bends and shapes the rules of his religion to justify his comfortable life and to satisfy every bodily desire.'

'But your family has given permission?' said the Major.

Abdul Wahid looked at him, and the Major was concerned to see a gaunt misery in his face. 'I do not want to be the cause of my family stooping to hypocrisy,' he said. 'They took me away from her because of faith. I didn't like it but I understood and I forgave them. Now I fear they withdraw their objection in order to secure financial advantage.'

'Your aunt has offered to support the union?' said the Major.

'If faith is worth no more than the price of a small shop in an ugly village, what is the purpose of my life—of any life?' said Abdul Wahid.

'She will give up the shop,' said the Major. He did not phrase it as a question, because he already knew the answer. That Abdul Wahid should slight, in one sentence, both the sacrifice of his aunt and the pastoral beauty of Edgecombe St Mary incensed the Major to the point of stuttering.

'She will give up the shop, which is a huge and generous gift from her,' added Abdul Wahid, spreading his hands in a gesture of conciliation. 'There is only the question of where she will live that is to be determined. But what will I give up in accepting?'

'Your absolute arrogance might be a welcome start,' said the Major. He could not prevent the caustic anger in his words. Abdul Wahid widened his eyes and the Major was maliciously happy to have shocked him.

'I don't understand,' he said, frowning.

'Look here, it's all very tidy and convenient to see the world in black and white,' said the Major, trying to soften his tone slightly. 'However, philo-sophical rigidity is often combined with a complete lack of education or real-world experience.'

Abdul Wahid looked confused, which was an improvement over the frown. 'Are you saying it is wrong, stupid, to try to live a life of faith?'

'No, I think it is admirable,' said the Major. 'But I think a life of faith must start with remembering that humility is the first virtue before God.'

'I live as simply as I can,' said Abdul Wahid.

'I admire that about you, and it has been refreshing to see a young man who is not consumed by material wants.' As the Major said this, he thought bitterly of Roger and his shiny ambition. 'I am just asking you to consider whether your ideas come from as humble a place as your daily routine.'

Abdul Wahid looked at the Major with some amusement and gave another of his short, barking laughs. 'Major, how many centuries must we listen to the British telling us to be humble?'

'That's not what I meant at all,' said the Major, horrified.

'I'm only joking,' said Abdul Wahid. 'You are a wise man, Major, and I will consider your advice with great care—and humility.' He finished his tea and rose from the table to go to his room. 'But I must ask you, do you really understand what it means to be in love with an unsuitable woman?'

'My dear boy,' said the Major. 'Is there really any other kind?'

THE SUN WAS RED, haloed in mist and barely showing over the hedgerows as the Major crunched across the frost-stiffened field to the manor house, intending to arrive before the rest of the shooting party. It was not that he feared that his Rover would make an inadequate impression among the luxury four-by-fours of a London crowd. He simply preferred to enjoy the ritual of the walk. He felt the balance of his guns, cracked open and cradled in the crook of his elbow. Bertie's gun was now oiled to a deep shine, almost a match for his own gun's patina. He enjoyed the creaking seams of his old shooting coat and the weight of his pockets. The waxed cotton bulged with brass cartridges laden with steel shot, and his old game bag was buckled across his chest and flopped on one hip.

On the edge of what remained of the manor house parkland, he entered a short *allée* of elms, fuzzy with tangled branches, which constituted the truncated remains of what had once been a mile-long ride. Between the trees, crude wire cages and a plastic contraption attached to a small generator bore evidence of the gamekeeper's duck-raising. The cages were empty now. They would be refilled with hand-raised chicks in the spring. The Major was disappointed that the gamekeeper was nowhere to be seen. He had hoped to discuss the layout of the line today. He had entertained a mild thought that after such a talk, he might approach the main gravel courtyard with the gamekeeper in tow and so show the London types immediately that he was a local expert. A rustle in an overgrown wall of rhododendron revived his hopes, but as he assembled a smile and appropriate words of greeting, a small pale boy of about five or six dressed in school uniform popped out of the hedge and stood staring, transfixed by the Major's guns.

'Hullo, who are you?' said the Major. 'Not a good idea to be playing hide-and-seek when there's a shoot about to happen.'

The boy screamed. It was a scream like a power saw through corrugated iron. The Major almost dropped his guns in fright.

'I say, there's no call to go on so,' he said. Overhead, a cloud of ducks flew up like a feathered elevator straight from the pond into the sky.

'Quiet, now,' said the Major, trying for a raised tone of calm authority. 'Let's not frighten the ducks.' The boy's face began to turn purple.

'What's going on?' asked a voice that he recognised from the other side of the hedge. After some rustling, his neighbour, Alice Pierce, pushed her way through, a few twigs catching at the knobby orange and purple yarn flowers that made up an enormous woolly poncho. Beneath the poncho the Major caught a glimpse of wide green trousers over scuffed black sheep-skin boots.

'What are you doing here, Thomas?' she asked the boy as she took him gently by the arm. The boy clapped shut his mouth and pointed at the Major. Alice frowned.

'Thank goodness you're here, Alice,' said the Major. 'He just started screaming for no reason.'

'You don't think a strange man with a pair of huge shotguns might con-stitute a reason, then?' She raised an eyebrow in mock surprise, hugging the boy hard to her ample poncho. The boy whimpered under his breath and the Major hoped he was being comforted rather than suffocated.

'Why aren't you on the bus, Thomas?' Alice asked, and stroked his hair.

'I'm so very sorry, young man,' said the Major. 'I had no intention of frightening you.'

'I didn't know you'd be here, Major,' said Alice. She looked worried.

'What are *you* doing here, Alice?' asked the Major. 'Are you chaperon-ing the children?' He knew she taught a few art classes at the boarding school that Lord Dagenham had been forced to set up at his home for mon-etary reasons.

'Not really,' said Alice, with an obvious vagueness. 'That is to say, I had better get Thomas back to Matron right away.'

There was a further rustling in the hedge and Lord Dagenham and the keeper popped out.

'What the hell was all the racket?' asked Dagenham.

'The Major here frightened Thomas with his guns,' said Alice. 'But it's all right now—we've made friends, haven't we, Thomas?' The boy peeked at the Major from under Alice's arm and stuck out his tongue.

'They were all supposed to be on the bus ten minutes ago,' said Dagenham. 'My guests are arriving now.'

'No harm done,' offered the Major.

'I'm sure it's not as easy as all that,' said Alice, drawing herself up. 'The children are all understandably upset this morning.'

'Good God, I'm giving them a trip to the bowling alley and an ice cream party on the pier,' said Dagenham. 'What on earth are they upset about?'

'They know about the ducks,' she whispered, leading the boy away. 'They're not stupid, you know,' she added in a louder voice.

'There'll be duck soup for dinner,' said Dagenham under his breath. Alice gave him a look of pure poison as she and the boy disappeared through the hedge again. 'I really thought the school would be preferable to a nursing home but I was wrong,' he added. 'Thank God it was only you, Major. Could have been rather embarrassing otherwise.'

'Glad to have headed them off, then,' said the Major, deciding to take Dagenham's remark as a compliment.

'Thought it might be protesters from the damn "Save Our Village" picket line, down the road,' said Dagenham. 'Shall we get along up to the house?'

AS THE THREE MEN EMERGED into the courtyard of the mellow stone Georgian manor house, the Major realised he had obtained his wish. There was a small group of men, drinking coffee and munching on plates of food, and the last of the luxury cars were pulling in at the driveway just in time to see him arriving with both the keeper and the master of the house. The moment would have been perfect, but for two incongruities. One was the old green bus pulling away through the same gates, the windows filled with the glass-squashed faces of small, angry children. The other was the sight of Roger, emerging from someone's car dressed in a stiff new shooting jacket with a small tag still swinging from the hem. Roger did not appear to see his father but busied himself greeting a second car full of guests. The Major gratefully decided not to see Roger, either; he had a vague hope that in the next half-hour Roger's coat and breeches might at least develop a few respectable creases round the elbows and knees.

'Good morning, Major. You will step in and get a cup of tea and a bacon roll before we start, won't you?' The Major found Dagenham's niece at his elbow. She pulled him into the lofty entrance hall, where a buffet table overflowed with pyramids of bacon rolls. A huge tea samovar and several Thermos jugs of coffee were arrayed as if awaiting a crowd several times the size of the gathering party, which looked to number about twenty in all. 'My uncle seems to think it's a bit lavish, given that there'll be a full breakfast after the shooting,' said Gertrude.

'They seem to be tucking in,' said the Major. Indeed, the London bankers were filling up their plates as if they had not eaten in recent days. The Major wondered how they intended to swing a heavy gun barrel on such a full stomach; he accepted only a cup of tea and the smallest bacon roll he could find. As he savoured his roll, a cream-coloured Bentley pulled up at the open door and disgorged Ferguson, the American. The Major ceased to chew as he took in the sight of him shaking hands with some people on the steps. The American was dressed in a shooting jacket of a blinding puce tartan, crossed with lines of green and orange. With this he wore reddish breeches and cream stockings tucked into shiny new boots. He wore a flat shooting cap in too bright a green and a yellow cravat tucked into a cream silk shirt. He resembled a circus barker, thought the Major. There was a momentary hush as he swept into the room; even the bankers paused in their foraging to stare. Ferguson took off his cap and gave a general wave.

'Good morning, all,' he said. He spotted Dagenham and shook the cap at him like a dog showing off with a rabbit. 'I say, Double D, I hope that wasn't our ducks I just saw taking off towards France?' There was a general murmur of laughter round the room as the assembled men seemed to make a group decision to ignore Ferguson's outlandish get-up and return to their small groups of conversation. Dagenham was slightly slower than the rest to wipe the look of astonishment from his face as he shook Ferguson's hand.

'So how d'you like the new duds?' Ferguson gave a half-turn to allow a better view of his outfit. 'I'm reviving the old family tartan.'

The Major swallowed his tea the wrong way and began to choke.

'Ah, there's the Major,' said Ferguson, taking two large strides and sticking out his hand. The Major was forced to control his coughing, move the bacon roll to his saucer, and shake hands all in one move. 'Say, how do you like my neoprene sweat panels?'

'Do they assist one in swimming after the ducks?' asked the Major.

'That's what I love about this guy,' said Ferguson. 'His dry sense of humour. Major, you're an original.'

'Thank you,' said the Major, who could not help but be aware that there were many ears tuned in to the conversation. He felt a vibration of approval in the room. He noticed Roger frowning at an enquiry from an older man. He hoped his son was being asked about the distinguished gentleman who was laughing with Dagenham and Ferguson.

'Speaking of originals, how about giving me a look at those Churchills of yours?' said Ferguson.

'Oh, yes, we're all dying to get a look at the famous Pettigrew Churchills,' said Dagenham. 'Shall we get started, gentlemen?'

The Major, who had dreamed of such a moment for years, found himself surrounded by a small crowd following him out to the temporary rack where they had left their guns. He was offered many hands to shake, not that he had any hope of distinguishing one waxcoated banker from the next, and at one point found himself shaking hands with his own son.

'Father, why didn't you tell me you were so friendly with Frank Ferguson?'

A LINE HAD BEEN ESTABLISHED behind a waist-high hedge that ran along a narrow field to the east of the pond's edge. Thick woods shaded the opposite side of the field. The field itself provided an open flightway for the ducks to the small dew pond, which was fringed on the western side by a straggly copse of trees. As they walked down to the hedge, the Major could see that both the pond and the copse were thick with ducks. Green ropes divided the stands and little wooden stakes showed each man his position. As etiquette demanded, conversation ceased as the men came towards their spots in front of the young men drawn from local farms, who stood ready to act as loaders.

'Good luck,' whispered a nervous Roger, from his own spot near the pond. The Major continued down the line towards the more favoured end, where he found his name on a prime spot next to Ferguson's. He was not altogether pleased by the prospect of having Ferguson's beady eyes fixed on his Churchills all morning. He feared the American might be so crass as to ask to borrow them. The Major nodded at his red-haired young loader and passed him one gun and a box of cartridges.

'Comfy there, are you, Pettigrew?' asked Lord Dagenham, clapping him on the back. 'Show our American friend how it's done, will you?'

As the assembled guns waited quietly, the Major inhaled cold air and felt his spirits soar. The grass of the field had begun to steam in the strengthening sunlight and the adrenaline of the impending sport began to sing in his extremities. He thought of Mrs Ali still tucked up in bed, and allowed himself to imagine striding into her shop at the end of the day, a magnificent rainbow-hued drake spilling from his game bag. It would be a primal offering of food from man to woman and a satisfyingly primitive declaration of intent. However, he mused, one could never be sure these days who would be offended by being handed a dead mallard full of tooth-breaking shot and sticky about the neck with dog saliva.

A loud rattling sound from behind the pond launched the ducks, almost vertically. It was Morris, the keeper, thrashing the inside of an old oil barrel with a cricket bat—an alarm from which all the ducks had been trained to fly. South behind the wood they disappeared, their cries growing faint. The Major loaded cartridges into his gun and as he raised it to his shoulder, he felt as if the whole world were holding its breath.

The sound of ducks began again in the distance and grew until a chorus of calls came in waves down the field, followed by the urgent flapping of wings. The whole squadron curved over the wood and began their descent along the field, heading for their home pond. The first gun barked and soon the entire line was popping at the blur of wings. The Major lost his shot at a fat drake as Ferguson, having missed it, took an extra shot well out of his own line. The Major waited a fraction of a second for the next duck to come by. Sighting at the target he moved his gun smoothly into the lead, squeezed the trigger, and watched with satisfaction as the bird fell dead. Ferguson potted a second duck flying at the lowest limit of what any man would consider a sporting height. The Major swung his own gun high and squeezed off a difficult shot at a bird soaring up and slightly away. The bird fell on the far side of the field and the Major marked it before reaching back to hand his empty weapon to his loader and retrieve his second gun, Bertie's gun. His third shot missed but the gun worked smoothly and felt perfectly balanced in his hands. He thought of how much these guns had meant to his father. He thought of Bertie and how the two of them had perhaps been as separated as these two guns in the last, wasted years. He tracked another duck but did not fire; whether because the flock was thinning out or because he was overcome with strong emotion, he could not say.

A great splashing on the pond indicated that many ducks had made it through the barrage and were quarrelling over their options like politicians. In a matter of a few minutes, Morris would bang the oil can again and send them all aloft to repeat their suicidal mission. Meanwhile the hired youths went out to collect the small bodies and toss them over the hedge to the right gun. The red-haired youth gave the Major a wink as he tossed Ferguson's drake at the Major's feet.

'I think this was actually your kill,' the Major said, picking it up by the neck and handing it to the American.

'Afraid I poached your airspace on that one,' said Ferguson, his face alight with cheer as he took the dead bundle and tossed it in a crate.

'Not a problem. We keep things fairly informal down here,' said the Major, who wished to be polite while also delivering a clear rebuke.

'You'll have to come shoot with me in Scotland in January and show them how to keep it loose,' said Ferguson. 'I've had my own ghillie scream at me in front of my guests for shooting over the line.'

'My father is very knowledgeable about shooting,' said Roger, appearing out of nowhere, and sticking out his hand. 'Roger Pettigrew. I'm with Chelsea Equity Partners. We did an underwrite for you on the Thames effluent plant deal.'

'Oh, one of Crazy Norm's boys,' said Ferguson, shaking hands. 'Well then, I think you're just the man to negotiate my next acquisition for me.'

'I am? I mean, whatever you need,' said Roger, beaming.

'The seller's pretty stubborn,' said Ferguson, grinning at the Major. 'I don't think it's just gonna be about the price.' Roger beamed as if he was being put in charge of buying a small country and the Major was irritated by both of them.

'I think Mr Ferguson is hoping you can persuade me to sell him my guns,' said the Major. 'I can assure you, Mr Ferguson, you'll have Roger's full cooperation on that score.'

'What—oh, of course.' Roger blushed. 'You're the American buyer.'

'I sure hope to be,' said Ferguson. 'Bring me home that deal, son, and I'll make sure Crazy Norm puts you in charge of his entire deal team.'

The cricket bat sounded in the barrel again and in the cacophony of fleeing ducks, men all along the line dropped their conversations abruptly.

'Of course, I would be delighted to help you with anything you need,' said Roger, hovering as Ferguson struggled to stuff cartridges into his gun.

'Roger, get to your position,' said the Major in a terse whisper. 'Talk later.'

'Oh, right, must bag another couple of ducks,' said Roger, hurrying away.

'Here they come,' said the Major.

As the guns were raised and the squawking cloud of ducks wheeled in over the far trees, the Major caught sight of movement at the lower edge of his vision. Refocusing he saw, with horror, that small figures were emerging all along the woods and beginning to run across the field.

'Hold your fire, hold your fire!' shouted the Major. 'Children on the field!' Ferguson pulled his trigger and blasted a duck from the sky. One or two other shots rang out and there were screams from the field as uniformed children ducked and zigzagged. A separate group of people, some carrying signs, came marching, in a flanking action, from the direction of the copse. Alice Pierce, in all her orange and purple glory, broke from the group and began shouting and waving her hands as she ran towards the children.

'Hold your fire!' bellowed the Major again. 'Children on the field!'

'What the devil is going on?' asked Dagenham, from his place in the line. 'Morris, what on earth are they doing?' The gamekeeper gave a signal and the farm hands ran out and began trying to corral the children like unruly sheep. The Major saw a beefy young man tackle a skinny boy to the ground in none too gentle a fashion, and there followed a general cry of outrage from the adults on the field who began chasing the farm youths, jabbing about with their signs like pitchforks. A woman the Major now recognised with horror as Grace flapped at a young man with her sign, which read 'Peace, Not Progress'. Hanging back by the pond stood two figures who the Major was almost sure were the vicar and Daisy. They did not carry signs and they seemed to be arguing with each other.

'Morris, tell those people they're trespassing,' cried Dagenham. 'I want them all arrested.'

'Maybe we should just shoot them,' said a banker somewhere down the line. A chorus of approval followed and one or two levelled their guns.

'Steady there, gentlemen,' said Morris, walking the hedge.

'Too many idiots wanting to shut down our way of life these days!' shouted a loud voice. Someone fired both barrels of his shotgun into the air. There were screams from the field as farm workers and protesters ceased battling to throw themselves to the ground. The Major heard cheers and jeers from along the line of guns. The children continued to wander about, most of them crying.

'Are you quite mad?' shouted the Major. He laid down his gun and began to cross the green ropes, waving his hands and grabbing by the arm men who had not uncocked their guns. 'Put up your guns. Put up your guns.' Morris was doing the same thing from the opposite side of the hedge.

'Morris, I want those trespassers arrested now,' said Dagenham, red in the face with anger. 'Don't just stand there waving, man, get it done.'

'Until these gentlemen put away their guns, I can't hardly be calling the constable,' said Morris. He turned to the field and gave a piercing whistle. 'Come away, boys, leave them children alone now.'

'May I suggest a prompt retreat to the house,' said Ferguson, coming up to Lord Dagenham. 'Cool tempers and so on.'

'I'll be damned if I'll be forced to retreat from my own land,' said Dagenham. 'What the hell is Morris doing?' he added as the gamekeeper headed off to meet his men. The protesters sent up a feeble cheer and began to pick themselves up from the ground.

'If I may agree with Mr Ferguson, returning to the house would not be a question of retreat,' said the Major. 'Completely the moral high ground—ensuring the safety of women and children, and so on.'

'They killed our duckies,' came a wail from a child holding up a bloody carcass.

'Oh, very well,' said Lord Dagenham. 'Everybody down to the house, please. Breakfast is served.' The bankers trotted away, looking grateful for the excuse. The Major saw Roger was at the front of the departing crowd.

'Major Pettigrew, are you there?' came the distinct cry of Alice Pierce, who was advancing on the hedge waving a grubby white handkerchief.

'I'm here, Alice, and so is Lord Dagenham,' said the Major. 'You're quite safe.' Lord Dagenham gave a snort but did not contradict him.

'Oh, Major, the poor children,' she said. 'The matron says they escaped from the bus and she had no idea they were going to come here.'

'Oh, please,' said Lord Dagenham. 'I'll have you all brought up on negligence charges for letting innocent children join in such a riot.'

'Negligence?' said Alice. 'You shot at them.'

'We did not shoot at them,' said Dagenham. 'For God's sake, woman, they ran into the guns. Besides, you're all trespassing.'

'The children are not trespassing; they live here,' said Alice.

Matron hurried up to say that they needed to get the children home right away. 'We stopped only a moment for the picket line,' she said. 'Then Thomas started being sick, so we got out for a minute and before we knew it, they all just ran from the bus and scattered.'

'Someone put them up to it,' said the bus driver, who had just arrived.

'I'll help you get them back in the school,' said Alice to the matron, hurriedly.

'Can't have them in the house. I'm hosting a breakfast for my guests,' said Dagenham, blocking the path. 'Put them back on the bus.'

The Major cleared his throat and caught Dagenham's eye. 'Might I suggest, Lord Dagenham, that you allow the children, under the good care of their matron, to take some food in their rooms and have a rest?'

'Oh, very well,' said Lord Dagenham. 'But for goodness' sake, Matron, take them in the back door and keep them quiet.'

As Alice and the matron escorted the children to the house, Dagenham was surveying the field, where the protesters had begun to advance on the hedge, chanting, 'Don't pillage our village.'

'Where are the police?' said Dagenham. 'I want these people arrested.'

'If it's all the same to you, Double D, better to keep the cops out of it,' said Ferguson. 'That kind of publicity isn't what the project needs right now.' He clapped Dagenham on the back. 'You gave us a dash of excitement. Now come and give us a good breakfast. My guys'll keep 'em away from the house and take plenty of pictures. Generally I find it best to let people protest a bit, then they think they're making a difference.'

'You sound as if you've had plenty of experience,' said the Major.

'Can't build a billion square feet these days without riling up the local hornets' nest,' said Ferguson, oblivious to the slight distaste in the Major's voice. 'I have a whole system of control and containment.'

'Major, you're a good man to have around,' said Dagenham. 'I think, Ferguson, that we should invite the Major to the private briefing after breakfast. You'll stay behind, won't you, Major?'

'I'd be happy to,' said the Major.

'I'm with you on that,' said Ferguson. 'And maybe the Major'd like to have that bright son of his sit in, too?'

As they walked back to the house for breakfast, they passed two security guards dressed in black and sitting in a large black four-by-four. Ferguson nodded and the idling car pulled across to block the path behind them. Containment of the locals had obviously begun.

THE BREAKFAST, eaten in an elegant parlour overlooking the terrace, was hearty, and fuelled by large quantities of Bloody Marys and hot punch. On the long buffet table in the hall, the bacon rolls had been replaced with steaming globes containing bacon, sausage and scrambled eggs, along with an entire side of smoked salmon and a marble board of cold meats and pungent cheeses. The bankers were so loud, outstripping each other in the length and ribaldry of their anecdotes, that there was no disturbance to the party at all from the presence of children overhead.

Gertrude did not sit down to breakfast but stomped in and out checking on the service from the temporary waiters, and shaking hands here and there. After a while she came over and said, 'The villagers in the lane said thank you very much for the ham sandwiches and hot toddies, Uncle.'

'What the devil do you mean sending them food?' asked Dagenham.

'It was Roger Pettigrew, actually, who mentioned that it might be a nice gesture given the earlier confrontation,' she said, smiling down the table towards Roger. Roger raised a glass in her direction.

'Shrewd operators those Pettigrews,' said Ferguson, winking at the Major.

'The constable thought it was a sign of great consideration,' added Gertrude. 'He's down there having a sandwich, and whoever called him is too polite to make any complaints while eating.'

'I told you Gertrude was a smart girl, Ferguson,' said Dagenham.

As breakfast bled on imperceptibly into lunch, and most of the bankers left, Roger came over to the Major. 'I'm to stay for some hush-hush business with Ferguson,' he said. His chest seemed to puff up and the Major thought he might pop with delight. 'Do you have a lift home?' he added.

'I'm invited to stay myself, thank you,' said the Major, careful not to claim credit for Roger's invitation in case it spoiled his son's pleasure.

'Really? I can't imagine you'll understand much of it,' said Roger. 'Stay close to me and I'll explain the technical terms to you if you like.'

'That's exactly what I told Lord Dagenham and his American colleague when they asked me if you should be invited,' said the Major, feeling slightly ashamed that his good intentions had been so quickly abandoned. But he told himself that the fleeting glance of dismay on his son's face was for Roger's own good. 'Shall we join the others?'

THE TABLE in the middle of the old stone dairy wore a lumpy nylon cover, concealing something large and horizontal. The remaining guests were squeezed along the edges of the small room.

'Sorry about the accommodations, gentlemen, but this is more private than the house,' said Lord Dagenham. 'With Mr Ferguson's approval—or should I say with the approval of Lord Ferguson, Laird of Loch Brae'— here Ferguson winked, and waved away the honour with a modesty that did not conceal his delight—'I give you the Twenty-first Century Enclave at Edgecombe.'

He and Ferguson gripped the fabric cover and drew it gently off the table. What was revealed was a model of the village. The Major could see at once the folds and creases of the familiar landscape. He could see the village green and the pub, which seemed to have been painted pale green and to have developed some carbuncular buildings on one side. He could see the lane leading up to Rose Lodge and even pick out his own garden, edged with fuzzy miniature hedges and trees. The village, however, seemed to have sprouted a few too many versions of Dagenham Manor, each identical and sporting a long carriage drive, squares of formal gardens, stable blocks, and even a round pond, complete with five mallards each. There was one such manor in the field behind his own house and another where the bus stop should have been. The bus stop and the main road seemed to have disappeared, removed to the edge of the model, where they disappeared into the farmland. The Major peered closer at the village green, looking for the shop. The plate-glass window was gone and the shop, faintly recognisable behind a new bowed window, was called 'Harris Jones and Sons, Purveyors of Fine Comestibles and Patisserie'. A wicker basket of apples and an old iron dog cart containing pots of flowers stood at the door. A tea shop, a milliner's and a tack and gun shop had been added. The Major felt frozen to the spot.

'In looking to the future of the Dagenham estate,' said Ferguson, 'my good friend Lord Dagenham and I have come up with a vision of the highest-end luxury development, unparalleled in the UK. Taking advantage of the availability of planning permission for new, architecturally significant country estates, my company, St James Homes, will build an entire village of prestigious manor homes and redevelop the village to service those estates.' As he paused to draw breath, the bankers bobbed and squatted to view the tabletop village from closer angles. 'I have info packets for all back in the house, so may I suggest we gather back there to talk numbers as soon as you've finished looking at the model?'

THE MAJOR LINGERED around the model after the last of the bankers had left. Alone with his village, he kept his hands inside his jacket pockets in order to resist the temptation to pluck off all the little manor houses and cover the resulting empty spots by moving round some of the wire-brush trees.

'Cigar?' He turned to find Dagenham at his side.

'Thank you,' he said, accepting a cigar and a light.

'You are, of course, appalled by all this,' said Dagenham matter-of-factly, while squinting at the model like an architect's apprentice.

'It is quite—unexpected,' said the Major in a careful tone.

'I saw your letter to the planning chappie,' said Dagenham. 'I told Ferguson, the Major will be appalled. Fact is, I'm appalled myself.' He looked at the Major with a wry smile. 'Trouble is, even if I were prepared to bury myself here all year round I couldn't save the old place, not long term.'

'I'm sorry?' said the Major.

'Estates like mine are in crisis all over the country,' said Dagenham. His sigh seemed to contain genuine defeat and the Major, watching his profile, saw his jaw tighten and his face grow sad. 'Can't keep up the places on the agricultural subsidies, hunting is banned, and shooting is under attack from all sides as you just saw. We're forced to open tea shops or theme parks or nursing homes or schools, or host rock festivals on the lawn.'

'What about the National Trust?' asked the Major.

'Oh, yes, they used to be there, didn't they? Always hovering, waiting to take one's house away and leave one's heirs with a staff flat in the attic,' said Dagenham, with bitterness in his voice. 'Only now they want a cash endowment, too.' He paused and then added, 'I tell you, Major, very soon the great country families will be wiped out—extinct as the dodo.'

'Britain will be the poorer for it,' said the Major.

'You are a man of great understanding, Major.' Dagenham clapped a hand on the Major's shoulder and looked more animated. 'You may be the only one who can help me explain this to the village.'

'I understand the difficulties, but I'm not sure I can explain how all this luxury development saves what you and I love,' said the Major. 'Won't people be tempted to insist that this is similar to the kind of new-money brashness that is killing England?' He wondered if he had managed to express himself politely enough.

'Ah, that's the beauty of my plan,' said Dagenham. 'This village will be available only to old money. I'm building a refuge for all the country families who are being forced out of their estates by the tax man and the politicians and the EU bureaucrats.' He pointed at a large new barn on the edge of one of the village farms. 'We'll have enough people to maintain a proper hunt kennel and a shared stables here,' he said. 'And over here, behind the existing school, we're going to found a small technical college where we'll teach the locals all the useful skills like stable management, hedging, butlering and estate work so there will be a ready pool of labour. Can you see it?' He straightened a tree by the village green. 'We'll get the kind of shops we really want in the village. Get rid of that dreadful minimart-style shop and add a proper chef at the pub.'

'What about the people who already live here?' asked the Major.

'We'll keep them all,' said Dagenham. 'We want the authenticity.'

'What about Mrs Ali at the shop?' asked the Major. His face felt hot as he asked; he looked very hard at the model to disguise his feelings. Dagenham gave him a considering stare.

'You see, this is just where you might advise me, Major. You are closer to the people than I am and you could help me work out such nuances,' said Dagenham. 'We were looking for the right multicultural element, anyway, and I'm sure we could be flexible wherever you have—shall we say—an interest?' The Major recognised, with a lurch of disappointment, the subtle suggestion of a quid pro quo.

'I assure you none of this is set in stone yet,' continued Dagenham. He laughed and flipped one of the model houses onto its roof with a fingertip. 'Though when it is, it'll be the best white limestone from Lincolnshire.' He picked up the cover from the floor. 'Ferguson doesn't want to reveal anything before we have to.' The Major was grateful to watch the ruined village being swallowed in the tide of grey fabric.

'Is there really no other way?' asked the Major.

Dagenham sighed. 'Maybe if Gertrude weren't so plain, we might have tempted our American friend to the more old-fashioned solution.'

'You mean marriage?' asked the Major.

'Her mother was such a great beauty, you know,' he said. 'But Gertrude's happiest in the stables shovelling manure, and these days men expect their wives to be as dazzling as their mistresses.'

'That's shocking,' said the Major. 'How will they tell them apart?'

'My point exactly,' said Dagenham, missing the Major's hint of irony. 'Shall we go and see if Ferguson has nailed down any offers of financing?'

'They're probably securing houses for themselves,' said the Major as they left. He felt gloomy at the prospect.

'Oh God, no banker is going to be approved to live here,' said Dagenham. 'Though I'm afraid we will have to swallow Ferguson.' He laughed and put an arm round the Major's shoulder. 'Support me in this, Major, and I'll make sure he doesn't end up in the house behind yours!'

Chapter 8

He had planned to bring Mrs Ali a dozen long-stemmed roses, swathed in tissue and a satin bow. But now that he was to pick her up with Grace, at Grace's cottage, the roses seemed inappropriate. He settled for bringing each of them a single rose of an apricot colour on a long brown stem.

Straightening his bow tie and giving a final tug to his dinner jacket, the Major knocked on Grace's front door. It was Mrs Ali who opened it, the light spilling out onto the step around her and her face in partial shadow. She smiled and he thought he detected the shine of lipstick.

'Major, won't you come in,' she said and turned away in a breathless, hurried manner. Her back, receding towards the front room, was partly revealed against the deep swoop of an evening dress. Under a loosely tied chiffon wrap, her bronze skin glowed between the dark stuff of the dress and the low bun at the nape of her neck. In the front room, she half pirouetted on the hearth rug and the folds of the dark-blue silk velvet dress billowed round her ankles and came to rest on the tips of her shoes. The deeply cut décolletage was partially hidden by the sweep of the chiffon wrap, but Mrs Ali's collarbones were exquisitely visible several inches above the neckline. The material fell over a swell of bosom to a loosely gathered midriff where an antique diamond brooch sparkled.

'Is Grace still getting ready, then?' he asked, unable to trust himself to comment on her dress and yet unwilling to look away.

'No, Grace had to go early and help with the set-up. I'm afraid it's just me.' Mrs Ali almost stammered and a girlish blush crept into her cheek-bones. The Major wished he were still a boy, with a boy's impetuous nature. A boy could be forgiven a clumsy attempt to launch a kiss but not, he feared, a man of thinning hair and faded vigour.

'I could not be happier,' said the Major. Being also stuck on the problem of how to handle the two drooping roses in his hand, he held them out.

'Is one of those for Grace? I could put it in a vase for her.' He opened his mouth to say that she looked extremely beautiful and deserved armfuls of roses, but the words were lost in committee somewhere, shuffled aside by the parts of his head that worked full-time on avoiding ridicule.

'Wilted a bit, I'm afraid,' he said. 'Colour's wrong for the dress anyway.'

'Do you like it?' she said. 'I lent Grace an outfit and she insisted that I borrow something of hers in fair trade.'

'Very beautiful,' he said.

'It belonged to Grace's great-aunt, who was considered quite fast and who lived alone in Baden-Baden, she says, with two blind terriers and a succession of lovers.' She looked up anxiously. 'I hope the shawl is enough.'

'You look perfect.'

'I feel quite naked. But Grace told me you always wear a dinner jacket, so I just wanted to wear something to—to go with what you're wearing.' She smiled, and the desire to kiss her welled up in the Major again.

He reached a spontaneous compromise with himself and reached for her hand. He raised it to his lips and closed his eyes while kissing her knuckles.

She smelled of rose water and some spicy clean scent that might, he thought, be lime blossom. When he opened his eyes, her head was turned away, but she did not try to pull her hand from his grasp.

'I hope I have not offended you. Man is rash in the face of beauty.'

'I am not offended,' she said, blushing again. 'But perhaps we had better go to the dance now?'

THE GOLF CLUB had abandoned its usual discreet demeanor and now it blazed and sparkled on its small hill. Lights filled every door and window; floodlights bathed the plain stucco façade and strings of fairy lights danced in trees and bushes.

'Looks like a cruise ship,' said the Major as they walked up the gravel driveway, which was outlined in flaming torches. Rounding a corner, they were startled by a half-naked man in a mask wearing a large python round his neck. A second man capered at the edge of the drive, swallowing small sticks of fire with all the concern of a taxi driver eating chips.

'Good God, it's a circus,' said the Major as they approached the floodlit fountain filled with violently coloured water lilies.

'Mr Rasool has loaned the lilies,' said Mrs Ali. She choked back a giggle.

The Major heard a waltz strike up in the Grill and was relieved that there was to be real music. 'Shall we throw ourselves into the festivities?'

'I suppose that is what comes next,' she said. She did not move, however, but hung back just on the edge of where the lights pooled on the gravel. 'I didn't know I would be so anxious.'

'My dear lady, what is there to fear?' he said, gently taking her hand. 'Except putting the other ladies quite in the shade.' A murmur like the sea swelled from the open doors of the club, where a hundred men were no doubt already jostling for champagne at the long bar, and a hundred women discussed costumes and kissed cheeks. 'It does sound like it's a bit of a crush in there,' he added. 'I'm a little frightened myself.'

'You're making fun of me,' said Mrs Ali. 'I don't even dance,' she said. 'Not in public.' She was trembling, he noticed. She was like a bird under a cat's paw, completely still but singing in every sinew with the need to escape. He dared not let go of her hand.

'Look, it's slightly gaudy and horribly crowded, but there's nothing to be nervous about,' he said. 'Personally I'd be happy to skip it, but I've promised to be there to accept the silly award thing as part of the entertainment.' He stopped, feeling that this was a stupid way to encourage her.

'I don't want to burden you,' she said.

'Then don't make me go in there alone,' he said. 'When they hand me my silver plate, I want to walk back and sit with the most elegant woman in the room.' She gave him a small smile and straightened her back.

'I'm sorry,' she said. 'I don't know why I'm being such a fool.' He tucked his arm under her elbow and she allowed him to lead her up the steps, moving fast enough that she would not have time to change her mind.

THE DOORS to the Grill had been pinned back by two large brass planters containing palm trees. Scarlet fabric looped from the door surround, caught up in swags by gold braid, fat tassels and strings of bamboo beads.

In the centre of the vestibule, Grace was handing out dinner cards and programmes. She was dressed in a long embroidered coat and pyjama bottoms in a deep lilac hue, and her feet were tucked into jewelled sandals. Her hair seemed softer around her jaw than usual, and for once she seemed to have left off the creased caking of face powder she habitually wore.

'Grace, you really look enchanting this evening,' said the Major, and he felt the joy of being able to offer a compliment he actually meant.

'Daisy tried to ruin it with a garland of paper flowers.' Grace appeared to be speaking more to Mrs Ali than him. 'I dumped them in a flowerpot.'

'Good move,' said Mrs Ali. 'You look perfect.'

'So do you,' said Grace. 'I wasn't sure about adding a shawl, but you've made the dress even more seductive, my dear. You look like a queen. Now do go in and let our Grand Vizier announce you.'

Mrs Ali gripped the Major's arm and gave him a smile that was more determination than happiness. As they crossed the Rubicon of the crimson entrance carpet he whispered, 'Grand Vizier—good God, what have they done?'

At the end of the carpet Alec Shaw stood waiting for them, frowning in a large yellow turban. An embroidered silk dressing gown and curly slippers, from which his heels hung out at the back, were complemented by a long braided beard. He looked unhappy.

'Don't speak,' he said, raising an arm. 'You're the last people I'm doing. Daisy can get some other idiot to stand around looking ridiculous. Alma's glued this beard on so tight I may have to shave it off.'

'Perhaps if you soak it in a glass of gin, the glue will soften,' said Mrs Ali.

'Your companion is obviously a lady of intelligence as well as beauty.'

'Mrs Ali, I believe you know Mr Shaw,' said the Major. Mrs Ali nodded, but Alec peered from under the slipping turban as if unsure.

'Good heavens,' he said, and turned a red that clashed with the yellow of his gown. 'I mean, Alma said you were coming, but I would never have recognised you—out of context.' Then, taking up a small brass megaphone he bellowed an announcement over the sound of the orchestra: 'Major Ernest Pettigrew, costumed as the rare Indian subcontinental penguin, accompanied by the exquisite queen of comestibles from Edgecombe St Mary, Mrs Ali.' The orchestra embarked on a choppy segue into its next tune and, as the dancers paused to pick up the new rhythm, many turned their heads to peer at the new arrivals.

The Major nodded and smiled as he scanned the blur of faces. Two couples he knew from the club nodded at him, but then whispered to each other from the sides of their mouths and the Major felt his face flush.

The room was uncomfortably full. To the east, the folding doors had been flung back and the small orchestra sawed away on the stage set against the far wall. Around the edge of the dance floor, people were packed in tight conversational clumps between the dancers and the rows of round tables, each decorated with a centrepiece of yellow flowers and a candle lantern in the shape of a minaret. Waiters squeezed in and out of the jostling crowd, carrying tilting trays of hors d'oeuvres.

Mrs Ali waved to Mrs Rasool, who could be seen dispensing waiters from the kitchen door as if she were sending messengers to and from a battlefield. As they watched, she dispensed Mr Rasool the elder; he wobbled out with a tray held dangerously low and made it no farther than the first set of tables before the tray was picked clean. Mrs Rasool hurried forward and, with practised discretion, pulled him back to the safety of the kitchen.

The Major steered Mrs Ali in a slow circle round the dance floor. As the main bar, next to the kitchen, was invisible behind the battalion of thirsty guests waving for drinks, he had decided to head for a secondary bar, set up in the lee of the stage, hoping that he might then navigate them into the relative quiet of the enclosed sun porch.

A rather unhappy-looking Sadie Khan and her husband, the doctor, were standing at the bar. The doctor was a handsome man with thick short hair and large brown eyes, but his head was slightly small and was stuck well into the air as if the man were afraid of his own shirt collar. He wore a white uniform with a short scarlet cloak, and a close-fitting hat with a military badge. Mrs Khan wore an elaborately embroidered coat and several strands of pearls.

'Jasmina,' said Mrs Khan.

'Saadia,' said Mrs Ali.

'My goodness, Mrs Ali, you look quite ravishing,' said the doctor, giving a low bow.

'Major Pettigrew, may I present my husband, Dr Khan.'

'Delighted,' said the Major, and leaned across to shake Dr Khan's hand.

'Major Pettigrew, I believe we are all to be seated together this evening,' said Sadie. 'Are you at table six?'

'I can't say I know.' He fumbled in his pocket for the card that Grace had handed him and peered with disappointment at the curly 'Six' written on it in green ink.

'Would anyone care for champagne?' said one of Mrs Rasool's catering waiters, who had glided up with a tray of assorted glasses. 'Or the pink stuff is fruit punch,' he added in a quiet voice to Mrs Ali.

'Fruit punch all round, then, and keep 'em coming?' asked the Major. He assumed none of them drank and wanted to be polite, though he wondered how he was to get through the evening on a child's beverage.

'Actually, I'll get another gin and tonic,' said Dr Khan. 'Care to join me, Major?'

'Oh, you naughty men must have your little drink, I know,' said Sadie, smacking her husband's arm lightly with a large alligator clutch bag. 'Do go ahead, Major.' There was a pause as the drinks were poured.

'You must be very excited about the "dance divertissement",' said Sadie at last, waving the thick white programme labelled 'A Night at the Maharajah's Palace Souvenir Journal'. She held it open for the Major to read:

COLONEL PETTIGREW SAVES THE DAY

An interpretive dance performance incorporating historic Mogul folk dance traditions, which tells the true story of the brave stand in which hero Colonel Arthur Pettigrew, of the British Army in India, held off a gang of murderous thugs while stranded on a train, to rescue a local maharajah's youngest wife.

For his heroism, the colonel was awarded a British Order of Merit and personally presented with a pair of fine English sporting guns by the grateful maharajah.

After the dance, a silver tea tray of recognition will be awarded to the family of the late colonel by our distinguished Honorary Event Chair, Lord Daniel Dagenham.

'Relative of yours?' asked Dr Khan.

'My father,' said the Major.

'Such an honour,' said Mrs Khan. 'You must be very thrilled.'

'The whole thing's a bit embarrassing,' said the Major, who could not quell a small bubble of satisfaction.

'It is absurd the fuss they make,' said Mrs Khan. 'My husband is quite appalled at the way they've splashed the sponsors all over the cover.' They all looked at the front cover, where the sponsors were listed in descending type size, beginning with 'St James Executive Homes' in a bold headline and finishing up with a tiny italic reference to 'Premiere League Plastic Surgery'. This last was Dr Khan's practice, the Major surmised.

'Who on earth is "St James Executive Homes"?' asked Dr Khan. The Major did not feel like enlightening him. However, the mystery of the decorative extravagance was now clear: Ferguson had made another shrewd move towards controlling the locals.

A small drumroll interrupted their conversation. Alec Shaw, turban quivering on his head, announced the arrival of the maharajah himself, accompanied by his royal court.

The crowd pressed to the sides of the dance floor as two waiters carrying long banners entered from the lobby. Lord Dagenham and his niece followed behind, dressed in sumptuous purple costumes. Gertrude had obviously been instructed to wave her arms about to display her flowing sleeves, but she clumped down the length of the room as if still wearing wellies. Two lines of dancing girls—the lunch ladies—trudged after them, led by the light-footed Amina in a peacock-blue pyjama costume. She had hidden her hair under a tight satin wrap and though her face, below kohl-ringed eyes, was obscured behind a voluminous chiffon veil, she looked surprisingly beautiful.

Two drummers and a silent sitar player followed the girls, then the fire-eater, and finally a tumbling acrobat, who did a few spins in place to give the procession time to exit through the door stage left.

Lord Dagenham and his niece mounted the stage from opposite sides and came together behind Alec, who gave them a low bow.

'I declare this wonderful evening officially open,' Lord Dagenham said. 'Dinner is served!'

TABLE SIX was placed in a very visible spot along the window side of the dance floor, and towards the middle of the room; the Khans seemed satisfied with their prominence.

Grace arrived at the table and introduced Ferguson's assistant, a dapper American whose name was Sterling. He was wearing a long antique military coat in yellow with black lace and frogging and a black cap.

'What a charming costume,' said Mrs Khan, holding out her hand.

'The Bengal Lancers were apparently a famous Anglo-Indian regiment,' said the young man, pulling at his thighs to display his white jodhpurs. 'Though how they conquered the Empire wearing clown pants is beyond me.'

'From the nation that conquered the West wearing leather chaps and hats made of dead squirrel!' said the Major, extending a hand.

'And where is Mr Ferguson?' asked Grace.

'He likes to come late for security reasons,' said Sterling. 'Keep things low-key.' Just then, Ferguson appeared at the door. He was dressed in a sumptuous military uniform topped with a scarlet cloak trimmed with ermine. Under his left arm he carried a tall cocked hat. Sandy, in a column of dove-grey chiffon, was holding his elbow.

'Oh, look, Major, isn't that Roger coming in with Mr Ferguson?' asked Grace. Indeed he was: buttoned too tight into his grandfather's old army jacket—the Major had wondered why Roger had turned up asking to go into the attic some days earlier—and conversing in an eager terrier manner with Ferguson's broad back. Sandy seemed to be struggling to keep her pale, diplomatic smile.

'Mr Ferguson has quite outdone even our maharajah in magnificence,' said Mrs Khan.

'Isn't it fabulous?' said Grace. 'It's Lord Mountbatten's viceroy uniform.'

'How historically appropriate.' A slight stiffness crept into Mrs Ali's voice. 'You are joking, I hope.'

'Not the real thing, of course,' said Sterling. 'Borrowed it from some BBC production, I think.'

'Major, is that your son playing Mountbatten's man?' asked Dr Khan.

'My son—' began the Major, making a serious attempt to control the urge to splutter. 'My son is dressed as Colonel Arthur Pettigrew, whom he will portray in tonight's entertainment.' There was a small silence round the table. Across the room, Roger continued to shuffle behind Ferguson in a way that did suggest an orderly more than a leader of men.

'Roger looks so handsome in uniform,' said Grace. 'You must be so proud.' She caught Roger's eye and waved. Roger smiled and started across the dance floor towards them.

'So your grandfather was a colonel?' asked Mrs Khan as Roger was introduced. 'How wonderful that you are following the family tradition.'

'Tradition is so important,' added the doctor, shaking hands.

'Actually, Roger works in the City,' said the Major. 'Banking.'

'Though it often feels like we're down in the trenches,' said Roger. 'Earning our scars in the fight against the markets.'

'Banking is so important nowadays,' said Dr Khan, switching gears with the poise of a politician.

'I saw Marjorie,' said the Major, pulling Roger to one side.

'Ferguson invited her, sent her a lovely note apparently, asking her to be his guest. I expect he's looking to pressure her over the guns,' Roger replied.

They watched as Lord Dagenham's table assembled in the centre of the room, after which dinner proceeded as an exercise in barely contained chaos. Waiters forced their way through the aisles as guests wandered from table to table, greeting friends and promoting their own self-importance. Even the Khans, who excused themselves for a cha-cha, were to be seen hovering in the small group round Lord Dagenham. The crowd was so thick that the Major could see Sandy, sitting between Dagenham and Ferguson, signal a waiter to hand her dinner across the expanse of table rather than try to serve over her shoulder. And it soon became clear that the waiters were far too busy pouring wine to bother fetching fruit punch for Mrs Ali, so the Major made a dash for the bar to get her some.

On his way back, the Major paused in a quiet spot behind a palm fern and took a moment to observe Mrs Ali, who sat quite alone, dwarfed by the large expanse of the table. As he watched, Alec Shaw leaned in to talk to her and, to the Major's surprise, she rose from her chair, accepting an invitation to a rather fast foxtrot. As Alec passed his arm about her slender waist, someone slapped the Major's shoulder and demanded his attention.

'Having a good time, Major?' Ferguson was carrying a glass of Scotch and chewing on an unlit cigar. 'I was glad your sister-in-law could make it.'

'I'm sorry—what?' asked the Major, looking at the dancers. She was as light on her feet as he had dreamed, and her dress flew round her like waves.

'She told me all about her plans to take a cruise when she has the money,' Ferguson said.

'What money?' asked the Major. He was torn between a sudden urge to throttle Alec and a small voice that told him to pay attention to Ferguson. With great difficulty, he dragged his eyes from the dance floor.

'You might want to grab those guns quick after the show,' Ferguson continued. 'She did seem very interested to know they were here, and there are plenty of interested buyers around.' He smiled slyly as he moved away.

Dazed, the Major sank back into the shadow of the door's curtain just in time to escape the notice of Daisy, who promenaded by with Alma. She, too, had noticed Alec and Mrs Ali dancing, for she paused and said, 'I see she's ensnared your husband.'

'Oh, doesn't she look pretty,' said Alma. 'I asked Alec to make sure she wasn't left out.'

'I'm just saying that maybe if Grace showed a bit more cleavage, he wouldn't have been led on by more exotic charms.'

'You mean Alec?' asked Alma.

'No, of course I don't mean Alec, you ninny. Let's hope it's just a last fling.'

The two women moved away deeper into the hot, crowded room.

It was a moment before the Major could move; his body was strangely numb. A brief thought that perhaps he should not have invited Mrs Ali to the dance made him ashamed of himself and he instantly changed to being angry at Daisy and Alma for gossiping about Mrs Ali and him.

Returning to the table, he was in time to see Alec depositing Mrs Ali in her seat with a flourish.

'Now, remember what I told you,' said Alec. 'Don't you pay them any attention.' With that he added, 'Your lady is a wonderful dancer, Ernest,' and disappeared to find his dinner.

'What was he talking about?' asked the Major as he set down their drinks and took his seat at her side.

'I think he was trying to be reassuring,' she said, laughing. 'He told me not to worry if some of your friends seemed a bit stiff at first.'

'What friends?' asked the Major.

'Don't you have any?' she asked. 'Then who are all these people?'

'Blessed if I know,' he said and added, 'I didn't think you danced, or I would have asked you myself.'

'Will you ask me now?' she said. 'Or are you going to have seconds of the roast beef?' Mrs Rasool's waiters were circling with vast platters.

'Will you do me the honour?' He led her to the floor as the dance band struck up a slow waltz.

Dancing, the Major thought, was a strange thing. He had forgotten how this vaguely pleasant exercise and social obligation could become something electric when the right woman stepped into one's arms. He felt the small of her back and her smooth palm under his hands, and his body felt a charge that made him stand taller and spin faster than he would have ever thought possible; there were no people beyond the two of them in the gliding circle they made.

A drumroll at the end of the dance and an enthusiastic flashing of the main chandeliers announced the after-dinner entertainment. The Major did his best to navigate Mrs Ali smoothly back to their table.

Once everyone was seated, the lights dimmed and a crash of cymbals gave way to the flat squeal of recorded music and the whistle of a train. In the darkness, a single slide projector lit up a white screen with sepia-toned images of India flickering and cascading almost too fast to register actual scenes. The Major felt a horrible sense of familiarity build until a brief image of himself as a boy, sitting on a small painted elephant, told him that Roger had indeed raided the tin box in the attic and put the family photographs on public display.

A scatter of applause hid the muffled jingling of ankle bells; as the lights came up again a lurid green spotlight revealed the dancers, swaying in time to a train's motion and waving about an assortment of props including baskets, boxes and a number of stuffed chickens. Roger sat on a trunk smoking an absurdly curly pipe as he perused a newspaper, apparently oblivious to the colourful chaos around him. At one end of the ensemble, Amina made flowing gestures towards some wide and distant horizon. With the music, the train whistle and the flickering screen, the Major thought it looked much more effective than he would have imagined.

'It is the End of Empire, end of the line . . .' As Daisy Green's shrill voice narrated the story of the young, unsuspecting British officer returning to his barracks in Lahore on the same train as the beautiful new bride of the maharajah, Amina danced a brief solo, her flowing veils creating arcs of light and movement.

'She's really good, isn't she?' said Grace as a round of applause greeted the end of the solo. 'Like a real ballerina.'

'Of course, only courtesans would have danced,' said Sadie Khan to the table. 'A maharajah's wife would never have so displayed herself.'

'The line is blocked! The line is blocked!' shrieked Daisy. As the dancers stamped their jingling feet and swirled their chickens and baskets with more urgent energy, Roger continued to peruse his newspaper, oblivious. The Major was sure his father would have been quicker to pick up on the change of mood and was tempted to cough, to attract Roger's attention.

'A murderous mob rains terror on the innocent train,' cried Daisy. From all the doorways of the Grill room staggered the hastily recruited boyfriends of the lunch girls, dressed in black and flailing large sticks.

'Oh, dear,' said Grace. 'Perhaps it wasn't a good idea to give them the beer and sandwiches before the performance.'

'I probably would have thought twice about the cudgels,' joked the Major. He looked to Mrs Ali, but she did not smile at his comment. Her face, fixed on the scene, was as pale as alabaster.

As the images flickered ever faster on the screen, the men set about a series of exaggerated slow-motion attacks on the writhing women. The Major frowned at the muffled shrieking and laughter from the dancers, which was not entirely covered by the wailing music. Amina engaged in a frantic dance with two attackers, who did their best to lift her and throw her away whenever she grabbed their arms. At last she broke free and, leaping away, spun right into Roger's lap. Roger raised his head from the newspaper and mimed suitable astonishment.

'The maharajah's wife throws herself upon the protection of the British officer,' said Daisy's voice again. 'He is only one man, but by God he is an Englishman.' A round of cheers broke out in the audience.

'Isn't it exciting?' said Mrs Khan. 'I've got goose bumps.'

'Perhaps it's an allergic reaction,' said Mrs Ali in a mild voice. 'The British Empire may cause that.'

'Disguising the maharani as his own subaltern . . .' continued Daisy. The Major did not want to be critical, but he could not approve of Roger's performance. To begin with, he had assumed a stance more James Bond than British military; furthermore, he was using a pistol, having handed Amina his rifle. The Major thought this an unforgivable tactical error.

The sound of gunshots mingled with the music and the squealing. The spotlights flashed red and the screen went dark.

'When help arrived, the brave colonel, down to his last bullet, still stood guard over the princess,' said Daisy. The lights rose on a mass of inert bodies, both male and female. Only Roger still stood, pistol in hand, the maharani fainting in his arms. Though one or two girls could be seen to be giggling, the Major felt the whole room go quiet, as if everyone were holding their breath. The momentary hush gave way to a burst of applause as the lights went down again.

When the lights rose for the final time, a glittering final tableau featured Lord Dagenham and Gertrude on thrones, Amina at their feet. Alec Shaw, as the vizier, was holding out an open box containing the Churchills; Roger, standing to attention, saluted the royal court.

Then a series of photo flashes exploded in the room, loud Asian pop music with a wailing vocalist blared over the loudspeakers, and, as the audience clapped along, the female dancers broke into a Bollywood-style routine and spread up and down the edges of the dance floor, picking men from the audience to join them in their gyrations. As he blinked his dazzled eyes, the Major became dimly aware of a small man climbing onto the stage, shouting in Urdu and reaching for Daisy Green's microphone.

'Isn't that Rasool's father?' asked Dr Khan. 'What on earth is he doing?'

'I have no idea,' said Mrs Khan. 'This could be a disaster for Najwa.' She sounded very happy.

Mr Rasool Senior had the microphone now and was wagging his finger in the face of a shocked Daisy Green. 'You make a great insult to us,' he shouted. 'You make a mock of a people's suffering.'

'What is he doing?' asked Grace.

'Maybe he is upset that the atrocities of Partition should be reduced to a dinner show,' said Mrs Ali. 'Or maybe he just doesn't like bhangra music.'

'Why would anyone be insulted?' asked Grace. 'It's the Major's family's proudest achievement.'

'I'm so sorry,' said Mrs Ali. She pressed the Major's hand and he flushed with a sudden shame that perhaps she was not apologising to him but for him. 'I must help Najwa's father-in-law—he is not a well man.'

'I can't see why it should be your responsibility,' said Sadie Khan in a malicious voice. 'I think you really should leave it to the staff.' But Mrs Ali had already risen from the table. The Major hesitated, then hurried after her.

'Let go of him before I break your arm,' said a voice from the stage. The Major arrived in time to see Abdul Wahid at the front of a group of waiters, advancing on a couple of the band players, who were holding the senior Mr Rasool by the arms. 'Show some respect for an old man.'

Amina tried to grab Abdul Wahid by the arm, and the Major heard her say, 'What are you doing here? You were supposed to meet me outside.'

'Do not speak to me now,' said Abdul Wahid. 'You have done enough damage.' Dancing couples began to back away from the commotion.

'The old man is crazy,' said Daisy Green in a faint voice. 'Someone call the police.'

'Oh, please, no need to call the police,' said Mrs Rasool, collecting her father-in-law's arm from a scowling trombonist. 'He is only a little confused. His mother and sister died on such a train. Please forgive him.'

'He's a lot less confused than most people here,' said Abdul Wahid.

'He wants you to know that your entertainment is a great insult to him.'

'Who the hell does he think he is?' said Roger. 'It's a true story.'

'Yeah, who asked him?' jeered a voice in the crowd. 'Bloody Pakis.' The waiters swivelled their heads and a pale, thin man ducked behind his wife.

'I say, that's not on,' called out Alec Shaw from underneath his turban.

The Major knew, even as he witnessed the event, that he would be hard-pressed later to relay the details of the fight that now erupted. He saw a short man with large feet shove Abdul Wahid, who fell against one of the waiters. He saw another waiter slap a male dancer across the face with his white arm towel, as if to challenge him to a duel. He heard Daisy Green call out, somewhat hoarsely, 'People, please remain civilised,' as a riot erupted in the middle of the dance floor. Things became a blur as women screamed, men shouted, and bodies hurled themselves at one another.

The fight might have organised itself into something actually dangerous had not someone found the appropriate switch and killed the music. In the sudden quiet, heads popped up from the heaving mass of bodies and punches hesitated in midair. The fight began to lose steam.

'I am terribly sorry,' said Mrs Rasool to Daisy as she and her husband held up the elder Mr Rasool. 'My father-in-law was only six years old when his mother and sister were killed. He didn't mean to cause a fuss.' The old man was as translucent as parchment paper.

'He's ruined everything!' shrieked Daisy.

'He's obviously quite ill,' said Mrs Ali, casting round for an easy exit. 'He needs to get out of here.'

'Mrs Rasool, why don't we squeeze through and bring him to the porch?' said Grace, taking charge. 'It's quieter out there.'

'It's probably dementia, wouldn't you say?' Mrs Khan asked loudly.

'Oh no, Daisy is always that way,' said the Major without thinking.

'I SUPPOSE we call it a night and get a cleaning crew in here,' said Lord Dagenham, surveying the damage. Five or six overturned tables complete with broken dishes, a palm tree cut in half, and curtains down in the entranceway seemed to be the only major damage.

'Nonsense! No one's leaving until we have dessert and then make our presentation to Major Pettigrew,' said Daisy. 'Where is that caterer?'

'I am here and ready to get my team back to work,' said Mrs Rasool, appearing at Daisy's side. 'We will finish the job in the same professional manner we began.' She turned to the waiters. 'Do you hear me, boys? Get straightened up and start resetting those tables, then we'll start the dessert procession. No more nonsense now, please.'

The band gathered and began a particularly objectionable polka; to the Major's surprise, the waiters began to move. There were some muttered words among them, but they obeyed Mrs Rasool, some picking up tables and the rest disappearing out into the kitchen. The lunch girls were less inclined to leave their injured friends, but half of them complied while the others led away their aggrieved warriors to be comforted in the backstage room. The guests began to filter towards the bars, while a groundskeeper two-stepped his way across the dance floor with a huge wet mop.

'Mrs Rasool, you should have been a general,' said the Major, deeply impressed as the room began to assume normality and a parade of lunch ladies entered bearing tiered stands of petits fours.

'Major Pettigrew, my apologies for the disturbance,' said Mrs Rasool. 'The sight of all the dead bodies came as a shock to my father-in-law.'

'Why do you apologise?' said Abdul Wahid, startling the Major, who had not seen him approach. 'He spoke nothing but the truth. They should be apologising to him for making a mockery of our land's deepest tragedy.'

'You have no right to call it a mockery,' said Amina angrily. 'I worked like crazy to make a real story out of this piece.'

'Abdul Wahid, I think you should take Amina home now,' said Mrs Ali. Abdul Wahid looked as if he had plenty more to say, and Amina hesitated. 'Both of you will leave now. We will not discuss this further,' added Mrs Ali, and the steel in her tone caused them to do as she said.

'Look here, normally I'd say the show must go on,' said Lord Dagenham. 'But maybe we just drop it and avoid any further controversy? Give the Major his tray on the quiet.'

'That would be fine with me,' said the Major.

'Nonsense!' said Daisy.

'If you let an old man's aspersions drive you from the stage, people may think there is some kind of truth to his view,' said Ferguson. 'But if there is a picture of us all in the paper with that silver tray, then this dance will have been a big success and the contretemps never happened.'

'So let's get the tray and the guns, and round up the dancers,' agreed Dagenham. 'Then we make sure we include the doctor and his wife here, and Mrs Ali who looks so lovely, and we'll have a fine story.'

'I will not appear in the picture,' said Mrs Ali firmly. 'I am disinclined to be paraded for authenticity.'

'Oh, how very tiresome,' said Daisy Green. 'It really isn't polite to come to our party and then complain about everything.'

'There's no need to be rude,' said Grace. 'Mrs Ali is my good friend.'

'Well, Grace, that should tell you that you need to get out more,' said Daisy. 'Next you'll be having the gardener in for tea.'

There was an instant of stunned silence and the Major felt compelled to interject a rebuke. 'I think Grace is entitled to have anyone she likes to tea,' he said. 'And it's no business of yours to tell her otherwise.'

'Of course you do,' said Daisy with an unpleasant smile. 'We are all aware of your proclivities.'

The Major felt despair strike him like a blow to the ear. He had defended the wrong woman. Moreover, he had encouraged Daisy to further insult.

'Major, I wish to go home,' said Mrs Ali in an unsteady voice. She looked at him with the smallest of painful smiles. 'My nephew can drive me. You must stay for your award.'

'Oh, no, I insist,' he said.

'You can't leave now, Dad,' said Roger, in an urgent whisper. 'It would be the height of rudeness to Dagenham.'

'At least let me walk you out,' said the Major as Mrs Ali walked away.

Out in the cold night, the stars were abundant in a way that increased the pain of the moment. Mrs Ali paused on the top step and the Major stood at her shoulder, mute with humiliation at his own foolishness.

'I made a mess of everything, didn't I?' he said. Below them, Amina and Abdul were arguing as they walked down the driveway. Mrs Ali sighed.

'I was in danger of doing the same,' she said. 'Now I see what I must do. I must put an end to the family squabbling and see those two settled.'

'Then may I come and see you tomorrow?' he asked.

'I think not,' she said. 'I think I shall be busy, preparing to go to my husband's family.'

'You can't be serious. Just like that? What about our Sunday readings?'

'I will think of you whenever I read Mr Kipling, Major,' she said, with a sad smile. 'Thank you for trying to be my friend.' She offered her hand and he again put it to his lips. After a few moments, she tugged it gently away and stepped down to the driveway.

'Go back to your party, Major,' she said. 'You'll catch cold standing in the dark.' She hurried down the driveway and as she disappeared, blue dress into deep night, he knew he was a fool. Yet at that moment, he could not find a way to be a different man.

Chapter 9

Mrs Ali left the village. The Major did not see her go. He had meant to visit her, but his anger and despair at having made such a mess of the evening seemed to help bring on the full-blown cold she had so carelessly predicted, and he lay in bed for three days. As he dozed in rumpled pyjamas, Mrs Ali went north to her husband's family and, by the time he was well enough to walk down to the village, it was too late.

The Major put his head down and prepared to battle through the tinsel storm that passed for Christmas now. Holiday preparations seemed to elbow aside all other concerns in the village. Even the campaign against St James Homes seemed to be muted and the 'Save our Village' posters that had sprung up after the shooting party were hardly noticeable amid all the flashing fairy lights and lurid lawn displays of inflatable Santas.

At the village shop, which the Major had avoided for as long as possible, Christmas decorations helped obliterate any trace of Mrs Ali. There were none of her homemade samosas next to the packaged meat pies in the cold case. The large caddies of loose tea behind the counter had been replaced by a display of chocolate assortment boxes of a size guaranteed to cause acute happiness followed by acute gastric distress. The modest, hand-wrapped gift baskets had been replaced by large, cheap, commercial baskets painted in garish colours and crowned with yellow cellophane. The Major stood staring at the poor things until a hard-featured old woman who was knitting behind the counter asked him if he wanted to buy one.

'Good heavens no, no, thank you,' he said. The old woman glared at him without a pause in the furious clicking of her needles. Abdul Wahid, appearing from the back, greeted him rather coldly and introduced the woman as his great-aunt.

'Pleased to meet you,' lied the Major. She inclined her head, but her smile retracted itself almost at once.

'She doesn't speak much English,' said Abdul Wahid. 'We have only just persuaded her to retire here from Pakistan.' He retrieved a bag from under the counter. 'I am glad you came in. I have been asked to return something to you.' The Major looked in the bag and saw the little volume of Kipling poetry that he had lent to Mrs Ali.

'How is Mrs Ali?' asked the Major, and the aunt released a torrent of language at Abdul Wahid, who nodded, then smiled apologetically.

'We are all very nicely settled, thank you,' he said and his voice continued to brick up a barrier of cold and indifference between them. 'Is there anything I can get for you this morning, Major?'

'Oh, I don't need anything, thank you,' said the Major. 'I just popped in to—er—see the decorations.'

'I will not forget your hospitality this autumn, Major,' said Abdul Wahid. His voice at last offered some hint of recognition, but it was combined with an unanswerable finality, as if the Major were also planning on leaving the village for ever. 'You were very kind to extend your assistance to my family and we hope you will continue to be a valued customer.' The Major felt his sinuses contract and tears begin to well at the loss of connection even to this strange and intense young man. He dug in his pocket for a handkerchief and blew his nose loudly, apologising for his lingering cold. The aunt and Abdul Wahid both drew back from the invisible menace of his germs and he was able to escape the shop without embarrassing himself.

CHRISTMAS WAS STILL PRESENT, he hoped, in the church, where he went one morning to lend some carved wooden camels for the crib by the altar, as his father had begun doing many years ago.

The church was blissfully bare of any manufactured decoration. The simple crib was supplemented by two brass urns of holly flanking the altar and an arrangement of white roses draping the font. Still tired from his cold, the Major dropped into the front pew for a few moments of quiet reflection.

The vicar, emerging from the sacristy with a handful of leaflets, gave a small start—almost a hesitation—and then walked over to shake hands.

'Brought the dromedaries, I see,' he said and sat down. The Major said nothing but watched the sunlight pour across the ancient flagstone floor. 'Glad to see you out and about,' the vicar went on. 'We heard you were laid up after the dance, and Daisy kept meaning to check on you.'

'Entirely unnecessary and so no apologies required,' said the Major.

'Bit of a shambles, that dance,' said the vicar. 'Daisy was very upset.'

'Was she?' said the Major in a dry tone.

'Oh, she worries about everyone so much, you know.' The vicar took an obvious deep breath, then said, 'We heard that Mrs Ali has moved away to be with family?' His eyes were nervous and probing.

'That's what I'm told.' The Major felt a choke of misery rise into his voice.

'It's good to be with family,' said the vicar. 'Among your own people.'

'We could have been her people,' said the Major in a low voice. There was a silence as the vicar shifted his bottom on the hard pew. He opened his mouth a few times, to no effect. Then he set his hands in his lap and looked at the Major directly.

'Look, I know you feel you've lost—a friend,' said the vicar, hesitating over the word, as if the Major had been engaged in a steamy affair. 'But it's for the best, believe me.'

'What are you saying?'

'Nothing, really. All I'm trying to tell you is that I see people get into these relationships—different backgrounds, different faiths, and so on—as if it's not a big issue. They want the church's blessing and off they go into the sunset as if everything will be easy.'

'Perhaps they're willing to endure the hostility of the uninformed.'

'Oh, they are,' said the vicar. 'Until it turns out the hostility is from Mother, or Granny cuts them out of the will, or friends forget to invite them to some event. Then they come crying to me.' He looked anguished.

'I've never heard you talk like this, Christopher,' said the Major.

'Might as well get it all on the table, then, Ernest,' he said. 'My wife was in tears after that stupid dance. She feels that she may have been unkind.' He stopped and they both understood that this admission, while pathetically short of the mark, was nonetheless extraordinary coming from Daisy.

'I am not the one to whom any apology is owed,' said the Major at last.

'That will be the burden my wife will have to bear,' said the vicar. 'But as I told her, the best way to prove our remorse is not to compound the injustice with a lie.' He looked at the Major with a determination in his tightened jaw that the Major had never seen. 'Therefore I will not sit here and pretend that I wish things had turned out differently.'

The silence seemed to reach to the very walls of the sanctuary and hum against the rose window. Neither man moved. The Major supposed he should feel angry, but he felt only drained.

'I've upset you,' said the vicar at last, rising from the pew.

'I will not pretend that you haven't,' said the Major.

'I thought you deserved honesty,' said the vicar. 'People never speak of it directly, but you know that these things are difficult in a small community.'

'I take it, then, that you won't be giving a sermon on this subject of theological incompatibility?' asked the Major. He felt no rage, only a calm and icy distance, as if this man, who had been both a friend and an adviser, was now talking to him on a bad phone line from an ice floe in the Arctic.

'Of course not,' said the vicar. 'Since the Bishop's office did market research on the devastating impact of negative or unduly stern sermons on the collection plate, we're all under orders to stick with the positive.'

'Well, since we're being candid, I'd rather welcome a stern sermon, vicar, since what you usually deliver puts me to sleep.' He was gratified to see the vicar flush even as he kept a smile fixed on his face. 'I thought your honesty deserved reciprocity,' he added.

Upon leaving the church, the Major found himself walking towards the lane on which Grace lived. He felt an urgent need to talk over his sense of permanent estrangement from the vicar, and he felt cautiously optimistic that Grace would share his sense of outrage. At her front door, he paused, remembering the night of the dance and how everything had seemed possible in the sparkling hours of anticipation. After he rang the bell, he placed his fingertips on the door and closed his eyes as if he might conjure Jasmina in her midnight-blue dress, but the door stayed stubbornly real and the hall behind it now sounded with Grace's footsteps. She would give him tea and agree with him that the vicar was being absurd and she would talk to him about Jasmina and be sorry that she was gone. In return, he now decided, he would invite her to join him at Roger's cottage for Christmas dinner.

'What a nice surprise, Major,' Grace said as she opened the door. 'I hope you're feeling better?'

'I feel as if the entire village is against me,' he burst out.

'Well then, you had better come in and have a cup of tea,' she said. She did not bother to pretend she did not understand what he meant. As he stepped into her narrow hallway, he was very glad that England still created her particular brand of sensible woman.

The Major, with Grace's complete agreement, decided that he would look more ridiculous, and be more talked about, if he avoided the village shop, so he continued to pop in though every visit was painful. Amina, who worked during school hours, had lost the spiky tufts from her hair and no longer wore bright colours or wild footwear. She maintained a subdued, noncommittal tone when Abdul Wahid's ancient auntie was around.

'How's little George?' he asked during a moment when she was alone. 'I never see him.'

'He's fine,' she said, ringing up his bag of cakes and two oranges. 'Two kids were mean to him his first day at school and there was a rumour that one family was taking their kids out.'

'You seem very accepting.' Where had her usual prickliness gone?

She looked at him squarely, and for a moment her eyes flashed with the old anger. 'Look, we all make our own beds,' she said in a low voice. 'George lives here now, and he has a father who makes a solid living in his own business.' She looked round to check the shop was empty. 'If that means biting my tongue and not chewing the heads off the customers, well, I know what I have to do.'

'I'm sorry,' he said, feeling a little nibbled.

'But as soon as we're married, I'm going to make Abdul Wahid send that old bat home. She gives me the creeps.'

'You don't get along?' asked the Major.

'They say she was a midwife in her village. But if you ask me, I think that's code for some kind of witch.' Anger burned in her dark eyes. 'If she pinches George one more time, I'm going to slap her silly.'

'Do you ever hear from Mrs Ali—Jasmina?' he asked, desperate to bring her name into the conversation. 'Perhaps she might return to help you.'

Amina hesitated, but then said in a rush, 'They say if Jasmina doesn't like where she is, she'll go to Pakistan and live with her sister.'

'But she never wanted to go to Pakistan,' said the Major, appalled.

'I can't say for sure. It's not really my place to get involved.' Here Amina looked away with what the Major took to be a consciousness of guilt.

'Your happiness was important to her,' said the Major, hoping to suggest a similar responsibility in Amina.

'You can't reduce life to something as simple as happiness,' she said. 'There's always some bloody compromise to be made—like having to work in a godawful shop for the rest of your life.'

'I admire your tenacity, young lady,' he said, turning towards the door. 'You are the kind of person who will succeed in making your own happiness. George is a lucky boy.'

When he got home to Rose Cottage, the Major glanced at the little book of Kipling poems, which he had left on the mantelpiece. There had been no note tucked inside (he had shaken out the pages in hope of some brief parting message) and it was foolish to keep it out as if it were a talisman. He would put it away, and then later he would pop over to Little Puddleton and buy Grace a Christmas present and call in on Roger and let him know he would be bringing a guest for Christmas dinner.

HE THOUGHT for a moment that Roger and Sandy were not home. A single lamp burned in the window of Apple cottage, but the front hall was dark and no flicker of television or sound of a stereo gave any sign of life.

The Major knocked anyway and was surprised to hear the scraping of a chair and feet in the passage. Several bolts were drawn and the door opened to reveal Sandy, dressed in jeans and a white sweater. She seemed pale and unhappy. Her skin was scrubbed bare of make-up, and her hair escaped in wisps from the rolled-up scarf she wore as a headband.

'Come on in,' she said, letting him into the warm hallway. 'Roger didn't tell me you were coming over.' She gave him a hug, which he found disconcerting but not unpleasant.

'He didn't know,' said the Major, hanging up his coat on a hook made from some bleached animal bone. 'Spur-of-the-moment visit.'

'Roger's not here,' she said. 'But you and I can have a drink, can't we?'

'A dry sherry would be welcome,' he said, advancing into a very sparsely furnished living room. He stopped in his tracks to peer at a giant, black, bottle brush that he supposed must be a Christmas tree. It reached the ceiling and was decorated only with silver balls. It glowed in waves of blue light from the fibre-optic tips of its many branches.

'Good heavens, is it Christmas in Hades?' he asked.

'Roger insisted. It's considered very chic. I was prepared to go more traditional down here, but since it cost a fortune and it'll be out of fashion by next year, I threw it in the car and brought it down with me.'

'I am usually all in favour of domestic economy,' he said doubtfully as she poured him a large sherry.

'Yeah, yeah, it's hideous.'

'Perhaps you can rent it out in the spring to clean chimneys?'

'I'm sorry we didn't get the chance to have you over before.' She waved him to the low white leather couch. 'Roger wanted everything to be done before he showed it off.' Her voice was low and uninflected and the Major worried about whether she was feeling unwell. She poured herself a large glass of red wine and curled her long legs onto a metal chaise that seemed to be covered in horse skin.

The Major looked around. 'Saves on the dusting I suppose, keeping things minimal,' he said. 'The floors look very clean.'

'We scraped off seven layers of linoleum and sanded off so much varnish, I thought we were going right through the boards,' she said, looking at the pale honey of the wide planks.

'It's a lot of effort for a rented place.' The Major had wanted to say something more complimentary and was annoyed that the same old critical language had come from his lips. 'I mean, I hope you get to keep it.'

To his surprise, she started crying. The tears ran down her cheeks in silence as she cupped one hand over her face and turned away towards the fire. The Major could see misery in the hunch of her back and the shadowed edge of her frail collarbones. He put his glass very quietly on the coffee table before speaking.

'Something is the matter,' he said. 'Where is Roger?'

'He's gone to the party at the manor house.' Bitterness clipped her words short. 'I told him he should go if that's what he wanted, and he went.'

The Major considered this as he shifted his weight on the uncomfortable leather. It was never wise to get sucked into taking sides when a couple were having a domestic squabble, but he feared, in this case, that his son must be at fault, if such a self-possessed woman had been reduced to the fragility of glass.

'What can I do to help you?' he asked, removing a clean handkerchief from his breast pocket and offering it to her. 'Can I get you some water?'

'Thank you.' She took the handkerchief to wipe her face with slow measured strokes. 'I'll be fine in a minute. Sorry to act so stupid.'

When he came back from the kitchen, she looked strained but controlled. She drank as if she had been thirsty for a while.

'Feeling any better?' he asked.

'Yes, thank you. Sorry to put you in such a position. I promise not to start telling you everything that's wrong with your son.'

'Whatever he's done, I'm sure he'll be sorry directly,' said the Major. 'I mean, it's Christmas Eve.'

'It won't matter, anyway. I won't be here when he gets back,' she said. 'I was just packing a couple of boxes of my stuff to be sent on later.'

'You're leaving?' he said.

'I'm driving back to London tonight and flying home tomorrow.'

'But you can't leave now,' he said. 'It's Christmas. Can't you stay and work things out? I thought you were—fond of each other,' he said, choosing to tread lightly over any mention of love or marriage.

'We are.' She looked round her, not at the stylish furnishings but at the heavy beams and the smooth floor and the old slats of the kitchen door. 'I just forgot what we started out to do, and I got kinda carried away with the thought of this place.' She turned away again and her voice trembled.

'You have no idea, Major, how hard it is to keep up with the world some-times—just to keep up with ourselves. I guess I let myself dream I could get out for a while.' She wiped her eyes again and stood up and smoothed her sweater. 'A cottage in the country is a dangerous dream, Major. Now, if you don't mind, I'd better finish my packing.'

'Is there nothing I can do to fix this?' asked the Major. 'Can I go and fetch him home? My son is an idiot in many respects, but I know he cares for you and—well, if you let him go, then we have to let you go and that's three of us made all the lonelier.' He felt as if he were being left behind on the dock while all around him others chose to embark on journeys without him.

'No, don't go after him,' she said. 'It's all decided. We both need to get back to doing what we do.' She held out her hand and as he took it, she leaned in to kiss him on both cheeks.

'I hope you find a way to be happy in the world one day,' he said.

'I hope you find someone to cook your turkey. You do know not to rely on Roger, right?'

THE MAJOR AWOKE on Christmas morning with a feeling that the day was to be a low point of his world, an Antarctic of the spirit. Getting out of bed, he went to the window and leaned his head against the cold glass to look at the dark drizzle over the garden. It did not seem like a day to rejoice in a birth that had promised the world a new path to the Lord.

The morning began with the awkward question of how early to tele-phone Roger. It had to be done soon, because he had no idea how large a bird Roger and Sandy might have purchased. Hazarding a guess that they would have been intimidated by anything over fifteen pounds, he waited until the last possible moment, eight thirty, to pick up the phone. He had to redial two more times before a hoarse voice answered.

'Hurro,' whispered the ghost of Roger, voice desiccated and distant.

'Roger, have you put the turkey in yet?'

'Hurro,' came the voice again. 'Who, who the . . . what day is it?'

'It's Christmas Day and it's already past eight thirty,' said the Major. 'You must get up and put on the turkey, Roger.'

'I think it's in the garden,' said Roger. The Major heard a faint retching and held the phone away from his ear in disgust.

'Roger?'

'I think I threw the turkey out of the window,' said Roger. 'Or maybe I threw it through the window. There's a big draught in here.'

'So go and fetch it,' said the Major.

'She left me, Dad.' Roger's voice was now a thin wail. 'She wasn't here when I got home.' The Major heard a sniffling sound from the phone and was annoyed to feel rising in his chest a sense of compassion for his son.

'I know all about it,' said the Major. 'Take a hot bath and some aspirin and get into clean clothes. I'll come and take over.'

HE CALLED GRACE, just to let her know he would drive over and pick her up at noon as arranged. But after he had sketched briefly what had happened, mostly in case she would like to withdraw from the festivities, she insisted on going with him to Roger's to help prepare the dinner.

A few hours later the Major was sipping a glass of champagne and staring out the window of Roger's kitchen at the wilting garden. Behind him, a large saucepan jiggled its lid as the pudding simmered; Grace was straining gravy through a sieve. The turkey, rescued from under the hedge, was missing a wing but, well washed and stuffed lightly with brown bread and chestnuts, it was now turning a satisfying caramel colour atop a pan of roasting vegetables. Roger was asleep again; the Major had peeked in and seen him, hair sticking up all over and mouth open on the pillow.

'It was lucky you had a spare pudding.' The Major had searched Roger's cupboards but found only assorted nuts and a large bag of biscotti.

'Thank my niece for always sending me a hamper instead of visiting,' said Grace, lifting her glass of champagne. She had brought a large tote bag filled with the pick of the hamper and had already spread crackers with smoked oysters, tipped cranberry sauce into a cut-glass dish, and set the Cornish cream to chill on the scullery windowsill. The Major had even managed to work out how to use Roger's stereo system, which was now playing a Christmas concert performed by the Vienna Boys' Choir.

The Major did not have to go and wake his son: the phone rang and he heard Roger pick it up. He was putting the finishing touches to the table, while Grace was busy in the kitchen, when Roger appeared, neatly dressed in a navy sweater and slacks and smoothing down his hair.

'Thought I heard you earlier,' said Roger, looking with some queasiness at the table. 'You didn't make dinner, did you?'

'Grace and I made it together,' said the Major. 'Are you up for champagne, or would you like a plain club soda?'

'Nothing for me just yet,' said Roger. 'I can't really face it.' He shifted from foot to foot in the manner of a hovering waiter. 'Only the thing is,

I didn't realise you'd be going to all this trouble.' He was looking out of the window now and the Major felt a slow but familiar sinking feeling. 'I thought it was all cancelled.'

'Look, if you can't manage to eat, just sit and relax and maybe later you'll feel like having a turkey sandwich.' Even as he said this, the Major felt as if Roger was slipping away from him somehow. There was a look of absence in his eyes and the way he stood, balanced on the balls of his feet, suggested that either Roger or the room was about to shift sideways. A small car pulled up outside, the top of its roof only just visible over the gate.

'It's just that Gertrude is here to pick me up,' said Roger. 'I was awfully cut up about the row with Sandy, you see, and Gertrude was so understanding . . .' He trailed off. The Major, feeling rage stiffen the sinews of his neck and choke his speech, said quietly, 'Grace has made you Christmas dinner.'

At that moment, Grace came in from the kitchen.

'Oh, hello, Roger, how do you feel?' she asked.

'Not too bad,' said Roger. 'I'm very grateful about the dinner, Grace, only I don't think I could eat a thing right now.' He looked out of the window and waved at Gertrude. 'My father didn't tell me you were here, you see, and I promised Gertrude I'd go to the manor and play bridge.' A faint redness about the ears told the Major that Roger knew he was behaving badly.

'You can't go,' said the Major. 'Out of the question.'

'I wouldn't go if Grace wasn't here to keep you company.' Roger went round the couch, took Grace's hand, and gave her a loud kiss on the cheek. 'You and Grace deserve to enjoy a nice dinner together without me groaning in the background.' He dropped her hand and sidled towards the hallway. 'I'll be back in a few hours, tops.' With that, he disappeared into the hall and the Major heard the front door open.

'Roger, you're being an ass,' said the Major, hurrying after him.

'Make sure you leave me all the cleaning up,' said Roger, waving from the gate. With that he jumped in Gertrude's car and they drove away.

'That's it,' said the Major, stamping his way back into the living room. 'I am done with that young man. He is no longer my son.'

'Oh, dear,' said Grace. 'I expect he is very unhappy and not thinking straight. Don't be too hard on him.'

'That boy hasn't thought straight since puberty,' he said acidly. 'What say you we wrap the food in foil and organise a relocation to Rose Lodge, where we can have a real fire, a small but living Christmas tree, and a nice dinner for the two of us?'

'That would be lovely,' said Grace. 'Only perhaps we should leave something here for Roger when he returns?'

'I'll leave him a note suggesting he find the turkey's other wing,' said the Major darkly. 'It'll be like dinner and party games all in one.'

SOON AFTER the New Year, the Major admitted to himself that he was in danger of succumbing to the inevitability of Grace. Their relationship had developed a gravitational pull, slow but insistent, as a planet pulls home a failing satellite. After their Christmas dinner, at which he offered a profusion both of champagne and apologies, he had accepted her invitation to 'just a quiet, early supper' on New Year's Eve and invited her to tea twice in return.

Tonight, however, would be the second time this week he had been asked to dinner at her house and had accepted. This, he realised, merited closer examination of his own intentions.

After a meal of steamed haddock and buttered potatoes he sat in an armchair while she clattered dishes and made tea in her small kitchen. She would not let him help, and it was difficult to make conversation through the small pine-shuttered hatch in the wall, so he dozed, hypnotised by the fierce blue cones of the gas fire's flames.

'Anyway, Amina says Jasmina's not coming to the wedding,' said Grace through the hatch.

He raised his eyes abruptly, knowing that he had heard but not registered a much longer sentence of which this was merely the footnote. 'I'm sorry,' he said. 'I couldn't hear.'

'I said I met Amina and little George at the mobile library this morning, and she told me Jasmina's not coming to the wedding. Such a pity, I really hoped to see her,' said Grace. 'When she wrote to me, I wrote back right away and asked her to please come and see me.' The Major could hear the dishwasher being set into operation.

'She wrote to you?' he asked the room at large. Grace did not answer at first, being engaged with manoeuvring a silver tea tray too large for her narrow, sharp-cornered hallway. He went to the door and received the tray from her, angled to squeeze in at the doorjambs.

'Yes. She wrote to me right after she left and apologised for running off without saying goodbye. I wrote back, and I sent a Christmas card, but I haven't heard from her since. Have you heard from her?' she asked as he concentrated on placing the tray on the coffee table.

'I never heard from her,' he said.

'It's all a bit strange,' she said, and, after a long moment of quiet, 'You still miss her.'

'I'm sorry?' he asked, fumbling for a suitable reply.

'You miss her,' repeated Grace, her eyes firmly fixed on his. His own gaze wavered. 'You are not happy.'

'It is a moot point,' he said. 'She made her choice very clear.'

'I have a feeling she is not happy where she is,' said Grace. 'You and Roger should look in on her on your way to Scotland. Didn't you say you're going up for some shooting with Frank Ferguson?'

'It's not my place to interfere,' he said.

'It's a pity you can't just storm in and fetch her back,' said Grace. 'She could be your very own damsel in distress.'

'Life is not a Hollywood film,' he snapped. He wondered why on earth she was pushing at him like this. Couldn't she tell he was ready to declare his affection for her? 'I didn't come here tonight to talk about Mrs Ali,' he said. 'She made her choice and it is high time I moved on and made some choices of my own. Do come and sit down, dear Grace.' He patted the armchair next to his and she came over and sat down.

'I would like you to be happy, Ernest,' she said. 'We all deserve that.'

He took her hand and patted the back of it. 'You are very good to me, Grace,' he said. 'You are intelligent, attractive and supportive. You are kind and not a gossip. Any man would be happy to call you his own.'

She laughed, but her eyes seemed to be brimming. 'Oh, Ernest, you just listed the perfect qualities in a neighbour and the worst possible qualifications for passion.' He was shocked for an instant by the word 'passion', which seemed to crash through several conversational boundaries at once.

'At our age, surely there are better things to sustain a marriage, than the brief flame of passion?'

A tear made its way down Grace's cheek and he thought that she looked quite beautiful, even in the overly bright room.

'You are mistaken, Ernest,' she said at last. 'Without passion, two people living together may be lonelier than if they lived quite alone.' Her voice had a gentle finality, yet some contrary spirit made him stubborn in the face of what he knew to be true.

'I came here tonight to offer you my companionship,' he said. 'I had hoped it would lead to more.'

'I will not have you, Ernest,' she said. 'I care for you very much, but I won't compromise the rest of my years.' She wiped her eyes with the back of her hand, like a child, and smiled. 'You should go after her.'

'She will not have me either,' he said, and his gloom betrayed the truth of everything Grace had said.

'You won't know that if you don't ask her, will you?' said Grace. 'I'll go and get you her address.'

TELLING ROGER that the journey to Scotland would include a detour to visit Mrs Ali was not the sort of thing one could successfully manage on the telephone. So, on the Sunday before the shoot, the Major tapped lightly on the door at Roger's cottage. There was a frost, and the sun was only a vague promise in the midmorning sky; he blew on his hands and stamped his feet against the cold.

He tapped again, the sound reverberating like a pistol shot, then heard footsteps, banging and a muttered curse before Roger opened the door wrapped in flannel pyjamas.

'Aren't you up?' asked the Major, feeling cross. 'It's eleven o'clock.'

'Sorry, bit of a hangover,' said Roger, leaving the door wide open and trailing back into the living room, where he collapsed onto the couch. 'What are you up so early for, anyway?'

The Major explained, in as vague a way as possible, that he needed to leave earlier on Thursday in order to visit a friend on the way to Scotland and so he would need Roger to be up with the dawn.

'Not a problem,' said Roger.

'Considering the difficulty I just had in rousing you from your slumbers at eleven o'clock,' said the Major, 'I'll need some more reassurance.'

'It's not a problem because I'm not going to drive up with you,' said Roger. 'Gertrude's going up early and she wants me to go with her.'

'You're going with Gertrude?' asked the Major.

'I ordered a picnic for the trip,' said Roger. 'I'm going to whip out my hamper of mini pasties and duck confit and seal the deal with a split of chilled champagne.' He rubbed his hands with anticipatory glee. 'Nothing like a road trip to advance romantic activities.'

'But you asked to drive up with me. I was counting on two drivers so we wouldn't have to stop. And besides, don't you think it's unconscionably soon to be pursuing another woman? Sandy's only just left.'

'She made her choice,' said Roger. The Major recognised, with a rueful smile, that his son's words sounded familiar. 'I'm not going to let the grass grow,' he added. 'Mark to market and move on, as we say about a bad deal.'

'Sometimes it's a mistake to let them go, my boy,' said the Major. 'Sometimes you have to go after them.'

'Not this time, Dad,' said Roger. He looked at his father with some hesitation and then lowered his head, and the Major understood that his son did not believe he welcomed awkward confidences.

'I would like to know what happened,' he said.

'I screwed it all up and I didn't even know it,' said Roger. 'How was I supposed to know what she wanted if she didn't know herself?'

'What did she want?'

'I think she wanted to get married, but she didn't say.'

'And now it's too late?'

When Roger spoke again, his usual bravado was replaced with a note of seriousness. 'We had a little mishap. No big deal. We agreed on how to handle it. I went with her to the clinic and everything.'

'A clinic?' The Major could not bring himself to ask more plainly.

'Don't make a face like that,' said Roger. 'It's absolutely acceptable these days—woman's right to choose and all that. It's what she wanted.' He paused. 'Well, we talked about it and she agreed. I mean, it was the responsible thing to do at this stage of our careers.'

'When was this?' asked the Major.

'We found out right after the dance,' said Roger. 'Took care of it before we came down for Christmas, and she never told me she didn't want to go through with it.'

'You are not the first man to miss a woman's more subtle communication,' said the Major. 'They think they are waving when we see only the calm sea, and pretty soon everybody drowns.'

'Exactly. I think,' said Roger, and then he added, 'I asked her to marry me, you know. On Christmas Eve, before the party at Dagenham's. I felt bad about the whole thing and I was prepared to move our plans along.' He tried to sound nonchalant, but a crack in his voice betrayed him. 'I mean, I told her maybe we could even try again next year, if I got promoted through this Ferguson deal.' He sighed and his eyes assumed a dreamy look that might have been emotion. 'Maybe a boy first, not that you can really control these things. I told her we could use the little bedroom here as a nursery and then maybe build on a playroom.' He looked with confusion at the Major. 'She slapped me, and screamed that I'm so shallow that only a minnow would drown in my depths. What does that even mean?'

The Major wished he had known, coming upon Sandy in the darkened house that night. He might have really done something then. Was it his fault that Roger had the perceptiveness of concrete, he wondered. 'I think perhaps your timing was not sensitive, Roger,' he said.

'Anyway, who needs that kind of drama,' said Roger. 'I've had plenty of time to consider and now I'm serious about making a go of things with Gertrude.' He looked more cheerful. 'There's a lot of mileage in leveraging an old country name like hers, and she's always adored me. Under the right conditions, I might be prepared to make her very happy.'

'You can't negotiate love like a commercial transaction,' said the Major, appalled. 'If you don't feel any real passion for Gertrude, don't shackle yourselves together. You'll only be dooming both of you to a life of loneliness.' He smiled wryly to hear himself repeating Grace's words as his own.

As he was preparing to leave, Roger suddenly asked him, 'Where are you diving off to, anyway? Who's this friend you're off to visit?'

'Just someone who relocated up north.'

'It's that woman again,' said Roger, narrowing his eyes.

'Her name is Jasmina Ali,' replied the Major. 'Please show enough respect to remember her name.'

'What are you doing, Dad?' said Roger. 'Wasn't the golf club fiasco enough to warn you off? She's a bad idea.'

'Receiving romantic advice from you is a bad, if not horrendous, idea. Spending an hour dropping in on an old friend is a good idea and also none of your business.'

'Old friend, my arse,' said Roger. 'I saw how you looked at her at the dance. Everyone could see you were ready to make a fool of yourself.'

'And "everyone" disapproved, of course,' said the Major. 'No doubt because she is a woman of colour.'

'Not at all,' said Roger. 'As the club secretary mentioned to me in private, it's not remotely a question of colour but merely that the club doesn't currently have any members who are in trade.'

'The club and its members can go to hell,' said the Major, spluttering in anger. 'I'll be glad to watch them throw me out.'

'My God, you're in love with her.' Roger rolled his eyes. 'What on earth would Mother think about you chasing all over England after some shopgirl?'

The Major felt a rage unlike anything he had felt towards his son before.

'If you say "shopgirl" ever again, I shall punch you,' said the Major. 'And speaking of your mother, you were there when she begged me not to remain alone if I found someone to care for.'

'She was dying,' said Roger. 'She begged you to marry again and you swore you wouldn't. Personally, I was furious that we wasted so much valuable time on deathbed promises both of you knew were untenable.'

'Your mother was the most generous of women,' the Major said. 'She meant what she said.' They were silent for a moment and the Major wondered whether Roger was also smelling again the carbolic and the roses on the bedside table and seeing Nancy's face, grown as thin and beautiful as a painted medieval saint, with only her eyes still burning with life. He had struggled in those last hours, as had she, to find words that were not the merest of platitudes. Words had failed him in the awful face of death, which seemed so near and yet so impossible.

'Are you all right, Dad? I didn't mean to be harsh,' said Roger, bringing him blinking to his senses.

He focused his eyes and braced one hand on the back of Roger's couch. 'Your mother is gone, Roger,' he said. 'Your uncle Bertie is gone. I don't think I should waste any more time.'

'Maybe you're right, Dad,' said Roger. He seemed to think for a moment, then held out his hand. 'Look, I wish you luck with your lady friend,' he said. 'Now, how about you wish me luck at Ferguson's shoot? You know how much this deal means to me.'

'I appreciate the gesture,' said the Major, shaking hands. 'It means a lot to me. I do wish you luck, son. I'll do what I can to support you up there.'

'I was hoping you'd say that,' said Roger. 'Since I'm going up early, there may be some wildfowling, Gertrude says. So how about letting me take up the Churchills?'

As the Major drove away from Roger's cottage, leaving his gun box with his delighted son, he had a sinking feeling that he had been manipulated once again.

THE MAJOR STOOD on the doorstep of the Ali family's semidetached house, which had a small two-seater sports car parked on the drive, quite certain that today would be a disaster. What if Mrs Ali wasn't even home? The siren call of Ferguson's castle in Scotland and shooting in the heather almost made him make a run back to his car. A young man passed slowly on a bicycle, chewing gum and staring at him. The Major nodded and, feeling too embarrassed to shuffle away, turned back to knock at the door.

A young pregnant woman answered. Her face was attractive but blunt, and bore more than a passing resemblance to Abdul Wahid's.

'Yes?' she said.

'Good afternoon, I'm Major Ernest Pettigrew. I'm here to see Mrs Ali,' said the Major in his most authoritative tone.

'Are you from the council?' said the woman.

'Good heavens, no,' said the Major. 'I'm a friend of Mrs Ali's.'

'My mother's stepped out to the shop,' said the woman. 'Do you want to wait?' She did not open the door further or step aside as she said this.

'Oh, I don't want your mother,' said the Major, understanding her mistake. 'I'm here to see Mrs Jasmina Ali, from Edgecombe St Mary.'

'Oh, her,' said the woman. 'You'd better come in and I'll phone my dad.'

'Is she here?' asked the Major as he was shown into the kind of spare, formal front room that is kept exclusively for guests. Two sofas faced each other across the small gas fireplace, each dressed in crimson flocked silk in a pattern of roses. Good-quality fabric blinds hung at the bay window; opposite the window, frosted French doors led to another room. The room's finest decorative feature was an oriental rug, a glorious riot of pattern hand-woven from a thousand different blue silks.

'I'll get you some tea,' said the woman. 'Please wait here.' She left, shutting the door behind her. The Major sat down and the silence in the room settled round him. The street noises were muffled through the double glazing and no clock ticked on the mantel. There was not even a television, though he seemed to hear the jingling of a game show coming from deeper in the house.

He stood up when the door to the hall opened. It was the young woman, coming back with a brass tea tray that held a teapot and two glasses set in silver cup holders.

'My father will be home right away,' said the young woman, indicating that the Major should sit. She poured him a cup of tea. Then, instead of pouring one for herself, she left, shutting the door again behind her.

A few more silent minutes passed, then, all at once, there was a key in the front door and movement in the hallway. Urgent voices and fierce whispers accompanied the usual hallway noise of coats and shoes being deposited.

The door opened again to admit a broad-shouldered man with black cropped hair and a neat moustache. He wore a shirt and tie and his breast pocket bore a name tag that identified him, unexpectedly, as Dave.

'Major Pettigrew? I'm Dave Ali and it's an honour to have you in my humble home,' he said in a tone that, the Major had observed over the years, was used by those who believe their home superior to most. 'I have heard all about you from my son, who considers himself greatly in your debt.'

'Oh, not at all,' said the Major, finding himself waved back to his seat and offered more tea. 'Your son is a very intense young man.'

'He is impetuous. He is stubborn. He makes his mother and me crazy,' said Dave, shaking his head in mock despair. 'I tell her I was the same at his age, but she tells me I had her to whip me into shape, while Abdul Wahid— well, *insha'Allah,* he, too, will find his way once he is married.'

'We were all looking forward to seeing Jasmina—Mrs Ali—when she came for the wedding,' said the Major.

'Yes, I'm sure,' said Dave in a noncommittal voice.

'She has many friends in the village,' said the Major, pressing him.

'I'm afraid she will not be coming,' said Dave Ali. 'My wife and I are going in the Triumph and can barely fit our luggage. And then someone must take care of my mother, who is very frail, and Sheena is due any day.'

'I appreciate that there are difficulties,' the Major began. 'But surely, something as important as a wedding . . .?'

'My wife, who is the soul of kindness, said, "Oh, Jasmina should go and I will stay with Mummi and Sheena," but I ask you, Major, should a mother miss her only son's wedding?'

'I suppose not,' agreed the Major.

'Besides, we feel it is important for our Jasmina to make a clean break with the past if she is to be happy in her future.'

'A clean break?' asked the Major. Dave Ali sighed and shook his head in what appeared to be pity.

'She insisted on taking on a large burden when my brother died,' he said slowly. 'A burden no woman should carry. And now we want only for her to lay down such responsibilities and allow us to take care of her.'

'That is very generous of you,' said the Major.

'In time we hope she will learn to be content here in the heart of family. She is already indispensable to my mother and she is reading the Qur'an to her every day.'

'She is used to a certain independence,' the Major said.

Dave shrugged. 'She is coming round. She has stopped suggesting to my poor wife new ways to run our inventory systems. Instead, she is obsessed with getting her own library card.'

'A library card?' asked the Major.

'If she wants one, I tell her she is welcome to it. We are very busy right now, what with the wedding and opening a SuperCentre next month, but my wife has promised to help her establish proof of her residency and then she will be able to sit home and read all day.'

They were interrupted by a commotion in the hallway, and the Major heard a familiar voice cry out, 'This is ridiculous. I will go in, if I please,' and then the door opened and there she was, Mrs Ali, still wearing a coat and scarf and carrying a small bag of groceries. Her cheeks were flushed, either from the argument or from having been outside, and she looked at him as if she were hungry to see all of him at once.

'It is you,' she said. 'I saw a hat in the hallway and I knew it was yours.'

'We did not know you were back from your errands,' said Dave.

'I had to come and see you,' said the Major. He wanted desperately to take her hand but he restrained the impulse.

'I was just telling the Major how much you enjoy your reading,' said Dave. 'My brother used to tell me, Major, how Jasmina was always buried in reading. "So what if I have to do a little more so she can read. She is an intellectual," he would say. I'm only sorry he worked himself so hard.'

'That is despicable even for you,' said Mrs Ali in a low voice. 'Sheena told me you had a business meeting.'

'Sheena is very cautious,' said Mr Ali, addressing the Major.

'Grace wanted me to come and see you,' the Major said to Mrs Ali. 'I think she was expecting you to write.'

'But I did write, several times,' she said. 'I see I was right to worry when I received no reply.' She gave her brother-in-law a look of disdain. 'Is this not strange, Dawid?'

'Shocking, shocking—the post office is very bad these days,' agreed her brother-in-law, pursing his lips as if he did not like being addressed by his real name in front of an outsider. 'And I speak as someone who has three sub-post offices. We can only put the mail in the bag, but after that . . .'

'I would like to talk to the Major alone,' said Mrs Ali. 'Should we speak here, or should I take him on a walk to show him the neighbourhood?'

'Here will be fine, just fine,' said Dawid Ali in a hurried tone. He went to the frosted doors and slid them open. In the back room, a television played low and an old lady sat slumped in a wing chair. The Major saw her black eyes swivel towards them. 'If you don't mind, I will not ask Mummi to turn out of her chair.'

'I don't need a chaperone,' said Mrs Ali in a fierce whisper.

'Of course not,' said Dawid. 'Don't worry,' he added to the Major, 'she's as deaf as a post.'

'I must thank you for your hospitality,' said the Major.

'I doubt we'll see you again, clean break and all that,' said Dawid Ali, holding out his hand. 'It was a pleasure to meet such an acquaintance of my brother and an honour that you should come so far out of your way.'

AFTER DAWID ALI had left the back room, the Major and Mrs Ali moved as far away as possible from the open doors and sat on a bench in the bay window.

'I feel like I'm just dreaming that you're here,' she said.

'I don't think they'd like it if I pinched you,' he replied. They sat in silence for a moment.

'That stupid dance,' he said at last. 'I never got the chance to apologise.'

'I do not blame you for the rudeness of others,' she said.

'But you left,' he said. 'Without saying goodbye.' She looked out of the window and he took the opportunity to study again the curve of her cheek and the thick lashes of her brown eyes.

'I had allowed myself to daydream.' She smiled at him. 'I woke up to find myself a practical woman once more.' Her smile faded. 'I threw in my lot with the Ali family a great many years ago and I realised it was time to pay that debt.'

'When you sent back the Kipling, I thought you despised me.' He was aware that he sounded like a wounded child.

'Sent it back?' she asked. 'But I lost it in the move.'

'Abdul Wahid handed it to me,' he said, feeling confused.

'I thought it was in my small bag with all my other valuables, but after I got here I couldn't find it.' Her eyes widened. 'She must have stolen it.'

'Who?'

'My mother-in-law, Dawid's mother,' she said, nodding towards the back room. The Major tried to share her outrage, but he was too happy to discover that she had not meant to return his book.

'Your letters go missing, you are kept from your nephew's wedding, you are asked to leave your home,' he said. 'You cannot stay here, my dear lady. I cannot allow it.'

'What would you have me do?' she said. 'I must give up the shop, for George's sake.'

'If you'll allow me, I will take you away from here right now, today,' he said. 'Under any conditions you like.' He turned and took both her hands in his. 'Simply tell me what I have to do to get you out of this room and take you somewhere where you can breathe. And do not insult me by pretending that you are not suffocating in this house.' His own breath came heavy now, his heart seeming to knock about in his chest like a trapped bird. She turned on him eyes wet with tears.

'Are we to run away to that little cottage we once talked about? Where no one knows us and we send only cryptic postcards to the world? I should like to go there now and be done with everyone for a while,' she said.

He gripped her hands tightly and did not turn when he heard a wail from the old lady, gabbling in Urdu and calling, 'Dawid! Come quick!'

'Let's go now,' he said. 'I shall take you there, and if you want we'll stay for ever. I promise, whatever happens, I will not abandon you.'

'I will go with you,' she said. She got up and picked up the bag of groceries. 'We must leave now, before they try to stop me.'

'Shouldn't you pack a bag?' he asked, flustered for a moment by the transformation of a momentary passion into cool reality.

'If we stop now, I will never leave here,' she said. 'It is too sensible to stay. Am I not to help with dinner and then read the Qur'an aloud? Is it not raining in England?' It was in fact now raining, and the fat drops splattered on the window like tears.

'I am expected in Scotland,' he said. He had forgotten all about the shoot and now, glancing at his watch, he saw that he would likely not make it in time for dinner. He turned to see her teetering on her feet. At any moment she would sink onto the bench and the madness of running away would be gone. He recognised the tiny moment before his failure would be understood and accepted. He hung in the space of the room. Feet pounded in the hall. Then the Major leaned forward, reached out a hand, and fastened it round her wrist, hard. 'Let's go now,' he said.

Chapter 10

The old fishing lodge belonged to his former CO, Colonel Preston, who was wheelchair-bound now with a combination of Alzheimer's and neuropathy of the legs. The Major had phoned the Colonel's wife, Helena, who had told him that the key was under the stone hedgehog by the shed and that the paraffin lamps were kept in the washtub for safety. Helena had been graciously uncurious about his sudden need to use it.

The lodge was more a tumble-down sheep shed, its thick stone walls topped with a crooked slate roof and its original openings crudely filled with an assortment of odd windows and doors, salvaged from other properties. The front door was heavy oak and carved with acorns and a medallion of leaves, but the neighbouring window was a ramshackle blue casement, with missing glass in one of the panes.

The light had all but gone from behind the mountains looming in the west, and a gibbous moon was making its humpbacked way into the sky. Below the lodge, a rough lawn led down to a narrow cove on a lake that seemed to open out like a sea in the darkness. The Major was about to embark on a grid-by-grid search for the stone hedgehog, when it occurred to him that the broken window might allow entry.

It was cold now and Mrs Ali stood shivering in her thin wool coat, the tail of her scarf flapping in a sharp wind off the lake. She had her eyes closed and breathed deeply.

'Cold enough for a frost tonight,' he said. He moved towards her, worrying that she was horrified at the state of the place. 'Perhaps we ought to go back to the village we passed and see if there's a bed and breakfast?'

'Oh, no, it's just so beautiful here,' she said.

'I don't know if you'll feel that way if we find squirrels in there,' he said, worried about the broken casement. He tightened his grip on the pencil-thin torch he had extracted from its place in his car's glove compartment. 'I suppose we'd better mount an expedition to the interior.'

He was able to reach the lock through the broken window; he pushed open the door and stepped into the deeper cold of the lodge. The torch gave only a thin bluish beam that danced over glimpses of table and chairs, a wicker sofa and an iron sink with cotton-curtained cabinets. A large fireplace loomed sooty and dark in one corner, smelling of damp coal. An arched opening showed the briefest glimpse of a bedroom. Through another strange arrangement—one patio slider and one French door jumbled together—the lake shone silver, and a broad triangle of moonlight fell across the floor showing large baskets stuffed with fishing gear, dropped as casually as if the owner were going out on the lake again directly. The Major found matches in a tin on the mantelpiece, and, in the low-ceilinged laundry room past the sink area, the promised zinc washtub filled with three paraffin lamps.

'I hope you're not expecting this place to look any better in the light,' he said as he struck a match and lit the nearest lamp.

She laughed and said, 'I haven't smelled a paraffin lamp since I was a small child. My father would tell us how it was discovered by an alchemist in ninth-century Baghdad who was trying to distill gold.'

'I thought it was a Scotsman who invented it,' said the Major, burning his thumb and dropping the match as he fumbled with the second lamp. 'But then the most amazing things were being made in the east while we were still getting the hang of wattle and daub and trying to find our runaway sheep.' He struck a new match. 'Unfortunately, none of it counted in the end unless you got your patents in ahead of the Americans.'

WITH THE LAMPS offering their wavering yellow light and a coal fire leaping in the hearth, the room began to lose its damp crypt smell.

'It's quite charming in here if one squints.' He was opening a bottle of claret that had been meant as a gift to his Scottish host.

'Luckily I bought some food,' Jasmina said, looking in the shopping bag. 'I didn't know what I was doing at the time, but apparently I'm making us a chicken balti.'

The rickety stove was powered by a rusty tank of bottled gas just outside the kitchen window. 'The dust seems to be years thick. I'll have to wipe everything before using it.'

'The owner has been frail for a couple of years now,' said the Major, looking at the assembled fly rods on the wall. 'I doubt he'll ever visit here again.' He walked to the hearth and tested the water heater built into the chimney with the back of his hand. He stood with his back to the blaze and sipped wine from a mug, looking at how her hands chopped tomatoes with a smooth twist and fall of the knife, and how she cocked her head in concentration.

'Pity, really; he talks about this place as if it was the most important place in the world to him. On some days, days that his wife thinks are bad but which perhaps are good, my friend is quite convinced that he is back here,' said the Major.

'So he dreams himself the life he cannot have?'

'Exactly. But we, who can do anything, we refuse to live our dreams on the basis that they are not practical. So tell me, who is to be pitied more?'

'There are real-life complications,' she said, laughing. 'Can you imagine if the whole world decided tomorrow to move to a fishing lodge in the English countryside?'

'It's Wales, actually,' said the Major. 'And they do get a bit funny if there are too many visitors.'

THEY ATE the chicken balti, mopping up the sauce with sweet almond rolls, and when they had finished he gave her the nicer of his two pairs of pyjamas, navy cotton piped in white, as well as his camel robe and a pair of wool socks for her feet. He was glad he had packed the extra set after all. Nancy had often chided him for what she called his meticulous overpacking and his insistence on carrying a hard-sided leather bag for all trips.

From a separate compartment, the Major produced a leather wash kit and, with some embarrassment at the intimacy, laid out soap, shampoo, toothpaste and a small Egyptian cotton towel.

'I'll just run out to the car,' he said. 'I have an extra toothbrush in my breakdown kit.'

'Along with a barrel of brandy and a spare Shakespeare?' she asked.

'You're laughing at me,' he said. 'But if I didn't have a blanket in the car I'd be pretty cold tonight on that couch.' He thought she blushed, but it might have been the candle flickering on her skin.

WHEN HE RETURNED she was dressed in his pyjamas and robe and was combing out her hair with his small, inadequate comb. The wool socks flopped round her slender ankles. The Major felt his breath falter and a new tension vibrate through his limbs.

'It's a very uncomfortable couch,' she said. Her eyes were dark in the lamplight and as she raised her arms to flip her hair back, he was aware of the curves of her body against the smooth cotton of the borrowed pyjamas and the soft robe.

'Lucky thing the blanket is cashmere. I'll be perfectly comfortable,' he said, trying to keep his composure.

'You must at least take back your robe.' She stood and slid the robe off her shoulders and the Major found this so sensual that he dug his fingertips into his palms to keep the heat from rising in his face and body.

'Very kind of you.' Panic threatened to overwhelm him just from being close to her. He backed away towards the bedroom and the tiny bathroom beyond. 'I'd better say good night now.'

'It's so beautiful I'd like to lie awake and watch the moon on the water all night,' she said, advancing on the bedroom.

'Much better to get some rest,' he said. He stumbled away from her, found the bathroom door with some effort, and clawed his way in, wondering just how long he might have to hide out in the bathroom pretending to wash before she would be safely asleep.

THE SOAP AND WATER revived him and also made him feel foolish. 'At your age you should be perfectly able to share a small cottage with a member of the opposite sex without getting all carried away like a pimply teenager,' he lectured the face in the dim mirror. He resolved to march through to the sitting room, uttering a cheery good night as he went, and to allow no more nonsense from himself.

As he walked out into the small bedroom, carrying the lamp, she was sitting up in bed with her knees hugged to her chest and her hair spilling round her shoulders. When she looked up at him, he could see her eyes shining at him.

'I was thinking about being practical,' she said. 'Thinking of how everything is uncertain once we get back to the world.'

'Do we have to think of that?' he asked.

'So I was wondering whether it might be best if you just made love to me now, here, while we're enjoying this particular dream,' she said. She looked at him with a steady gaze and he saw his ache for her echoed in the high colour of her cheeks. There was no panic or fluster in his mind now. He would not diminish her declaration by asking her if she was sure. He merely hung the lamp on a hook in the beamed ceiling and went down on his knees at the bedside to take both her hands in his and kiss them, backs and palms. As he lifted his face to hers, he found words suddenly irrelevant and so he said nothing at all.

IN THE EARLY MORNING, he stood with a foot raised on a smooth granite boulder by the empty lake and watched the sun dazzle on the frosted reeds and melt the lace of ice on the muddy edge. It was bitterly cold, but he felt the sear of air in his nose as something exquisite and he lifted his face to the sky to feel the warmth of the sun. The mountains across the lake wore capes of snow on their massive rocky shoulders, and Mount Snowdon pierced the blue sky with its sharp white ridges. A lone bird, falcon or eagle, with fringed edges to its proud wings, glided high on the faintest of thermals, surveying its kingdom. The Major raised his own arms to the air, stretching with his fingertips, and wondered whether the bird's heart was as full as his own as he braced his legs against an earth made new and young. A pleasant glow, deep in his gut, was all that remained of a night that seemed to have burned away the years from his back.

He looked back to the lodge, which slept under eaves crusted with ice. A lazy curl of smoke rose from the chimney. He had left her asleep, sprawled on her stomach, her hair in knots and her arms flung carelessly round her pillow. Too full of energy to remain in bed, he had, as silently as possible, dressed, built up the fire, and set a kettle of water over a low flame so it would boil slowly while he took a walk.

As he gazed, the French door was pushed open and Jasmina came out of the house, squinting at the brightness. She had dressed and was carrying two mugs of tea, which steamed in the air. Smiling under her tangle of hair, she picked her way carefully down the stony path, while he held his breath as if the slightest move might cause her to shy away.

'You should have woken me,' she said.

'I needed to do a little capering about,' he said. 'Some beating of the chest and a spot of cheering—manly stuff.'

'Oh, do show me,' she said, laughing while he executed a few half-remembered dance steps, jumped on and off a tussock of grass and kicked at a large stone with a wild hooting. At the sound of his yelling, a flight of hidden ducks launched themselves into the air and she laughed and waved as they flew low across the water. Then she turned and kissed him while he spread his arms wide and tried to keep his balance.

They found two large rocks to sit on and slowly savoured their tea and munched on the last two, slightly stale almond rolls as the lake lapped at their feet and the sky flung its blue parachute over their heads. He thought then how wonderful it was that life was, after all, more simple than he had ever imagined.

FOR THE FIRST TIME EVER, the drive back to Edgecombe did not seem like the drive home. Instead it seemed that the closer they got, the more his hopes sank and his stomach tightened, squeezing bile he could taste. He had promised to get Jasmina home for the wedding and they had risen early, before the dawn, rather than go back the night before.

'I do hope Najwa has remembered to get me the clothes.' She had called on her mobile phone and arranged to have Mrs Rasool let the family know she was coming to the wedding and to have a complete set of suitable clothes waiting for her. 'She is very upset with my sister-in-law, who keeps changing the dinner menu, so she is very happy to know that we will add a pinch of subversion to the feast.'

'Are you sure I should come with you?' he asked. 'I'd hate to be their excuse to back out.'

'Najwa has arranged it so we can wait until we see the imam arrive before we go in,' she said. 'Then they will not be able to make a fuss. It will drive them all crazy, which will be of great satisfaction to me, but they will get their final papers signed and the shop will belong to Abdul Wahid, so what can they do?'

They took a small back lane into the village. Rose Lodge looked welcoming in the pale sunshine and they hurried inside to avoid being seen by the neighbours.

There was a still-warm teapot on the kitchen table, together with the remains of a ham sandwich and the day's newspaper.

'Someone's been here,' said the Major in some alarm, and he looked round for the poker, intending to check the whole house for intruders.

'Hullo, hullo,' said a voice from the passageway and Roger appeared with a plate of toast and a tea mug. 'Oh, it's you,' he said. 'You could have let me know you were coming. I'd have cleared up.'

'I should have let you know?' asked the Major. 'This is my house. Why on earth aren't you in Scotland?'

'I felt like coming home,' said Roger. 'But I suppose I shan't be welcome here any more.' He glared at Jasmina.

'Your welcome here will depend entirely on your own ability to keep a civil tongue in your head,' said the Major, angrily. 'I don't have time for your petulance today. Mrs Ali and I have a wedding to attend.'

'I don't suppose it matters to you that my life is in ruins,' said Roger.

'Why don't you sit down?' said the Major, examining the contents of the teapot to see whether it was still fresh. 'Then we'll have some tea and you can quickly tell Jasmina and me all about it.'

'It's Jasmina now, is it?' said Roger as the Major poured tea and handed round the cups. 'I can't believe my father has a lady friend—at his age.'

'I refuse to be referred to by a term so oily with double entendre,' said Jasmina, as she hung her coat on one of the pegs by the back door and came to sit at the table. 'I prefer "lover",' she said.

The Major choked on his tea and Roger actually laughed. 'Well, that'll make the village speechless,' he said.

'Which would be truly wonderful,' she said, and sipped her tea.

'Forget about us,' said the Major. 'What happened in Scotland, and where are my guns? Did you sell them?'

'No, I did not sell them,' Roger said. 'I told Ferguson where he could shove his all-cash offer and I brought them home on the train.'

'You came on the train? What about Gertrude?'

'Oh, she drove me to the station,' said Roger. 'It was quite an affecting goodbye, considering she had just refused to marry me.'

'You asked her to marry you?'

'I did,' said Roger. 'Unfortunately, I was the second bidder and my terms were not up to par. She's going to marry Ferguson.'

The Major listened in some disbelief as Roger told them how Gertrude had quite won the day in Scotland. It sounded as if she had taken over the place, even getting the head ghillie to agree to a restocking plan for the grouse moor. She had found a new cook at short notice through the ghillie's wife, and together they had produced a bountiful menu of feasts and lunches such as Loch Brae Castle had not seen for years. She strode round in her boots and her mackintosh like she'd been living there for ever, and she had got more done in a week than Ferguson had been able to get his workers to do in a year.

'I suppose it was just her competence,' said Roger miserably, 'but she seemed to get prettier as the week went on. It was positively weird. And after a few days, Ferguson took to following her around.'

'She found the right setting,' said the Major. 'A place where she belongs.' He could see her quite clearly walking thigh-deep in heather, her paleness perfect for the misty-grey light of the north, the slight stockiness of her figure perfectly proportioned for the low, rugged landscape.

'I really blew it,' said Roger. 'I should have got in right away, but she was so besotted with me I thought I could take all the time I wanted.'

'And she fell in love with someone else,' said the Major. 'I did warn you love was not to be negotiated.'

'Oh, they're not in love. That's what stings,' said Roger. 'It's a mutual under-standing. She gets to stay in the country and run the estates, and he gets the acceptance he was looking for.' He sighed. 'It's quite brilliant, actually.'

'What about my guns?' asked the Major.

'I told Ferguson he couldn't have them,' Roger said. 'He got the girl. He cancelled the Edgecombe deal like he was cancelling an order for curtains. Now he's marrying Gertrude, he fancies a long line of his heirs being lords of the manor here.' Roger sniffed. 'Suddenly it's sacred ground and to be protected at all costs.'

'But he already has a title,' said Jasmina.

'A Scottish title isn't really the same thing at all,' the Major said.

'Especially when you buy it over the Internet,' added Roger.

'I can't believe it,' said the Major. 'This is wonderful news.'

'Glad you're happy,' said Roger. 'But what about me? I was going to get a big fat bonus out of being in charge of this deal, but right now I doubt I'll keep my job.'

'But you came home to Edgecombe St Mary,' said Jasmina. 'Why did you come?'

'I suppose I did,' said Roger, looking round the kitchen as if surprised. 'I felt so low I just wanted to go home and I guess—I guess I always think of this as home.' He looked bewildered, like a lost child discovered under a bush at the bottom of the garden.

The Major looked at Jasmina and she gripped his hand and nodded.

'My dear Roger,' said the Major. 'This will always be your home.'

There was a moment of silence in which Roger's face seemed to work through a range of emotions. Then he smiled. 'You have no idea how much it means to me to hear you say that, Dad,' he said. He stood up and came round the table to envelop the Major in a fierce hug.

IT TOOK THE MAJOR a fraction of a second to understand the scene as something other than a mere impediment to his own car's forward passage. An ambulance with its lights flashing stood open and empty at the front door of the village shop. Parked next to it, a police car also flashed its lights, its doors flung open and a young redheaded policeman was speaking with urgency into his radio.

'Something has happened,' said Jasmina and she jumped out of the car as soon as it stopped and ran to the policeman. By the time the Major caught up with her, she was pleading with him to let her in.

'My sergeant said to not let anyone in, ma'am.'

'For God's sake, this lady is the owner of the place,' said the Major. 'Who's hurt?'

'A lady and her son,' said the policeman.

Just then an older policeman, a sergeant with eyebrows as unkempt as a hedge but a kindly expression, came out holding George, who had a large bandage on his left arm and was crying. He was accompanied by Amina's aunt Noreen, who was dressed in a shalwar kameez of white and gold that was ruined with a large bloodstain and several smudged bloody hand prints about George's size. George saw Jasmina and let out a wail.

'Auntie Jasmina!'

'This is her family's doing,' said Noreen, pointing at Jasmina. 'They are criminals and murderers.'

'What happened here?' asked Jasmina. 'I demand to know.'

'Far as we can make out from the boy, ma'am,' said the younger police-man, 'an old lady stabbed his mum with some kind of knitting needle. Must have missed the heart or she'd be a goner. The auntie's done a runner with a man believed to be the boy's father. Don't know where they went.'

A stretcher appeared, pushed by two ambulance men. Amina lay covered in a sheet, an IV in her arm and an oxygen mask on her face. She made a faint sound when she saw them and tried to raise her hand.

'Mummy!' called George, and Noreen and the kindly sergeant struggled to hold him back.

The Major stepped over to the stretcher and took Amina's hand.

'Please find Abdul Wahid,' whispered Amina. 'He thinks it's his fault.'

'Do you know where your nephew might go, ma'am?' the sergeant asked, writing on a notepad.

'I have no idea,' said Jasmina. She smoothed George's tear-stained face with her hand as the men loaded the stretcher into the ambulance and asked, 'George, where did your daddy go?'

'He said to Mecca,' said George. 'I want my mummy.'

'Mecca—is that a restaurant or something?' said the young policeman.

'No, he means the city, I think,' said Jasmina. The Major felt her look at him.

'He said walking to Mecca,' repeated George, through his tears.

'Well, if he's walking they won't get far,' sneered the policeman.

'Is Daddy with old auntie?' asked Jasmina.

George broke into fresh wails. 'She hurt my mummy with her knitting and scratched my arm.' He showed the bandage and his body trembled.

'You never know, he might try to slip the country.' The sergeant turned to his companion. 'Better warn the airports and get out a description. Does he own a car, ma'am?'

'No, he does not own a car.' The Major noticed that Jasmina did not men-tion her own blue Honda, which was not parked in its usual spot. He saw her sway as if she might faint and grabbed her round the waist.

'This has been a big shock, officers,' he said in his most authoritative tone. 'I think I need to take Mrs Ali home to sit down.'

'Are you in the village, sir?' asked the sergeant, and the Major gave them his address and helped Jasmina back to the car.

'Stay home once you get there,' added the younger policeman. 'We may need to talk to you again.'

OUTSIDE ROSE LODGE, the Major left the car running while he hurried inside to the scullery. He retrieved his gun box and slipped one of the guns into a canvas carrying-slip. Taking a box of shells from the locked cabinet, he shook out a few and stuffed them in his trouser pocket. Then, for good measure, he unhooked a pair of binoculars and a water flask, too. He put them in his leather game bag and patted it, hoping he was adequately armed and provisioned to face an insane woman. As he left, he met Roger in the passageway.

'Where are you going? I thought you were dancing it up at a wedding.'

'Got to try and find the groom first,' said the Major. 'Abdul Wahid may be trying to walk off a cliff.'

THE MAJOR KNEW he was driving faster than was safe in the growing darkness of the lanes, but he felt no fear, only a soldier's pride at an assignment well executed.

'What if we're too late?' whispered Jasmina, shivering beside him. The anguish in her voice threatened to tear his composure to shreds.

'We must refuse to imagine it and concentrate only on the next step and then the next,' he said, swinging the car into the empty car park.

The cliff on which they had strolled so happily with little George lay in gloom under grey clouds that streamed and feathered at the edges in the growing wind. Out in the Channel, curtains of rain already brushed the choppy sea.

'We need coats,' the Major said, and hurried to the back of the car.

'Ernest, there's no time,' she said, but she got out and hovered at the edge of the road waiting for him. He strapped his game bag across his chest, slung his gun slip over one shoulder, and picked up his shooting coat and hat. When he handed Jasmina the coat, he hoped she wouldn't notice the gun.

She was scanning the endless grass for signs of Abdul Wahid. 'How will we find them?'

'We'll head up to that vantage point,' he said, looking at a small knoll with its low stone wall and pay telescope. 'Always see more from high ground.'

'Oi! Where d'you think you're going?' A short man emerged from one of the small buildings adjacent to the darkened public house. 'Too windy to be safe out there tonight.' He wore stout boots and jeans with a short work coat and a large reflective vest that made his ample torso resemble a pumpkin. Some sort of harness jingled its loosened buckles at his waist.

'I'm sure you're right,' said the Major, 'but we're searching for a young man who may be despondent.'

'Jumper, is he?' said the man, consulting a clipboard. Jasmina moaned slightly at the word. 'I'm with the Volunteer Suicide Emergency Corps so you've come to the right place. What's his name?'

'His name's Abdul Wahid. He's twenty-three and we think his elderly great-aunt is with him.'

'Not many people jump with their auntie,' said the man. 'How d'you spell Abdool?'

'Oh, for pity's sake, just help us look for him,' said Jasmina.

'We'll start searching,' said the Major. 'Can you round up more help?'

'I'll put out the call,' said the man. 'But you can't go out there. It's not safe for the general public.'

'I'm not the general public, I'm British Army, rank of major,' said the Major. 'Retired, of course, but in the absence of any proof of your authority, I'll have to demand you step aside.'

'I see someone down there, Ernest.' Jasmina dodged sideways and began to cross the road. The Major created a diversion by saluting the clipboard man and receiving an uncertain hand waggle in response, then followed her.

A man became visible, running towards them up the incline from an area of thick scrub. It was not Abdul Wahid. This man also wore a reflective vest and the Major prepared to avoid him but he was waving his mobile phone in a way the Major understood as an urgent signal for help.

'Oh, no, it's Brian,' said the clipboard man, from behind them.

'No bloody phone reception again,' said Brian. Although he was a compact, fit-looking man, he put both hands on his knees and bent over to catch his breath after the uphill climb. 'Got a jumper south of Big Scrubber,' he went on. 'Can't get near to talk him in. Some old lady with a weapon and a foul mouth threatened to stick me in the gonads.'

'It's Abdul Wahid,' said Jasmina. 'He's here.'

'We're not to approach people with visible weapons or psychiatric disorders,' said the clipboard man. 'We have to call for police back-up. Reception's better at HQ, but I can't go unless you all come with me.'

'Please, I have to go to my nephew,' cried Jasmina.

'Brian, you seem to me to be a man of action,' said the Major, unsleeving his gun as casually as possible and breaking it gently over the crook of his elbow. 'Why don't you take Jim to get reinforcements, and the lady and I will go down and quietly persuade the elder lady to behave.'

'Shit,' said Jim, staring mesmerised at the shotgun. Jasmina gasped and then used the opportunity to turn and run down the slope.

'Shit,' said the Major. 'I have to go after her.'

'So go,' said Brian. 'I'll make sure Clipboard Jim makes the right calls.'

'It's not loaded, by the way,' called the Major as he began to hurry after Jasmina. 'Only, the old lady's already stabbed one person with that needle.'

'I didn't see any shotgun,' said Brian, and the Major broke into a run, heading for the bank of gorse and scrub trees.

BEHIND THE SCRUB, he saw Jasmina's small Honda half buried in gorse; a great furrow of mud behind it indicated that it had slid and swerved before coming to a stop.

Abdul Wahid was kneeling close, but not dangerously close, to the edge of the cliff some 200 feet away. He seemed to be praying, bending his head to the ground as if unaware of any drama in his surroundings. Closer to the car, two islands of gorse created a narrowing of the grass and here the old lady stood guard, her knitting needle pointing at Jasmina.

'Auntie, what are you doing?' called Jasmina, spreading her hands in a gesture of placation. 'Why must we be out here in the rain?'

'I'm doing what none of you knows how to do,' said the old lady. 'No one remembers what it is to have honour any more.'

'But Abdul Wahid?' Jasmina said. Then she raised her voice and called out to him, 'Abdul Wahid, please!'

'Don't you know better than to disturb a man at prayer?' asked the old woman. 'He prays to take the burden on himself and restore our honour. This is how it has always been done, child,' continued the old woman in a dreamy voice. 'My mother was drowned in a cistern by my father when I was six years old. I saw him push her down with one hand and with the other he stroked her hair because he loved her very much. She had laughed with the man who came selling carpets and copper pots and handed him tea from her own hands. I was always proud of my father and his sacrifice,' she said.

'This is insane. This is not how things are resolved, Auntie. We are civilised people, not some rural peasant family stuck in the past,' said Jasmina, her voice choked with horror.

'Civilised?' hissed the old woman. 'You are soft. Soft and corrupted. My niece and her husband are weakened by decadence. They might complain, but they offer only indulgence for their son. And I, who should be eating figs in a garden of my own, must come and set things right.'

'Did they know you would do this?' asked Jasmina.

The old lady laughed, an animal cackle. 'They will cry and rant and pretend to be ashamed but you will see, they will give me my own small house in Pakistan and I will grow figs and sit all day in the sun.' She ran her fingers slowly up the shaft of the needle and began to creep forward across the grass, waving the tip of the needle as if to hypnotise.

The Major stepped from behind the bushes and planted his feet firmly apart, resting his right hand on the stock of the shotgun still broken across his arm. 'This has gone quite far enough, madam,' he said. 'I'll ask you to throw down your needle and wait quietly with us for the police.'

The old woman fell back a few steps but regained her composure, and a leer crept slowly up the left side of her face.

'Ah, the English Major,' she said. 'So it is true, Jasmina, that you ran away to fornicate and debauch yourself.'

'How dare you,' said the Major, stepping forward and snapping the shotgun together.

'Actually, you're quite right, Auntie.' Jasmina's eyes flashed with anger. She stepped forward, too, and held her chin high, her hair whipping about her face in the wind. 'And shall I tell you how delicious it was, you with your shrivelled body and your dried-up heart, who have never known happiness? Would you like to hear how it is to be with a man you love and really breathe the sensuality of life itself? Should I tell you this story, Auntie?'

The old woman howled as if racked with pain and leaped towards Jasmina, who planted her feet and held out her arms and showed no intention of dodging. Quick with fear, the Major swung up his gun and, running forward, butted the edge of the stock against the old woman's head. It was only a glancing blow, but her own momentum made it enough. She dropped the needle and crumpled to the ground. Jasmina sat down abruptly in the grass and began to laugh, an ugly robotic laugh that suggested shock. The Major picked up the needle and slid it into his bag.

'What were you thinking?' he said. 'You could have been killed.'

'Is she dead?' asked Jasmina.

'Of course not,' said the Major, but he was anxious as he felt the old lady's leathery neck until he found a pulse. 'I do try to avoid killing ladies, no matter how psychotic they may be.'

'You're a useful sort in a fight,' came the now-familiar voice of Brian, who was advancing from behind a bush. He bent down to peer at the old woman. 'Good work,' he said. 'Jim's waiting for back-up. Shall we go and have a bit of a chat with your nephew now and see what he wants? Main thing is to act casual and not make any sudden moves.'

Together they walked cautiously down the slope towards Abdul Wahid. He had finished his prayers and was gazing with unnatural stillness out to sea, as the embroidered hem of his long tunic snapped in the wind.

'He put on his wedding clothes,' said Mrs Ali. 'Oh, my poor, poor boy.' She stretched out her hand and the Major reached to catch her arm, fearing she might run the last hundred yards or so.

'Easy, now. No sudden moves,' said Brian. 'Let me get his attention.' He stepped forward and gave a low whistling sound as if, thought the Major, he were calling a gundog to heel. Abdul Wahid turned slightly.

'Hullo there,' said Brian. He held a hand up in a slow wave. 'I was just wondering if I could talk to you a minute.'

'I suppose you want to help me?' asked Abdul Wahid.

'As a matter of fact, I do,' said Brian. 'What do you need?'

'I need you to get my aunt away from here,' said Abdul Wahid. 'She should not have to endure this.'

'So you don't want to talk to her?' asked Brian. 'That's fine. If I have the Major here take her away, will you agree to talk to me—just for a bit?' Abdul Wahid seemed to consider this option carefully.

'I would prefer to talk to the Major,' said Abdul Wahid.

'So if I get your aunt away to somewhere dry and warm you'll sit tight and chat with this gentleman?'

'Yes,' said Abdul Wahid.

'He's got a gun, you know,' said Brian. 'You sure you can trust him?'

'What are you doing?' whispered the Major in fierce anxiety. 'Are you trying to provoke him?' Abdul Wahid, however, actually produced one of his short barking laughs.

'It would not exactly spoil my plans if he shot me, would it?'

'OK, then,' said Brian. 'I think we can make that deal.' He turned to the Major and whispered. 'His laughing is a good sign. We should play along, give him what he wants, within reason.'

'I won't leave,' said Jasmina. She turned her tear-stained face to the Major. 'If I leave him in your hands and you can't keep him safe . . .' she began. She turned her face away, unable to continue.

'You may very well never forgive me,' finished the Major. The words tasted bitter in his mouth. 'I do understand.' She looked at him and he added, 'Whoever stays, whoever goes, I fear his death would come between us just the same, my dear.' He took her hand in his and squeezed it. 'Let me play the man's part now and fight for Abdul Wahid and for us, my love.'

H<small>E WAITED WHILE BRIAN</small> and Jasmina climbed the slope, stopping to collect the dazed but conscious old woman on their way. Out of the corner of his eye he watched Abdul Wahid, who remained motionless. Finally, he turned and walked slowly downhill, flanking left to come parallel to the young man while maintaining a respectful distance.

'Thank you,' said Abdul Wahid. 'This was no place for a woman.'

'This is no place for any of us,' said the Major, peering into the abyss of churning whitecaps and jagged rocks that seemed to suck at his feet from hundreds of feet below.

'Did you see Amina?' asked Abdul Wahid. The Major nodded. 'Will she live?' he added.

'She asked for you in the ambulance,' said the Major. 'I could take you to her. I have my car.'

Abdul Wahid shook his head and rubbed the back of his hand over his eyes. 'It was never meant to be,' he said. 'Every day more complication, more compromise. I see that now.'

'That's just not true,' said the Major. 'You're talking like a fool.' He felt the note of desperation in his own voice.

'So much shame,' Abdul Wahid continued. 'It hangs round me like chains. I ache to scrape it all off and be clean for . . .' He stopped and the Major sensed he felt unworthy to even mention the name of his creator.

'If you want to talk of shame,' began the Major, 'look at this gun of which I'm so proud.' They both considered the rain beading on its polished stock and dull steel barrel. 'My father, on his deathbed, gave one of these guns to me and one to my younger brother and I was consumed with disappointment that he did not give me both and I chewed on my own grievance as he lay dying before me and I chewed on it while I wrote his eulogy and damn me if I wasn't still chewing on it when my brother died this autumn.'

'It was your right as the eldest son.'

'I was more proud of these guns than I was of your aunt Jasmina. For the sake of these guns, I let down the woman I love in front of a whole community of people, most of whom I can barely tolerate. I let her leave, and I will never get rid of that sense of shame.'

'I let her leave so that I could acquire all her worldly possessions,' said Abdul Wahid quietly. 'With death, this debt will also be wiped out.'

'This is not the solution,' said the Major. 'The solution is to make things right, or at least to work every day to do so.'

'I have tried, Major,' he said. 'But in the end I cannot reconcile my faith and my life. At least this way, the debt of honour is paid and Amina and George can go on with their lives.'

'How is suicide to be reconciled?' asked the Major, because he knew that suicide was not allowed in Islam.

'I will not commit suicide,' said Abdul Wahid. 'It is *haram*. I will merely pray at the edge and wait for the wind to carry me where it will. Perhaps to Mecca.' He opened his arms and the heavy shirt billowed in the wind like a sail. 'You have kept me too long, Major,' he said. 'I must go to my prayers.'

As he stepped forward, the Major fumbled in his pocket for cartridges and stuck two in the barrels, snapping the shotgun closed. Abdul Wahid stopped and looked at him as the Major took two long steps downhill and began to sidle up between Abdul Wahid and the crumbling cliff edge. Abdul Wahid smiled gently at him and said, 'So, Major, you do intend to shoot me after all?'

'No, I do not intend to shoot you,' said the Major. He stepped uphill and turned the gun round in his hands, presenting the stock end to Abdul Wahid. 'Here, take this.' Abdul Wahid caught the gun as it was pushed into his stomach. He held it, puzzled, and the Major stepped back, uncomfortably aware of the barrels pointing at his chest. 'Now I'm afraid you are going to have to shoot me.'

'I am not a man of violence,' said Abdul Wahid, lowering the gun.

'I'm afraid you have no choice,' said the Major, stepping forward again. 'I intend to spend all night, if necessary, standing between you and the edge. Thus you will not be blown over by accident at any point. Of course, you can always jump, but that was not your plan, was it?'

'This is silly. I could never hurt you, Major,' Abdul Wahid stepped back.

'You see, if you die here today, your aunt Jasmina will be lost to me, and I do not want to live without her.' The Major struggled to keep his voice even. 'Also, I will not face your son, George, and tell him I stood by and let his father kill himself.' He stepped forward again, pushing Abdul Wahid back. Abdul Wahid moved his hands to grip the gun more comfortably. The Major prayed his fingers were not near the twin triggers.

'You must see that your sense of shame will not die with you, Abdul Wahid. It will live on in your son and in Amina and in your aunt Jasmina. Your pain will haunt their lives. I do not want to live to see that happen.'

'I will not shoot you.' Abdul Wahid was almost crying now, his face twisted with anguish and confusion.

'Either shoot me or choose to live yourself,' said the Major. 'I can't face your aunt any other way.'

Abdul Wahid gave a bellow of anguish and threw the gun away from him onto the ground. The butt end hit first and the gun gave a roaring boom and discharged what the Major registered as a single barrel.

He felt a white-hot sear of steel shot through his right leg. The force of the close range spun him round and he fell heavily, slipping in the grass. As he rolled, he felt the ground disappear under him. His legs slipped over the edge of the chalk into empty air. There was no time to feel any pain as he scrabbled above his head with his hands and felt his left elbow bump a metal stanchion that had once held a wire fence. He grabbed the stanchion. It held briefly against the tug of his body then it began to move, the metal squeaking like a dull knife. In an instant, a body landed on his left lower arm and fingers dug at his back to find any grip. His legs jackknifed and his knee struck the cliff with a pain that flashed like a light in his head. It was so fast there was no time for thought. There was only a brief feeling of surprise and the smell of cold white chalk and wet grass.

Chapter 11

The Major was keen to push away the nagging idea of pain, which started to seep into his head along with the light. It was comfortable in the warm darkness of sleep and when he felt his eyelids flutter he tried to squeeze them shut. It was his attempt to roll over that shocked him awake with a tearing pain in his left knee that made him gasp.

'He's waking up.' A hand held his shoulder down and the voice added, 'Don't try to move, Mr Pettigrew.'

'Isss Major . . .' he whispered. 'Major Pettigrew.' His voice was a hoarse whisper in a mouth that seemed to be made of brown paper.

'Here's something to drink,' said the voice as a straw snagged on his lip and he sucked at lukewarm water. 'You're in the hospital, Mr Pettigrew, but you're going to be fine.'

He slipped away again into sleep, and when he awoke he saw Roger sitting beside him. 'How long have I been here?' whispered the Major.

'About a day,' said Roger. 'Do you remember what happened?'

'I was shot in the leg, not the head. Is it still there?'

'The leg? Of course it is,' said Roger. 'Can't you feel it?'

'Yes, of course I can,' said the Major. 'But I didn't want any nasty surprises.' He found it quite exhausting to speak but he asked for some more water. Roger helped him sip from a plastic cup.

'They dug a whole lot of shot out of your leg,' said Roger. 'Lucky for you it missed any arteries, and the doctor said it only clipped the edge of the right testicle, not that he expected it mattered much to a man your age.'

'Thanks very much,' said the Major.

Roger leaned over and, to the Major's surprise, squeezed his hand and kissed him on the forehead. 'You're going to be fine, Dad.'

'If you kiss me like that again, I'll have to assume you're lying.'

'You gave me a fright, what can I say? It was all quite nasty.'

'Nastier still for me,' said the Major. He struggled a moment to ask the questions to which he was not sure he could bear the answers. It must be bad, he thought, since there was no sign of other visitors.

'I want to know,' he began, but he seemed to choke on his own voice. 'I must know. Did Abdul Wahid jump?'

'Considering he shot my father, I wouldn't have cared if he had,' said Roger. 'But apparently he threw himself down as you went over and grabbed you just in time. It was touch-and-go, they said, what with the wind and the slippery rain, but some guy named Brian threw himself on Abdul and then some other guy came with a rope and stuff and they dragged you back and got you on a stretcher.'

'So he's alive?' asked the Major.

'He is, but I'm afraid there's some bad news—'

'Amina's dead?' asked the Major. 'His fiancée?'

'Oh, the girl who got stabbed?' said Roger. 'No, she's going to be fine. They're all with her one flight up in Women's Surgical.'

'All who?' said the Major.

'Mrs Ali, Abdul Wahid and that George who keeps dunning me out of coins for the vending machine,' said Roger. 'Half of Pakistan is there.'

'Jasmina is there?' the Major asked.

'When she can bear to be away from you. I can't seem to get rid of her.'

'I intend to ask her to marry me,' said the Major, his voice curt. 'No matter what you think.'

'Don't get all excited. That testicle is still in traction,' Roger said.

'What's in traction?' asked a voice and the Major felt himself blush as

Jasmina came round the curtain wearing a big smile and a shalwar kameez in a yellow as soft as butter. She smelled of soap and lemons.

'You finally went home and took a shower, then?' asked Roger.

'The matron said I was frightening all the visitors with my bloodstained clothes.' She came to the side of the Major's bed and he felt as weak as the day she had held him up, faint from hearing about Bertie's death.

'He didn't jump,' was all he managed to say as he clutched her hand.

'No, he didn't,' she said. She gripped his hand and kissed him on the cheek. 'And now he owes you his life and we can never repay you.'

'If he wants to repay me, tell him to hurry up and get married,' said the Major. 'What that boy needs is a woman to order him around.'

'Amina is still quite weak. My brother and sister-in-law have vowed to stay on as long as it takes to see them settled.'

'It all sounds wonderful,' said the Major. He turned to Roger, who was fiddling with his mobile phone. 'But you told me there was bad news?'

'He is right, Ernest,' said Jasmina. 'You must prepare yourself.' She looked at Roger, and he nodded as if the two of them had spent some time discussing how to tell him. The Major held his breath and waited for the blow.

'It's the Churchill, Dad,' said Roger at last. 'I'm afraid in all the commotion it slid over the edge and Abdul Wahid says he saw it smashing on the rocks.' He paused and lowered his head. 'They haven't found it.'

The Major closed his eyes and saw it happen. He smelled again the cold chalk, felt the agonising slow slipping of his body as if the sea were a magnet pulling at him and, at the edge of his vision, he could see the gun slipping faster, smooth against the wet grass as it inscribed one slow circle on the edge and then went ahead of them over the cliff.

'Are you all right, Ernest?' said Jasmina. He blinked away the scene, not sure whether it was a real memory or just a vision. The smell of chalk faded from his nostrils and he waited for the pangs of sorrow to overwhelm him. He was surprised to find that he could summon no more than the kind of faint disappointment one might feel upon finding a favourite sweater accidentally shrunk in the wash to a felt mess sized for a small terrier.

'Am I medicated with something?' he asked from behind his closed lids. 'I don't seem to feel as upset as I should.'

'You've longed for that pair since I can remember,' Roger said.

'I longed for the day when I could look important to a lot of people whom I felt were more important than I,' said the Major. 'I was arrogant.'

'I'm sorry you lost the gun your father gave you, Ernest,' said Jasmina.

'But you lost it saving a life, and you are a hero to me and to others.'

'Actually, I lost Bertie's gun,' said the Major. He yawned and felt himself growing sleepy. 'Happened to be the closest one to grab.'

'Are you serious?' said Roger.

'And I'm glad,' said the Major. 'Now I won't have to be reminded that sometimes it might have been more important to me than my brother.'

'Oh, shit!' said Roger. 'Now we have to pay Marjorie fifty thousand pounds and have nothing to show for it.'

'I expect the insurance company will take care of that,' said the Major. He struggled to stay awake so he might keep looking at Jasmina's face smiling at him.

'You had them insured all this time?' asked Roger.

The Major closed his eyes. 'When my father died, my mother kept paying the premiums, and when she died, so did I. I take great pride in never leaving a bill unpaid—it makes the filing messy.'

'You are tired, Ernest,' Jasmina said. 'You should rest after all this excitement.' She laid her hand along his cheek and he felt as a small child feels when the night's fever is cooled by the touch of a mother's hand.

'Must ask you to marry me,' he said as he drifted away. 'Not in this dreadful room, of course.'

Epilogue

The view from the book-lined room that now went by the name 'The Squire's Morning Room' took in the comings and goings on the terrace and lawn of the manor house. The Major had a full view of Mrs Rasool, resplendent in saffron coat and silk trousers, who seemed to be arguing loudly and happily into a tiny black headset. The microphone part rested on her cheek like a fat fly. She waved a clipboard and two tuxedoed helpers rushed to assist more guests to the semi-circle of white folding chairs arranged in front of a low dais. The Major, half hidden behind the pale linen drape, was glad to have a moment of silent reflection before the wedding.

He heard the door open; turning, he watched Jasmina slip into the room and gently close the door. She was dressed in a coat and trousers of old silk that glowed with the ruby-dark softness of fine port. A spider's web of a scarf in a pale blue was spun about her head like a vision. She trod softly across the carpet in low slippers and came to stand at his shoulder.

'You're not supposed to be here,' he said.

'I thought it wrong to leave even one small tradition unbroken,' she said, smiling. She took his arm and they both watched for a while in silence as the guests gathered.

Roger was talking with the musicians—a harpist and two sitar players—and the Major assumed he was opining on the music selections. The groom's side of the chairs was filling up, the men largely invisible between large bobbing hats. The Major spotted Grace talking to Marjorie, while the vicar hung about looking lost. Daisy had refused to attend. Alec and Alma were here, not speaking to each other in the front row. The Major was very grateful to Alec for standing up for their friendship and quite demanding that his wife accompany him, despite her sighs of mortification. As they watched, Alice from next door arrived wearing some kind of batik tent and a pair of hemp sandals. She was accompanied by Lord Dagenham, who had sent word that he would like to receive an invitation but who now seemed rather bewildered to find such strange people waiting on his back lawn.

'Do you suppose Dagenham likes what the Rasools have done with the place?' asked the Major.

'After that incident with the schoolchildren and the ducks, he should think himself lucky things have arranged themselves so profitably,' replied Jasmina. The local authorities had come to hear of the duck-shooting fiasco and had promptly closed the school. It was only recently, as part of a long-range plan instituted by Gertrude, now wife of the Laird of Loch Brae, that the Rasools had quietly leased all but the east wing as a country house hotel, allowing ample funds for Lord Dagenham to go back to dividing his time between Edgecombe and other society haunts. It seemed only appropriate that this eclectic affair should be their first catered wedding.

The bride's guests—a very small party made up of an assistant imam named Rodney, Amina and her auntie Noreen and Mrs Rasool's parents—now began to cluster on the terrace as if held behind an invisible rope. Abdul Wahid was to lead them to their chairs in a small traditional procession at the appropriate time. He stood to one side with his usual frown, as if he disapproved of all the chattering frivolity round him, and tousled the hair of his son, who leaned comfortably against him, knotted tie askew.

The Major sighed and Jasmina laughed at him and took his arm.

'They are a motley and ragged bunch,' she said, 'but they are what is left when all the shallow pretence is burned away.'

'Will it do?' said the Major, laying his hand over her cool fingers. 'Will it be enough to sustain the future?'

'It is more than enough for me,' she said. 'My heart is quite full.' The Major heard a catch in her voice. He turned to face her and pushed back a stray tendril of hair from her cheek, but he said nothing. There would be time to speak of Ahmed and Nancy in the ceremonies to come. At this moment, there was only the pause of quiet reflection pooling between them like sunlight on carpet.

Outside, the harpist improvised a wild glissando. Without looking, the Major could sense the guests sitting taller and gathering their attention. He might have preferred to stay in this room for ever and gaze at this face that wore love like a smile about the eyes, but it was not possible. He straightened his shoulders and offered her his arm with a formal bow.

'Mrs Ali,' he said, delighting in using her name one last time, 'shall we go forth and get married?'

helen **simonson**

RD: Where were you born and what is your strongest memory of your childhood?

HS: I was born in Slough, west of London and, as a small child, lived in the nearby suburb of Woodley, which was surrounded by pockets of countryside. Our house backed onto an abandoned World War II airfield. Although we kids were banned from playing there, we had our hole in the fence and we spent long summers squishing about in swampy lowlands, daring each other into the dank air-raid shelters and dodging strange adults who sometimes wandered through the straggling copses. Our mothers never asked where we found the buckets of blackberries and the armfuls of fat velvety bulrushes—and we never told.

RD: What did you study at college, and are you still happy with your choice?

HS: I thought I'd be a politician and, like my local councillor parents, help make the world better. So, I went to the LSE to study economics and politics. I quickly discovered that politics is much more about horse-trading than idealism. I am still thrilled to have studied at such a legendary college, though. Plus, I met my American husband there!

RD: You now live in America. In what part, and have you enjoyed it?

HS: I lived in New York City for over twenty years, mostly in a leafy enclave of historic homes known as Brooklyn Heights. My husband and I chose New York as a young married couple and it is the most exciting of cities. One night Broadway, the next an avant-garde dance performance in an East Village garage. New York has everything. If I wrote a coming-of-age novel, it would end with a small-town girl getting on a Greyhound bus to New York. Now that work has relocated us to the DC area, we are enjoying the grace and elegance of America's capital city. Here, the culture comes with cherry blossoms, a host of international friends and a welcoming community of writers.

RD: You say you have a deep connection to England still—a yearning to come home. What is it that you love so much about the country?

HS: I love the voice over the loudspeaker that says 'Welcome to Gatwick'. I love the thick silver dew on the grass along the M25 as I drive home to Sussex in the early morning, from the airport, in my rental car. I love the greasy full English breakfast and thick orange tea at a motorway service station. As a young person, I perhaps discounted the pull of home and the feel of belonging. The attachment to England has never gone away and now I know there is a cost to even the most willing self-exile.

RD: Does the Major live on in your imagination?

HS: I picture him out on tour in the world. Even now, he may be catching a train across Australia to another book signing! I do carry a warm sense of him with me; it's like having a very pleasant uncle. We do not talk, however, and he is getting on with his own life while I observe a new set of characters who are considering whether to let me in on their plans.

RD: It's interesting that you say that the Major teaches us that the world is what we make of it. Do you believe that we create our own happiness?

HS: Well, look at me—one small book in print and, already, I'm pontificating about personal happiness. Please don't pay me any attention. I'm personally a big fan of a country walk on a sunny day (with maybe a pub lunch) as the epitome of personal happiness. For group happiness, I think a dash of altruism, a pinch of tolerance and a hint of compromise might make all our neighbourhoods better places to live.

RD: Are there other professions you would have liked to have experienced?

HS: At eleven, I was told I was too tall to be a ballet dancer. At twelve, that women did not become airline pilots. Why do we listen to people who tell us what we *cannot* do?

RD: How would you describe yourself, as a person?

HS: I would like to describe myself as willowy and impeccably groomed, but you might come to a bookstore reading and actually meet me. Good friends have been nice enough to describe me as 'generous' and I would like to deserve that description.

RD: Did you know of Reader's Digest Condensed Books before we requested permission to condense your novel?

HS: At my maternal grandparents' house, when I was a child, dinner at lunchtime was often followed by an imposed quiet period (so the adults could snooze). I usually retreated under the dark oak dining-room table with a Reader's Digest Condensed Book, of which there was an entire neatly organised bookcase. It was an amazing feeling to luxuriate in novel after novel, ranging over vast distances of geography and genre. I was never in a hurry to have the grown-ups wake up for tea.

RD: Finally, what does it feel like to see the glittering reviews for *Major Pettigrew's Last Stand*?

HS: It is so exciting to see the Major receive such a warm reception in the world. I had my doubts that a book with humour, social comedy, and a slightly optimistic view of the future, would find favour among reviewers. But they have all been extremely kind to a debut author and I am very grateful. I am especially happy whenever someone emails to complain that my book has kept them up late into the night.

ROBERT CRAIS

THE FIRST RULE

Frank and Cindy Meyer and their family
are living the American dream—until they
are raided by thieves and murderers. The
police believe that Frank had been
harbouring money or drugs. But Joe Pike
worked with Frank Meyer, back when they
were both young and in the military, and he
knows that his buddy was innocent.
So Joe has decided that those who killed
Frank must be taught a lesson . . .

The organised criminal gangs from the fifteen republics of the former Soviet Union are bound by what they call the 'Vorovskoy Zakon'—the thieves' code—which is comprised of eighteen written rules. The first rule is this:

A thief must forsake his mother, father, brothers, and sisters.
He must not have a family—no wife, no children.
We are his family.

If any of the eighteen rules are broken, the punishment is death.

FRANK MEYER CLOSED his computer as the early winter darkness fell over his home in Westwood, California. Westwood was an affluent area on the west side of Los Angeles, resting between Beverly Hills and Brentwood, in a twine of gracious residential streets and comfortable, well-to-do homes. Frank Meyer—more surprised about it than anyone else, considering his background—lived in such a home.

Work finished, Frank settled back in his home office, listening to his sons crash through the far side of the house like baby rhinos. They made him happy, and so did the rich scent of braising beef that promised stew or boeuf bourguignon. Voices came from the family room, almost certainly the sound of a game show on television. Cindy hated the nightly news.

Frank smiled because Cindy didn't much care for game shows, either, but she liked the background sound of the TV when she cooked. Cindy had her ways, that was for sure, and her ways had changed his life. Here he was with a lovely home, a growing business and a wonderful family—all of it owed to his wife. Frank teared up, thinking how much he owed that woman. He was like that, sentimental and emotional. As Cindy always said, Frank Meyer was a softy, which is why she fell in love with him.

Frank worked hard to live up to her expectations, beginning eleven years ago when he realised he loved her and committed to reinventing himself. He was now a successful importer of garments from Asia and Africa which he sold to wholesale chains throughout the United States. He was forty-three years old, still fit and strong, though not so much as in the old days. OK, well—he was getting fat.

Frank didn't miss that earlier life, and if he sometimes missed the men with whom he had shared it, he kept those feelings to himself. He had re-created himself, and, by a miracle, his efforts had paid off. Cindy. The kids. The home they had made. Frank was still thinking about these changes when Cindy appeared at the door, giving him that lopsided, sexy grin.

'Hey, bud. You hungry?'

'Just finishing up. What am I smelling? It's fabulous.'

Pounding footsteps, then Little Frank, ten years old and showing the square, chunky build of his father, caught the doorjamb beside his mother to stop himself, stopping so fast his younger brother, Joey, six and just as square, crashed into Little Frank's back.

Little Frank shouted, 'Meat!'

Joey screamed, 'Ketchup!'

Cindy said, 'Meat and ketchup. What could be better?'

Frank pushed back his chair. 'Nothing. I'm dying for meat and ketchup.'

Cindy rolled her eyes and turned back towards the kitchen.

'You've got five, big guy. I'll hose off these monsters. Wash up and join us.'

The boys made exaggerated screams as they raced away, passing Ana, who had appeared behind Cindy. Ana was their nanny, a nice girl who had been with them almost six months. She had bright blue eyes, high cheekbones, and was a fantastic help with the kids. Another perk of Frank's increasing success.

Ana said, 'I'm going to feed the baby now, Cindy. You need anything?'

'We've got it under control. You go ahead.'

Frank finished putting away his paperwork, then pulled the shades before joining his family for dinner. Frank Meyer had no reason to suspect that something unspeakable was about to happen.

As FRANK ENJOYED DINNER with his family, a black Cadillac Escalade slow-rolled onto his street, the Escalade stolen earlier that day from a shopping centre in Long Beach, Moon Williams swapping the plates with an identical black Escalade they found in Torrance. This was their third time round the block, clocking the street for pedestrians, and witnesses in parked cars.

This time round, the rear windows drooped like sleepy eyes, and street-lights died one by one, Jamal shooting them out with a .22-calibre pistol.

Darkness followed the Escalade like a rising tide.

Four men in the vehicle: Moon driving; Moon's boy, Lil Tai, riding shot-gun; Jamal in the back with the Russian. Moon, eyes flicking between the houses and the white boy, wasn't sure if the foreigner was a Russian or not. What with all the Eastern Bloc assholes runnin' around, boy coulda been Armenian, Lithuanian, or a Transylvanian vampire, and Moon couldn't tell'm apart. All Moon knew, he was makin' more cash since hookin' up with the foreigner chillin' behind him than any time in his life.

Still, Moon didn't like him back there, money or not. All these months, this was the first time he had come with them.

Moon said, 'You sure now, homeboy? That house right there?'

'Same as last time we passed, the one like a church.'

Lil Tai twisted round to grin at the white boy.

'How much money we gettin' this time?'

'Much money. Much.'

Moon killed the headlights and pulled into the drive, the doors opening as soon as he cut the engine. The Escalade's interior lights had been removed, so nothing lit up. Only sound was Lil Tai's eighteen-pound sledgehammer, clunking the door panel as he got out.

They went directly to the front door, Jamal first, Moon going last, walk-ing backwards to make sure no one was watching. Jamal popped the entry lights, just reached up and broke'm with his fingers. Moon pressed a folded towel over the deadbolt to dull the sound, and Lil Tai hit it with the hammer as hard as he could.

FRANK AND CINDY were clearing the table when a crash jolted their home as if a car had slammed through the front door. Joey was watching the Lakers in the family room and Little Frank had just gone up to his room. When Frank heard the crash, he believed his older son had knocked over the grandfather clock in the front entry. Little Frank had been known to climb the clock to reach the first-floor landing.

Joey ran to his mother. Frank was already hurrying towards the sound. 'Frankie! Son, are you all right—?'

Then four armed men rushed in, moving with the loose organisation of men who had done this before.

Frank Meyer had faced high-speed, violent entries before, and had known how to react, but those situations had been in his former life. Now, eleven years and too many long days at a desk later, Frank was behind the play.

Four-man team. Gloves. Nine-millimetre pistols.

First man through had average height, espresso skin, and heavy braids to his shoulders. Frank knew he was the team leader because he acted like the leader, his eyes directing the play.

A shorter man followed, angry and nervous, with a black bandanna capping his head, shoulder to shoulder with a bruiser showing tight corn rows and gold in his teeth. The fourth man was a step behind, more like an observer than part of the action. White, and big, almost as big as the bruiser, with a bowling-ball head, wide-set eyes, and thin sideburns that ran down his jaw like needles.

Two seconds, they fanned through the rooms. Frank realised they were a home-invasion crew. He raised his hands, shuffling sideways to place himself between the men and his wife.

'Take what you want. We won't give you any trouble.'

The leader came directly to Frank, holding his pistol high and sideways like an idiot in a movie, bugging his eyes to show Frank he was fierce. 'Damn right. Where is it?'

Without waiting for an answer, he slapped Frank with the pistol. Cindy shouted in panic, but Frank had been hit harder plenty of times. He waved towards his wife, trying to calm her.

'I'm OK. It's OK, Cin, we're gonna be fine.'

'Gonna be dead, you don't do what I say!'

He dug the pistol into Frank's cheek, but Frank was watching the others. The bruiser and the smaller man split, the bruiser charging to the French doors to check out the back, the little guy throwing open cabinets. Their movements were fast. Fast into the house. Fast into Frank's face. Fast through the house. Only the man with the strange sideburns moved slowly, floating outside the perimeter.

Frank knew from experience you had to be ahead of the action to survive. He tried to buy himself time to catch up.

'My wallet's in my office. I've got four hundred dollars—'

The leader hit Frank again. 'You take me for a fool?'

The man with the sideburns finally stepped out of the background, appearing at the table. 'See the plates? More people are here. We must look for the others.'

Frank was surprised by the accent. He thought it was Polish, but couldn't be sure.

The man with the accent disappeared into the kitchen just as the bruiser charged out of the family room and went directly to Cindy and Joey. He held his pistol to Cindy's temple, shouting at Frank, 'You want this bitch dead?'

The bruiser suddenly backhanded Cindy with his pistol. Joey screamed, and Frank Meyer suddenly knew what to do.

The man with Frank was watching the action when Frank grabbed his gun hand, rolled his wrist to lock the man's arm, and jointed his elbow. The moves were burned into his muscle memory from a thousand hours of training. He had to neutralise his captor, strip the weapon as he levered the man down, recover with the pistol in a combat grip, put two into the big man who had Cindy, then turn, acquire and double-tap whoever was in his field of fire.

The moves flowed out exactly as Frank had trained for them, and, back in the day, he could have completed the sequence in less than a second. But Frank was still fumbling with the pistol when three bullets slammed into him, the last shot hitting the heavy vertebra in Frank's lower back, putting him down.

Frank opened his mouth, but only a hiss escaped. Cindy and Joey screamed, and Frank fought to rise with the fierce will of the warrior he had been, but will was not enough.

The man with the accent said, 'I hear someone. In the back.'

A shadow moved past, but Frank couldn't see.

Frank's world grew dark, and all he had left were feelings of failure and shame. He knew he was dying, exactly the way he had always thought he would die, only not here, and not now. All of that should have been behind him.

He tried to reach for his wife, but could not.

He wanted to protect her, but had not.

His index finger was the only part of him that moved.

Twitching as if with a life of its own.

His trigger finger.

Pulling at empty air.

Part One—The Professionals

1

At ten fourteen the following morning, approximately fifteen hours after the murders, helicopters were dark stars over the Meyer house when LAPD Detective-Sergeant Jack Terrio threaded his way through the tangle of marked and unmarked police vehicles, and vans from the Medical Examiner's office. He phoned his task force partner, Louis Deets, as he approached the house. Deets had been at the scene for an hour.

'I'm here.'

'Meet you at the front door. You gotta see this.'

'Hang on—any word on the wit?'

A slim possibility existed for a witness—an Anglo female had been found alive by the first responders, and identified as the Meyers' nanny.

Deets said, 'They brought her over to the Medical Centre, but she's circling the drain. One in the face, one in the chest.'

'Hold a good thought. We need a break.'

'Maybe we got one. You gotta see.'

Terrio snapped his phone closed, annoyed with the dead-end case. A home-invasion crew had been hitting upscale homes in West LA for the past three months, and this was their seventh score. All of the robberies had taken place between the dinner hour and 11 p.m. Most of the homes had been occupied. A litter of 9mm cartridge casings and bodies had been left behind, but nothing else—no prints, DNA, video or witnesses. Until now, and she was going to die.

When Terrio reached the plastic screen that had been erected to block the front door from prying cameras, he waited for Deets. Across the street, he recognised two squats from the Chief's office, huddled up with a woman who looked like a Fed. Terrio thought, 'Now what?'

She was maybe five foot six, and sturdy with that gymed-out carriage Feds have when they're trying to move up the food chain to Washington. Navy blazer over outlet-store jeans. Wraparound shades. A little slit mouth that probably hadn't smiled in a month.

Deets came up behind him. 'You gotta see this.'

Terrio nodded towards the woman. 'Who's that with the squats?'

Deets squinted at the woman, then shook his head.

'I've been inside. It's a mess in here, man, but you gotta see. C'mon, put on your bootees—'

They were required to wear paper bootees at the scene so as not to contaminate the evidence.

Deets ducked behind the screen, so Terrio hurried to catch up, steeling himself for what he was about to see. Even after eighteen years on the job, the sight of blood and rent human flesh left him queasy.

They reached a large, open dining area where a coroner investigator was photographing the crumpled form of an adult white male.

Deets said, 'OK we touch the body?'

'Sure. I'm good.'

'Can I have one of those wet-wipes?'

The CI gave Deets a wet-wipe, then stepped to the side.

The male victim's shirt had been cut away so the CI could work on the body. Deets pulled on a pair of latex gloves. The body was lying in an irregular pool of blood almost six feet across.

Deets lifted the man's arm, cleaned a smear of blood off the shoulder with the wet-wipe, then held the arm for Terrio to see.

'What do you think? Look familiar?'

Lividity had mottled the skin with purple and black bruising, but Terrio could still make out the tattoo. He felt a low dread of recognition. 'I've seen this before.'

'Yeah. That's what I thought.'

'Does he have one on the other arm, too?'

'One on each side. Matching.'

Deets lowered the arm, then peeled off the latex gloves. 'Only one guy I know of has tats like this. He used to be a cop here. LAPD.'

A blocky, bright red arrow had been inked onto the outside of Frank Meyer's shoulder. It pointed forward.

Terrio's head was racing. 'This is good, Lou. This gives us a direction. We just gotta figure out what to do.'

The woman's voice cut through behind them. 'About what?'

Terrio turned, and there she was. Wraparounds hiding her eyes. Mouth so tight she looked like she had steel teeth.

'I asked a question, Sergeant. Do about what?'

Terrio glanced at the arrow again, then gave her the answer.

'Joe Pike.'

THE FIRST TIME Joe Pike saw the tattooed woman, she was struggling up the eastern ridge of Runyon Canyon, Pike running down, both of them blowing steam in the chill before dawn. Seeing her in the murky light that first morning, the young woman appeared to be wearing tights, but as they drew closer, he realised her legs were sleeved with elaborate tattoos. More ink decorated her arms. Pike had only two tattoos. A red arrow on the outside of each deltoid, both pointing forward.

He saw her two or three times each week after that. They had never exchanged more than a word or two.

The day Pike learned about Frank and Cindy Meyer, he and the tattooed woman left the park together. They had not run together, but she had been at the bottom when he finished, and fell in beside him. Pike wondered if she had planned it that way, and was thinking about it when he saw the first man.

The first man waited beneath a jacaranda tree on the opposite side of the street, jeans, sunglasses, cotton shirt tight at the shoulders. He openly stared as Pike passed, then fell in behind at a casual jog.

The second man was leaning against a car with his arms crossed. He watched Pike and the woman pass, then he, too, fell in behind. Pike knew they were plain-clothes police officers, so he decided to give himself room. He grunted a goodbye and picked up his pace.

The woman said, 'See you next time.'

As Pike drifted to the centre of the street, a blue sedan pulled out from a cross street two blocks behind. One block ahead, a tan sedan pulled from the kerb, boxing him in. Two men were in the front of the tan car, with a woman in the back. Pike saw her turn to see him. Short brown hair. Wraparound sunglasses. Frown. The man in the passenger seat dangled a badge.

Pike eased to a stop. The sedans and trailing officers stopped when Pike stopped, everyone keeping their distance.

The tattooed woman realised something was happening and nervously danced on her toes. 'Dude, what is this? You want me to get help?'

'They're police. They just want to talk to me.'

If they wanted to arrest him, they wouldn't have approached in the middle of a residential street. If they wanted to kill him, they would have already tried.

The man with the badge got out of the lead car. He was balding, with a thin moustache that was too dark for the rest of his hair. His driver got out too, a younger man with bright eyes. The woman remained in the car, twisted round to watch. She was on her cell phone.

The man with the badge said, 'Jack Terrio, LAPD. This is Lou Deets. OK if we come over there?'

'Sure.'

Pike unshouldered his rucksack. He ran with a weighted ruck, and also wore a bumbag, a sleeveless grey sweatshirt, New Balance running shoes, blue shorts and government-issue sunglasses.

When Terrio and Deets reached him, Deets stood to the side.

'That's some nice ink you have there, Pike, the red arrows. Don't see many like that, do we, boss?'

Terrio ignored him, and said, 'You know a man name of Frank Meyer?'

A chill spread through Pike's belly. He had not seen Frank Meyer in years, though he frequently thought about him, and now his name hung in the midmorning air like a frosty ghost.

'What happened?'

Deets said, 'Have you seen him in the past week or so?'

'Not in a long time. Ten years, maybe.'

'What if I told you I have a witness who claims you were with Meyer recently?'

Pike studied Deets for a moment, and read he was lying. Pike turned back to Terrio. 'You want to play games, I'll keep running.'

'No games. Meyer and his family were murdered in their home two nights ago. The boys and the wife were executed. A woman we've identified as their nanny survived, but she's in a coma.'

No part of Joe Pike moved except for the rise and fall of his chest until he glanced at the tattooed woman. An older woman had come out of her house, and now the two of them were watching him.

Pike faced Terrio again. 'I didn't kill them.'

'Don't think you did. We believe a professional home-invasion crew killed them. We believe that same crew has hit six other homes in the past three months, murdering a total of eleven people.'

Pike knew where they were going. 'You don't have any suspects?'

'Nothing. No prints, pix, or witnesses. We don't have any idea who's doing this, so we started looking at the victims.'

Deets said, 'Turns out we found something the first six have in common. Three were drug traffickers, one was a pornographer who laundered money for the Israeli mob, and two were jewellery merchants who fenced stolen goods. The first six were as dirty as yesterday's socks, so now we're seeing what's up with Meyer.'

'Frank wasn't a criminal.'

'You can't know that.'

'Frank had an import business. He sold clothes.'

Terrio fingered a photograph from his jacket. The picture showed Frank, Pike and a chemical-company executive named Delroy Spence in the El Salvadorian jungle. Spence was dirty, lice-ridden and wearing the remains of a tattered blue business suit. Meyer and Pike were wearing T-shirts, faded utility trousers, and M4 rifles slung on their arms. Meyer and Spence were both smiling. Spence was smiling because Pike, Meyer and a man named Lonny Tang had just rescued him after two months of captivity at the hands of a band of narcoterrorists. Meyer was smiling because he had just cracked a joke about retiring to get married.

'You and Meyer were mercenaries.'

'So?'

Terrio studied the picture. 'He's all over the world, hanging out with the wrong kind of people. Maybe he started importing more than clothes.'

'Not Frank.'

'No? None of his friends or neighbours knew what he used to do. This little picture is the only thing from those days we found in his house. Why do you think that is?'

'Cindy didn't approve.'

Terrio slipped the picture into his pocket. 'This home-invasion crew doesn't pick homes at random. Sooner or later, we're going to learn Meyer had something they wanted—dope, cash.'

Terrio returned to the tan sedan without another word. Deets didn't follow.

Deets said, 'So you haven't seen this guy in ten years?'

'No.'

'Why is that? You have a falling-out?'

Pike thought how best to answer. 'Like I said, his wife.'

'But it was your picture he kept. And your tattoos. What's up with that, Pike? Some kind of unit thing?'

Pike didn't understand. 'The arrows?'

'Yeah, here and here, like you.'

The last time Pike saw Frank, on the day Frank left the contract service for good, Frank Meyer had no tattoos.

Pike said, 'I don't know what you're talking about.'

Deets made a stiff smile, then lowered his voice. 'I never met someone who's killed as many people as you, still walking free.'

Pike watched Deets walk away. Terrio was already in the car. Deets got in behind the wheel. The woman in the back seat was talking to Terrio. They drove away.

Everything was normal except Frank Meyer was dead.

The tattooed woman trotted up, excited. 'What did they want?'

'A friend of mine was murdered.'

'Oh, I'm sorry. That's awful. They think you did it?'

'Nothing like that.'

She made a ragged laugh. 'Dude, listen, they *do*. I'm tellin' you, man, those cats were scared of you.'

'Maybe.'

'I'm not.'

Pike studied her for a moment then shouldered his ruck. 'You don't know me.' He settled the pack, and continued his run.

WHEN PIKE REACHED his Jeep, he drove directly to Frank Meyer's home. Pike had lied to Terrio. He had seen Frank three years ago, though they had not spoken. A mutual friend told Pike about Frank's new house in Westwood, so Pike cruised by. Meyer had been on Pike's team, so Pike liked to make sure he was doing OK.

The Westwood house was taped off as an active crime scene. A black and white radio car was out front, along with two SID wagons, an unmarked sedan and a single TV news van. Two female officers posted to protect the scene were slumped in the radio car.

Pike parked a block behind their car, then studied Frank Meyer's house. He wanted to know how Frank died, and was thinking he would break in that night when a tall, thin criminalist named John Chen came down the drive to an SID wagon. Chen was a friend.

Chen's vehicle was directly in front of the radio car. If Chen left, Pike would follow. If Chen returned to the house, Pike would wait.

Pike was waiting to see what Chen would do next when his phone rang. The caller ID read JOHN CHEN.

Pike said, 'Hello, John.'

Chen was a paranoid. Even though he was alone in his vehicle, his voice was guarded, as if he was worried about being overheard.

'Joe, it's me, John Chen. I'm at a murder scene in Westwood. The police are coming to—'

'I'm behind you, John. Look behind you.'

Chen emerged from his wagon. He stared at the radio car as if the officers would jump out to arrest him.

Pike said, 'Farther back. I'm on the next block.'

Chen finally saw him, then shrivelled back into his wagon. 'Did the police already come see you?'

'A detective named Terrio.'

'I was calling to warn you, bro. They found a picture of you with the vic. I'm sorry, man. I only heard about it this morning.'

'I want to see what happened in there.'

Chen hesitated, then sighed. 'OK, listen—two dicks from West LA are inside. I don't know how long they'll be.'

'I'll wait.'

'All right. OK. I'll call when it's clear.' Chen re-emerged from his wagon, then slouched back to the house.

Pike studied Frank's house. The house looked stable, traditional and strong, and was suited to the Frank Pike knew. Pike liked that. Frank had done all right for himself.

After a while, a man and a woman who were most likely the West LA detectives came out, got into the unmarked sedan and drove away. Chen called as Pike watched them. 'You still out there?'

'Yes.'

'I'll come get you. We won't have much time.'

Pike met Chen on the sidewalk, then followed him to the house. The two uniforms in the car appeared to be dozing, and no one was visible in the media van. When they reached the front door, Chen handed Pike a pair of blue paper bootees.

They slipped on the bootees, then stepped into a large circular entry with a winding staircase up to the first floor. A towering grandfather clock stood guard at the stairs, standing tall over a rusty crust of blood footprints that dotted the floor.

Pike felt odd, entering Frank's home, as if he was intruding into a place where it was understood he would never be welcomed. He had glimpsed Frank's life from the outside, but never from within. He had never met Cindy, or the boys, and now here he was.

Pike followed Chen through the entry to a large, open family room adjoining a dining area. An irregular pool of drying blood covered the floor midway between the dining table and the hall. Bright green yarn had been stretched from a metal stand centred in the blood pool to two stands set up about ten feet apart in the living room. These stands marked the probable location of the shooters. A second, smaller stain was visible across the family room.

Chen nodded towards the stain at their feet. 'Mr Meyer was here. His wife and one of the boys there by the French doors. The nanny was in her room.'

A three-ring binder was open on a table where Chen had been making sketches. He flipped to a scaled floor plan showing the location and position of the bodies, along with recovered shell casings.

'The family was probably having dinner when the shooters broke in. Meyer probably advanced on them, brief struggle, boom, boom—he had cuts on his face, like they hit him with a hard object, probably a gun—and that's when they killed him.'

Two strands of green yarn stretched from the large bloodstain to the metal stand on the far side of the room almost thirty feet away. A third strand stretched to a closer stand. Three strands of green.

Pike said, 'They shot him three times?'

'Yeah, once high on his hip, once in the side, and once in his back. Two shooters, like they were trying to put him down fast. This suggests he was fighting. The others were shot once in the forehead at close range, which suggests a deliberate execution.'

The others. Cindy and the boys.

'How many men altogether?'

'Four distinct shoe prints. Casings from four different guns. All nine millimetres.'

'Fingerprints?'

'They were gloved. We didn't find anything at the earlier crime scenes, either. C'mon, I'll show you where we found the nanny.'

Chen led Pike across the dining room, through the kitchen, to a tiny bedroom where the door and jamb were split.

'See how they crunched the door? It was locked. She was probably trying to hide.'

Chen glanced at his notes. 'Ana Markovic, aged twenty-two. Two shots close range, one in the face, one in the chest, two casings here in the room.'

The room was a small place to die, filled by a bed and a desk, with only a casement window for light. Pictures of a smiling young woman hugging Frank's boys were taped over the cluttered desktop, part of a birthday card the kids had made of construction paper. *We love Ana.*

Pike said, 'Her?'

'Uh-huh. An au pair.'

Smears of blood on the floor and the door indicated she tried to crawl away after being shot.

Pike said, 'Did she describe them?'

'Uh-uh. She was unconscious when the uniforms found her. They got her over to UCLA, but she's not going to make it.'

'Does Terrio have any suspects?'

'No one we've identified.'

'How many people have they killed?'

'Eleven. Hey, that's why they set up a task force.' Chen suddenly glanced at his watch. 'Listen, I gotta get busy.'

Pike followed Chen back to the dining room, but he still wasn't ready to leave. He said, 'Let me see the pictures.'

Chen would have photographed everything when he arrived at the scene, before he made the sketches.

'Bro, these people were your friends. You sure?'

'Let me see.'

Chen went to his case and returned with a digital camera. He scrolled through the images, then held it so Pike could see.

The image was tiny, but Pike saw Frank splayed on the floor. He was on his back, his left leg straight and right leg cocked to the side. Pike had wanted to see if the red arrows were inked on his arms like Deets said, but Frank was wearing a long-sleeved shirt, rolled to his forearms.

'I want to see his face. Can you zoom it?'

Chen adjusted the picture. Frank was cut beneath his right eye in two places. Pike wondered if he had been trying to disarm the man or men closest to him when the men across the room shot him.

Pike said, 'Was a time, he would have beat them.'

'You want to see the wife and kids?'

'No.'

Chen looked relieved.

'You knew him pretty well?'

'Yes.'

'What was he holding?'

'Frank wasn't a criminal.'

'All the other vics in the string were dirty. That's part of the pattern.'

'Not Frank.'

Chen read something in Pike's voice. 'Sorry,' he said. 'They probably made a mistake. Assholes like this, they probably hit the wrong house.'

'Yes,' Pike said. 'They made a mistake.'

Chen said, 'I gotta get back to work. I gotta get you outta here.'

Pike followed the hall to the front door, but he did not leave. On the way in, they had passed what appeared to be a home office.

Photographs of Frank and his family hung on the walls. Pike studied the pictures, comparing the Frank he had known with the Frank who had lived in this house. When Pike met Frank for the first time, Frank was fresh out of eight years in the Marine Corps, having seen service in Central America and the Middle East. He had been young and lean, but had the chunky build of a kid who would put on weight quickly if he stopped working out. The Frank in these pictures had gained weight, but looked happy and safe.

Pike found a picture of Frank and Cindy, then moved to a picture of Frank and Cindy with the two boys. Cindy was squat and sturdy, with short brown hair, happy eyes, and a crooked nose that made her pretty. Pike studied more pictures. The two boys, then the four of them together, father, mother, children, family.

Pike came to a space on a shelf with an empty frame. The frame was the right size for the El Salvador picture. Pike took a breath, let it out, then found Chen back in the dining room.

'Show me his family.'

'You want to see what they did to his wife and his kids?'

Pike wanted to see. He wanted to fix them in his mind, and have them close when he found the men who killed them.

PIKE LIVED ALONE in a two-bedroom condo in Culver City. He drove home, then stripped and showered away the sweat. He let hot water beat into him, then turned on the cold. Pike didn't flinch when the icy water fired his skin. He rubbed the cold over his face and scalp, and stayed in the cold much longer than the hot, then towelled himself off.

Before he dressed, he looked at himself in the mirror. Pike was six foot one. He weighed 205 pounds. He had been shot seven times, hit by shrapnel on fourteen separate occasions, and stabbed or cut eleven times. Scars from the wounds and resulting surgeries mapped his body like roads. Pike knew exactly which scars had been earned when he worked with Frank Meyer.

Pike leaned close to the mirror, examining each eye. Left eye, right eye. The irises were a deep, liquid blue. The skin surrounding the eyes was lined from squinting into too many suns. Pike's eyes were sensitive to light, but his visual acuity was amazing. They had loved that in sniper school.

Pike dressed, then put on his sunglasses.

Lunch was leftover Thai food nuked in the microwave. Tofu, cabbage, broccoli and rice. He drank a litre of water, then washed the one plate and fork, all the while thinking about what he had learned from Chen and Terrio, and how he could use it.

Jumping him in broad daylight on a residential street to ask questions was a panic move. This confirmed that after three months, seven invasions and eleven homicides, Terrio had not developed enough evidence to initiate an arrest. But a lack of proof did not necessarily mean a lack of suspects or usable information. Professional home-invasion crews were almost always comprised of career criminals. If caught, they would be off the streets for the period of their incarceration, but would almost always commit more crimes when released. Terrio knew this, and would compare the date of the original robbery to release dates of criminals with a similar history, trying to identify suspects. Pike wanted to know what they had.

He went upstairs to his bedroom closet, opened his safe and took out a list of telephone numbers in code. He found the number he wanted, then brought it downstairs and made the call.

Jon Stone answered on the second ring. Stone must have recognised Pike's number on the caller ID. 'Well. Look who it is.'

'Got a couple of questions.'

'How much will you pay for a couple of answers?'

Jon Stone was a talent agent for professional military contractors. Stone used to be a PMC himself, but now placed talent with the large private military corporations and security firms favoured by Washington and corporate America. Safer that way, and much more profitable.

Pike didn't respond.

Stone said, 'Tell you what, let's table that for now. You go ahead, ask, we'll see what develops.'

'Remember Frank Meyer?'

'Fearless Frank, my man on the tanks? Sure.'

'Has he been on the market?'

'He retired ten years ago, at least.'

'So you haven't heard any rumours? Like Frank getting involved with people you wouldn't expect.'

Jon snorted. 'Fearless Frank? Get control of yourself.'

Pike went on. 'Less than two hours ago, a police detective named Terrio told me Frank was dirty. He believes Frank was using his import business for something illegal.'

'Why was a cop talking about Frank?'

'Frank and his family were murdered.'

Stone was silent for a time, and when he spoke again, his voice was low. 'For real?'

'A robbery crew broke into their home two nights ago. Frank, his wife, their kids. They zero in on targets with a cash payoff—dope dealers, money launderers, people like that. Frank wasn't their first.'

'I can't believe Frank went wrong,' Stone said, 'but I'll ask around.'

'Another thing. You have juice with Fugitive Section or Special Investigations?'

Now Stone grew wary. 'Why?'

'You know why, Jon. If Terrio's task force has any suspects, Fugitive Section or SIS will be trying to find them. I want to know what they have.'

Fugitive Section detectives specialised in tracking down and apprehending wanted felons in high-risk situations. Special Investigations Section were elite operators who ran long-term, covert surveillance on criminals suspected of committing violent serial crime. Retired Fugitive Section and SIS operators commanded top dollar at private security firms, and Jon Stone had placed more than a few into fat corporate jobs.

Stone hesitated. 'I might have a friend who has a friend.'

'I need this information before they make an arrest. Frank was one of my guys.'

Stone lapsed into silence, and seemed thoughtful when he spoke. 'I have an idea. Ask Lonny. Lonny might know.'

Lonny Tang. The man who had taken the picture in El Salvador. Thirteen days later, on a job in Kuwait, Frank Meyer had saved Lonny Tang's life on what would turn out to be Lonny's last job.

Pike said, 'Why would Lonny know?'

'Frank kept in touch with him. If Frank was mixed up in something, he'd tell Lonny if he was gonna tell anyone.'

'That's a good idea, asking Lonny. I will.'

'You gotta set it up through his lawyer. You want the number?'

'I have it.'

'I'll let you know about the other thing after I talk to my guys.'

'Thanks, Jon. How much do I owe you?'

'Forget it. Frank was one of my guys, too.'

Pike hung up, cleared the appointments he had that afternoon, then called Lonny Tang's attorney, a man named Carson Epp.

Pike said, 'I need to speak with him. Can you set it up?'

'May I tell him what this is about?'

Pike decided Lonny should hear about Frank from him, and not Epp or someone else. Lonny had been one of Pike's guys, too.

'Frank the Tank. He'll know. Let me give you my cell.'

Pike gave him his number, then lowered the phone, thinking he couldn't wait for Stone to come up with something. He wondered if Ana Markovic was still alive, and if she had managed to speak. Chen said she hadn't, but Chen was only repeating what he had heard from the cops. Pike wanted to talk to the nurses. She might have mumbled something after the cops had gone. A word or a name could give him an edge. Pike wanted the edge.

Pike changed into a pale blue dress shirt to make himself presentable, then bought a bouquet of daisies and drove to the hospital.

2

The intensive care unit was on the sixth floor of the UCLA Medical Centre. Pike stepped out of the elevator and followed signs to an octagonal command post at the end of a hall lined by glass-walled rooms. Curtains could be pulled for privacy, but most of the rooms were open so the staff could see the patients from the hall.

Pike walked the length of the hall checking for officers, but any who had been present were gone. He returned to the nurses' station, and waited until a harried nurse turned to him. Her name tag read BARBARA FARNHAM.

'May I help you?'

Pike and his dress shirt held out the flowers. 'Ana Markovic.'

The nurse's expression softened. 'I'm sorry. Are you a relative?'

'I know the family.'

'We limit our visitors in ICU. Her sister's here now, but I'm sure she wouldn't mind.'

Pike nodded. 'That's fine. Thank you.'

'Room twelve, but you can't leave the flowers. If a patient has an allergic reaction, it could weaken their immune system.'

Pike had expected this, and handed over the flowers.

'You can pick them up when you leave or we can send them to another part of the hospital. We usually send them to maternity.'

'Before I see her, I'd like to speak with her primary nurse. Is that possible?'

'Well, that's all of us, really. We work as a team.'

'The police told me she wasn't able to make a statement when they found her. I was wondering if she came round after surgery.'

'No, I'm sorry, she hasn't.'

'I don't mean a conversation. Maybe she mumbled a name. Would you ask the other nurses?'

'I'll ask, but I'm sure she hasn't spoken.'

A light mounted outside a nearby door came on. The nurse hurried away, so Pike went down the hall to room twelve. He expected to find the sister, but room twelve was empty except for the bandaged figure in the bed.

Pike went to the bed. The left side of her face and head were hidden beneath bandages, but the right half of her face was visible. She seemed to be trying to open her eye. Her eyelid would lift, the eye beneath would drift and roll, then the eyelid would close.

Pike knew she had not spoken as soon as he saw her, and thought it unlikely she would regain consciousness. The shape of the bandage on her head suggested a bullet had entered beneath her left eye. Pike lifted the sheet enough to see the incisions taped across her chest and abdomen, which were still orange from the Betadine solution used to clean the area. He lowered the sheet, and tucked it beneath her. The upper chest wound had done the most damage. The bullet had most likely deflected off her ribs or clavicle, and punched through the diaphragm into her abdomen. Ana Markovic had bled out internally, and now she was dying.

Pike touched her cheek. 'Ana, we need your help.'

The eye rolled, then drooped, an autonomic move without conscious thought.

He took her hand. He stroked it, then pinched the soft flesh between her thumb and index finger. 'Who shot you?'

A female voice cut him from behind. 'Move away from her.'

Pike calmly turned. A woman in her late twenties who was probably the sister stood framed in the door. Eyes like flint chips, black hair pulled tight, and a pronounced East European accent.

Pike said, 'I was trying to wake her.'

'Leave go her hand, and move away.'

She wore a suede jacket over designer jeans, and cradled an oversized leather shoulder bag with one hand. The other hand was inside the bag, and ominously still.

Pike placed Ana's hand on the bed. 'I'm sorry. I came to see if she was awake. The Meyers were friends of mine.'

The woman's eyes narrowed. 'The people she worked for?'

'Frank and Cindy. Ana cared for their boys.'

The woman's eyes charted his face, his build, his shades and cropped warrior hair. She didn't like what she saw. Not even the shirt. She stepped aside to clear the door. 'You should leave now.'

Her hand stayed in the bag.

Pike said, 'Has she said anything that could help us? A name. A word. Something that could identify the people who did this.'

'She tells us who did this thing, I will tell the police.'

Pike went to the door. 'I understand. I'm sorry about your sister.'

As Pike left, he glanced back, and saw her watching from the door as if sizing him for a coffin.

He waited at the nurses' station until Barbara Farnham returned, then asked if she had checked with the other nurses. She had. Ana Markovic had made no sounds, or showed any signs of recovery.

'Thanks for checking.'

When Pike reached the elevator, Ana's sister was waiting. He nodded, but she looked away. The elevator arrived with three other people aboard, so they rode down in silence. The sister exited the elevator first, but stopped at a lobby newsstand as Pike continued to the parking structure. He saw her watching him as he passed.

Pike crossed to the parking garage, then stopped on the ground floor for the elevator. Pike always took the stairs, but now he waited for the elevator. He was not surprised when Ana's sister stepped up beside him, just as she had before.

She made a tight smile. 'We are destined to see each other.'

Pike said, 'Yes.'

The elevator was empty when it opened. Pike held the door, letting her go first. The woman moved to the back corner. Pike followed her, as certain of what she was about to do as if he could see it on a Sunset Boulevard billboard. Her hand was still in her bag.

Pike said, 'Which level?'

'Six.'

As the doors closed, her hand came out of the bag with a small black gun that Pike twisted away even before she raised it. She swung at him, but Pike caught her arm. She tried to knee him, but he leaned in just enough to pin her with his hip. He pulled the button to stop the elevator. A loud buzzer went off, but not for long.

'I didn't come here to hurt her.'

She was trapped. Breathing hard, eyes cut to slits, she looked as if she wanted to rip his throat out with her teeth.

Pike said, 'Calm down. Look.'

Keeping her pinned, he one-handed the clip from the pistol, and jacked the slide to clear the chamber. A nice little Ruger .380.

'Frank Meyer was my friend.' Pike held out the unloaded gun. 'You see?'

She straightened, maybe not altogether convinced. She clutched the gun, her back pressed to the wall. 'How did you find her?'

'The police told me.'

'Those bastards might find her, too.'

'So you're standing guard?'

'They leave her here with no one! I do what I have to do.'

Pike's phone vibrated. Pike would have ignored it, but he was expecting Carson Epp, and that's who it was. Pike took the call, staring at her as he spoke. 'Pike.'

'I'll have Lonny on the line in twenty minutes. Will you be able to take it?'

'Yes.'

Pike returned the phone to his pocket, then tipped his head at her pistol. 'Put it away.'

She put the Ruger into her bag. Pike added the clip and the loose cartridge, then offered his hand.

'My name is Pike. Joe.'

She stared at him. Her cheekbones were high and prominent, her cheeks were lean. Pike's hand had been cooked dark by the sun, but her skin was pale as milk. She gripped his hand.

She said, 'Rina.'

'Karina?'

'Yes.'

'Russian?'

'Serbian.'

'Leave the gun at home. They won't come here. Their risk would be larger than the chance she could identify them. They know that, so they won't take the chance. The police know the same thing, which is why they didn't post a guard.'

The elevator buzzed again, anxious to move.

Pike said, 'Which floor?'

'Here. I am not parked in this building.'

Pike reached for the button to open the door.

'When we got on, what were you going to do, shoot me?'

'I thought you might be one of them. If you were, then, yes, I would have shot you.'

Pike opened the door. Rina Markovic stepped off.

She said, 'Perhaps someone will find these bastards, yes?'

'Someone will find them. Yes.'

She studied him. 'I am sorry for your friend.'

She walked away as the door closed. Pike took the elevator up to his Jeep. He took off the blue dress shirt, slipped on the sleeveless grey sweatshirt he'd been wearing earlier, then wound his way down to the exit.

Eight minutes later, he was parked in a Best Buy parking lot when Lonny Tang called.

Pike said, 'I'm here.'

Carson Epp said, 'Lonny, can you hear him OK?'

Lonny's voice was high-pitched, and soft.

'Yeah, I hear him fine. Hey, Joe.'

Epp said, 'Lonny, when you're finished, just hang up. I'll check back with you to make sure everything is all right.'

'OK. Thanks, Carson.'

Pike heard a click as Epp left the line, then the soft hush of Lonny Tang's voice. 'Must be bad, you calling like this.'

Pike gave it to Lonny head-on. 'Frank's dead. He was murdered two nights ago. Frank and his family.'

Lonny was silent, but then Pike heard a soft sobbing. Pike let him cry. If any of them had a right to cry, it was Lonny.

Lonny got himself together. 'Thanks for letting me know. I appreciate it, Joe. The bastard who did it, they get him?'

'Not yet. The police think it's a home-invasion crew. Frank's house was the seventh home they've hit.'

Lonny cleared his throat. 'OK, well, I don't know what to say. When they get these pricks, will you let me know?'

'I have to ask you something.'

'What's that?'

'This crew, they work on good intelligence. Their first six targets were all people like dope dealers and money cleaners. You see where I'm going?'

'Frank had an import business. He imported clothes.'

'If Frank was importing something else, he was in business with someone who gave him up. That person knows who killed him.'

'This is Frank, man. Are you serious?'

'Did he tell you something I should know?'

Lonny was quiet for a while, breathing, and his voice was calm. 'He came to my trial. Not every day, but a couple of times. This once, I asked him if he was sorry he saved me, you know—because if he hadn't saved me, those men I murdered would still be alive. So I asked if he regretted it. He told me guys like us had each other's back, so he had my back. He didn't have any choice.'

'C'mon, Lonny, yes or no. Did Frank tell you he was into something? Maybe say something that left you wondering?'

'You think if I could help get the pricks who killed him, I wouldn't be all over it? I'd kill them myself.'

'You're sure?'

'*Yes*. He was the same Frank we knew. Being an Eagle Scout was in his DNA.'

Pike felt the tightness in his chest ease, bringing a sense of relief.

'OK, Lon. That's what I thought, but I had to be sure. You're the only one he stayed in contact with.'

Pike wanted to hang up, but he hadn't spoken with Lonny in a long time, and now he felt guilty. Lonny Tang had been one of his guys for eleven years, on and off, until Lonny got hurt.

Pike asked the obvious. 'How you doing in there?'

'You get used to it. I get all the meds and medical care I need.'

On the day Frank Meyer saved Lonny Tang's life, an RPG explosion sent a piece of shrapnel the size of a golf ball through Lonny's abdomen. Lonny lost his left kidney, a foot of large intestine, his spleen, part of his liver and his health. He was left with a growing addiction to painkillers and no way to pay for them. The Percocets led to harder drugs, and finally to a bar in Long Beach, which Lonny robbed. He shot and killed the bar's owner and an innocent bystander and was arrested less than three hours later. Convicted on two counts of first-degree murder, he was currently serving twenty-five years to life at the Corcoran State Prison in California.

Pike was about to hang up when he remembered something else. 'One more thing. The police told me Frank had my ink.'

'You didn't know?'

'No.'

'That was years ago, man. This time he came to visit, he showed me. He'd just had 'm done. Big ol' red arrows like yours. Cindy damn near threw him out of the house.'

Lonny laughed, but Pike felt embarrassed. 'He say anything?'

'Why he got them?'

'Yeah.'

'Remember all the trouble she gave him about being a contractor, and how she wouldn't marry him unless he settled down?'

'Sure.'

'The rest of us were all over him to dump her. But Frank said you told him to go for it. He really appreciated that, Joe.'

Pike considered that for a moment. 'Was he happy?'

'Yeah, brother. Hell, yeah, he was happy. It was like he woke up in someone else's life. What's the word? He was content, man.'

Pike said, 'Good.'

'Joe? Thanks for calling about Frankie. I don't get many calls.'

'I have to go.'

'Joe?'

'I gotta get going.'

'You were a good leader. You really took care of us, man. I'm sorry I let you down.'

Pike closed his phone.

THE EARLY-EVENING SKY purpled as Pike turned towards Frank Meyer's house for the second time that day. Pike drove slowly, buying time for the twilight sky to darken. Pike loved the night. He felt safe in the darkness. Hidden, and free.

Frank's house was dark when Pike drove past. The SID wagons and criminalists were gone. A radio car remained out front, but Pike recognised the car as a scarecrow vehicle, left to discourage intruders, but posted without a crew. This made his task easier.

Pike parked in the deep shadow of a maple tree two houses away. He moved without hesitation, sliding out of his Jeep and into a row of hedges. He crossed the neighbour's yard, then hoisted himself over a wall. He followed the side of Frank's garage into the back yard, then stood for a moment, listening. The neighbourhood was alive with normal sounds. A watchful owl, a faraway siren.

Pike went to the French doors, popped a pane near the lever, and stepped into the deeper black of the family room. Pike listened again, then turned on a small flashlight that produced a dim, red light. He covered the lens with his fingers, letting out only enough light to reveal the room. His hand glowed as if filled with fire.

The heart-shaped stain where Cindy Meyer and her youngest son died was a smudge on the dark floor. Pike studied it for a moment, but Pike wasn't looking for clues. He was looking for Frank.

Pike circled the family room, the dining room and the kitchen, moving as silent as smoke. He noted the furniture, toys and magazines, as if each was a page in the book of the family's life, helping to build their story.

A hall led to the master bedroom. Photographs of the kids and Frank and Cindy dotted the walls like memories, captured and frozen in time. An antique desk sat opposite a king-sized bed with a padded headboard, a plaque on the desk reading: *Empress of the World*. Cindy's desk.

Something about the bed bothered Pike, and then he realised the bed was made. The family room and Frank's office had been upended, but the bed here in the master was undisturbed. This suggested the home invaders had either been frightened away before searching the master, or had found what they wanted.

Pike played the red light over Cindy's desk, and saw more snapshots. Frank and the kids. An older couple who might have been Cindy's parents. And then Pike found the picture he was looking for. He had not known he was searching for it, but felt a sense of completion when he saw it. The snapshot showed Frank in a swimming pool with one of the boys. Frank had heaved his son into the air, his arms extended. This picture was the only photograph that showed the red arrows inked onto his deltoids. Pointing forward, just as the arrows on Pike's delts pointed forward. Identical.

He studied the picture for a long while before he left the bedroom. He moved back along the hall, thinking how different his own home was from Frank's. Pike did not have a family, so he had no pictures of family on the walls, and he did not keep pictures of his friends. Pike's life had led to blank walls, and now he wondered if his walls would ever be filled.

When Pike reached the entry, the outside of the house was lit like a blinding sun. Pike closed his hand over the tiny red light, and waited.

A patrol car was spotlighting the house. They had probably been instructed to cruise by every half-hour or so. Pike was calm. The light worked over the house, then it died abruptly.

Pike followed his crimson light upstairs, where a stain on the carpet marked the older son's murder. Little Frank. Pike counted the years back to a deadly night on the far side of the world when big Frank told Pike that Cindy was pregnant.

That time, they were protecting a collective of villages in Central Africa. A group called the Lord's Resistance Army had been kidnapping teenage girls, whom they raped and sold as slaves. Pike brought over Frank, Jon Stone, a Brit named Colin Chandler and Lonny Tang. They were tracking the LRA to recover sixteen girls when Frank told him that his girlfriend, Cindy, was pregnant. Frank wanted to marry her, but Cindy had stunned him with an ultimatum—she wanted no part of his dangerous life or the dangerous people with whom he worked, so either Frank would leave his current life and friends behind, or Cindy would never see him again. Frank had been shattered, torn between his love for Cindy and his loyalty to his friends. He had talked to Pike for almost three hours that night, then the next, and the next.

Those African nights led through the intervening years like a twisting tunnel through time to this spot on the floor. Pike covered the red light, turning the world black.

He went downstairs to Frank's office.

The drapes had been left open by the SID crews, so the office was bright with outside light. Pike turned off his red flash. He sat at Frank's desk, his back to the window. Frank the Tank's desk. A long way from Africa.

THE NIGHT IN AFRICA when Frank decided to change his life, he had thirty-one days remaining on his contract, but was still thirteen days from earning his nickname. Two days after Africa, Joe, Frank and Lonny Tang flew to El Salvador. Frank had not been able to reach Cindy until they landed, but that's when he told her. She wanted him to fly home immediately, but Frank explained he had made a commitment for the duration of his contract, and would honour that commitment. Cindy didn't like it, but agreed. Joe and his guys spent five days in El Salvador, then flew to Kuwait.

It was a British contract, providing security for French, Italian and British journalists. That particular assignment was to transport two BBC journalists and a two-person camera crew inland to a small village called Jublaban, well away from hostile forces.

Pike gave the Jublaban run to Lonny, Frank, Colin Chandler and an ex-French Foreign Legion trooper named Durand Galatoise. Two Land Rovers, two operators per Rover, the journalists divided between them. A fast thirty-two miles over the mountains, leave in the morning, back after lunch.

They left at eight that morning, Lonny and Frank in the lead truck, Chandler and Galatoise in trail, and reached Jublaban without incident. There to do a story on rural medical care, the journalists were interviewing Jublaban's only physician when an incoming RPG hit the second Rover, flipping it onto its side. The operators and journalists immediately came under small-arms fire.

Galatoise was killed within the first sixty seconds, the remaining Rover was hit, then Lonny Tang caught the piece of shrapnel that tore him inside out. Frank and Chandler realised they were facing eight or ten men, then noticed an approaching nightmare: four armoured vehicles and two full-sized battle tanks were rumbling towards them across the desert. With both Rovers disabled, the operators and their journalists were trapped.

Frank pushed Lonny Tang's intestines back into his body, then wrapped him with pressure bandages and belts. While Chandler laid down cover fire, Frank ran to his burning Rover for radios, more ammunition, and a thirty-pound, .50-calibre Barrett rifle they used for sniper suppression. The Barrett could punch through engine blocks at more than a mile.

Chandler herded the journalists to a more defensible location, but Lonny Tang could not be moved. Frank stashed him in a stone hut, then moved forward with the Barrett gun. Pike heard much of it through his radio, with Chandler broadcasting a play-by-play as Pike coordinated a rescue effort with a British air controller.

Frank Meyer fought for almost thirty minutes, running and gunning with the Barrett even when the tanks and armoured vehicles crunched into the village, Frank banging away like a lunatic to draw them from Lonny Tang.

Everyone later assumed the big boomers turned back into the desert after they picked up their troops, but Chandler and the BBC journalists reported that a young American named Frank Meyer had shot it out toe-to-toe with four armoured vehicles and two heavy tanks, and had driven the bastards away.

Frank's contract expired five days later. He wept when he shook Pike's hand for the last time; he boarded an airplane, and that had been that, changing one life for another.

Pike officially retired from contract work sixty-two days later, and maybe Frank's decision had something to do with Pike's decision, though Pike never thought so. Pike had told Frank to do it. Build the family he wanted. Leave the past. Always move forward.

PIKE WAS STILL at Frank's desk when his cell vibrated.

Jon Stone said, 'All right, listen. They're watching a guy named Rahmi Johnson. They've been on him for almost a month. I've got an address for you.'

'If they're on him for a month, he didn't murder Frank.'

'Rahmi isn't the suspect. Cops think his cousin might be involved, a dude named Jamal Johnson.'

'Might be, or is?'

'Gotta have proof for *is*, but he looks pretty good. He was released from Soledad two weeks before the first score. He crashed with Rahmi when he got out, but moved out after the score. Four days after the second score, Jamal dropped by with a sixty-inch plasma to thank Rahmi for putting him up. A week after the third score, Jamal tools up in a brand-new black-on-black Malibu with custom rims. He gives that to Rahmi, too.'

Pike said, 'Where's Jamal?'

'Nobody knows, bro. That's why they're sitting on Rahmi.'

'Maybe Rahmi knows. Have they asked him?'

'That's where they messed up. A couple of task force clowns rolled by two months ago, when Jamal was first identified as a person of interest. They heard he was crashing with Rahmi, so they went by. Rahmi played stupid, but he warned Jamal the second those cops were out the door. Jamal dropped off the map.'

Pike thought about it. 'So SIS are covering Rahmi, hoping Jamal will come round again.'

'They got nothing else, man. Jamal's their only good suspect.'

Pike grunted. SIS were good. They would shadow their target for weeks, but Pike didn't want to wait that long. The police were trying to build a case, but Pike didn't care about a case. His needs were simpler.

'What's that address?'

Stone cleared his throat. 'OK, now listen, we can't have any blowback here. You go barging in and it comes back to me, the SIS guys will know who gave them up.'

'No blowback. They'll never see me.'

Stone was giving Pike the address when light exploded into the office.

The patrol car had returned. Then the light snapped off. The yard plunged into darkness. The chatter faded. The patrol car rolled on.

Pike heard Stone swallow. Heard the glass tink the phone. Stone had been drinking.

'You think it's true, he went bad?'

'Lonny thinks the people who did this got the wrong house.'

Stone sighed, then he had another sip of whatever he was sipping.

'What are you drinking?'

'Scotch, in honour of Frank. I would rather rip off a twenty-one-gun salute out in the back yard, but my neighbours prefer the drinking.'

Pike said, 'Jon? Do you have photographs on your walls?'

'What, like naked chicks?'

'Pictures of your family. Friends.'

'Yeah. I take pictures of everything. Why?'

'No reason. Get some sleep.'

Stone was silent for so long Pike thought he had fallen asleep. 'Jon?'

'None of us had families. You never married. Lonny, Colin, not them, either. I've been married six times, man, what does that tell you? None of us had kids.'

Pike didn't know what to say, but maybe Stone voiced it for him, soft, and hoarse from the booze.

'I really wanted Frank to make it. Not just for him.'

Pike closed his phone. He sat in Frank's office for almost an hour, alone with himself and the silence, then walked back along the hall to Cindy's desk. He took the framed picture of Frank in the pool, then let himself out the way he had entered, and drove home for the night.

Part Two—The First Rule

3

Pike returned home after leaving Frank's house and found a message waiting from Elvis Cole, who was Pike's friend and partner in a detective agency.

Cole said, 'Hey. A cop named Terrio came by the office today, asking about you and someone named Frank Meyer. Felt like he was fishing, but he said this guy Frank Meyer was murdered. Call me.'

Pike deleted the message, then looked up Rahmi's address on his computer. Google Maps was like having a spy satellite. Pike typed in Rahmi's address, and there it was—all of Compton spread out thousands of feet below. Pike zoomed in for a closer look, then went to the street view.

Rahmi Johnson lived in a two-storey apartment building in Compton. His building was shaped like a shoebox, with three units on the bottom, three on the top, and a flat, featureless roof. He had the centre, ground-floor apartment. Single-family homes lined his side of the street, on lots so narrow that some of the homes were turned sideways. Rahmi's building was sideways. Almost every yard had a chain-link fence, and almost every house had security bars on its windows. The opposite side of the street was lined by single-storey commercial buildings.

Because of the sideways orientation, the side of Rahmi's building faced the street and the fronts of the apartments faced the next-door neighbour's property. Residents entered through a chain-link gate, then went along the length of their building to reach their doors. This sideways orientation made it difficult for Pike to see Rahmi's door from the street. He considered this, and knew the police would have the same problem.

Pike noticed that neither Rahmi's building nor the other apartment buildings had driveways or spaces for off-street parking; residents parked on the street. This meant Rahmi's new Malibu would probably be parked in front of his building.

No building in the area was more than two storeys. With no overlooking vantage point, the SIS spotter would have to be close. The high density of residents, the on-street parking, and the long-term nature of the surveillance meant the spotter was in a nearby building. After forty-five minutes, Pike believed he had a pretty good idea where the SIS would place their spotters, and also how he could reach Rahmi without being seen. He would have to see the area at night and during the day to be sure, but he knew what he had to do.

Pike changed into his workout gear, stretched to warm himself, then eased into the meditative state he always found through yoga. He moved slowly, working deeply through asanas from hatha yoga. He breathed, and felt himself settle. Peace came with certainty, and Pike was certain.

When Pike finished, he eased awake like a bubble rising to the surface of a great flat pond. Dinner was rice and red beans, mixed with grilled corn and eggplant. After dinner, he showered, then dressed in briefs and a T-shirt. He returned Cole's call, but Cole didn't pick up, so he left a message.

After a while, Pike went to bed. He was asleep almost at once.

His eyes opened two hours later. Pike rolled out of bed, dressed, got together his things, then drove south to Compton across a landscape brilliant with unwavering lights.

PIKE KNEW RAHMI was home the first and only time he drove past in his Jeep because the shiny black Malibu was wedged to the kerb. Three in the morning on a weeknight, the streets were dead. Pike slumped behind the wheel. Everyone else in the world might be sleeping, but SIS would be watching. One pass, they would ignore him. Two passes, they would wonder. A third pass, they would probably call in a radio car to see what was going on.

Pike drove to a park-and-ride by the freeway, parked, then called a cab service. He stood in the vapour light until a lime-green cab showed up.

The cab driver was a young African-American with suspicious eyes, who did a double take when he saw his fare was a white man.

He said, 'Car trouble?'

'I have a friend nearby. You can take me to her place.'

'Ah.' Her. A woman made everything better.

Pike gave the nearest major intersection, but not Rahmi's address. Pike didn't want the cabby to know it if he was later questioned. When they reached Rahmi's street, Pike told him to cruise the block. 'Go slow. I'll know it when I see it.'

'I thought you knew this girl?'

'It's been a while.'

Pike knew the SIS spotters would be watching the cab. This time of morning, they didn't have anything else to watch, but Pike wanted to see how Rahmi's building was lit. The lighting was crucial in helping Pike determine where the spotters were hiding, and in planning how to defeat them.

The entry side of Rahmi's building was lit by yellow bulbs, one outside each of the three doors on the ground level, but only one outside a door on the first floor. The others appeared to be out. Pike was more interested in the back of the building. The Google images showed that the back of Rahmi's building was very close to the neighbouring home, and now Pike saw the area caught only a small amount of glow from the neighbour's porch light. This was good for Pike. The narrow separation between the two buildings meant the area behind Rahmi's apartment was a tunnel of darkness. Pike would be able to disappear into the tunnel.

The cabby said, 'Which one?'

'Don't see it. Let's try the next block.'

Pike had the cabby slow in front of two more buildings to throw off the spotters, then headed back to his Jeep.

He took another cab past the apartment just before dawn to check the lighting again from the opposite direction, and made six more cab rides before noon, different cabs each time.

Pike now believed the primary SIS spotter was located in one of two commercial buildings directly across from Rahmi's building. The only other building with a view of Rahmi's door was the house it faced, but Pike had seen a woman herd three children out of the house for school. The two commercial buildings were the only remaining possibilities.

Rahmi's Malibu was parked outside his building almost directly in front of the chain-link gate. Every time Rahmi drove away, SIS would follow. They would have placed a GPS locator on the car, and they would use at least three vehicles to maintain contact.

The Malibu was Pike's key. SIS had to watch Rahmi's apartment, but Pike only needed the Malibu, and a place where he could watch it without being seen.

Pike picked up his Jeep, then drove north into East LA. A friend of his had a parking lot there, where he kept vehicles he rented to film companies. Pike rented a taco truck with faded paint, a heavy skin of dust and a cracked window.

He left his Jeep, then drove the taco truck back to Compton. He parked three blocks from Rahmi's on the opposite side of the street in front of a row of abandoned storefronts. Pike shut down the engine, then moved back into the kitchen bay where he would be hidden from people on the street. Three blocks away, the SIS spotters would ignore him. They were busy watching Rahmi's apartment.

Pike couldn't see the apartment, but he had a good view of the Malibu, and the Malibu was all he needed. Pike settled in.

AT EIGHT FIFTY that night, the Malibu pulled away, came towards Pike until the first cross street, then stopped. A dark blue Neon approached on the cross street as the Malibu signalled to turn. The Neon was dirty, and missing the left front hubcap. When the Malibu turned, the Neon continued across the intersection behind it. Pike figured the Neon was SIS.

Pike waited five minutes before he slipped out of the taco truck.

For the first time in hours, the spotters would be relaxing. They wouldn't be staring at Rahmi's door because Rahmi was gone.

Pike trotted up to the intersection, then rounded the corner to the next street, and vaulted a fence into the yard butting the back side of Rahmi's building. He then lifted himself over another chain-link fence directly behind Rahmi's apartment.

Each of the apartments had only a single window on the back of the building, one of those high, small windows you find in bathrooms, but the windows were caged by iron bars. Rahmi's window and the window in the street-side apartment were lit, but the rear apartment was dark.

The bathroom door was open, the bathroom light was off, but lights and the television were on in the outer room. The television being on, Pike figured Rahmi would return soon, but couldn't be sure.

Pike examined the security bars. The bars were vertical rods welded to a frame, like a catcher's mask. Pike ran his fingers along the bottom frame plate and found four screws.

Pike had come prepared with a crowbar. He jemmied the crowbar under the frame, used his SOG knife to pop the heads off the screws, then levered the cage from the window. Pike placed it on the ground, pushed open the window, and lifted himself through.

Rahmi had a studio apartment, with the bathroom in one corner sharing a wall with his kitchen. The furnishings were ratty and cheap. The sixty-inch flat-screen hung opposite the couch like a glittering jewel, as out of place as a human head.

The police had almost certainly been inside the apartment and left a listening device. Pike didn't want them listening when Rahmi came home.

He put away the crowbar and knife, and took out a small RF scanner the size of an iPod. Pike used it often in his security work. If the scanner picked up an RF signal, which pretty much all eavesdropping bugs emitted, a red light would glow.

Pike swept the main room, the kitchen and the bathroom, then checked the big-screen components and furniture without finding anything. Then he studied the shades covering the windows. The rollers were fuzzy with dust. Pike scanned them, and found the bug on the second roller. Pike removed it, and placed it on the floor behind the door. This would be his position when Rahmi came home.

Pike put away the scanner, but continued his search. He found a 9mm Smith & Wesson wedged between the cushions on the couch, a blue glass bong the length of a truncheon on the floor, and a baggie containing two joints. Pike unloaded the 9mm, pocketed the bullets, then tucked the gun under his belt. He found nothing else of interest, so he returned to his position behind the door.

Twenty-five minutes later, Pike heard the chain-link gate, and drew Rahmi's pistol.

Then the door swung in. Pike stepped on the bug as the door opened. Rahmi Johnson entered carrying a white paper bag, closed the door, and saw Pike just as Pike hit him with the pistol. The police would have resumed their watchful positions, and would be wondering why the sound went dead, but would assume the closing door had somehow knocked it loose.

Rahmi staggered sideways. Tacos spilled out of the bag, smelling of grease and chilli sauce. Pike twisted Rahmi's arm behind his back, clipped his knees, and rode him down. He held the gun out.

Rahmi probably thought Pike was a cop. 'What you want, man? I ain't done nothin'.'

Pike tapped him again. 'Sh.' He went through Rahmi's pockets. He found a cellphone, a fold of cash, a pack of Parliaments, and a Bic lighter. No wallet. He pulled Rahmi to his feet, and pushed him to the couch. 'Sit.'

Rahmi sat, trying to figure out who Pike was and what was in store. Pike didn't want Rahmi to think he was a cop.

He stuffed Rahmi's cash into his pocket.

Rahmi jerked forward. 'Yo! That's my money!'

'Not any more. Jamal owes me cash. Where's Jamal?'

'I don't know where Jamal is.'

'Jamal has my money. I'll get it from him, or from you.'

'I don't know you, man. I don't know anything 'bout no money.'

Rahmi was thinking if Pike wasn't a cop, maybe it wasn't as bad as he thought, but Pike wanted him to think it was worse.

Pike threw the cellphone at him. 'Call him.'

'Man, get outta here. Jamal in prison.'

Pike swung the Smith backhand, hitting the sixty-inch plasma dead in the centre of the screen. The safety glass split, and multicoloured blocks danced and shimmered where the image had been. Rahmi lunged up from the couch, eyes trembling like runny eggs.

Pike aimed the Smith at Rahmi's forehead, and thumbed back the hammer. 'Call.'

'I'll call. I'll call all you want, but we ain't gonna get no answer. I been leavin' messages. His message box full.'

Rahmi fumbled with the phone, then held it out for Pike to see.

'Here. Listen here. You'll see. I called him right now.'

Rahmi tossed the phone over. Pike caught it in time to hear a computer voice say the recipient's message box was full.

Pike then brought up the call log. The last call out showed as 'Jamal'. Pike closed the phone, then put it into his pocket.

'He told me he was crashing here. How else would I have your address?'

Now Rahmi appeared confused. 'Man, that was weeks ago. I don't know where he cribs now, and I don't wanna know.'

'Why not?'

'Aw, man, you know. The police came around looking, so he's gotta stay low. He didn't say where he went and I didn't ask. If I don't know, I can't say.'

Pike decided Rahmi was telling the truth, but Jamal was only one of the people he wanted to find.

'I think you're lying. I think he left my money with you and you spent it.'

Pike aimed the Smith at Rahmi's left eye. Rahmi flinched.

'He ain't said nothin' 'bout no money, you, or anything else. How much he owe you?'

'Thirty-two thousand dollars. I'm getting it from him, or you.'

'I ain't got no thirty-two grand.'

'You were driving it. Now I'm driving it.'

Rahmi blinked at what was left of his big-screen television, then slumped in defeat. 'Jamal, he gave me these things 'cause he doin' so well. We family, dog.'

'How'd he get to be doing so well?'

'He got in with a good crew.'

'Who? Maybe I can find him through them.'

'Jamal never told me no names.'

Pike raised the gun again, and this time Rahmi pleaded.

'It's true, bro. They hooked up with this Serbian cat, lays off one fat score after another. They makin' the bank!'

Pike lowered the gun. 'Serbian?'

'They in with this dude set'm up with the scores. Tell'm who to hit, they split the cash. He say it the easiest money he ever made.'

Ana Markovic was from Serbia. Dying in the hospital with her sister standing guard.

Pike thought for a moment, then went to the bag of tacos. He stepped on it. Crunch. Rahmi looked pained.

He picked up Rahmi's keys, then tossed them to him. 'Get some more tacos.'

'What?'

Pike held up the fold of bills.

'Take your car. Go get more tacos.'

Rahmi wet his lips as if he was expecting a trick, then snatched the bills and went to the door.

'How you know Jamal?'

'He murdered me.'

Rahmi froze with his hand on the knob.

Pike said, 'You see Jamal before I find him, tell him Frank Meyer is coming.'

Rahmi let himself out. Pike stood by the door, listening. He heard the gate. He heard the Malibu rumble, and the tyres screech. Just as before, the SIS detail would scramble to follow.

Pike slipped out of the bathroom window, and returned to the night.

PIKE WENT BACK to UCLA the next morning. When he stepped off the elevator onto the ICU floor, he saw Rina outside her sister's door with a doctor and a nurse. Pike stepped back onto the elevator, and rode down to the lobby. He wanted to speak with her alone.

Pike repositioned his Jeep so he could watch the lobby entrance, then turned on the phone he had taken from Rahmi Johnson.

Pike scrolled through the list until he reached Jamal's number, then pressed the button to dial. Pike had called the number twice last night, and now again, but Jamal's message box was still full.

Pike stared at the lobby. Rina emerged a few minutes later. Same jeans and jacket. Same shoulder bag clutched to her chest.

Pike moved through a row of cars as she crossed into the parking lot. She didn't see Pike until he stepped from between the cars, then she gasped.

Pike said, 'Do you know who did this?'

'How could I know?' She edged away, keeping the bag close.

Pike stepped in front of her and caught her arm.

'The crew who shot your sister bought the score from a Serbian gangster. They bought information about a house where your sister worked. And now here you are, afraid, with the gun.'

She glared at his hand. 'Leave go of me.'

Pike let go because he saw her look past him. Pike drifted to the side, and saw a large, burly man approaching. He was jumbo large, with sloping shoulders, a big gut, and a dark, unshaven face.

He stopped when Pike turned, and said something Pike did not understand. Rina answered in the same language.

'My friend, Yanni. He see you grab me. I tell him we're fine.'

Yanni was probably six foot five and weighed close to 300 pounds. He was scowling at Pike like a Balkan grizzly, but Pike wasn't impressed. Size meant little.

Pike turned back to the woman. 'If you know who did this, tell me. I can protect you better than him.'

'I don't know what you mean, Serbian gangster.'

'How did Frank and Cindy meet your sister? How did she get the job with them?'

'I don't know.'

'Who are you afraid of?'

She studied him a long time, then shook her head. 'Ana is dead now. She died this morning. I have much to do.'

She turned and walked past Yanni, the two of them exchanging words Pike could not understand.

Pike returned to his Jeep. He watched them cross the parking lot to a small white Toyota. The woman got in behind the wheel. Pike followed them, several cars back, rolling north, then east to Studio City. He drove after them into the parking lot of a large apartment complex. It was one of those complexes with gated entries and visitor parking.

Pike parked at the kerb and trotted after her on foot, staying along the edge of the building. He stopped when her brake lights flared. Yanni got out, then climbed into a metallic tan F-150 pick-up truck. The Toyota continued into the residents' parking lot.

Pike noted the F-150's licence plate, but stayed back until Yanni drove away, then jumped the gate into the parking structure. He found Rina's Nissan. It was parked in a space marked 2205. Pike thought it likely that 2205 would also be Rina's apartment number.

Pike returned to his Jeep, wrote down the licence plates and numbers before he forgot them, then phoned a friend.

He wanted information about Ana and Rina Markovic, and the phone numbers in Rahmi Johnson's phone. Pike was a warrior. He could hunt, stalk and defeat an enemy in almost any environment, but detective work required relationships Pike did not possess.

A man answered on the second ring.

'Elvis Cole Detective Agency. We find more for less.'

Pike said, 'I need your help.'

ELVIS COLE PUT down the phone, feeling even more concerned than he was before Pike called. Cole couldn't count the times Pike had saved his life. But he could count on one hand the times Joe Pike had asked for help.

Cole hadn't felt right since Detective-Sergeant Jack Terrio hit him with questions about a multiple homicide he knew nothing about, and now Cole was irritated he had to wait to find out what was going on. Pike hadn't explained anything over the phone. Just said he was on his way. Ever the mannered conversationalist.

The Elvis Cole Detective Agency maintained a two-office suite, four flights up, great little deli on the ground floor and an elevator that Cole rarely used. The selling point had been the balcony, where, on a clear day, he could see all the way down Santa Monica Boulevard to the sea. Sometimes, the seagulls flew inland, floating in the air outside like white porcelain kites. Sometimes, the woman in the next suite stepped onto her balcony to sun herself. Her selection of bikinis was impressive.

Cole's name was on the door, but Joe Pike was his partner, as well as his friend. They bought the agency the same year Pike left the LAPD and Cole was licensed by the state of California as a private investigator.

That morning, the sky was milky, but bright, cool, but not chilly. Cole was wearing a killer Jams World aloha shirt (colours for the day: sunburst and lime) and khaki cargo pants.

Twenty minutes later, Pike arrived. Cole didn't hear the door open or close. This was just how Pike moved. As if he was so used to moving quietly he no longer touched the earth.

Cole let Pike see his irritation.

'So I'm sitting here yesterday, the door opens, and these cops walk in, badge, badge, badge. Three of them, so I know it's important. They say, what do I know about Frank Meyer? I say, who? They say, Meyer was a merc with your boy, Pike. I say, OK, and? They say, Meyer and his family were shot to death. I don't know what to say to that, but that's when the alpha cop, a guy named Terrio, asked what I knew about your personal relationship with Meyer, and whether you had a business relationship. I said, brother, I have never heard that name before.'

Cole watched as Pike settled into a spot against the wall. Pike rarely sat when he was at their office. He leaned against the wall.

Pike said, 'No reason you would. Frank was one of my guys. From before.'

'Terrio told me they had reason to believe this crew hit Meyer because he had cash or drugs at his home.'

'Terrio's wrong. He believes the other six victims were crooked, so he's gunning for Frank.'

Cole frowned, feeling even less in the know. 'Other six?'

'Frank's home was the seventh hit in a string. Same crew, working the Westside and Encino. They've been ripping off criminals.'

'Terrio left out that part. So did the paper.'

After Terrio left, Cole had searched the LA *Times* website and local news stations for their coverage of the murders. The *Times* had provided the most information, describing Frank Meyer as a successful businessman. No mention was made of his past as a military contractor. A detective was quoted, saying he believed a professional home-invasion crew numbering between three and four men entered the home between 8 and 10 p.m., with robbery as the likely motive. He provided no details about what might have been stolen.

Cole had printed out the article, and now pushed it towards Pike. 'If Terrio's wrong, then what did these people go there to steal?'

Pike took a sheet of notepaper and a cellphone from his pocket, and placed them on Cole's desk.

'I found a connection Terrio doesn't know about.'

Cole listened as Pike told him about a recently released criminal named Jamal Johnson, and his cousin, Rahmi. Pike told him about a new Malibu, and that Jamal told Rahmi his crew bought scores from someone in the Serbian mob. Pike tossed the phone to Cole.

'Rahmi's phone. Jamal's number is in the memory. Maybe you could ID the service provider, and back-trace Jamal's call list. We might be able to find him through his friends.'

Cole put the phone aside, and picked up the sheet of notepaper. 'I'll see what I can do. How are these people connected?'

'Ana Markovic was the Meyers's nanny. She died this morning. Rina was her sister. She has a friend called Yanni. I'm not sure how he spells it. Rina was at the hospital before her sister died. She was standing guard because she believed the people who shot her sister might come round to finish the job.'

'You think she knows something?'

'They're Serbian. Rahmi says his cousin hooked up with a Serbian gangster. What are the odds?'

Cole thought about it. Los Angeles had always had a small Serbian population, but the Serbian and expatriate Yugoslavian populations shot up after the conflicts in the nineties. Criminals and organised gangsters arrived along with everyone else, and LA now had significant numbers of criminal sets from all over Eastern Europe.

'Your pal Rina, you think she'd talk to me?'

'No.'

'Where did Ana live?'

'With Frank.'

'Maybe she had another place for the weekends.'

'I don't know.'

The classic Pike conversation.

'What I'm getting at is that talking to people who knew this girl might be a good place to start. I'll need the names of her friends. If the sister won't talk to us, can we get into the crime scene?'

'I'll take care of it. Also, John Chen is on the SID team.'

Cole nodded. Chen was good. Cole would call him after Pike left.

Two seagulls appeared in the empty blue nothing outside the glass. Cole watched them float. One of them suddenly dropped out of sight. His partner folded his wings and followed.

Cole said, 'And Terrio knows nothing about Jamal and the Serbian connection?'

'No.'

'You going to tell him?'

'No. I want to find them before the police.'

Pike was staring at him but his face was as empty of expression as always, the dark glasses like two black holes cut into space. The stillness in him was amazing.

Cole looked for the gulls, but they were still gone. He glanced at the news story again, the one Pike had not touched. The second paragraph, where the names of the murder victims were given. Frank, Cindy, Frank Jr, Joey. The youngest was Joey. Executed. The word chosen by the journalist to describe what had happened. *Executed.* Cole wondered whether or not the youngest boy, Joey, had been named after Pike.

Who was Frank Meyer?

One of my guys.

Cole had learned enough over the years to know what was meant. Pike had been able to handpick his guys, which meant he chose people he respected. Then, because they were Pike's guys, he would have taken care of them, and they would have taken care of him, and he would not have let them sell their lives cheaply.

Cole studied Pike, and thought that Pike was studying him back. He never knew what Pike was thinking.

Cole said, 'I want you to hear this, and think about it. I don't think Terrio is necessarily wrong. If I were him, I would be looking at Meyer, too. What if it turns out Frank isn't the man you knew. What if Terrio's right?'

The flat black lenses seemed to bore into Cole as if they were portholes into another dimension.

'He's still one of my guys.'

The seagulls reappeared, drawing Cole's eye. They hung in the air, tiny heads flicking left and right as they glanced at each other. Then, as one, the two birds looked at Cole, then banked away. Gone.

Cole said, 'You see that?'

But when Cole looked over, Pike was gone, too.

4

When Pike cruised past Frank's drive, no official vehicles were present. Four days after the murders, the lab rats had found everything there was to find. Pike knew the house would remain sealed until the science people were certain they wouldn't need additional samples.

Pike parked across from Frank's. Then he walked up the drive, and entered through the side gate. Someone had taped a piece of cardboard over the broken pane in the French door. Pike pushed the cardboard aside and let himself in. He went to Ana Markovic's room.

The handmade birthday card made by Frank's boys, the tiny desk with its clutter and a laptop computer all remained as Pike remembered. He unplugged the power cord, and placed the computer by the door. He searched through the drawers and clutter, hoping for some kind of address book or cellphone, but found neither. Instead, he found a high-school yearbook, and some birthday and holiday cards. He put the cards in the yearbook, and the yearbook with the computer.

Pike was bothered by the absence of a phone. He looked under and around the desk, then pulled a mound of sheets and a quilt from the bed. He found rumpled clothes, two open boxes of cookies, an open box of Pampers, some magazines, but no phone.

He realised he had not found a handbag or wallet, either. It occurred to him that Ana's phone had been in her bag, and the paramedics might have taken her handbag along when they rushed her to the hospital. Cole could check to see if this was what happened.

The tiny room held a closet smaller than a phone booth. The closet floor was deep with clothes, shoes and an empty backpack, but a corkboard had been tacked to the inside of the door, and the corkboard was covered with snapshots, cards, pictures cut from magazines, and ticket stubs. Ana was in most of the snapshots, posing with people her own age, everyone smiling for the camera.

Pike selected pictures that appeared the most recent, and those with handwritten notes and names, and tucked them into the yearbook. He had just crossed the hall into the bathroom when he heard a car door. He picked up the computer and yearbook, ran to the front of the house, and saw two unmarked Crown Vics.

Terrio and Deets were already out of their car, and two more detectives were climbing out of the second car. Terrio and Deets went to Pike's Jeep, then scowled towards the house.

Pike left the way he had entered, went round to the side of the house, then slipped through the hedges to the wall. He didn't go over. He stripped a .25-calibre Baretta from his ankle and a Colt .357 Python from his waist, then chinned himself up to see what was on the other side. He dropped the computer, yearbook and guns into a soft cushion of calla lilies, then let himself out through the side gate.

Terrio and the others were halfway up the drive when Pike stepped out, letting them see him.

Terrio said, 'You forget what that yellow tape means?'

'I wanted to see what happened.'

'Did you enter the premises?'

'Yes.'

Deets grinned at the other detectives. 'I like it. We have breaking and entering, illegal entry, interfering with a lawful investigation. How about adding burglary, Pike? Did you take anything?'

Pike spread his arms to let them search. 'See for yourself.'

Deets moved behind Pike. 'Good idea. I've heard about this guy, Jack. Never know what he might be packing.'

The younger detective ran his hands over Pike's legs, pocket and belt line, but his grin collapsed when he found nothing.

Terrio didn't look so happy about it, either, but he tipped his head towards the house, speaking to the other detectives.

'I'll catch up with you. I'm going to walk Mr Pike to his car.'

Terrio didn't say anything more until they reached the street.

'Why'd you come here?'

'To see. Like I told you.'

'That why you went to the hospital?'

Pike wondered how Terrio knew. 'That's right.'

'The girl died this morning. That makes twelve homicides. If you think I'm spending my resources digging up dirt on your friend, you're wrong.'

Pike didn't respond. He figured Terrio would make his point soon enough.

'I've got the mayor, the police commissioner and the brass on my arm. I've got a rising body count, and no certain suspects. If you know something that could help, you should tell me.'

'Can't help you.'

Terrio stared at Pike, then laughed. 'Sure. Sure you can't.'

Pike's cellphone buzzed. Pike didn't move. The buzzing stopped when the call went to voicemail.

Terrio said, 'Get out of here.'

Pike watched him head towards the house. Pike got into his Jeep, and pulled away. He drove far enough so he couldn't be seen from Frank's house, then jogged back through the neighbour's yard to the calla lily bed, recovered his guns and the things he had taken, and walked away.

PIKE DROVE to the far side of the park before he pulled over to check his phone. Cole had left a message, asking him to call.

When Cole answered, Pike said, 'Me.'

'You wanted to know how a gangster could be connected to the nanny?'

Cole was being dramatic, and continued without waiting for an answer. 'Here's a hint. Your girl Rina works for the Serbian mob.'

'You've been on this less than two hours.'

'Am I not the World's Greatest Detective?'

Pike glanced at his watch. 'Ninety-two minutes.'

'Karina Markovic, aged twenty-six, arrested twice for prostitution, once for assault, and once for robbery. Total jail time served is nine days. She was busted in a Serbian sex crib up in the Valley. She's been in this country for at least eight years, and she's probably here illegally.'

The San Fernando Valley was the porn capital of the world, and the Russian gangs discovered it as soon as they arrived. The sex trade was an easy moneymaker, but American women were difficult to control, so the Russians brought Russian girls over, and each new wave of East European gang sets followed the pattern, from the Ukranians to the Armenians to the Serbs.

Pike said, 'Does she have any warrants?'

'None at this time, but that doesn't mean there won't be. Her licence plate came back as inactive.'

'Her car is stolen.'

'Stolen, or built from stripped parts. The Eastern Bloc gangs are into that. She might not know it was stolen. But the apartment address you gave me? The registered tenant is Janic-with-a-J Pevich.'

Cole pronounced Janic as if it was spelled with a 'y'. Yanni.

'He have a record?'

'Nothing that I found, but the day is young.'

Pike lowered the phone. He thought that now he understood why Rina Markovic was afraid. The Serbian mob owned her, and someone in the Serbian mob had killed her sister. Pike wondered if this was the fourth man.

Either way, Pike now believed Rina knew who pulled the trigger.

Pike made his way towards Yanni's apartment, wondering if Rina was there or if she had moved on. Pike wasn't worried. Even if she had gone, he could make Yanni tell him where to find her.

Pike cruised through the small visitors' parking lot where Yanni's truck had been parked before, but now it was gone. He took a space at the end of the lot, and tucked the Python under his belt. He didn't bother to hide the crowbar. He hopped the gate into the residents' parking lot. Rina Markovic's car was still in apartment 2205's parking spot.

He made his way along a sidewalk between the buildings. The grounds were large, with eight separate three-storey buildings laid out like four 'equal' signs end to end in a line.

Pike searched almost ten minutes before he realised the apartment number wasn't 2205, but was apartment 205 in building number 2. He climbed a flight of stairs, found 205, and listened at the door. The apartment was silent, so he covered the peephole and knocked. When no one answered, he knocked again, harder.

He checked to make sure no one was watching, then wedged the end of the crowbar into the jamb where the deadbolt was seated. He gave the crowbar a hard shove, and the jamb gave way. Pike stepped inside, then closed the door, forcing it past the splintered jamb. He found himself in the living room, facing a kitchen to his right and a bedroom to his left. The kitchen and bedroom were separated by a door that was probably a bathroom. The bathroom door was closed. The shower was running.

Pike drew the Python as he made sure the bedroom was empty, then moved to the kitchen as the shower stopped. Quick glance into the kitchen, then he turned towards the bathroom, waiting.

The door opened an inch, then suddenly opened wider with a billow of steamy air. Rina came out with her eyes down, vigorously towelling her hair. She was naked, with very white skin and a fleshy body. Pike studied her, seeing that corded pink scars crisscrossed her belly as if she had been clawed. The scars were so deep they puckered, and Pike knew by their faded colour they were old.

Then she saw him. She shrieked and lurched sideways, bunching the towel to cover herself.

Pike raised the gun enough to make sure she saw it, but did not point it at her. 'Who killed them?'

She was as still as an ice sculpture. She stood with the towel, water dripping across her shoulders and down her legs. 'Get out of here. I will call the police.'

She glanced at the door just as Pike heard the knob, and Yanni stepped through carrying what looked like a large gym bag. A scowl flickered on the big man's face even as he dropped the bag and charged. Pike simply waited as he watched Yanni come.

Pike let Yanni reach him, then slipped to the side, pushing Yanni's hand down to hook his arm. Pike dropped under and brought the arm with him, rolling the big man over his hip, and put Yanni flat on his back. Pike hit him hard on the forehead with the Python. The skin split deep and Yanni's eyes turned glassy.

It took less than two seconds, but when Pike glanced up Rina was already in the bedroom.

He reached her as she turned from the bed with the pistol. He caught it, and twisted it away. She punched at him and tried to claw his eyes as Pike dragged her backwards to the living room so he could see Yanni. Her elbows cut into him, and she stomped at his feet.

Pike said, 'Stop.'

Yanni was blinking in confusion at the blood filling his eyes.

'I know you know. The mob owns you. You know who did this.'

She fought even harder. Pike's arm around her, he squeezed so tight that something in her cracked. He hammered-back the Python.

'I won't ask you again.'

'Yes.'

'Yes what?'

'I *know*. I know who killed them. I know who did this.'

'Who?'

'My husband.'

PIKE TOLD HER to wrap herself in the towel, then put her on the couch. She glanced at Yanni, still flat on his back.

'What about him? We should do something.'

'After you tell me.'

She didn't like that, and said something to Yanni in Serbian.

Pike said, 'English.'

He slipped her pistol into his pocket, then positioned himself so he could see both of them at the same time. Pike said, 'Who's your husband?'

'Michael Darko. You know this name?'

'No. He's a thief?'

She smirked, as if Pike was an idiot.

'Please. He is a boss of thieves.'

'OK, the boss. Was he your boss when you were arrested for prostitution?'

A tint of pink coloured her cheeks. 'Yes. He bring me here to America. I work for him then.'

'This boss sent a crew to Frank's house?'

'Yes.'

'Did he go with them?'

'Maybe he go, maybe not. I was not there.'

'What did he go there to steal?'

'My baby.'

Her answer hung in the air. Pike stared, thinking about what she had said. 'Frank and Cindy had your baby?'

'My sister. I gave him to my sister when I find out Michael is going to take him. I hide him with her until we can leave.'

Pike tried to get his head round it. Then he remembered seeing the box of Pampers in Ana's room. He had thought nothing of it. There had been no crib or baby food—just the one box of Pampers.

'A baby. How old?'

'Ten months.'

'Michael and his crew, they've invaded six other homes. They've killed other people. He have kids in those places, too?'

Her eyes flashed. 'I don't know nothing about other things. All I know is this. Michael want his child. He take him back to Serbia.'

Terrio hadn't mentioned a kidnapping. Neither had Chen. Then Pike realised why. 'You didn't tell the police, did you?'

'Of course not. They cannot help me.'

Yanni was waking up. Pike waved the gun towards him.

'This one your boyfriend?'

'No. He want to be, but, no. I hide with him when I hear Michael wants the baby, but then I get scared and I have much to do, so I give the baby to Ana.'

Yanni stirred. He rolled onto his side, trying to rise.

Pike said, 'Tell him if he gets up, I'll shoot him.'

She spoke the language, and Yanni turned towards Pike. Pike showed him the gun. Yanni rested his head on the floor. His face was a mess.

Pike said, 'I want to be clear. Your husband, this guy Michael Darko, he went to Frank's house to steal his kid from your sister?'

'Yes.'

'What happened that night, it had nothing to do with Frank? It was all about taking your kid?'

'Michael is going back to Serbia. He wants to raise his son there. Me, he wants to kill. I am nothing. Do you see? He does not want his son to be the child of a whore.'

'So he murdered your sister and an entire family?'

'My sister was nothing to him. Your friends, nothing. I am nothing, too. He will kill me if he can. He will kill you, too.'

Pike said, 'We'll see.'

He closed his eyes and saw the bodies: Frank, Cindy, Little Frank, Joey. He saw the oily, irregular pools of blood. Collateral damage. Bystanders in a domestic dispute.

Pike took a slow breath, and felt as if his world had gently shifted. Everything realigned itself into a more comfortable and familiar arrangement, but Frank and his family were still dead. Someone had hurt them. Someone would pay.

Pike considered the woman on the couch, and realised Frank had not been expecting what happened.

'Frank didn't know this lunatic was after your kid?'

She glanced away for the first time. 'No. We lie to them.'

Then she went on. 'We tell them I have emergency, and the lady there, she is nice. I was making arrangements for to get to Seattle. No one know Ana work for these people. How could he find out?'

Collateral damage.

'Stay on the couch.'

Pike went into the kitchen. He found ice in the freezer, and plastic garbage bags under the sink. He cracked a tray of cubes into a garbage bag, then dropped it on Yanni.

'Put this on your face. Tell him to put it on his face.'

Yanni said, 'I know what you say.'

Pike returned to the woman. 'Is Darko still in Los Angeles?'

'I think yes. It is hard to know.'

Pike wasn't thrilled by her uncertainty, but at least she seemed willing to cooperate. 'Let's say he is. Where can I find him?'

'I don't know. If I knew where he was, I would have the boy, yes? I would shoot him, and take back the boy.'

'How can you not know where your husband lives?'

She closed her eyes. 'He has not been my husband for many months.'

Pike waved the gun at her belly. 'He do that?'

She looked down and opened the towel, not giving a thought that she was naked. Or maybe she had. She was a good-looking woman. A little too hard and cold, but maybe that came from the belly. These weren't surgical scars. Someone had most likely been trying to kill her. Pike wondered who, and why. She considered herself before closing the towel. 'Not Michael. He make me pregnant after the scars. They turned him on.'

'You have a picture of him?'

'No. He does not have his picture taken. He has no pictures.'

'How about a phone?'

'No.'

Pike frowned. 'What if the kid got sick? What if you needed something?'

'These things are paid for. There are other people I tell.'

Pike thought hard, trying to come at it from a different direction. 'Where would he take the kid?'

'Serbia.'

'Before he goes to Serbia. He has to keep a baby somewhere. Does he have a girlfriend? Is he living with another woman?'

'I don't know. I am going to find out.'

'It was a mistake not to tell the police. You still can. You should.'

'What will they do, deport me? I have been arrested many times. I am not here with the papers.'

'They won't ask if you're a citizen. Your child was kidnapped. The kidnappers murdered five people. Michael's crew has murdered twelve people, altogether. That's what the police care about.'

'You don't know anything.'

'I know the police. I used to be a policeman.'

'Well, let me ask you this, Mr Policeman-Used-To-Be. When I find this man, you think the police will let me shoot him in the head? That is what I am going to do.'

Pike thought, this woman means it.

Rina seemed to read his thoughts. 'This is how we do it, old-school, where I am from. Do you see?'

Pike holstered the Python. He took her gun from his pocket. He took out the magazine, then worked the slide to unload the chamber. He thumbed the loose cartridge into the magazine, then tossed the gun and magazine onto the couch. They bounced against her thigh.

She said, 'You aren't going to call the police?'

'No. I'm going to help you.'

When he took out his cellphone, Rina jumped up.

'You say no police!'

'I'm not calling the police.'

Pike called Elvis Cole.

MICHAEL DARKO. Pike now had a name, but he needed to know more. It was important to understand the enemy before you engaged him, and impossible to find him without knowing his patterns.

When Cole arrived, Yanni was seated on a dinette chair, holding a bloody towel to his head. Rina was dressed, but the gun was still by her on the couch. Pike introduced them.

Cole eyed Yanni, then the gun, then Rina. Rina eyed him back, cool and suspicious.

'What is this one, another Mr Policeman-Used-To-Be?'

'He's a private investigator. He's good at finding people.'

Cole took a seat near the couch as Pike sketched out everything Rina had told him about Darko, how the baby came to be with Ana, the kidnapping, and Rina's intention to take back her child. When Pike was recounting that part of it, Cole looked over at Rina.

Cole said, 'What's your son's name?'

'*Petar*. Peter.'

'You have a picture?'

Pike thought her face darkened, but she stared at Cole glumly until Yanni mumbled something in Serbian.

Pike said, 'English. I'm not going to tell you again.'

Rina pushed up from the couch. 'Yes, I have picture.'

She went into the bedroom, dug through her bag, then returned with a snapshot. It showed a smiling baby with wispy red hair. The baby was on a green carpet, reaching towards the camera.

She said, 'When I leave apartment, I leave fast. This is only picture I have. You cannot have it.'

Pike said, 'He doesn't look almost a year old.'

She scowled like he was an idiot. 'You are stupid? He is ten months and three days now. In picture, he is six months, one week and one day. Is only picture I have.'

Cole arched his eyebrows at Pike. 'What's wrong with you? Can't you tell how old a baby is?'

Pike wasn't sure if Cole was joking or not.

Cole turned back to the woman. 'I can scan a copy on my computer, and give this one back. Would that be OK?'

She nodded. 'That would be OK.'

Cole put the picture aside. 'Why did you have to leave so fast?'

'Michael was coming. Michael say he want the boy. I know what he thinks. He kill me, he take the boy, he pretend I never exist.'

'So you stashed Peter with your sister while you went to find a place to live in Seattle.'

'Yes.'

'How did Michael find them?'

'I don't know.'

'Would Ana have called him, maybe trying to work things out for you?'

Rina laughed, but it was bitter and wise. 'She would never do that. She is scared of these people. I keep her away from all that.'

Cole glanced at Pike, not understanding. 'These people?'

Yanni spoke again, and another brief, incomprehensible conversation ensued. Pike stood, and Yanni immediately raised both hands. 'She means the thieves. Ana is little girl when they come. Rina keep Ana away from these men.'

Rina picked up where Yanni left off. 'She is not to work for Michael. I make her go to school, and have normal friends, and to be a good girl.'

Pike said, 'You protected her.'

Rina glanced out of the window. 'Perhaps not so well.'

Cole cleared his throat, pulling them back. 'Who knew Ana had the baby?'

'No one. I don't know how Michael find her there. I cannot understand.'

'This guy is your husband, but you don't know where he lives?'

'Nobody knows. That is how he makes his life.'

'No address, no picture, not even a phone?'

'He get new phone every week. The numbers change.' Rina scowled at Pike. 'When is he going to start all this finding he is so good at?'

Pike said, 'Michael hides. We get that. But you know more about him than anyone else here. We need information so we have something to work with.'

Cole said, 'Who are his friends?'

'He has no friends.'

'Where does his family live?'

'Serbia.'

'OK. What about *your* friends? Maybe one of them can help.'

'I have no friends. They are all afraid of Michael.'

Cole looked over at Pike. 'I can't write fast enough to keep up.'

Rina squinted at him. 'Is the great finder of people making fun of me?'

Pike cleared his throat again. 'We need some names. Who does Michael work with? Who works for him? Even if you don't know them, you must've heard the names mentioned, time to time.'

Rina frowned at Yanni as if looking for guidance. Yanni glanced at Pike, afraid to say anything. Pike nodded giving permission. They had a brief conversation that sounded more like an argument, and then they both started spitting out names. The names were difficult to understand, and even more difficult to spell, but Cole scratched them into his notebook.

When Cole finished with the names, he looked up and seemed hopeful. 'Has Darko ever been arrested? In LA?'

'I don't know. I don't think so, but I don't know. He has been here much longer than me.'

Cole glanced over at Pike. 'I'll check out Darko and these other guys, see if they're in the system. If Darko's been arrested, we might get lucky here.'

Cole continued the questioning, but Rina didn't know very much more. Darko paid for everything in cash, and made Rina pay all the bills for herself and the baby from her own current account, which he then reimbursed in cash. Phones changed, addresses changed and cars changed. He was a man who left no trails.

Pike said, 'How were you planning to find him?'

She shrugged as if there were only one way. 'I would watch for the money.'

Cole looked at her. 'How does he make his money?'

'He has the girls. He has the people who steal the big trucks—'

'Hijackers? Trucks filled with TVs, clothes, things like that?'

'Yes. He has the people who steal the credit-card information. He sells the bad gasoline. He has the strip clubs and bars.'

Pike said, 'You know where these places are?'

'Some. I don't know to say the address. I can show you.'

Cole stood. Pike followed him to the far side of the room, where Cole lowered his voice. Both Rina and Yanni were watching.

'Did you find anything of her sister's?'

Pike told him what he found—the laptop, the yearbook, a few other things. All out in the Jeep.

Cole said, 'Good. I want to check out her story. Just because she tells us this stuff doesn't make it real.'

'I'll put everything in your car when I leave.'

'Also, I want to see what I can find out about this guy, Darko. If she's giving it to us straight about him, then I probably know someone on LAPD who can help.'

Pike knew someone, too, though not on LAPD, and now Pike wanted to see him.

From the couch, Rina said, 'I don't like all these whispers.'

Pike turned to face her. 'You're going to take a ride with him. Show him whatever you know about Darko's businesses, and answer his questions.'

'Where are you going? What are you going to do?'

'I'm going to answer his questions, too.'

Pike glanced at Cole. 'You good?'

'Living the dream.'

Pike let himself out.

PIKE PLACED THE LAPTOP and other things he had taken from Ana's room in Cole's car, then headed back to his Jeep. As he was crossing the visitors' parking lot, a brown Nissan Sentra slowed by the entrance. Two Latin men in the front seats seemed to be looking at Pike's Jeep. Then the driver saw Pike. There was a slight hesitation, then the driver sped up.

Troops in the desert called it 'spider-sense', after the movies about the *Marvel* comic book character, Spider-Man, how he senses something bad before it happens.

Pike's spider-sense tingled, but then the Sentra was gone. He was in no hurry to leave. If the Sentra was waiting round the corner to follow him, they might get tired of waiting and come back to see what he was doing. Then Pike would have them. He spent the next few minutes thinking about Michael Darko. Learning that Darko belonged to an Eastern European gang set was a major break, mostly because it gave Pike direction.

Pike called Jon Stone. 'Is Gregor still in LA?'

'It's George Smith now. You have to be careful with his name.'

'Is he here?'

'Got a new place over on La Brea. What do you want with George? This thing with Frank?'

'An Eastern European organised crime gang is involved.'

Stone was silent for a moment, then gave Pike an address.

'Take your time getting there, OK? I'll talk to him first. You walk in cold, he might get the wrong idea.'

'I understand.'

La Brea Avenue starts at the foot of the Hollywood Hills, and runs south through the city. A ten-block stretch of its length between Melrose and Wilshire was known as decorators' row because it was lined with everything from high-end custom furniture boutiques to Middle Eastern rug merchants to designer lighting and antique shops. The people who owned the stores came from all over the world, and sold to customers from all over the world, but not all of them were what they seemed.

Pike found a spot for his Jeep outside a florist shop a block south of Beverly Boulevard. He checked for the Sentra again when he got out of his

Jeep. The Sentra had probably been nothing, but he still had the creeped-out sensation of cross hairs on his back.

He walked south one and a half blocks to an antique-lighting store. A chime tinkled when Pike entered.

The interior of the shop was cluttered; the walls festooned with sconces, and chandeliers and pendant lamps dripping from the ceiling. A man's voice said, 'Hello, Joseph.'

George Smith materialised from between the lamps. Pike hadn't seen him in years, but he looked the same—shorter than Pike, and not as muscular, but with the sleek, strong build of a surfer, a surfer's tan, and pale blue eyes. George was one of the deadliest human beings Pike knew. A gifted sniper. An immaculate assassin.

George was Gregor Suvorov in those days, but had changed his name when he moved to Los Angeles. George Smith sounded as if he had grown up in Modesto, having what broadcasters called a 'general American' accent, but Gregor Suvorov had grown up in Odessa, Ukraine, where he enlisted in the Army of the Russian Federation, and spent a dozen years in the Russian Special Purpose Regiment known as the Spetsnaz GRU—the Russian version of the US Army's Special Forces—that was run by the KGB.

After combat tours in Chechnya and Afghanistan, Gregor cashed into the private contractor market, and enjoyed his new-found money and freedoms. He moved to Los Angeles, where he enjoyed the sun, sold collectible lamps, and worked for the Odessa Mafia.

George offered his hand, and Pike took it. Warm iron. 'Man, it's been for ever. You good?'

'Good.'

'I was surprised when Jon called. But pleased. Watch your head. That's a deco Tiffany, circa 1923. Eight thousand to the trade.'

Pike dipped sideways. He said, 'Business good?'

'Excellent, thank you. I wish I had come to America sooner.'

'Not the lamp business. Your other business.'

George smiled. 'I knew what you meant. That business is good, too, both here and abroad.'

George still accepted special assignments outside of the Odessa work, though his clients these days were almost always governments or political agencies. No one else could afford him.

Pike followed George to a desk where they could sit.

'Jon tell you why I'm here?'

'Yeah. Listen, I'm sorry about Frank. Really. I never met the dude, but I've heard good things.'

'You still involved with Odessa?'

George's smile flashed again. 'Would you like a cup of tea?'

Pike didn't want his tea and didn't want to chat. 'I'm good. You still in with the ROC, George?' Russian Organised Crime.

George pursed his lips. Annoyed. 'It's Odessa, and I'm not *in* with them. I'm not a *member*. I consult on a freelance basis. I'm my own boss.'

This seemed important to George, so Pike nodded. 'I understand.'

'That said, if you want to discuss Odessa business, I can't.'

'I don't care about Odessa. I want to know about the Serbs.'

'So Jon told me. A hard people. Very tough.'

'Can you talk about the gang sets here in Los Angeles?'

George nodded. 'Shouldn't be a problem. They do their thing, Odessa is something else. Like with the Armenians. The same, but different.'

'You know of a Michael Darko?'

'He killed your friend, Frank Meyer?'

'Looks that way.'

George grunted. 'I know who he is. A hard man. You understand the word, *pakhan*?'

'No.'

'A boss. Middle management for now, but he's on the way up. These people aren't given their promotions, they take them. Like cannibals eating each other.'

Pike saw disdain in the pale eyes, and realised George felt superior to the gangsters who employed him. Maybe this was why he wanted Pike to understand that he was an independent contractor.

'What kind of crime does he do?'

'A finger in many pies, like all these guys. Girls and sex, hijacking, extorting his own people. He's aggressive, and trying to expand. Quick with the trigger.'

Pike said, 'Know where I can find him?'

'I don't. This man is just a name to me. Like I said, different circles. I'm a lamp salesman.'

A lamp salesman who could put a bullet through your head from a thousand metres away. Then George continued. 'They have a nickname for him, the Shark. Did you know this?'

'No.'

'He is the Shark because he never stops moving, and he moves so no one can find him. This is not a loved man, even among the Serb sets.'

Pike grunted, now understanding why Rina didn't know where to find him. So far, her description of Darko matched with George's.

'He's been using a home-invasion crew to take out his competition. He used the same crew on Frank. I want to find them, and I want to find him.'

George laughed, full-bodied and deep. 'You got part of that wrong, buddy. He isn't taking out his competition. He's ripping off his partners. Why do you think he has to keep moving?'

'You know about this?'

'Enough to keep tabs. If he wants to rip off his own business partners, good riddance. If he sends a crew to Odessa, they'll have to deal with me.'

Pike wondered if Darko was ripping off his partners because he was returning to Europe—get some quick cash, grab his kid, go.

'The tabs you keep include his crew?'

George shrugged, no big deal. 'Bangers from Compton.'

'Jamal Johnson?'

'Never heard of him. A D-Block Crip banger called Moon Williams runs Darko's crew. Darko feeds him the targets and they split the take.'

Pike felt a burn of excitement. 'Moon Williams. You sure?'

George cupped a hand behind his ear as if he was listening.

'The KGB is everywhere. Also, Mr Moon has been making much money recently, too. He spends it in a club owned by Odessa. Cristal champagne and beautiful Russian women. He loves the Russian women. He loves to tell them what a badazz he is.'

Pike said, 'Uh-huh. Does the KGB know where I can find him?'

George considered, then lifted his phone, and punched in a number. George spoke Russian to whoever answered, had a conversation, and hung up. When he looked at Pike again, he was sombre.

'Jon told me you and Frank were close.'

'Yes.'

'So you have business with Mr Darko?'

'If he's good for Frank's death, yes. Is that a problem?'

'So long as you stay with the Serbian sets, go with God, my friend.' George told him where to find Moon Williams, then stood. They shook again.

'Good luck, my friend.'

When Pike reached the door, he glanced back, but George was hidden by the lamps, wrapped in so many shadows the light could not reach him.

EVEN WITH HIS SUNGLASSES, Pike squinted against the glare, scanning the cars parked along both sides of La Brea. He walked up the street to his Jeep. No Sentra.

Pike located Moon Williams's address on his Thomas Guide map, then pulled into traffic. According to George, Earvin 'Moon' Williams was a D-Block Crip banger with a harsh reputation, two felony strikes, and five 187s tattooed in a neat column on his right forearm. Moon bragged to the Russian strippers that each 187 represented a body he had put in the morgue. The LAPD code for homicide was 187.

Operatives of the Odessa Mafia, who followed him home on at least three occasions, determined that the stone-cold killer lived with his grand-mother, a woman named Mildred Gertie Williams.

Pike found the address in a weathered, residential neighbourhood in Willowbrook, at the bottom of a freeway off-ramp. A small stucco house had probably sat on the property at one time, just like all the other houses lining the street, but now a double-wide mobile home sat on blocks in its place, with three ancient Airstream trailers shoehorned behind it. Pike figured the no-doubt-illegal trailer park was how Mildred Williams paid her bills.

The trailers were faded, and scabbed with freeway dust. The double-wide had a small porch set up with a sun awning and potted plants, but shrivelled brown threads were all that remained of the plants, and the yard had gone over to sand, dirt and litter. The litter hugged the inevitable chain-link fence as if it was trapped, and trying to escape.

Pike turned round on the next block, then pulled to the kerb. Three girls on bikes pedalled past, swung round and rode past again. Eyeing the white man. They probably thought he was a cop. He watched the mobile homes for a few minutes, but saw no signs of activity. An ancient Buick Riviera was illegally parked alongside the fence, so wide it covered the sidewalk. Pike didn't necessarily expect to find anyone home, but he wanted to con-firm that Moon still lived here. If he found evidence that Moon lived here, he would wait until he returned, then use him to reach Darko.

The girls rode past again, and this time Pike rolled down the window. The first girl wore a blue short-sleeved shirt, the second a baggy white T-shirt, and the third was wearing a red sweatshirt. Red, white and blue. Pike wondered if they had planned it that way.

'Need some help, ladies. You live on this street?'

The blue girl said, 'Are you a policeman?'

'No. I'm a salesman.'

The girl laughed. 'You're a plain-clothes policeman. My Uncle Davis is a plain-clothes officer, so I know. Also, you're white. We don't get many white people except for the police.'

Pike said, 'Do you know Ms Mildred Gertie Williams, up there in the trailers?'

The girl said, 'You here for Moon?' Just like that.

Pike said, 'Yes.'

'I live right over there, that yellow house? Uncle Davis warned us about that Moon Williams. He said don't never go over there. He said if Moon ever makes a problem, we should call him right away.'

Pike tipped his head. 'Those your sisters?'

'No, sir. That's Lureen and Jonelle. They're my friends.'

'Which one of those trailers does Ms Williams live in?'

'The one up front. That's the big one.'

'Does Moon live with her?'

'He's in the back trailer, the one with the dogs.'

Pike hadn't seen dogs when he passed the yard. 'You know who lives in the other trailers?'

She shook her head. 'Was a lady in one and Jonelle's cousin lived there for a while, but they moved out after Moon came home.'

'Have you seen Ms Williams or Moon today?'

'No, I sure haven't. I was at school, and then I was at Jonelle's, and Lureen just came over so we're going to her house.'

Pike said, 'OK, then. You have a nice time at Lureen's.'

He decided he didn't have much time as the three girls rode away. They would probably tell Lureen's mother, and Lureen's mother would probably call the blue girl's mother, who would call Uncle Davis. Uncle Davis would probably send a patrol car by to take a look.

Pike waited until the girls disappeared, then parked alongside the Riviera. He saw no dogs, though the last trailer was surrounded by its own fence. He slipped his .45 Kimber under his belt at the small of his back, clipped the Python to his belt under his sweatshirt, then hopped the first fence into Mildred Williams's yard.

He went to the big double-wide, listened at the door, then went to the nearest window. He stretched on his toes to peek inside, and saw a basic living room with an old-fashioned console television. The room was neat, and the television was off.

Pike was trying to see through an interior door when a grey and white cat jumped against the window, as if it was lonely and wanted to escape.

Pike returned to the door. He tapped three times, then decided Ms Williams had probably gone out. He drew the Python as he moved to the second trailer. The second and third trailers were both empty, the tenants long since gone to escape Moon and his crew.

The fourth trailer sat by itself, caged by a six-foot chain-link fence. A gate in the centre of the fence was latched but not locked. There wasn't much of a yard. Just a few feet of dirt on either side of the Airstream and a few feet behind. Two large metal bowls were under the trailer, one filled with water. A chain stretched from the tow hitch to disappear behind the trailer, but Pike could not see what was attached to the other end. The trailer was still. He made a tsk, tsk, tsk sound.

A dog inside the trailer barked. Not behind. One dog inside.

Pike let himself through the gate. The dog inside was barking so loudly, Pike doubted anyone was home. He latched the gate, then walked behind the trailer, and that's when he saw the dog. A ragged, male pit bull lay on its side, swarming with black bottle flies, but the dog wasn't the only dead thing behind the trailer. An African-American man was sprawled face down a few feet beyond the dog. His shirt was heavy with dried blood.

Pike checked the body, but found no identification. He had been shot twice in the back. A black 9mm Ruger pistol lay by his hand. Pike left the man and the gun, and went to the window. The barking inside grew louder as he approached, then abruptly stopped.

The old Airstream contained only three small rooms—a kitchenette, a living room, and a single bedroom with a bath. Pike looked into the kitchen first, saw nothing, then looked into the living room.

The inside pit bull had stopped barking because it was eating. The dog tore a strip of flesh from a man's neck, and gulped the meat down. A second male body was half on a couch and half on the floor. The flesh on the second man's left forearm had been partially eaten, but his right forearm was intact. The numbers tattooed there were easy to read.

187

187

187

187

187

One for each of the people he put in the ground.

Pike said, 'Good night, Moon.'

PIKE STOOD at the window, deciding what he needed to do. He wouldn't leave the dog trapped in the trailer, and he wouldn't leave the bodies where the red, white and blue girls could find them. Pike would call the police, but he wanted to search the premises first. While Pike was thinking, the dog looked at him and lunged against the window.

Pike found a length of two-by-four by the double-wide. He unclipped the chain from the tow hitch, fashioned a noose, then looped it around the two-by-four. When Pike approached the trailer's door, the dog slammed into the interior side like a linebacker.

The door was hinged to open out. Pike pressed his shoulder against the door, unshipped the latch, and the big dog immediately tried to push the door open.

Pike let it open enough to offer the end of the two-by-four. The dog crunched into the wood. Pike let the noose slip off the board over the dog's head, then pulled the noose tight, and dragged the dog out of the trailer. The dog spat out the two-by-four and twisted and snapped.

Pike worked the dog to the tow hitch, and wrapped off the chain so the dog's head was held close to the steel. The dog's head and shoulders were blistered with scars. A fight dog, tossed in the pit with similar dogs because Moon and his friends dug watching them rip each other apart.

Pike said, 'Guess you had the last laugh.'

He entered the trailer. The stink was terrible. Pike pulled on a pair of latex gloves, then noticed that Williams's right elbow appeared injured. The inside of the elbow above the 187s was badly discoloured, showing a prominent lump under the skin. Pike felt the lump and realised it was bone. Moon's elbow had been broken. Pike thought Frank Meyer might have done the deed, and the corner of his mouth twitched, Pike's version of a smile.

Pike found a 9mm Glock in Williams's back pocket. Pike counted thirteen cartridges in a magazine designed to hold seventeen. With one remaining in the chamber, this meant three shots could have been fired. Pike wondered if the bullets found in Frank's house had come from this gun. SID would test-fire the weapon, and run a comparison, and then they would know. Pike put the clip back into the gun, and the gun in Moon's pocket.

Moon's remaining pockets produced a wallet, a ring of keys, a bandanna, a pack of Kools, two joints, a Bic lighter and a Payday candy bar. The wallet contained $342 and seven Visa cards in seven different names. Pike examined the keys, and found one bearing the Buick emblem. He kept the keys.

The second body yielded another 9mm Glock, this one missing two bullets, but no wallet or cellphone. Neither Moon nor the man outside had cellphones, either.

Pike moved to the door for some fresh air, and looked back at the scene. Open beer bottles and two crack pipes on a ceramic ashtray—these guys were chilling when they were shot. Moon had been shot twice in the face. The other man had been shot once in the chest and once in the head. Neither had drawn their weapons, suggesting they had been caught off guard by someone they knew. The third man probably bailed when the shooting started, but was chased down outside and shot.

He studied the floor, wondering if the murders had been committed by more than one person. The dog had been trapped for days, endlessly moving from door to windows, in and out of each room, and on the furniture, obliterating any footprints.

Pike found three shell casings. He examined each one without touching it, noting that all three were 9mm casings. He wondered if the bullets in Moon and his friends would match the bullets in Frank, and if Michael Darko had killed them. He quickly searched the rest of the trailer, but found nothing useful, and no evidence that a small child had been present. He decided to check the Buick.

Moon's key opened the Riviera perfectly, but Pike did not get in. He pulled on a fresh pair of latex gloves, then searched the glove box and under the front buckets, hoping for some link to Michael Darko. He found it on the back seat—a baby's bib. Made of a soft white cloth with a pattern of blue bunnies. Orange and green stains streaked the front. Pike held it to his nose, and knew the stains were recent. The orange smelled of apricots, the green of peas.

Pike tucked the bib into his pocket, wondering what Moon Williams had done with the baby. Then Pike remembered Moon's grandmother. Multiple gunshots had been fired. The woman should have heard. Her grandson and the other two bodies had been here for at least three days. She would have discovered them.

He locked the Riviera and went to the double-wide. This time he didn't knock. The grey and white cat raced out when he opened the door, and the same terrible smell seared his throat. As soon as he entered he saw the broken door at the end of the hall, and heard the upbeat melody of game-show music. Pike found Ms Mildred Gertie Williams dead on her bedroom floor. A small television on her dresser was showing a rerun of *The Price is Right*. Ms Williams was wearing pyjamas, a thin robe and furry pink slippers, and had been shot twice in the body and once in the forehead.

Pike turned off the television. Ms Williams's bed was rumpled and unmade, with a TV remote by the pillows. She was probably watching TV when she heard the shots, and got up to see what had happened. Pike pictured her standing as she would have been before she was murdered. He placed himself where the shooter would have stood, and aimed. The spent casings would have ejected to the right, so he looked right, and found them between the wall and an overstuffed chair. Two 9mm, same brand as the casings in Moon's trailer. Pike went outside. He sat in one of the lawn chairs under the awning. The air was good and cool, and not filled with death.

Pike phoned John Chen, who answered from the lab at SID in a hushed, paranoid whisper. 'I can't talk. They're all around me.'

'Just listen. In a couple of hours, SID will roll to a murder site in Willowbrook. You'll find three deceased males, a deceased female, three 9mm pistols, and spent casings from a fourth gun.'

Chen's voice grew even softer. 'Did you kill them?'

'Comp their guns and the casings against what you have from the Meyer house. I think they'll match.'

'You got the crew who killed the Meyer family?'

'If the results pair up, then three of the four. The fourth man probably committed the Willowbrook murders.'

'Wait a minute. One of their own guys killed them?'

'Yes.'

Pike broke the connection, then phoned Cole. 'You alone?'

'Yeah. I'm at the office. Just dropped her off.'

'She have anything?'

'She showed me three condo complexes, and gave me a lecture on how Darko runs his call-girl business. I'm having a title and document search run. I'm about to get started on her sister.'

'You won't need to trace Rahmi's calls.'

'You found Jamal?'

Pike did not mention George Smith by name, but described how someone with inside information connected Michael Darko with a D-Block Crip banger named Moon Williams. Then Pike described what he found.

'We'll know if these are the same guns when Chen runs the comps, but they're going to match.'

'You think it was Darko?'

'Yes.' Pike told him about the bib.

Cole said, 'But why would he kill them after they delivered his kid?'

'Maybe they didn't deliver the kid. These guys were used to stealing cash, but now all they had was a kid. Maybe they tried to hold him up for a bigger payoff.'

Cole said, 'What are you going to do?'

'Call the police. I can't leave these people like this.'

Even as Pike said it, he saw two LA County Sheriffs' cruisers coming up the street. An unmarked car was behind them.

Pike said, 'Looks like I won't have to call.'

'How did the cops get there?'

'I don't know.'

A third cruiser appeared from the opposite direction, the three of them blocking his Jeep. Uniformed deputies and the plain-clothes people climbed out of their vehicles, and no one seemed in much of a hurry. Almost as if they knew what they'd find.

Pike remembered the bib. 'Don't tell her what I found here, OK?'

'OK.'

Pike put away his phone, and raised his hands. The deputies saw him. An older dep approached the gate. 'You Joe Pike?'

'I am. I was just about to call you.'

'Sure you were. That's what they all say.'

The deputy drew his gun, and then the other deps fanned out along the fence, and they drew down on him, too.

The dep said, 'You're under arrest. You do anything with those hands other than keep them up, I'll shoot you out of that chair.'

The pit bull went into a frenzy trying to break free. Pike studied the two plain-clothes cops who got out of the unmarked car. Middle-aged Latin guys. The last time he saw them, they were driving a Sentra.

5

Ana Markovic graduated from high school in Glendale two years earlier. Cole knew this from the yearbook Pike took from her room. First thing Cole did, he found her picture among the senior class— a thin girl with clean, bright features, and a large nose. The yearbook claimed that Ana's class consisted of 1,284 graduating seniors.

Pike had tucked three snapshots in the yearbook. One showed Ana with Frank Meyer's two little boys, so Cole put it aside. The second showed Ana with two girlfriends, the three of them on a soccer field, arms round each other with happy smiles. In this picture, one of the girls had short black hair with purple highlights and the other was a tall girl with long, sandy-brown hair, milky skin and freckles. The third photo showed Ana and the brown-haired girl at what appeared to be a Halloween party. They wore identical flapper costumes.

The background in the soccer-field picture suggested a school campus, so Cole went back to the yearbook. He started at the beginning of the senior-class pictures, hoping to get lucky. He did. The brown-haired girl was named Sarah Manning.

Cole phoned Information, and asked if they had a listing for that name in Glendale. 'I'm sorry. We have no listing by that name.'

'What about Burbank and North Hollywood?'

'Sorry, sir. I already checked.'

Cole examined Ana's computer. It took for ever to boot up, but the desk top finally appeared. Cole studied the icons for an address book, and found something called *Speed Dial*. He typed in *Sarah Manning* clicked *Search*, and there she was.

Cole said, 'The World's Greatest Detective strikes again.'

The entry for Sarah Manning showed an address in Glendale, an 818 phone number, and a gmail Internet address. Cole called the number, and was surprised when she answered.

'Hello?'

'Sarah Manning?'

'Yes, who is this, please?'

She sounded breathy, as if she was in a hurry. It occurred to Cole she might not know that Ana Markovic had been murdered, but she did, and didn't seem particularly upset.

Cole said, 'I'd like to sit down with you for a few minutes, Sarah. I have some questions about Ana.'

'I don't know. I'm at school.'

'East Valley High?'

'Cal State Northridge. High school was two years ago.'

'Sorry. This won't take long, but it's important.'

'Did they catch the people who did it?'

'Not yet. That's why I need your help.'

'Well, OK, like what? I'm really busy.'

'You're on campus? I can be there in fifteen minutes.'

Sarah described a coffee shop on Reseda Boulevard not far from campus, and told him she would meet him in twenty minutes.

Twenty-two minutes later, he found her seated at an outside table. She was wearing pale blue shorts, a white T-shirt and sandals.

'Sarah?' Cole gave her his best smile and offered his hand. She took it, but was clearly uncomfortable. He nodded towards the deli.

'Would you like something?'

'This is just weird, that's all. I don't know what I can tell you.'

'Well, let's see where the answers take us. When was the last time you spoke with her?'

'A year. Maybe more than a year. We kinda drifted apart.'

'But you were close in high school?'

'Since seventh grade. We all came from different elementaries. We were the three musketeers.'

Cole flashed on the picture of the three girls on the soccer field.

'Who was the third?'

'Lisa Topping. You should talk to Lisa. They stayed in touch.'

'Black hair, purple highlights?'

Sarah cocked her head. 'Yeah. How'd you know?'

'Ana had a picture of the three of you in her room.'

Sarah stared at him for a moment, then looked away. She suddenly reached into her bag and came out with her cellphone. She punched in a number, then held the phone to her ear. Voicemail.

'Hey, honey, it's me. There's this guy here, his name's Elvis Cole and he wants to know about Ana. Call him, OK—'

She covered her phone. 'What's your number?'

Cole told her, and she repeated it. Then she put away her phone.

'She'll call. She goes to school in New York, but they stayed in touch.'

'Great. But you're here, and you've known her since the seventh grade, too, so I'll bet you can help. My understanding is she lived with her sister. Is that right?'

Sarah stared at the street. 'That's right. Her parents were dead. They died when she was little. Back in Serbia.'

'Uh-huh. And what was her sister's name?'

Cole made as if he was poised to take notes. He had two objectives. He wanted to see if Rina's story checked out, and, if so, he was hoping to learn something that might help find Darko.

Sarah said, 'Rina. I think her full name was Karina, with a K, but we called her Rina.'

So far so good. 'You knew the sister?'

'Well, yeah. They lived together. Kinda.'

'What's the "kinda" mean?'

Sarah shifted and grew irritated. 'Dude, I'm not an idiot. I know you know. Rina was a prostitute. That's how she paid the rent.'

Cole put down his pen. 'Did everyone know?'

'Just me and Lisa, and we had to swear. Ana only told us because she had to tell *someone*. We were kids. We thought it was cool. But after a while, when you thought about it, it was just gross.'

Cole sensed this was probably why they had grown apart.

'Did Rina see clients at home while Ana was there?'

'No, nothing like that. She would go away for a few days. I guess she worked at one of those places.'

'You ever hear them mention the name Michael Darko?'

'I don't know. Who's Michael Darko?'

'How about where she worked, or who she worked for? You remember anything like that?'

'Nothing to remember. Rina wouldn't tell her anything about that part of her life. It was like an open secret they had. Ana knew, but they didn't talk about it.'

'How did Ana know if Rina wouldn't talk about it?'

'Rina got arrested. Ana always thought Rina was a waitress or something until this time Rina called her from jail. Ana got really scared. That wasn't until, like, ninth grade. She was really scared, 'cause she didn't know what was going to happen, like, what if Rina went to prison?'

Cole counted backwards to ninth grade, and compared it with Rina's arrest record. The year matched with the date of her first arrest.

He sighed. Ninth grade meant she would have been fourteen. A fourteen-year-old girl, not knowing whether her only family and sole support was ever coming back. She would have been terrified.

'Who were her Serbian friends?'

'She didn't have any. Rina wouldn't let her.'

'So all she had was you?'

Sarah nodded, looking lonely and lost.

Cole said, 'Hey. Sounds like Rina was trying to protect her. I think you were trying to protect her, too.'

'I should've told someone. We should have told.'

'You didn't know, Sarah. None of us ever know. We just try to do our best.'

'She might be alive.'

Sarah Manning stood and walked away without looking back.

PIKE WATCHED the two Latin cops. They did not approach him. They left the scene while he was being searched.

The senior dep was named McKerrick. While his officers spread through the trailers, McKerrick placed Pike under arrest, cuffed him, and went through his pockets. He placed the things he found in a green evidence bag. These included Pike's watch, wallet, weapons and cellphone, but not the baby's bib. McKerrick probably thought this was Pike's handkerchief.

At no time did McKerrick Mirandise Pike, or question him. Pike found this curious. He also wondered how the two Latin guys had followed him since he left Yanni's apartment.

When the search was complete, McKerrick walked Pike to a Sheriff's car, placed him in the back seat, then climbed in behind the wheel.

Pike looked back at the dog. The dog was watching him go.

McKerrick brought him to Parker Center, the Los Angeles Police Department headquarters. They drove round to the processing entrance, where three uniformed LAPD officers were waiting. Two men and a woman. The female officer opened the door. 'Get out.'

They brought Pike inside without processing him, directed him onto an elevator, then up to the third floor. When the elevator opened, the officer carrying the evidence bag split off, and the other two steered Pike to an interview room. A small table jutted from the wall, with a cheap plastic chair on either side.

They uncuffed Pike, then cuffed his right hand to a steel bar built into the table. Then they stepped out, and closed the door.

Pike looked around. The interview room smelled of cigarettes. Pike considered the camera bolted to the wall in the corner up by the ceiling, and wondered if Terrio was watching. They would probably let him wait for a while, but Pike didn't mind. He emptied his mind of everything, and breathed. After a few breaths, he felt himself float. His heart rate slowed. Time slowed. Pike had spent days like this, waiting for the perfect shot in places that were not as comfortable as an LAPD interview room.

Pike wondered why they had pulled him in. He knew they weren't going to charge him because they had not Mirandised him or booked him. Hence, they wanted to talk, but the question was why? He also wondered why they bounced him at Williams's home. If they were on him all day, they could have bounced him at any time, yet they waited until he found Williams.

He was still pondering these things two hours later when Terrio and Deets came in. Maybe now he would get answers.

Terrio unlocked the cuff from the metal bar, then from Pike's wrist. He pocketed the handcuffs, then took the remaining chair. Deets leaned into the corner and crossed his arms.

Terrio said, 'OK, listen. You are not under arrest. You don't have to talk to us. I'm hoping you will, but you don't have to. If you want a lawyer, here'—Terrio took out a cellphone, slid it across the table—'you can use this. We'll wait.'

Pike flicked it back. 'I'm good.'

Deets in his corner. 'Did you kill those people?'

'No.'

'You know who did?'

'Not yet.'

Terrio pushed closer to the table. 'What were you doing there?'

Pike had already decided what he would tell them. 'I was looking for a two-time felon named Earvin Williams. Williams might have participated in or had knowledge of Frank's murder.'

'Why did you think Williams was involved?'

'Williams was a D-Block Crip banger. He put together a crew of his homies, some of whom have shown a sudden increase in personal wealth.'

'You know other D-Blocks who were involved?'

'Jamal Johnson.'

Terrio turned white, and Deets snapped a glance at him as fast as a nail gun. 'How do you know about Jamal Johnson?'

'His cousin, Rahmi.'

Deets shifted in the corner. 'No way. SIS is on Rahmi Johnson. They're on him right now. You couldn't have spoken with him.'

Pike shrugged. 'Williams and Johnson were both D-Block. I don't know about the other guy. Was Jamal Johnson one of the vics?'

Deets said, 'We ask, you answer. This isn't a conversation.'

Terrio cut him off. 'Johnson was confirmed as one of the vics.'

'Who was the third male?'

'Samuel "Lil Tai" Renfro. He goes back to the D-Block with Williams and Johnson. How was it you came to believe this is the crew who hit Meyer's home?'

Terrio was staring at Pike intently and Pike realised that Jamal Johnson had still been only a suspect, and Williams hadn't even been on their radar. They hadn't brought Pike in to find out what he knew—they wanted to know how he knew it.

Pike said, 'I came to believe Williams was running the crew. We'll know for sure after you run their guns.'

Terrio said, 'We have no physical evidence tying these people with what happened to Meyer, or the earlier six robberies.'

'You do now. Run their guns.'

'How did you come to identify Williams as a person of interest?'

'Sources.'

Terrio slipped a spiral notepad from his pocket, and read an address. 'One of these sources live in Studio City?'

Pike didn't respond. He was at Yanni's apartment building in Studio City when he first saw the Sentra.

'How about on La Brea just south of Melrose? Maybe we'll find one of your sources there, too.' Terrio slipped the pad back into his pocket, then leaned forward again. 'Who killed these people?'

'Don't know.'

Terrio leaned back in his chair, studying Pike as he tapped the table. 'These three idiots—Williams, Johnson and Renfro—they weren't in this alone. Someone was pointing them in the right direction. You and I on the same page with that?'

'Yes.'

'Your sources tell you who they were working for?'

Pike studied Terrio. Something about Terrio's inflection suggested he already knew, and wanted to find out if Pike knew.

'Williams was working for a Serbian OC gangster named Michael Darko. Darko or someone working for Darko probably killed Williams and his crew.'

Terrio and Deets stared at him, and for a few seconds the interview room was quiet. Then a large, balding deputy chief opened the door. Darko was the magic word.

'Jack, let's clear the room, please,' said the chief.

Terrio and Deets left. The chief followed them, and the woman Pike had seen in the back seat of Terrio's car on the day they told him about Frank entered and closed the door. Blue blazer over a white shirt. Dark grey slacks. An angry slash for a mouth.

She studied Pike as if he were a lab specimen, then glanced up at the camera. She went to the camera, unplugged it, then turned back to Pike. She held up a federal badge.

'Kelly Walsh. I'm with the ATF. Do you remember me?'

Pike nodded. The Bureau of Alcohol, Tobacco and Firearms.

'Good. Now that we've met, you're going to do exactly what I say.'

Part Three—It's Personal

6

Kelly Walsh stood twelve inches from the table, close enough so Pike was forced to look up, but not so close as to touch the table. He recognised this as a controlling technique.

Then she said, 'Was Frank Meyer smuggling guns?'

This was the first time one of them asked a question that surprised him. 'No.'

'You sure? Or you just want to believe he wasn't?'

Pike didn't like this business about guns. He studied her face, trying to read her. Her eyes were light brown. No laugh lines, but no frown lines, either. Pike didn't like her certainty.

She made an offhand shrug. 'OK, you're sure. Personally, I don't know, but I need a reason Darko killed him, and that one makes sense.'

'Guns.'

She pointed at herself. 'ATF. The "F" is for firearms.'

She studied him a moment longer. 'You don't know about the guns. You're just in this to get some payback. OK, I get it.'

Pike knew she was trying to decide what to tell him, and how to play him. Same things he was thinking about her.

'Terrio lied about our not having anything that ties Williams to the earlier six invasions. We found a woman's bracelet in his grandmother's trailer that puts him with the Escalante invasion, and an antique Japanese sword that puts him with the Gelber invasion. The gun comps will be the icing, but these boys are our killers.'

Pike knew that Escalante was the second of the six home invasions. Gelber was the fifth.

'If you found these things only now, then you didn't know Williams was involved.'

'No. You did a good job there, Pike, finding these guys so fast. We hadn't even come up with names for them, but you found them. I like that a lot.'

She reached into her inside jacket pocket, and fingered out a four-by-six-inch photograph. Pike saw a clean-cut African-American man, early thirties.

'Special Agent Jordan Brant. Jordie was one of my undercovers. He was murdered twenty-three days ago trying to identify a takeover crew employed by one Michael Darko. This is Darko.'

She produced a second picture showing a big man in his late thirties with wide-set eyes in a round face. He had black hair pulled into a short pony-tail, a thick moustache, and long, thin sideburns. The man who would not let himself be photographed had been captured on a security camera at the Bob Hope Airport in Burbank.

Pike stared at the picture, and Walsh read the stare.

'Yeah, baby, that's him. Killed your boy, Frank. Killed those little kids. The young one, Joey? Was he named after you?'

Pike sat back, and said nothing.

'You know where he is?'

'Not yet.'

'Jordie was found behind an abandoned Chevron station in Willowbrook. They used a box cutter on him. Wife and a child. You can relate to that, right? Me losing my guy. You losing your guy.'

'You believe Williams killed him?'

'Considering that Williams and his crew were Willowbrook homies, I'd say yes, but all we knew at the time was that a Crip set was involved. Jordie was trying to identify them.'

'What does this have to do with guns?'

'Darko works for a man named Milos Jakovich.' She arched her eye-brows, the arch asking if he recognised the name. Pike shook his head, so she explained.

'Jakovich heads up the original Serb set here in LA—the first of the old bosses to come over in the nineties. Jakovich is bringing in three thousand Chinese-made AK-47 assault rifles.'

The number stopped Pike. He tried to read if she was lying, but decided she was telling the truth.

'Full-auto combat rigs that pirates stole from the North Koreans. So if Darko sends his killers to murder a man who used to be a professional mercenary, and who probably knows how to buy and sell weapons anywhere in the world, pardon me if I see a connection.'

Pike took a breath. A new element had entered the field, and now Pike felt a stab of doubt. He felt bad for having it, as if he were betraying Frank's memory. 'Frank wouldn't do that.'

'Tell you what. Let me figure out whether he would, since that happens to be my job. Here's what's more important—you're going to help me get those guns.'

Walsh leaned forward, resting her hands on the table. 'Darko works for Jakovich, but he's trying to take over the deal, pick his own buyer, and force a regime change. That buys me time to find the guns, but if you keep dogging this guy, and he feels the heat.' She snapped her fingers. 'Poof! The guns disappear. So, first, you're going to drop your search-and-destroy.'

She didn't give Pike time to respond, but pushed on. 'These East European sets haven't been in this country long enough for us to develop informants. My guy died trying to bust that lock, Pike, but you—I think you have someone inside with the Serbs. So—second—I want your contact.'

This was why she bounced him. Williams was the break point. A Crip connected to Darko. When Pike reached Williams, Walsh must have realised Pike had inside help, and that triggered the bust. She was with Terrio and Deets on the day they told him about Frank, and now he wondered if she had been using him to get inside from the beginning.

Pike wondered if someone as far down the food chain as a prostitute would have information about an important deal. It was doubtful, but Rina might be able to find out. Pike said, 'I'll see.'

Walsh shook her head. 'You don't understand. We have three thousand automatic weapons coming into this country, so I am not asking you. You *will* put me together with your informant.'

'I hear what you're saying, Walsh. I told you I would talk to my source. I will, but there's a risk. I didn't know about these guns. If I bring it up now, and word gets to Darko, you're in the weeds.'

Walsh glared, but only for a moment, as Pike went on.

'There are people in the EEOC community who know I'm on the hunt, and they know why. They won't be spooked by a civilian working out a grudge. It's something they understand.'

Walsh shook her head to stop him. 'Don't even think about it, Pike. I am not going to allow you to murder this man.'

'I suddenly stop, the people who know are left hanging. They want things in this, too. That's why they're helping me. If I go back with this gun thing, and tell them I'm talking to you, they'll disappear as fast as your guns.'

Now Walsh didn't seem so confident. 'What are you saying?'

'You don't have someone inside—I do. They're inside—and they want me to find Darko—badly. Whatever I learn, I will pass back to you, and I can start by giving you something right now—Darko is going back to Europe.'

She stared at him, and now her tanned face paled. 'When?'

'Don't know.'

'Why is he going back?'

'Don't know. Maybe his deal is closing. Maybe he wants to go back after it's finished.'

Pike decided he could not mention the child, or Rina, or the true reason Darko sent his killers to Frank Meyer's home. Not without Rina's permission.

Walsh's face hardened as she struggled with the new information. When she spoke again, her voice was soft. 'I can take you out of the play. You don't want that.'

'No. I want Darko.'

'I've got three thousand weapons being brought into this country by a foreign national. That's a terrorist act. By the law as written in the Homeland Security Act, I could make you disappear. No trial, no lawyers, no bail—just gone.' She stared at him. 'If I lose those weapons because I couldn't find them, I can live with it, but I am not going to trade the guns for Darko. Do you understand that?'

'Yes.'

'I want him, but on my terms, not yours, alive, so I can testify against him in open court. So Jordie Brant's wife can sit in the front row, and watch him squirm. I want that, Pike, and I will have it. Guns or not, the only way you're leaving here is if you agree.'

Pike studied her face, and knew she meant it. He nodded.

'You agree? Darko is mine?'

'Yes.'

She put out her hand, he took it, and, for a moment, she did not let go.

She said, 'If you kill him, I swear I will devote the rest of my life to putting you in jail.'

'I won't kill him.'

She walked him downstairs. His Jeep was waiting. So were his weapons.

PIKE TURNED OFF his cellphone as soon as he was alone. He stopped at the first large shopping mall he reached, cruised up to the top floor of the parking structure, then down, looking for tails. He found none, but he had found none before. He still didn't understand how they followed him.

He parked on the second floor of the parking structure, then he inspected the underside of the Jeep with his flashlight. He found nothing. He cleaned himself off, then went into the mall. He bought a throwaway cellphone, batteries, and a prepaid calling card good for two hours. Pike called Elvis Cole.

'It's me. Where's Rina?'

'With Yanni. I brought her back after our tour.'

'Do me a favour, and go get them. The ATF knows I was at their building today, and suspects I was seeing a source. They want the source.'

Cole made a soft whistle. 'How do you know?'

'I just spent three hours with them.'

Pike sketched out what he found at Willowbrook, what happened when Walsh had picked him up, and the information she gave him about Darko. 'This is no longer about some gangster murdering people in their homes—they're bringing three thousand Kalashnikovs into the country. That's why the Feds are involved.'

Cole said, 'You want me to bring them to my place?'

'For now. I'll have a place for them by the time I get there.'

Pike phoned Jon Stone next. 'Someone's been able to find me without following me, Jon. I think the Jeep might be bad.'

'You driving it now?'

'Yes.'

'Don't come here. I'll meet you.'

Twenty minutes later, Pike arrived at a car wash in West Hollywood, and pulled round back to the detailing bays as Stone had instructed, where they couldn't be seen from the street.

Stone pointed at the empty bay on the far side of his Rover, and that's where Pike parked. Stone opened the back of the Rover, and took out a long aluminium tube with a movable mirror jointed to a pod containing sensors and antennas. Jon was a pro.

He swept the pod under the Jeep, talking to Pike as he watched a dial in the handle. 'You find these creeps?'

'Found the crew. They were dead.'

'Who bagged them?'

'Their boss.'

'No honour among scumbags. What was the butcher's bill?'

'Three. Their boss is still up, but these three are down.'

Stone paused between the Jeep's headlights and studied the dial. After a moment, he continued on round the Jeep, making a full sweep of the vehicle until he returned to the front end. Then wiggled under the engine.

'Here you go.'

He rolled to his feet, and showed Pike a grey box the size of a pack of cigarettes. 'GPS locator. High-end piece made by Raytheon under a National Security Agency contract. This is top-dollar equipment. Federal?'

'ATF,' Pike said. 'Kill it, and I need you to do something else.'

'For Frank?'

'Yes.'

'I'm there.'

Pike told him about the guns—3,000 Chinese AKs stolen from the North Koreans. 'Jakovich didn't steal them. He bought them from someone. See what you can find out.'

Stone hesitated, but made a slow nod.

'I know a guy who knows a guy, but I want a piece of the hunt. I'll help, but I want some trigger time. For Frank.'

'You got it.'

PIKE DROVE to Cole's house when he left the car wash. He decided Walsh had planted the locator on his Jeep the day they stopped him at Runyon Canyon.

Pike wondered now if she bugged him to follow his own investigation, or because she believed Frank was involved with the guns. There would have been no reason for her to believe Pike was involved in an arms deal, but maybe she knew something Pike didn't yet know.

The sky was deep purple when Pike pulled up in front of Cole's A-frame, and let himself into the kitchen. Pike liked Cole's home. Perched high in the canyons where it was surrounded by trees, it felt removed from the city. Pike took a bottle of water from Cole's fridge. A dish of cat food sat on the floor beside a small bowl of water. The house smelled of eucalyptus, wild fennel and the flora that grew on the canyon's steep slopes.

Cole, Rina and Yanni were in the living room, watching the news. They glanced over when Pike entered, and Cole muted the sound. Yanni's face was swollen and purple where Pike had hit him.

Rina squinted at Pike as if she were sizing him up for target practice. 'We are not going to stay here. It smells like cats.'

Cole arched his eyebrows, the arch saying you see what it's like?

Pike motioned Cole over. 'See you a minute?'

When Cole joined him, Pike lowered his voice.

'You were going to check out her story. What do you think?'

Cole shrugged. 'I located one of Ana's friends, and have a call into another. Everything checked.'

Rina stood, then raised her voice. 'I don't like this whispering. I told you already once. Yanni and I, we are going to go.'

Pike said, 'Yanni's building is being watched by the police.'

Rina said, 'The police don't care about Yanni. Why would they watch?'

'They followed me earlier today. They know I'm trying to find Darko, so now they believe someone in Yanni's complex has information about him. They will look for that person.'

Rina and Yanni launched into Serbian, and Yanni didn't look happy.

Pike asked Cole, 'Did you find anything running the check on Darko's condos?'

'Yeah. They're not his—not in his name or any name I've been able to connect to him. This guy is hidden, man—he does not exist, so he's almost certainly here illegally.'

Cole ticked off the points.

'No one named Michael Darko appears in the Department of Motor Vehicles, the Social Security rolls, or the California state tax rolls. No one by that name has an account with any of the major credit card companies, the public utilities here in Los Angeles County, the telephone company, or any of the major cellphone service providers. Michael Darko has no criminal record that I've been able to find.'

Cole continued, 'His hookers rent their condos in their own names. Darko supplies them with a credit and rental history for the application, and kicks back cash to cover their rent, but they have to write the cheques. Same with other expenses. Everything is in their names, and they pay the bills. That way he avoids a paper trail to the girls.'

Rina said, 'Yes. That is why we follow the money. The money will give us the man.'

Cole nodded. 'He has women spread from Glendale to Sherman Oaks. A collector stops by every day to pick up their cash.'

Pike glanced at Rina. 'You know the man who picks up the money?'

'I will know him to see him unless the man change. He will be there between four and six. This is always the way.'

Pike said, 'Will he know how to find Darko?'

She shook her head. 'No, no, no. He is an outcast.'

Pike and Cole traded a look, not understanding. 'Why? He's being punished?'

Rina tried to explain. 'Outcast is like someone learning.'

Cole said, 'Starting at the bottom?'

'Yes! The men who want to be accepted, but must prove themselves. The *pakhan* is the boss—that is Michael. Below him, his close friends are what we call the authorities. These are the men who make sure everyone do what Michael say.'

Pike said, 'Enforcers.'

'Yes. They make the men obey. The men, they are the ones who do the work and earn the money. The outcasts help the men.'

'OK, so the guy who collects the money, he's an errand boy. He brings the money to Michael?'

'He brings it to his boss. Michael does not touch the money.'

Cole said, 'Then how do we find Michael?'

She glanced at Yanni. Yanni mumbled, and Rina shrugged.

'Depends. If boss is authority man, then maybe he know. If boss is only one of the men, then no. We won't know until we see. Is like a sergeant, and Michael is a colonel. The sergeant does not talk to the colonel. He talks to the captain.'

Pike thought for a moment, then looked at Cole. 'Maybe there's a way to turn this around. Maybe we can make Darko find us.'

'Steal the money?'

'Follow these people from business to business, and hit him. Hit him so hard he has no other choice.'

Cole thought for a moment, then nodded. 'Sounds like a plan. You ready for something to eat?'

Cole stepped past him into the kitchen. Pike looked at Rina and Yanni. They whispered to each other, and then Rina glanced over.

'We will go to motel. Here smells like cats. It is making me ill.'

Pike said, 'Eat. I have a place you can stay. We'll go after dinner.' He took his new phone and stepped out onto Cole's deck.

THE NIGHT AIR was clear, and chill, and the canyon below Cole's home was quiet of man-made sounds. A wooden deck jutted from the back of Cole's house, hanging out over the night-filled canyon like a diving board to nowhere. Pike went to the rail. The air felt good. Out here on the deck, at the edge of the glow from within Cole's home, Pike enjoyed the solitude.

He turned to face Cole's home, the wide glass face of the house an invisible wall. Rina and Yanni were still huddled together on the couch. Cole was in the kitchen, busy with cooking.

Pike fished out the new phone and called George Smith.

George answered on the first ring. 'This is George.'

'Williams was dead. Williams, and two of his crew. Jamal Johnson and Samuel Renfro.'

George laughed. 'Well, there you go. Justice is swift.'

'Wasn't me. Someone killed them four days ago. The same night they murdered Frank. I thought you should know in case your friends in Odessa ask.'

'Then *muchas gracias.*'

'Something else. The ATF was tracking my vehicle when I came by this morning. They might come round, knocking on doors.'

George was silent for several seconds. When he spoke, his tone was edged with something dark. 'You brought them to my store?'

'I don't know. They were tracking my vehicle. They know where I parked, and how long I parked there. I don't know if they had eyeballs on me or not.'

'Where did you park?'

'A block north.'

'There are many shops within a block of my place.'

Pike didn't bother to say anything. George was shaking the facts to see if he could live with them, just as a terrier shakes a rat.

Inside, Rina stood. She peered outside, trying to find Pike at the edge of the light, then said something to Yanni.

George said, 'Why might they knock on doors, Joseph?'

'Darko. They know I have inside information on the Serbians. They want my source. They'll probably retrace my route today.'

George suddenly laughed, giving it his best Modesto twang.

'Why, hell, George Smith ain't some Bosnian refugee. If they come round, I'll tell 'em you wanted a lamp.'

Rina was heading for the deck. Pike would have to go, but he still needed a favour from George. 'One more thing. I'm going to hit Darko's business, and I want him to know it's me. Maybe Odessa can drop my name in the Eastern Bloc neighbourhoods.'

George grew serious again. 'This would put a target on your chest.'

'Yes.'

George made a little sigh. 'Well, we do what we do.'

Rina stepped out onto the deck as Pike put away his phone.

She said, 'It's dark out here. Why do you stand in the dark?'

Pike hesitated, wondering whether he should tell her what he had found in Willowbrook, and finally decided he should. He had been feeling the bib in his pocket as if it were a living thing, alive and pulsing, and wanting to come out. 'Darko's crew is dead.'

She visibly stiffened, then joined him at the rail.

'You found them?'

'Yes. Men named Jamal Johnson and Moon Williams. Have you heard of them?'

She shook her head.

'Samuel Renfro?'

She shook her head again.

'They were killed the same night they took your son and murdered my friends.'

Her mouth shrunk to a tight knot. 'Were Michael or Petar with them?'

'No. But I found this.'

Pike took the bib from his pocket. He smelled the apricots.

Rina took it, and seemed to marvel at it just as Pike had.

Pike decided to feel her out about Jakovich. 'I found another line I can follow—a man named Milos Jakovich. Do you know him?'

She stared into the dark for a moment. 'The old one. Michael, he work for him.'

'Do they have business together?'

A shrug. 'I do not know. The blood is not good.'

'They don't like each other?'

'I don't think so. Michael never tell me these things, but I hear.'

'Maybe Jakovich or someone who works for Jakovich knows how to find Michael. Is there someone you could ask?'

She shrugged again. 'I would be scared, I think.'

Pike let it go, thinking she was probably right in being scared.

They stood in silence, then she leaned over the rail to peer down into the black canyon. She said, 'It is so dark.'

Pike didn't answer.

'Do you have children?'

'No.'

'You should have children. You should make plenty of babies, and be a strong father.'

Rina held the bib to her nose, and Pike could feel her draw in the deep apricot smell and the scent of her child.

Pike said, 'We'll find him.'

'Yes. I know we will find him.'

'Get Yanni. I have a place where the two of you can stay. I'll take you.'

Pike went out without eating, and took them away.

7

The next morning, Pike had Cole take him to check out the building in Sherman Oaks. It was a three-storey structure a few blocks south of Ventura Boulevard, across from a gourmet food store.

Pike said, 'How many prostitutes does he have in there?'

'She says he had four, two on the top floor and two on the first, but that could have changed.'

'The pick-up happens between four and six?'

'Yeah, but that's only approximate. We should set up early, plan on staying late, and be ready to wait a few days.'

They circled the building to see the surrounding residential streets, and finished their tour in the food store's parking lot.

Pike said, 'How many stops does he make before here?'

'Three. Darko has buildings in Glendale, Valley Village, and this one. This was always the last stop.'

'So he should be carrying the full day's take?'

'Should be. If this is still the last stop.'

Pike was going to steal the money. He was going to steal it, and leave the pick-up man so scared he would run straight to his bosses. Then Pike would take whatever his bosses had, too.

Pike said, 'I've seen enough. Let's go.'

They would need Rina to identify the bagman, so Pike picked her up a little while later. He had brought them to an empty guesthouse the night before. It was small, but nice, with a lovely courtyard and neighbours who wouldn't pry. Pike had used it before.

Rina was waiting on the street when he arrived.

Pike brought her to Cole's, where they reviewed the plans and maps of the location with Jon Stone. When Stone first arrived, Rina squinted at him, and tugged at Pike's arm. 'Who is this?'

'A friend. He was a friend of Frank's, too.'

'I don't trust these people I don't know. I would rather have Yanni.'

'Not for this, you wouldn't.'

At one thirty that afternoon, they climbed into their cars and returned to Sherman Oaks, Pike and Rina in his Jeep, Cole in his Corvette, and Stone in his Rover. They looked like a caravan winding their way along the spine of the mountains.

When they reached the gourmet food store, Pike and Cole turned into the parking lot, but Stone continued past to set up on one of the nearby residential streets. Pike found a parking spot in a row facing the apartment building's entry, and Cole parked three spaces away.

Pike said to Rina, 'The guy who's coming to pick up the money, does he know you?'

'I don't know. Probably he would know me, yes.'

'Then get in the back seat. You won't be as easy to see in the back.'

She scowled, but got out and climbed into the back seat. Pike adjusted the mirror so he could see her. 'Can you see the entry?'

'Yes.'

'Watch.'

They watched for an hour and ten minutes, silent. Rina did not move or speak for the entire time, but then she suddenly pulled herself forward and pointed past his chin.

'That window on the top floor, on the side there away from the freeway. That was mine.' Then she settled back and said nothing more.

An hour and twenty minutes later, she abruptly pulled herself forward again. 'That girl. She is one of the girls there. In the green.'

A young woman in black spandex shorts and a lime-green top came round the corner and went to the glass door. She looked very young. The girl let herself into the lobby.

Fifteen minutes later, Rina pulled forward again.

'There. In the black car.'

A black BMW convertible with the top down turned off Sepulveda and crept past the building as if looking for a parking place. The driver was a white male in his twenties, with long, limp hair. He wore a white shirt with the sleeves rolled, a day-old beard, and sunglasses.

Pike hit the speed dial for Cole.

Cole glanced over as he raised his phone. 'What's up?'

'The black convertible.'

Cole glanced at the street. 'I'll get Jon.'

Pike lowered the phone, but didn't end the call. Cole was using a second phone to put Stone in the loop. They had planned on multiple phones to maintain constant contact.

The BMW turned into the parking lot.

'Get down.'

Rina slumped down in her seat without question.

The Beemer passed behind Pike's Jeep and Cole's Corvette, then turned onto the next row and parked by the sidewalk. The driver got out, stepped over a low hedge, then crossed the street. He let himself into the building with his own key.

Pike said, 'Here's where you leave.'

Rina went directly to Cole's Corvette, and got in as they had planned. She did not stare or draw attention to herself. Pike liked that about her.

Cole's voice came from the phone. 'You want Jon to come in?'

'I'm good. Get her gone.'

Cole backed away, and cruised out of the parking lot.

The bagman was inside for less than ten minutes.

When he emerged from the building, Pike stepped out of the Jeep. The bagman passed in front of Pike within ten feet and swung round the Beemer's rear end. As he opened the door, Pike closed the gap. When the bagman slid in behind the wheel, Pike came up along the passenger's side, and lifted himself over the door and into the passenger's seat.

The bagman lurched in surprise, but by then it was too late. Pike showed him the .357, down low so no one could see. 'Sh.'

The man lunged for Pike's gun, but Pike rolled his hands down and away, and snapped the Python up hard into the bottom of the man's chin, popping his jaw like a rat trap. The Python flicked again, and this time Pike hit him in the Adam's apple. The bagman clutched at his throat, choking.

Pike took the key from his hand and fitted it into the ignition. He pushed the console button to raise the convertible top. He had to keep the button depressed throughout the process, but that was OK. His arm was a steel bar with his tattoo in the runner's face. Pike wanted him to see the red arrow.

When the top was in place and the windows were closed, Pike said,

'Grab the wheel. Both hands. Try to escape, I'll kill you. Try to grab this weapon again, I'll kill you. Do you understand?'

'This is a mistake, my man. I don't know what you—'

Pike backfisted him hard on his temple, striking so fast the man had no time to react. His head bounced off the window.

Pike jerked him upright. The man moaned, and pushed weakly at Pike's hand, so Pike hit him again. Pike said, 'Grab the wheel.'

The man grabbed the wheel with both hands. Blood from his mouth dripped onto his shirt and his temple was swelling.

Pike said, 'What's your name?'

'Vasa.'

'I'm going to search you, Vasa. Don't let go of the wheel.'

Pike went through Vasa's pockets, finding a black wallet, a cellphone and four vinyl billfolds. Pike said, 'One from each girl?'

'Yes.'

'They have the money ready? You stop by, they give it to you?'

Vasa wet his lips. 'You know who this belongs to?'

'Me.'

Pike thumbed through the bills and counted out $3,800. He tucked the money into his pocket.

'Where's the rest?'

Vasa blinked at him. 'What rest? That's it.'

Pike stared into his eyes, and finally Vasa sighed. 'Under the seat.'

Pike found $7,300 under the seat. That made $11,100 of Darko's money. He stared at Vasa. The man turned away.

'Why are you staring at me. Who are you?'

'My name is Pike. Say it.'

'You are Pike?'

'Say the name. Say it.'

'Pike. I say it. You are Pike.'

Pike touched the arrow on the outside of his arm. 'See this?'

Vasa nodded. 'I see it.'

'Where is Michael Darko?'

Vasa's eyes grew into saucers. 'How would I know?'

'Call him.'

'Bro, I don't have his number. He is the boss. Why are you taking his money? This is crazy. He will kill you.'

Pike studied Vasa a moment longer. 'Tell Darko I'm coming.'

Pike got out, taking the money, the wallet, the keys and the cellphone. He returned to his Jeep, and circled the parking lot until he pulled up behind the Beemer. He wanted Vasa to see his Jeep, too. He motioned for Vasa to roll down his window.

Inside the BMW, Vasa couldn't roll down the window without the keys, so he opened the door.

Pike tossed out his keys, then drove away. He drove exactly two blocks, then pulled to the kerb and lifted his cellphone. 'What's he doing?'

'Getting on the freeway. Jon's three cars behind him and I'm behind Jon,' Cole said.

Pike pushed hard to catch up.

THEY FOLLOWED THE BEEMER east across the bottom of the San Fernando Valley, Pike watching Cole and Jon Stone take turns behind the Beemer. The BMW drove steadily, in no great hurry to get where it was going. Vasa probably wasn't looking forward to explaining what happened to Darko's money.

They stayed on the Ventura Freeway past the Hollywood split, but took the first exit. Cole tightened up on the Beemer when they left the freeway, and Jon fell back. Ten minutes later, Cole once more spoke in Pike's ear.

'We're turning up ahead on Victory.'

Neither Pike nor Stone responded.

Three minutes later, Cole spoke again. 'Turning again. A place called the Glo-Room. We're going past to the first cross street.'

Two blocks ahead, Pike caught a glimpse of the BMW turning, and spoke to Cole. 'Does Rina know the place?'

'She's heard of it, but never been here.'

When Pike passed, he glimpsed Vasa's convertible parked in a narrow lot alongside a black single-storey building. A sign jutted out from the front of the building, saying GLO-ROOM GENTLEMEN'S CLUB. Pike continued past to the first cross street. Cole and Rina were already waiting in Stone's Rover. Pike pulled in behind them, then climbed into the Rover's front passenger seat. Stone turned down an alley to circle around behind the bar.

Pike said, 'Stop short.'

Stone stopped three doors away, parking behind a pet supply store. A white delivery van was parked behind the Glo-Room.

Pike turned so he could see Rina. 'Darko owns this place?'

'One of his men own it, but Michael he get the money.'

'You know the people who work here?'

She shook her head. 'No, I don't think so. I never been here.'

They started rolling again. They drove all the way to the next cross street, turned round and came back from the opposite direction. This time they stopped with an easy view of the side lot and delivery truck. A back door used for deliveries and service help was cracked open on the alley. The BMW was parked outside the bar's main entrance. A dark grey Audi sedan and a silver Mercedes were parked near the Beemer, and now three men were standing outside the door. Two of the three were large guys wearing loose shirts. The third man was younger, with hard, muscular shoulders.

Pike turned enough to see Rina. 'Know them?'

'That one in the middle, maybe, but maybe not. Other two, no.'

Stone said, 'You see it?'

Pike nodded.

Rina said, 'See what?'

Cole said, 'The muscle has a gun in his belt.'

The three men finished their conversation, then the two big men went into the bar and the muscular guy walked back to the delivery van. He slapped the side twice, and the van's rear door opened. A burly guy climbed out, showing a mat of dark hair on his arms and neck. He hoisted three cases of Budweiser, and brought them into the bar. The muscular guy leaned into the van, came out with three more cases, and followed him inside.

Rina said, 'They steal the beer to sell, you see? He buy some, but he have people who steal.'

That fitted with what George described. Darko resold most merchandise stolen by hijack crews. Alcohol went to his clubs.

Pike tapped Jon's leg, and Jon rolled on, cruising back to their cars. Everything moved quickly after their brief reconnoitre, which was how Pike liked it. In armed confrontations, speed was the difference between life and death.

Cole put Rina in his car and left the area. Stone motored away, but would circle the block to approach from the front. Pike returned to his Jeep, pulled into the alley, and parked behind the bar. By the time he got back, the van and the back door were both closed, but the door was unlocked.

Pike hit the speed dial on his phone for Jon Stone, and Stone answered with a single word. 'Go.'

Pike stepped inside, and found himself in a hall crowded with stacked boxes. A larder to his left was filled with more beer, tap kegs, booze and other supplies. Pike shut and locked the door behind him.

Further along the hall was a small dressing room for the dancers, a couple of rest rooms, and a swinging door. The rest rooms and dressing room were all empty. Pike heard voices coming from the front of the club, but no music or other sounds.

Pike pushed through the swinging door. The three men from the parking lot were crowded round bar tables with a fourth man and Vasa. The furry man was behind the bar, manoeuvring a beer keg into place. Pike had entered so quietly the men at the tables did not hear him, but the furry man caught the movement, and turned.

He said, 'We're closed. You'll have to leave.'

The men at the tables all looked over, and Vasa saw Pike. He lurched to his feet as if someone had kicked him. 'That's him.'

Pike said, 'I'm looking for Michael Darko.'

The oldest of the men was in his fifties, a heavy man with small eyes. Three of the four wore short-sleeved shirts, two showing skin that had been inked up with Eastern Bloc prison tats back in the old country.

The oldest man said, 'I have never heard of this man.'

Two vinyl billfolds identical to the ones Pike took from Vasa were on the bar, along with a brown leather briefcase. Just sitting there, as if someone was in the middle of business when Vasa rushed in to tell his story. Pike moved towards the bar.

When Pike reached the end of the bar, the furry man behind the bar charged, but Pike slipped to the side, pushed the man's elbow down and away, caught his twisting head, and rolled him into the floor. Third of a second once contact was made, and Pike was on his feet, calmly watching the muscular man rush towards him as the three other men jumped to their feet.

The muscular man reached under his shirt even as he pushed past the tables. Pike did not try to stop the gun; he rolled his hand under the man's wrist, drove the man's arm over and back, and pulled him backwards and down. Pike had the gun before the man slammed into the floor, and hit him on the forehead with it two hard times, even as Jon Stone's voice cut through the gloom.

'Freeze!'

The three men at the tables, on their feet now, raised their hands.

Jon stood just inside the door with an M4 carbine. Never taking his eyes from the men, Stone closed and locked the door. He grinned at Pike. 'Always wanted to say that.'

Pike checked the man's pistol, then went through his pockets. He found a wallet, keys, and cellphone, then stood away. He waved towards the floor with the pistol. 'Knees. Fingers laced behind your head.' The men hurried into position.

Pike returned to the furry man. His eyes were open, but unfocused. Pike came away with a neat little .40-calibre pistol. He put everything on the bar with the vinyl billfolds, then searched the others as well. None were armed.

When Pike finished, he returned to the bar and checked the billfolds. They were filled with cash. He opened the briefcase. More cash, a metal skimmer used to steal credit card information, and some business papers. He put the two pistols and the other things he had taken from the men into the briefcase, then closed it.

Pike said, 'Darko?'

The older man shook his head. 'You are making a mistake.'

Pike said, 'Vasa, do you remember my name?'

'You are Pike.'

The older man said, 'You are dead man.'

Stone snapped the M4 into the back of his head. The man fell like a bag of wet towels. Vasa and the other men stared at his unconscious form for a moment, and now their eyes were frightened.

Pike dangled the briefcase, showing them.

'Everything Darko owns is mine. Darko is mine. This bar is mine. If you're here when I come back, I'll kill you.'

The other big man, the one still conscious, squinted as if Pike was hidden by fog. 'You are insane.'

'Close this place now. Lock it. Tell him I'm coming.'

Pike left with the briefcase, and Stone followed him out. They went directly to Pike's Jeep, then drove round the corner to Stone's Rover. When they stopped, Stone opened the briefcase. He pushed the cash packs aside, and frowned.

'Hey, what is this?'

Pike fingered through the pages, clocking the columns of numbers organised by business, and realised what they had.

'Our next targets.' He opened his phone to call Cole.

THEY MET BACK at Cole's house to go through the papers. Rina recognised them immediately.

'They are gas stations. You see? He make much money there.'

Stone said, 'How much dough can he make selling gas?'

Cole said, 'It's a skimmer rip-off. He's doing credit-card fraud.'

Cole explained how it worked. Darko's people connected a skimmer sleeve to the card reader inside each gas pump, along with an altered keypad over the pump's actual keypad. This allowed them to collect credit card and PIN information every time a customer swiped a credit card or debit card to pay for gas. Darko's fraud crew then used this information to create new credit and debit cards, with which they could drain the victims' debit accounts or run up huge charges before the victims or credit-card companies froze the accounts.

'Each of these skimmers is worth anywhere from a hundred thousand to one-fifty a month in goods and cash, times however many skimmers he has in each of the three stations, All-American Best Price Gas, Down Home Petroleum and Super Star Service.'

Now Jon Stone made a little whistle. Then he frowned. 'But wait a minute—if there's no cash, what are we gonna steal?'

Pike said, 'His machines.'

Cole nodded. 'Bust them right out of the pumps. Pop out the skimmers and keypads, he's bleeding big money.'

Stone said, 'Now you're talking, bro. Let's get it going.'

Pike stopped him. 'Tomorrow. We want to give him time to hear about what happened today, let him get angry about it. Tomorrow, we take him down one by one, pace it out over the day.'

'And sooner or later the enforcers show up.'

'That's the idea.'

ALL-AMERICAN BEST PRICE GAS was a ragged dump in Tarzana. Six pumps, no service bays, little minimart with a middle-aged Latina holed up behind a wall of bulletproof glass.

Cole and Stone went in first, Cole scouting the surroundings, Stone pretending to put air in his tyres while he checked out the people around the station. Pike waited until they called. Pike heard them through his Bluetooth earbud, which he would wear while he did what he had to do, Cole and Stone providing security.

Cole told him about the woman. 'Strictly counter personnel.'

'Will we have a problem with her calling the police?'

'Rina said no. The employees are schooled to call their manager, not the police. That's the front man who runs it for Darko. Listen, they're selling diluted gas and they have skimmers on all the pumps. They don't want the police sniffing around.'

Pike said, 'I'm rolling.'

He pulled up to the pumps, giving the woman inside a clear view of his Jeep. He wanted her to be able to describe it accurately.

Pike went inside. He gave the woman his name, then told her he was there to give Mr Darko a message.

She looked confused. 'Who's Mr Darko?'

'Doesn't matter. I'm going to adjust the pumps. Mr Darko will explain.'

The emergency cut-off switch for the pumps was on the wall outside the door. Pike cut the power, then crowbarred the cover off each pump register. The woman behind the glass simply picked up her phone, and made a calm call.

Six pumps, two sides to each pump, twelve card readers.

Pike tore off the skimmer sleeves and circuit boards, and stowed them in a plastic bag. He left the pump registers broken, and open.

Eight minutes later, the skimmers were stripped from the pumps and Pike was finished.

They took a long break for breakfast, and hit the next station three hours later. Down Home Petroleum was a cheesy little station in North Hollywood that was older and smaller than the All-American Best Price, and so dirty it looked like a smudge.

Cole and Stone rolled in first, just as they had before, and this time it was Stone who spoke in Pike's ear.

'Two dudes inside, bro. Young and white, but that doesn't mean they aren't packing.'

Cole, listening in, said, 'Surrounding streets clear.'

'I'm in.' Pike rolled, once more pulling up to the pumps.

A tall Anglo kid sat behind a counter, unshaven, shaggy, and looking as if he'd rather be anyplace else. Had a friend keeping him company. Pike heard them talking when he entered, and recognised accents similar to Rina's. A flicker of recognition flashed in their eyes when he mentioned Darko. The kid behind the counter raised his hands. 'Hey, man, I just work here.'

His friend smiled, incredulous. 'Dude. Are you *robbing* us?'

Civilians, or so far out of the loop they might as well have been.

Six pumps, twelve skimmers, eight keypads rigged to steal PIN numbers. Pike was gone in seven minutes.

They killed two hours at Cole's house, then rolled down through the

422 | ROBERT CRAIS

canyons to Hollywood. Super Star Service was located on a seedy part of Western Avenue. It was smaller than the Tarzana station, having only four pumps, and shared its property with a taco stand.

As Pike waited for Cole and Stone to recon the area, it occurred to him that this was their last target. If Darko's enforcers didn't show, they would have to come up with something else. That's when Cole spoke in his ear. 'Well, Joseph, I think we have company. Dark blue Navigator parked across the street, and a silver BMW alongside a little taco stand they have here.'

Stone's voice came in. 'I make two guys in the Beemer, and at least two in the Nav.'

Pike said, 'What about the station personnel?'

Cole again. 'One male at the counter, but he's nothing like the last kids. Don't get out of the car this time. These boys are ready. Come in. Let them see you. Then leave. Make them follow you.'

'Rog. I'm rolling.'

Pike slipped his .357 from its holster, and set it between his legs.

He approached the station slowly, seeing both the Navigator and the BMW without looking directly at them. They had to believe he did not suspect they were waiting.

Pike eased into the station, but stopped short of the pumps. He counted to ten, then slowly turned back to the street, and out into traffic. He didn't speed away, and never once looked in his mirror.

Cole said, 'Here we go. Nav's pulling out.'

Now Pike glanced in his rearview and saw the dark blue Navigator swing through a hard one-eighty, looping into the gas station and out, jumping into traffic four or five cars behind him. The BMW followed the Navigator, cutting across oncoming traffic.

Stone said, 'Groovy. This is gonna be like shooting fish, bro.'

Pike's mouth twitched. 'Shoot them later. Right now, watch them.'

Pike led them into a bottleneck where construction had forced three lanes of traffic into two. When Pike popped out the other side, they were trapped by the quicksand of congestion.

A few minutes later, Cole reported. 'The one dude jumped out and chased after you on foot. That didn't work so well.'

'What are they doing?'

'They split up. I'm with the Navigator, northbound on Vine.'

Stone said, 'Beemer's north on Gower. We're probably heading for the same place.'

This was what Pike wanted. The authority men had sent the enforcers, and now the enforcers had to explain how they blew it. They might even lead him to Darko.

Pike caught sight of Stone's Rover at the bottom of Laurel Canyon, just as it turned between a pair of pretentious Greek columns to enter the Mount Olympus housing development.

Cole, ahead of Stone and already climbing the side of the canyon, called again to warn that their caravan would stand out in the residential neighbourhood. 'I'm approaching a construction site here on the right. Let's dump two of these cars.'

Pike and Cole left their cars at the construction site, and jumped into Stone's Rover. Stone barrelled away.

Palatial homes of dubious architecture lined the steep streets. They climbed hard, catching glimpses of the cars they followed higher on the mountain.

They reached the crest of the ridge, rounded a tight curve, and saw the Navigator and Beemer parked outside a dark grey home on the downhill side of the street. The cars were empty. The house was set on the kerb with almost no setback. Low-slung and contemporary, the face of the house was a windowless, monolithic wall with a buffed-steel entry and a matching three-car garage.

'Drive past, and drop me in front of the next house.'

Jon slowed enough for Pike to slide out. Pike glanced at the surrounding houses to see if anyone was watching, but all the homes were still and closed to the world.

Pike walked back to the grey house's mailbox, and found a thin stack of magazines and envelopes. He saw that everything was addressed to someone named Emile Grebner. He returned the mail, then set off after the Rover. It had turned round at the far intersection and was waiting at the kerb. As he walked, Pike phoned George Smith.

George answered right away. 'My friends tell me you're a one-man wrecking crew. Odessa is loving this.'

'I'm not doing this for Odessa. What do you know about Emile Grebner?'

George thought for a moment. 'If this is the same Grebner, he works with Darko, yes. I do not recall his first name.'

'An authority man?'

'That's what they call them. Darko will have three or four like Grebner, each running cells of their own at street level—the people who do the crime. Secrecy is everything with people from our part of the world, my man. They may not even know each other.'

'A cell system.'

'Yes. Like these gas stations you hammered—they're probably Grebner's responsibility, so you're his problem to handle. Is that how you know him? He sent people for you?'

'That's how I know him.'

'Ah. Then pity for them.'

Pike put away his phone as he reached the Rover. He got into the Rover, and filled them in on what he had learned from George Smith. As he went through it, the front door of the house opened and the two big men from the Navigator came out. They didn't look happy. The Navigator squealed away in a wide, screaming U-turn.

Pike wondered if Darko was holed up with Grebner. Pike thought this unlikely, but knew it was possible. There might be only one or two men inside, but there could be a dozen, or a family.

Cole said, 'So what are we going to do?'

'Take a look. Me and you. Jon, you're out here. Let us know if someone comes.'

As Cole and Pike slipped out, Stone said, 'Want the M4? It's ideal for urban assault.'

Cole frowned at Stone. 'You have an M4?'

'Shit, yeah, man. Suppressed. Frangible bullets so you don't kill a buncha people in the next house. Straight from the Delta Armory.'

Cole looked at Pike. 'Is he kidding?'

'Let's go.'

Pike jogged away, and Cole fell in behind him. They slowed as they neared the house, then lingered at the nearest side gate to let a car pass. Neither spoke, and neither needed to. Pike had been on missions as long as a week, and never uttered a word.

Pike went over the gate first, then slipped along the side of the house. When he reached the corner, Cole was at his shoulder.

The back yard was small, but had an outdoor bar, cabana seating around an elevated fire pit, and an infinity pool. The view past the pool encompassed the Los Angeles basin from downtown to the Pacific, and south all the way to Long Beach.

Pike heard the drone of faraway voices, and realised he was hearing the television. ESPN, someone going on about the Lakers.

Cole touched his shoulder, and pointed. The service walk ran behind the bar to an area walled off for the pool equipment. Cole touched his shoulder again, then pointed at his own eyes, telling Pike the pool equipment store would be a good vantage point.

Pike slipped past the bar to the pool, and squeezed in behind the pool equipment. Cole joined him a moment later.

The entire back of Emile Grebner's house was open. Floor-to-ceiling glass sliders had been pushed into pockets. Two younger men and a shorter, bulky man in his fifties were in the living room, but none of them was Michael Darko. The older man was doing all the talking, so Pike decided he was Grebner. Grebner was angry.

One of the younger men made the mistake of speaking, and Grebner slapped him. The younger man came outside, where he lit a cigarette, and leaned against the bar. Sullen.

Grebner finally ran out of gas. He picked up a phone to make a call and the other young man hurried into the kitchen. Grebner threw down the phone, then stalked into a bathroom off the living room. He slammed the door.

Pike touched Cole, then pointed at the man in the kitchen—that man is yours. He touched himself, then pointed at the man by the bar—that one is mine.

Cole nodded, and both moved without hesitation.

Pike slipped up behind the man at the bar, hooked his left arm round the man's neck, and lifted. Pike said, 'Sh.'

The man struggled, but Pike compressed the carotid artery to cut off the blood to his brain, and in a few seconds the man went to sleep. Pike laid him behind the bar, and bound his hands behind his back with a plasti-cuff.

Pike glimpsed Cole putting the other man down as he moved for the living room. He reached the bathroom and placed himself behind the door only a second before it opened, and Grebner stepped out.

Pike slapped him behind the right ear with the .357, and Grebner hit the terrazzo hard on his hip, but didn't go all the way down. Pike hadn't wanted him out. Pike wanted him awake.

Cole stepped out of the kitchen, glancing at Grebner but otherwise ignoring him. 'I'll clear the house.' Cole disappeared.

Pike cuffed Grebner's hands behind his back.

Grebner's eyes went to the Python, to Pike. 'Who the hell are you?'

Pike could see he was scared, which was good.

Grebner shook his head. 'You got no idea, I am telling you. No idea what kind of hell you have unleashed.'

Pike said, 'Where's Darko?'

'Kiss my ass.'

Pike hit him again. The barrel of the .357 caught him on the temple.

Grebner made a growling sound. 'I know you want Darko. You been telling everyone you want Darko. Here, you can call him.'

Grebner tipped his head towards the couch. 'You see the phone there on the couch? Get it. Scroll for Michael. Call him.'

Pike saw the phone. He picked it up, then scrolled through the directory until he found the name.

Outside, Cole dragged the man from the kitchen next to his friend. Both men were now awake, and bound hand and foot. Cole hurried away to another part of the house, his gun out.

Pike called the number, and a female computer voice said, 'Enter your callback number at the tone, followed by the pound sign.'

A paging system. Pike hung up when the tone sounded, and brought up the phone's call list. The call list revealed the same number had been dialled a few minutes earlier, which would have been the call Grebner placed before he went to the bathroom. Grebner was telling the truth.

Pike slipped the phone into his pocket. 'Where is he?'

Grebner glanced at the pocket. 'There. This is where Michael is. You page him, and he calls. He lives there in the phone.'

Pike holstered the .357, then squatted so he and Grebner were only a few inches apart. He said, 'This will hurt.'

Pike dug the point of his thumb behind Grebner's right collarbone, probing for a bundle of nerves. He found it, and pinched the bundle into the bone. Grebner screamed. Pike let go. 'It will hurt worse next time.'

Grebner sucked deep breaths. 'I do not know. I call the number. That is all I know. He tells no one his whereabouts for this very reason. You can beat me all you like, but I cannot say.'

'Jakovich?'

Grebner's eyes narrowed as if Pike had finally surprised him.

'How about if I say "Kalashnikov"?'

Grebner slowly opened his mouth, staring as if Pike were mystical. 'How can you know these things?'

'Are the rifles in Los Angeles?'

Pike reached for his shoulder, and Grebner jerked. 'Yes! Yes, this is what

I hear. I don't *know* this, but this is what I am told.'

Cole reappeared as Grebner answered. Cole was carrying a grocery bag tucked under his arm. He motioned Pike over, and spoke so Grebner couldn't hear. 'The guns are here?'

'That's what he says.'

'How about Darko? He have a location?'

'He has a pager number. That's it.'

Cole patted the bag. 'I scooped some billing records and files, but it's lame. I don't know if this will help.'

They returned to Grebner. Pike said, 'Where are the guns?'

'How would I know? The old one. He has them.'

'Jakovich?'

'You do this for the guns? You want to steal them, buy them, what? Who are you working for?'

'Frank Meyer.'

'I don't know a Frank Meyer. Who's that?'

'Darko sent a crew to a house in Westwood six nights ago. Do you know about that?'

'Of course, I know. This was Frank Meyer's house?'

'Frank, his wife Cindy, their two little boys. Darko's crew murdered them when they snatched his son.'

Now Grebner's eyes narrowed again. 'Michael's son?'

Pike nodded, but this seemed to confuse Grebner even more.

'Michael has no children. This was the old man's child he took.'

Cole and Pike shared a glance, then Cole took the picture of Rina's son from his pocket and held it out. The baby with the wispy red hair. 'Peter. *Petar*. Is this the kid you're talking about?'

'I have not seen the child. All I know is what Michael tell me.'

'Which is what?'

'Michael took the child to get the guns. He thinks if he have the child he can force the old man to make a deal, but the old man is crazy. You would have to be Serbian to understand. He tells Michael he will kill his own child to show he cannot be threatened, and he will kill Michael.'

Cole said, 'Jakovich's child? Not Michael's?'

'Yes.'

'Who's the mother?'

'Who can say? I don't know these people.'

The phone in Pike's pocket rang with a high-pitched jangle. Grebner's phone. Pike glanced at the incoming number, but it meant nothing. Pike answered, but said nothing. Pike heard breathing, then the person hung up.

Pike slipped the phone into his pocket, and saw that Grebner was smiling. Grebner said, 'This will be Michael, yes?'

'Probably.'

'I am sorry for your friend, but he should not have involved himself in our affairs. Neither should you. We are terrible enemies.'

Pike glanced at Cole and said, 'We're done.'

Cole headed for the front door, and Pike turned back to Grebner. When Cole was gone, Pike drew the .357, then thumbed back the hammer. The locking steel spring was a breaking bone in the quiet house. Grebner wet his lips, and began to breathe faster.

Pike said, 'Where did Jakovich get the guns?'

'I got no idea. I don't know.'

'The man who owned the house. Frank Meyer. Was he involved in the deal for the guns?'

'I don't know. How could I know?'

Pike pressed the muzzle into Grebner's head. 'What did Darko tell you?'

'He said nothing about this Frank Meyer. He told me he knew where the old man had hidden his son. That's all he said.'

'Darko went with the crew to the Westwood house?'

'That's what he say. To make sure they not mess it up. Please—'

Pike looked out over the white terrazzo floor and the fine white furniture and beyond the two trussed men with their frightened, watching eyes, to the infinite, hazy sky. Knowing was good.

'Deliver a message.'

Grebner stared at him. He had expected Pike to kill him.

'Tell Michael nothing he does or can do will stop me.'

Grebner slowly nodded, staring into Pike's invisible eyes.

'I think maybe you are a terrible enemy, too.'

Pike holstered his gun, and left.

PIKE FLAGGED JON to pick them up, Cole tugging his arm as soon as they were out of the house. 'Refresh my memory. Whose kid is this we've been trying to find?'

'Your memory's fine. She said Darko is the father.'

'Only Darko tells this guy that Jakovich is the father.'

'Yes.'

'I don't get it. Everything she told us checked out when I spoke with Ana's friend.'

In the car, Pike explained about Grebner, and asked Jon to stay at the scene to follow Grebner in case he left for a face-to-face with Darko. Stone told him it would be no problem, then had a few questions.

Stone said, 'This guy Grebner, was he in on killing Frank?'

'No. Says he knew about it, but it was Darko's play.'

'So he didn't know if Frank was involved?'

'He doesn't think so, but he doesn't know.'

Cole said, 'The guns are in Los Angeles, and Jakovich has them. Way these people keep secrets, Darko may not even know how he got them. He just wants them.'

They drove the rest of the way in silence. The field of fire was growing confused. Rina hid her baby with her sister to keep him from Michael, or Jakovich hid his child with Ana or Frank for the same reason, which meant Jakovich had a relationship with Rina's sister or with Frank. Frank and his family were either innocent collateral damage, or Frank was somehow involved with Jakovich.

Pike said, 'Let's talk to Rina again.'

They took their own vehicles to the guesthouse while Jon Stone returned to Grebner's. The drive to the guesthouse at the far end of the Sunset Strip took only minutes. Yanni's truck was gone.

Pike waited for Cole at the gate, then they eased along the stubby drive past the front home into the tiny courtyard. Pike tried the knob, found it unlocked, and went in with Cole behind him. The little guesthouse was cool and pleasant. The single studio was empty.

Pike called anyway. 'Rina?'

'They're gone. Look. Their things are gone.'

Cole set the bag on the table. 'I'll see if this stuff gives us anything.'

He dumped the contents of the bag, then began organising a jumble of phones, wallets and papers.

Pike phoned Kelly Walsh as Cole worked, putting the phone on speaker. Walsh seemed distant and wary. 'Where are you? You were supposed to keep me advised.'

Pike knew she was trying to bait him into admitting he found the bug, so he ignored her. 'The guns are in Los Angeles.'

'Where?'

'Don't know, but the deal is close.'

'Don't just leave me hanging. *Where are those guns?*'

'Jakovich has them. You want me to leave it at that?'

'No.' She sounded defeated.

'Does Jakovich have any children?'

'What does that have to do with anything?'

'Darko caused a one-year-old male child to be kidnapped, and I have conflicting information about the child's identity. One of my sources tells me the child is Darko's child. The other says Jakovich is the father. If Darko kidnapped this kid to force the old man's hand, it's blown up in his face. This source tells me the old man has ramped up the war, which means he could unload the guns faster just to get rid of them.'

'OK, wait—how has he ramped up the war?'

'He's vowed to kill the kid himself. This takes the child off the table as a bargaining chip, and sends a message to the other Serb sets. The source told me they're big on messages.'

Pike heard Walsh take a deep breath. 'Is this source reliable?'

'I had a gun to his head, Walsh. How reliable could he be? That's why I'm calling you—to see if any of this is possible.'

Her voice was thoughtful. '*Vorovskoy Zakon.* You know what that is?'

Pike glanced at Cole, but Cole shook his head. 'No.'

'Started with the Russian gangs, but it's all through the East European gangs now. It translates as "thieves in law". *Vory v Zakone.* What they call the thieves' code. These people live by eighteen rules, Pike—actual written rules. The first rule is that their families don't matter. Mom, dad, brother, sis—those people do not matter. They are not supposed to have wives or children. It's written like that.'

Pike thought about Rina. 'What about girlfriends?'

'Girlfriends are fine. Marriage is out. These guys swear a blood oath on this crap, and I have interrogated enough of them to tell you they mean it. So if you're asking me whether Jakovich would sacrifice his own child, I have to say yes. They have these rules, and the rules are enforced. If the rules are broken, the punishment is death.'

Pike nodded, thinking about a man who could do such a thing, and then he continued. 'I need to know about Darko, too. If the child is Darko's, then my other source is solid. If not, then not, and what I told you about him leaving the country is probably wrong.'

'I'll check with Interpol. They might have something on Jakovich, but you're on your own with Darko.'

'OK. Let me know.'

She said, 'Pike? Don't get second thoughts about killing him. Don't make that mistake. Darko is mine.'

Pike said, 'Sh.'

He ended the call as Cole glanced up from the things he had spread on the table. Cole said, 'I think we have something.'

Pike went to see, thinking he had rules of his own.

8

Jon Stone dropped off Pike and Cole at their cars, then drove back up the hill, but he didn't return to his observation point.

He parked outside Grebner's house. Stone got out, and opened the hatch. He dug in his gearbox, selecting a sweet little 9mm Sig, along with its matching suppressor tube. He screwed the suppressor in place, then closed up his Rover and let himself into Grebner's house.

Stone figured the three guys Pike described would still be trying to get loose, and, sure enough, there they were, the two outside, and the older one there in the living room—Grebner.

Grebner was on his feet, stumbling around in a circle as he tried to see his back in a mirror. He had scored a pair of scissors, and was trying to cut the plastic ties binding his wrists.

When Jon walked in, Grebner looked over, saw the Sig, and froze.

Jon said, 'That guy who was here, with the dark glasses? He's the nice one.'

Stone stripped the scissors from Grebner's hand, kicked his legs out from under him, and dropped him to the terrazzo.

'You got a message to deliver. You'll do that, won't you?'

'Yes!'

'Now let me ask you a question—does Jakovich have a buyer?'

'I don't know. Michael say no, but I don't know.'

'How about Michael? Why's he hot for so much heavy metal?'

Grebner glanced away. Stone snapped a hard fist into his nose. He punched him again, then a third time.

Grebner snorted out streamers of blood, now spitting the words.

'He have a deal with the Armenians. Way over market price. Three million dollars. He think maybe more.'

Stone patted Grebner's head, admired the distant view for a moment, and left the house. He broke down and stored his weapon, then resumed his position at the end of the street. He took out his cellphone, and called a friend of his who often dealt in illegal arms.

'Hey, bruddah-man! What's the word on those AKs?'

COLE WENT THROUGH the call log on Grebner's phone, and made notes in a spiral notebook. When he finished, he brought up the most recent incoming call number on Grebner's phone, and held it out. Pike saw a number in the 818 area code.

Cole said, 'This is the call you answered when the caller hung up. The incoming number.'

'Darko.'

'I think so. This is the last outgoing call, which is the pager number programmed to Darko's name.'

Cole showed him a number with a 323 area code, then scrolled back through the outgoing call log.

'The second-to-last outgoing call went to the same number, which is the call we saw Grebner make before he threw the phone.'

'That's why I think it was Darko. Grebner paged him, so he was probably answering the page.'

'Uh-huh, so check it out.' Cole turned the notebook so Pike could see. Cole had listed the call numbers in two columns, along with the times and dates the calls were made or received. Cole had drawn a small 'x' next to almost half of the incoming numbers, indicating the calls were received from blocked numbers. Cole had drawn lines connecting three of the outgoing calls with three incoming calls. He pointed out the outgoing calls.

'Here's Grebner paging Darko. See the times?'

'Yeah.'

Cole pointed out the corresponding incoming calls.

'OK, over here he receives an incoming call within twenty minutes of making the page. One of the callbacks was from a restricted number, but two come from the same number as the call you answered up at the house.'

'Different locations?'

'That's what I'm thinking. But why use a listed number? Twice?'

'No cell service. Nothing else available.'

Cole picked up his phone. 'Let's see what we get.'

Cole dialled the number, then listened for a very long time.

'No answer. I counted twenty rings, but nada. That usually means a phone is unplugged.'

Pike said, 'Can you get an address?'

Two calls and twelve minutes later, Cole had an address. The phone number was listed to something called Diamond Reclamations in Lake View Terrace, up in the San Fernando Valley.

'It fits. Lake View is in the foothills up by Angeles Crest. Mountains mean bad cell service, so land lines are the way to go.'

Pike said, 'Good start. How about I check out Lake View?'

Cole pushed the papers back into the grocery bag.

'How about I try to find Rina and Yanni? There are way too many conflicting stories here—' Cole was still talking when they heard the outside gate, and Pike went to the door. Rina stopped when she saw him, shielding the sun from her eyes with a hand. She had a big bag slung over one shoulder.

She said, 'What you find?'

'Where's Yanni?'

She scowled at him, then pushed past him into the guesthouse. She glanced at Cole as she put her bag on the table. 'He work for a living. They don't give him time off to help find stolen children.'

Cole said, 'Where were you?'

She upended her bag, dumping out freshly washed clothes.

'I went to wash. My clothes, they smelled like feet.'

Pike said, 'You know Emile Grebner?'

'Of course. He have the big house in the hills, and would have girls for the parties. He like only Serbian girls. He trust the Serb girls. That is where Michael first see me. Why you want to know?'

Pike said, 'Grebner told us the baby's father is Milos Jakovich.'

He watched her carefully. A frown cut lines between her eyebrows as if she was struggling with the language. She glanced at Cole, who was watching her just as carefully, then turned to Pike.

'Grebner, he lies. Why he say this? Where you see him?'

Pike said, 'Grebner believes it. Darko and Jakovich are at war over some illegal arms. Rifles. Do you know anything about that?'

'Michael hate the old man, this I know, but I don't know nothing about this other thing. Why he say Michael not father?'

'Probably because this is what Michael told him. Is Jakovich the father?'

Rina looked at Pike. 'This makes no sense. Michael is father, not this old man I have never seen. I am mother. Petar is mine.'

Cole frowned at Pike. 'This is making my head hurt.'

Rina ignored him. 'Does Grebner say where is my boy?'

'He doesn't know, but we might have a lead on Darko. Have you heard of Diamond Reclamations?'

She shook her head. 'No. This is a jewellery store?'

Pike said, 'We're going to find out.'

Rina started for the door. 'Good. Let's find out.'

Pike stopped her. 'Not you. Me.'

He left Cole at his car, and headed for the valley.

COLE THOUGHT about Yanni as he left the guesthouse.

Janic 'Yanni' Pevich had come back clean. But after leaving Grebner, Cole had begun to have second thoughts. They now had two divergent and different stories, which meant one of the principals was lying.

Cole returned to Yanni's apartment. Rina had said he was at work, but Cole didn't know if he was working, or care. Yanni's pick-up truck was missing. Cole parked in the visitors' parking lot and made his way back to Yanni's apartment. He knocked first, then rang the bell. When no one answered, he slipped the deadbolt and let himself inside.

He locked the door, then made a quick search of Yanni's bedroom. He found nothing to suggest Yanni had lied. He also found nothing of a particularly personal nature, which he found odd—no pictures of family or friends, no souvenirs. He went into the kitchen. The counter and sink were cluttered with unwashed dishes. Cole found a box of ziplock bags, then selected a glass tumbler, placed it in one of the bags, and let himself out. Yanni Pevich had no record, but maybe Yanni Pevich was someone else.

Cole phoned John Chen from his car, and explained the situation.

Chen said, 'How am I going to sneak it in with everyone here?'

'You'll think of something. I'm already on my way.'

'You're *coming* here? Don't come *here*!'

'Meet me outside.'

The trip down to SID only took fifteen minutes, and John Chen had probably been waiting out front for the entire time. Chen relaxed when he saw the glass.

'Hey, that's a pretty good sample. You want an Interpol check?'

'Yeah, Interpol. I'll be in my car.'

Chen scurried away. All he would have to do was dust the glass with latent powder, lift the fingerprints with tape, then scan them into the Live Scan system. He would have a hit, or not, in minutes.

When Cole reached his car, he phoned Sarah Manning. He had not heard from the girl with the purple hair. He was disappointed when Sarah's voice-mail picked up.

'Hey, Sarah, it's Elvis Cole. I never heard from Lisa Topping. Would you please give me her number? Thanks.'

Cole left his cell number, and hung up.

Cole couldn't think of anything else to do, so he thought about Grebner. Grebner had really blindsided them with that business about Jakovich, which seemed all the more believable because Rina had so readily admitted she knew him. They both seemed believable, but Cole knew from experience the best liars are always believable, and the very best lies were mostly the truth. Here was Grebner with his party house in the hills, and here was Rina, who claimed to have attended his parties, along with other Serbian girls.

Cole wondered if there was a way he could find out if this was true, and thought he might be able to get the information from one of the other pros-titutes. He had copied the dates of Rina's arrests, and now he phoned the district attorney's general administration office. He spent almost twenty minutes on the phone before he found someone to identify the deputy dis-trict attorney who handled the case.

'That would be Elizabeth Sanchez.'

'Could I have her current posting and number, please?'

Deputy District Attorney Elizabeth Sanchez was currently posted to the Airport Courthouse in Playa del Rey.

Cole thought he would probably get a voicemail, but a woman picked up the call.

'Liz Sanchez.'

Cole identified himself, gave her the date and the case number, and said he needed the names of the other prostitutes scooped up in the sting.

Sanchez laughed. 'That was almost six years ago. You can't really expect me to remember their names.'

'I thought it might stand out because of the nature of the arrest. A Serbian sex ring. They worked for a Serb gang set.'

'Ah. OK, that sounds familiar. NoHo Vice took down thirteen or four-teen girls. A joint task force deal with OCTF.'

Organised Crime Task Force.

'That's the one. I want to talk to them about events occurring at or about that time.'

Sanchez said, 'You mind if I ask what this is about?'

'A gang *pakhan* named Michael Darko heads up the set that owned these particular girls. One of his lieutenants probably ran the operation, but Darko was the man. I have some questions about Darko these girls might be able to answer.'

The silence from Sanchez was thoughtful.

'I don't think that was it. I don't think that was the name.'

Now it was Cole's turn to hesitate.

'Darko?'

'Well, I'm thinking.'

'Was it Grebner? Might have been Grebner.'

'Hold on. The OC guys weren't happy with the way it turned out. The Vice coppers were fine—they took down thirteen hookers—but the OC dicks wanted to move up the food chain, but none of the girls would roll. I remember it now—his name was Jakovich. That's who they wanted. His set ran the girls.'

'You're telling me they worked for Milos Jakovich.'

'Absolutely. That's why OC planned the sting. They wanted Jakovich. We had thirteen prostitutes coming out of a prelim, and none of them—not one—would roll.'

'Thanks, Liz. You've been a big help.'

Cole put down the phone. He stared at the empty sky, and knew, once more, how well some people could lie.

His phone rang, and he answered, feeling dull and slow.

A young woman's voice came from far away. 'Mr Cole? This is Lisa Topping. Sarah Manning called. She said you want to speak with me?'

Lisa was Ana's best friend, and knew things no one else knew.

PIKE FOUND Diamond Reclamations on a four-lane boulevard at the foot of Little Tujunga Canyon, fenced between a Mom's Basement public storage location and a stone yard. A huge Do-It-Yourself home improvement centre sat directly across, surrounded by a couple of hundred parked cars. Dozens of men were clustered at the entrances to the Do-It-Yourself, come up from Mexico and Central America, ready and willing to work.

Pike pulled into the Do-It-Yourself centre. Diamond Reclamations was a scrap-metal yard. A yellow single-storey building sat at the street with eight-foot red letters painted across the front: SCRAP METAL WANTED. A gravel drive ran past the front building to a small parking lot. Behind the parking lot was a larger, two-storey corrugated-steel building. Pike could see that the grounds were crowded with stacked auto chassis, rusting pipes and other types of scrap metal. Two new sedans were parked out front on the street, and two more sedans and a large truck were in the parking lot, but the gravel drive was chained off, and a sign in the front office window read CLOSED.

As Pike watched, a man in a blue shirt came out of the front office building, and crunched across to the corrugated-steel building. As he reached the door, he spoke to someone Pike didn't see, and then a big man stepped out from behind the parked truck. The two men laughed, then the man in the blue shirt went into the building. The big man returned to his place behind the truck.

Darko probably travelled with bodyguards, and this man was probably one of his guards. Darko might be in either one of the buildings. The man who murdered Frank and Cindy Meyer, Little Frank and Joey.

Pike said, 'Almost there, bud.'

Three of the Latin workmen broke away from the group by the entrance, and came towards Pike. He rolled down his window and motioned them over. Pike spoke Spanish pretty well. 'Excuse me. May I ask you a question?'

The youngest man answered in English. 'My cousin is a very good mason, but we can also do rough carpentry.'

Pike said, 'I'm sorry, but I am not looking for workmen. I have a question about the business across the street.' He pointed.

'The scrapyard?'

'Yes. I have metal to sell, but the sign says closed.'

The three men spoke among themselves in Spanish. The younger man finally answered. 'The people are there, but the chain is up. It has been like this four or five days.'

Since the murders in Westwood.

'Before that, the chain was down and the business open?'

'Yes, sir. Before the chain, the trucks come to bring or take the metal, but now, they no longer come. My cousin and I, we go there to see if they need good workers, but they tell us to leave. Now the trucks do not come, just the men in their nice cars.'

'The men you spoke with, they were here in the front? The little building is the office?'

The men nodded. 'There were two men. We see other men in the back, but we were scared to ask them.'

'Did they have Americano accents?'

'No, sir. They speak with a different flavour.'

'*Muchas gracias, mis amigos.*'

Pike offered a twenty-dollar bill for their help, but the men refused and continued on their way. As they were leaving, the man in the blue shirt reappeared and returned to the front building.

It occurred to Pike to see if the business had a second number. He opened his cellphone to call Information, but his phone could not find a signal. This confirmed the reason behind the land line.

Pike brought a handful of quarters to a payphone hanging beside the centre's entrance to make the call, and asked if they had a listing for Diamond Reclamations in Lake View Terrace. They did. It was different from the number he had.

Pike copied the new number, then called Information again for the same listing, and asked if Diamond had more than one number. The operator now read off two numbers and the second number was the number from Grebner's phone. Pike dialled the new number.

A male voice answered. East European accent. 'Hello.'

'Is this Diamond Reclamations?'

'Yes, but we are closed.'

'I have ten Crown Victorias for sale. I need to get rid of them, and I will let you have them cheap.'

'I am sorry. We are closed.' The man hung up.

Pike was walking back to his Jeep when three men came out of the corrugated-steel building. The first man out held the door. The last man was a big man. The corner of Pike's mouth twitched.

The big man was Michael Darko.

Pike kept Darko in sight at all times. Crossing the parking lot, moving between and round the parked vehicles, Pike did not look at anyone or anything else. Pike was locked on.

Pike slipped behind the wheel of his Jeep, then started the engine. He used a pair of Zeiss binoculars to confirm the man was Darko. He was. Darko was thinner than in the picture Walsh showed Pike. His moustache was gone, and his hair was shorter, but the wide eyes and sharp sideburns were unmistakable.

As Pike watched, Darko lit a cigarette, then waved the cigarette angrily, pacing with stop-and-go bursts in front of the other men.

Pike wondered if Darko had spoken with Grebner, and if he was preparing to change locations. If so, Pike would have to act quickly. Pike wanted Rina's kid, and he wanted the truth about Frank. Darko knew the answer to these things, and Pike was certain he could make Darko talk.

Darko flicked away his cigarette and stalked back into the corrugated building. The other two men followed. Pike pulled out of the Do-It-Yourself lot, drove two blocks, then swung round and went back to the Mom's Basement, where an eight-foot cinder-block wall separated the storage location from the scrapyard.

People who rented space drove through a security gate that required a swipe card. Behind the gate, storage units ran along the eight-foot wall.

Pike clipped on his .357 Python and his .45 Kimber, pulled off his sweatshirt, then strapped into his vest. He left his Jeep at the street, scaled the gate, and trotted along the storage units built against the wall.

When he was beyond the corrugated building next door, Pike hoisted himself up onto the low roof, then peered over the wall. Pike saw no one, so he moved along the top of the wall to inspect the building. Several casement windows were cut into the back of the corrugated building, but the windows were too high to reach.

Pike chose a path through the scrap that would allow him a view of the other side of the building, then dropped over the wall. He drew his Python and followed the path to the far side of the yard.

From his new position, Pike saw the office, part of the gravel parking area, and the long side of the corrugated building. A row of windows suggested a series of rooms on the first floor. A single large overhead garage door was open, revealing a large service bay outfitted with tools, hoists and bins. A man sat on a lawn chair in the open door. A black shotgun leaned against the wall beside him.

Pike slipped behind a row of fenders. When he had a view of the service bay again, the man in the chair was now on his feet. A second man had appeared at a door, and the two were talking. The chair man picked up his shotgun, and the two of them disappeared.

Pike moved fast to the building. He pressed his back flat to the wall outside the big door, then cleared the service bay and saw it was empty. Darko would either be in the rooms beyond the door or upstairs, but someone close to Darko would do, if they could tell him what he wanted to know.

He stepped into the service bay when he heard the baby crying. Pike realised it was coming from one of the windows overhead. Making for Darko was the play to make, but the kid was upstairs.

Pike made his decision. A metal stairway at the back corner of the service bay led up to the first floor. Pike made for the stairs.

THE STAIRWELL OPENED to a long, narrow hall. The first door in the hall was open, and the baby sounds were loud, but now Pike heard a woman's irritated voice. Pike couldn't understand her language. Male voices came from the far end of the hall.

Pike entered the room, moving so quietly the woman did not hear. The woman was bouncing a baby. A bassinet was against the wall, along with a small table spread with a blanket and a wooden desk. Disposable diapers and jars of baby food were stacked on the table and desk.

Pike made a ss-ss-ss sound to draw the woman's attention. When she turned, Pike touched the gun to his lips. 'Sh.'

The woman was so still she might have stopped breathing.

Pike whispered, 'Whose baby is this?'

'Milos Jakovich. Please do not kill me.'

Pike said, 'Don't speak. Don't move.'

The baby frowned at Pike. Its red hair was wispy and fine, and its blue eyes seemed large for its head.

Pike moved past the woman to look out of the window. The drop was about fourteen feet. The impact would be similar to a hard parachute landing, but Pike could make the drop with the baby.

Pike holstered the Python. He was opening the window when the same man who summoned the chair guard appeared, and saw him.

The man shouted, and was pulling a pistol when Pike snapped his neck.

The woman was shouting out of the window, and now the baby was screaming, too, its face a vivid red. Pike pulled her backwards. She shoved the baby into his arms, and ran down the hall. Pike took the baby back to the window, but now three men were running towards them, one of them pointing up at the window.

Pike stepped back and listened. He heard footsteps, voices, but nothing on the stairs. This meant they were talking to the woman. They would spend a few minutes trying to figure out who he was and whether or not he was alone, and then they would come. Men would be outside to cover the window, one team would come up the far stair, and another team would come up the near stair. Then they would fight.

The baby was screaming, tiny legs kicking, fists clenched for battle, tears squeezed from eyes clenched tightly closed.

Pike held up the baby so they were face to face. 'Boy.'

The screaming stopped, and the angry blue eyes opened.

The close-quarters fight would be loud and vicious, and it occurred to Pike he had to protect the kid's ears. He spotted the cotton wool in the baby supplies, pinched off two bits, and pushed a plug into each of the baby's ears. The baby fought fiercely. 'Gonna be loud, boy.'

Pike heard movement in the building, and knew the fight was approaching. Pike jerked a blanket from the bassinet, wrapped it around the baby, then pulled a drawer from the desk. He placed the baby inside. The baby immediately stopped crying.

'You good?'

The baby blinked.

'Good.'

Pike closed the drawer with the baby inside, and hurried back to the door. Shooters were probably in both stairwells by now. They would have made up some kind of plan, and would now feel confident they had Pike trapped. They were wrong. Pike attacked.

He crushed the near stairwell door from its jamb. The two men on the stairs were caught off-guard. Pike shot them, and immediately heard shouting below in the service bay.

Pike did not continue down because that is what the men below expected. They would cover the bottom door, thinking that Pike was trying to fight his way out. The men at the far end of the first floor would probably advance, believing they could trap Pike on the stairs. They couldn't. He was already gone.

Pike blew back up the stairs. He was braced in the doorway and ready when the door at the far end of the hall opened, and two more men charged out. Pike shot the first man, and the other fell back, kicking the door closed, leaving his partner moaning. Pike put three fast rounds into the door, then popped the Python's wheel and fed it a speed-loader. He ducked through the baby's room and swung out of the window. The three men seen earlier were gone, drawn inside by the gunshots.

Pike hit sand, then ran, always moving forward. He slipped into the same service bay he entered earlier, only now four men were jammed at the base of the far stairwell, focused on the door. Pike shot the nearest man in the back, moved to cover, and shot a second. The remaining men fired blindly as they fled. Pike heard fading shouts and engines rev.

A short hall led towards the front. Pike paused, but heard only silence, then approached the open door. The parking lot was empty. Darko and his people were gone.

Pike found the front stair and hurried up to the first floor. He worked his way down the hall, clearing each doorway until he was back where he started, then put away his gun and opened the drawer.

The baby looked angry as hell. The little fists swung and the legs pumped, and the red face was slick with tears.

Pike said, 'You good?'

He lifted the baby out, and snuggled it to his chest. He took out the cotton-wool plugs. The crying stopped. The baby settled against him. Pike rubbed its back. 'That's it, buddy. I got you.'

Pike headed back along the hall to the front stair, then down. Someone would have called the police, and the police would be rolling.

Pike was only five feet from the door when Rina Markovic came in from the service bay. She was holding her little black pistol, but it was her eyes that gave her away, and he knew she was Jakovich's killer. They were cold, and dull, like the eyes of fish on ice.

'You find him. Good. There is Petar. Yanni, he have Petar.'

Yanni stepped in from the gravel. Yanni's gun was stainless steel, and found Pike as if it could see him.

Pike knew his best chance was now, in the opening second, before they got to the killing. And as before, Pike took immediate action. He spun to the left, shielding the baby with his body. Pike thought he would take at least two bullets in the back before he could return fire, and either the vest would save him or it wouldn't. If those first two shots didn't kill or cripple him, he thought he could beat them even if he had to fight wounded.

Pike did not hear the shot when Yanni fired, but the bullet hit his back like a big man throwing a good hook. Pike staggered, but still managed to draw his weapon and turn to fire, when Jon Stone appeared in the door. Jon forearmed the M4 into Yanni's head, and the big man dropped as Cole hit the woman from behind, stripping her weapon, then riding her down, his own gun out, eyes crazy and wide.

Cole said, 'You all right?'

Pike checked the kid, who was screaming so hard he might have a stroke. Petar was fine.

'We're good.'

Part Four—Guardian

9

They tied off Yanni and Rina with plasti-cuffs, then dragged them out to the cars, clearing the area before the police arrived. The kid was screaming like a banshee, and Rina was screaming, too.

'Is not what you think. Petar is mine! I was trying to save him!'

Stone's Rover was in the parking lot. They shoved Yanni into the rear. Cole pushed Rina into the back seat, and climbed in after her.

Pike said, 'Up in the canyon. Angeles Crest. Jon?'

'I know where.'

Cole held out his hands for the boy. 'Here, I'll take him.'

'I got him.'

'How you going to drive, just you?'

'Go.'

Stone ripped away before the door was closed, throwing up gravel.

Pike ran hard to his Jeep, and saw the oncoming flashers as he pulled into traffic. Three Sheriff's cars flashed past a quarter of a mile later, so Pike pulled to the right like everyone else. The kid was scared, and screaming. Pike repositioned the little guy on his shoulder, and patted his back.

'It's OK, buddy. Gonna be fine.'

They climbed into the Little Tujunga Wash. The road rolled through the bottom of the ravine, and something about the motion settled the boy. He stopped crying, and lifted the big head to look around.

Pike drove exactly 6.2 miles up the canyon, then turned onto a gravel road. He made the drive often, coming up to the middle of nowhere to test-fire weapons he had repaired or built. He followed the gravel over a gentle rise, and saw Stone's Rover parked on the flat crest of the hill. Stone and Cole were already out. Yanni was belly down on the ground, and Rina was crosslegged beside him, hands still cuffed behind her back.

Cole came over as Pike got out with the boy. 'We could be professional baby sitters. I hear there's good money in that.'

'He's loud.'

The boy arched his back, and turned to see Cole. Cole wiggled his fingers and made a face like a fish. 'Cute kid.'

The baby broke wind.

Pike glanced at Rina, and lowered his voice. 'Is she the mother?'

'None of that was true. They work for Jakovich. I don't know who his parents are. Maybe Grebner was telling the truth.'

'Is Darko the father?'

'All I know is she isn't the mother. Ana told a friend named Lisa Topping that Rina couldn't have children because she was cut.'

Pike watched Rina while Cole described what he knew and how he knew it. Rina had told the truth about being a prostitute for Serbian mobsters, but she worked for Jakovich, not Darko.

Pike nodded towards Yanni. 'What about him?'

'Real name is Simo Karadivik, originally from Vitez. That's Jakovich's hometown. Karadivik is one of Jakovich's enforcers.'

Pike realised he had a long way to go before the kid was safe. Everything he thought he knew was lies, and the only truth seemed to be that Darko and Jakovich hated each other, and were willing to murder a ten-month-old baby to further that hate. Pike sensed this was something he could use.

Pike thought for a moment. 'We need to get some stuff for Petar.'

'Are you serious? We can't keep this kid.'

'I'm going to keep him until he's safe.'

Pike rubbed the boy's back, then held him out to Cole. 'Take him, OK? He's getting cold. Get whatever he needs, and we'll hook up back at your place. Take my Jeep. I'll ride with Jon.'

Cole glanced at Yanni and Rina, and Pike saw he was worried.

'What are you going to do with them?'

'Use them to meet Mr Jakovich. I have something he wants.'

Cole considered Pike for a moment, then took the boy. Pike watched them go. He wanted Cole gone, and now he was, so Pike walked over to his prisoners. He and Stone pulled Yanni into a seated position.

Rina said, 'You are making mistake. Petar is mine.'

Pike didn't say anything. There was no point. He stretched his back where Yanni shot him. It hurt. He thought the impact had probably cracked a rib. 'Whose baby is it?'

'Is mine. I am saying the truth. Why are you acting like this?'

Stone prodded Yanni with the M4. 'Maybe because he shot him.'

'That was a mistake. He got confused.'

Pike looked at Yanni. 'Was shooting me a mistake, Simo?'

Yanni's eyes fluttered. 'I get confused. Who is this Simo?'

'A soldier for Jakovich. From Vitez. Ran your prints, Simo.' Pike drew the .357, put it to Yanni's head, and pulled the trigger. The blast echoed off the surrounding hills like a sonic boom.

Rina jerked sideways, and shrieked, but Yanni simply slumped.

Jon Stone said, 'Ouch.'

Pike thumbed the hammer, but he did not have to ask Rina again.

The words spewed from her like lava. 'No, no, no, no—is not mine, isn't, but is Milos's. That is why Darko take him. It is true.'

'You work for Jakovich?'

'Yes!'

'Jakovich is the father?'

'No, no! The grandfather! He is the boy's grandfather!'

The newest story rattled out, but this time Pike believed her. Milos Jakovich's actual and only son was a forty-two-year-old man who had been incarcerated in a Serbian prison. Petar had been conceived during a conjugal visit, only to have his mother die in childbirth. Two months later, the boy's father, Stevan, was murdered in his cell by a Bosnian-Croat. This left Petar Jakovich as the old man's sole remaining male heir, so he had the boy shipped to the US.

Rina said, 'When he find out what Michael going to do, he say we must hide the baby. He give Petar to me, and I give him to Ana. Then Michael take, and Milos tell us to find the boy, and show them.'

Show them. Murder his own grandson to show them.

Stone spat in the sand.

Pike thought through what he had, and what he needed. Protect the boy. The man who killed Frank. Three thousand combat weapons. In that order. 'Where is Jakovich? Right now, where is he?'

'On his boat. He have a boat. The Marina.'

'You can reach him? Call him?'

'Yes! He is not like Michael. He does not hide.'

Pike jerked her to her feet and cut the plasti-cuffs, freeing her wrists. 'Good. We're going to see him.'

Pike shoved her towards the Rover. He now had something that both men wanted, and a plan was coming together.

THE LONG DRIVE from Angeles Crest to Marina del Rey gave Pike time to find out what Jakovich knew. Rina had told him about Pike, and Frank Meyer, and what Pike was trying to do. Pike decided this was good. It would make Pike's play more believable, especially with what Jon Stone had learned about the guns.

'Does he know I tracked Darko to the scrapyard?'

'Yes. I tell him after you leave.'

'Does he know you and Yanni followed me?'

'Yes. He the one tell us to go.'

Which meant Jakovich was wondering what happened, and expecting Rina to call.

Rina did not know the name of his yacht, but she knew where it was berthed. 'He have to let us in.'

The marina was surrounded by restaurants and hotels open to the public, but the yachts were protected by high fences, electric gates and security cameras. Rina directed them to the far side of the marina, and onto a street with yachts on one side and apartment buildings on the other. It was like driving onto a long, narrow island, and when they reached the end of the island, they found a hotel.

She said, 'Is behind the hotel. Where they keep the big boats.'

Stone cruised through the hotel's parking lot until they found a view of the yachts. Rina searched the rows of yachts, and finally pointed. 'That one. The blue. You see it there, on the end?'

Pike made the boat for an eighty-footer; a fibreglass-and-steel diesel cruiser with a dark blue hull and cream decks.

'Take us back to the gate, Jon.'

When they reached the gate, Pike gave Rina her phone. He had already told her what to say and how to say it. 'Remember—you're alive as long as you help me.'

Rina made the call. 'Is me. I have to speak with him.'

They waited almost three minutes, and then she nodded. 'No, we did not get him. No, not Michael, either. Pike got the boy. Yes, he has the boy now, but Michael escape.'

Pike could hear a male voice on the other side of her conversation. She talked over him. 'We are here, Milos. He is here. Pike.'

She glanced at Pike.

'He is sitting here with me. He want to see you.'

She glanced away. 'Yanni is dead.'

Pike took the phone. 'I shot him. I will do the same thing to Michael Darko, but I need your help to do it.'

The phone was silent for several seconds, but then the male voice spoke.

'Go to the gate. We will buzz you in.'

Pike was at the gate less than thirty seconds when the lock opened. He let himself through, walked down a long ramp to the wharf, then followed the wharf past the row of yachts. The sky was beginning to colour, but the afternoon was still bright, and people were out.

Two large men were waiting, one on a lower fantail deck, and one a short flight of steps above on an upper deck. Pike decided he would be safe as long as he stayed on deck, and in the open. No one would pull a trigger with so many people nearby.

A balding man who appeared to be in his seventies was seated at a table on the upper deck. He had been a big man once, but his skin was beginning to hang like loose fabric. He motioned Pike aboard.

'Come on. Let's see what you have to say.'

Pike went aboard. The big man on the lower deck moved to search him, but Pike pushed his hand away.

The older man waved again. 'Come on. It's fine.'

Pike climbed to the upper deck, but did not join Milos Jakovich at the table, and wasn't invited. A salon behind the old man was visible through sliding glass doors. A young woman was inside watching television. Naked.

Jakovich said, 'OK. So here we are. What is this business with Michael Darko, and why would I help you?'

Pike said, 'Three thousand Kalashnikovs.'

Jakovich tapped the table. His finger was the only part of him that moved. Tap tap tap. 'I don't know what you are talking about, these guns. Is this a joke?'

He was concerned that Pike was wired. Pike raised his hands to the side. 'We have to speak plainly. Have your boy search me.'

Jakovich considered it for several seconds then searched Pike himself.

Pike said, 'One on my right hip, and another on my left ankle. You can touch them, but if you try to pull either one, I'll kill you with it.'

The search was thorough. When Jakovich had finished, he returned to the table.

He said, 'OK, we will speak plainly.'

'Do you know why I'm going to kill Michael Darko?'

'Your friend.'

'Yes. My friend and I were military contractors. Professional soldiers. Did my friend help you buy the guns?'

The question Pike had been waiting to ask.

'I knew nothing about this man. Rina's sister, she worked for him. I didn't know anything about these people.'

Pike did not show his relief. Frank was clear.

'I didn't think so. If he was helping you, you would have had a buyer.'

Jakovich tried to act offended. 'I have many buyers.'

'If you had a buyer, the guns would be gone, and Darko would have no play to jam you. I want to buy them, and I can eliminate Darko, or I can give him to you, whatever you like.'

Milos Jakovich cleared his throat. 'This isn't what I expected.'

'No. I probably know more about the guns than you. They were stolen by Indonesian pirates from a container ship bound for Pyongyang. They're brand-new, fully automatic weapons, but they won't be easy to sell because of how they came to the market.'

Jakovich looked irritated. 'How do you know these things?'

'I'm a professional,' Pike said. 'I want to buy them. If you agree, I'll throw in Darko and your grandson as an incentive.'

'What kind of money are we talking about?'

'Three thousand rifles, five hundred per, that's one-point-five million, but only if they're free of rust and corrosion. I will check each weapon, all three thousand. If they're missing bolts or receivers, I'll still buy them, but at a reduced price.'

Pike could see Jakovich was thinking. He was convinced Pike knew what he was talking about, but afraid. He was desperate enough to consider it.

'You have the cash?'

'I can have it by this time tomorrow.'

'And how will you give me Michael?'

'He wants the rifles, too. If you make a deal with me, I'll bring Darko when I pick up the guns.'

Jakovich decided. 'I will let you know sometime tomorrow.'

'Don't wait too late in the day. I can only get the cash during business hours.'

Pike left his cell number, then walked off the boat. He let himself through the gate, and climbed back into the Rover.

Stone looked disappointed. 'I didn't hear anything blow up.'

Pike said, 'Can you put your hands on a Chinese AK? New, still in the wraps? Has to be Chinese. A battle rifle.'

Stone shrugged. 'I know a guy who knows a guy.'

'Call him. Let's go see Grebner.'

THERE WAS ONLY ONE guard this time, a short, muscular man who answered Grebner's door with a scowl. Pike disarmed him, and marched him through the house to where Grebner was sitting. Pike made the guard lie on his belly, and told Grebner to stay put.

Pike said, 'Call Darko. I have the boy now, and that changes things.'

'How you mean changes?'

'I can get Milos Jakovich, and that means I can get his rifles. I will sell Jakovich to Darko for one third of the guns—two thousand rifles for him, one thousand for me.'

'You will sell him? What are you talking about?'

'It means if Darko and I can put our disagreement behind us, Darko can get rid of his competition. I wrote my phone number on the floor in your living room. Tell Darko to call. If he doesn't call, Jakovich will sell them to someone else, and he can kiss his Armenian deal goodbye.'

Pike walked out of the house, and filled Stone in as they headed for Cole's. They parked across the drive, and Pike let them in through the kitchen. Stone hung on to Rina like she might try to run.

Cole had the boy in his arms, watching the Lakers. Cole was set up nicely. Food for the boy. Pampers and lotions, and a spoon set. Pike saw the stuff in the kitchen as they entered.

Cole stood as they entered and arched his eyebrows because he expected to see four people, and Yanni was missing.

'I shot him.'

Cole came over with the boy. The little kid swivelled his head round, saw Pike, and smiled. He flapped his hands. Excited.

Cole said, 'He wants you.'

Pike took the boy, and propped him on his chest.

Cole lowered his voice so Rina wouldn't hear. 'What happened?'

Pike explained what he now believed to be the truth, and described the play he was making on Jakovich and Darko.

He said, 'I'll have to call Walsh. They'll find Yanni's car up in Lake View, so they'll know he was at the scene. When the IDs come back on the stiffs at the scrapyard, and everyone shows a gang-set connection, the police will be all over it. I'm going to need her cover, and her cooperation pulling this off.'

Pike jiggled the boy. The boy laughed, then pulled off Pike's sunglasses. The last person who took Pike's shades bought a three-week stay in the hospital. He waved them like a rattle.

Cole said, 'What about the baby?'

'He needs someone who'll take care of him.'

'And that's you?'

'Not me, but someone. Everyone needs someone.'

'Even you?'

Pike studied his friend, then gently took back his glasses. He didn't put them back on. The boy seemed to like him without them.

They handcuffed Rina to the bed in Cole's guest room, then made a bassinet in the living room. The boy didn't like the food Cole bought, so they made scrambled eggs. He liked the eggs fine.

Pike phoned Kelly Walsh that night, but kept it vague. He told her he might soon know where the guns were located, and promised to call her tomorrow. His true purpose was to make sure he could reach her in case he heard back from Jakovich or Darko. If either of them went for it, he would have to move quickly, and he would need Walsh to move quickly, too.

Later, Cole went for a run, so Pike and Stone stayed with the boy. Pike held him, and after a few minutes the boy fell asleep. Stone got drunk and passed out on the floor, so Pike woke him and told him to sleep in the car. Pike didn't want the snoring to disturb the boy.

Groggy, Stone said, 'I gotta go see that guy.'

Cole returned an hour later, shut the lights, and went up to his loft for a shower. A few minutes later, Pike heard Cole climb into bed, and the last light went off. Pike listened to the house settle.

Sometime after two that morning, a thin layer of clouds masked the full moon, filling the room with blue light. Pike had been holding the boy for almost three hours. Then the boy squirmed.

Pike said, 'I got you, bud. You're OK.'

The boy woke, arched his back, and saw Pike watching. He stared into Pike's eyes as if he had never seen eyes before, looking from one eye to the other, as if each view was fascinating.

The little body was solid and warm. Pike felt the boy's heart beat, delicate and fast, and his chest move as he breathed. It felt good, holding a tiny living person. Pike whispered, 'Hey.'

The boy smiled. He kicked his legs and pumped his arms with excitement. He reached a hand towards Pike, his fingers spread.

Pike touched the centre of the little hand with his index finger. The boy's hand closed on his fingertip. Pike wiggled his finger, just a little, and the boy, still hanging on, gurgled with a sloppy smile as if Pike's finger was a wonderful toy.

Pike whispered again. 'You're safe. I won't let them hurt you.'

The feet kicked, and Pike sat, and held the baby for the rest of the night, until a golden light brightened the world.

LATER THAT MORNING, just after full-up sun, Jon Stone crept into the house. He made a thumbs up, indicating he had the rifle. Pike eased the baby onto the makeshift bed, and followed Stone out.

Stone led him behind the Rover. When he opened the rear door, Pike saw a long, narrow cardboard box printed with Chinese characters. Stone opened it. The rifle was wrapped in a plastic wrapper. Stone slid the rifle from its wrapper, and placed it on the box. 'Never been fired. The factory preservative is still on it.'

Pike opened the bolt to inspect the receiver and breech. They were flawless.

'Good work, Jon. Perfect.'

They put the box into Pike's Jeep, and went back inside.

Michael Darko called at ten minutes past seven. Both the baby and Stone were sleeping, and Cole was checking on Rina. Pike was doing pushups when the phone buzzed.

'Pike.'

'You been trying to kill me for days. Why should I talk to you?'

'We both want the guns.'

'I want the guns. What you want, I don't care.'

'You can't get the guns. I can. My deal is in place, and I have a buyer.'

Darko hesitated. 'You are lying.'

'No, I'm not lying, but I need you to make it happen.'

'You think me a fool.'

'I have his grandson. That got you nowhere because he hates you. Me, he doesn't hate. I met him yesterday at his boat to see the guns. I did, we dealt, they're mine.'

Another hesitation. 'You saw the arms?'

'A sample. He gave it to me when we closed the deal, but now there's a way to make even more money. I'll show you. Hollywood Boulevard outside Musso's in one hour. You'll see my Jeep.'

Pike hung up. He knew he couldn't convince Darko with more talk, and now he would either show or he wouldn't.

Cole was back in the living room when Pike put down the phone. Stone was still sleeping. Pike explained what he was going to do, and Cole offered to come, but Pike turned him down.

Pike wanted to be alone when he faced Darko. Later, he realised this was because he had not fully decided whether or not to kill the man even though he had made the agreement with Walsh.

Pike drove down through the canyon, and was in front of the restaurant in less than ten minutes.

Twenty minutes later, a heavy young man who needed a shave came round the corner, heading towards Pike. Just another pedestrian except he was watching the Jeep, and turned up the next cross street.

A few minutes later, the same man and another man appeared in the mirror. They looked around, then the first man took out a cellphone. Pike watched him talk. He put away his phone, and moved close, approaching Pike and the Jeep as if they were radioactive. The other man stayed on the corner.

When the first man arrived, he looked in at Pike.

'Why don't you come out here? Come stand with me.'

Pike got out, and stood with the man on the sidewalk. A few minutes later, Michael Darko came round the corner.

Pike stared at the man who sent Earvin Williams and his crew to Frank's house. Here he was, the man responsible for Frank, Cindy, Little Frank, and Joey. Pike was not angry or filled with hate. More like he was an observer. Pike waited until Darko arrived, then motioned towards the Jeep.

'In back. Take a look.'

Pike lifted the hatch, and swung the box round so Darko could see the Chinese characters. Then he opened it. Darko leaned close, but did not touch. He finally straightened.

'All right, he will make the deal with you, but still you call me.'

'He wants the money in cash. I don't have it. I can buy them for five hundred each—that's one-point-five million dollars. But I have a buyer in place who will pay a thousand.'

'But you don't have enough to buy them.'

'No. He wants half the cash before he will take me to the guns. That's seven-fifty. I don't have it, but I thought of you. Maybe you have it, but he won't deal with you. So we partner.'

'I don't like being partners with you.'

'I don't like being partners with you, but business is business. This is why I offered a bonus.'

'Jakovich.'

'Once he sees the cash, Jakovich, the gun and the money will be in one place. Then you can solve your problem, we can keep all the money, and you can be the head *pakhan*.'

'So what you're saying is we will steal the guns?'

'It saves us a lot of money.'

Darko studied him, and Pike knew he was considering it.

'What of your friend?'

'I miss him, but this is three million dollars, a third for me, that's a million. I don't have to like you.'

'I will think about it.'

'You're either in or you're not.'

A flash of irritation shadowed Darko's face, but then he nodded.

'All right. When it is time, call me. I will have the cash.'

Darko motioned to his men and walked away.

Pike closed the Jeep, and watched Darko leave. Darko had done these things, and Pike had an obligation to Frank. The obligation existed because they had each other's back, and trusted their teammates to pick them up if they fell. No one was left behind. Pike felt a stab of regret he made the deal with Walsh, but he needed something from her even more than he needed to kill Darko.

Pike climbed back into his Jeep, and called her as he pulled into traffic. 'I need to see you.'

'A red Jeep Cherokee was seen leaving a scrapyard in Lake View Terrace yesterday. Was that you?'

'Yes.'

'Damn it, did you kill five people up there?'

'Six. I need seven hundred and fifty thousand dollars.'

'What the hell are you doing?'

'I met Jakovich. I just left Darko. Do you want the guns?'

They met in a Silver Lake parking lot on Sunset Boulevard. Pike arrived first, and stayed in his Jeep until he saw her pull in. She was driving a silver Accord. Her personal car. He went over and climbed into the passenger seat. She seemed cool.

'The police want to arrest you, and they're blaming me for getting them involved. You want to explain how six people came to be dead?'

'They were holding Milos Jakovich's grandson hostage. Now I have him.' Pike told her about Petar Jakovich, and Rina and Yanni, and the rest of it. She had been completely out of the loop.

'Frank didn't have anything to do with the gun deal. Jakovich told me that himself. Frank and his family were collateral damage. Darko went in because of the nanny.'

'Ana Markovic?'

'Her sister stashed the old man's grandson with Ana to hide him from Darko, but Darko found him anyway. Darko thought he could use the kid to force Jakovich into a deal, but he was wrong.'

Walsh finally nodded. 'OK. I'm listening.'

'Jakovich wants Darko. Darko wants the guns. I have something they both want, and I'm using it to play them against each other. I believe I can put them together with the weapons.'

'How?'

'Jakovich thinks I'm going to buy the guns, and Darko thinks we're going to steal the guns. They each think I'm going to double-cross the other.'

'What's our timeline here?'

'Later today. Darko's on board. I'm waiting to hear from Jakovich. I need three things to make it happen.'

'Let's hear it.'

'I haven't been working alone. The people who are helping me, they get a pass. In writing. I get a pass, too. In writing. Absolution from any and all charges arising out of our activities in this matter, now and in the future.'

'This isn't a double-O licence to kill.'

'I'm not finished. I need seven hundred and fifty thousand dollars, and I'll need it in a few hours. Darko promised to front the cash, but he may or may not deliver. If he doesn't, I can still make the play on Jakovich, but he needs to see cash.'

She nodded. 'OK. I understand. I think I can make it happen.'

'One more thing. I get the boy. You're going to supply him with a US birth certificate and full citizenship, so I can place him with a family of my choosing. This placement will not be a matter of state or federal record. No record will exist that his biological family can use to find him.'

Walsh was silent on this point even longer than when he asked for a pass on the killings. She finally shook her head.

'I don't know if that's possible. I mean, even if I wanted to, I don't know if it's legal.'

'I don't care if it's legal. I just want it done.'

Walsh let out a sigh. She finally nodded. 'I'd better get started.'

Pike returned to his Jeep, and drove back to Cole's. Cole, Stone and Pike spent the rest of the morning getting together their gear. When it happened, it would happen fast, and it started at ten minutes before noon.

Pike's cell vibrated, and now it was Jakovich.

He said, 'You have this money?'

'I can get it in four hours.'

'Cash. And Michael. I will want Michael.'

'If I get the guns, Michael is yours. Where do I meet you?'

'Here. On the boat. I will be here.'

They agreed on a time, then Pike hung up and immediately called Kelly Walsh. 'It's on.'

WALSH AND FOUR AGENTS from the Bureau of Alcohol, Tobacco and Firearms arrived at Cole's house an hour later. Two stayed with their cars, but two agents came in with Walsh—a tough-looking Latin guy named Paul Rodriguez and a tall lanky guy named Steve Hurwitz. Hurwitz was wearing an olive-green Special Response Team jumpsuit. SRT was the ATF's version of SWAT. Jon Stone had brought in his surveillance gear, and Cole was helping him set up. Cole was shirtless, but had strapped on a bullet-resistant vest.

Seven hundred and fifty thousand dollars in cash didn't take up much room. Walsh carried the money in a gym bag slung over her shoulder. She hefted it onto Cole's dining-room table, and opened it, letting Pike see why the package was small. The bills were in vacuum-packed bricks, bound in clear plastic wrap.

Walsh placed a form on the table, and handed a pen to Pike.

'You have to sign for it. If Darko delivers, don't use it.'

Pike signed, and pushed back the form.

Walsh said, 'Where's the girl's sister?'

Cole brought Rina from the guest room. She looked shrunken, and even more pale. Rodriguez placed her under arrest. Hurwitz repeated everything Rodriguez told her in Serbian.

Pike said, 'For what it's worth, at the end, she helped.'

Rina looked at Pike as Rodriguez led her out, and said something in Serbian, but Pike didn't know what she said.

Hurwitz looked at him. 'You speak it?'

'No.'

'She hopes you do it for Ana.'

Walsh looked irritated as if they were wasting time. 'What about the kid? Where is he?'

'Someplace safe.'

'OK, let's go through this. What are we doing?'

Pike said, 'Jon.'

Stone held up the GPS locator from Pike's Jeep. 'Remember this?'

Walsh reddened as Stone went on. 'We canned the one you put on his Jeep. This one's mine. White-burst digital ceramic, no RF, will not show on airport scanners or wands. It's better than yours.

'One on Pike, one on Cole—they're going together—and one on their vehicle, Pike's Jeep. We link through a receiver that repeats on my laptop. I can email the software to you, and slave the repeater.'

Pike went through how he planned to bring Jakovich and Darko together with the guns. It would be up to Walsh and her people to follow, and make their entrance when the guns were confirmed.

She said, 'What about Darko?'

'Elvis and I will meet him in Venice. We picked a location close to the marina.'

Walsh looked at Cole. 'Both of you?'

Pike said, 'He's going to have people. It'll look better if I have people, too.'

Cole pointed at himself. 'I'm his people.'

Pike went on with it. 'He thinks we're meeting to pick up the money. The real reason is to give him this.'

Stone showed them a handheld GPS locator. 'He thinks he's getting this to follow Joe and Elvis to the guns, but we're going to use it to follow him. You'll be able to track him when you download the software.'

The SRT agent said, 'So Venice will be our start point?'

'Only to meet Darko. From Venice, we're going to the marina. That's the true start.'

They spent the next hour going over their plan and setting up their equipment. Stone fitted locators on Pike and Cole, one in Cole's hair, and the other on Pike's belt buckle. Both Walsh and Hurwitz made multiple calls, coordinating the SRT team and additional agents.

At 12.45, the agents left, heading for Venice to rendezvous at their staging area. Walsh was the last agent to leave. She said to Pike, 'Nobody likes what happened up at Lake View, buddy. Just remember, Michael Darko belongs to me.'

At exactly one o'clock, Pike and Cole climbed into Pike's Jeep, and drove down the hill. Stone had already gone. They had left the kid with Cole's neighbour, Grace Gonzalez.

Michael Darko was waiting for them at the end of Market Street in Venice. Two black Beemer sedans and a black Escalade were hunkered together, taking up most of the parking spaces.

Cole said, 'Don't these guys know any colour but black?'

Pike pulled up beside the Beemers, and got out. Cole stayed in the Jeep. As Pike got out, both Beemers opened, and Darko and three of his men emerged.

Darko stared at Cole. 'Who is this?'

'He's going to help me check the rifles. Jakovich expects it.'

Pike gave him the handheld locator, and showed him how it worked. It showed a circle of green light on a map.

'See the light? That's us. Don't follow too close because Jakovich might see you. Hang back. Use this to stay with us.'

Darko and two of his men had a conversation about the device Pike didn't understand, and then Darko opened the Beemer's back door. He took out a gym bag that was much larger than the one Walsh delivered. 'The money. Count it, you want.'

Pike didn't bother to count. 'Don't need to count it. We take the guns, you're getting it back.'

Darko smiled. 'So tell me something. How are you going to deliver me to Jakovich?'

Pike stared at him for a moment, then answered. 'I told him you think I'm going to sell the guns to you. I told him I would set up the meet with you, and when you showed up, his guys could kill you.'

Pike made a pistol of his hand, pointed at Darko, and pulled the trigger.

Darko seemed to realise what Pike had said, and slowly looked around at the surrounding buildings.

Pike said, 'We'd better go. He's waiting.'

Pike got back into the Jeep, and headed for the marina.

PIKE COULD SEE them in the rearview, eight or ten cars back, but the three black vehicles bunched together looked like a freight train.

Cole phoned Stone and described their cars. 'Two Beemer sedans and an Escalade, all black. You reading us OK?'

Cole listened for a minute, then closed his phone. 'They're clear. We're clear. He'll pass it to Walsh.'

They drove south along the beach, then turned inland at Washington, heading for the Palawan Way marina entrance. It was close, and getting closer. The SRT and Special Agent teams were set up on both sides of Palawan Way outside the marina. At least one SRT car had taken a position inside on the island.

They turned onto Palawan, drove to the hotel at the end of the finger, and parked in exactly the same spot Pike had parked in the day before. Pike said, 'You ready?'

'I'm good.'

Pike called Walsh. 'Calling him now.'

Pike broke the connection, then called Jakovich. A man who wasn't Jakovich answered.

'Pike. For Mr Jakovich.'

Pike expected them to buzz him in, but they didn't.

The voice said, 'We'll be right out.'

Five minutes later, Jakovich and his two bodyguards came through the gate. Jakovich hesitated when he saw Cole, but the three of them finally approached. Jakovich said, 'Who is this?'

'He's going to help me check the weapons.'

'I'm not going to wait while you inspect three thousand rifles.'

'I don't care if you wait or not, but I'm going to check them. This isn't a surprise. I told you I would.'

Jakovich was clearly irritated. 'Let me see the money.'

Pike showed him Darko's gym bag. 'Seven hundred and fifty.'

Jakovich rifled a few of the packs, then pulled a bill at random and examined it, then put the bill back into the bag.

'OK. We go.'

He raised his hand, and two dark grey Hummers rumbled out from either side of the hotel. Jakovich said, 'We go in my cars.'

Pike did not look at Cole or hesitate. He followed Jakovich to the closest Hummer. One of the bodyguards brought Cole to the second Hummer. Separation was bad, but showing fear was worse.

As soon as he was in the back seat, a man in the front passenger seat pointed a pistol at him.

Jakovich said, 'We're going to take your gun this time.'

The other big man patted for his guns. 'He is wearing a vest.'

Pike said, 'Precaution.'

Jakovich tugged at his shirt. 'We take the vest.'

They took his Python and the .25-calibre he kept on his ankle, and told Pike to take off his sweatshirt. Pike removed the vest, then was allowed to

put on the sweatshirt. The same big man ran a wand over him, searching for
RF devices. Pike kept himself relaxed, planning what he would do if they
found Stone's bug.

The wand passed over his buckle without beeping.

Point for Jon Stone.

They pulled away, and the second Hummer fell in behind.

Two points for Stone.

The Hummers never left the marina. They circled past the green glass
towers and restaurants, and kept circling until the street ended. Then they
turned back towards the water. They passed the final row of slips, then the
last leg of the channel before it reached the ocean. Here, the channel was
lined with maintenance buildings, nautical-supply shops, storage facilities
and boat-rental businesses.

The Hummers pulled up outside a long, low industrial building, and
Jakovich opened the door. 'The guns are here.'

It had taken only five minutes to reach the weapons, but there was only
one road in or out. Jakovich's guards would be able to see Walsh and her
back-up units coming from a quarter of a mile away.

THE METAL BUILDING reminded Pike of an airplane hangar, with hangar-
sized doors, but now the doors were closed. Two oversized fork-lifts were
parked nearby, along with yachts on metal frames.

A large slip cut into the dock allowed boats to be floated onto a sling.
They were then lifted from the water and placed on a metal frame. The
fork-lifts then carried them into the building for secure, long-term storage.

Jakovich said, 'We have the place to ourselves.' He unlocked the door
and entered the building. Two of his men followed, but the others stayed by
their cars.

Pike stopped at the door. 'You should have your men come in with us.
They'll attract attention out there.'

'There is no attention to attract, and who cares? I own it. I have every
right to be here.'

The lights flickered to life. The ceiling was almost three storeys high,
and lined with parallel steel girders the length of its width. More girders
were built onto the long walls, each facing the other. They reminded Pike of
the Hollywood Squares. Most of the squares were filled with yachts.

Jakovich and his two watchdogs set off down the length of the building.
Cole and Pike walked behind. Cole glanced at Pike, arching his eyebrows to

send a message. If Darko and Walsh followed their signal to the end of the marina, a caravan of vehicles would appear.

Cole ran his hand through his hair, palming the bug. He broke it, then flicked the tiny pieces away. Pike did the same.

A metal storage container the size of a two-axle truck sat at the far end of the building. It was just sitting there, secured by a single lock. Jakovich removed the lock and pushed open the door. It scraped the concrete floor with a high squeal.

Jakovich said, 'There.'

Wooden crates stamped with Chinese characters filled the container. Jakovich mumbled something, and one of his goons pulled out a crate. It hit the floor with a bang that cracked the wood.

Jakovich toed the crate. 'You want to inspect, you better get started. You gonna be here for ever.'

Pike opened the crate. Cardboard boxes matching Jon's box were packed inside. Pike tore open the cardboard, and slid out the rifle in its plastic wrapper. 'Forget it. We don't need to inspect.'

'You like my rifles?'

'Yes.'

'Good. So do I. I'm going to keep them. I'm going to keep your money, too.' The watchdogs drew their guns.

Pike felt Cole move more than saw him, shifting to the side, and Pike shook his head. 'You're giving up Darko?'

'I will get Darko on my own. This way, I get three-quarters of a million dollars.'

'Let me ask you something. Everything Rina told you about me, you think I'd give you seven hundred and fifty thousand in cash, and come here unprotected?'

Jakovich reached under his shirt, and came out with a pistol. 'Yes, I think maybe you did. Now we'll take you for a boat ride.'

He was saying something in Serbian when a voice outside shouted, followed by a soft pop like a champagne cork. Pike didn't know if it was Darko or Walsh, and did not wait to find out. He stepped into Jakovich, stripped his pistol, and shot the two closest guards. They dropped their guns when they fell, and Cole scooped up the nearest. Pike locked his arm round Jakovich's neck, and fell back, using him as a shield. 'There a way out behind us?'

Cole said, 'I'm looking.'

Three men ran through the far door. They stopped long enough to fire several shots, then noticed the two men Pike shot, and then they saw Pike holding Jakovich. Jakovich shouted something, but Pike cut off his wind before he finished. The men disappeared between the yachts as more men came through the door.

Cole shouted, 'Back here. The big doors.'

The gunfire out front exploded into a fire-fight. Pike dragged Jakovich to the doors, then pushed him away to help Cole open them.

Pike said, 'Here comes Walsh.' An SRT wagon appeared at the far turn, followed by several unmarked cars.

Two men ran into the building. The first man was Michael Darko. He stopped just inside the door, saw Jakovich, and shot him. He ran closer, and shot him twice more. He shouted something in Serbian, and shot Jakovich a fourth time. Then he saw Pike, and gave a big smile. 'You had a good plan.'

Pike saw him shooting Frank Meyer in exactly the same way. Pike raised his gun, and shot the man who had run in with Darko. Darko stood slack-jawed for a moment, as if he didn't understand, then lifted his gun and fired.

Pike pushed Cole out, and followed, ducking behind the big door as the SRT teams identified themselves over their PA systems and demanded that everyone surrender.

Cole said, 'He's out the side door. He's running.'

Darko.

Pike ran hard along the front of the building through the chaos of the fight. The SRT operators and arriving ATF agents were spreading along a perimeter, taking men into custody. Pike ran past them.

He saw Darko halfway down the length of the building. Pike started after him. Darko suddenly turned towards the street. He saw Pike following, and popped off two shots, but Pike didn't slow.

Darko ran across the street, jumped high onto the chain-link fence, and clawed his way over. He dropped into the sandy brush, staggered to his feet, and fired three more shots.

Pike kept running.

He hit the fence at a hard run, and crashed down into dead scrub. Pike couldn't see Darko or hear him, so he traced the fence until he found the spot where Darko climbed over. The signs were easy to follow, even as Hurwitz's voice echoed over the PA.

'Stand down, Pike. We are moving into the area. We'll get him.'

Pike picked up his pace.

The footprints and trail scuffs led up a rise, then down into a depression overgrown with chaparral and sage. The ground rose, and tabled out into a small clearing. Darko's footprints continued across. Ballona Creek was visible about three hundred yards ahead. It was a wide creek with concrete walls, and current that pushed to the sea. They were very close to the ocean. If Darko made it to the creek, there was a good chance he could escape.

Pike set off across the clearing. He was less than halfway across when Michael Darko exploded from a ball of chaparral, and crashed into him. He had circled back to wait in the brush. Pike spun with the contact and pushed him hard. Darko staggered sideways. He was winded and out of shape. He wasn't holding a gun. Dropped it, fighting his way through the brush.

Darko stared at Pike's gun, still sucking wind like a bellows.

Pike tossed the pistol to the ground at Darko's feet.

Darko dropped for the gun. His hand was on the grip when Pike hit him with a roundhouse kick that snapped his humerus like a wet stick. He made a deep grunt, then Pike swept his legs from under him. Darko landed on his side, then rolled onto his back.

The pistol was next to him, but Darko made no move for it.

Pike was staring at him when the brush moved, and Cole stepped out. Cole took in the scene. 'You got him. We're done here, Joe.'

Pike picked up the gun, still looking at Darko. He held it with a relaxed grip and jiggled it.

Cole said, 'You good?'

Pike didn't know if he was good or not. He thought maybe he was, but wasn't sure.

More crashing came up the hill, then Walsh burst into the clearing. She had her service piece, and she immediately beaded up on Pike. 'Put it down! Move away from him and put it down, Pike!'

Cole stepped between them, putting himself in front of her gun. 'Take it easy, Walsh. We're cool.'

She shouted, angling sideways to see her target. 'He's mine, damn it! You step away from there, Pike! That bastard is *mine*!'

Pike tossed the little pistol towards her. It landed in the sand.

'You can have him.'

Pike glanced down at Darko again, but saw Frank and Cindy. Frank, Cindy and their two little boys.

Cole stepped up beside him, and put a hand on Pike's shoulder.

'We're done. You got him.'

Pike followed his friend out of the brush.

Part Five—Rest
10

Cindy's sister arranged the memorial. She did not know Frank's friends from that earlier time, so Pike was not invited. Cole saw a notice for the memorial when he read the Meyer family's obituary. The obituary was published as a sidebar to an article in the *Los Angeles Times* about East European gang wars, the death of Milos Jakovich, and the conviction and sentencing of Michael Darko to three consecutive life sentences for the murders of Earvin Williams, Jamal Johnson and Samuel Renfro, as well as the murders they committed on Darko's behalf. Darko did not stand trial. He accepted a plea agreement which let him escape the death penalty. The obituary noted that a memorial for the Meyers was going to be held at the United Methodist church in Westwood that coming Sunday.

Cole pointed out the memorial. 'You should go.'

'I don't know.'

Pike told Jon Stone about it, and asked if he would go, but Stone refused, not because he didn't care about Frank, but because he hated funerals. They made him depressed.

Pike decided to go. He wore a black suit over a black shirt and black silk tie. Frank, Cindy, Little Frank and Joey were represented by poster-sized photographs set up on easels.

The people in attendance were mostly Cindy's family, but a significant number were people who knew the Meyers from school, business and church. Two cousins from Frank's side showed up.

When people asked, Pike told them he knew Frank from the service, but didn't say where or when. These people knew the Frank they wanted to know, and the Frank that Frank and Cindy wanted them to know. Pike was fine with it.

Pike left in the middle of the service, and turned up the coast towards Malibu. The ocean was grey, and crowded with sailboats and surfers, come out on the weekend to play.

Pike turned up into Malibu Canyon, and drove for a while, until he came to a bluff deep in the hills with no one else around. Pike shut off his Jeep, then got out.

One night four men you do not know and to whom you have no connection enter your home. They kill you, your family, and everything you hold dear. You are left with nothing except how you lived, and how you died.

Frank Meyer's fingerprints were found on Earvin 'Moon' Williams's pistol. A post-mortem examination of Williams's elbow revealed that the ulnar collateral ligament was ruptured, along with cracks in both the ulna and radius bones in the forearm.

This was how Pike wanted to remember his friend. Out of shape, and a dozen years out of the game, Frank had moved to defend his family and lost his life in the effort. Frank the Tank to the end.

Pike returned to the Jeep and opened a gun case on the back seat. He took out his pistol, and three speed-loaders, two of which were already charged with six bullets, and one which was only half loaded. He raised the Python, fired six times, then reloaded. He fired six more shots, reloaded, then did it again, and finally a last time, firing only three shots. Twenty-one shots, in all.

'Goodbye, Frank.'

Pike put his gun away, and drove the long road home.

THREE WEEKS LATER, one day after they removed the cast from his arm, Michael Darko scowled at the flat, dry fields as they approached Corcoran State Prison. Darko had spent the past two weeks at Terminal Island, a federal facility he thought would be his home for many years. He asked why he was being transferred, but no one offered an answer.

Even as the prison grew in the van's dusty windows, Darko was planning to establish contact with other East European inmates. These associations would be useful in building an empire.

Ten minutes later, the van entered the facility through a rolling gate, then drove into a parking area where several guards waited. Darko and the two inmates sharing the ride had to wait for the guards to enter the van and unlock them. Darko was taken off last.

The three new inmates were herded through the admitting process. Michael Darko was assigned a cell in Level Three Housing, a facility for homicidal offenders deemed free of drug problems, mentally stable, and capable of self-restraint. Two guards walked him to his new home. More guards processed him into their facility. He was then given fresh bedding, and led to his cell.

He arrived during the afternoon break, a time at which the cells on the main block were open, and main block prisoners were allowed to mingle in the common areas.

The two guards pointed out a sheetless bunk.

'This side. Your bunkie's a brother named Nathaniel Adama-bey. He's in for two homicides, but he ain't so bad.'

'I am sure we will become great friends.'

The guards left, and Darko turned to his bunk. He unrolled the mattress, straightened it, then picked up his sheet. It was coarse, and stiff with plenty of starch.

Darko unfolded the sheet, and shook it into the air to open it. The sheet billowed out, and floated for a moment like a great white bubble. The bubble was still in the air when Michael Darko slammed face-first into the wall, breaking his nose. Then an arm as hard as steel locked round his throat, and something stung his back like an angry wasp, low on his side over his kidney—*stickstickstick, stickstickstick, stickstickstick*—a sharp pricking that happened too fast to hurt, and moved from his side to his ribs—*stickstickstick, stickstickstick*.

Michael Darko tried to rise, but the man kept him off-balance—*stickstickstick*—until a hissing, hot breath scalded his ear.

'Don't die yet, not yet.'

Darko was flipped over. He saw a short Asian man with tremendous shoulders and arms, whose face was dimpled with scars as if from horrible wounds. Michael Darko tried to raise his hands, but couldn't. He tried to defend himself, but was beyond all that. The man's arm moved as furiously as a needle on a sewing machine—*stickstickstick, stickstickstick*—punching Darko in the chest with an ice pick.

Michael Darko watched himself being killed.

The man suddenly grabbed Darko's face, and leaned close with his rage, close enough for a kiss. 'You're gonna meet Frank Meyer. Tell'm Lonny sends his love.'

The man shoved the ice pick hard into Darko's chest, all the way to the hilt, and abruptly walked away.

TRAFFIC AT A STANDSTILL. Someone lost control of his vehicle, and now the southbound 405 was a parking lot. Kelly Walsh didn't mind. Windows up, AC blowing, the horns outside muted. CD player. Roy Orbison kissed her heart with longing and pain.

Michael Darko had cut a deal, which meant there had been no trial.

Jordie Brant's wife lost the chance to confront her husband's killer, and Walsh herself lost the vengeance of offering testimony to nail Darko's conviction. That lack of closure left her feeling as if she had somehow failed him again. And lost him again.

Her cellphone buzzed and she checked the incoming ID, then stopped the music to answer. 'Kelly Walsh.'

'Have you heard?'

'I get promoted?'

'Better. Michael Darko was murdered.'

Walsh was caught off guard and left feeling surprised. She had expected this call sooner or later, but not this soon, and not today. A mixture of warmth and fear blossomed in her belly.

She said, 'Couldn't happen to a nicer guy.'

'These things happen.'

'Yes. Yes, they do. They know who did it?'

'Uh-uh. Someone got in his cell during a free period. No video, either. The DVR was down.'

Walsh smiled, but kept the smile from her voice. 'That's a bad break. How'd they kill him?'

'Looks like an ice pick.'

Walsh smiled a warm, soft smile all the way from Jordie Brant's grave. 'Thanks for letting me know.'

Walsh closed her phone. She knew how she would do it since she learned Lonny Tang was sitting in Corcoran. Walsh had called in big favours to have Darko transferred to Corcoran, and would owe a big favour in return, but Special Agent Kelly Walsh had fulfilled her obligation. Jordie Brant had been one of her guys. You have to take care of your own, and that's what she did.

COLE FOUND THE FAMILY. They were good people, a young couple from Sierra Madre who had already adopted two children. Cole had checked them thoroughly, and interviewed them several times, and Pike had watched how they related to the boy and their other children. He thought they would do a fine job.

Walsh had come through on the paperwork. Documents would be created that established the boy was a natural-born citizen of the United States, born to a fictitious couple in Independence, Louisiana, and adopted through a private attorney.

Pike held the boy for the last time on a bright sunny morning outside a federal office building in downtown Los Angeles. A private social worker employed by the attorney was going to deliver the boy to his new parents, who were waiting across the street.

The boy liked the sun, and he liked being outside. He flapped his arms and made the gurgling laugh. Pike said, 'You good?'

The boy flapped his arms harder, and touched Pike's face.

Pike stroked his back, then handed him off to the social worker. Pike watched her deliver him to the young couple. The young woman took the boy in her arms, and the young man made a silly face. The baby seemed happy to see them.

Pike turned away, went into the building, and found the office. A woman there was going to generate the necessary paperwork. She told Pike to have a seat, then faced her computer.

'I have to fill in the name, place of birth, things like that. Most of these things will change with the adoption—like his name—but we need something right now to create his place in the system.'

'I understand.'

'I was told you're the one who has that information?'

Pike nodded.

'OK. Let's get started. What's his first name?'

'Peter.'

'Spell it, please.'

'P-E-T-E-R.'

'Middle name?'

'No middle name.'

'Most people have a middle name.'

'I don't. Neither does he.'

'OK. His last name?'

'Pike. P-I-K-E.'

robert **crais**

Robert Crais is one of those people who radiates fixity of purpose, a deep-seated certainty that he can cope with whatever life may fling at him. Were he to ever find himself on the mean streets of LA, working alongside his two unforgettable campaigners for justice, Elvis Cole and Joe Pike, he'd probably be right up to the job. Like them, he has forged his path through life with grit and determination, overcoming all vulnerability as though it were his worst enemy. Perhaps he picked up some clear sense of right and wrong, too, from the various members of his extended family who worked in law enforcement.

As with so many crime writers, discovering the works of Raymond Chandler helped to set Crais on the path to a writing career. In the hard-boiled stories about Chandler's private eye, Philip Marlowe, he no doubt found a compelling expression of that justice-focused determination that he had grown up with, and it set fire to a latent spark of creativity. Despite his family's wish for him to follow a safe career in engineering, he took the path less travelled, dropping out of Louisiana State University in 1976, to head for Hollywood and LA, the City of Dreams. He found work writing scripts for major television series such as *Hill Street Blues*, *Cagney & Lacey* and *Miami Vice*. But, ten years on, he began to find the collaborative working requirements of Hollywood too constricting and branched out on his own.

A key turning point that he has often touched on in interviews, was his father's death in 1985. It shook his world to the core but also gave him the impetus to reach for the stars. 'I had wanted to be a novelist for so long,' he remembers, 'but I didn't have a story. That story came from the death of my father, and wrestling with how to help my mother. Writing it allowed me to work through my fears, frustrations and desires. I wanted control over the situation. And I wasn't sure I would have any in real life. But through the character of Elvis Cole, I could exercise a measure of the control and resolution I wanted. He's me, idealised.'

The Monkey's Raincoat (1987) won the Anthony and Macavity Awards and was nominated for the Edgar Award. It was also later selected as one of the 100 Favourite Mysteries of the Century by the Independent Mystery Bookseller Association. Crais initially considered the work to be a stand-alone novel, but realised that the character of Elvis Cole resonated strongly with readers and has since written twelve more novels based around him.

If the character of Elvis Cole is Crais's alter ego, it's fair to say that Elvis's often silent partner, Joe Pike, reflects an even deeper and more private self. 'Joe Pike does embody some of my inner traits. Joe says: "I don't like people with no will, no commitment, no pride." I'm more tolerant than Joe. But I know that if you don't have those things, you are hampered.'

Crais has termed Joe Pike a 'dragon slayer', because, like a character out of a Viking saga, Pike faces down whatever enemy comes his way, be it gangsters on the mean streets of LA, or the debilitating effects of grief. Crais believes that there has been a basic human need for such indomitable fictional heroes ever since mankind began. 'We have always needed stories through which we can exorcise our fears. You have close calls. You may almost get taken, but in the end, you set the trap, and you kill the sabretooth. Whether you're talking crime fiction, fantasy, romance, whatever, it's about story. I think people have always created story, and there is, in fact, a sameness to the emotional payoff. But that sameness is defined by what it means to be a human animal. That's why people want to tell stories and to read stories. It's how we make sense of our lives, how we say there is some fulfilment here. It isn't simply a shadow in the darkness—gone and it meant nothing. There is closure. We can find peace.'

> 'We have always needed stories through which we can exorcise our fears . . . That's why people want to tell stories, and to read stories. It's how we make sense of our lives.'

It is also true that however we may try to render ourselves invincible, we all share a basic human vulnerability and a need for affection. Crais recently described a sudden vision he had of Joe holding a baby. 'My books come to me in images . . . In *The First Rule*, the image that came was Joe and this small child alone in the desert and on the run. As soon as I saw it, I realised it was Joe who was the parent here. I knew I wanted to write that story, because I think that's his ultimate desire. He isn't simply a terminator—a double-Y-chromosome, stereotypical tough guy—he's so much more than that. Joe is a guy who deals with loneliness. What he really wants, like so many of us, is someone to love.

Hannah's Choice

HANNAH & KIRSTY JONES

If I could have any wish, what I'd like is to have just one day without having to rest when my heart gets tired. But I can't, and I've learned that feeling unhappy is a waste of time. Being happy gives me energy—so much so that sometimes I want to do a cartwheel even though I can't actually manage it. So, you see, my decision to say no to the transplant wasn't about dying. It's about living.

Hannah x

In these pages, Hannah Jones, 13, and her mother, explain the extraordinary journey of courage that lead to the biggest and bravest decision of Hannah's young life.

CHAPTER ONE

Seize the Moment

Hannah

So what are the really important things you need to know about me? Well, first there's the fact that if I ever have a boyfriend I want him to look like Zac Efron. At the moment, though, I don't want a boyfriend. My friend Simone has one called Tiago and we've nicknamed them Barbie and Ken. But I'm not interested because I don't want anyone tagging on to me. I've got more important things to do.

Simone is one of my school friends. Others are Laura, Becky, Kelcea, Brigitta and Zoe. They're all nutters and we're always in touch, even though I don't see them much because at the moment I'm not well enough to go to school a lot. When I'm at home, though, they message me to find out how I am or to tell me what's happening because there's usually something going on—like when two of them stopped speaking and I just wanted to bang their heads together. But I had to wait until I got back to school and by then they'd made up again. Mostly, though, we get on really well and do girly stuff like trying out make-up on each other or having sleepovers. Once I stayed up until 11 p.m. on a school night and felt like a zombie the next day.

Then there's my family. First off is my dad, Andrew, who's forty-three and really big and round so you get better cuddles. Mostly he smiles and winds me up by making jokes. But sometimes he blows his top and shouts the house down so we have to leave him alone until Mum puts him on the right path again. That doesn't happen often, though, because he's usually in a good mood. He's a really nice dad.

My mum, Kirsty, is forty-two. Small with long red hair, she has twinkly eyes and loves horses almost as much as she loves my brother, sisters and I.

She's a really good mum and on the days I'm feeling well we'll do things like bake cakes and biscuits. But if I'm feeling tired we'll stay quiet and she'll sometimes go to the shop to get me juice and magazines. The best thing she did recently, though, was deciding to have a week when we didn't answer the phone. Our house can get really busy sometimes and I just wanted it all to slow down because I felt so tired. That was when Mum took the phone off the hook and I really enjoyed it.

Then there are my younger brother and sisters. First comes Oli, who's twelve and will hit you if he's in a bad mood. But if he's in a good one he'll help you get past the hard levels on your Nintendo DS—sitting for ages working out how to get past obstacles or putting in cheat codes if he can't. Mostly Oli is quiet and shy but he's chatty with me when he wants to be.

Next comes Lucy, who's ten. She's outgoing, always wants to beat every-one to be the best and is almost as horse-mad as Mum. In fact she's so good at showjumping that she's hoping to go to the Olympics some day. She competes in shows at weekends and I miss her because I can't go. There's no heating in the horse trailer and I'd get too cold if I did, which isn't good when your heart is bad. But when she is at home we talk about horses—looking at pony magazines and deciding which ones we'd buy if we had loads of money—and I love it when I do get to go to shows because we eat loads of burgers. I've tried riding myself but I'm scared of heights and have a weak ankle which isn't a good combination to have on a horse.

Finally there's Phoebe, who's four and wild. Mum sometimes says she could swear she was given the wrong baby at hospital because Phoebe will run round the house again and again and never get tired. She goes at fifty miles an hour—banging the lounge doors so you know where she is—which is amazing because when she was born she weighed less than two bags of sugar. Phoebe also loves riding, but while most girls her age have a leading rein she doesn't have one because she's so brave. She'll always put up a good fight with me but she's kind too and will share her chocolates or give me a one pence piece which she thinks is a lot of money.

Then there are our animals: a dog called Ted, a cat called Tails McFluff, some goldfish (although Tails ate some of them) and ponies called Roxie, Buddy and Mr Minty for Mum, Lucy and Phoebe to ride. We also have chickens for eggs but aren't allowed to play with them because we put one on the trampoline in the garden once and laughed as it bounced up before flying away. Mum really told us off so we knew we couldn't do that again.

Then there's me. I'm thirteen and don't spend nearly so much time running around as Oli, Lucy and Phoebe because I've got a bad heart and get tired easily. That's why I only go to hospital school in the mornings and come home at lunchtime to rest. I spend a lot of time in bed because I pick up any little infection going like colds or stomach upsets which can get boring because when I feel ill my energy goes and all I can do is lie quietly.

But when I get well I get busy again, though I call it 'lazy busy' because I can't run around or climb trees. Instead I read, go on my laptop, watch TV or play DS in my bedroom. It's my favourite place in the world, pink with a four-poster bed, and my room at Acorns, where I go once a month, is cool too. Acorns is a place where children who are really ill can have a rest.

The films I like are *Enchanted* and *High School Musical*. I know it's not cool for someone as old as me to enjoy films like that. So I don't tell my friends. But I prefer happy stuff. That's why I like those films and the music in them. On TV I enjoy detective programmes like *Poirot* because I try to work out the case before the policeman does. I also like *The Apprentice* when Sr'Alan tells the contestants where they're going wrong, and *Strictly Come Dancing*. The other thing I watch is *Masterchef* because it makes me laugh. Like the time when John picked up a piece of black salmon and said, 'That's one well-cooked piece of fish.' What an understatement.

Maybe my favourite thing is a game called Boggle. It's a box full of letters that you jumble to make words. I love it because it feels like there are lots of them inside me which I can see in the game. That's why I also enjoy reading because books are full of words you can lose yourself in. One I really like is Enid Blyton's *The Magic Faraway Tree*. It tells of a group of friends who climb an enchanted tree and find a different land at the top each time. They visit places like the Land of Spells, where they accidentally make a child shrink, the Land of Magic Medicines, where they buy a potion for their mum who's ill, and the Land of Presents (that one's obvious).

The place I like the sound of best, though, is the Land of Do As You Please where the children get to do whatever they want—drive a train, ride elephants and swim in the sea. A lot of people think you stop having fun if you get sick, which means you never get to go to the Land of Do As You Please. But it's not like that. Sometimes you have to have fun in a different way, but mostly you have it just like other kids. It's important to have fun and I don't understand adults who think their life is really bad. You've only got one and if you don't enjoy it then you've blown it, haven't you? That's why I try to get to the Land of Do As You Please as often as possible.

If I could have any wish it wouldn't be a year in Disneyland (that would be nice) or a walk-on part in *High School Musical* (that would be unreal). What I'd like is to live just one day without having to stop and rest when my heart gets tired: I'd go out and just waste my energy—visit Lucy's horses, ping all over the place doing stuff with friends, dance to *Mamma Mia!*

But I can't do that, and I've learned that feeling unhappy about it is a waste of time. Being happy gives me more energy—so much that sometimes I want to cartwheel even though I can't manage it. So that's how I try to feel each day. I think I've always been like that. But I can't really remember that far back, so Mum will have to tell you how everything started.

Kirsty

I don't know how I knew it was the day on which our world would fall apart. Call it a mother's intuition or my medical training, but that day in December 1999 I knew I couldn't listen to another doctor telling me there was nothing wrong with Hannah.

'I want a second opinion,' I said to the young A&E doctor standing in front of me at Worcester Hospital.

Hannah was lying on a bed between us, pale and listless, so quiet. Not the bubbly, chatty four-year-old I knew. It was 11 p.m. and she'd woken up a couple of hours before, crying and complaining of a tummy ache.

The doctor looked at me as exasperation washed across his face.

'You just need to give her some Calpol,' he said.

'I have,' I lied. I didn't want to be dismissed with paracetamol. I wasn't simply an overprotective mother. Something was terribly wrong. I knew it.

'I think you should take her home and see how she is in the morning,' the doctor replied slowly.

'I want a second opinion,' I said, trying to keep my rage under control.

'Well, I'm afraid there's no paediatric consultant on duty tonight. You'll have to take her to Birmingham or Hereford to be seen.'

Scooping up Hannah in my arms, I ran out of A&E towards the car. Putting her into her seat, I ran around the car, got in and started the engine. Hereford was closest—forty-five minutes' drive away.

'My tummy hurts, Mummy,' Hannah moaned.

'I know, darling, and we're going to make it better,' I said softly.

Hannah shut her eyes as I drove. Why wouldn't the doctor listen to me? Why hadn't I done something more before? Hannah hadn't been well for a few weeks but the GP had told me it was just a virus and I had told myself she was tired at the end of her first term at school. When she hadn't perked

up, I'd gone back to the GP again and was told she had one of those unspe-
cific childhood bugs that every under-five gets and she'd soon shake it off.

So when Hannah had refused to eat on a visit to my great-aunt Kitty, I'd
told her off. When bruises had appeared on the top of her feet, I'd explained
them away by a bang she'd got when she opened a cupboard door. I told
myself I was being overindulgent—the kind of mother who won't listen to
good medical advice. The kind of mother I didn't want to be. But what kind
of mother was I now? I'd known deep down that something was wrong and
hadn't trusted my own judgment. Now I knew I must.

Fear turned inside me as I pressed my accelerator foot closer to the floor.
Hedges and trees rushed by in the blackness as we neared Hereford.

'Nearly there, Han,' I said in the singsong voice mothers use to calm fear,
anger or anything in between.

But Hannah did not reply and I turned to glance at her beside me. She
looked as if she was sleeping. I grabbed her leg and shook it.

'Han?' I said. 'Han?'

She didn't open her eyes. I pushed my foot down harder, trying to stave
off a rush of panic. Was she breathing? Should I stop to check? No. I had to
get her to hospital. They could do more for her there than I could.

Driving into the entrance of Hereford Hospital, I headed for the children's ward. I'd done some nursing shifts there before so I knew where it
was. It was quicker than trying to find A&E. Hannah was limp in my arms
as I pulled her out of the car. Quick, quick. Hurry. Let me in.

I hit the doorbell to the unit, the door opened and I dashed in. Running
along the corridor towards the children's ward, I hit the bell on another
door. It seemed for ever until it opened and I ran into a long corridor.

'I need help,' I pleaded as I reached the nursing station. 'Please. My
daughter is unconscious.'

Nurses burst into life in front of me and Hannah was taken out of my
arms. I followed as she was carried into a room. Her breathing was fast and
shallow as a doctor started examining her. 'We'll need to put a line up,' he
said as the nurses peeled off the top of Hannah's sleep suit.

I stared in horror at her tiny body. It was covered in tiny red marks—
more appearing with each second—livid spots popping under her skin as if
an invisible person was pricking her. The doctor pressed a needle into her
right arm to take some blood.

'We'll send this straight off to the lab,' he said as he slipped the syringe
into a plastic bag.

Hannah was semiconscious as she was put onto a saline drip. Now all we could do was wait for the blood-test results. I sat by her bed waiting. Her breathing was still shallow and rapid and her skin looked almost grey.

'Mrs Jones?' a voice said. 'The doctor wants to speak to you.'

I was taken into a room where the doctor was waiting with a nurse. She walked towards me as if to put her arm round my shoulders but stopped as I stared at her. I knew what this meant. I'd seen it a lot during twelve years of nursing. But I'd always been on the other side before, one of the people waiting to gently break bad news to a stunned relative.

I sat down opposite the doctor.

'We've had the results back,' he said. 'Hannah has tummy ache because she's bleeding into her stomach and is now beginning to bleed everywhere. We need to work quickly to save her life. This is very serious, Mrs Jones. Hannah is a very sick little girl. We think she has leukaemia.'

IT WAS QUIET on the ward, past midnight, as I opened my eyes and looked at Hannah. A small light above her bed threw soft beams and shadows across it. Standing up, I tucked her yellow knitted blanket round her. We'd brought it from home—something familiar in all that was so new.

Turning round, I stared at the plastic chair that I'd earlier folded out flat before wrapping a hospital sheet and blanket round it. This was my bed now, but I knew I wouldn't be able to switch off as I heard the hushed sounds of the hospital at night—the clip of nurses' footsteps, the rumble of trolley wheels and the soft beeps made by machines. I felt as I had in the first few weeks after becoming a mother—too scared to fall properly asleep as I listened to Hannah breathing.

Hours after arriving at Hereford, we'd been transferred to Birmingham Children's Hospital and already the map of our world was unrecognisable. Gone were pre-school and nursery pick-ups, bath times and stories before bed. Instead there were lumbar punctures and central lines, HB levels and platelets.

We'd been plunged into our new world during our first meeting with Hannah's oncology consultant, Dr Williams. Young, smiling and rounded, he'd told us that she had probable acute myeloid leukaemia (AML)—an aggressive and rarer form of the blood cancer. This morning Hannah had gone down to the operating rooms to be anaesthetised for a lumbar puncture to confirm the diagnosis and identify the specific type of leukaemia by drawing spinal fluid to test for cancer cells. A central line had also been inserted—

an intravenous catheter that snaked through her chest wall and into her jugular vein ready to deliver chemotherapy drugs straight to her heart.

Andrew and I sat quietly as Mr Williams explained AML to us. In healthy adults and children, bone marrow produces red blood cells to carry oxygen round the body, white blood cells to fight infection and platelets to knit blood together and control bleeding. But in Hannah this system had gone out of control. Deep in her bones, her marrow was overproducing imperfect cells. Healthy blood was not being made, which was why Hannah had started bleeding internally. Without treatment she would certainly die.

For a moment fear had engulfed me as the doctor talked. But I'd pushed it down as I listened to every word he said, knowing I must keep calm as we prepared to fight for Hannah's life. Working for many years at the extreme end of nursing—intensive care and cardiac transplant wards, major injuries units and paediatric ICU transfer—had taught me how to do this. In the rush and panic of acute medicine I'd learned to keep still in the eye of a storm. Sick and infirm, young and fit, death was a random enemy which didn't make allowances as it took lives. But it was only now as it tried to take my own child that I knew what fear really tasted like.

It had all felt unreal during those first anxious hours in Hereford Hospital as we waited to be transferred to Birmingham by blue-light ambulance. After the doctor had spoken to me, I'd phoned Andrew and he'd arrived desperate for news. Until then we'd had an ordinary life: Andrew working as an auditor and me doing twenty hours a week as a junior sister on a coronary care unit in Worcester, juggling my shifts round our three children, baby sitters and nursery. We lived in a new house on a little estate and went on holiday once a year. It was a busy, run-of-the-mill life until we stepped out of the lift into the long corridor leading through Birmingham's paediatric oncology unit and I knew nothing would ever be the same again.

Hannah was lying on a stretcher and I looked up to see a little girl walking towards us. She must have been about ten and was stick thin—a pair of shorts hanging from her hips and a white T-shirt dropping in folds round her body, her head bald. She looked like a ghost. Just the day before I'd been planning for Christmas because it was only a week away. What toys to buy? What food to cook? But now that world had disappeared completely.

Mr Williams talked us through Hannah's diagnosis and treatment. Her leukaemia would be treated by six rounds of chemo that would last about a month each and all follow the same pattern—after an initial burst of intensive drugs over several days, Hannah would continue on a lighter cocktail of medication for another ten before being given a 'rest' of about another ten days to allow her body to recover from the onslaught.

'We hope Hannah will quickly go into remission,' Mr Williams had told us. 'But even if she does she will have to complete all six chemo courses to give her the best possible chance of long-term remission.'

Andrew and I had listened as Mr Williams warned us of the side effects the powerful chemo drugs could trigger because they would attack the healthy fast-growing cells in Hannah's skin and digestive tract as well as the cancerous ones. The chemo might cause anything from hair loss and nausea to skin changes and tiredness. Hannah's immune system would be so depleted by the highly toxic drugs that any tiny infection could be serious.

There was also the possibility of more extreme side effects like an increased risk of thrombosis or heart damage. But they were remote, the stuff of warnings listed on an aeroplane safety card that you barely glance at as you settle back in your seat. We didn't have a choice. If Hannah didn't have the drugs, we would certainly lose her.

As soon as Hannah started chemotherapy, it became clear just how much the treatment was going to affect her. The chemotherapy drugs had to be administered day and night through two bags that hung from drip stands beside her. Each ran in turn down the central line into Hannah's heart, which was washed out with saline whenever the drugs were switched to ensure they did not mix. Within days, she had started passing blood clots or vomiting them up as the skin on her inner digestive tract disintegrated.

It is one thing knowing your child must have life-saving treatment but another to watch it being administered. The cries of children too young to understand what was happening cut razor-sharp through me, and at nights the buzz of the day disappeared and soft sobs filled the silence. But the only time Hannah cried out was when the drips and lines going into her veins caught as they were moved. Otherwise she lay still and her silence was almost worse than screams. It was as if she was too weak to express her pain.

Time disappeared. I didn't think of the next chemo cycle, next month or even next week. I knew Oli and Lucy were being looked after at home by Andrew and his parents so I focused on Hannah. My days were lived waiting for her latest blood results: white and red blood-cell counts, platelet levels and HB ratings. Leucocytes, basophils, eosinophils, creatinine levels . . . the list of blood cells and other physiological markers was endless. Each morning a blood sample was taken, and when the results came back soon after lunch I'd write down the figures in a pocket-sized book, lines of numbers running down the page. The tiny figures became my talismen and I'd wait anxiously each day until the small hand hit the number two on my watch face and it was time to walk to the nurses' station to ask for news.

'Must be busy in the labs,' someone would smile. 'They'll be here soon.'

Pushing down my impatience, I'd walk back to Hannah's bed. But in my desperation for news I wasn't any different from every other mum on the ward who also pored over the figures when they got them. Did their child have an infection? Was their red blood count coming back up? Or their white count going down? Some couldn't decipher the list of intricate numbers and asked me to explain after realising I could help. The figures were the one piece of fact we could hold on to amid so much uncertainty, and understanding the numbers felt like some small practical way to help our child at a time when there was so little else we could do.

Otherwise I spent hours sitting beside Hannah, longing to get onto her bed and lie beside her but unable to because she didn't want to be touched. Hannah's senses were so heightened that her skin was incredibly sensitive and I found it hard not to physically reassure her. I wanted to cradle her just as I had when she was a baby, feel her weight against me and soothe her. But Hannah did not want to be hugged and she did not cry out for me either. She lay in a cocoon of silence, as if willing herself to live, while I sat within arm's reach, close enough for her to feel my presence. The hours slipped by with the television on low as she slept and when she woke I would colour in a picture so that she could watch, or read a story for her to listen to.

Too ill to eat, Hannah was fed by a high-calorie feed that dripped into her nasogastric tube from a bag on a drip stand beside the bed. Thick and sticky, the feed had to be covered in brown paper to protect it from the sun because light could alter its delicate chemical balance, and we quickly got used to this strange kind of nourishment, just as we did the rest of our new life. After that first shocking sight of the little girl walking towards me, it soon became normal to see children with no hair; after a few nights in the chair beside Hannah's bed I knew other parents in the ward were lying awake just like me and occasionally I could hear their sobs. We smiled at each other during the day and silently accepted each other's grief by night.

LIFE ON THE UNIT wasn't just about sadness—there was hope and light too. Doctors walked around in white coats splattered with water shot from pistols by the children who were well enough to play, and the nurses were endlessly cheerful. Christmas also worked its magic on the ward just as surely as it did in any other place filled with children. Decorations were strung across the walls, nurses played carols on the radio and Father Christmas visited the children each day to hand out presents. If Hannah was sleeping when he came, she'd wake to see a Barbie car or a colouring book, a doll or a fairy wand, in the stack of presents that slowly piled up beside her bed.

I liked the fact that the doctors who clustered round her each morning to assess her progress were followed by a man with a red jacket and a huge smile. Just like every other four-year-old, Hannah loved Father Christmas, and although she was too sick to express her excitement I knew she enjoyed his daily visits.

He was something comfortingly familiar—just like the duvet, sheets and pillows Andrew had brought from home after Hannah had told me the hospital ones were too scratchy. To minimise the risk of infection on a ward full of children who were so weak, I had to wash the linen each day to stop bugs breeding and soon realised we needed more supplies to keep up with the constant flow of clean laundry. But I knew the familiar smell of our washing powder would comfort Hannah, just as Father Christmas would.

Then, after nearly a week in hospital, a nurse came to deliver bad news just as Andrew arrived with Oli and Lucy. 'There won't be a visit from you-know-who this afternoon,' she said in a low voice. 'There's no one to do it.'

I looked at Andrew—with his big belly and smiling eyes he'd be perfect.

The nurse took Andrew off to get dressed as I turned to Oli, a toddler of nearly three, and Lucy, a bouncing baby of fifteen months. I had missed them so much, and seeing the energy and life shining out of them was like seeing shards of light glittering across water.

'Where's Daddy?' Oli asked as he looked up from a colouring book.

'He's gone to the car to get something. Shall we draw a picture for him?'

Oli picked up some crayons as I jiggled Lucy, happy to feel her in my arms again, and waited for Andrew to come onto the ward. But as I watched him walk up to the first bed I realised that I might have made a mistake. Would Hannah recognise her father? She was an intelligent child, advanced beyond her years in many ways after being diagnosed with dyspraxia when she was two and a half. The condition was a bit like dyslexia but affected movement and coordination. It meant that Hannah had been late learning to walk and dress herself, but her language, as if in compensation, had developed quickly and she was also very sensitive to other people's emotions.

But it was too late to do anything now because Andrew was walking up to Hannah's bed and all I could do was hope that she didn't recognise him as he chuckled, 'Ho, ho, ho'.

'Father Christmas!' Oli squealed as he jumped up.

I got up with Lucy as Andrew sat down on the chair beside Hannah's bed and Oli climbed onto his knee, listing the presents he wanted while Lucy sat in my arms, refusing to go anywhere near the strange man in red. When Andrew had finished with Oli, he turned to Hannah and held out his left hand towards her. She looked at him silently and I held my breath.

Very slowly, she lifted her right arm and pushed her hand into the space between the bed and chair where her father's was waiting for hers.

'You're being a very good little girl,' Andrew said softly.

Hannah's mouth curved into a tiny smile as she looked at Father Christmas and I knew this one piece of magic was still safe for her.

NEW YEAR'S EVE 1999—millennium night. After two weeks in hospital the intensive phase of Hannah's first cycle of chemotherapy drugs had ended a few days before. But while I could hear people getting ready to celebrate outside on the streets of Birmingham, inside the hospital everything was quiet as Hannah lay almost unconscious. Two mornings ago the nurses had noticed her vital statistics weren't normal when they did her usual observations—her pulse was rising, her blood pressure and oxygen saturation were dropping. The doctors knew immediately that Hannah's heart was struggling, and a cardiologist who'd seen her had told me she might be suffering a side effect of the chemo. She'd been put on new medication but Hannah was still dangerously ill and was now on morphine to control her pain.

She was lying still on the bed with her eyes closed, oblivious to the nasal canula running underneath her nose to give her oxygen, the feeding tube running up it or the central line attached to her chest. Three sticky electrode pads were attached to a heart monitor which beeped softly, and a 'sats' probe on her finger constantly checked her oxygen levels.

After the rush of emergency when we had first arrived in hospital, the silence now felt overwhelming, and all the questions I had been asked since that day rolled in a constant stream through my mind. There had been so many of them. Did I breastfeed? What type of bottled milk did I use? Did I warm it in the microwave? None are proven links to leukaemia, but as I searched for a reason why Hannah was now even sicker I focused on the questions I'd been asked and why. Surely I should have been able to stop the unseen enemy that had sneaked into our life? I must have made some mistake and allowed it in. Hannah was my child. My job was to protect her.

I remembered how I'd only breastfed Hannah for a couple of weeks because I'd gone back to work. I hadn't had a choice, but now I wondered if I'd harmed her in some unthinking way at the very beginning of her life.

I'd longed to be a mother when I'd met Andrew eight years before. I was twenty-five and knew I was ready to fall in love and start my own family after a year travelling in Australia. I'd been brought up by my grandmother after my mother had died when I was five, and though my childhood had been strict but loving, the loss had implanted in me a need to create the bustling family life I hadn't had. My childhood was one of such stillness and routine that I craved a big, messy family full of life and laughter.

I'd met Andrew in a village pub where he'd stood out in his suit. Quiet and kind, he was a big man who made me feel safe, and when I got home after our first date, I told my grandmother I was going to marry him—even if he didn't know it yet. I proposed four months later but Andrew refused because I was being typically impetuous. So we waited another year to get engaged, and I was over the moon when we started trying for a baby.

But two years had passed and I hadn't fallen pregnant. No one could explain why, and I felt hopelessness seep into me. Feeling more and more overwhelmed, I gave up my job and stayed in bed for weeks until realising I couldn't lie there for ever. So I forced myself back out into the world, where I got a job on a production line at a cake factory—repetitive, undemanding work that I didn't need to worry about—and told myself I would fall pregnant when the time was right. Two months later I did, and was overjoyed. My family was finally starting and I knew I'd do anything to protect it.

So when Andrew had been made redundant, weeks before Hannah was born, I had found a job to support us and returned to work when she was just three and a half weeks old. I ached every day for Hannah, who was being looked after by Andrew and my grandmother, and was overjoyed when Andrew found a new job. It meant I could go home again, and I'd stayed there ever since, working part-time as a nurse to help pay the bills.

But now, as I thought back to those first few weeks of her life and tried to make sense of what was happening, I wondered if leaving Hannah was just the first mistake I'd made without even knowing it.

THREE DAYS into New Year, Hannah was transferred to the high-dependency unit—a halfway house between the oncology wards and intensive care. She was semiconscious and still on morphine, and we lived in half darkness, with blinds closed and wave sounds playing softly to soothe her. Various types of therapy were offered to children by aromatherapists and reflexologists who came onto the ward, but all they could do for Hannah was give her crystals—pebble-smooth stones that we put in the palms of her hands.

No one knew why Hannah had weakened and, desperate to make sense of the chaos inside me, I had asked for a priest to perform the Anointing of the Sick—prayers said for the dangerously ill. I had been brought up with a strong Catholic faith, and Hannah had always enjoyed church. She'd also liked the nuns who visited the children's ward so much that she'd ask where they were if we hadn't seen them for a few days. Hannah liked routine, and they always came on time before reading the same prayers, exuding a quiet stillness which calmed her.

Now the priest traced the sign of the cross on Hannah's forehead.

'Through this holy anointing, may the Lord in His love and mercy help you with the grace of the Holy Spirit,' he said softly.

Hannah did not move or speak but her eyes were open as she watched. The familiar words and phrases of the prayers felt soothing—just as knowing other people were praying for us was. When Hannah had first been admitted to hospital, my great-aunt Kitty, who had once been a nun, had contacted all the churches she knew and by now hundreds of people were praying for Hannah. It comforted me to know that we were not alone.

After the priest gave me communion and left, I sat down again, lost in thought as Hannah slept. Since becoming an adult, I'd been constantly busy, but now for the first time there was no shift to start at work, no cleaning to do, no food shopping to get or children to calm. All I could do was concentrate on tiny things: the feel of Hannah's right hand enclosed in my left one as it lay limply on the bed. It felt so small and fragile.

I clung to the little things I could still do—checking Hannah's feeding tubes, smoothing her sheets or wiping her hands clean of the blood spots running off the drips—but I knew it wasn't practical care she needed from me any more. Hannah and I had moved beyond an everyday world of yoghurt pots and finger painting, cut knees and spilt drinks. We'd fallen off the map into the lands where dragons lay.

But as I sat with her, I realised that I must conquer my fears if I was to be what I hoped for Hannah. I had to stop looking back at the past and searching for a reason where there was none. She needed my courage, reassurance and strength to draw on now—a fixed point in all the uncertainty. I could not dwell on making sense of the past or controlling the uncertain future. I must live in the moment, finding strength in it and living it with Hannah, knowing it was precious minute by minute, hour by hour and day by day.

I had always been so busy focusing on goals and the next plan. Upgrading cars, booking holidays, finding schools—like many people I'd been preoccupied with a future that was just beyond my reach, hardly taking any notice of the moment I was in. But as Hannah's life hung in the balance I finally saw what I could lose if I wasted the moment. Each one was precious, and I wanted her to feel loved in them all.

Hannah was helping me see this. Since she'd fallen ill she had quietly accepted what was happening, and her calmness had humbled me. She hadn't questioned the drugs or railed against the endless tests. She hadn't complained when in pain or screamed at the injustice of it all. She had simply submitted to what was happening and in doing so had guided me as much as I had guided her as we took uncertain steps through our new world.

CHAPTER TWO

Precious Time

Hannah

It was Dad's birthday a few days ago and we went out for a meal at a pub to celebrate, Mum and Dad, Oli, Lucy, Phoebe and me as well as Grandma and Granddad, my uncle Nigel and auntie Serena and cousins Katie, who is ten, and Toby, who's a bit younger than Phoebe. Becky, who used to live over the road from us, also came with her mum Lindy and sister Abby. We all gave Dad his presents when we got to the pub and I'd made him a card covered in hearts and flowers. I also got him a tie and some chocolates because he loves those.

I got to dress up especially to go out because earlier this week I went into town with forty pounds that I'd saved up from my pocket money. I'm awful at making up my mind, though, so I went from shop to shop before going back to the first place to buy the first thing I saw. I do that because I have to be sure what I think I like is what I really want. So when I was certain, I bought some gold sandals I'd seen in the first shop. It's only April and my feet might get cold when I wear them but they're really nice. I'd like to have heels but can only wear flat shoes because my balance isn't good.

Lucy and I were so excited about going out for Dad's birthday that we started getting ready yesterday afternoon. We've both got make-up and so I did hers before painting her nails. Then she did my toes but I did my fingers because she makes them too messy. Mum doesn't usually like us wearing make-up but we're allowed to on special occasions. The trouble was that we were ready by 3 p.m. and so Mum sent me to bed to have a rest. She said I'd be too tired if I didn't sleep and I knew she was right, but it was still boring.

I had roast chicken, chips, peas and a knickerbocker glory at the pub. We sang 'Happy Birthday' as a waitress brought Dad's pudding with a candle in it. Our friends Tina and Marco were on a big table behind us. They own an equestrian centre near our house where Lucy and Mum go riding.

Suddenly a rolled-up napkin landed on the table in front of Lucy and me. We looked round and Marco was laughing, so we lobbed one back. Marco threw another napkin, Mum chucked one back at him and then Marco flicked a pea that flew over my head and landed on the table. Lucy and I were really laughing by now as I threw a piece of bread. Then suddenly Tina, her daughter Emma and another little girl joined in. Everyone was at it until Dad got cross and told Lucy and me to stop.

'You should know better, Hannah,' Dad said.

Mum started clearing up bits of napkin and bread while Dad stomped off back to the car. But instead of feeling bad, I felt annoyed because I was the one getting all the blame even though it wasn't all my fault.

So I was feeling angry until I got in the car, and Dad was quiet. Then I started feeling bad because I realised that I'd ruined his party. I felt worse and worse until we got home and I went to bed, which was where Mum found me crying when she came in to say good night.

'I've messed everything up,' I told her. 'And I've been told off. I know when I've ruined things.'

Mum told me not to worry and that Dad was fine—everything had been cleared up and no harm had been done—which is when I got angry again. I knew Mum was trying to make me feel not too bad, which was nice of her, but everyone has to feel sorry sometimes and so do I. It annoys me when people treat me differently and that's why I didn't like Mum doing it because one of the best things about my family is that I'm normal to them which makes up for all the people who give me the Chitty Chitty Bang Bang look. Remember how scared the baroness was when the children took over her castle? How she screamed at the sight of them? Well, that's how some people look at me, and the reason I hate it is because I know that whoever is giving me that look doesn't see me as a normal teenager.

Now I know I'm not exactly average: I'm thirteen and I've been in and out of hospital all my life. But the Chitty Chitty Bang Bang look tells me I'm abnormal, and while I know I'm different I'm not a total weirdo. That's why I like my mates because they never look at me like that, and that's why I got angry when Mum tried to make me feel better because it made me feel like it does when a teacher gives out homework at school before saying to me: 'Do as much as you can.' They usually say it quietly but even if everyone has left the class I reckon people are still in the corridor so they can hear. When a teacher says that I'm like, 'Whatever! I can't run a race but I can do my schoolwork.' (I don't say that but I shout it in my head.)

It's not that I want homework. I hated homework from the moment I started school when I was nearly ten. I had not been to school since I was sick as a little girl, and me and homework didn't get on because when I got home it was dinner time, TV and bed. There was no time for homework. But though I hate it, I hate it more when a teacher makes out that I don't have to do it, because I don't want to be treated differently to anyone else.

So I was still angry when Mum left my room and Dad came to say good night. He told me he'd had a nice time and I promised I wouldn't throw napkins again when we went out, so I felt better. It's good when Mum and Dad tell me off. It shows that they're not going to tiptoe round me. Though I can't remember much about being in hospital with leukaemia, Mum has told me that she even got cross with me back then because I kicked a doctor. She's right to get angry sometimes, because if people were nice to me all the time I'd have them wrapped round my little finger. I'd be able to do what I want and there have to be rules otherwise I wouldn't get anywhere.

It's a bit like *Wind in the Willows*. Toad doesn't have any discipline, and look where he ends up. He has to learn that there are different kinds of discipline too: the bigger one that stops you chucking napkins because other people will get angry, and the smaller one that stops you doing things that aren't good for you. I had to learn that one when I came out of hospital after saying no to a heart transplant, because while I was in bed most of the time at first, my energy got bigger as I got stronger. But I realised that if I did too much I'd feel ill again, so I had to learn not to, even though I wanted to go mad. I had to save my energy so I could do stuff later otherwise my blood pressure would drop and I'd see funny lights in front of my eyes.

It was really hard because sometimes I wanted to get up so much that I almost had to ask Mum to pin me down. But eventually I taught myself to stay still even though being bored and tired is the worst thing in the world.

I've had to learn that I must lie down until the tiredness goes away because that's the only way I'm going to feel better, even if it takes days. That's why discipline is important, and that's why I'm glad Dad told me off last night. If he didn't do it sometimes then I'd run rings round him and Mum like I've seen some children do in hospital. I knew one girl who refused to eat anything except crisps and I realised that it's easy to get spoiled if you're sick and I'm glad I haven't been. My mum and dad have made me happy but I don't think I'm a spoilt child. Getting told off occasionally makes me feel normal, and I like that. It's really important.

Kirsty

Hannah regained consciousness soon after New Year; days later we learned she had gone into remission. There were no cancer cells in her blood. But five years of remission was the benchmark of true hope, five years before we could believe with any certainty that she was really well—and even though her remission was a good start, the problems with Hannah's heart had still not been solved. In fact, they had worsened during the second chemo cycle and were only just being controlled by medication.

The doctors knew for sure that a virus wasn't causing the problem and had adjusted Hannah's medications to keep her stable. But she had developed septicaemia which was putting extra pressure on her heart.

We'd stayed in the high-dependency unit for Hannah's second round of chemo to allow the doctors to keep a close eye on her, and this time the drugs had taken a greater toll on her body than before. As they worked their way into her system, Hannah was sick up to six times a day and had terrible diarrhoea. Her fingernails and toenails fell out to reveal raw red nail beds which I dressed each day with tiny pieces of paraffin gauze that had been chilled in the fridge. Wrapping them loosely round her finger and toe tips, I would bandage each one as she cried out softly. She also needed gauze pads under her heels, shoulder blades and bottom to stop sores developing because her skin was peeling—the new skin so painful that she had to be handled like a burns victim. For several days we could hardly touch Hannah because she was in too much pain, and even her mouth bled—blood caking her gums, teeth and lips that I tried to wipe gently away.

Hannah was wracked with pain. Doubt and distress filled me as I watched her suffer. Sick and exhausted, she lay in bed as the drugs worked their way through her body—her face the chalk white of marble, the only movement coming from pink tears which trickled from the corners of her eyes because her mucous membranes were so fragile that tiny spots of blood had seeped into them.

I bled too. After Christmas I'd discovered I was pregnant with my fourth child and was pleased despite everything. I knew it was a bad time, but felt that any life was a blessing. Soon after finding out, though, I had started bleeding and knew I was miscarrying. I told myself the baby had died for a reason and I needed all my strength to look after Hannah.

HANNAH SAT in the middle of the towel-covered bed. The drugs for her second chemo cycle had finished last week and the curtains were drawn round her bed as a nurse stood in front of us holding a pair of hair clippers.

The previous day Hannah had looked into a tiny pink Barbie mirror before turning to me. 'I look like Bert. Can I be like the others, please?'

Bert was one of her favourite *Sesame Street* characters, and I knew what Hannah meant. Many of the children on the oncology unit had completely lost their hair and she had obviously had enough of being only halfway through the process. I was glad she was telling me what she wanted again because it meant the little girl I knew was coming back to me.

'Of course we can give you a haircut, my darling,' I said. 'Shall we ask a nurse to do it?'

'Yes, please.'

I knew I couldn't do it. Hannah's pale gold hair had always framed her beautiful blue eyes and I didn't feel able to rid her of it when only weeks before I'd tied it back into bunches and plaits ready for school.

'This won't take a minute,' the nurse said with a smile.

Hannah had seemed excited as we'd planned her hair 'cut' but now didn't look so sure as the clippers' harsh metallic buzz filled the room. Her hair fell to the floor and tears ran down her face.

'I want my hair,' she said with a sob.

I longed to comfort her, to tell the nurse to stop even as I made myself smile brightly to try and calm her. 'Nearly there, Han,' I whispered. 'Soon you can try on your pretty hat.'

I'd bought a pink beanie made of soft sweatshirt material.

Hannah was quiet again until the clippers finally fell silent and I looked at my child transformed. Her head was completely bald and her eyes looked even bigger in her gaunt face as she lifted her hand to touch her naked skull.

I slipped the beanie onto her head.

'That's better,' Hannah said, and smiled. 'My head's not cold any more.'

OLI'S THIRD BIRTHDAY was in late January. After almost six weeks in hospital I was desperate to get home for it. I thought of him and Lucy all the time: as I woke in the morning and wondered if they were still sleeping; as I ate my lunch from a hospital tray and hoped Andrew had persuaded them to eat their vegetables; when I heard the sounds of a TV programme Oli liked and imagined him watching it; or when a baby brother or sister came onto the ward and I thought of Lucy's smiles.

We saw them every other weekend. They'd also come to stay with us for a night. But it wasn't a success because Lucy had been in Hannah's bed and Oli was beside me on the pull-out so no one was comfortable. But I couldn't bring myself to use the family suite because it meant leaving Hannah on the ward overnight and we both felt anxious if we were apart too long.

I was aware that children's lives move fast because things had already changed. I had been sitting by Hannah's bed one day when I looked up to see Lucy toddling towards me. She'd been on the cusp of walking for a while but my heart missed a beat as I realised I had not been there for her first steps. It was a moment that could never be recaptured, which was why I wanted to be at home for Oli's birthday. Hannah was going to make the journey with me because, though weak, the doctors thought she could manage the short trip, and I'd been on the phone all week organising Oli's party. He'd asked for a pirate theme. I'd arranged for a bouncy castle to be put up in the garden and I'd slipped out of the hospital for a couple of hours to buy pirate hats and party bags.

Hannah seemed as excited as I was that we were going home. 'What presents will Oli have?' she kept asking as we waited for Andrew to pick us up.

'Pirate ones!' I exclaimed with a smile.

We were quiet on the ninety-minute journey home. After pulling onto the drive, Andrew lifted Hannah out of the car to take her inside. I followed and stepped over the threshold to smell a different home. Everything was spotless—even the black and white checked kitchen floor that was usually covered in paint splashes and crumbs. I knew Andrew and his parents had gone to a lot of trouble, but I felt like an animal that's gone back to its lair to find the scent of a stranger there. My home felt different now that I was not in it.

'Mummeeeeeee,' Oli shouted as he ran towards me. 'Look at the food. Have you got my present? When does the party start?'

I felt a rush of pleasure to see him so excited as he took my hand to lead me into the garden and look at the bouncy castle. But as we walked outside I felt anxious. Was Hannah OK? I told myself she would be fine. Andrew was looking after her now. This was my time with Oli. He deserved that.

The house filled with children and parents and I went to get Hannah from the lounge to carry her into the kitchen. I wanted her to feel part of the day, and I sat her on the work surface so she could look out of the window at the children in the garden—a gaggle of three-year-olds oblivious to the chill as they flung themselves on and off the bouncy castle.

Hannah sat on the kitchen worktop beside me. Tiny veins covered her bald head, a transparent feeding tube snaked across her pale cheek up her nose, an oxygen tube ran under it and two drip stands stood like sentinels beside her. There were moments when she looked almost old and wizened.

'It's too cold for me in the garden, isn't it, Mummy?' Hannah said.

I knew how much she wanted to play, to be a little girl again.

'Yes, my darling. But you can stay here with me and I'll watch with you.'

Hannah gazed at her brother playing with his friends. But before we set off back to the hospital, Andrew cleared the bouncy castle and I carried her out. It was freezing as I stepped gingerly across the garden with Hannah in my arms. She felt so fragile, like a baby wrapped up against the elements. Lifting her gently, I sat her on the edge of the bouncy castle and kneeled down. She didn't have the strength to make herself bounce and I knew she wouldn't want to. But Hannah was smiling as she sat quietly—staring at the grass, feeling the wind on her face and breathing in the world.

It wasn't just the doctors and nurses on the oncology ward who were filled with energy, kindness and patience. Others worked with them to make life on the ward more bearable, and perhaps the most inventive were the play leaders. They seemed to possess a never-ending treasure chest of ideas to help children smile, and Hannah always looked forward to their visits.

There was one in particular, though, who could always make her laugh, and Hannah's favourite game with Sarah involved dipping sponges into water before lying in wait for a doctor to pass the bed.

'Go on!' Sarah would shriek and Hannah would toss the wet sponge.

'You got me again!' the doctor would exclaim with a smile as the missile hit him or her and Hannah started to giggle.

But the one thing she didn't want to do, even with Sarah, was talk about her treatment. The only person Hannah spoke to about it was me and, as she remained in remission, her inquisitive nature began to show itself.

'Why are they cleaning my wiggly again, Mummy?' she'd ask as the nurses flushed out her central line, something that had to be done every day to ensure the site was kept completely sterile.

'To make sure there are no bugs, Han.'

She became impatient when blood was taken from her thumb on every visit to the weekly clinic where in-patients being treated for leukaemia were seen. Unlike the routine blood tests, which were done each morning using a syringe in her central line, this one involved making a knick on the pad of her thumb with a small blade before a nurse squeezed long and hard enough to collect a few millilitres of blood.

One day she firmly refused to have a thumb test done. 'You can use my wiggly,' she said to the nurse as she pointed to her central line.

There was no point in fighting with her because Hannah could be very sure if she made up her mind and, as she remained in remission, her explanations about how she wanted things done only increased.

'Please use just a tiny bit of sticky,' Hannah would say as a nurse changed her dressings because the tape securing them irritated her skin.

At other times Hannah would refuse to let the nurses remove all the tape securing her central line because it was just too sore. 'I think you'll have to wait until tomorrow,' she'd tell whoever had come to see her.

Although medical advice was always given with the best possible intentions, there were times when I, too, rebelled against it: 'forgetting' to brush Hannah's teeth when her mouth was bleeding during chemotherapy and too painful to disturb; or asking the nurses to wait a couple of hours so that medications, blood samples and dressing changes could be done together rather than spread out, which only prolonged the discomfort.

I found my voice more and more because I wanted to make sure the quality of the life Hannah lived each day was the best it could be. It was a question of balancing my child's long-term good with the short term. Sometimes that meant the rules had to be respected for Hannah's sake—but at others they had to be broken.

'SHE SHOULDN'T GO into theatre with her nail varnish on,' the nurse said.

Hannah was getting ready to go down and have her central line changed. It was the time both of us dreaded most—she hated being put to sleep, and watching her slip into unconsciousness always made me afraid. She had to have a lumbar puncture every month for detailed blood tests to be done, and we both went quiet when the time came. Hannah would be lifted onto a trolley and I'd walk beside her to theatre.

'I don't want to go to sleep,' Hannah would cry.

'It will just be for a little while,' I'd reassure her. 'And I'll be there until you go to sleep.'

Hannah would go quiet as we travelled through the hospital, but as soon as we got to the anaesthetic rooms leading to the theatres she would cry. Scrabbling for me with her hands, the doors would open and she would be pushed feet first into the tiny room.

'Mummy, Mummy, I don't want to sleep,' she'd sob.

'I'm here,' I'd whisper. 'I'm with you.'

As a mask was slipped over her face or the anaesthetic was connected to her central line, Hannah would struggle to stay awake even as she started falling into unconsciousness. 'Help me, help me,' she would cry as her body twitched and I had to leave the room so the staff could intubate her.

It was only when I got back into the corridor that I would start to cry.

Now I looked at Hannah's toenails as the nurse held out the nail varnish remover and I wondered what to do. Hannah loved having her nails painted, each one a different colour so that she could stare at the rainbow on her toes—pink, blue, green, red, yellow—as she lay in bed. Even when she couldn't speak, she'd wiggle her toes so the nurses could admire them.

I knew what I had to say. 'I can't take the varnish off,' I said to the nurse.

She looked at me—sympathy and routine wrestling across her features. Nail varnish was supposed to be removed during a general anaesthetic so the patient's nail bed colour could be checked as an indicator of circulation.

'If you have to take it off then I want you to do it while she's asleep,' I said. 'And if you do then I would like someone to draw a chart with every one of her fingers and toes written on it so that you can reapply the varnish before she wakes up. I know it's a lot of work but it's important to her.'

'We'll see what we can do,' the nurse said with a smile.

As the nurse left the room, I looked at the colours sparkling on Hannah's toes and breathed a sigh of relief. If I was going to let the doctors do what they must to save my child's life, then they had to listen to me when it came to making it slightly easier for her.

CRIES CUT THROUGH the stillness of the ward. It was the early hours of the morning. I sat up to check that Hannah was asleep. The sobs echoed down the corridor and cut through me—a haunting lament for a son or daughter lost, an animal howl of grief that made my heart twist. Somewhere nearby, a child had lost its fight against the illness we were all trying to conquer.

These were the darkest moments—the time when my hope was stretched to its limit. Each day I clung on to it, knowing what might happen if Hannah's treatment was unsuccessful but believing it would be successful. Only the sight of an empty bed, which hours before had been filled by a dangerously sick child, or the quiet sadness that curled round the unit when a girl or boy died, threatened to dent the dam of hope I'd built inside.

'Mummy?' I heard Hannah whisper. 'What's that noise?'

I got out of bed and sat beside her. Looking at her pale face, I wondered how I could explain what had happened without showing my fear.

'I think one of the children is very poorly and their mummy is sad,' I said softly.

'Have they died?'

Death was a concept Hannah had become familiar with in hospital. It was part of life here and she knew that children who were there when she fell asleep had sometimes gone by the time she woke in the morning.

'I don't know, Han.' I smoothed her forehead, soft strokes to try and soothe her back to sleep. I didn't want these sounds to frighten her.

'What does heaven look like, Mummy?' she asked.

'Heaven is a beautiful place where God lives,' I said. 'There are no bad people there, or medicines. Instead there are lots of apples on the trees and daisies in the fields.'

'Do you have to go to school in heaven?'

'No. You can play.'

'How do you get to heaven, Mummy?'

'If you're really, really poorly then you fall asleep and wake up there.'

'Will I go to heaven?'

'Not now, Han. You only go when you're very, very sick.'

'I'm not poorly enough?'

'No, darling. You're not poorly enough. I promise that you'll wake up tomorrow for a whole new day.' I kissed her. 'Now close your eyes and I'll stay right beside you.'

I pulled Hannah's duvet round her and waited until she was sleeping. I shivered as I thought of those parents for whom bereavement came in an instant. Even though I had watched Hannah walk a road I had wished many times that I could travel for her, I was glad I had been given the chance to walk by her side. I'd had time to comfort and soothe her, prepare her in whatever way I could for whatever lay ahead.

As I listened to the steady breathing of Hannah's sleep, I knew that once again she'd taught me just how much I had to be thankful for.

CHAPTER THREE

Not Ours to Keep

Hannah

It's Easter 2009. We went to Cornwall for a week and I really enjoyed myself because there have been loads of times in the past when I haven't got to go away with Dad, Oli, Lucy and Phoebe during the school holidays. I went last year but didn't enjoy it much because I was ill so I spent most of the time in my wheelchair and kept getting cold, which meant Mum had to put me back in the car with a rug. We spent ages sitting in there together while the others did stuff, which really annoyed me.

But this time I felt much better and wondered what my doctors would say if they could see me playing on the arcade machines and eating candy floss. They thought I wasn't going to get any better when I left hospital two years ago after saying no to a transplant. I knew that not having the operation would limit my life but I just didn't want it. Instead I was given a pacemaker, and though my heart still doesn't work properly and I have to spend a lot of time in bed, I'm stronger now and no one expected that.

We left Mum at home so she could have a rest while we went to Cornwall. It was brave of Dad to take us away on his own. Oli, Lucy and I can look after ourselves most of the time but you have to keep an eye on Phoebe, which is hard because she never stops. We stayed in a caravan in a town called Looe and played bingo, ate fish and chips and even went gold panning in a river. I found a gold chip but not enough to make a ring or anything.

I was a bit worried before we went away because my wheelchair didn't fit in the back of the car. But I was also happy we weren't taking it because although it's pink, which means it's as nice as it can be, I still like to walk. I shouldn't have worried, though, because I didn't need my chair in the end. That's what seems to happen when I'm really excited about something—somehow I find the energy to do it. It's only afterwards that I feel ill.

Now I'm home again but I'm not back at school. I've been trying to go for months but I've been ill or something else has happened and I'm missing my mates. One of the reasons I like being with my friends is they don't look at me all worried or go quiet as they wonder if I'm tiring myself out. They know if I've done too much the colour will drain from my face, I'll see spots in front of my eyes and have to lie down until I pick up again.

They trust me to know when I need to slow down and leave me to get on with it, which I like.

But since I came out of hospital after having the pacemaker I haven't been able to get to proper school a lot. Instead I go to the one at Hereford Hospital where the day only lasts the morning and we have our lessons in a classroom at the end of the children's ward. There are usually four pupils and two teachers, which is great because I get help with maths which is my hardest subject. I don't get numbers and my mind wanders when I don't understand something so I usually end up staring out of the window. But it's not so easy to daydream when you've got a teacher sitting right next to you.

I like going to hospital school, though, because at least it means I'm well enough to do something. When I first came out of hospital two years ago, after saying no to the transplant, I just lay in bed. I was so ill the doctors had said I wouldn't get any better. But I knew I would, even though my heart wouldn't. I had the pacemaker and a drug called dobutamine to make my heartbeat stronger. Most of all, I knew I'd get well because I hate being in hospital so much that being at home always makes me feel better.

The dobutamine gave me really bad headaches, though, and was a real pain because I had to have it through a central line attached to a syringe driver that went everywhere I did. So I was really happy when I stopped taking the dobutamine last year, and I've been getting stronger ever since.

I know exactly where my pacemaker is because it's underneath a scar on my chest, just across from my heart. It's got four wires, one going into each chamber of my heart, and sometimes I can feel it zapping. The worst, though, is having it tested, because when one side of the pacemaker is switched off, I can feel my heart beating really hard against my chest until they turn it back on, and I can feel the difference immediately.

Most of the time, the problems with my heart mean I just have to make sure I don't get too tired, because that's how a bad heart makes you feel—so tired you can't even lift your head off the pillow sometimes. There are four chambers in everyone's heart—two on the left and two on the right—and the ones on the right side of mine don't pump properly.

If my heart gets tired and slow the pacemaker says, 'Jump to it.' My heart can also beat too fast and the pacemaker slows it down as well. Occasionally I can feel it when I'm ill in bed and my blood pressure has dropped. Sometimes it's like a vibration but at others it's more like a ping! Sometimes it stops me going to sleep but most of the time I can't feel it.

The doctors know what's going on in my heart because they do scans. I can see the blood going in and out of my heart on the screen. I can see the valves aren't closing properly and one side of my heart is leaking. Though I feel better now, the doctors have told me my heart has not improved.

Now we're home after our holiday and Oli, Lucy and Phoebe have started school again, I get lonely sometimes. But I also quite like being quiet because though I love my brother and sisters, they can annoy me too. Oli and Lucy know the best hiding places in my bedroom so if I try to keep something secret they'll always find it. Phoebe is also in and out all the time and if I'm feeling tired I just want her to leave me alone.

Being on my own again means I've lots of time to think. I've been wondering why people are still so interested about me not having the transplant. Everyone went mad when they found out about my decision after a newspaper did a story about it. That was last year but journalists still ring up to see how I am and ask the same things. Why didn't you have the transplant? Will you reconsider? One asked me once how I wanted my funeral. It's not that I hate mentioning it but I don't like going on about it. I can talk about it to a certain extent but then I go quiet.

I just wish people would accept that I don't want the transplant. I want to be at home even though the doctors have said I won't get better. It was a big decision but I wanted to make it even though I felt scared and sad and anxious at the same time. Mum and Dad said they'd choose if I wanted them to but I didn't because they might feel guilty if something went wrong. It was my decision. No one else's. And I made it for the right reasons.

Now the summer term has started, I'm looking forward to September because I hope I'll be well enough to start Year 10. It's scary because it seems like yesterday that I was in Year 7. I've picked my GCSEs. I'm doing the five main subjects plus ICT and something I can't remember. I'm doing a bit of everything because I need to learn as many different things as I can. At the moment there are three jobs I'd like to do: mostly I want to be like Cheryl Cole but I also want to be a fashion designer and make pink clothes because there aren't enough of them, or be the boss of a company like Alan Sugar in *The Apprentice*—really rich and in charge of everyone.

To keep myself 'lazy busy' now everyone else is back at school, I've been watching my new favourite film—*Mamma Mia!* It's brilliant, cool and fab. I've been sitting in my room reading the words of the songs on the CD cover and singing along. Sometimes I dance a bit too. Headbanging is my favourite thing because it makes me feel dizzy, though I have to sit down if I do too much. But it feels great while I'm doing it, and that's what counts, isn't it?

Kirsty

Since New Year we'd known Hannah's heart wasn't pumping as it should have been. But it had become clear that the problems were not being solved by medication. Hannah was still tired, weak and out of breath, and I was terrified when the doctors told me she was suffering mild heart failure.

As she rested after her second round of chemotherapy, Dr Williams and our cardiologist Dr Wright decided they needed to do a more in-depth scan to give them a fuller picture of what was happening.

A couple of days later we were taken to the X-ray unit, where Hannah lay on a bed as Dr Wright smeared gel onto her chest before pushing a probe across it. Working round the central line coming out of her chest, he guided it until a picture appeared on the monitor beside Hannah's bed. Andrew stood close to me as we watched her heart expanding and contracting, blood rushing in and out of it in waves of blue and red across the screen.

As he moved the probe across Hannah's chest, Dr Wright freeze-framed images to take detailed measurements. Lines and shapes, trapezoids and rectangles appeared on the images to give an exact assessment of Hannah's heart rate and function. Numbers popped up on the screen.

When the scan was over the doctors went away to talk before calling Andrew and me back to see them. Their faces were serious as we sat down.

'I'm afraid the results were not what we'd hoped,' Dr Wright told us. 'The scan has shown that Hannah has cardiomyopathy. This means the muscles of her heart are damaged, and she also has problems with her fractional shortening, the amount her heart expands and contracts with each beat. The bigger it is, the better the heart is pumping, but I'm afraid we've discovered that Hannah's heart function is low.'

'How low?' Andrew asked softly.

'Seventeen per cent.'

Andrew slumped back in his chair, stunned. Hannah's heart was struggling to beat at less than a fifth of the capacity of a healthy child's.

'There is a lot of medication we can give Hannah to help her body cope,' Dr Williams said gently. 'There are drugs to make her heart beat more efficiently or increase her blood pressure.'

'But she will get better?' Andrew cried.

'This is a situation which happens in only a tiny percentage of children who undergo chemotherapy,' Dr Williams said. 'We can't be sure what will happen to Hannah's heart. It is possible that new muscle will grow as she gets older and her heart function will improve, but we cannot say for certain.'

'But what caused this?' I said, the words feeling thick in my mouth.

'We think Hannah has had a very rare reaction to the chemotherapy, and the drugs given to combat the leukaemia have damaged the muscles to her heart,' Dr Williams replied. 'As you know, we would usually complete all six courses of chemotherapy to maximise Hannah's chances of continuing in long-term remission from the leukaemia. But given that we believe the chemotherapy is responsible, it means there is a risk of further damage to her heart if we continue Hannah's treatment.'

'Does that mean Hannah has to stop treatment?' Andrew asked.

'If she does have another round of chemotherapy, it should be her last,' Dr Williams replied. 'We do not want to run the risk of causing further and catastrophic damage.'

Hannah had only completed two chemo cycles and we'd been told she needed six to maximise her chances of beating the cancer. How could we deny her that? But how could we risk further damage to her heart?

'You will need to decide quickly what you want to do because Hannah is due to start treatment again in a few days,' Dr Williams continued quietly.

I knew he had children Hannah's age. 'What would you do?' I asked.

'I'm afraid I can't tell you,' the doctor replied softly. 'This really is a decision that only you can make.'

HANNAH WAS THE PERSON who would be affected by whatever we decided for her, and I knew we must talk to her. Although the decision about whether to continue with the chemotherapy or not belonged solely to Andrew and me, I wanted Hannah to understand what was happening.

The doctors agreed to speak to her with us. We walked to Hannah's room where we gathered round her bed and I sat down beside her.

'Han,' I said as I stroked her feet, 'Dr Williams thinks if you have more medicine to kill the leukaemia bugs then your heart might get more poorly. But if you don't have more then the leukaemia bugs might grow bigger. Mummy and Daddy have to decide whether to give you more medicine.'

She looked up at me. 'I don't want any more,' she said.

'I know they're horrible, Han,' I said slowly. 'But the medicines are killing the bugs in your blood and the doctors will make sure they don't hurt too much when you have them again.'

'But they do hurt,' she cried.

'I know, but we all want you to get better.'

Hannah looked at Dr Williams. 'I'll have to think about it,' she said.

HANNAH WAS WEARING a soft cotton top with buttons down the front, and the tubes leading to her central line spilled out of it. To stop them pulling, they'd been put into a 'wiggly' bag, which hung on a satin ribbon round her neck. The strap on the small material bag was padded with pieces of foam that I'd stitched on because Hannah was still so thin everything had to be soft or padded to make it comfortable on her skin.

A drip bag was clamped to one side of the wheelchair and a syringe driver to the other. The box measured six inches by eight and contained syringes that pumped Hannah's medications into her bloodstream at one mil every hour. She was wearing a fleece jacket with a fur-lined hood and three rugs round her legs to protect her from the February chill because we were going to High Mass at St Chad's, Birmingham's Catholic cathedral. It was very close to the children's hospital and I wanted to take Hannah out now that she was in the rest period before her third round of chemotherapy.

Andrew and I had decided to give Hannah one final round of chemotherapy—knowing it would be her last. One last chance at making sure the cancer didn't return.

'I'm tired of being in hospital, Mummy,' Hannah had said as she lay in bed after we'd spoken to Dr Williams. 'I want to go home.'

The more time we spent in hospital, the more regularly Hannah asked for this now, and it worried me that her longing for home might make her resistant to more treatment.

'I want you to go home too,' I said as I sat beside her. 'And we will as soon as the doctors have given you all your medicines. But we have to make sure the bugs in your blood are really gone first.'

The next morning Dr Williams came back to see us. After he'd examined Hannah and checked her charts, she'd looked at him with a serious face.

'I have decided that I will have some more medicine,' she said solemnly.

Dr Williams turned to me. 'Is this what Mum thinks too?' he asked.

'Yes,' I said.

'We'll start again next week.'

All we could do was inch forward, hoping we had made the right choice. I thought about it for the thousandth time as I stopped to tuck the rugs more closely round Hannah's legs, and a picture of Andrew, Oli and Lucy flashed into my head. Sometimes it felt as if the life we'd all lived together was so far away we might never get back to it. Hannah and I had slipped so completely into the rhythm of hospital life that it was a shock when I'd first left the building and the real world had burst in again. A wall of sound had surrounded me—sirens wailing, people shouting and cars beeping their horns. Now I walked towards the cathedral entrance and wondered how Hannah felt to be outside again. Apart from the visit home for Oli's birthday, she had only glimpsed the world when I'd pushed her to the front door of the hospital to smell the fresh air. I knew it must be strange for her now and pushed a little harder to get us more quickly into the quiet of the cathedral where we sat down near the altar—me on the end of a pew and Hannah in her chair in the aisle beside me.

I drank in the stillness of the cathedral, letting it take root inside. I would need all the strength my faith could give me for the next stage of our journey.

ONCE AGAIN Hannah's immune system was reduced to almost nothing as the chemotherapy drove her white blood-cell counts down to stop her immune system attacking the drugs. As they fed into her system, I counted down the days until the most intensive phase ended.

Because of her heart problems, Hannah could no longer have regular lumbar punctures to check she was still in remission. Instead her blood was sent to Italy where specialised tests were run on it. It took two weeks to get the results, and it was an anxious time as we waited. But just as she'd done after the previous two chemo cycles, Hannah recovered quickly and started growing stronger as her blood counts rose days after the intensive phase of drugs ended. Soon we learned that she was still free from cancer. Her heart had also not worsened during this treatment cycle.

As her health improved, I tried to take her out of her room in the high-dependency unit a little and we made trips round the hospital to the café or to see a man who brought snakes and spiders in for the children to look at.

Hannah's chemotherapy came to an end, and as soon as her blood counts were high enough and the doctors were sure she was free of infections, we would be free to go home to see what the future held.

My excitement about returning to normal life had been tinged with fear, though, after an overnight trip home showed me how difficult it might be. I went because Oli in particular was missing me and I wanted to tell him that I'd soon be back. After almost three months away I was longing to see Andrew and the children, but it was the first time I'd left Hannah for any length of time and I felt anxious as I got on the train home. I knew she would be well looked after, but what about all the tiny things that only I knew? Like the way her duvet had to be smooth on the bed or the fact that she liked a few toys but not too many on her feet?

My hands itched to pull the emergency cord. I shouldn't have left her. I should be with her. I felt confused as I watched houses and trees rush by. How could I feel so desperate that my journey was taking me away from Hannah when it was also bringing me nearer to Oli and Lucy?

When the train finally pulled into the station, I got off and saw Andrew with Oli and Lucy. The children smiled and shrieked as they saw me. A rush of love filled me as I ran towards them. I'd missed them so much and their smiles told me I was right to be here.

But as I scooped them into my arms, doubt seeped over the edges of my joy. As I was reunited with one part of myself, I felt I'd left another behind, and wondered how I was going to reconcile them when we got home because Hannah's needs were so different to Oli and Lucy's—on oxygen twenty-four hours a day, she still wasn't eating, her feed had to be administered by a nasogastric tube and her drug regime was also very complicated.

But all Hannah wanted was to leave hospital, and so I set my worries aside and urged the doctors to release us as soon as possible. At first, they weren't keen, but they soon realised that my will was as strong as my daughter's when I wanted something. Hannah hated it in hospital and I felt sure she would get stronger once we left. It seemed logical that the happier she was, the healthier she would be.

CHAPTER FOUR

Look for the Love

Hannah

I've been in bed for a few days because I went to a horse show last weekend and it flattened me. I wasn't feeling that well before I went but going really knocked it out of me. I knew Mum and Dad were worried but I don't get to visit horse shows often so I really wanted to go. For ages after my heart got worse it was too cold for me during the winter and I wasn't well enough. But it's spring now, I'm stronger and Lucy is such a good rider that her bedroom is covered in rosettes and I want to see her win some for myself.

'We'll see how you feel nearer the time,' Mum kept telling me.

Lucy and I got excited as the time to leave for the show got closer. She was going to ride Mr Minty, who is a grey, which means his coat is white, and another pony whose name is Gunner. He was too much of a handful for the girl who had him, so her parents lent him to Lucy because she's not afraid of anything.

We counted down the days until the one before we were due to leave, when Mum drove the horse lorry from the garage where it's kept and parked it outside our house. It's old but there's room in the front for three people to sit next to the driver. Behind is a living area with a tiny kitchen, a big bed on a platform above the driver's seat that you have to climb up a ladder to get to and a door through to the horses at the back.

As soon as the lorry arrived, I got in and asked Lucy to get everything we needed—duvets, pillows, food and drinks. Though I still didn't know what Mum was thinking, I knew she must be coming round when I saw her put my medicine box and oxygen cylinder into the van. When everything was ready, she told me I could go, and I jumped up and down I was so happy.

We left early on Friday morning and the journey took so long that I felt really tired by the time we arrived and couldn't get up the ladder to bed. Luckily we'd brought a camp bed for Mum so I went on that and she went up top with Lucy. The next morning I stayed in bed late before Mum put me in our friend Tina's lorry. It's heated and better than being outside because my circulation is bad and I feel ill if I get too cold. So I sat in the van which was parked right next to the arena and watched the jumping from there. Lucy looked really smart in her white shirt, blue jacket, gloves and boots.

I stayed in Tina's lorry until the jumping was over and then went back to ours where Mum covered me in blankets and duvets to warm me up because I'd still managed to get cold even in the warm lorry. Just as I was going to sleep, a karaoke started somewhere and it felt as if the people were singing right next to our van. Then the lorry started shaking because of the wind and that's when I got a bit cross, which I do sometimes when I feel really ill. Mum gave me a pill to help me sleep, though, and I got up again late on the Sunday before going back to Tina's lorry to watch the jumping.

Lucy ended up winning two classes, coming second in two and fourth in one. She pretended to be pleased but I knew she wanted to win them all. Though I was tired by the time we got home on Sunday night, I was glad I'd been. The horse show was an adventure and I don't get many of those.

I learned about adventures from the *Famous Five* books. I like the way the Five look for adventures even when told not to, and I wish I could do what they do—live in a cottage by the sea and not care about anything.

I've only had one real adventure but didn't even realise I was having it until it was over. It happened when I was in hospital after my heart got bad, but it was only when I got home that I realised I'd had it. I'd seen so many different things on the ward, had X-rays taken and drains put in. I'd even had a pacemaker fitted, which is unusual for someone as young as me.

To be honest, I didn't enjoy my adventure much, though, so I'd like to have another by flying round the world to see the Eiffel Tower, the Leaning Tower of Pisa and the Statue of Liberty. I also want to go to China and see how different chow mein tastes there, find out what coffee is like in Brazil and eat pasta in Italy. Then I'd go to Australia to find out how tall the roof of the Sydney Opera House is. I'm not sure about Africa because it might be too hot for me but I'd like to go on safari.

I think about what I'd like to do and the places I'd like to go. Maybe I do it more than other kids my age because I'm different. I can't do as much. But the main thing that makes me different is that I've had to think about dying. I've learned to push those thoughts away because it's no good keeping them in my head. Mostly I manage to, but it's hard if I've been very ill. Sometimes my heart can get suddenly worse and I'm so poorly that I can't really remember what's happened when I get better. That's when I feel very scared because I wonder why there weren't more signs before I got really ill. And if I didn't think I was too bad when my heart was getting worse then maybe I'm sicker than I think right now?

At times like those I make myself think about something else so I read a book, go on the computer or watch TV. There's no point wasting time feeling bad and so I remind myself about all the good things there are, like:

NATURE: my cat, dog, chickens and hamster (I also like fish because you can eat them and keep them in a tank); I like red and pink roses, the blue climber that was at the bottom of the garden in our old house, summer when it's hot but not too hot, and winter because I like snow even though it makes my fingers go numb.

FOOD: chocolate, watermelon, spaghetti Bolognese, Sunday roasts, salami, tortilla chips, sausage rolls and pork pies. I love Dad's stew. Once I had two bowlsful, followed by a big plate of tiramisu, and had to go to hospital when I got a pain in my chest. After loads of tests, the doctors told us it was indigestion. I think Dad felt bad about giving me so much, but I was the one who'd asked for second helpings.

MUSIC: *High School Musical*; The Saturdays; *Love Machine* by Girls Aloud; Cheryl Cole because she does *The X Factor* and you can tell she's pretty even when she's got too much make-up on; and ABBA.

SMELLS: Moroccan Rose shower gel from the Body Shop, the Ocean candle from there too. Gwen Stefani's perfume, and Top Model. Dad's stew would also have to be one of my favourite smells—even if it did make everyone think I was really ill.

Kirsty

Oli and Lucy giggled as I spread out huge white sheets of paper on the living-room floor, tucking them under the sofa to make sure everything was covered. The red carpet disappeared as the floor became a sea of white with five margarine tubs full of brightly coloured paint sitting in the middle.

'Can we start, Mummy?' Oli asked as Lucy tottered towards the tubs.

I nodded as he plunged his fingers into the paint—blue first and then yellow, the colours smearing together on his skin.

'Squoosh hard, Oli,' I urged as he pressed his hands onto the paper.

He laughed as he stared at the two mottled prints he'd made.

I grabbed Lucy. 'How about one at a time?' I laughed as she thrust her hands into every colour.

Hannah was watching us from the sofa where she sat with her drip stand.

'Why don't you have a go too?' I asked as I let go of Lucy and crawled across the paper to put two tubs of paint at Hannah's feet.

She bent forward slowly, dipping her fingers into green and red before leaning down and dragging her fingers across the paper.

'Why don't we try using our feet?' I exclaimed, and the children laughed even harder.

I grabbed Lucy and undressed her—leaving her in just a nappy—while Oli pulled off his T-shirt and trousers. The two of them sat in the middle of the paper, plunging hands and feet into the margarine tubs with relish.

'How about you, Han? Do you want another go?'

'Yes, please, Mummy.'

I tiptoed towards her across the paper, careful not to smudge the pictures that Oli and Lucy had made. I could see Lucy heading for the wall and knew there would soon be a messy handprint on it. Paint was smeared across a coffee table I'd pushed to the side of the room. I'd leave a few marks when I cleaned up—reminders of memories made on a happy day.

'Can you carry the drip bag for me, please?' I asked Oli as I lifted up Hannah underneath her arms.

He took the bag I'd unhooked and held onto it tightly, carrying it like a precious relic as I lowered Hannah's feet into the paint.

'It's cold,' she squealed as I lifted her out of the paint and we walked across the paper. 'Look, Mummy!' she exclaimed as she stared at the pictures she'd left. 'It's like footprints in the sand.'

It was a prayer Hannah knew. In it, a narrator talks about a dream they've had. Walking across a beach, scenes from their life replay, but as they look back they notice that the two sets of footprints representing God walking beside them dwindle to one at times—particularly during the most difficult periods of the narrator's life. So they ask God why He left when He was needed most, and God replies that He didn't—He was carrying them at their hardest moments when they were too weak to keep on walking.

A KITCHEN CUPBOARD summed up how different our life was now: on one shelf stood packets of cereal, jams and baked beans, on the other boxes of swabs and syringes, dressing packs and a sharps box to store used needles.

Hannah was too weak to eat or walk. A wheelchair sat by the front door and a feeding pack was housed in a metal box about a foot long, which she was connected to day and night, four hours on, three hours off, via a nasogastric tube. She needed oxygen constantly and liquid medications every two hours, which I gave via her central line or nasogastric tube: captopril for blood pressure, furosemide to combat fluid retention, digoxin to make her heart beat efficiently, ranitidine to stop ulcers forming in her stomach.

Because the central line gave direct access to Hannah's heart, it was vital that it was kept clean and so I had to be scrupulous about 'flushing' the line once a day. This involved cleaning the three smaller lines which ran off the main one. Each of these had a cap on the end to which syringes could be attached, and it took me up to forty-five minutes to complete the process.

Just getting Hannah up and down the stairs to bed was difficult because I couldn't carry her as well as a heavy oxygen cylinder. So I'd disconnect her from it before moving her as quickly as possible, knowing she would soon get breathless. After putting her on the sofa or back into bed, I'd run back for the oxygen so that I could reconnect her to it.

Taking off the pieces of tape securing Hannah's nasogastric tube had to be done regularly but they chafed her skin and left it raw. I would try to gently ease the tape away from the raw spots on Hannah's cheek, but however careful I was I sometimes couldn't stop her pain.

But it wasn't just Hannah I had to look after now, there were Oli and Lucy to consider, too, and something as simple as taking Oli and Lucy to nursery or the park for a walk was impossible because I couldn't leave Hannah.

Andrew did as much as he could but he'd taken so much time off work while Hannah was in hospital that he couldn't have any more. Mountains of washing-up slowly grew and piles of dirty clothes inched upwards. Or I'd open the fridge door and realise we had nearly run out of food before ringing Andrew to give him a hurried list.

Each day I counted down the minutes to 5.30 p.m., almost holding my breath until the moment he walked through the door. When I saw his face I would feel like crying with relief knowing that he would now look after Oli and Lucy. As I got Hannah ready for bed, he would feed and bath the others before putting them into bed, clearing up the house and cooking for us.

Even when Oli and Lucy were asleep, though, I hardly saw Andrew. As soon as I'd soothed Hannah to sleep I would lie down exhausted on the mattress I used on the floor by her bed, snatching some rest in the hour before preparing her next set of medication. It was hard, but Andrew and I understood that we had to get through the days one by one if we were to hold our family together. In those first few weeks at home, I didn't bath or wash my hair or look in a mirror. All I could do was complete the most crucial tasks.

Days passed and I hardly slept, because when I did lie down I felt too agitated to relax. When I finally dropped off I'd soon wake to find the house quiet. Feeling my stomach gnaw, I sometimes went to find the food that Andrew had left for me.

But even as I began to realise I wasn't coping, I felt too ashamed to admit it. I felt inadequate that I couldn't do everything. Then, about two weeks after Hannah came home, I finally rang the A&E at Worcester Hospital.

'I need help,' I pleaded. 'I need someone to come to my house.'

'I'm afraid we can't just send someone out,' a voice said. 'You have to make an appointment before we can assess you.'

'If you don't send someone now then I will bring my daughter to you,' I said as I steadied my voice. 'I cannot cope any more.'

Within an hour my GP, a social worker and two nurses had arrived at my house and arranged for an auxiliary nurse to come to the house for an hour each morning and evening. They couldn't be left alone with Hannah because they weren't trained to look after her central line, but at least I would be able to do some jobs while they were there. It was a start, but I still tried to deny what was happening as I got more and more exhausted. It took a few more weeks for things to finally reach rock bottom and for me to realise that unless I changed they would never move back up again.

It happened one morning after I'd decided to take Oli and Lucy to the sweet shop. We hadn't been out before and I don't know why I wanted to do it that particular day. Maybe I was desperate to do something normal for them, maybe I wanted to prove that our life could resume the rhythm it had once had—walks in the park, feeding the ducks—a tiny straw to clutch onto as I felt things slip out of my control.

I told the children what we were going to do and Oli started planning what sweets he wanted. Two hours later we were ready to leave the house and I opened the front door with Hannah and Oli in a buggy and Lucy in a backpack. Hannah's feeding pack was clamped to the pram and there was a small oxygen cylinder in the sling underneath the seat. I also had digoxin, furosemide and codeine with me in case Hannah deteriorated.

Our house was at the end of a cul-de-sac, and almost as soon as we stepped outside we reached a pavement. Easing the pushchair down it, I walked across the road to tip it back up onto the pavement at the other side.

'Ow!' Hannah cried as her feeding line pulled.

'It's OK, Han,' I soothed. 'It won't take long.'

'But I don't want sweets,' she cried. 'I want to go home.'

I leaned down to Hannah. 'We'll go quickly and then straight home.'

I walked down to the main road. Four side streets to cross—four times down a pavement and four up the other side. Each time, Hannah winced.

I carried on pushing until we reached the top of the hill that led down to the sweet shop. I looked at it below us.

'I'm tired, Mummy,' Hannah wailed. 'I want to go home.'

I stared at the shop. To get there I would have to cross a main road. I could see people going in and out—the door closing and opening, people leaving with bags, mothers with children clutching sweet wrappers. The shop was close but it might have been on the other side of the Sahara.

'Please, Mummy,' Hannah sobbed. 'Take me home.'

'No!' Oli shouted at her. 'We're going to the shop.'

'Please, Mummy,' Hannah shrieked. 'I want to go home.'

I bent down to kiss her, and as I looked at her tear-stained cheek, reality jolted me. Why was I doing this? When would I accept that life had changed? I wasn't going to do any good by trying to paste a carbon copy of our old life over the new. Everything had changed and I must accept it.

I had to give up my expectations and 'rules' about being the perfect mother and wife, giving my children the perfect upbringing. Things had to change and I must discover how best to let that happen. Our old life was a skin we had shed and we had to make a new beginning.

As I turned the pram back towards home, I remembered the splashes of paint on the sitting-room coffee table. There were challenges to overcome now, but there were also joys to be tasted more fully.

I PUSHED HANNAH through the door of the village hall. Inside, mothers and children who'd attended the playgroup I'd run with my friend Karen until Hannah got sick were waiting for us. Although I knew Hannah wouldn't be able to stay long, I wanted her to be here today.

We'd just got back home after ten days in hospital. Hannah had been readmitted after coming down with severe shingles and quickly becoming very poorly. I felt desperately sorry that she'd had to return to hospital when she'd only just left. For Hannah, it was a bad place and, however kind the doctors and nurses were, neither they nor I could erase her memories.

Now a burst of noise surrounded us as everyone started singing 'Happy Birthday'. I could see a table laid with party plates and hats, balloons above it on strings, presents in colourful paper and a birthday cake.

'Who's party is it, Mummy?'

'Yours, Hannah.'

'But it's not my birthday. My birthday isn't until July.'

It was three months away but Karen knew that with only three rounds of chemotherapy and such a low heart function, nothing was sure for Hannah. I spoke to Karen on the phone every day, and she was the person with whom I came closest to letting my terror tumble out, because while Andrew and I drew strength from each other's constancy we didn't confront our fears together. It was as if speaking them to each other might overwhelm us.

Andrew and I had recently travelled to London to meet doctors at Great Ormond Street in case Hannah needed a transplant. They'd told us that she couldn't be considered for one until she had been in remission from cancer for five years. All that was certain was that keeping the white blood cells low after a transplant to minimise the risk of organ rejection increased the risk of the cancer returning, and if that happened Hannah could not undergo chemotherapy because a new heart would not be strong enough to cope.

So Andrew and I had quietly focused on letting the days and weeks unfold, hoping we might have months and years, knowing nothing was sure. This is what Karen understood and why she had organised today's party.

'I know it's not your birthday, Han,' I said as I pushed her wheelchair towards our waiting friends. 'But everyone wanted to give you an extra one this year because you've been so brave.'

'Does that mean I won't have my real birthday?'

'No. It means you'll have two.'

She grinned as mothers and children surged around us, smiling and cooing words of encouragement. I felt surrounded by love.

In April I took Hannah to our local pub where Andrew was a regular. His friends wanted to raise money to send Hannah to Disneyland in Paris, and after doing sponsored cycle rides and darts matches some of them were now going to have their heads shaved.

'Will their hair grow back?' Hannah asked as she stared at the huge men whose soft skulls looked as pink as newborns.

'Yes,' I told her.

'Does that mean my hair will grow back too?'

'Yes, Han. It will take a little bit longer, but it will, I promise.'

The trip to France was scheduled for June, but just before we were due to leave, Hannah had to go back into hospital. It was three months since she'd finished her chemotherapy, but after the shingles she'd been in with infections—two in her chest and one in her toe. Each had to be taken seriously.

By the time we left for Disneyland she was better but still on antibiotics, so I got onto the ferry carrying a tin filled with syringes, needles, glass phials of antibiotics and saline packs. When I asked if there was a first-aid room we could use, Hannah was delighted to be shown to the captain's cabin where I syringed the drugs into her line as she chatted about our trip.

We arrived at Disneyland late in the day and put Hannah and Oli into separate beds in the hope that they'd fall asleep quickly. But as we turned off their lamps, the lights in the park suddenly came to life. Outside our windows, Disneyland stretched out into the distance, lights twinkling.

'Look, Mummy!' Oli cried as he leapt out of bed.

I lifted up Hannah as Andrew grabbed her oxygen cylinder and we walked to the window. I could almost hear her sigh with relief.

'It's Cinderella's castle,' she gasped.

In the days that followed, Hannah decided what she loved most were the daily parades when her favourite Disney characters came to life. The one she particularly liked was led by furry chipmunks, and each day we'd go to the main square where we'd wait for them to walk up Main Street, leading a procession that ended with huge floats on which more characters sat.

But one afternoon, two chipmunks stopped and held out their huge furry hands as they beckoned her to join the parade. As Hannah tried to stand, I unclipped the lines to her feeding pack even as I wondered how she was going to walk. She could still only manage a few steps at home and was so unsteady on her feet that we always used a wheelchair when we went out. But Hannah didn't look back as the chipmunks took her hands and she got slowly to her feet. Step by tiny step, she walked away from me.

Teetering forwards, Hannah melted into the parade: Mickey Mouse danced, Minnie bobbed her head and furry animals jigged. Hannah looked tiny amid it all but the chipmunks didn't let go of her hands. They walked at a snail's pace with her as Snow White glided into the square on a huge float, greenery tumbling from its sides and a tiny house perched on the top.

The procession came to a halt and Hannah watched in wonder as Snow White got off the float, walked across to Hannah and kissed her cheek. A minute later, she climbed back onto the float again and it started its journey as the chipmunks helped Hannah walk back to us.

She sat down in her buggy. 'I was the only child Snow White said hello to, Mummy,' she said in a rush. 'Wasn't she beautiful?'

Snow White didn't know what she'd done that day, just as the mothers at my playgroup couldn't have either. But together they taught me that if you look for love you will find it in many places.

CHAPTER FIVE

Magic in the Air

Hannah

I'm sitting on my bed in my room. My bed is a total sticker. I'd never get rid of it. It's four-postered with white wood and pink curtains on the top. I could have a bed that moves up and down to help when I'm ill because my pillow riser, which lifts me up to help my breathing when it gets bad, can be really uncomfortable. But there's no way I'm having a different bed.

When we left our last house, I thought I'd never like my new bedroom as much as the one I was leaving because it had more than fifty stickers on the wall. But we had to move because my bedroom was upstairs, which meant I was a bit cut off from everyone whereas now my room is next to the front door so I can hear them coming and going. Mum also got tired going up and down the stairs all the time. One day she counted she'd done it sixty-two times because I was so ill that I could not even turn on the TV. When I moved into my new bedroom the walls were blue and there was a brown carpet on the floor. I wasn't looking forward to spending much time in it but then a charity called 'Make a Wish' offered to decorate it for me and asked me to choose paint colours and fabrics. What did I pick? PINK, of course!

I forgot all about my room when I went to Acorns. I go there at the end of every month. The longest I've stayed was two weeks, though it's usually four nights. The nurses and carers there are really nice and I really enjoy it. I can rest and Mum and Dad have a rest too, which is important because while I'm away they get to do what they want.

Acorns is a hospice and a lot of the children who go there are in wheel-chairs or on food pumps. Most of them are little although there are some older kids who bash the walls with their wheelchairs when they race up and down the corridors. Some children die there; one was a baby girl who I liked very much. I missed her when she died. I also thought a lot about her mum and dad, and the great loss they must have felt.

It made me feel sad, but Acorns isn't usually like that and I laugh all the time there—especially with Paul who does night shifts and is a nutter. There's lots of things to do like go in the pool, which is so warm you can never get cold. In the summer we have a sports day—just a bit easier—and water fights. There are also PlayStations, Sing Stars and an art room. But the best thing is the food which you can smell cooking because the kitchen is next to the sitting room and the door is always open. The cooks are really nice because though you're not allowed in the kitchen when they're making lunch you can ask to cook things when they're not busy. I made a chocolate cake. The best thing, though, is that you can ask for something else if you don't like what's been made and have whatever you want—even pizza.

When I first went to Acorns, Mum went with me for weekend stays. But then I decided I wanted to go for longer and Mum wasn't sure she could come because there was Oli, Lucy, Phoebe, Dad, the horses, chickens, Ted and Tails McFluff to look after as well as me. At first I was worried about going on my own but then I realised Acorns is like being at home. There are TVs, comfy sofas and always someone to talk to. They listen to what you say and I've even helped pick new duvet covers for the rooms. I also suggested they got some lava lamps because I like having a light on in my room at night if I'm not well so I thought other kids might too.

The only thing I don't like about Acorns is that no one else my age seems to go there, so I play with a girl who's ten, which is a lot younger. She's nice but I wish there was another thirteen-year-old to muck around with. If I feel like that, I have a chat with Yasmin, who's my link carer and nice, or one of the Clares or the Helens, or Andrea or Sharnie, and I feel all right again.

Anyway, I was having so much fun at Acorns that I'd forgotten all about my room by the time Mum, Oli, Lucy and Phoebe came to pick me up. But when they walked in, Phoebe shouted that they had come in a big white car.

Mum's car is blue so I wondered what she was on about.

'And the man driving it has a big hat,' she yelled.

I went to the front door and what did I see? A massive white stretch limo!

'What's this for?' I asked Mum.

'Well, you've always wanted to ride in one so today's the day,' she told me, and I couldn't believe it.

We piled into the car where there were disco lights flashing and music playing which was brilliant until Oli felt sick halfway home and we had to stop. He'd drunk all the Coke on the way to Acorns so it was his own fault.

But I still didn't realise what was happening when we got home and I walked into the house. Then I opened the door to my room and saw what Make a Wish had done. The whole room had been decorated—pink walls, pink carpet, pink curtains. That was a year ago and I'm still really pleased.

That day is one of my best memories, and another is meeting Prince Charles after I got picked to go with some other children to Clarence House. His house was smaller than I thought it would be. I'd put on my smartest clothes—a long purple skirt with flowers on it and a white top with fake fur round the wrists. I kept thinking there would be trumpets or something to let us know he'd arrived. Instead I turned round and there he was.

Mum was with me and we'd bought a present. I felt nervous as I handed over what we'd brought—biscuits, jam and some kind of alcohol. (I wouldn't want to be given alcohol because I had a sip of sherry once and it gave me a headache but Mum thought Prince Charles would like it.)

'Is this good?' he asked as he looked at the bottle.

I didn't know what to say because I hadn't tasted it so I told him Mum liked it and he laughed. Then he chatted to me and I was surprised because I thought he'd be strict and not say much. But he was nice and looked smart in his uniform with buttons, a chain and coloured stripes. He was wearing it because he'd been doing investitures before he met all the children and the only thing that surprised me about Prince Charles was that he was much shorter than I thought he'd be. In fact he was only a bit taller than Mum and his hands were really big with fingers as fat as sausages.

But my best memory is of Christmas just gone. The year before, I'd only had my pacemaker in for six months and was still so ill that I couldn't eat.

I was much better by last Christmas and had turkey with all the trimmings, then a Christmas pudding that Dad covered in whisky and set alight and blue flames flickered round it. Mum told me to wait before I had some. She knows I'll get stomach pains if I eat too much. When I finally had the pudding it tasted so good that I'll never forget it.

Kirsty

Our new life got better the longer we lived it together, and by the time Hannah turned five in the July after we got home from hospital she and I had developed a routine about her medications and care. My confidence slowly grew and I knew I had to listen to the instinct that was telling me more and more strongly that I could not constantly watch over her.

Early on, I realised that Hannah's illness could make or break our family. Just as many marriages crack under the strain, so do the childhoods of many siblings of sick children, as parents pour everything into those children and leave little for those who are well. Of course there were days when Hannah was particularly ill, when my focus was solely on her. But I also knew I must save some of my energy for Oli and Lucy.

Bit by bit I started spending a few minutes with them in the two hours when Hannah was off her feeding pack during the afternoon. Gradually this built up to about half an hour. After putting Hannah in front of a favourite television programme, I'd go up to Oli's room. I knew my full attention was worth a whole day of treats to him, and I'd take crisps, cheese and apples up to his room before tucking sheets around the bottom of his bed on stilts to make Lucy a fairy castle to play in. Then Oli and I would build towers of Lego or he whizzed up and down the ladder to his bed as I watched.

We also started making short trips to the park, where I would play with Oli and Lucy as Hannah sat in her buggy. I wanted her to carry on learning the lessons that any other child her own age would, and patience was one of them. I was ready to drop everything if Hannah needed me urgently, but I made myself stop responding to every call. The need to constantly comfort her could become almost overwhelming if I wasn't careful, and I knew it would not help her, Oli or Lucy to cosset her in my constant attention.

Hannah and I had an ongoing conversation about her illness, and while she never complained about it I knew she didn't always like watching her brother and sisters venture out bit by bit into the world.

'Am I still poorly, Mummy?' she'd ask as we sat at the kitchen table drawing. 'Why isn't anyone else poorly too? Will I go to school soon?'

'We hope so. Your heart is poorly but we hope it's going to get better.'

Hannah stopped what she was doing and looked at me.

'You know that if I go to heaven I will be with Grandma and Grandpa until you come and there will be lots of sweeties, animals and trees?'

'Yes, my darling.'

However often we had the conversation, it made me inexpressibly sad to hear her talk in such a way, but Hannah was as quietly accepting as she always had been. She knew she couldn't run around with Oli and Lucy, because she had to live a different kind of life. But although she could easily have thrown a tantrum or sulked about it, she never did.

There were moments, though, when her vulnerabilities shone through, as did mine. One day I felt so exhausted that I started crying in front of the children. I remember sitting at the top of the stairs with the three children around me.

'Mummy's very tired,' I sobbed. 'And I want you to go to bed now.'

Their eyes were wide as they looked quizzically at my tears. They knew it was far too early for them to go to bed. The sun was still shining. We had not eaten tea or had a bath yet. This was not how things usually were.

'It's all right, Mummy,' Hannah said. 'I'll help you.'

She was wearing her oxygen line, attached by a long thin tube to the converter in her room that had replaced the cylinders she had come home from hospital with. The converter was a box that sucked oxygen out of the air and delivered it to Hannah through a tube under her nose. She wore it constantly because her heart wasn't strong enough to properly oxygenate her blood.

But now Hannah slipped off the oxygen line as she took Oli's hand.

'I'm going to put you into bed while Mummy puts Lucy in hers,' she said softly to her brother.

As Hannah walked slowly away with her brother, I wiped my face and took Lucy into her room where I settled her before walking back to Oli's. He was lying on his raised bed and Hannah, who couldn't make the climb, was sitting at the bottom in a plastic chair. A book was open in her hands and Oli was leaning out of the side of the bed to look at the pictures as she read to him—the words coming out in breathy chunks.

I went back into the hallway to pick up Hannah's oxygen line before going back into Oli's room and putting it on her again. She breathed deeply as the oxygen hissed softly through the line.

'Why don't I help you finish the story?' I said as I sat down beside her.

I PRESSED MY FACE to the glass panel in the top of the door as it closed. Six months after leaving hospital, Hannah was on the other side being led into a classroom by a teacher for her first day back at school. I'd registered her at a tiny primary in a village called Whitbourne, about ten miles from Worcester, where we were looking for a house to buy.

Whitbourne was a village with a school that was surrounded by stone walls, a village hall on a green, a pub, river and shop. I wanted my children to walk to school, run barefoot on grass, eat boiled eggs for breakfast from chickens that roamed in the garden. It was a dream that I'd always had, but Hannah had taught me that we couldn't put it off. Andrew and I were going to create the life we wanted today instead of waiting for a tomorrow that might never come.

So while I house-hunted, Hannah was going to go to school for a few hours on as many mornings as she could manage. For the first few weeks, at least, I was going to attend school with her, and although we'd been 'practising' for school so she could be off her oxygen for a few hours, a cylinder would be stored in her classroom just in case she needed it.

Still very skinny, Hannah was dwarfed by the backpack she was carrying which contained her feed. Her nasogastric tube was stuck to the side of her cheek and she wore a bobble hat to keep her head warm. I wanted to cheer as I watched her sit down at a table with two other children.

A couple of hours later I arrived back at the class to take her outside for break time. At the start of the day I'd pushed Hannah to the school steps in her wheelchair, but now she wanted to walk. We edged our way twenty feet into the playground and sat down on a bench near the door as children peered shyly before getting braver and walking up to talk to Hannah.

'What's that?' a little boy asked, as he pointed to her feeding tube.

'It's my food. I can't eat enough.'

'Where does it go?'

'Into my tummy.'

'What's that?' another child asked, pointing to the wiggly bag which hung round her neck holding the tubes from her central line.

'It's for my medicine,' Hannah told them. 'I have a poorly heart.'

'Where's your hair?' a little girl asked.

'It fell off,' said Hannah.

'Oh.'

Soon all the questions had been asked and Hannah became just another classmate. My heart leapt with joy.

Hannah pressed her face to the window of the plane.

'Where's Father Christmas?' she said. 'I can't see him.'

We were coming in to land on a trip to Scotland with a group from Birmingham Children's Hospital. Hannah's fifth birthday had been spent in hospital so this was our first chance to celebrate something as a family.

'This is Captain Christmas!' a voice had boomed out of the cabin speakers soon after we'd boarded. 'I'm going to need your help to get off the ground because Santa Claus is waiting! So I want everyone to make a big noise to get the plane into the air.'

Children cheered as we soared into the sky, and soon Oli, Lucy, Hannah, Andrew and I were invited to go and meet Captain Christmas. We walked into the cockpit to find him waiting—snow on the dashboard, lights twinkling, and an elf sitting in the seat next to Captain Christmas .

'He might look like Father Christmas but he's not,' the elf said as he gestured at Captain Christmas's red coat and white beard. 'He's his brother and he's taking you to see Father Christmas because he knows that some of you might not be in your own beds on Christmas Eve.'

Wide-eyed and even more excited, the children had gone back to their seats, and now Hannah watched as we came in to land. On the runway below she could see dozens of figures in fancy dress standing in a line.

'Where is he?' she cried again.

'He'll be here soon,' I told her. 'Captain Christmas will make sure of it.'

After the plane had come to rest, Oli, Lucy and other well siblings walked down the steps to be greeted by the volunteers in costume who were going to look after them for the day. Then Hannah and other sick children were taken off the plane in an armchair lift before being driven to a hall.

Inside were tables laden with food, 'snow' on the ground and streamers tumbling from the ceiling. Andrew, me and the other parents were ushered to seats and told we didn't have to do a thing for the rest of the afternoon because doctors and nurses from Birmingham were on hand. Brothers and sisters dug into bowls of sweets and crisps, while sick children were given morsels of food specially prepared for their tiny appetites. If, like Hannah, they couldn't eat, the volunteers helped them colour in pictures or 'dance' to the disco music. Laughter and shouts filled the air, and within an hour the hall was strewn with debris as the children clustered round a huge English Shepherd which had tinsel in his tail and was giving them rides.

'The reindeers are coming,' a voice boomed out, and children rushed to the windows.

Far in the distance, at the other side of the airfield, were six reindeers pulling Father Christmas in a sledge. The sledge drew closer and closer before Father Christmas finally strode into the hall.

'Happy Christmas, children,' he cried. 'Did my brother bring you here?'

Hannah looked overwhelmed. I remembered last year when she had been too weak to sit up when Father Christmas came to see her. Now she held on to the 'mouse' and 'fairy' looking after her as children rushed at him.

'You need to come up to see me one by one,' he said with a laugh as he sat down on a throne. 'Because though I don't normally give out presents before Christmas Day, you've been all good enough to have one early.'

Each child was given a present before some of the well ones were put into a fire engine, water cannons firing as they drove round the airfield, while others patted the reindeers. It was too cold for Hannah to go outside, but she sat and watched the others until dusk finally began to fall and a voice shouted that Father Christmas had to leave.

The lights of the sleigh shone as Father Christmas galloped across the airfield, then they gradually dimmed as he disappeared into the darkness. Seconds later, lights rose into the air and the children stared in wonder as Father Christmas 'flew' into the night sky.

Now it was time to get back on the plane as Captain Christmas appeared in his flight helmet to welcome us all back on board. We looked out of the windows. In the darkness the fancy-dress figures had lined up on the runway, each wearing a glove with tiny lights embedded that twinkled as we rose into the air—scores of hands waving us goodbye, ordinary people who had given their time to wish us a Happy Christmas.

CHAPTER SIX

Live the Life You Love

Hannah

The news is full of stories about MPs' expenses and it's got me thinking about what I'd do if I was Prime Minister. The first thing would be to sack all the MPs who fiddled their expenses. But these are some others:

- Make the government pay for children's hospice care like Acorns because they don't and I think that's really bad.

- Stop charging for parking at hospitals.

- Stop hospital parking attendants being so fussy. The taxi that takes me to hospital school can hardly stop to let me out before the driver gets in trouble.

- Give children good homes. I see children at Acorns who can't move or talk but they've got good mums and dads. That's a lot compared to some who are living in homes with parents who don't love them.

I thought that last one up after visiting the British Heart Foundation to meet other kids like me. I thought it was going to be boring and we'd all sit around telling each other what was wrong with us. But instead we did activities and just chatted, which was good. I met one girl about my age who'd had a heart transplant and told me she'd had to go back into hospital because her body was trying to reject her heart, which made me feel a bit funny. Mostly, though, I liked meeting other kids who were as different as me. It reminded me I'm not the only one with a bad heart, and the world opened up a bit. It was also good because we talked about the here and now, not the future; that's what I like to do—take every day as it comes.

Sometimes I think about the transplant, but it's usually when I've been feeling ill, like after I went to the horse show. I had not been that ill for a long time and it took ages to feel better. I'm still a bit tired but I'm back to being me, and even though I've been told I'll get sicker if I don't have the operation, and my illness might go away if I do, I'm still not having it. When people ask why I said no, I wonder if they understand what it's like to be ill when you're a child, because if they did then I don't think they'd go on about my decision so much.

My earliest memory is of going to Disneyland. After that I can remember being at home and doing my school work while Mum was in the kitchen. But other than that a lot of my memories are about hospitals: having blood tests; Mum taking the tape off my nasogastric tube, which hurt so much that I screamed; the Vitamin K injections I had to have in my leg after my heart got worse, which really hurt; that kind of thing. I also remember having to go to hospital all the time for check-ups, which I didn't like.

Anyway, when you've been ill you think about things because you have so much time. I know that if my heart gets worse I will probably get more tired, short of breath, and go to bed. I don't think about it all the time because if I did I wouldn't do anything. I don't go around thinking, 'Oh my gosh, I might die this week,' because if I did there would be no point in living and that's what I want to do. I made my decision to suit me and I knew Mum and Dad were happy with it. I wanted to be back at home. I did not want another operation or to have to stay in hospital for ages.

When I was finally allowed to come home I was happy that the whole hospital thing was over. But even then I had to take meds all the time. At the moment I take seven pills in the morning, two at lunchtime and five in the evening. It's not that much compared to what I've taken before—sometimes more than thirty pills a day at 8 a.m., 10 a.m., 12, 2, 4, 6 and 8 p.m.—it might not sound a lot, but, believe me, if you have to do it every day then it gets to be a real pain. The meds remind me I'm ill and it's one of the things that puts me off having a transplant because I'd have to take antirejection drugs for the rest of my life.

All I'm saying is that being in hospital for a short while is OK and there's a lot to play with if you're a young child, but it gets harder as you get older. You see the same walls every day and know what's going to happen. The worst thing, though, is that you know what you're missing.

Kirsty

Nerves filled me as I stared at the paper I'd just signed. It was a letter telling Hannah's headmaster I was taking her out of school to educate her at home.

We'd moved to Whitbourne days before Christmas 2000 into a semi-detached house that stood on a hill overlooking fields. The house needed work but the view was beautiful and the garden was perfect for the children.

In the months that followed, Oli and Lucy had been registered at the nursery attached to the village school and Hannah had continued to go as often as she could. She'd also come off permanent oxygen and got a little stronger. But as much as I wanted her to be well enough for school, she became increasingly tired and anxious about her limits.

'Will I feel too sick in class today, Mummy?' she'd ask. 'Will someone knock me over? I don't want to fall down.'

After months with other sick children, returning to school made Hannah aware of how difficult she found it to keep up. It didn't surprise me that she sometimes got angry as she watched Oli and Lucy exploring the world around us. Soon after moving, we'd bought a pony because I'd ridden as a child and wanted Oli and Lucy to learn. Learning to ride, though, was just one of the new things that they were doing. They were also beginning to ride scooters and bikes, and skip, hop and jump on the trampoline in the garden. Hannah had to be put on it and bounced gently, and although she was beginning to walk more she still couldn't go far.

But it was only after her calm nature erupted into a terrible rage that I knew I had to do something. It happened as Hannah stood in a doorway beside Lucy while I did up their shoes before school. I don't know what provoked Hannah but suddenly she lashed out and I looked up to see Lucy's head smash into the door frame. Springing forward, I reached up to push Hannah away from her sister and she stumbled, crashing into the other side of the door. Blood spurted from a cut on Lucy's head as I turned to Hannah.

'What are you doing?' I shouted. 'Why did you hurt your sister?'

I took Lucy to the bathroom to butterfly stitch her cut.

'Mummy knows she was wrong to grab you and I promise never to do it again,' I said to Hannah later. 'But you must also promise me that you will never hit Lucy like that.'

'I won't,' she said.

'Why did you do it, Han?'

'I don't know,' she said, as if bewildered by my question.

Hannah's calm acceptance of her illness was being pushed to its limits, and I knew I had to stop trying to fit her life into a box that it didn't suit. Much as I wanted her to be at school, it was too much. It was then that I heard about a small but growing number of parents across the UK who were choosing to home educate their children, and I wondered if this was what Hannah needed.

Although Andrew thought the idea was too way out at first, the more I thought about it, the more sure I felt. At home, Hannah could learn at her own pace and gain strength rather than having her confidence knocked by not keeping up at school. She faced challenges other children didn't and I had to trust my judgment that this decision was right for her. When I explained how I felt, Andrew had agreed and I took a deep breath now as I picked up the letter and slipped it into an envelope. I would take it with me to school when I took Hannah in to pick up Oli and Lucy.

Walking to the front door, a feeling of liberation filled me as I wrapped my fingers round the envelope. This was another lesson that Hannah was going to help me learn and now we were going to live the life we loved, however different it might be to the one we had had before.

'Are you ready?' I called to her as I opened the front door. Soon we would start on the next stage of our journey together.

To ME, EDUCATION MEANT not just sitting with a pen and paper, so as Hannah's sixth birthday approached I taught her to look after the chickens and put plates in the dishwasher. I tried to make lessons come alive, so if we were doing history I would take her to see the Hereford Mappa Mundi—a medieval map of the world that we stared at together in the city's cathedral. To help with maths I gave her coins to count or asked her to double the quantity of flour we were using in a recipe.

Food was a big part of our learning because it remained a problem for Hannah, and I tried to re-engage her interest in it. Months after coming out of hospital, she would only eat 'easy' foods like yoghurt and ice cream and still needed the feeding pack. But Hannah had to learn how to eat again because children can become phobic about food after going so long without it during chemotherapy. Eating also required a lot of energy for someone with a weak heart, so I had to find ways to make it easier for Hannah.

To help with chewing and swallowing, I minced her food into purées before putting them on a plate—a tiny brown pile of puréed mince, another of orange carrot and another of green peas. She could see the 'meal' she was trying to eat, and slowly but surely Hannah started to eat a little more. Soon her strength had improved, and within months of starting home schooling she was able to walk outside instead of using her wheelchair and had come off the feeding pack during the day. She would still need it at night for another year as she progressed through eating small chunks to whole food, and Hannah would be about nine before I could take her for her first pizza.

But in the meantime I sparked her interest in food by making vegetable growing a big part of our home tuition. Hannah watched as I cut turf in the garden to create a vegetable plot before helping me to plant potatoes, peas, broccoli, carrots, cabbage and cauliflower. In the greenhouse we grew tomatoes, cucumbers, peppers, squash and spaghetti fruits.

We picked plums and apples from trees in our garden, fed the chickens every day and Hannah helped water the plants. After moving to Whitbourne we'd had an extension built that housed a kitchen overlooking the garden. In it was a pine table, blue-and-white checked curtains, an Aga, and a sofa where Hannah rested during the day. She still needed a lot of sleep and, sometimes, when I put Lucy down for a rest on a soft, blue-mesh swing seat in the afternoon, I'd put Hannah in with her. Having pegged sheets round it to protect them from the sun, I'd swing them both to sleep.

When they woke up they'd potter round the garden together and I'd watch them through the French windows in the kitchen. Standing by the vegetable plot, they'd reach up to snaffle peas in their pods. Then the two of them would teeter across the lawn to the water butt, where they'd dip the peas for a quick wash before popping the whole pod into their mouths.

Hannah seemed to thrive on being at home with me and our unusual lessons. Perhaps her favourite was to watch me digging potatoes, and she knew there was one enemy in particular who might spoil her fun—slugs. So at night we'd go outside in our dressing gowns and wellies, holding a paraffin lamp to light up the ground and kitchen tongs to pick up the slugs.

'If we throw them over the hedge they'll come back again tomorrow, won't they?' Hannah would ask, just to make sure that we really had to consign the slugs to their demise in a jar of beer that I was carrying.

'Yes, Han,' I'd tell her.

'OK, Mummy,' she'd say and I'd hear a plop as the slug hit the beer.

TODAY WAS A DAY that Hannah had spent two years longing for. In the months after her central line had been put in, it had been in almost constant use. But as time had passed, Hannah had grown stronger and learned to take her heart medications in tablet form so it was needed less. Her heart function had also improved a little, and when the line went unused for three months her doctors had decided it could be removed.

We'd gone into hospital to have it done just before her seventh birthday, but because the central line had been in place for so long, it had embedded into the skin on Hannah's chest and we'd had to stay in for the site to be monitored after the line was removed. The procedure also involved a general anaesthetic—something Hannah hadn't had since her heart was damaged and which was extremely risky for her. But she was anaesthetised with a cardiac team on standby and the operation was a success.

Hannah hated being in hospital for her birthday, but having the line removed was important because she had never been able to get it wet, which had stopped her from doing so many things she wanted to. For two years she hadn't had a splashy bath or gone swimming, run through the sprinkler in the garden or played in the paddling pool. Removing it also meant she was finally free of the line coming out of her chest and the 'wiggly' bag holding the connecting tubes that had constantly hung round her neck.

Part of me dreaded the removal of the line even though I was happy for Hannah. It had been there if she got an infection or her heart worsened. An entry point for Hannah to receive rapid and powerful treatment, a safety net that had always been there to catch her. Now I knew it was time to move on from the red-alert mode I'd been in for so long—constantly watchful, ready to drop everything if she got worse, on the look-out for signs of a recurrence of leukaemia or a worsening of her heart—to amber; from a state of high anxiety to a place where I could dare to hope the crisis had passed. Hannah was moving into a new stage of her recovery, which meant I must, too, because our lives were moving on in more ways than one. Andrew had got a new job that would take him away from home a lot during the week and I would be alone with the children. It was a new phase for all of us.

Now, after several days at home, during which Hannah had constantly examined the incision site to check it was healing, her scab was finally starting to transform into a pink scar and it was time for her to have what she'd been longing for—a bubble bath.

'Can Oli come in with me?' she'd asked me that morning.

'Of course.'

'And will you let us shut the door?'

'Maybe. But you must promise not to stand up in the bath.'

'I won't. Do you mind if we make a mess?'

'No. Just try not to flood the kitchen, Han.'

I ran the bath and filled it to the brim with bubbles. After standing Oli in the bath, I sat Hannah down because she was still so wobbly on her feet.

'Will you shout for me if anyone slips?' I asked Oli.

'Yes, Mummy,' he yelled in excitement.

I wondered what I was doing leaving a five-and-a-half-year-old and his seven-year-old sister in a bath full of bubbles. But I couldn't stop smiling as I went downstairs and heard peals of laughter and howls of hysteria. It sounded like pure joy crystallised, and as I watched water stain the kitchen ceiling I didn't care if it came down.

'Can you get me out of the bath, please, Mummy?' Hannah shouted about half an hour later. 'Oli's done it but I can't.'

I walked upstairs. Opening the door, I saw Hannah's eyes looking at me from just above the edge of the bath. There were bubbles everywhere, streaks of coloured soap up the wall and water all over the floor. Oli had disappeared, leaving his big sister to face the music, and Hannah's eyes were anxious as she peered at me, her hair sitting up in tufts on her head.

'I'm sorry, Mummy,' she said.

I smiled. 'It's OK, Han,' I said as I wapped her in a towel and lifted her up. 'I said you could have a big bath and you've had it. Did you have fun?'

'It was great,' she said, her eyes shining. 'Can we do it again?'

CHAPTER SEVEN

Everyone is Equal

Hannah

It is June and Phoebe was five last week so we had a party for her at home.

I'd helped Mum get everything ready while Phoebe was at school. I wasn't very well though and had been in bed because I had too much fluid in me, which is what happens when my heart isn't pumping fast enough and my liver is suffering. So I got up late on Phoebe's birthday, helped Mum lay the table and make a trifle, and then went back to bed again. Mum only has to tell me to lie down when I'm excited. Otherwise I know when I need to go to bed, just like I know what to do with my medicines.

Mum let me take them when I came out of hospital after the pacemaker because I wanted to know what I was taking and when. In the morning I take captopril, furosemide, carvedilol, spironolactone, digoxin, aspirin and Q10; at lunchtime it's captopril and furosemide; then in the evening I finish with captopril, furosemide, carvedilol, spironolactone and Q10.

I got up when Phoebe, Lucy and Oli came back from school and the party started. I'd bought Phoebe a ra-ra skirt, sweets and a colouring book. By 5.30 p.m., though, I felt really tired again and had to go back to bed.

I didn't feel like doing much for a few days after that. If I get ill then our GP, Dr Knight, comes to see me and talks to Mum about giving me a bit more furosemide or something. If it's bad then I have to go into Hereford Hospital to see Dr Meyrick, who's looked after me ever since I was little.

Now I'm out of bed again because I'm feeling better; yesterday I went up to the horse field with Lucy. Before my heart got worse we used to go together a lot. We'd wash the ponies, play in the long grass and then wait for Mum to come and see what we'd done—she was always surprised when the ponies were immaculate. Lucy could be a bit annoying because she'd run off to play, so I'd have to tell her to come back and finish helping me. But now she does the ponies on her own most of the time and even gets up early on school mornings to do them if I'm ill and Mum can't leave the house.

Yesterday, though, I felt OK and helped Lucy as she washed Mr Minty with special shampoo. It's purple and we sponged it on before rubbing out the grass stains on his coat and washing the shampoo off. By the time we'd finished, Mr Minty looked as white as white can be. I liked doing it because

Mum was pleased with us. It was also good to be out of the house because I'd been there for too long. I like the freedom of being outside, the sound, the light, the noise of grass under your feet as you walk.

It was good to go out with Lucy, too. Even though she's three years younger than me, we're good mates.

Phoebe's too young to understand what's wrong with me, and Oli and Lucy find it hard to imagine being in my place. I wonder if they think it's easy being ill, because I get things like my own TV. I saved up my pocket money to buy a flat screen because I spend so much time watching stuff in bed. I asked Dad to take me into town to help me pick. But then I saw how much the televisions cost and realised I didn't have enough. Luckily Dad said he'd lend me some extra as long as I saved up to pay him back later.

That's the kind of thing that makes Oli and Lucy jealous, though, and I could tell when we got home that they wished they had a TV too. But although I know they think my life is easy, I wish I could ride as well as Lucy or go on the school bus like Oli does every day.

The other thing that really gets to them is when they think I'm not being told off as much as they are. They're right, but it's got nothing to do with being ill. I'm just not as naughty as they are. I was sent to my bedroom a lot when I was eleven but I'm not so bad now I'm thirteen.

Kirsty

I listened to the sound of the children downstairs. Nearly six months pregnant with my fourth child, I was suffering from morning sickness and had started getting labour pains a week ago before being given drugs to stop them. Now I was in bed resting and could hear Hannah as she shooed her brother and sister around to make sure they got ready for school.

In the two years since her central line had been removed Hannah had grown stronger, and now, as she approached her ninth birthday, the five-year anniversary of her remission was just months away.

At first I'd worried that my morning sickness was making it impossible for me to do as much as usual around the house. But I'd soon realised that it meant Hannah did more for herself, and I was glad because I wanted her to become as confident and independent as Oli and Lucy were.

They had had to start learning from a young age because as much as I'd tried to make sure that Oli and Lucy got enough of my attention, I'd had to trust them to do things. They had learnt a great deal because of it, and by the age of five could take Hannah's medications to her. Counting the pills into their hands, I'd tell them to count them back into Hannah's. When they started school, I left them to clean their own teeth and faces while I gave Hannah her morning medications and cooked the breakfast.

Lucy's independent streak had showed itself by the age of four, when she got sick of Oli putting lopsided bunches into her hair and taught herself to do it, while her brother's trustworthiness was apparent when I started letting him walk her to school. We were lucky because Whitbourne was a quiet village with little traffic, but I also knew that even at the age of seven Oli would make sure his sister followed the pavement on the four-minute walk.

Now I heard the front door open and the children clatter outside.

'Bye, Mummy,' Lucy yelled.

I couldn't even raise my head off the pillow to say goodbye, and I lay still in bed until Hannah appeared at the door a few minutes later.

'I walked Oli and Lucy to the garden gate and watched them to the end of the road,' she told me. 'Now would you like some water, Mummy?'

'Yes, please, Han,' I murmured gratefully.

OUR THIRD DAUGHTER, Phoebe, was born sixteen weeks prematurely and weighed just one pound nine ounces.

I'd wanted to fight my body, to force it to keep my baby safe inside me, after I went into labour. But I couldn't stop what was happening and was rushed by ambulance to Bristol for an emergency delivery. By the time I woke up from the anaesthetic, Phoebe had been taken to intensive care and the nurses told me to rest. But I asked Andrew to push me to the baby unit in a wheelchair. A row of identical incubators lined each side of the room, but something made me stop at the second cot on the right.

Staring into it, my heart turned as I saw Phoebe for the first time—so small that the tiny teddy lying in her crib dwarfed her. Just six inches long, her eyes were still fused shut and she had no fingernails, hair or eyebrows. But as I looked I felt a familiar feeling—an intertwining of love and protection so strong it took my breath away. Once again, one of my children was fighting for her life and I had to do all I could to help her survive.

The doctors had warned me that the risk of a brain haemorrhage or fatal infection was high in such a premature baby. Things as simple as breathing and eating were hard for Phoebe, and because she was so premature I was not yet producing milk properly. So I would collect it, drop by drop, because all she needed was one millilitre an hour in her tiny stomach. Her lungs, like many premature babies, were undeveloped and so I would sit for hours with her lying naked against my bare chest because I knew such kangaroo care could help a baby's breathing. Watching her nestle against me, with a ventilator tube up her nose, an oxygen probe on her toe and a nasogastric tube for feeding, Phoebe looked as if she was hovering on the edge of our world, and I marvelled at how strong the will to live can be.

For six weeks I lived in a bubble with her. Andrew and his parents had picked up everything at home and Phoebe was all that mattered now. When the children came in to see us, they would look in wonder at their tiny sister lying in the incubator. Hannah was a little scared of the intensive-care unit at first. But gradually she started to help me when she came in for a visit.

'I can do it,' she'd say as I went to make sure the tubes connected to Phoebe were lying comfortably or to turn her every twenty minutes to even out the pressure on her tiny skull.

Then I would watch as she reached into the incubator, her small hands holding her sister gently as she moved her.

Phoebe got stronger until she was well enough to be moved to Worcester and I had to leave her at night. I hated not being there but Andrew had had so much time off work that I had return home to do the school run and pack lunch boxes, hang clothes on the line and prepare food. But my mind was constantly with Phoebe, and I drove to see her twice a day. Hannah came with me and would sit quietly as I fed Phoebe.

By the time Phoebe arrived at Hereford for the final weeks of her three-and-a-half-month hospital stay, she was off the ventilator and the nasogastric tube. She was so close to home now that I could drive in to breastfeed her five times a day, and by the time she came home she weighed four pounds one ounce.

At first I wondered if it might unsettle Hannah when Phoebe came home because it had been just the two of us during the school day for so long. But she relished the chance to help and be an older sister—fetching nappies and bottles, or making me a cup of tea which she'd bring as I breastfed.

I soon realised, though, that things couldn't stay as they had been. I'd been thinking about sending Hannah back to school—undecided about whether it would be too much physically but knowing it would be good for her in other ways. Now the decision had been taken out of my hands because I didn't have time to educate Hannah and look after a new baby.

Six months after Phoebe was born we moved to a village between Hereford and Worcester called Burley Gate, where Hannah started primary school. She attended gradually—building up from mornings to full days—and was ready to start the school year properly by September 2005.

More and more now I could live without worrying over every cough and cold she had. Each time we saw Hannah's doctors they told us that her heart function was stable; over the years it had even increased to 25 per cent. When we went for four-monthly check-ups it was a question of monitoring rather than increasing her treatment.

As she took her first steps into the world at school, I realised just how much Hannah's illness had shaped her character. She was fearless about expressing herself in classroom discussions and could be as implacable in her actions when she'd made her mind up. I cherished her strength because Hannah could so easily have been a frightened and hesitant child. But all the months and years of doctors and nurses asking her to do things she didn't necessarily like had made Hannah far more definite than most children about what she was—and wasn't—prepared to do.

There would be mornings when she would refuse to take her tablets and once again I knew it was a battle that I couldn't fight because I would certainly lose it. I reasoned with her and sometimes became so desperate that I'd resort to almost frightening her into taking the medicines as I told her how much her heart needed them. But Hannah wouldn't say a word as she sat silently with her lips clamped shut.

Hannah wasn't the only one, though, who had been deeply affected by her illness—Oli and Lucy's school reports often mentioned how considerate and patient they were with less able children, and both of them had learnt well how to stick up for someone who stood out. I wanted all my children to live their lives bravely and know that no matter our differences, weaknesses or strengths, everyone is equal.

I GOT UP and walked to the living-room window to stare down the road for the hundredth time. It was 4.30 p.m. on an average October afternoon—dusk was falling and Oli and Lucy were watching TV after coming home from school. But this was an extraordinary day and one that had made me anxious and overjoyed in equal measure.

Hannah had started at secondary school a few weeks before in a large village about a fifteen-minute drive from our home. After a year at primary school, she was blossoming. She'd made friends and was full of stories about them. School discos, GCSEs, sleepovers, and becoming a teenager, were all rushing closer and closer. Life finally felt dependable again with three children at school and two-year-old Phoebe growing up fast.

Each step Hannah had taken into her new life was important, but today was the first time she'd gone on the school bus. Ever since she'd started back at primary school, I'd either driven Hannah or walked in with her.

I knew the travelling might tire her. Still on about six types of heart medication, which she took in three doses over the day, Hannah could get run down if she did too much. But she wanted to be the same as her classmates.

'I'll walk you to the bus stop and then pick you up when you get back,' I'd told her as we talked about it.

'No, Mum,' she insisted. 'I don't want you to meet me. The other mums don't go to the bus. My friends just walk home. Why can't I?'

This wasn't about Hannah's limits but testing mine and letting her go.

'Will you let me walk you there on the first morning if I promise not to meet the bus again?' I asked.

'All right, but will you let me get home late? I want to go to the shop.'

So Hannah and I had made a deal and this morning I'd walked her to the bus stop and watched as she got on. I knew she was looking forward to telling her school friends about her journey and she smiled at me before waving as the bus pulled away. My heart had tugged as I'd watched her go.

Now I glanced at my watch and told myself I had to do something other than stare out of the window. I walked into the kitchen and put on the kettle. The bus would have dropped her off about twenty minutes ago, more than enough time to get to the shop and back. Should I go and look for her?

Suddenly I heard the thud of the front door slamming and a bag being dropped on the hallway floor. Footsteps padded towards the kitchen and Hannah appeared at the door. I wanted to run at her and start firing questions. Instead, I poured some water onto a tea bag and tried to look relaxed.

'Hi, Mum,' she said as she walked in.

'Hello, darling.'

'What's for tea?'

'Spaghetti Bolognese.'

'Great.'

She sat down at the kitchen table and I gave her a mug of tea.

'Thanks,' she said.

'So how was the bus, Han?' I asked as I sat down.

'Fine.'

'Did you get to school and back OK?'

She looked at me in exasperation. 'Of course! I'm here, aren't I, Mum?'

'So where have you been?' I asked.

'To the shop, like I said.' She pulled a white paper bag out of her pocket. 'I bought us all some sweets. Where are Oli and Lucy?'

She picked up her mug and walked out of the kitchen. I smiled to myself as I heard her call her brother and sister.

CHAPTER EIGHT

The Right to Choose

Hannah

St Mary's seemed massive on my first day there—full of kids rushing round and Year 8, 9, 10 and 11s who all knew each other. This time I really was on my own and felt weird in my brand-new uniform—a blazer with electric blue, yellow and white stripes, a white shirt with long sleeves, and a navy skirt. I'd never worn anything like it and some of the other girls' skirts looked really short so I wondered if mine was wrong.

But then I met Simone and everything changed because I realised that people who are really different can be good friends. Simone is bubbly and I'm quieter, she's tall and I'm short, she looks fifteen, I look younger because I'm little. But there was one important thing that was the same— we both laughed at things we weren't supposed to.

She is my true friend. Simone understands everything, doesn't question me about things I don't want to talk about, and if I don't get to school then she phones me up to tell me what's going on. For a long time I'd wished I could have a best friend—someone to muck around with and to talk to about normal stuff. A proper, hundred-per-cent friend who I could tell secrets to.

The other people we made friends with were Becky, Brigitta, Laura, Kelcea and Zoe, and they're all brilliant too. Every morning before school we'd sit on a windowsill near our form rooms and chat about random things like *Twilight*, which boy was most annoying, homework and stuff. It was great but what I liked most was that no one knew about my heart. I'd told Simone a bit, but otherwise people didn't know until they saw me on the news after I'd said no to the transplant, and the secret was out.

When I first started at St Mary's only the teachers knew, and my friends just saw me as one of them. All I could think was 'Great!' I was at school full-time, not taking too many pills, and I didn't get too tired.

I loved school. I was up for everything except PE. The best bits were:

- Someone blowing up their oven in cookery class. The teacher had to use the fire extinguisher on the flames.

- My maths teacher, Mr Robinson. I'd always hated maths and he was really nice so it got a bit easier.

- When people mucked around and played up so we missed a bit of a lesson. I liked watching other people be naughty.

- My first sleepover at Simone's when I was in Year 7.

- History lessons with Mr Carter because he made us laugh. Once we had a lesson about Roman architecture and ended up singing the *Bob the Builder* theme tune. How random is that?

But if I had to pick one best bit then it would be my friends, because I've realised that, although I love my family, everyone needs people of their own age to mix with. At first it scared me a bit to go up to people I didn't know and chat to them, but then I made friends and really appreciated them.

That's the main reason why I hated it when I got ill again. I was normal, I was at school, I had mates, I was like everyone else. And then one day I went to school in the morning and by that night I was in hospital again.

Kirsty

In the first months of 2007, Hannah had complained of stomach ache and feeling tired. But blood tests, chest and abdominal X-rays were fine and I didn't consider that Hannah's heart might be worsening because she had been well for so long. Then a phone call in the middle of an ordinary day taught me for the second time that life can fall apart in one sentence.

Andrew had taken Hannah to the GP that day after she'd become unwell at school. Now they were at Hereford Hospital where Hannah had collapsed.

'They think it's her heart,' he said, his voice clipped with fear.

Another car journey made too quickly, another dash through hospital corridors, until I reached Hannah who was lying semiconscious in a bed.

Dr Meyrick, the consultant who'd known Hannah since she fell ill with leukaemia, told us that she was dangerously sick. Her heart was enlarged and not beating powerfully enough, which meant she was struggling to get enough oxygen. Vital organs like her kidneys and liver were suffering.

'Hannah is in acute heart failure,' he said gravely. 'She is going to be transferred to Birmingham's intensive-care unit immediately. She needs intravenous drugs to act directly on her heart. Time is of the essence.'

He could not tell us why Hannah's heart had suddenly deteriorated, and Andrew and I could only watch numbly as she was put into an ambulance. Andrew went home to arrange for someone to look after Oli, Lucy and Phoebe, while I got into the car to follow the ambulance up the motorway.

I SAT BY Hannah's bed. The doctor beside me held an anaesthetic consent form that I needed to sign to give permission for Hannah to undergo surgery. For three days medics at Birmingham Children's Hospital had been trying to stabilise her after an echocardiogram had revealed that Hannah's heart function had dropped to just ten per cent. Her liver and kidneys were failing and she needed a central line inserted to make sure she got enough of the drug called dobutamine, which was keeping her alive.

It acted like adrenaline to stimulate Hannah's heart contractions, but getting enough dobutamine into her body was difficult. Hannah's heart was pumping so weakly that her veins weren't being opened by sufficient blood flow and they kept collapsing. She also needed a range of drugs to counteract other symptoms and deal with the side effects of so many medications.

Semiconscious, Hannah had become increasingly distressed as the days had passed. Allergic to local anaesthetic, she felt every needle as it punctured her body—sometimes as many as eight sticking into her hands and feet—just as pain shot through her when an inch-long cut was made in her elbow to thread a line under her skin. It travelled via her armpit along a vein to her heart, but the site went septic within twenty-four hours as the dobutamine burned a hole the size of a one-pence piece into her elbow. The only option left for administering dobutamine was a central line.

But the anaesthetic she would need to put the line in place was a huge risk for someone whose heart was so weak. I took the form, and the anaesthetist traced his finger along a line of words: 'This procedure can result in death.' I signed my name. Hannah's heart failure had not been caused by an infection that could be cured in a few days with antibiotics and neither was it a problem that could be solved with surgery. The doctors did not know why her health had so suddenly deteriorated, but the only thing keeping her alive now was the dobutamine. She needed the central line.

Hannah was taken to theatre. All I could do was wait. I'd known that the heart damage caused by the chemotherapy was irreversible and had accepted that Hannah may not live as long as a healthy child. But I'd dared to imagine her growing into adulthood, and now nothing was sure.

I counted down the thirty minutes I'd been told she would be in theatre. It was two and a half hours before the surgeon came to tell me she was waking up.

'We had to put the line into her neck because of the scarring from older procedures,' he told me. 'It's running across her chest wall, which might be a bit more uncomfortable, and her veins were also very narrow so it was a bit tricky at times. She was poorly on the table but she's waking up now.'

I knew enough to read between the doctor's reassurances.

'Was there an emergency?'

'Yes.'

My whole body jolted as I heard those words. Hannah must have had a cardiac arrest, and though I knew this was not uncommon in heart patients undergoing surgery, terror gripped me as the doctor started to leave.

'She's fine now, Mrs Jones,' he said softly as he opened the door. 'We've done what we had to and she's through it.'

MACHINES CLICKED AND BEEPED as Hannah lay on the bed. A doctor was standing beside her and I tensed as I heard the crackle of a sterilised needle pack being opened. Even though the central line was in place now, Hannah still required a cocktail of other drugs to keep her stable, and the doctor was going to insert a needle into the top of her foot to give her saline.

'No!' Hannah moaned as the needle slid underneath her skin and her body tensed in pain.

'That's it now, darling,' I said. 'It's all over.'

But even as I comforted Hannah and the saline bag was suspended from a drip stand, I knew she would soon need another needle inserted. Once the fluid had gone into her system, Hannah's heart would not be able to pump it properly to her weakened kidneys. She would then need albumin to suck the saline through her system before a third needle was inserted to give her furosemide, a drug to help her kidneys pass it out of her body.

'Don't let them,' she'd say softly, as a nurse or doctor came to put another needle in. 'Please, Mummy.'

'But they have to,' I would reply, hardly knowing if it made sense any more when I saw how much pain she was in.

Then her eyes would close and doubts would fill me as she fell into a troubled sleep. How long could her body cope with this? And, more importantly, how long could her spirit?

Hannah hated being back in hospital. As days turned into a week and the dobutamine kept her heart beating, she began to be more wakeful, but her distress hung round her like a shadow.

And it was clear that Hannah could not cope without the dobutamine. Any change to her dosage—even a decrease of just half a millilitre over twenty-four hours—would make her heart gallop as it tried to beat, her breathing become shallow and her kidneys start to shut down as fluid collected in her tissues. As I watched her struggle, I knew just how fragile Hannah's grip on life was.

When the dosage was increased again she became more alert, but every touch or movement seared into her as the doctors monitored vital signs and gave drugs, the nurses changed dressings and tried to soothe skin raw from needles. Her senses were heightened, and Hannah would moan if a light shone too brightly or cry if someone spoke too loudly. Even the sound of a bin being emptied in a corridor outside was enough to unsettle her, and she didn't like to be touched because her skin was painful. Her room had to be dark and quiet, a cocoon in which she fought to live.

Andrew and his parents looked after Oli, Lucy and Phoebe while I stayed in hospital. So the days passed, until Hannah was strong enough to have the television or some music on for a few minutes. The only thing that punctured the time were her pleas to go home, because in the moments when Hannah felt just a shred more energy she would beg me to take her.

'I want to go home,' she whispered as tears trickled down her cheeks.

Her words cut into me as I tried to soothe her.

'But you can't, Han. You're poorly. We must wait until you're stronger.'

'Please, Mummy. Please.'

Soon the effort of just a few words would exhaust her and Hannah would fall silent again. But day by day I could sense her despair growing.

Hannah did not argue or get angry. She was too weak to do anything other than retreat into herself.

THE WATER FELT WARM as I soaked the flannel before wringing it out. Was it soft enough? I'd hunted through every one in the shop to find the softest and would use this just a couple of times before discarding it. It would be too harsh for Hannah's skin after a couple of washes.

I opened out the warm flannel and dabbed at her face. I would start at her forehead and move down. I had to be quick but not too quick. I must make sure she was clean but also keep her warm while I washed her.

'It won't take long, darling,' I said softly.

Hannah was propped up by pillows. Her neck muscles were so weak that she could not lift her head for more than thirty seconds without help. Her weight had halved over the past month and her muscles had also wasted. Hannah did not have the energy to eat and weighed just over three stone.

'I'm going to do your mouth now, Han.' I picked up a jar of Vaseline.

I rubbed some onto her cracked lips before wrapping cotton wool round the tip of a cotton bud and soaking it in water. The hospital gave me sponges on sticks to use for Hannah's mouth care, but they were too hard. I pulled back her bottom lip, tiny bit by bit, before easing the cotton bud into her mouth to clean it.

When her face was clean, I unscrewed the top of a bottle of moisturiser. The sweet smell cut into the clinical hospital air, opening a window onto another world—of perfumes and music, make-up and friends. But Hannah was quiet as I massaged the moisturiser into her skin.

I lifted the basin of water and walked to the bottom of her bed where I balanced it on a table. Rolling up the sheet and blanket covering Hannah's legs, I left her top half covered to make sure she stayed warm. Over her legs lay one half of a pair of pyjama bottoms that I'd cut in two. Hannah was too weak to get in and out of clothes, and something as small as lying on a crease of fabric was too much for her. But she didn't like it if the doctors pulled back her covers and saw her naked, so I draped clothes across her to make her feel dressed.

I folded one half of the pyjama bottoms to the side before lifting Hannah's foot and rolling it in ever widening circles. We tried to do exercises like these twice a day. The joint in her knee looked huge, incongruous, in her tiny, withered leg as I lay it back down on the towels. Quickly I washed her leg before covering it up again and moving on to the other one.

When her bottom half was clean, I pulled back the blankets covering her from the waist up. I pulled back the soft cotton top with buttons that lay across her bare chest, and washed one arm before covering it and doing the other. I tried not to see her collarbones or rib cage, her breast- or hipbones, jutting out from skin so paper thin it looked as if it might break.

When Hannah was finally washed and covered in towels, I moved to the side of the bed to turn her over and do her back.

'It hurts too much,' she whispered.

I thought of the livid red bedsore that had developed on Hannah's coccyx. I bent to kiss her. I would stop now. There was always tomorrow.

As THE WEEKS went on, it became more and more important for Hannah to put on weight because she needed food and calories to give her precious energy. But eating was too much for her most days—it required energy she just didn't have—and she hated the high-calorie build-up soups and drinks she was given so much that a dietician was called in to try to find out if there was anything that might tempt her to eat.

'My mummy knows how I like things,' was all she would say.

It was arranged for me to show a hospital chef how I cooked her food at home in the hope that she might eat it. After going to the local shops to buy the ingredients I cooked with, I went to the kitchens and explained how she liked her Bolognese: well-browned mince, no fat, and tinned tomatoes.

'No herbs or onion?' the chef asked, a little surprised by its blandness.

'Nothing except spaghetti cooked so well you can mash it,' I told him.

Hannah's preference for soft food had stayed with her ever since chemotherapy, but she just looked at the meal listlessly later that day when it was delivered to her room.

'Have a taste,' I said. 'Please.'

She opened her mouth without a word and I slid some food into it. She chewed slowly and deliberately, forcing herself to swallow, but kept her mouth closed when I lifted the next spoonful to it.

'Please, Han,' I said softly. 'Just a little bit more?'

Hannah's eyes began to fill with tears. 'No, Mummy,' she whispered.

'But I showed the chef how to make it.'

'It's not the same. You didn't make it at home.'

'WILL YOU lift me up, Mummy?' Hannah asked.

I looked out of the window at the bright blue sky that Hannah could only glimpse as she lay in bed. Still too weak to walk or even stand, she longed to see it and I knew that lifting her onto her feet for even just a few seconds would exhaust her. But such tiny moments were precious and so I sat her up before moving her pillows out from behind her.

Sitting down, I wriggled to a kneeling position behind Hannah and put my arms underneath hers. Pushing her up, I knelt on one knee as I raised her to her feet. She felt like a rag doll in my arms, tiny and fragile as I supported her to make sure she didn't have to bear any of her own weight. She leaned against me as she lifted her head to stare out of the window. Drip lines ran from her arms to several bags of medication, and fluid hung on stands beside the bed. Her central line poked out of the side of her neck and an oxygen tube ran under her nose. Sats and oxygen monitors were attached to her fingers and toes, and machines beeped softly around us.

Hannah smiled as she looked out of the window. 'It's a lovely day.'

The view was mostly the concrete and bricks of Birmingham's skyline, but Hannah drank in the sight of the world outside. Today was fine, but she didn't mind what the weather was: sun made the sky blue, wind sent clouds scudding across the horizon, rain sent silver drops bouncing off a flat roof below her window. She liked to see the world outside—particularly on Friday and Saturday nights when the entrance to the police station opposite got busy with lights flashing, cars pulling up, and people going in and out.

Soon Hannah had decided that the policemen and women who spent their nights working so hard deserved a treat and asked me to buy them some chocolates. I delivered them one afternoon to a duty sergeant who looked at me in amazement when I gave him Hannah's present. But to her the giving of a gift was a precious link to life, and her desire to be part of it again would almost crackle off her as she slumped back onto her pillows.

Day after day she asked me when she could go home. I didn't know. The dobutamine was not a long-term solution for her heart failure because patients were not kept on it indefinitely. But as it continued to keep her alive I told myself that we just had to keep hoping. Heart failure is not always permanent, and I believed that Hannah could get stronger—just as she had done when her heart first weakened and she was dangerously ill as a child.

I knew how much Hannah missed her school friends, and pupils and staff from St Mary's had sent cards and letters, which I'd stuck across her walls along with those from other friends and family. For Hannah it was a vital reminder of all the people who were thinking of her, and she'd been pleased when I'd told her that a teacher was bringing three of her friends up to Birmingham to visit. Hannah was in a room on the high-dependency unit, and the three girls arrived, bristling with energy and life, to find her lying quietly in bed. Their eyes widened as they saw all the machines that monitored her breathing, pulse and medications. They left after an hour, as Hannah was too exhausted to talk much.

She wasn't improving, and when a month turned into five weeks, then six, I was not surprised when Dr Wright, the cardiologist who had looked after Hannah since she was small, asked to talk to me privately.

'We have been thinking about more long-term options for Hannah,' Dr Wright said. 'Her heart function is so low that we must consider the possibility of some other intervention. If we don't do something, she could die.

That is why I wanted to talk to you about a heart transplant. A successful one could offer Hannah several more years of healthy life. Patients are now surviving postoperatively for ten or twenty years. This is an area of medicine where advances are being made all the time.'

I struggled to understand what Dr Wright meant. I'd nursed patients on transplant units before, and I knew that organs were only given to patients for whom hope was fading. Did he mean that Hannah was one of them?

'You need to think carefully, Mrs Jones,' Dr Wright continued. 'This is something you should consider. I'm afraid that Hannah will not recover without a heart transplant.'

The day after I spoke to Dr Wright, he came back to see me.

'There might be something else we can try,' he told me. 'A multi-site pacemaker. They are usually given to adults, but we think this device might work for Hannah. There is no guarantee, but we have given them to a handful of children and think Hannah might be suitable.'

The pacemaker would strengthen the electrical impulses that governed the contractions of Hannah's heart. While most pacemakers had two wires, a multi-site device contained four—one running into each chamber of the heart—which, unlike other pacemakers, would send out continual electrical impulses. This might help strengthen the muscle tone of Hannah's heart, and although it would take several months until we knew for sure, she could stay on the dobutamine in the meantime.

I wanted to do as Dr Wright suggested. I still felt unsure about a transplant because I wondered if we had quite yet reached this final frontier of hope. A transplant was a place of no return because if it failed there was nothing else that could be done. There were also extra risks for Hannah because the antirejection drugs could trigger a return of her leukaemia. At least the procedure to fit the pacemaker would be far less invasive than a transplant and the postoperative recovery much easier.

Andrew agreed immediately when I phoned him, but both of us knew that the person who would need to be convinced was Hannah. I thought of her lying in bed and wondered how I could tell her she needed surgery, that she wouldn't be able to go home any time soon.

I walked into Hannah's room. All I knew as I sat down beside her was that, if anything was going to help her, then Hannah had to want it to.

'I spoke to Dr Wright today, Han,' I said.

The television was on in the corner of the room and I turned it off as she looked at me.

'You know you're very sick, don't you?' I asked gently. 'Dr Wright thinks you might need something more to help your heart than the dobutamine. He thinks you might need an operation.' I reached out to take her hand.

'What kind?' she asked.

'Either a heart transplant or a pacemaker, which is a little box that sits inside your chest and helps your heart to beat.'

'Which one would work better?'

'No one can be sure, Han. A heart transplant is a big operation and doesn't always work but you could live many years if it did. The doctors aren't certain either that the pacemaker will work but they are willing to try it.'

'How long would I be in hospital if I had a transplant?'

'We can't be certain because it might be a long time if you had to wait for a heart, or it could be just a few weeks.'

'And how long would I be in hospital if I had the pacemaker?'

'I think the operation would take less time to recover from.'

'If the pacemaker doesn't work could I have the transplant?'

'Yes.'

'And if the transplant didn't work could I have the pacemaker?'

'No.'

'And what would happen if I didn't have either?'

I faltered for a second before speaking again. 'You could die.'

She started crying softly. 'But I don't want another operation,' she sobbed. 'I've had enough. I want to go home.'

'I know.' I put my arms round her as she buried her head in my chest.

Hannah pulled away to look at me again, our faces both wet with tears.

'What do you think?' she asked.

I could see how strong the urge inside her was to say no to anything else. Hannah had had enough of hospital, doctors, operations and anaesthetics.

'Whatever you want is fine by me, Han, but I think we should listen when the doctors say you need more than dobutamine,' I said gently. 'I know you don't want an operation but I think we should try.'

Hannah lay back on the pillows, almost too weak to say any more.

'I need to know what you think, Han. If you want to have the pacemaker we can do that, but if you want to have the transplant that's fine too.'

'I'll have the pacemaker,' she said softly.

'Are you sure?'

'Yes. Can I go home when it's done?'

'I hope so, Han.'

DAYS LATER, Hannah went down to theatre to have the pacemaker fitted by a cardiologist called Dr de Giovanni. Andrew and I had been told the procedure should take about two hours, but once again the time dragged by—one hour, two hours, two and a half, three hours, four—until Dr de Giovanni came to see us, his face exhausted and sweat dappling his forehead.

'Hannah is out of theatre but we've had a problem,' he said. 'Her veins and arteries are so narrow that we only managed to get the pacemaker box and one of the wires inserted. We still have to place the other three.'

'But how will you do that?' Andrew asked.

Dr de Giovanni told us he had read about pacemaker wires that had been developed abroad for premature babies. He hoped they might fit Hannah's small veins and arteries but they were not yet being manufactured. Andrew and I waited nervously as an urgent phone call was made and were relieved when the company agreed to make three wires and fly them over to England with a technician to advise the surgical team on how to insert them.

But it would take a couple of weeks until the wires were ready, and for now I had to tell Hannah that she would need another operation.

'We can't go home quite yet,' I told her quietly as we sat together. 'The doctors need to do another operation to put some more wires into the pacemaker because they couldn't do it all today.'

'But I want to go home,' Hannah whispered. 'Please, Mummy. Please.'

'I will take you home when the pacemaker is fitted,' I said softly. 'I will make sure we leave here.'

'OK,' she whispered.

IT TOOK ABOUT ten days for the new pacemaker wires to be flown over to the UK, and Hannah was in surgery for several gruelling hours as they were fitted. When it was finally over she asked once again when she would go home.

At first her doctors were doubtful whether she could be discharged on IV dobutamine. The drug worked directly on her heart so any mistake in administering it could mean life or death for Hannah: she could die if her central line got blocked or the solution was too concentrated or weak. Flushing a line containing the drug was also more complex than anything I'd had to do when she was young, because the dobutamine was so powerful that her condition could deteriorate if she was without it as the line was cleaned. Because of this, I would have to attach her to a second line when I wanted to flush the first one, and switch her between the two at exactly the right time to make sure she received a continuous dose. The drug was also measured in half-millilitres and because of all this only specialist nurses and doctors normally attended lines containing it.

The only thing in my favour as I tried to persuade the doctors was my years of experience as a nurse. I had worked in intensive care looking after cardiac patients in the past and knew I could look after Hannah.

'Are you sure?' her doctors would ask as we talked it over. 'You will be completely responsible for her day and night.'

'I know, but I can do it,' I insisted. 'I want to.'

The doubts in their eyes didn't scare me because I was sure of what I had to do. I felt certain that if Hannah was at home she would be happier, eat better and sleep more comfortably—and those things together would give the pacemaker the best chance of success. The team at Birmingham had done all we could ask for but I had seen Hannah's will at work throughout her childhood and believed it would sustain her again if we went home. I knew there was a risk that Hannah's body might be too weak to keep fighting, but I could not let my own fears overrule her wishes. She was a girl on the cusp of becoming a woman and she knew what she wanted.

I TOOK A deep breath as the door closed and I was left in the room alone. Dr Wright, a specialist from Great Ormond Street, nurses and a social worker had just left to go and talk to Hannah again about a transplant. We were due to leave hospital in just a few days after Dr Wright had agreed to let her go home. But first the people looking after Hannah wanted to make sure that she had had no second thoughts about the transplant.

I understood why they needed to. Ever since a transplant had first been mentioned, the weight of medical opinion was behind it. The pacemaker was an unknown and we would have to wait for several months to see if it was effective. Hannah was so weak that no one could be sure she would have that time, and only a successful transplant could offer her a certain solution. It was the choice most people would have made, and Hannah's decision not to was highly unusual.

The doctors had just spoken to Andrew and me about what a heart transplant would mean: the healthy life that children enjoyed after successful surgery and the fact that half of all heart-transplant patients were still alive ten years after having surgery. But we were also told that a transplanted heart would not last for ever and most patients suffered from chronic long-term rejection, which meant their arteries hardened quicker than usual. A heart transplant could certainly be a gift of many extra years of healthy life, but it was not a certainty or a cure.

I knew Hannah might change her mind today but didn't think she would. She'd been distraught a few days earlier to still be in hospital for her twelfth birthday. But light had at last flickered in her eyes again when Andrew, Oli, Lucy, Phoebe and Andrew's parents had arrived to celebrate and Hannah had sat on her bed wearing a crown with the words 'Birthday Girl' spelled out in glittering pink stones, surrounded by the people she loved. She would soon return to them after three long months away.

In some ways I didn't think Hannah was strong enough to cope with so many strangers asking her such an important question. But I also knew the doctors had to be sure she wasn't being pressed into saying no to a transplant. I wanted them to understand that Hannah knew her own mind, which was why I trusted her to make this decision.

When Hannah was young, I'd done what I thought was best for her. But now she knew for herself, and however closely I had walked by Hannah's side I had not walked in her shoes: she was the person who had lived with this for so long—and now could die with it too. If a transplant was too high a price for her to pay then I would accept that, however hard it was for me. Most importantly, I knew that I could not force her to have an operation she did not want or make her live on my terms.

CHAPTER NINE

Face Your Fears

Hannah

Doctors from Great Ormond Street came to see me about a transplant. They talked to me for ages and I understood what they were saying. I've had to think about my body all my life and knew they meant that I wouldn't get better without a transplant. But I didn't want to see any more doctors or have anyone else looking in on my life. I'd had enough of that.

Dad was with me when the doctors showed me pictures of children who'd had successful transplants. But they also told me there was a risk that my body could reject the heart and I'd need to take medicines for ever to stop that happening. So it seemed to me that there were good and bad bits about a transplant, but I knew what I wanted. I'd listened to the doctors carefully but was sure a transplant wasn't for me: it involved too many risks and I might be worse off than before. I didn't want that but most of all I wanted to be at home, not in a hospital bed. I'd spent long enough in one of those and wanted to be somewhere I could smell fresh air and see the sun, hear Oli, Lucy and Phoebe playing and see Mum and Dad. I didn't want to be stuck in hospital even longer having an operation that might not even work. I wanted to live my life. So I told the doctors what I wanted.

They were a bit shocked. But I thought of the drains, the medicines and the biopsies and knew I'd rather go home than have all of those again. I wanted to be where I was happy even though I understood I might die.

But it was hard choosing because I didn't know what would happen if I said no—whether I'd be told off or forced into having it. But I didn't want anyone interfering in my decision or for Mum and Dad to make it for me. I knew they could if I wanted them to, but what would happen if it turned out wrong and they felt guilty if I died? I didn't want that to happen.

It's not up to me to say that all children should choose for themselves like I did because they might not want to—they might want their parents to do it for them. But I wanted to choose and I'm glad my mum and dad let me.

I'm glad my mum trusts me too because if she didn't then I'd feel like I wasn't important. Another reason I wanted to choose was because if we all relied on our parents too much then we wouldn't learn anything.

So I'm glad Mum trusted me and I'm happy she and Dad let me decide for myself. I didn't say no to the transplant because I was scared. I thought about everything and decided. I'm not going to give up without a fight.

Kirsty

When the doctors had gone, I opened the door to Hannah's room and walked inside. 'What did they say, Han?' I asked as I sat down beside her.

'They talked to me about a transplant,' she said, her voice quiet but steady. 'They asked if I would like one. They say my life might be shorter if I don't have the transplant. But I don't want to take a heart that someone else wants more than me. It's better they give it to a child who really wants it, Mummy.'

I took her hand. 'I want you to know that Mummy and Daddy support your decision, but if you ever decide that you want us to choose for you or change your mind then we'll take you straight down to Great Ormond Street. You must always remember that.'

'I won't. The doctors don't know everything, Mummy. I proved them wrong when I was little, and I'll do it again. I'll get better.'

THE PAGE WAS livid red as I stared at it, the colour of danger. It was a document formalising Hannah's decision, and its bright red urgency was an immediately identifiable signal to anyone looking at her medical notes. The 'Do Not Resuscitate' order was a legally binding instruction which explained that if Hannah's heart failed she was not to be artificially resuscitated. There would be no ventilators, defibrillators or respirators. She would be allowed to die naturally if her heart gave up its fight. Hannah's decision to say no to a transplant had signalled to everyone involved in her care that she was prepared to die. She knew it was a possibility, and now, if the worst happened, no one would fight to bring her back.

Even as the wheels had ground into motion for giving Hannah palliative care at home—the kind given to relieve symptoms rather than cure a life-threatening illness—I'd resisted thinking about her possible death. And as she was assigned a social worker to liaise with home support services and given a place at Acorns Children's Hospice on the outskirts of Worcester, I'd told myself that Hannah's life was limited but her illness was not definitely terminal. Even so, when I met Dr Wright a few days before we left hospital, I knew I had to ask the question I'd been putting off.

'How long do you think she has?' I asked him as we sat together.

He looked at me steadily. 'Nothing is certain, but if I had to I would say Hannah has three months, possibly six.'

My tears ran slowly at first, coming thicker and faster as I shook, physically shocked at hearing out loud what I almost knew, and an even greater urgency to take Hannah home filled me. The only thing I could be sure of was that I would help Hannah to live as she wanted and make sure she was happy while I hoped for a miracle. Other people might think we were going home to die, but I knew that we were not.

What gave me the strength to sustain this tussle between realism and hope? Hannah. She had taught me to seize the day and embrace it. She had made a choice and now I would live it with her. Hannah was so much more than her illness. We would let each day unfold one by one as we gleaned as much pleasure as possible from them.

After the Great Ormond Street team had come to see her, I'd talked to Hannah again about her decision. But while I wanted her to understand what it meant, I didn't want her to be afraid of death, counting down time instead of enjoying it. I wanted her to be positive, because if she didn't have that then there was little else for us to cling onto. Everything concrete was stacked against Hannah. But life isn't just about what we can see, measure and touch, it is about how we feel, and being positive would not only help Hannah to enjoy her life but would maybe prolong it.

'They don't know it all, do they, Mum?' she'd say. 'I'll get better when I go home, won't I?'

'I hope so, darling.'

'The doctors think I might die, but they don't know, do they?'

'Not always, Han. We need to let your pacemaker settle so we're going home to enjoy ourselves and we'll see what happens.'

The only concern Hannah expressed was that I would not be able to cope with her at home because her care was still very intensive.

'I don't want to make you work too hard,' she would tell me.

'I will have lots of help and we can go to Acorns for a rest. I don't want you to worry that looking after you is too difficult for me. It never will be.'

A few days later we left hospital and arrived at Acorns, where we were going to stay for two weeks as a transition from hospital to home. Hannah was stretchered inside and I walked beside her into the 'hub' area at the building's heart. It was a light room with windows along one side which opened into the garden. Shelves lined with films and books filled one wall and there were huge sofas covered in cushions. It was a home from home.

Running off the hub were the kitchen and dining area, an art room and more windows overlooking a play area. Two corridors led to the hospice's bedrooms, and the whole building was full of light and colour. But it was in Hannah's bedroom that the thoughtfulness of the care at Acorns was most obvious. The soft duvet had been made up with a pink cover, just as the staff knew she liked, and a lavender bag hand-embroidered with the letter 'H' was lying on her pillow. Pink roses stood in a jar on the bedside table, and a door opened onto the garden. Through large windows Hannah could see the sun shining, grass, flowers and sky, and as she was put into bed a shard of the worry that had made her face drawn for so long began to fade.

'It's beautiful, Mummy,' she said as she looked around. 'Oli, Lucy and Phoebe can visit me now. When are they coming?'

'Tomorrow, I think. Daddy too.'

'I can't wait to see them.'

Over the next few days we settled in at Acorns, and the help and support offered by everyone there soothed both Hannah and me. After months in hospital, little things meant a great deal—soft carpet, newly washed clothes, doors wide enough to let wheelchairs pass through easily, and fresh food served by the half-spoonful to tempt a sick child. Most important of all, though, was being in a place surrounded by people who either had a sick child or were expert in dealing with life-limiting conditions.

We had been due to stay at Acorns for two weeks but ended up staying a month after floods made roads impassable and shut down electricity supplies. Hannah was content but still wanted to make the final journey back home. I drove there one day to get Hannah's room ready before stopping off for petrol on the way back to the hospice.

'What do you think you're doing?' a man shouted, as I got out of the car in a daze. 'You've come in the wrong way. You've jumped the queue.'

'I'm sorry,' I said. 'I didn't realise.'

'Well, that's no use to me, is it? Move your car.'

I looked at him blankly, unable to understand how someone could get so angry about something so small. But I said nothing as the man let his anger stream out of him. I knew more than ever now that some battles weren't worth fighting. But there were some I would do anything to win.

I COULD SEE their faces as we turned into the drive. Andrew, Oli, Lucy and Phoebe were watching at a window for us, waiting for us to come home, and the children ran outside as I pulled up the car.

'Mummy!' Phoebe cried, and I lifted her into my arms. 'Where have you been? Grandma has bought me a bag of clothes and I want to show you.'

She carried on chatting, a stream of words tumbling out of her mouth, as Lucy pulled open Hannah's door.

'You're here!' she exclaimed. 'We've got a DVD and Dad has got pizza.'

Hannah smiled as her sisters chatted and Oli stood quietly, trying to get a word in edgeways but unable to find a gap in the girls' excitement.

'Welcome home,' Andrew said with a smile.

He reached into the car to put his arms round Hannah and she blinked in the sunlight as he lifted her out. She looked pale and slight in her father's arms. The dobutamine line peeped out of her jumper and a nasogastric tube ran under her nose. Reaching into the car, I took out her syringe driver and followed Andrew as he started carrying Hannah inside.

'We've done lots to your room,' Lucy cried. 'We've got you flowers too.'

The children crowded behind us as Andrew carried Hannah to her room. Pointing out the welcome banners they'd made and the pictures they'd painted for their sister, the children talked excitedly as Andrew sat Hannah down on the edge of the bed and she looked around.

'My room smells nice,' she said, and smiled.

Her hands flitted up to her face, curling round her nose and mouth. It was a gesture Hannah made whenever she was happy or excited, and I hadn't seen her do it for so long. She was happy. She was home.

LUCY SAT beside Hannah, who was lying on her bed stroking Tails McFluff. The sun was shining outside and I'd just opened Hannah's bedroom window to let the smell of early autumn into the room. I'd just changed her sheets and brought a pair of warm pyjamas from the kitchen where I'd ironed them. Lucy was chatting to Hannah as I left them again.

'Did I tell you what Mr Minty did yesterday?' I could hear her say. 'He tried to buck me off after clearing a three-foot jump, but I didn't let him!'

The girls giggled and I smiled to myself.

This was how Hannah had spent most of her time since coming home from Acorns. Still weak, she struggled with the side effects of the drugs she was taking and often had diarrhoea or sickness. The medication also affected her eyesight so she couldn't read and got bad headaches.

But, even so, Hannah was part of our family life again: she could hear the door bang when Lucy went out to ride her pony, a shout of triumph as Oli won his computer game, or Phoebe's cries as she played. The girls in particular brought the outside in to Hannah. Lucy came home from riding with brightly coloured leaves or a handful of blackberries, while Phoebe literally dug her heels in to get fresh flowers for her sister.

'Stop!' she'd shouted one day as she left the house for school. 'Look!' She was pointing to tiny crocuses that had flowered overnight on the lawn.

A taxi was waiting to take her to school because I couldn't leave Hannah.

'She won't be long,' I said to the driver

Phoebe picked the flowers and put them in an egg cup. 'Look what God grew for you last night,' she said to Hannah, who smiled when she saw the purple splashes that spoke of a new season.

Moments like this made Hannah happy, just as stroking the cat or eating a morsel of food she particularly liked did, and it comforted me to know that pleasure found in the tiniest moments can make a life worth living.

Our days were unpredictable. On good ones, Hannah could get out of bed while I carried the heavy syringe driver containing her dobutamine so that she could watch some television in the lounge or just sit with us. Within a couple of months of coming home she'd also started going to the local hospital school for a few hours on the morning of days when she felt well enough.

Otherwise our routine was like it had been when Hannah came home following the chemotherapy. I was with her constantly—giving her medication every two hours from 7 a.m. to 10 p.m. and checking on her throughout the night. District nurses visited every day, but they could only do observations or check up on Hannah rather than care for her. So other than the hours when she was at hospital school, it would be three months before I could leave Hannah in someone else's care. When nurses trained to look after the dobutamine started making a four-hour round trip from Bristol three times a week, I was finally able to do the school run, catch up on washing and look after the thousand details of caring for everyone.

Once again, looking after my well children and a sick one was more of a juggling act than a properly executed plan. Oli, Lucy and Phoebe learned that on days when Hannah was poorly, my attention was focused on her and we all switched into 'sick' mode—Phoebe sitting in front of the television, Lucy getting her sister ready for bed or preparing some simple food and Oli helping out as well. On a day when Hannah was barely conscious, he had helped me carry her to the bathroom, where he'd sat with her as she lay in the water, quietly keeping watch over his big sister, while I went to change her sheets. He was just ten years old, and his quiet kindness humbled me.

There were times when I wanted to split myself in two so that I could look after everyone. But if Hannah was short of breath or in pain, my physical presence was the only thing that reassured her. Some nights felt like for ever as I sat with her and waited to see if her body would win or lose its fight, and these were the only moments when Hannah became scared.

'I'm frightened, Mummy,' she would moan breathlessly as her hands reached out for me.

On nights like those the question of a transplant would press into the front of my thoughts again, and I would talk to Hannah about it when she had recovered a little.

'You know you can always change your mind about the transplant, don't you, Han? And if you decide you want it I can let the doctors know.'

'I don't,' she would tell me before turning over, signalling to me that she didn't want to talk about it any more.

I wasn't the only one who asked her. Many of the professionals we came into contact with—doctors, specialists, nurses, carers and a social worker—questioned Hannah about the transplant, and I understood why. But it also frustrated me because I wanted Hannah's choice to be respected, not doubted. I wished people could accept it.

'I don't want to talk about it any more,' she would tell me. 'Why does everyone keep asking?'

'Because they want to be sure that you know you can change your mind.'

'But I do,' Hannah would say. 'I want everyone to stop asking.'

But after a particularly bad night or day, Hannah would stabilise and I would breathe a sigh of relief as our life slipped back into the pattern we had created. When the children were at school I would do household jobs before sitting in Hannah's room to brush her hair or read stories until everyone else came home and Oli, Lucy or Phoebe tumbled into her room to chat. On the Sundays when Hannah felt well, Andrew took us all to the pub, which was an outing she particularly loved.

We were all pleased to be together again, and each of my children told me how they felt: Oli, by sitting closer as we watched TV, and Phoebe, by hanging on to me for a moment longer than necessary as we cuddled.

But, as ever, it was Lucy who was the most outspoken. 'It's lovely to have you home,' she said. 'I missed you and Hannah when you weren't here.'

I WAS SITTING OUTSIDE with my friend Lindy. It was about 1 a.m., and although it was cold, we'd been sitting out here ever since I'd finally got Hannah to sleep. Lindy had understood when I'd called to ask her to come over and had waited for me to come downstairs before handing me a mug of tea.

'Did I tell you who I saw at the horse sales?' she said, and slipped into a stream of chatter as I sipped.

This was what Lindy always gave me—a comforting glimpse of the everyday world which I needed after a particularly dark day. She told me about the village, school and any gossip she'd heard as I sat with my thoughts. Lindy had lost her husband and knew what it was like to grieve—the aching emptiness, the physical feeling of heaviness that filled me on days when Hannah was at her weakest and I knew how close we were to the edge of the unknown. In the rush of emergency I could lose myself in practical tasks. But when Hannah was stable again and asleep, my fears crept out of the darkest corners of my mind and I cried as I sat outside and stared up at a dark sky, trying to make sense of it all.

There were moments now when I was more afraid than I ever had been, and I felt very alone after leaving the safety of the hospital. I was the one who sat with Hannah and gave her pain relief or turned on her oxygen to help ease her breathing when her skin went grey. Andrew was often away with work during the week, and although I knew I could call him at any time, it was hard to know when to phone to say that Hannah was dangerously ill. It happened frequently, and Andrew was working hard to support us all and his efforts outside the home were as important as mine within it.

When Andrew was away I almost dreaded the quiet hours when Hannah had finally fallen asleep and the house was quiet. So I would call Lindy and we would sit together—sometimes talking about small, everyday things, at others quietly discussing some of my doubts and fears.

Hannah never spoke about her fears, but I knew what they were because I shared them. Being told that your child might die is something that takes just a few seconds; accepting it is a process that never ends. The thing that scared me most was the thought of Hannah suffering. I wanted her to feel peaceful and unafraid whatever happened.

'Dying is like going to sleep,' I told her one night. 'It doesn't hurt. I'll be with you. I'll always be here.'

But I was afraid that I wouldn't be strong enough for her.

Lindy didn't speak as she slipped her hand over mine. She would wait until I felt ready to talk. For now we would sit together. Just like Hannah, it comforted me to have someone close by.

HANNAH WAS LYING unconscious. I was waiting to see if she would stir, wondering if now was the day, hour or minute when I would lose her. Three days ago she had suddenly and severely deteriorated, and I'd phoned the doctor in the middle of the night. Hannah had been put onto morphine, but even with it she was still distressed and I'd asked if she wanted to go to Acorns.

'Yes, Mummy,' she'd replied, her face drawn. 'I'm very tired now.'

An ambulance had brought us here, and within hours Hannah had fallen unconscious. The days had blurred one into another, hours slipping by in the silence of the room as I talked to Hannah, telling her what we were going to do at Christmas, just a few days away.

'Will Hannah wake up soon, Mummy?' Phoebe had asked when Andrew, Oli, Lucy and Phoebe had arrived to see us earlier that day.

'I don't know, darling,' I replied.

They left the room to go to the Acorns carol service and I stood up as I heard the music start. Walking down the corridor, I went into the hub and stood beside them as the first carol was sung. Phoebe slipped her hand into mine. It felt warm, solid, and I thought of Hannah lying so quietly.

'Are there any children too sick to be here today?' a woman who had played the harp asked as the concert came to an end.

'My sister is asleep in her room,' Lucy told her. 'I think she'd like to hear a carol. She likes music very much.'

'Do you know what carol she would like?' the woman asked gently.

Lucy thought for a moment. 'Little Town of Bethlehem.'

We walked with the harpist to Hannah's room and stood round the bed.

Soon the sound of the music filled the room. I thought of the notes, weaving their way into the darkest recesses of Hannah's mind as she lay unconscious. Would they tell her that Christmas was nearly here?

I will never know if she heard the music or not, but within twenty-four hours Hannah started moving. Over the next day she woke up gradually.

'Is it Christmas yet?' she asked drowsily when she could finally speak.

'No. Not yet.'

'My presents.'

I thought of them lying in shopping bags underneath her bed.

'They're waiting for you, Han. They're still where you left them.'

'I need to wrap them,' she said, her voice weak but audible.

Late on Christmas Eve, we arrived home to find that Andrew, Oli, Lucy and Phoebe had decorated a tiny tree in the corner of Hannah's bedroom. They had also strung fairy lights round her window, which shone as she sat, propped up on pillows in bed the next morning, while Oli, Lucy and Phoebe opened the presents she'd given them.

'Thanks, Hannah,' Oli said as he looked at his Nintendo game. 'Shall we do yours for you?'

They all started ripping paper as Hannah watched and a weak smile stole across her face. Later that day she got out of bed for long enough to join us at Christmas lunch, unable to eat but wanting to be part of the day. I hurriedly had my food before carrying her into the sitting room, where we sat together. Drops of coloured light shone on the Christmas tree and bounced off the tinsel strewn all over it. All I could do was wonder at the strength of spirit that had brought her home to us. Hannah's determination to carry on living had willed her back from the very edges of life.

THE PHONE RANG as darkness fell on a Friday afternoon in late January 2008. The day before, I'd taken Hannah into Hereford Hospital, where she'd had an echocardiogram to check her progress after coming off the dobutamine. She'd wanted to stop taking it because the heavy syringe driver made it impossible to do something as simple as get a drink or reach up to get a book from a shelf.

It wasn't the life that she'd wanted when she'd decided to come home. dobutamine wasn't a long-term treatment for her heart failure, and it was six months since she'd left hospital. So at a meeting attended by doctors, nurses and social workers involved in her care, it was agreed to let Hannah come off the drug, and a few days ago I'd taken her into hospital where the dobutamine had been slowly reduced as her vital statistics were monitored.

It was an anxious twenty-four hours, but Hannah's pulse had stayed exactly where it was, her breathing was easy and she was pain free. It was now a question of taking it day by day, and although no one knew exactly how Hannah was coping without the dobutamine—whether the pacemaker had strengthened her heart muscles or her body had just learned to deal with such low cardiac function—it was clear that she was indeed coping.

But yesterday we'd seen a locum doctor we didn't know well for a follow-up scan, and the question had been raised whether she wanted to go back onto the dobutamine. I didn't understand why this doctor was asking about it again, so I'd confronted him angrily after Hannah had left the room.

'This has only just been decided,' I told him. 'I don't understand why you are questioning her.'

I had gone home simmering that this doctor seemed unable to accept a decision so many people had agreed on. But we were having Oli's birthday party at the weekend and by the next day I'd almost forgotten the locum doctor as I walked to pick up the phone when it rang.

'Mrs Jones,' a voice said. 'I'm sorry to call late but the doctor you saw yesterday has some concerns about Hannah.'

'What do you mean? She's here with me and she's fine.'

'He'd like to see her again.'

'But we came in yesterday. It's late, it's cold. I don't want to make her go out again.'

'So you don't want to bring Hannah back in?'

'No. I don't. She's fine. We can come in next week if you need us to.'

Soon Andrew arrived home, and it must have been about 5 p.m. when the phone rang again. I walked into the living room to see the colour draining from Andrew's face as he spoke.

'No,' he kept saying again and again. 'She's here. We're fine.'

'It was the hospital,' he said. 'They want us to take Hannah back in to start the dobutamine again. If we don't agree they're thinking of applying for a court order to make sure Hannah is treated. They said she could be forcibly removed from our care.'

A court order? How could this be? Hannah was doing well without the dobutamine. How could people talk about Hannah's choice and now try to foist another on her? My hands shook as adrenaline rushed through me.

'We need a lawyer,' Andrew said.

We started searching through phone books. But late on a Friday evening answering machines clicked on at the end of every number we tried.

I slammed down the phone. The children knew something was wrong because my friend Tina had come over to look after them.

The phone rang and I snatched the receiver.

'Kirsty?' a voice said.

It was a nurse we knew well and who Hannah liked.

'A bed has been prepared for Hannah,' she told me, and my hands started shaking. 'But if an ambulance is sent for her with the police, I've offered to come with it so at least Hannah will see a face she knows.'

I thought of the hospital managers and lawyers, locked in rooms discussing the case of a girl they didn't know. Maybe I should have been afraid all along that something like this would happen. Maybe I should have prepared myself for it because I had always known that there were those who couldn't under-stand Hannah's choice—and my support of it perhaps even more so. Over the past few months, I had looked into eyes that had silently questioned me at best, accused me at worst. The doctors who knew Hannah well—like Dr Wright at Birmingham and Dr Meyrick at Hereford—had always respected our decisions. But on a few occasions I'd seen distrust deep in a person's gaze and had to steel myself against their doubts. What kind of woman did these people see? A mother who wanted her child to die?

I understood how people who did not know us could wonder why I did not coax my child into having an operation that could give her years of good health. But Hannah knew what she wanted and I knew that I could never force her to have an operation she didn't agree to. Neither I, nor her doctors at Birmingham or Great Ormond Street, would countenance that.

But not everyone knew us as well as they did, and how to explain years of ill health and dashed hopes to strangers who didn't know our story? How to encapsulate in neat conversation the experience of watching Hannah during all this time and understanding why she had had enough of hospital? How to describe the experience of learning that what she wanted was the most important thing? Not my grief, dreams or fears, but Hannah's wishes?

Late in the evening the hospital rang back. After talking to Great Ormond Street, who had explained how vital both Hannah's and our views were, the hospital had decided not to seek a court order that night. It was a comfort to know that Great Ormond Street was speaking reason, but I knew I had to agree when the hospital asked if a child-protection nurse could come to see Hannah the next day before the matter was reconsidered by a barrister acting for the health authority on Monday morning.

CHAPTER TEN

Know Your Strength

Hannah

I didn't like the look of the doctor we went to see just before the hospital decided a court might have to take me away, and that never helps. You have to like someone to trust them, and he looked stern to me. Like a traffic warden who wants to stick a ticket on your car. So I went home thinking I didn't like him. I was in my bedroom when Mum told me the hospital said they might make me go back. I cried when I found out. I didn't understand why the hospital wanted to make me have the dobutamine again, but when I asked Mum if she'd make sure they didn't she only said that she'd do her best. I knew it meant that she wasn't sure she'd be able to, because when Mum knows she can do something she always says 'Yes'.

That's why I felt nervous when the nurse came to talk to me. Mum, Dad, Grandma and Grandpa were in the kitchen, but it was just me with the hospital woman for the talk. We sat in my bedroom for an hour as she asked me questions. I found it hard to talk about it all again. But it was easy in another way because I can't always say all the things that are in my head if I'm with someone I know. I don't want someone I like or love to feel sad about what I say, so it was good that I didn't know the hospital woman because I could tell her everything I felt about the operation and anaesthetic, needles and drains. How boring it was in hospital, how much I wanted to be able to do what I wanted at home, why I didn't want to go back on the dobutamine or have a transplant even though I knew I could die. I also told her that I didn't want Mum and Dad to decide for me and I was happy to be off the dobutamine because the syringe driver was so heavy that I couldn't move anywhere.

When she left Mum came in and told me the woman had said I was 'remarkable'. But Mum said we had to wait until a judge decided what was to happen. It was horrible not knowing. I couldn't stop thinking about it.

Kirsty

It was about 11 a.m. on the Monday morning when the phone finally rang.

'Mrs Jones?'

My hands began to shake as I heard the child-protection nurse's voice.

'Yes.'

'The hospital's legal advisers have met and a decision has been reached,' she said. 'They know that Hannah is very clear about not wanting to go back on the dobutamine or have a transplant. She is sure of what she wants, and because of this no more legal action will be taken.'

I felt relieved at first, but then angry as Hannah cried when I told her the news. And when the child-protection nurse came back to see us I asked for letters of apology to be written to the children because I did not want any of them to worry it might happen again in the future.

But the pointlessness of the hospital's actions had been proved every day since because Hannah had got stronger after coming off the dobutamine, slowly gaining stamina as the weeks passed, and starting to get out of bed on more days than she did not. I believed it was partly because she could move around more and also eat properly now that she was free of the dobutamine syringe driver. Mostly, though, I was sure it was down to contentment as Hannah challenged herself to do more, and began to learn the new limits of her body after being so weak for so long.

THE HORSE LORRY shuddered as it came to a stop, and I jumped out.

'We've got to hurry!' I called to Lucy. 'We won't get you entered in all your classes if we don't do it soon.'

Lucy, strangely slow today, didn't seem to want to get out of the lorry.

'Will you catch me up?' I called as I got out and started walking towards the indoor school where the jumping competition was being held.

We were at a riding school fifteen miles from our home. Andrew was at home with Hannah, Oli and Phoebe. But as I walked I heard giggles behind me and turned to see Lucy walking to join me—with Hannah by her side.

'What are you doing here?' I asked. 'Did Daddy bring you?'

'No!' shrieked Hannah. 'I hid! I was in the bed right above your head!'

With peals of laughter, they explained how Lucy had helped Hannah hide under a duvet in the lorry's sleeping area.

I didn't have any oxygen with me, and for a moment I wondered what might happen if Hannah got short of breath. But I didn't want to spoil the moment as I looked at her expectant face.

'You won't send me home, will you?' Hannah asked, suddenly anxious as she realised that I might be angry. 'You won't phone Daddy?'

'Doesn't he know you're here?'

'No.'

'I think I'd better tell him, don't you?'

I rang home to let Andrew know where Hannah was, and the girls looked at me hopefully as I finished the call.

'Hannah can stay,' I said, and they cheered. 'But you have to promise that you'll never stow away again. Daddy was really worried.'

'We promise,' they cried.

I was not completely surprised that Hannah had dared to make this trip: she probably had four good days when she was up and about each week now, and I was pretty sure that Lucy had also encouraged her. For the first time in many months Hannah's illness completely receded into the background of our everyday life. Lucy entered her jumping classes and returned to us clutching rosettes while Hannah organised her—helping her fill out entry forms and sitting clutching a wooden spoon with a number on it to make sure the chips she ordered for them during breaks arrived safely.

'Isn't this great?' Hannah said, as she turned to me late in the day. 'I want to come all the time from now on, Mum.'

Lucy started laughing as she looked at Hannah who, in her eagerness to eat her chips, had smeared her face with ketchup.

'You are so greedy!' Lucy exclaimed.

'You can talk!' Hannah cried.

As I looked at them I thought of the precious lesson I had learnt with them during recent months: that focusing on the good in life, the here and now, can give you a strength you never knew was there. Children can quickly cast off unhappiness, and they had taught me to do the same. Hannah had refused to let her illness define her. And, as I looked at her laughing with Lucy, I knew there was joy to be found in even the most ordinary moments—a streak of sunshine in a grey sky, the sound of laughter or the sight of a sister's face smeared with ketchup.

BY LATE 2008 Hannah had started doing two mornings a week at school. Too tired to manage it most of the time, she went in on the days when she felt strong enough, and her teachers at St Mary's did everything possible to help her—including reorganising Hannah's class timetable for the first three lessons of the day to make sure they were downstairs. She loved being part of school life again, however irregularly, and Simone would push her in a wheelchair from class to class as they chatted.

Other than school, Hannah continued to go to Acorns once a month, which had become a much-loved second home, and when she was well enough she helped me cook supper, groom the horses and even went to the dentist—something she hadn't done for years. Hannah's determination to live life to the full was proved every day.

It was more than a year now since she had left hospital, and Hannah had achieved the almost impossible—she was stronger, the pacemaker was doing its job, and although her heart function remained at just 10 per cent, her body had somehow adapted. But while she was still adamant whenever the subject of the transplant was mentioned, no one could be sure when the spell that was keeping her strong might break. So when a charity offered us a once-in-a-lifetime opportunity, I knew we had to take it.

Caudwell Children were taking forty children to Disney World Florida—a place we could never have visited without the paramedics, volunteers and doctors who would accompany the party—and at first I wasn't sure if Hannah was strong enough for such a long flight. But after talking to Dr Wright we decided that this was a unique opportunity for us as a family.

Shortly before we were due to leave, though, I got a phone call to say that Hannah was the only child on the trip who had been refused insurance. Every company approached had told Caudwell she was too big a risk.

When the charity asked if they could issue a press release appealing for help, I agreed. I just hoped that a small piece in a local paper might encourage someone to put up the surety the insurance company needed to cover Hannah, and an article soon appeared in a couple of local papers.

After the first story appeared, we were contacted by a news agency who asked to do another, and I agreed, thinking that the more coverage Hannah's plight got, the greater the chances of persuading someone to help with the insurance. As the journalist interviewed Hannah and me, we talked of all that had happened—the leukaemia, her decision about the transplant and the legal action that had been dropped—and thought nothing more of it.

A couple of days later I left Hannah at home with a carer while I went to drop Oli, Lucy and Phoebe off at school and arrived home to find cars and vans parked all along the country lane where we lived. I saw people holding cameras and others talking into mobile phones. There was even a van with a satellite dish parked on the side of the road, and as I pulled the car onto the drive and got out a woman rushed at me with a microphone.

'Mrs Jones?' she said, and I stared at her, unsure of what to say or do.

The group of reporters moved forward like a swarm as they pushed towards me. Cameras started clicking, microphones were switched on.

'Yes,' I said.

'I'd like to talk to you about Hannah's decision. The transplant.'

'We want to talk about Hannah's decision to say no to a transplant—her right to die,' another voice said as the cameras got closer. '

It was the start of a media storm. The story of Hannah's decision was covered by every newspaper and television station in the UK, as well as the world. Television stations and newspapers from Spain, Germany, Australia, Russia and France to Norway, Portugal, America, South Africa and New Zealand covered the story, and Hannah's choice sparked a furious debate about a child's ability to make such an important decision.

The phone rang every minute of every day, interview requests poured in, and I allowed Hannah to do some because she was so excited at the thought of being filmed and photographed by newspapers and television. I also felt quietly proud that she could speak her mind so eloquently, and the coverage seemed like a tribute to her stoicism and bravery. If Hannah's decision inspired another parent to have the courage to make the right one for their child, even if it meant going against the collective wisdom, then she would make a mark on the world few children had the opportunity to create.

Soon letters were pouring through our door, some simply addressed to *Hannah the girl with the poorly heart*, written by ordinary people who had been moved by her bravery. On some days ten letters arrived, on others there were as many as eighty, and we ended up receiving more than a thousand. Hannah wanted to reply to them all, and on one single day we wrote 120 letters of thanks.

But I was unprepared for the storm of controversy her decision would create as journalists, commentators and the general public debated her decision in the pages of newspapers, on television and on internet sites. Although there was mostly an upswell of support for Hannah's choice, there were those who didn't think she should have been able to make it.

Negative reactions aside, though, the publicity did what I'd hoped it would, and soon an anonymous company had agreed to put up the money for Hannah's insurance. Their kindness, and that of everyone who supported Caudwell Children, gave us a unique experience, because the real world seemed another place when we flew to Disney World in December.

HOWEVER MANY MEMORIES I was given during the two precious years after Hannah left hospital having had the pacemaker, I still couldn't feel grateful when I began to realise that time might be running out. In May, Hannah had a scan at Birmingham that showed her heart function was slightly lowered, and I greedily wished that the world could stop and leave us where we were. I'd always known this might happen but I didn't feel ready for it.

I told myself that maybe this was a blip, maybe Hannah's heart function would increase by the time we went back for another scan in three months. Although weaker, she was still up and about and looking forward to a trip we were making in a few days to a horse show that Lucy was competing at. I felt unsure about whether to allow her after the scan because we would be away for the weekend, which would take a lot out of her. But as she excitedly prepared with Lucy, I couldn't bring myself to dash her hopes.

As I feared, though, the journey exhausted Hannah, and she had to go to bed by the time we arrived. She and Lucy had planned to sleep in the alcove above the driver's seat, but she wasn't strong enough to get up the ladder to it, so I settled her down to sleep on a camp bed, covered in blankets.

The rest of the weekend was the same—trying to keep things as normal as possible, but sensing that something was changing. Hannah had had bad days before, but they were getting more frequent and took longer to recover from. It was a week before she was out of bed again. I was desperate to keep positive but knew that a day would come when Hannah's will was no longer enough to sustain her heart—and I feared it would be soon.

'WOULD YOU LIKE some oxygen?' I asked Hannah as she prepared to sleep.

'No,' she insisted.

'Just have it on for a while. I'll turn it off later when I go up to bed.'

'I'm fine, Mum. It's uncomfortable. I can't sleep with the line on. It hisses.'

It was six weeks since the horse show, and Hannah had been getting slowly weaker. The changes were so small that someone who didn't know her well might hardly notice them. But I did. Each extra hour in bed, each additional dose of antidiuretics or anticoagulants told me her heart was weakening.

I bent to kiss her and turn off her light, knowing that when she finally fell asleep I would creep back into her room and switch on the oxygen cylinder. Then I would push a mask as close to Hannah's face as I dared without waking her up and switch it off a few hours later so that she would never know what I had done. I wanted her to have the few moments of possible relief that the oxygen might give her even if she didn't.

The question of a transplant was hanging heavier in the air around us than it had for months. The longer she had been at home, the more important it had become to me that if she lost her fight she would do it peacefully in a place she loved. I felt afraid that if she had the operation she might reject the heart and die in hospital. But another part of me understood why Hannah might change her mind. Two years ago in hospital she had been too weak and afraid, too tired of being ill, to say yes. Now she had seen life again, tasted all it had to offer and might feel ready to make a new decision.

I wanted to know what Hannah was thinking, sensed that the transplant was in her mind again, but was afraid to push her and make her feel pressured to have one. She was still adamant every time it was mentioned, but I knew she had been talking to a paediatric nurse who had started visiting. It wasn't until late June that she spoke to me as I sat on her bedroom floor while she rested and we watched television together.

'Mum?' she asked. 'I have been thinking about the transplant. About things like the medicines and how long I'd be in hospital. I think I'd like to go and see the doctors at Great Ormond Street.'

'OK, darling,' I replied softly, fear and relief welling up inside me.

THE COLOURS GLARED on the screen. Hannah and I were at Great Ormond Street and had talked to a transplant nurse about what the operation would entail if Hannah decided to have it. Now a consultant was giving her a heart scan and Hannah lay on a bed as the probe was run over her chest.

I stared at the image of her heart. Blood rushed blue and red across the screen as the valves on the left side of her heart pumped weakly.

But the ones on the right were not moving at all. Those valves were still.

When the scan was finished, I pushed Hannah out of the room in her wheelchair before stopping in the corridor. 'I just want to ask the doctor a couple of questions, Han,' I said. 'I won't be a minute.'

I left her with a nurse as I walked back to see the doctor.

'How bad is it?' I asked him quietly.

'Very,' he said. 'Hannah's heart is very, very weak. In fact the right side of it is not working at all. There is also a very significant area of clotting at the top of Hannah's heart, which is pooling at the bottom of it. I'm afraid that one of those clots could break off at any moment.'

'What would happen if it did?'

'Hannah could go into arrhythmia because the beat of her heart would be affected, which might make her fall unconscious or cause her chest pain. The other possibility is that she could suffer a catastrophic stroke.'

'How long does she have?' I asked eventually.

'It's her fourteenth birthday next week, isn't it? I can't say for sure that she will not see it, but I am certain she won't make her fifteenth.'

A thousand contradictions filled me—my mind clicking into practicalities like morphine and oxygen, anything to make sure that Hannah did not suffer—even as I wanted to run into the corridor and plead with her to have the transplant.

'If Hannah decides to go ahead with the transplant then we will need to know straight away,' the doctor said. 'You must also know that if she leaves it too long and her other organs begin to fail then she would not qualify for a new heart even if she changes her mind.'

HANNAH WAS WALKING OUT of her bedroom as I opened the door.

'Can I have a word with you, darling?' I asked, and she stopped.

It was the day after we'd been to Great Ormond Street, and I had thought about this conversation ever since we had travelled back from London. Hannah had been quiet in the car and so had I. But now we must talk because she was leaving for a visit to Acorns tomorrow and the doctor's words were echoing in my mind. Time was running out.

'Your scan at Great Ormond Street was very bad,' I said softly.

Her gaze was steady. 'I know,' she replied.

'The doctors think that if you don't have the transplant then you are probably going to die very soon. Your heart is very weak now and you need to decide what you want to do.'

Tears pricked bright in Hannah's eyes and I put my arms round her.

'If you don't have a transplant then you will probably have your birthday next week but not your fifteenth,' I said, trying to keep my voice steady.

She was silent and I lowered my head next to hers.

'We can do whatever you want, Han, and if you decide that you still don't want the operation then I will make sure you don't feel any pain. I will always be with you. I will always be here. You will not be alone.'

Determination wrestled with fear on her face.

'If this is too hard then Daddy and I can make the decision for you,' I said softly. 'You don't have to decide anything, Han, if you don't want to. Would you like to know what we would choose?'

She nodded.

Last night, Andrew and I had talked about the transplant and agreed what we would decide if Hannah asked us to. I had never spoken to her like this before, but I could see she was struggling and I wanted to help her carry the burden of the decision.

'Daddy and I think we would say yes to the operation.'

Neither of us moved.

'If you don't want it then that is absolutely fine with us, Hannah. We just want what is best for you, and that is whatever you are comfortable doing.'

'I'm frightened,' she sobbed, 'of asking you and Daddy and something going wrong because then you'd feel guilty and I don't want that.'

I bent my head towards her. 'Hannah, you must never feel you can't ask us to decide. If you did then we would try our best to make the right decision, and we couldn't feel guilty if we tried our best.'

'Yes,' she said quietly. 'But I don't know what I want.' She looked tired, as if the weight of the world was resting on her shoulders.

'Well, you don't have to decide tonight, do you?' I said softly. 'I want you to go to sleep now and think about this tomorrow.'

CHAPTER ELEVEN

The Gift of Life

Hannah

I can't stop thinking about the transplant. I've been at Acorns for four days, but it's there in my head all the time. I know it's in everyone else's too. The Chitty Chitty Bang Bang looks are really bad now.

I know that if I don't have the transplant then I won't see fifteen. My fourteenth birthday is only five days away so it's only 370 days until my fifteenth. There have been 718 days since I left hospital, and that doesn't feel like long ago. So 370 days doesn't seem like much time.

I don't want to have my fourteenth and then nothing. I used to be sure, but now I don't know what to do. I feel too tired to think any more.

Mum and Dad have told me they can decide if I want them to, and I've nearly asked them loads of times. But I haven't because I still want to make my own decision. I know it would take the pressure off me if Mum and Dad chose, but they might feel guilty if I died after the transplant and I don't want them to live with that. I love them too much. They've got Oli, Lucy and Phoebe to look after so I don't want them to be sad if something happened to me after they had decided what to do. They've said they wouldn't, but even though they've promised me I still don't want to ask them.

Mum talked to me after we got back from Great Ormond Street and told me I wouldn't live long if I didn't have the transplant. That made me feel sad, but did I really want a massive operation? Could I promise to always take the pills I'd need? The next day she brought me here and asked me if I'd made up my mind. I told her I hadn't and she said that was fine and we'd talk about it when I got home. But I don't know how I'm going to choose, and I leave Acorns tomorrow. It's not a yes, it's not a no, it's a don't know. How do you work that out? Trying to decide between having a transplant and keeping going as I am is like being asked to pick between doing some hard maths or running a marathon. I don't really want to do either one.

I wish things could be like they were.

The doctors say a transplant will only work if I want it to and they won't do one unless I'm sure. I know I could die either way, but heaven doesn't scare me. When I think of it I see a place where you can do what you want and be with people you know who've gone before you. I'm not sure what it would look like, but if I had to guess I'd say there would be grass and sky and people playing table tennis. I know that when I arrived in heaven I'd be fine and if I could I would send my mum a message to tell her that.

But I am scared of getting to heaven. Would it hurt? What if something went wrong with a transplant? I'd also have to take tablets for the rest of my life. There have been days when I just couldn't take my pills, and if I had the transplant then I could never do that again.

I've been really tired this week. I've tried swimming or going on the computer but I feel so tired that I don't even want to talk or watch TV a lot of the time. All I can do is lie down. I wasn't even sure I wanted to see Simone when she asked to come and visit me. But then I was glad she had come because she brought flowers, chocolates, gum balls and giant strawberries. She also made me laugh.

At least I got my questions answered at Great Ormond Street. I wanted to know how long my recovery would be, how big my scar would be and what would happen after the operation. I also asked the transplant coordinator if there would be a time when it would be too late to change my mind, and she said yes. That really stuck in my head even though I didn't find out exactly when it would be. I'm glad I didn't ask that one.

But I know I don't have for ever.

I want to do everything I dream of doing.

When it's all running round my head I wonder if I have a choice anyway.

I want to have my Sweet Sixteen party, learn to drive and go on a ferry to France. We could eat croissants and try snails. I want to swim in the sea, run in a field and dance to loud music. I want to visit all the places I've read about in books. I want to be at home and play in the snow, go blackberry picking next autumn. I don't want to die. I want to live.

Kirsty

Hannah was quiet, just as she had been ever since I picked her up from Acorns four days ago.

'Maybe I'll have the transplant,' she'd told me as we drove home.

'Would you like me to ring Great Ormond Street?' I'd asked her.

'No. I'm not completely sure.'

I did not want fear or ignorance to hold Hannah back from making this decision and was sure that the fact that a donated heart would once have belonged to someone else was playing on her mind.

'You know you won't change if you have a transplant,' I told her. 'I know you've been thinking about it, Han, but it's your brain that makes you who you are, not your heart. It's your brain that gives you thoughts and feelings. And if you have the operation then I can't think of a little girl anyone would want to help more than you. When people decide to donate their hearts, or their relatives do, it's to help someone who's very sick. I can't imagine a more worthy person than you—kind and good, strong and brave.'

But still Hannah had waited, and I knew the final hurdle that stood between her and a decision was her fourteenth birthday tomorrow. She had missed so many birthdays over the years that they had become precious to her—unique days on which she could feel almost normal as she ate too much cake, opened presents and had fun just like her friends did. Nothing, not even the transplant, was going to stop her turning fourteen at home.

And so I'd waited for four long days since bringing her home from Acorns, refusing to let my fears or impatience rush Hannah—forcing myself not to think of what was happening inside her, telling myself that time was precious yet her peace of mind even more so. But her birthday was almost here—we had planned her party, wrapped her presents, invited her friends and bought a cake. Hannah could finally be sure that she would celebrate as she wanted to, and I knew that I must talk to her again. Both of us were increasingly restless, finding it hard to sleep and unable to relax.

'I want to talk to you, Han,' I said softly. 'I think you've made up your mind. If you have decided about the transplant then I'm going to ask you to tell Great Ormond Street.'

'I won't have to go back into hospital before tomorrow?'

'No, darling. We don't have to tell anyone except Great Ormond Street.'

'OK.'

I slowly dialled the number to talk to Nadine, Great Ormond Street's transplant coordinator.

'Hello?' she said as she picked up the phone.

'Nadine, it's Kirsty here. I think Hannah wants to talk to you.'

I handed her the phone. I held my breath as she began to speak.

'I've decided,' she said. 'I want to go onto the transplant list.'

When the call was finished, I bent to hug her.

'I want to go on holiday and do my GCSEs,' Hannah told me.

'I know you do, darling,' I whispered. 'And I want you to as well.'

MY EYES OPENED WIDE. It was 3 a.m. I was finding it hard to sleep now, fearful that Hannah might not be strong enough to wait for a heart. It was less than a week since her birthday but her health had deteriorated even more. Each night now I went down to check her every hour and give her medicines to ease her pain or oxygen to help her breathing if she needed them.

I got out of bed and walked downstairs. A light glowed softly in Hannah's room as I walked in and saw her—her face was grey, her hands were clasped to her chest and her breathing was ragged. She looked afraid.

'My chest hurts,' she gasped. 'It's like someone is sitting on me.'

The next morning, Hannah was taken into hospital where I was told her urea and creatinine levels were falling—her kidneys were beginning to fail and her blood pressure was low. Time was running out.

WAITING. HANNAH'S NAME is on the transplant list.

How long will it take? Will she die before someone else does, someone whose heart might save her life? Guilt and hope mix inside me. How can I hope for a heart from someone who was loved just as Hannah is?

It is three weeks since Hannah's birthday and we've been in and out of hospital ever since. The doctors have increased her drugs and now Hannah is back in hospital, too ill to be anywhere else. Her health is deteriorating.

Hannah is too tired to get out of bed or even talk much. She has been put back on dobutamine to keep her fragile heart beating.

Her blood pressure is dropping. The doctors have decided to space out her medications because her body is too weak to cope with large doses.

Her blood pressure is 49/22. A healthy pressure is 120/60.

Will she be too weak to survive the operation?

At midnight her consultant comes to see me. Hannah will have to be transferred to London in the morning. She needs life support. It's the only thing that will keep her alive now.

She lies sleeping. The door opens and her consultant walks back in.

'I have news,' she says. 'A heart has become available.'

THE BLADES of the RAF helicopter roared overhead. It was 4 a.m.—about two and a half hours since the call from Great Ormond Street. Hannah was too poorly to travel in an ambulance, and the helicopter was carrying a medical team from the Children's Acute Transport Service who had come to take her to London. The helicopter had landed outside Hereford Hospital, inching down into the available space just shy of the barriers to the car park. Fire-engine headlights flooded the area in beams as the doors opened and people jumped out. Adrenaline pumped through my body as I looked at them, and a tiny part of me wondered if Hannah was really so ill—a mother's desperate denial about losing her child still pricking inside me even as I knew she lay dangerously sick upstairs.

As the CATS team went up to Hannah's room to prepare her to be moved, I packed our belongings. About an hour later we were ready to go and I said goodbye to the nurses who had looked after us so well over the past weeks. Andrew was at home and would be on his way to London in the car as soon as his parents arrived to look after Oli, Lucy and Phoebe.

Hannah was stretchered outside and lifted into the helicopter. But even with all this activity, she had been too weak to be excited about the transplant or even frightened when I told her that a heart had become available.

'That's good,' she'd said, but nothing more.

She looked tiny as she lay on the stretcher with eight doctors and nurses sitting round her, their knees braced against the bed. Two drips stood beside her, she was connected to an oxygen mask and wore a helmet and ear defenders. My legs felt like jelly as I climbed into the helicopter and sat down before it took off into the dark. Was this the last journey that Hannah and I would make together? Was this the end of her life or a new beginning?

About fifty minutes later we landed in Regent's Park and Hannah was put into an ambulance—the final stage of her journey to Great Ormond Street.

She was quiet and self-contained within a shell of fear and anticipation as we arrived at Great Ormond Street, where we were taken up to the cardiac intensive-care unit. There we were told the surgeons were looking at the heart to make sure it was suitable. If it was, Hannah would go down for surgery within the hour.

When the transplant sister told us the heart was good, Andrew still hadn't arrived and I knew he would be devastated to miss seeing Hannah. But the doctors were ready and Hannah was put onto a stretcher and wheeled into the long hospital corridors and through double doors into a small anaesthetic room, where half a dozen doctors and nurses stood waiting for us.

I talked to her softly as the anaesthetic was connected to one of her drip lines. 'I love you, Han,' I said over and over, a mantra for her to keep within as she fell asleep.

'I love you too,' she replied.

As the anaesthetic pulsed into her veins, I bent towards her. 'I want you to think of all we are going to do together,' I said as she looked into my eyes. 'When you wake up from this sleep, there will be so many things to do, my darling. We are going to walk along the beach. Think of it, Han. Palm trees, white sand, water rushing onto the sand. That's where you are now. The air is warm, the sun is shining and you're walking into the sea. The blue, blue sea . . .'

Hannah smiled lazily as she drifted into unconsciousness.

'And when you are home, we will watch Oli play football, go to see the horses with Lucy, go for walks along the lane . . .'

I looked at her face. She was sleeping now, peaceful. She was finally ready. She had made her choice.

CHAPTER TWELVE

A New Beginning

Kirsty

The sunshine was the lazy yellow of early autumn as Hannah and I walked along the lane towards the fields.

'There's one,' I said, and pointed to the hedgerow.

She stepped towards the brambles and pulled a blackberry from a mass of tiny thorns. 'No good. Too small. Hasn't had enough rain.' She peered deeper into the hedge. 'That one looks better.' She pulled the blackberry from the bush and popped it into her mouth. 'I was right!' She giggled.

We walked on slowly in silence for a few moments as Hannah stopped to pull more blackberries from the bushes. The sun was warm today, and all around us the colours of early autumn were seeping across the countryside.

'What time do we have to leave tomorrow?' Hannah asked.

'Early, about six thirty, so you'll have to go to bed in good time.'

'OK.'

We were going to London for the weekly checkup Hannah had been having since leaving Great Ormond Street. After tomorrow's we hoped to go just once a fortnight because the doctors were pleased with her progress.

It was two months since Hannah had come home, and while she remembered only snatches of being in hospital, for me memories of the eleven days she'd spent in intensive care after her transplant were fresh. The surgeons had been unable to close her chest at first because the cavity wasn't big enough to cope with a healthy heart. Hannah had been unconscious for ten days until the wound had finally been sewn up, and every minute that she lay with her chest open had been a minute too long for me because of the high risk of infection.

Hannah was sealed in a room in intensive care and Andrew and I had had to put on gowns and aprons before opening the door. Computers stood round her bed and she lay in a pool of light hooked up to ventilators and other machines. There had been problems: Hannah's blood pressure was uneven, her kidneys were still weak, and she had not fully ingested her liquid feed.

After her chest was closed, Hannah had begun to wake up again, and I was thankful that she did not remember those awful days in intensive care. Her memories only began after she'd been transferred to a ward for the final nine days of her stay, and she'd started to move and eat, talk and even laugh.

On our final day before going home, Hannah's surgeon had come to see us and I had thanked him for all he had done, knowing that words were almost useless in expressing our gratitude for the dedication and excellence of the team at Great Ormond Street. After that we'd taken Hannah home, and although she had been tearful and weak initially, her body and emotions drained by all that had happened, she continued to get stronger.

Once again we measured our days by the most ordinary of things: Hannah getting out of bed and eating, sleeping well at night, feeling strong enough to walk a hundred yards down the road with me to visit a friend.

The doctors had told us she would need three months at home before she could go back to school, and during that time we had to be careful about going to restaurants, cinemas, or anywhere crowded with people who might pass an infection on to Hannah. So we had spent the time quietly at home, where her spirit gradually bubbled up inside her again as she did a little more each day. As Hannah realised she was growing stronger, her excitement and happiness about what she had to look forward to increased.

'Mum?' she said as we reached the field where the horses were waiting for us. She stood beside me as we got to the gate. Her cheeks were pink, her eyes were bright. 'Can we make blackberry jam when we get home?'

'Of course.'

'And then can I put on the *Mamma Mia!* soundtrack really loud?'

'We'll see.'

She giggled as she stood beside me, and I took her hand as we walked into the field. The green grass stretched ahead of us, the sky was blue overhead and I felt inexpressibly thankful for this day.

PHOEBE DREW ME a picture recently and I absent-mindedly put it down as I rushed around. But when I got into bed that evening I made myself study it—the eyes, the hair, the lopsided smile on the face of a stick person—and it reminded me that I must never forget all that Hannah has taught me. To take notice of the tiny details of my children's lives, to stop and appreciate them, to see who they are and love them for it.

Our life is already changing—when Hannah walked a few hundred yards from the car to a ward on Hereford Hospital for a blood-pressure check it felt like a hundred miles—and I am slowly learning to trust that it has. But it's a slow process and one that will take me some time. The most critical period for organ rejection is during the first six months after transplant, and although the children are desperate for us to book a holiday next summer I can't yet quite bring myself to go from living from minute to minute to planning a trip nine months away. In the New Year I'll sit down, make a booking and allow myself to believe.

But I know that, even as Hannah becomes stronger and our life slips back into a normal pattern, I will guard against falling into the trap of constantly looking forward and forgetting today. I want to honour the journey we have made because it taught me to live a life that is not as ferociously busy as so many people's. I don't want to run through days, weeks and months so fast that I don't have time to see them properly.

It wasn't always this way. Before Hannah fell ill I was caught up in the business of life, and I suspect I might have wasted a little of its joy if it hadn't been for her. But she showed me a different path, and I hope I have passed on to my children what I have learnt and taught them to enjoy every day.

When I think of Hannah, I believe that she is three miracles rolled into one: first, she was conceived when I'd almost given up hope of becoming a mother; second, she survived leukaemia; and third, she is alive today. Hannah has taught me more about life than I ever knew I had to learn and has shown me things I did not know I had not seen. Our journey took us to some of the darkest places, but it also took us into the light, to places we never expected to find. For that I will always thank Hannah, and her courage, determination and sheer love of life have shown me that it can be fully lived without necessarily being long.

It is one of the hardest things to remember when you fear your child is losing its battle against illness, and I have never forgotten a mother I met who told me she could never forgive herself if she didn't try every treatment, do everything possible to save her child, however tiny the chance it might work. I understood her desperation and respected her choice. But I have learned that it is also possible to make a different one—enjoy your child and accept that lives sometimes have limits, however painful they are. You must have peace inside you to give to a sick child, and that is what I wanted for Hannah—the knowledge that I was on her side for right or wrong because knowing that I would always respect and defend her wishes made her feel safe. I believe it was the right thing for her.

Now I look forward to our future together and feel grateful every day to the person or family who gave Hannah this gift. They will never know our joy, but I will honour it by teaching my children as best I can.

Hannah

I'll never be able to eat grapefruit again. It interferes with an antirejection drug called tacrolimus that I'll have to take for the rest of my life. That's just one of the things I can't eat now, and there are others. Sushi is one, but I'm not bothered about it because I don't want to eat raw fish. Also cheeses and salami I'd like to eat but can't because they might make me sick, which wouldn't be good for my medication. That's the only bad bit about having a transplant—and the fact that I'll have to do PE when I get back to school.

But other than that, having a new heart is brilliant because I've got so much energy I don't know what to do with myself. My scar is not too bad, and no one can see it if I wear a top with a high neck. There are more important things to worry about anyway. When I first got home I couldn't tie up the laces on my trainers because it made me dizzy to bend down or walk more than a couple of minutes before I got tired. I wondered if the transplant had worked properly. But then I got stronger and stopped watching the DVDs that everyone had given me. I just wanted to be up and about as soon as I could because I'd spent too much time lying in bed.

Now I can walk to the ponies, which are quite far down the road, and I've even been to school for a few hours. I had to rest when I got home but I was fine again quickly. These are the other things I've done: been to watch Oli play football, out for pizza, had Simone to stay, gone shopping and visited Grandma and Granddad. But that's nothing compared to what I'm planning to do: go to the theatre, learn to swim better because I never had enough energy to get far before, go to my friend Molly's Halloween party and stay with Simone at her house. I'm also going to a Christmas party that a friend of Grandma and Granddad's has in a barn every year, and next summer we're all going to Spain. I can't wait to jump in the pool with Lucy.

She's happy that we can do more stuff together now, and we've decided we want an Xbox or a Wii. Mum doesn't mind if we get the money ourselves, so we've collected all our old toys, books and DVDs, which we're going to sell at a car-boot sale this weekend.

I can't wait to go to St Mary's every day again. At the moment my hospital tutor comes to see me for an hour a day, but things will be just like they were before when I get back to school. The only thing that will have changed is the fact that I've gone off *High School Musical* because I've realised that everything is perfect in it and life isn't like that. So now *Mamma Mia!* is my favourite. I love it when Sophie says she's not going to get married at the end. She wants to see the world instead. That's what I'd like to do.

When I was first asked about the transplant I was sick and just wanted to go home. Sometimes you can't listen to doctors and have to go with what you want, whatever anyone else thinks. If I'd had the transplant when I was first asked about it I'd have been unhappy. What helped me change my mind was the fact that I'd had good years after coming out of hospital and I wanted to have more of them, so I felt happy when I said yes. I talked to my doctor at Great Ormond Street about it when I went for my last checkup, and he said I just needed to think more, and he was right. I wanted to live when I said no and I wanted to live when I said yes.

That's what everyone got wrong when the newspapers wrote about me, and although most people were kind, some weren't. 'I fear for Hannah's life,' one person wrote on a website. 'I fear she is too young and has made the wrong decision by refusing a heart transplant she obviously needs.'

It made me angry to read that. No one knows anyone else's life like they do, and I was young but I'd seen things most adults hadn't.

I was scared, though, when it happened. Everything seemed to happen so quickly, and though I knew one girl had waited just thirty-six hours for a new heart I'd also been told another boy had had to wait a year. But deep down I was sure. I feel thankful that someone gave me a new heart because that person saved my life, and what bigger thing can anyone do?

So now I'm going to keep getting better and be normal again. But when I am, I won't forget being ill because this is what I've learnt:

- Try not to be down every day or think your life is worse than anyone else's.
- Make yourself do something you've never done before.
- Prove someone wrong.
- Get good grades in school so you can get a good job.
- Think about people worse off than you.
- Enjoy what you've got.
- Love your family and friends.
- Break a rule but not the law.
- Be brave.

That's it really. I just want to keep on getting better and do all the things I've thought about for so long.

So I suppose there's just one other thing to say. But really, it's the most important thing of all.

Watch out, world . . . I'M COMING TO GET YOU!